NATHANAEL WEST

NATHANAEL WEST

NOVELS AND OTHER WRITINGS

The Dream Life of Balso Snell
Miss Lonelyhearts
A Cool Million
The Day of the Locust
Other Writings
Unpublished Writings and Fragments
Letters

THE LIBRARY OF AMERICA

The Dream Life of Balso Snell copyright 1931 by Moss and
Kamin; *Miss Lonelyhearts* copyright 1933 by Nathanael West.
Reprinted by permission of Farrar, Straus & Giroux, Inc.
A Cool Million copyright 1934 by Nathanael West; *The Day of
the Locust* copyright 1939 by the estate of Nathanael West.
Reprinted by permission of New Directions Publishing Corp.
Previously unpublished material: Copyright © 1997 by
The Estate of Nathanael West. Published by arrangement
with the Estate of Nathanael West, c/o Harold Ober
Associates Incorporated.

The paper used in this publication meets the
minimum requirements of the American National Standard for
Information Sciences—Permanence of Paper for Printed
Library Materials, ANSI Z39.48—1984.

Distributed to the trade in the United States
by Penguin Books USA Inc
and in Canada by Penguin Books Canada Ltd.

Library of Congress Catalog Number: 96–49007
For cataloging information, see end of Notes.
ISBN 1–883011–28–0
———
Second Printing
The Library of America—93

Manufactured in the United States of America

Sᴀᴄᴠᴀɴ Bᴇʀᴄᴏᴠɪᴛᴄʜ
ꜱᴇʟᴇᴄᴛᴇᴅ ᴛʜᴇ ᴄᴏɴᴛᴇɴᴛꜱ ᴀɴᴅ ᴡʀᴏᴛᴇ ᴛʜᴇ ɴᴏᴛᴇꜱ
ꜰᴏʀ ᴛʜɪꜱ ᴠᴏʟᴜᴍᴇ

Contents

THE DREAM LIFE
OF
BALSO SNELL

To A. S.

*"After all, my dear fellow,
life, Anaxagoras has said,
is a journey."*
                    Bergotte

WHILE walking in the tall grass that has sprung up around the city of Troy, Balso Snell came upon the famous wooden horse of the Greeks. A poet, he remembered Homer's ancient song and decided to find a way in.

On examining the horse, Balso found that there were but three openings: the mouth, the navel, and the posterior opening of the alimentary canal. The mouth was beyond his reach, the navel proved a cul-de-sac, and so, forgetting his dignity, he approached the last. O Anus Mirabilis!

Along the lips of the mystic portal he discovered writings which after a little study he was able to decipher. Engraved in a heart pierced by an arrow and surmounted by the initial N, he read, "Ah! Qualis . . . Artifex . . . Pereo!" Not to be outdone by the actor-emperor, Balso carved with his penknife another heart and the words "O Byss! O Abyss! O Anon! O Onan!" omitting, however, the arrow and his initial.

Before entering he prayed:

"O Beer! O Meyerbeer! O Bach! O Offenbach! Stand me now as ever in good stead."

Balso immediately felt like the One at the Bridge, the Two in the Bed, the Three in the Boat, the Four on Horseback, the Seven Against Thebes. And with a high heart he entered the gloom of the foyer-like lower intestine.

After a little while, seeing no-one and hearing nothing, Balso began to feel depressed. To keep his heart high and yet out of his throat, he made a song.

> Round as the Anus
> Of a Bronze Horse
> Or the Tender Buttons
> Used by Horses for Ani
>
> On the Wheels of His Car
> Ringed Round with Brass
> Clamour the Seraphim
> Tongues of Our Lord

Full Ringing Round
As the Belly of Silenus
Giotto Painter of Perfect Circles
Goes . . . One Motion Round

Round and Full
Round and Full as
A Brimming Goblet
The Dew-Loaded Navel
Of Mary
Of Mary Our Mother

Round and Ringing Full
As the Mouth of a Brimming Goblet
The Rust-Laden Holes
In Our Lord's Feet
Entertain the Jew-Driven Nails.

He later gave this song various names, the most successful of which were: *Anywhere Out of the World or a Voyage Through the Hole in the Mundane Millstone* and *At Hoops with the Ani of Bronze Horses or Toe Holes for a Flight of Fancy.*

But despite the gaiety of his song, Balso did not feel sure of himself. He thought of the Phoenix Excrementi, a race of men he had invented one Sunday afternoon while in bed, and trembled, thinking he might well meet one in this place. And he had good cause to tremble, for the Phoenix Excrementi eat themselves, digest themselves, and give birth to themselves by evacuating their bowels.

Hoping to attract the attention of an inhabitant, Balso shouted as though overwhelmed by the magnificence of his surroundings:

"O the Rose Gate! O the Moist Garden! O Well! O Fountain! O Sticky Flower! O Mucous Membrane!"

A man with "Tours" embroidered on his cap stalked out of the shadow. In order to prove a poet's right to trespass, Balso quoted from his own works:

"If you desire to have two parallel lines meet at once or even in the near future," he said, "it is important to make all the necessary arrangements beforehand, preferably by wireless."

The man ignored his little speech. "Sir," he said, "you are

an ambassador from that ingenious people, the inventors and perfectors of the automatic water-closet, to my people who are the heirs of Greece and Rome. As your own poet has so well put it, 'The Grandeur that was Greece and the Glory that was Rome' . . . I offer you my services as guide. First you will please look to the right where you will see a beautiful Doric prostate gland swollen with gladness and an over-abundance of good cheer."

This speech made Balso very angry. "Inventors of the automatic water-closet, are we?" he shouted. "Oh, you stinker! Doric, bah! It's Baptist '68, that's what it is. And no prostate gland either, simply an atrophied pile. You call this dump grand and glorious, do you? Have you ever seen the Grand Central Station, or the Yale Bowl, or the Holland Tunnel, or the New Madison Square Garden? Exposed plumbing, stinker, that's all I see—and at this late date. It's criminally backward, do you hear me?"

The guide gave ground before Balso's rage. "Please sir," he said, "please . . . After all, the ages have sanctified this ground, great men have hallowed it. In Rome do as the Romans do."

"Stinker," Balso repeated, but less ferociously this time.

The guide took heart. "Mind your manners, foreigner. If you don't like it here, why don't you go back where you came from? But before you go let me tell you a story—an old tale of my people, rich in local color. And, you force me to say it, apropos, timely. However, let me assure you that I mean no offense. The title of the story is

"VISITORS

"A traveler in Tyana, who was looking for the sage Apollonius, saw a snake enter the lower part of a man's body. Approaching the man, he said:

"'Pardon me, my good fellow, but a snake just entered your . . .' He finished by pointing.

"'Yes sir, he lives there,' was the astounding rejoinder.

"'Ah, then you must be the man I'm looking for, the philosopher-saint, Apollonius of Tyana. Here is a letter of introduction from my brother George. May I see the snake please? Now the opening. Perfect!'"

Balso echoed the last word of the story. "Perfect! Perfect! A real old-world fable. You may consider yourself hired."

"I have other stories to tell," the guide said, "and I shall tell them as we go along. By the way, have you heard the one about Moses and the Burning Bush? How the prophet rebuked the Bush for speaking by quoting the proverb, 'Good wine needs no bush'; and how the Bush insolently replied, 'A hand in the Bush is worth two in the pocket'."

Balso did not consider this story nearly as good as the other; in fact he thought it very bad, yet he was determined to make no more breaks and entered the large intestine on the arm of his guide. He let the guide do all the talking and they made great headway up the tube. But, unfortunately, coming suddenly upon a place where the intestine had burst through the stomach wall, Balso cried out in amazement:

"What a hernia! What a hernia!"

The guide began to splutter with rage and Balso tried to pacify him by making believe he had not meant the scenery. "Hernia," he said, rolling the word on his tongue. "What a pity childish associations cling to beautiful words such as hernia, making their use as names impossible. Hernia! What a beautiful name for a girl! Hernia Hornstein! Paresis Pearlberg! Paranoia Puntz! How much more pleasing to the ear [and what other sense should a name please?] than Faith Rabinowitz or Hope Hilkowitz."

But Balso had only blundered again. "Sirrah!" the guide cried in an enormous voice. "I am a Jew! and whenever anything Jewish is mentioned, I find it necessary to say that I am a Jew. I'm a Jew! A Jew!"

"Oh, you mistake me," Balso said, "I have nothing against the Jews. I admire the Jews; they are a thrifty race. Some of my best friends are Jews." But his protests availed him little until he thought to quote C. M. Doughty's epigram. "The semites," Balso said with great firmness, "are like to a man sitting in a cloaca to the eyes, and whose brows touch heaven."

When Balso had at last succeeded in quieting the guide, he tried to please him further by saying that the magnificent tunnel stirred him to the quick and that he would be satisfied to spend his remaining days in it with but a few pipes and a book.

The guide tossed up his arms in one of those eloquent gestures the latins know so well how to perform and said:

"After all, what is art? I agree with George Moore. Art is not nature, but rather nature digested. Art is a sublime excrement."

"And Daudet?" Balso queried.

"Oh, Daudet! Daudet, c'est de bouillabaisse! You know, George Moore also says, 'What care I that the virtue of some sixteen-year-old maiden was the price paid for Ingres' La Source?' Now . . ."

"Picasso says," Balso broke in, "Picasso says there are no feet in nature . . . And, thanks for showing me around. I have to leave."

But before he was able to get away, the guide caught him by the collar. "Just a minute, please. You were right to interrupt. We should talk of art, not artists. Please explain your interpretation of the Spanish master's dictum."

"Well, the point is . . ." Balso began. But before he could finish the guide started again. "If you are willing to acknowledge the existence of points," he said, "then the statement that there are no feet in nature puts you in an untenable position. It depends for its very meaning on the fact that there are no points. Picasso, by making this assertion, has placed himself on the side of monism in the eternal wrangle between the advocates of the Singular and those of the Plural. As James puts it, 'Does reality exist distributively or collectively—in the shape of *eaches, everys, anys, eithers* or only in the shape of an *all* or *whole*?' If reality is singular then there are no feet in nature, if plural, a great many. If the world is one [everything part of the same thing—called by Picasso nature] then nothing either begins or ends. Only when things take the shapes of *eaches, everys, anys, eithers* [have ends] do they have feet. Feet are attached to ends, by definition. Moreover, if everything is one, and has neither ends nor beginnings, then everything is a circle. A circle has neither a beginning nor an end. A circle has no feet. If we believe that nature is a circle, then we must also believe that there are no feet in nature.

"Do not pooh-pooh this idea as mystical. Bergson has . . ."

"Cezanne said, 'Everything tends toward the globular.'"

With this announcement Balso made another desperate attempt to escape.

"Cezanne?" the guide said, keeping a firm hold on Balso's collar. "Cezanne is right. The sage of Aix is . . . "

With a violent twist, Balso tore loose and fled.

BALSO fled down the great tunnel until he came upon a man, naked except for a derby in which thorns were sticking, who was attempting to crucify himself with thumb tacks. His curiosity got the better of his fear and he stopped.

"Can I help you?" he asked politely.

"No," the man answered with even greater politeness, tipping his hat repeatedly as he spoke. "No, I can manage, thank you . . .

"My name is Maloney the Areopagite," the man continued, answering the questions Balso was too well-bred to word, "and I am a catholic mystic. I believe implicitly in that terrible statement of Saint Hildegarde's, 'The lord dwells not in the bodies of the healthy and vigorous'. I live as did Marie Alacoque, Suso, Labre, Lydwine of Schiedam, Rose of Lima. When my suffering is not too severe, I compose verses in imitation of Notker Balbus, Ekkenard le Vieux, Hucbald le Chauve.

"In the feathered darkness
Of thy mouth,
O Mother of God!
I worship Christ
The culminating rose.

"Get the idea? I spend the rest of my time marveling at the love shown by all the great saints for even the lowliest of God's creatures. Have you ever heard of Benedict Labre? It was he who picked up the vermin that fell out of his hat and placed them piously back into his sleeve. Before calling in a laundress, another very holy man removed the vermin from his clothes in order not to drown the jewels of sanctity infesting them.

"Inspired by these thoughts I have decided to write the biography of Saint Puce, a great martyred member of the vermin family. If you are interested, I will give you a short précis of his life."

"Please do so, sir," Balso said. "Live and learn is my motto, Mr. Maloney, so please continue."

"Saint Puce was a flea," Maloney the Areopagite began in a well-trained voice. "A flea who was born, lived, and died, beneath the arm of our Lord.

"Saint Puce was born from an egg that was laid in the flesh of Christ while as a babe He played on the floor of the stable in Bethlehem. That the flesh of a god has been a stage in the incubation of more than one being is well known: Dionysius and Athene come to mind.

"Saint Puce had two mothers: the winged creature that laid the egg, and the God that hatched it in His flesh. Like most of us, he had two fathers: our Father Who art in Heaven, and he who in the cocksureness of our youth we called 'pop'.

"Which of his two fathers fertilized the egg? I cannot answer with certainty, but the subsequent actions of Saint Puce's life lead me to believe that the egg was fertilized by a being whose wings were of feathers. Yes, I mean the Dove or Paraclete—the Sanctus Spiritus. In defense of this belief antiquity will help us again: it is only necessary to remember Leda and Europa. And I must remind you, you who might plead a puce too small physically, of the nature of God's love and how it embraceth all.

"O happy, happy childhood! Playing in the curled brown silk, sheltered from all harm by Christ's arm. Eating the sweet flesh of our Saviour; drinking His blood; bathing in His sweat; partaking, oh how fully! of His Godhead. Having no need to cry as I have cried:

"Corpus Christi, salva me
 Sanguis Christi, inebria me
 Aqua lateris Christi, lave me.

"In manhood, fullgrown, how strong Saint Puce was, how lusty; and how his lust and strength were satisfied in one continuous, never-culminating ecstasy. The music of our Lord's skin sliding over His flesh!—more exact than the fugues of Bach. The pattern of His veins!—more intricate than the Maze at Cnossos. The odors of His Body!—more fragrant than the Temple of Solomon. The temperature of His flesh!—more pleasant than the Roman baths to the youth Puce. And, finally, the taste of His blood! In this wine all pleasure, all excitement, was magnified, until with ecstasy Saint Puce's small body roared like a furnace.

"In his prime, Saint Puce wandered far from his birthplace, that hairsilk pocketbook, the armpit of our Lord. He roamed the forest of God's chest and crossed the hill of His abdomen. He measured and sounded that fathomless well, the Navel of our Lord. He explored and charted every crevasse, ridge, and cavern of Christ's body. From notes taken during his travels he later wrote his great work, *A Geography of Our Lord*.

"After much wandering, tired, he returned at last to his home in the savoury forest. To spend, he thought, his remaining days in writing, worship, and contemplation. Happy in a church whose walls were the flesh of Christ, whose windows were rose with the blood of Christ, and on whose altars burned golden candles made of the sacred earwax.

"Soon, too soon, alas! the day of martyrdom arrived [O Jesu, mi dulcissime!], and the arms of Christ were lifted that His hands might receive the nails.

"The walls and windows of Saint Puce's church were broken and its halls flooded with blood.

"The hot sun of Calvary burnt the flesh beneath Christ's upturned arm, making the petal-like skin shrivel until it looked like the much-shaven armpit of an old actress.

"After Christ died, Saint Puce died, refusing to desert to lesser flesh, even to that of Mary who stood close under the cross. With his last strength he fought off the unconquerable worm." . . .

Mr. Maloney's thin frame was racked by sobs as he finished, yet Balso did not spare him.

"I think you're morbid," he said. "Don't be morbid. Take your eyes off your navel. Take your head from under your armpit. Stop sniffing mortality. Play games. Don't read so many books. Take cold showers. Eat more meat."

With these helpful words, Balso left him to his own devices and continued on his way.

H E HAD LEFT Maloney the Areopagite far behind when, on turning a bend in the intestine, he saw a boy hiding what looked like a packet of letters in a hollow tree. After the boy had left, Balso removed the packet and sat down to read. First, however, he took off his shoes because his feet hurt.

What he had taken for letters proved on closer scrutiny to be a diary. At the top of the first page was written, "English Theme by John Gilson, Class 8B, Public School 186, Miss McGeeney, teacher." He read further.

Jan. 1st—at home.

Whom do I fool by calling these pages a journal? Surely not you, Miss McGeeney. Alas! no-one. Nor is anyone fooled by the fact that I write in the first person. It is for this reason that I do not claim to have found these pages in a hollow tree. I am an honest man and feel badly about masks, cardboard noses, diaries, memoirs, letters from a Sabine farm, the theatre . . . I feel badly, yet I can do nothing. 'Sir!' I say to myself, 'your name is not Iago, but simply John. It is monstrous to write lies in a diary.'

However, I insist that I am an honest man. Reality troubles me as it must all honest men.

Reality! Reality! If I could only discover the Real. A Real that I could know with my senses. A Real that would wait for me to inspect it as a dog inspects a dead rabbit. But, alas! when searching for the Real I throw a stone into a pool whose ripples become of advancing less importance until they are too large for connection with, or even memory of, the stone agent.

Written while smelling the moistened forefinger of my left hand.

Jan 2nd—at home

Is this journal to be like all the others I have started? A large first entry, consisting of the incident which made me think my life exciting enough to keep a journal, followed by a series of entries gradually decreasing in size and culminating in a week of blank days.

Inexperienced diary-writers make their first entry the largest. They come to the paper with a constipation of ideas—eager, impatient. The white paper acts as a laxative. A diarrhoea of words is the result. The richness of the flow is unnatural; it cannot be sustained.

A diary must grow naturally—a flower, a cancer, a civilization . . . In a diary there is no need for figures of speech, honest Iago.

Sometimes my name is Raskolnikov, sometimes it is Iago. I never was, and never shall be, plain John Gilson—honest, honest Iago, yes, but never honest John. As Raskolnikov, I keep a journal which I call *The Making of a Fiend*. I give the heart of my Crime Journal:

Crime Journal

I have been in this hospital seven weeks. I am under observation. Am I sane? This diary shall prove me insane.

This entry gives me away.

Crime Journal

My mother visited me today. She cried. It is she who is crazy. Order is the test of sanity. Her emotions and thoughts are disordered. Mine are arranged, valued, placed.

Man spends a great deal of time making order out of chaos, yet insists that the emotions be disordered. I order my emotions: I am insane. Yet sanity is discipline. My mother rolls on the hospital floor and cries: "John darling . . . John sweetheart." Her hat falls over face. She clutches her absurd bag of oranges. She is sane.

I say to her quietly: "Mother, I love you, but this spectacle is preposterous—and the smell of your clothing depresses me." I am insane.

Crime Journal

Order is vanity. I have decided to discard the nonsense of precision instruments. No more measuring. I drop the slide rule and take up the Golden Rule. Sanity is the absence of extremes.

Crime Journal

Is someone reading my diary while I sleep?

On rereading what I have written, I think I can detect a peculiar change in my words. They have taken on the quality of comment.

You who read these pages while I sleep, please sign your name here.

John Raskolnikov Gilson

Crime Journal

During the night I got up, turned to yesterday's entry and signed my name.

Crime Journal

I am insane. I [the papers had it CULTURED FIEND SLAYS DISHWASHER] am insane.

When a baby, I affected all the customary poses: I "laughed the icy laughter of the soul", I uttered "universal sighs"; I sang in "silver-fire verse"; I smiled the "enigmatic smile"; I sought "azure and elliptical routes". In everything I was completely the mad poet. I was one of those "great despisers", whom Nietzsche loved because "they are the great adorers; they are arrows of longing for the other shore." Along with "mon hysterie" I cultivated a "rotten, ripe maturity." You understand what I mean: like Rimbaud, I practiced having hallucinations.

Now, my imagination is a wild beast that cries always for freedom. I am continually tormented by the desire to indulge some strange thing, perceptible but indistinct, hidden in the swamps of my mind. This hidden thing is always crying out to me from its hiding-place: "Do as I tell you and you will find out my shape. There, quick! what is that thing in your brain? Indulge my commands and some day the great doors of your mind will swing open and allow you to enter and handle to your complete satisfaction the vague shapes and figures hidden there."

I can know nothing; I can have nothing; I must devote my whole life to the pursuit of a shadow. It is as if I were attempting to trace with the point of a pencil the shadow of the tracing pencil. I am enchanted with the shadow's shape and want very much to outline it; but the shadow is attached to the pencil and moves with it, never allowing me to trace its tempting form. Because of some great need, I am continually forced to make the attempt.

Two years ago I sorted books for eight hours a day in the public library. Can you imagine how it feels to be surrounded for eight long hours by books—a hundred billion words one after another according to ten thousand mad schemes. What patience, what labor are those crazy sequences the result of! What starving! What sacrifice! And the fervors, deliriums, ambitions, dreams, that dictated them! . . .

The books smelt like the breaths of their authors; the books smelt like a closet full of old shoes through which a steam pipe passes. As I handled them they seemed to turn into flesh, or at least some substance that could be eaten.

Have you ever spent any time among the people who farm the great libraries: the people who search old issues of the medical journals for pornography and facts about strange diseases; the comic writers who exhume jokes from old magazines; the men and women employed by the insurance companies to gather statistics on death? I worked in the philosophy department. That department is patronized by alchemists, astrologers, cabalists, demonologists, magicians, atheists, and the founders of new religious systems.

While working in the library, I lived in a theatrical rooming house in the west Forties, a miserable, uncomfortable place. I lived there because of the discomfort. I wanted to be miserable. I could not have lived in a comfortable house. The noises [harsh, grating], the dirt [animal, greasy], the smells [dry sweat, sour mold], permitted me to wallow in my discomfort. My mind was full of vague irritations and annoyances. My body was nervous and jumpy, and demanded an extraordinary amount of sleep. I was a bundle of physical and mental tics. I climbed into myself like a bear into a hollow tree, and lay there long hours, overpowered by the heat, odor, and nastiness of I.

The only other person living on my floor, the top one, was an idiot. He earned his living as a dishwasher in the kitchen of the Hotel Astor. He was a fat, pink and grey pig of a man, and stank of stale tobacco, dry perspiration, clothing mold, and oatmeal soap. He did not have a skull on the top of his neck, only a face; his head was all face—a face without side, back or top, like a mask.

The idiot never wore a collar, yet he kept both a front and a back collar button in the neckband of his shirt. When he changed his shirt he removed the collar buttons from the dirty shirt and placed them in the clean one. His neck was smooth, white, fat, and covered all over with tiny blue veins like a piece of cheap marble. His Adam's apple was very large and looked as though it might be a soft tumor in his throat. When he swallowed, his neck bulged out and he made a sound like a miniature toilet being flushed.

My neighbor, the idiot, never smiled, but laughed continually. It must have hurt him to laugh. He fought his laughter as though it were a wild beast. A beast of laughter seemed always struggling to escape from between his teeth.

People say that it is terrible to hear a man cry. I think it is even worse to hear a man laugh. [Yet the ancients considered hysteria a woman's disease. They believed that hysteria was caused by the womb breaking loose and floating freely through the body. The cure they practiced was to place sweet-smelling herbs to the vulva in order to attract the womb back to its original position, and foul-smelling things to the nose in order to keep the womb away from the head.]

One night at the movies, I heard a basso from the Chicago Opera Company sing the devil's serenade from Faust. A portion of this song calls for a long laugh. When the singer came to the laugh he was unable to get started. He struggled with the laugh, but it refused to come. At last he managed to start laughing. Once started, he was unable to stop. The orchestra repeated the transition that led from the laugh to the next bars of the song, but he was unable to stop laughing.

I returned home with my head full of the singer's laughter. Because of it I was unable to fall asleep. I dressed myself and went downstairs. On my way to the street I passed my neighbor the idiot. He was laughing to himself. His laughter made me laugh. When he detected the strain in my voice he grew angry. He thought that I was making fun of him. He said, "Who you laughing at?" I became frightened and offered him a cigarette. He refused it. I left him on the stairs, struggling with his laughter and his anger.

I knew that if I did not get my customary amount of sleep, I would suffer when the time came for me to get up. I was certain that if I went back to bed I would be unable to sleep. In order to tire myself as quickly as possible, I walked to Broadway and then started uptown. My shoes hurt me and at first I enjoyed the pain. Soon, however, the pain became so intense that I had to stop walking and return home.

On regaining my bed, I still found it impossible to fall asleep. I knew that I must become interested in something outside of myself or go insane. I plotted the death of the idiot.

I felt certain that it would be a safe murder to commit. Safe, because its motives would not be comprehensible to the police. Policemen are reasonable men; they do not consider the shape and color of a man's throat, his laugh or the fact that he does not wear a collar, reasonable motives for killing him.

You also, eh, doctor, consider these poor reasons for murder. I agree—they are literary reasons. Reasoning your way, dear doctor—like Darwin or a policeman—I am expected to trace my action back to some such thing as the desire to live or create life. Because I want you to believe me, I shall say that in order to remain sane I had to kill this man, just as I had to kill, when a child, all the flies in my room before being able to fall asleep.

Nonsense, eh? I agree—nonsense. Please, please—here [please believe me] is why I killed Adolph. I killed the idiot because he disturbed my sense of balance. I killed him thinking his death would permit me to regain my balance. My beloved balance!

The fact that I had never killed made me uncomfortable. What was this enormous crime I had never committed? What were all the horrors attendant on this act? I killed a man and discovered the answers. I shall never kill another man. I shall never need to kill another man.

Let me continue with my confession. I decided not to plot an intricate killing. I was afraid that if I attemped a complicated crime I might get entangled in my own scheme. I decided to have the murder consist of only one act, the killing.

I even resisted the desire to look up certain books in the library.

Because the idea of the killing involved the dishwasher's throat, I decided to do the job with a knife. As a child I always took pleasure in cutting soft, firm things. I purchased a knife about fifteen inches long. The knife had only one cutting edge; the other edge or the back of the knife was about half an inch thick. Its weight made it a perfect instrument for the job.

I did not want to commit the murder too soon after purchasing the knife; but on the very night that I brought it home, I heard the idiot come up the stairs drunk. As I listened to him fumble with his key, I realized, for the first time, that he locked his door at night. This unlooked-for obstacle almost made me give up the idea of killing him. I rid myself of my misgivings by thinking of the torture I would have to go through if I frustrated my desire to commit murder. I decided to do the job that very evening and have it over with. I put on my bathrobe and went into the hall. His door was ajar. I went to it carefully. The idiot was stretched out on his bed, drunk. I went back to my room and took off my bathrobe and pajamas. I planned to do the murder naked, so that I should have no blood-stained things to wash or destroy. What blood I got on my body I could easily wash off. Naked: I felt cold; and I noticed that my genitals were tight and hard, like a dog's, or an archaic Greek statue's—they were as though I had just come out of an ice-cold bath. I was aware of a great excitement; an excitement that seemed to be near, but not quite within me.

I crossed the hall and entered the dishwasher's room. He had left his light burning. I walked to him and cut his throat. I had intended to do the cutting with several rapid strokes, but he awoke at the touch of the steel and I became frightened and sawed at his throat in a panic. When he lay still I calmed down.

I went back to my room and stood the knife up in the sink, like one does a wet umbrella, letting what blood was on it run into the drain. I dressed quickly, obsessed by the need for getting rid of the knife. While dressing I became conscious of a growing fear. A fear that as it grew seemed likely to burst me open; a fear so large that I felt I could not contain it without rupturing my mind. Inside of my head this expanding fear was like a rapidly growing child inside the belly of a mother. I felt that I must get rid of the fear or burst. I opened my mouth wide, but I was unable to give birth to my fear.

Carrying this fear as an ant carries a caterpillar thirty times its size, I ran down the stairs and into the street. I hurried west toward the river.

I let the knife slip into the water. With the knife went my fear. I felt light and free. I felt like a happy girl. I said to myself: "You feel like a young girl—kittenish, cuney-cutey, darlingey, springtimey." I caressed my breasts like a young girl who has suddenly become conscious of her body on a hot afternoon. I imitated the mannered walk of a girl showing off before a group of boys. In the dark I hugged myself.

On my way back to Broadway I passed some sailors, and felt an overwhelming desire to flirt with them. I went through all the postures of a desperate prostitute; I camped for all I was worth. The sailors looked at me and laughed. I wanted very much for one of them to follow me. Suddenly I heard the sound of footsteps behind me. The steps came close and I felt as though I were melting—all silk and perfumed, pink lace. I died the little death. But the man went past without noticing me. I sat down on a bench and was violently sick.

I sat on the bench for a long time, and then returned to my room, sick and cold.

Inside of my head the murder has become like a piece of sand inside the shell of an oyster. My mind has commenced to form a pearl around it. The idiot, the singer, his laugh, the knife, the river, my change of sex, all cover the murder just as the secretions of an oyster cover an irritating grain of sand. As the accumulations grow and become solidified, the original irritation disappears. If the murder continues to grow in size it may become too large for me to contain; then I am afraid it will kill me, just as the pearl eventually kills the oyster.

BALSO put the manuscript back into the tree and continued on his way, his head bowed in thought. The world was getting to be a difficult place for a lyric poet. He felt old. "Ah youth!" he sighed elaborately. "Ah Balso Snell!"

Suddenly he heard a voice at his elbow.

"Well, nosey, how did you like my theme?"

Balso turned and saw the boy whose diary he had been reading. He was still in short pants and looked less than twelve years old.

"Interesting psychologically, but is it art?" Balso said timidly. "I'd give you B minus and a good spanking."

"What the hell do I care about art! Do you know why I wrote that ridiculous story—because Miss McGeeney, my English teacher, reads Russian novels and I want to sleep with her. But maybe you run a magazine. Will you buy it? I need money."

"No, son, I'm a poet. I'm Balso Snell, the poet."

"A poet! For Christ's sake!"

"What you ought to do, child, is to run about more. Read less and play baseball."

"Forget it. I know a fat girl who only sleeps with poets. When I'm with her I'm a poet, too. I won her with a poem.

"O Beast of Walls!
O Walled-in Fat Girl!
Your conquest was hardly worth
the while of one whom Arras and
Arrat, Pelion, Ossa, Parnassus, Ida,
Pisgah and Pike's Peak never in-
terested.

"Not bad, eh? But I'm fed up with poetry and art. Yet what can I do. I need women and because I can't buy or force them, I have to make poems for them. God knows how tired I am of using the insanity of Van Gogh and the adventures of Gauguin as can-openers for the ambitious Count Six-Times. And how sick I am of literary bitches. But they're the only kind that'll have me. . . . Listen, Balso, for a dollar I'll sell you a brief outline of my position."

Balso gave the dollar to get rid of him and received in return a little pamphlet.

THE PAMPHLET

Yesterday, while debating whether I should shave or not, news of the death of my friend Saniette arrived. I decided not to shave.

Today, while shaving, I searched myself for yesterday's emotions. Searched, that is, the pockets of my dressing gown and the shelves of the medicine closet. Not finding anything, I looked further. I looked [first smiling, of course] into the bowels of my compassion, the depths of my being, and even into the receding vistas of my memory. I came from my search, as was to be expected, empty-handed. My "Open, oh flood gates of feeling! Empty, oh vials of passion!" made certain and immediate the defeat of my purpose.

That I failed in my search was for me a sign of my intelligence. I am [just as children choose sides to play "cops and robbers" or "Indians and cowboys"] on the side of intellect against the emotions, on the side of the brain against the heart. Nevertheless, I recognized the cardboard and tin of my position [a young man, while shaving, dismisses Death with a wave of his hand] and did not give up my search for an emotion. I marshalled all my reasons for grief [I had lived with Saniette for almost two years], yet failed to find sorrow.

Death is a very difficult thing for me to consider sincerely because I find certain precomposed judgments awaiting my method of consideration to render it absurd. No matter how I form my comment I attach to it the criticisms sentimental, satirical, formal. With these judgments there goes a series of literary associations which remove me still further from genuine feeling. The very act of recognizing Death, Love, Beauty—all the major subjects—has become, from literature and exercise, impossible.

After admitting to myself that I had failed, I tried to cover my defeat by practicing a few sneers in the bathroom mirror. I remembered that yesterday I had used Saniette's death as an excuse for not shaving and added in a loud voice, "Just as more than one friend will use the occasion of my death as an excuse for breaking an undesired appointment."

Heartened by my sneering reflection in the mirror, I pictured the death of Saniette. Hiding under the blankets of her hospital bed and invoking the aid of Mother Eddy and Doctor Coué: "I won't die! I am getting better and better. I won't die! The will is master o'er the flesh. I won't die!" Only to have Death answer: "Oh, yes you will." And she had. I made Death's triumph my own.

The inevitability of death has always given me pleasure, not because I am eager to die, but because all the Saniettes must die. When the preacher explained the one thing all men could be certain of—all must die—the King of France became angry. When death prevailed over the optimism of Saniette, she was, I am certain, surprised. The thought of Saniette's surprise pleases me, just as the King's anger must have pleased the preacher.

Only a portion of my dislike for Saniette is based on the natural antipathy pessimists feel for optimists, cowboys for Indians, cops for robbers. For a large part it consists of that equally natural antipathy felt by the performer for his audience. My relations with Saniette were exactly those of performer and audience.

While living with me, Saniette accepted my most desperate feats in somewhat the manner one watches the marvelous stunts of acrobats. Her casualness excited me so that I became more and more desperate in my performances. A tragedy with only one death is nothing in the theatre—why not two deaths? Why not a hundred? With some such idea as this in mind I exhibited my innermost organs: I wore my heart and genitals around my neck. At each exhibition I watched carefully to see how she received my performance—with a smile or with a tear. Though I exhibited myself as a clown, I wanted no mistakes to be made; I was a tragic clown.

I have forgotten the time when I could look back at an affair with a woman and remember anything but a sequence of theatrical poses—poses that I assumed, no matter how aware I was of their ridiculousness, because they were amusing. All my acting has but one purpose, the attraction of the female.

If it had been possible for me to attract by exhibiting a series of physical charms, my hatred would have been less. But I found it necessary to substitute strange conceits, wise and witty sayings, peculiar conduct, Art, for the muscles, teeth, hair, of my rivals.

All this much-exhibited intelligence is but a development of the instinct to please. My case is similar to that of a bird called the Amblyornis inornata. As his name indicates, the Inornata is a dull-colored, ugly bird. Yet the Inornata is cousin to the Bird of Paradise. Because he lacks his cousin's brilliant plumage, he has to exteriorize internal feathers. The Inornata plants a garden and builds a house of flowers as a substitute for the gay feathers of his relative. Of course the female Inornata loves her shabby artist dearly; yet when a friend passes, Mrs. Bird of Paradise can say, "Show your tail, dear," while Mrs. Inornata, to her confusion, has no explanation to give for her love. If she is in a temper she might even ask Mr. Inornata to exteriorize a few internal feathers. Still more, the Bird of Paradise cannot be blamed for the quality of his tail— it just grew. The Inornata, however, is held personally responsible for his performance as an artist.

There was a time when I felt that I was indeed a rare spirit. Then I had genuinely expressed my personality with a babe's delight in confessing the details of its inner life. Soon, however, in order to interest my listeners, I found it necessary to shorten my long out-pourings; to make them, by straining my imagination, spectacular. Oh, how much work goes into the search for the odd, the escape from the same!

Because of women like Saniette, I acquired the habit of extravagant thought. I now convert everything into fantastic entertainment and the extraordinary has become an obsession. . . . .

An intelligent man finds it easy to laugh at himself, but his laughter is not sincere if it is thorough. If I could be Hamlet, or even a clown with a breaking heart 'neath his jester's motley, the role would be tolerable. But I always find it necessary to burlesque the mystery of feeling at its source; I must laugh at myself, and if the laugh is "bitter", I must laugh at the laugh. The ritual of feeling demands bur-

lesque and, whether the burlesque is successful or not, a
laugh. . . . .

One night, while in a hotel bedroom with Saniette, I grew
miserably sick of the mad dreams I had been describing to
amuse her. I began to beat her. While beating her, I was unable to forget that strange man, John Raskolnikov Gilson, the
Russian student. As I beat her, I shouted: "O constipation of
desire! O diarrhoea of love! O life within life! O mystery of
being! O Young Women's Christian Association! Oh! Oh!"

When her screams brought the hotel clerk to our door, I
attempted to explain my irritation. In part I said: "This evening I am very nervous. I have a sty on my eye, a cold sore
on my lip, a pimple where the edge of my collar touches my
neck, another pimple in the corner of my mouth, and a drop
of salt snot on the end of my nose. Because I rub them continually my nostrils are inflamed, sore and angry.

"My forehead is wrinkled so hard that it hurts, yet I cannot
unwrinkle it. I spend many hours trying to unwrinkle my forehead. I try to catch myself by surprise; I try to smooth my
forehead with my fingers; I try to concentrate my whole mind
to this end, but I am unable to make smooth my brow. The
skin over my eyebrows is tied in an aching, unbreakable knot.

"The wood of this table, the glasses on it, this girl's woollen
dress, the skin under it, excites and annoys me. It seems to
me as though all the materials of life—wood, glass, wool,
skin—are rubbing against my sty, my cold sore and my
pimples; rubbing in such a way as not to satisfy the itch or
convert irritation into active pain, but so as to increase the
size of the irritation, magnify it and make it seem to cover
everything—hysteria, despair.

"I go to a mirror and squeeze the sty with all my strength.
I tear off the cold sore with my nails. I scrub my salt-encrusted
nostrils with the rough sleeve of my overcoat. If I could only
turn irritation into pain; could push the whole thing into insanity and so escape. I am able to turn irritation into active
pain for only a few seconds, but the pain soon subsides and
the monotonous rhythm of irritation returns. O how fleeting
is pain!—I cry. I think of sandpapering my body. I think of
grease, of sandalwood oil, of saliva; I think of velvet, of Keats,

of music, of the hardness of precious stones, of mathematics, of the arrangements of architecture. But, alas! I can find no relief."

Both Saniette and the clerk refused to understand. Saniette said that she understood the irritation I was talking about was one of the spirit; yet, she added, the only conclusion she could arrive at—a gentleman would never strike a lady—was that I no longer loved her. The clerk murmured something about the police.

In order to get him away from the door, I asked him if he had ever heard of the Marquis de Sade or of Gilles de Rais. Fortunately, we were in a Broadway hotel whose employees are familiar with the world. When I mentioned these names, the clerk bowed and left us with a smile. Saniette was also of the world; she smiled and went back to bed.

The next morning, remembering their smiles, I thought it advisable to explain my actions again. Not that it was necessary for me to differentiate between the kind of a beating alcohol inspires a temperance-cartoon drunkard to give his hard-working spouse, and the beating I had given Saniette; but, rather, that I found it difficult to illustrate the point I desired to make clear.

"When you think of me, Saniette," I said, "think of two men—myself and the chauffeur within me. This chauffeur is very large and dressed in ugly ready-made clothing. His shoes, soiled from walking about the streets of a great city, are covered with animal ordure and chewing gum. His hands are covered with coarse woollen gloves. On his head is a derby hat.

"The name of this chauffeur is The Desire to Procreate.

"He sits within me like a man in an automobile. His heels are in my bowels, his knees on my heart, his face in my brain. His gloved hands hold me firmly by the tongue; his hands, covered with wool, refuse me speech for the emotions aroused by the face in my brain.

"From within, he governs the sensations I receive through my fingers, eyes, tongue and ears.

"Can you imagine how it feels to have this cloth-covered devil within one? While naked, were you ever embraced by a fully clothed man? Do you remember how his button-covered coat felt, how his heavy shoes felt against your skin? Imagine having this man inside of you, fumbling and fingering your heart and tongue with wool-covered hands, treading your tender organs with stumbling soiled feet."

Because of the phrasing of my complaint, Saniette was able to turn my revenge into a joke. She weathered a second beating with a slow, kind smile.

Saniette represents a distinct type of audience—smart, sophisticated, sensitive yet hardboiled, art-loving frequenters of the little theatres. I am their particular kind of a performer.

Some day I shall obtain my revenge by writing a play for one of their art theatres. A theatre patronized by the discriminating few: art-lovers and book-lovers, school teachers who adore the grass-eating Shaw, sensitive young Jews who adore culture, lending librarians, publisher's assistants, homosexualists and homosexualists' assistants, hard-drinking newspaper men, interior decorators, and the writers of advertising copy.

In this play I shall take my beloved patrons into my confidence and flatter their difference from other theatre-goers. I shall congratulate them on their good taste in preferring Art to animal acts. Then, suddenly, in the midst of some very witty dialogue, the entire cast will walk to the footlights and shout Chekov's advice:

"It would be more profitable for the farmer to raise rats for the granary than for the bourgeois to nourish the artist, who must always be occupied with undermining institutions."

In case the audience should misunderstand and align itself on the side of the artist, the ceiling of the theatre will be made to open and cover the occupants with tons of loose excrement. After the deluge, if they so desire, the patrons of my art can gather in the customary charming groups and discuss the play.

WHEN he had finished reading, Balso threw the pamphlet away with a sigh. In his childhood, things had been managed differently; besides, shaving had not been permitted before the age of sixteen. Having no alternative, Balso blamed the war, the invention of printing, nineteenth-century science, communism, the wearing of soft hats, the use of contraceptives, the large number of delicatessen stores, the movies, the tabloids, the lack of adequate ventilation in large cities, the passing of the saloon, the soft collar fad, the spread of foreign art, the decline of the western world, commercialism, and, finally, for throwing the artist back on his own personality, the renaissance.

"What is beauty saith my sufferings then?" asked Balso of himself, quoting Marlowe.

As though in answer to his question, he saw standing naked before him a slim young girl busily washing her hidden charms in a public fountain. Through the wood of his brain there buzzed the saw of desire.

She called to him, saying:

"Charge, oh poet, the red-veined flowers of suddenly remembered intimacies—the foliage of memory. Feel, oh poet, the warm knife of thought swift stride and slit in the ready garden.

"Soon the hot seed will come to thwart the knife's progress. The hot seed will come in a joyous burst-birth of reeking undergrowth and swamp forest.

"Walk toward the houses of the city of your memory, oh poet! Houses that are protuberances on the skin of streets—warts, tumors, pimples, corns, nipples, sebaceous cysts, hard and soft chancres.

"Like the gums of false teeth, red are the signs imploring you to enter the game paths lit by iron flowers. Like ants under a new-turned stone, hysterical are the women who run there clad in the silk tights of pleasure, oiled with fish slime. Women whose only delight is to rub the jaded until it becomes irritated and grows new things, pimples of a . . . . "

Throwing his arms around her, Balso interrupted her recitation by sticking his tongue into her mouth. But when he closed his eyes to heighten the fun, he felt that he was embracing tweed. He opened them and saw that what he held in his arms was a middle aged woman dressed in a mannish suit and wearing hornrimmed glasses.

"My name is Miss McGeeney," she said. "I am a writer as well as a school teacher. Let's discuss something."

Balso wanted to bash her jaw in, but he found that he could not move. He tried to curse, but could only say: "How interesting. On what are you working?"

"At present I am writing a biography of Samuel Perkins. Stark, clever, disillusioned stuff, with a tenderness devoid of sentiment, yet touched by pity and laughter and irony. Into this book I hope to put the whimsical humor, the kindly satire of a mellow life.

"On the surface *Samuel Perkins: Smeller* [for so I call it] is simply a delightful story for children. The discriminating adult soon discovers, however, that it sprang from the brain of a kindly philosopher, that it is a genial satire on humanity.

"Under the title I intend placing as motto a verse from Juvenal: 'Who is surprised to see a goiter in the Alps? Quis tumidum guttur miratur in Alpibus?' I feel that this quotation strikes the keynote of the work.

"But who is Samuel Perkins, you are probably wondering. Samuel Perkins is the biographer of E. F. Fitzgerald. And who is Fitzgerald? You are of course familiar with D. B. Hobson's life of Boswell. Well, E. F. Fitzgerald is the author of a life of Hobson. The subject of my biography, Samuel Perkins, wrote a life of Fitzgerald.

"Sometime ago, a publisher asked me to write a biography, and I decided to do one of E. F. Fitzgerald. Fortunately, before commencing my study, I met Samuel Perkins who told me that he had written a biography of Fitzgerald the biographer of Hobson the biographer of Boswell. This news did not discourage me, but, on the contrary, made me determine to write a life of Perkins and so become another link in a brilliant literary chain. It seems to me that someone must surely take the hint and write the life of Miss McGeeney, the woman who wrote the biography of the man who wrote the biography of the man who wrote the biography of the man who wrote the biography of Boswell. And that, ad infinitum, we will all go rattling down the halls of time, each one in his or her turn a tin can on the tail of Doctor Johnson.

"But there are other good reasons for writing a life of Perkins. He was a great, if peculiar, genius with a character that lends itself most readily to biography.

"At an age when most men's features are regular, before his personality had been able to elevate any one portion of his physiognomy over the rest, Perkins' face was dominated by his nose. This fact I have ascertained from a collection of early photographs lent me by a profound admirer of Perkins and a fellow practitioner of his art. I refer to Robert Jones, author of a book called *Nosologie*.

"When I met Perkins for the first time, his face reminded me of the body of a man I had known at college. According to gossip current in the girl's dormitory this man abused himself. The source of these rumors lay in the peculiar shape of his body: all the veins, muscles and sinews flowed toward and converged at one point. In a like manner the wrinkles on Perkins' face, the contours of his head, the lines of his brow and chin, seemed to have melted and run into his nose.

"At this first meeting, Perkins said something that was later to prove very illuminating. He quoted Lucretius to the effect that 'his nose was quicker to scent a fetid sore or a rank armpit, than a dog to smell out the hidden sow.' Like most quotations, this one is only partially true. True, that is, of only one stage in Perkins' aesthetic development—the, what I have called quite arbitrarily, excrement period.

"It is possible to explain the powers of Perkins' magnificent sense of smell by the well-known theory of natural compensation. No-one who has ever observed the acuteness of touch exhibited by a blind man or the gigantic shoulders of a legless man, will question the fact that Nature compensates for the loss of one attribute by lavishing her bounty on another. And Nature had made in the person of Samuel Perkins another attempt at justice. He was deaf and almost blind; his fingers fumbled stupidly; his mouth was always dry and contained a dull, insensitive tongue. But his nose! His nose was a marvelously sensitive and nice instrument. Nature had concentrated in his sense of smell all the abilities usually distributed among the five senses. She had strengthened this organ and had made it so sensitive that it was able to do duty for all the contact organs. Perkins was able to translate the sensations, sound, sight, taste, and touch, into that of smell. He could smell a chord in D minor, or distinguish between the tone-smell of a violin and that of a viola. He could smell the caress of velvet and the strength of iron. It has been said of him that he could smell an isosceles triangle; I mean that he could apprehend through the sense of smell the principles involved in isosceles triangles.

"In the ability to interpret the functions of one sense in terms of another, he is not alone. A French poet, in a sonnet of the vowels, called the letter I red and the letter U blue. Another symbolist, Father Castel, made a clavichord on which he was able to play melody and harmony by using color. Des Esseintes, Huysmans' hero, used a taste organ on which he composed symphonies for the palate.

"But can you imagine, new-found friend and esteemed poet, how horrible was the predicament of this sensitive and sensuous man forced to interpret the whole external world through conclusions reached by the sense of smell alone? If we have great difficulty in discovering the Real, how much greater must his difficulty have been?

"In my presence, Perkins once called the senses a tread-mill. 'A tread-mill,' he said, 'on which one can go only from the odors of Indian-grass baskets to the sour smells of Africa and the stinks of decay.'

"Rather than a tread-mill, I should call the senses a circle. A step forward along the circumference of a circle is a step nearer the starting place. Perkins went, along the circumference of the circle of his senses, from anticipation to realization, from hunger to satiation, from naiveté to sophistication, from simplicity to perversion. He went [speaking in Perkins-esque] from the smell of new-mown hay to that of musk and vervain [from the primitive to the romantic], and from vervain to sweat and excrement [from the romantic to the realistic]; and, finally, to complete the circuit, from excrement he returned to new-mown hay.

"There is, however, a way out for the artist and Perkins

discovered it. The circumference of a circle infinite in size is a straight line. And a man like Perkins is able to make the circle of his sensory experience approach the infinite. He can so qualify the step from simplicity to perversion, for example, that the curve which makes inevitable the return to simplicity is imperceptible.

"One day Perkins told me that he was going to be married. I asked him if he thought his wife would understand him, and whether he thought he could be happy with a woman. He answered no to both questions, and said that he was marrying as an artist. I asked him to explain. He replied that the man who had numbered the smells of the human body and found them to be seven was a fool, unless the number was used in its mystic sense.

"After studying this strange conversation with the master, I discovered his meaning. He had found in the odors of a woman's body, never-ending, ever-fresh variation and change—a world of dreams, seas, roads, forests, textures, colors, flavors, forms. On my questioning him further, he confirmed my interpretation. He told me that he had built from the odors of his wife's body an architecture and an aesthetic, a music and a mathematic. Counterpoint, multiplication, the square of a sensation, the cube root of an experience—all were there. He told me that he had even discovered a politic, a hierarchy of odors: self-government, direct . . . "

By this time, Balso had gotten one of his hands free. He hit Miss McGeeney a terrific blow in the gut and hove her into the fountain.

THE WOODEN HORSE, Balso realized as he walked on, was inhabited solely by writers in search of an audience, and he was determined not to be tricked into listening to another story. If one had to be told, he would tell it.

As he hurried down the seemingly endless corridor, he began to wonder whether he would ever reach the Anus Mirabilis again. His feet hurt badly and his head ached. When he came to a café built into the side of the intestine, he sat down and ordered a glass of beer. After drinking the beer, he took a newspaper out of his pocket, put it over his face and went to sleep.

Balso dreamt that he was a young man again, lurking in a corner of the Carnegie Hall lobby among the assembled friends and relatives of music. The lobby was crowded with the many beautiful girl-cripples who congregate there because Art is their only solace, most men looking upon their strange forms with distaste. But it was otherwise with Balso Snell. He likened their disarranged hips, their short legs, their humps, their splay feet, their wall-eyes, to ornament. Their strange foreshortenings, hanging heads, bulging spinesacks, were a delight, for he had ever preferred the imperfect, knowing well the plainness, the niceness of perfection.

Spying a beautiful hunchback, he suddenly became sick with passion. The cripple of his choice looked like some creature from the depths of the sea. She was tall and extraordinarily hunched. She was tall in spite of her enormous hump; but for her dog-leg spine she would have been seven feet high. Moreover, he could be certain that, like all hunchbacks, she was intelligent.

He tipped his hat to her. She smiled and he snatched her from the throng, crying as he took her arm:

"O arabesque, I, Balso Snell, shall replace music in your affections! Your pleasures shall no longer be vicarious. No longer shall you mentally pollute yourself. For me, your sores are like flowers: the new, pink, bud-like sores, the full, rose-ripe sores, the sweet, seed-bearing sores. I shall cherish them all. O deviation from the Golden Mean! O out of alignment!"

The Lepi [for so did he instantly dub her] opened her mouth to reply and exhibited one hundred and forty-four exquisite teeth in rows of four.

"Balso," she said, "you are a villain. Do you love as do all villains?"

"No," he answered, "I love only this." As he spoke, he laid his cool white hands upon her beautiful, hydrocephalic forehead. Then, bending over her enormous hump, he kissed her full on the brow.

Feeling his lips on her forehead, Janey Davenport [the Lepi] gazed out over the blue waves of the Mediterranean and felt the delight of being young, rich, beautiful. No-one had ever before forgotten her strange shape long enough to realize how beautiful her soul was. She had never before known the thrill of being subdued by a male from a different land from that of her dreams. Now she had found a wonderful poet; now she knew the thrill she had never known before . . . had found it in the strength of this young and tall, strangely wise man, caught like herself in the meshes of the greatest net human hearts can know: Love.

Balso took her home and, in the hallway of her house, tried to seduce her. She allowed him one kiss, then broke away. From her lips—overhung by a moist eye and underhung by a heaving embonpoint—there came, "Love is a strange thing, is it not, Balso Snell?" He was afraid to laugh; he knew that if he even smiled the jig would be up. "Love," she said, "is beautiful. You, Balso, do not love. Love is sacred. How can you kiss if you do not love?" When he began to unbutton, she said with a desperately gay smile: "Would you want some one to ask of your sister what you ask of me? So this is why you invited me to dinner? I prefer music."

He made another attempt, but she fended him off. "Love," she began again, "love, with me, Mr. Snell, is sacred. I shall never debase love, or myself, or the memory of my mother, in a hallway. Act your education, Mr. Snell. Tumbling in hallways at my age! How can you? After all, there are the eternal verities, not to speak of the janitor. And besides, we were never properly introduced."

After half an hour's sparring, he managed to warm her up a bit. She held him to her tightly for a second, capsized her eyeballs, and said: "If you only loved me, Balso. If you only loved me." He looked her in the eye, stroked her hump, kissed her brow, protesting desperately: "But I do love you, Janey. I do. I do. I swear it. I must have you. I must! I must!" She shoved him away with a sad yet determined smile. "First you will have to prove your love as did the knights of old."

"I'm ready," Balso cried. "What would you have me do?"

"Come inside and I'll tell you."

Balso followed her into the apartment and sat down beside her on a couch.

"I want you to kill a man called Beagle Darwin," she said with great firmness. "He betrayed me. In this hump on my back I carry his child. After you have killed him, I shall yield up my pink and white body to you, and then commit suicide."

"A bargain," Balso said. "Give me but your stocking to wear around my hat and I'm off to earn the prize."

"Not so fast, my gallant; first I must explain a few things to you.

"After listening to Beagle Darwin recite some of his poetry, I slept with him one night while my folks were visiting friends in Plainfield, New Jersey. Unfamiliar as I was with the wiles of men, I believed him when he told me that he loved me and wanted to take me to Paris to live in an artistic studio. I was very happy until I received the following letter."

Here the Lepi went to a bureau and took out two letters, one of which she gave Balso to read.

Darling Janey:

You persist in misunderstanding me. Please understand this: It is for your own good that I am refusing to take you to Paris, as I am firmly convinced that such a trip can only result in your death.

Here is the way in which you would die:

In your pajamas, Janey, you sit near the window and listen to the gay clatter of Paris traffic. The highpitched automobile horns make of every day a holiday. You are miserable.

You tell yourself: Oh, the carnival crowds are always hurrying past my window. I'm like an old actor mumbling Macbeth as he fumbles in the garbage can outside the theatre of his past triumphs. Only I'm not old; I'm young. Young, and I never had any triumphs to mumble over; my only triumphs were those I dreamed of having. I'm Janey Davenport, pregnant, unmarried, unloved, lonely, watching the laughing crowds hurry past her window.

I don't fit into life. I don't fit into his life. He only tolerates me for my body. He only wants one thing from me, and I want, oh how I want, love.

The ridiculous, the ridiculous, all day long he talks of nothing else but how ridiculous this, that, or the other thing is. And he means me. I am absurd. He is never satisfied with calling other people ridiculous, with him everything is ridiculous—himself, me. Of course I can laugh at Mother with him, or at the Hearth; but why must my own mother and home be ridiculous? I can laugh at Hobey, Joan, but I don't want to laugh at myself. I'm tired of laugh, laugh, laugh. I want to retain some portion of myself unlaughed at. There is something in me that I won't laugh at. I won't. I'll laugh at the outside world all he wants me to, but I won't, I don't want to laugh at my inner world. It's all right for him to say: "Be hard! Be an intellectual! Think, don't feel!" But I want to be soft. I want to feel. I don't want to think. I feel blue when I think. I want to keep a hard, outside surface towards the world, and a soft, inner side for him. And I want him to do the same, so that we can be secure in each other's love. But with his rotten, ugly jokes he keeps me at arm's length just when I want to be confiding and tender. When I show him my soft side he laughs. I don't want to be always on my guard against his laughter. There are times when I want to put down my armor. I am tired of eternally bearing armor against the world. Love is a merging, not an occasion for intellectual warfare. I want to enjoy my emotions. I want, sometimes, to play the child, and to make love like a child—tenderly, confidingly, prettily. I'm sick of his taunts.

Pregnant, unmarried, and he won't marry me. If I ask him to, he will laugh his terrible horse-laugh: "Well, my little bohemian, you want to get out of it, do you? Life, however, is Life; and the Realities are the Realities. You can't have your cake and eat it too, you know." He'll tell his friends the story as a joke—one of his unexplainable jokes. All his smug-faced friends will laugh at me, especially the Paige girl.

They don't like me; I don't fit in. All my life I have been a misfit—misunderstood. The carnival crowds are always hurrying past my window. As a kid, I never liked to play in the streets with the other kids; I always wanted to stay in the house and read a book. Since my father's death, I have no one to go to with my misery. He was always willing to understand and comfort me. Oh, how I want to be understood by someone who really loves me. Mother, like Beagle, always laughs at me. If they want to be kind it is, "You silly goose!" If they are angry, "Don't be an idiot." Only father was sympathetic, and he is dead. I wish I were dead.

Joan Higgins would know what to do if she were in my position—pregnant and unmarried. Joan fits into the kind of a life he and his friends lead better than I do. Like the time Joan said she had gone back to live with Hobey because it was such a bore looking for healthy men to sleep with. Joan warned me against him; she said he wasn't my kind. I thought him just my kind, sad and a poet. He is sad, but with a nasty sadness—all jeers for his own sadness. "It's the war. Everybody is sad nowadays. Great stuff, pessimism." Still he is sad; if he would only stop acting we could be very happy together. I want so much to comfort him—mother him.

Joan's advice would probably be for me to make him marry me. How he would howl. "Make an honest girl of you, eh?"

You can see the Café Carcas from the window. You are living in the Rue de la Grande Chaumiere, at the Hotel Liberia.

Why don't I fit in well at the Carcas? Joan would go big there. Why don't they like me? I'm as good looking as she is, and as clever. It's because I don't let myself go the way she does. Well, I don't want to. There is something fine in me that won't let me degrade myself.

You see me come out of the café, laughing and waving my arms.

I hope he comes upstairs.

You see me turn, and come towards the hotel.

Just as soon as he comes in I'll tell him I'm pregnant. I'll tell him in a matter-of-fact voice—casually. As long as I keep my tone casual he won't be able to laugh.

"Hello darling, how are you this morning?"
"All right. Beagle, je suis enceinte."
"You're what?"
[Oh, damn my pronunciation, I spoilt it.] "I'm pregnant." Despite your desire to appear casual you let a note of heartbreak into your voice. You droop.
"We'll have a party tonight and celebrate." I leave the room, shutting the door behind me, carefully.
Perhaps he'll never come back . . . You run to the window—sick. You sit down and prepare to indulge your misery. Your misery, your misery—you roll, you grovel in it. I'm pregnant! I'm pregnant! I'm pregnant! You force the rhythm of this cry into your blood. After the first moments of hysterical anguish are over, you wrap your predicament around you, snuggling into it, letting it cover you completely like a blanket. Your big trouble shelters you from a host of minor troubles. You are so miserable.
You remember that "life is a prison without bars," and think of suicide.
No one ever listens to me when I talk of suicide. The night I woke up in bed with him, it was no different. He thought I was joking when I said that I had frightened myself by brooding on death. But I told the truth. Death and suicide are never far from my thoughts. I said that death is like putting on a wet bathing suit. Now death seems warm and friendly. No, death is still like putting on a wet bathing suit—shivery.
If I do it, I won't leave a note behind for him to laugh at. Just end it, that's all. No matter how I word a farewell note he will find something to laugh at—something to show his friends as a joke . . .
Mother knows I'm living with a man in Paris. Sophie wrote

that everybody is talking about me. If I were to go home—
even if I were not pregnant—mother would make an awful
stink. I don't want to go back to the States: a long dull trip
followed by a long dull life teaching elementary school.

What can I expect from him? He'll want me to have an
abortion. They say that on account of the decreasing birth
rate it is hard to get a competent doctor to do the operation.
The French police are very strict. If the doctor killed me . . .

If I kill myself, I kill my body. I don't want to destroy my
body; it is a good body—soft, white, and kind to me—a beautiful, happy body. If he were a true poet he would love me
for my body's beauty; but he is like all men; he wants only
one thing. Soon my body will be swollen and clumsy. The
milk spoils the shape of a woman's breasts after an abortion.
When my body becomes ugly, he will hate me. I once hoped
that having a child would draw him closer to me—make him
love me as a mother. But mother for him is always Mammy:
a popular Broadway ballad, Mammy, Mammy, my old Kentucky Home, put it all together, it spells Mother. He doesn't
see that Mother can mean shelter, love, intimacy. Oh, how
much I want, I need, love.

If I wanted to make a squawk, mother would force him to
marry me; but she would scold terribly and make a horrible
scene. I'm too tired and sick to go through with a shotgun
wedding.

Maybe I passed my period because of the wine—no, I know.
Where did I read, "In my belly there is a tangled forest of
arms and legs." It sounds like his stuff. When he left, he said
he'd give a party tonight in honor of the occasion. I know
what kind of a party it will be. He'll get drunk and make a
speech: "Big with child, great with young—let me toast your
gut, my dear. Here's to the pup! Waiters, stand erect while I
toast my heir." He and his friends will expect me to join in
the sport—to be a good sport.

He claims that the only place to commit suicide is on Chekov's grave. The Seine is also famous for suicide: " 'midst the
bustle of 'Gay Paree'—suicide." "She killed herself in Paris."
There is something tragic in the very thought. French windows make it easy; all you have to do is open the window and
walk out. Every window over the third floor is a door into

heaven. When I arrive there I can plead my belly—oh, how bitterly cruel the jest is. "Jest?" He would correct me—"not 'jest', my dear, but joke; never, never say 'jest'."

Oh, how miserable I am. I need love; I can't live without someone to treasure and comfort me. If I jumped from the third floor I might cripple myself—lucky this room is on the fourth. Lucky? [Animals never commit suicide.]

And mother—what would mother say? Mother would feel worse about my being unmarried than about my death. I could leave a note asking him, as a final favor, to write her and say that we were married. He would forget to write.

When I'm dead, I'll be out of it all. Mother, Beagle—they will leave me alone. But I can't blame my trouble on him. I got myself into this mess. I went to his room after he acted decently in mine. I was jealous of Joan; she had so much fun going to men's rooms, and all that sort of thing. How childish Joan and her follies seem to me now.

When I'm dead the whole world as far as I am concerned—Beagle, mother—will be dead also. Or aussi: I came to Paris to learn French. I certainly learnt French. I wasn't even able to tell him in French without turning my trouble into a joke.

What love and a child by the man I loved once meant to me—and to live in Paris. If he should come back suddenly and catch me like this, brooding at the window, he'd say: "A good chance for you to kill two birds with one stone, my dear; but remember, an egg in the belly is worth more than a bird in the bush." What a pig he is! He thinks I haven't the nerve to kill myself. He patronizes me as though I were a child. "Suicide," he says, "is a charming affectation on the part of a young Russian, but in you, dear Janey, it is absurd."

You scream with irritation: "I'm serious! I am! I am! I don't want to live! I'm miserable! I don't want to live!"

I'm only teasing myself with thoughts of suicide at an open window. I know I won't do it. Mother will call me away: "Go away from that window—fool! You'll catch your death-cold or fall out—clumsy!"

At the word "clumsy" you fall to your death in the gutter below the window.

Horrible, eh? Yes, Janey, it is a suicide's grave that I saved you from when I refused to take you to Paris.

Yours,

Beagle.

When Balso had finished reading, she handed him the other letter.

Darling Janey:

You did not take offence, I hope, at my letter. Please believe me when I say that I tried to make my treatment of your suicide as impersonal as possible. I did my best to keep the description of both our characters scientific and just. If I treated you savagely, I treated myself no gentler. It is true that I concentrated on you, but only because it was your suicide. In this letter I shall try to show, and so even the score, how I would have received your death.

You once said to me that I talk like a man in a book. I not only talk, but think and feel like one. I have spent my life in books; literature has deeply dyed my brain its own color. This literary coloring is a protective one—like the brown of the rabbit or the checks of the quail—making it impossible for me to tell where literature ends and I begin.

I start where I left off in my last letter:

As Janey's half-naked body crashed into the street, the usual crowds were hurrying to lunch from the Academies Colorossa and Grande Chaumiere; the concierge was coming out of the hotel's side door. In order to avoid running over her body, the driver of a cab coming from the Rue Notre Dame des Champs and going toward the Square de la Grande Chaumiere, brought his machine to a stop with screaming brakes. The concierge, on seeing the cab stop suddenly, one wheel over the body of a tenant of his, ran up, caught the chauffeur by the arm, and called loudly for the police. No one had seen her fall but the driver of the cab; he, bursting with rage, called the concierge an idiot, and pointed to the open window from which she had jumped. A crowd gathered around the chauffeur and shouted at him angrily. A policeman arrived. He, too, refused to believe the cab-driver, although he noticed that the dead girl was in her pajamas. "What would she be doing in the street in her night-clothes if she hadn't fallen from the window?" He shrugged his shoulders: "These American art students."

Beagle, on his way to the Café Carcas for a drink, turned to see where so many people were running. He saw the gesticulating group around the cab and went back, grateful for any diversion on what had been such a dull morning. As he joined them he kept thinking of Janey's announcement. "I'm pregnant." It reminded him of another announcement of hers. "It's about time I took a lover." "I'm pregnant" demanded for an answer, Life, just as "It's about time I took a lover" had been worthy of no less a reply than Love. She made a habit of these startling declarations: a few words, but freighted with meaning.

He knew what "I'm pregnant" meant; it meant canvassing his friends for the whereabouts of a doctor willing to perform the operation and writing frantic letters to the States for the necessary money. Through it all, Janey, having thrown the responsibility on him, would sit in one corner of the room: "Do with me what you will"—the groaning, patient, all-suffering, all-knowing, what has to be will be, beast of many burdens.

As he pushed into the crowd, someone told him a girl had been killed. He looked where the chauffeur was pointing and saw the open window of their room. Then he saw Janey under the cab; he could not see her face, but he recognized her pajamas.

This was indeed a solution. The problem had been solved for him with a vengeance. He turned away and hurried up the street, afraid of being recognized. It had become impossible for him to take his drink at the Carcas. If he went there some friend would surely come to him with the news: "Beagle! Beagle! Janey has killed herself." He wanted to go somewhere and prepare a reply. "Here today and gone tomorrow" would never do, even at the Carcas.

He went past the Carcas up the Rue Delambre to the Avenue de Maine. On this street he went into a café hardly ever visited by Americans and sat down at a table in the corner of an inside room. He called for some cognac and asked himself:

Of what assistance could I have been? Should I have gone down on my knees in the street and wept over her dead body? Torn my hair? Called on the Deity? Or should I have gone calmly up to the policeman and said: "I'm her husband. Allow me to accompany you to the morgue."

He ordered another cognac—Beagle Darwin the Destroyer. He pulled his hat down over his eyes and tossed off his drink.

She did it because she was pregnant. I would have married her, the fool. I hurt her when I made believe I didn't understand her French. "Je suis enceinte." My "what" was one of the astonishment, not the "what" of interrogation. No, it was not. You said "what" in order to humiliate her. What is the purpose of all your harping on petty affectations? Why this continual irritation at the sight of other peoples' stupidities? What of your own stupidities and affectations? Why is it impossible for you to understand, except in terms of art, her action? She killed herself because she was afraid to face her troubles—an abortion or the birth of a bastard. Absurd; she never asked you to marry her. You do not understand.

He crouched over his drink, Tiger Darwin, his eyes half shut—desperate.

I wonder if she was able to avoid generalizing before she killed herself. I am sure it was not trouble, that was uppermost in her mind, but the rag-tag of some "philosophy." Although I did my best to laugh away finita la comedia, I am certain that some such catch-word of disillusion was in her mouth when she turned the trick. She probably decided that Love, Life, Death, all could be contained in an epigram: "The things which are of value in Life are empty and rotten and trifling; Love is but a flitting shadow, a lure, a gimcrack, a kickshaw. And Death?—bah! What, then, is there still detaining you in this vale of tears?" Can it be that the only thing that bothers me in a statement of this sort is the wording? Or is it because there is something arty about suicide? Suicide: Werther, the Cosmic Urge, the Soul, the Quest; and Otto Greenbaum, Phi Beta Kappa, Age seventeen—Life is unworthy of him; and Haldington Knape, Oxford, author, man-about-town, big game hunter—Life is too tiresome; and Terry Kornflower, poet, no hat, shirt open to the navel—Life is too crude; and

Janey Davenport, pregnant, unmarried, jumps from a studio window in Paris—Life is too difficult. O. Greenbaum, H. Knape, T. Kornflower, J. Davenport, all would agree that "Life is but the span from womb to tomb; a sigh, a smile; a chill, a fever; a throe of pain, a spasm of volupty: then a gasping for breath, and the comedy is over, the song is ended, ring down the curtain, the clown is dead."

The clown is dead; the curtain is down. And when I say clown, I mean you. After all, aren't we all . . . aren't we all clowns? Of course, I know it's old stuff; but what difference does that make? Life *is* a stage; and *we* are clowns. What is more tragic than the role of clown? What more filled with all the essentials of great art?—pity and irony. Get it? The thousands of sweating, laughing, grimacing, jeering animals out front—you have just set them in the aisles, when in comes a messenger. Your wife has run away with the boarder, your son has killed a man, the baby has cancer. Or maybe you ain't married. Coming from the bathroom, you discover that you have gonorrhoea, or you get a telegram that your mother is dead, or your father, or your sister, or your brother. Now get the picture. Outside, after your turn, the customers are hollering and screaming: "Do your stuff, kid! We want Beagle! Let's have Beagle! He's a wow!" The clowns down front are laughing, whistling, belching, crying, sweating, and eating peanuts. And you—you are back-stage, hiding in the shadow of an old prop. Clutching your bursting head with both hands, you hear nothing but the dull roar of your misfortunes. Slowly there filters through your clenched fingers the cries of your brother clowns. Your first thought is to rush out there and cut your throat before their faces with a last terrific laugh. But soon you are out front again doing your stuff, the same superb Beagle: dancing, laughing, singing—*acting*. Finally the curtain comes down, and, in your dressing room before the mirror, you make the faces that won't come off with the grease paint—the faces you will never make down front.

Beagle ordered another cognac and washed it down with a small beer. The saucers had begun to pile up before him on the table.

Well, Janey's death is a joke. A young, unmarried woman

on discovering herself to be pregnant commits suicide. A very old and well-known way out of a very old and stale predicament. The moth and the candle, the fly and the spider, the butterfly and the rain, the clown and the curtain, all could be cited as having prepared one [oh how tediously!] for her suicide.

Another cognac! After this cognac, he would go to the Café Carcas and wait for a friend to bring him news of Janey's death.

How shall I receive the devastating news? In order to arouse no adverse criticism, it will be necessary for me to bear in mind that I come of an English-speaking race and therefore am cold, calm, collected, almost stolid, in the face of calamity. And, as the death is that of a very intimate friend, it is important that I show, in some subtle way, that I am hard hit for all my pretence of coldness. Or perhaps because the Carcas is full of artists, I can refuse to stop dreaming, refuse to leave my ivory tower, refuse to disturb that brooding white bird, my spirit. A wave of the hand: "Yes, really. You don't say so?—quite dead." Or I can play one of my favorite roles, be the "Buffoon of the New Eternities" and cry: "Death, what is it? Life, what is it? Life is of course the absence of Death; and Death merely the absence of Life." But I might get into an argument unbecoming one who is lamenting the loss of a loved one. For the sake of the waiters, I will be a quiet, sober, gentle, umbrella-carrying Mr. B. Darwin, and out of a great sadness sob: "Oh, my darling, why did you do it? Oh why?" Or, best of all, like Hamlet, I will feign madness; for if they discover what lies in my heart they will lynch me.

Messenger

"Beagle! Beagle! Janey has fallen from the window and is no more."

Patrons, Waiters, etc., at the Café Carcas

"The girl you lived with is dead."

"Poor Janey. Poor Beagle. Terrible, terrible death."

"And so young she was, and so beautiful . . . in the cold street she lay."

B. Hamlet Darwin

"Bromius! Iacchus! Son of Zeus!"

Patrons, Waiters, etc.

"Don't you understand, man? The girl you lived with is dead. Your sweetheart is dead. She has killed herself. She is dead!"

B. Hamlet Darwin

"Bromius! Iacchus! Son of Zeus!"

Patrons, Waiters, etc.

"He's drunk."

"Greek gods!—does he think we don't know he's a Methodist?"

"This is no time for blasphemy!"

"A little learning goes to the heads of fools."

"Yes, drink deep of the Pierian spring or . . . "

"Very picturesque though, 'Bromius! Iacchus!' very picturesque."

B. Hamlet Darwin

" 'O esca vermium! O massa pulveris!' Where is the rich Dives? He who was always eating? He is no longer even eaten."

Patrons, Waiters, etc.

"A riddle! A riddle!"

"He is looking for a friend."

"He has lost something. Tell him to look under the table."

Messenger

"He means the worms have eaten Dives; and that, in their turn dead, the worms have been eaten by other worms."

B. Hamlet Darwin

"Or quick tell me where has gone Samson?—strongest of men. He is no longer even weak. And where, oh tell me, where is the beautiful Appollon? He is no longer even ugly. And where are the snows of yesteryear? And where is Tom

Giles? Bill Taylor? Jake Holtz? In other words, 'Here today and gone tomorrow.' "

Messenger

"Yes, what he says is but too true. An incident such as the sad demise we are now considering makes one stop 'midst the hustle-bustle of our work-a-day world to ponder the words of the poet who says we are 'nourriture des vers!' Continue, dear brother in sorrow, we attend your every word."

B. Hamlet Darwin

"I shall begin all over again, folks.

"While I sit laughing with my friends, a messenger stalks into the café. He cries: 'Beagle! Beagle! Janey has killed herself!' I jump up, white as a sheet of paper, let us say, and shriek in anguish: 'Bromius! Iacchus! Son of Zeus!' You then demand why I call so loudly on Dionysius. I go into my routine.

"Dionysius! Dionysius! I call on the wine-god because his begetting and birth were so different from Janey's, so different from yours, so different from mine. I call on Dionysius in order to explain the tragedy. A tragedy that is not alone Janey's, but one that is the tragedy of all of us.

"Who among us can boast that he was born three times, as was Dionysius?—once from the womb of 'hapless Semele,' once from the thigh of Zeus, and once from the flames. Or who can say, like Christ, that he was born of a virgin? Or who can even claim to have been born as was Gargantua? Alas! none of us. Yet it is necessary for us to compete—as it was necessary for Janey to compete—with Dionysius the thrice born, Christ son of God, Gargantua born 'midst a torrent of tripe at a most memorable party. You hear the thunder, you see the lightning, you smell the forests, you drink wine—and you attempt to be as was Christ, Dionysius, Gargantua! You who were born from the womb, covered with slime and foul blood, 'midst cries of anguish and suffering.

"At your birth, instead of the Three Kings, the Dove, the Star of Bethlehem, there was only old Doctor Haasenschweitz who wore rubber gloves and carried a towel over his arm like a waiter.

"And how did the lover, your father, come to his beloved?

[After a warm day in the office he had seen two dogs in the street.] Did he come in the shape of a swan, a bull, or a shower of gold? No! But with his pants unsupported by braces, came he from the bath-room." . . .

B. Hamlet Darwin towered over his glass of cognac, and, in the theatre of his mind, over a cringing audience—tempestuous, gallant, headstrong, lovable Beagle Dionysius Hamlet Darwin. Up into his giant heart there welled a profound feeling of love for humanity. He choked with emotion as he realized the truth of his observations. Terrible indeed was the competition in which his hearers spent their lives; a competition that demanded their being more than animals.

He raised his hand as though to bless them, and the customers and waiters were silent. Gently, yet with a sense of mighty love, he murmured, "Ah my children." Then, sweeping the Café Carcas with tear-dimmed, eagle's eyes, he cried: "Yet, ah yet, are you expected to compete with Christ whose father is God, with Dionysius whose father is God; you who were Janey Davenport, or one conceived in an offhand manner on a rainy afternoon."

"Cognac! Cognac!"

After building up his tear-jerker routine for a repeat, he blacked out and went into his juggling for the curtain. He climaxed the finale by keeping in the air an Ivory Tower, a Still White Bird, the Holy Grail, the Nails, the Scourge, the Thorns, and a piece of the True Cross.

Yours,

Beagle.

W ELL, what do you think of them?"
Balso awoke and saw Miss McGeeney, the biographer of Samuel Perkins, sitting beside him at the café table.

"Think of what?"

"The two letters you just read," Miss McGeeney said impatiently. "They form part of a novel I'm writing in the manner of Richardson. Give me your candid opinion: do you think the epistolary style too old-fashioned?"

Refreshed by the nap he had taken, Balso examined his interrogator with interest. She was a fine figure of a woman. He wanted to please her and said:

"A stormy wind blows through your pages, sweeping the reader breathless . . . witchery and madness. Comparable to George Bernard Shaw. It is a drama of passion that has all the appeal of wild living and the open road. Comparable to George Bernard Shaw. There's magic in its pages, and warm strong sympathy for an alien race."

"Thank you," she said with precision.

How gracious is a woman grateful, thought Balso. He felt young again: the heel of a loaf, a piece of cheese, a bottle of wine and an apple. Clear speakers, naked in the sun. Young students: and the days are very full, and the nights burst with excitement, and life is a torrent roaring.

"Oh!" Balso exclaimed, carried away by these memories of his youth. "Oh!" His mouth formed an O with lips torn angry in laying duck's eggs from a chicken's rectum.

"Oh, what?" Miss McGeeney was obviously annoyed.

"Oh, I loved a girl once. All day she did nothing but place bits of meat on the petals of flowers. She choked the rose with butter and cake crumbs, soiling the crispness of its dainty petals with gravy and cheese. She wanted the rose to attract flies, not butterflies or bees. She wanted to make of her garden a . . . "

"Balso! Balso! Is it you?" cried Miss McGeeney, spilling what was left of his beer, much to the disgust of the waiter who hovered near.

"Balso! Balso! Is it you?" she cried again before he could answer. "Don't you recognize me? I'm Mary. Mary Mc-Geeney, your old sweetheart."

Balso realized that she was indeed Mary. Changed, alas! but with much of the old Mary left, particularly about the eyes. No longer was she dry and stick-like, but a woman, warmly moist.

They sat and devoured each other with looks until the waiter suggested that they leave as he wanted to close the place and go home.

They left arm-in-arm, walking as in a dream. Balso did the steering and they soon found themselves behind a thick clump of bushes. Miss McGeeney lay down on her back with her hands behind her head and her knees wide apart. Balso stood over her and began a speech the intent of which was obvious.

"First," he said, "let us consider the political aspect. You who talk of Liberty and cling to the protection of Dogma in the face of Life and the Army of Unutterable Physical Law, cast, I say, cast free the anchors, let go the moorings of your desires! Let to the breezes flap the standard of your revolt!

"Also we must consider the philosophical aspects of the proposed act. Nature has lent you for a brief time a few organs capable of giving pleasure. Among these are to be listed the sexual ones. The organs of sex offer in reward for their intelligent use a very intense type of pleasure. Pleasure, it is necessary to admit, is the only good. It is only reasonable to say that if pleasure is desirable—and who besides a few fanatics say it is not?—one should get all the pleasure possible. First it is important to dissociate certain commonplace ideas. As a thinking person, as an individualist—and you are both of these, are you not, love?—it is necessary to dissociate the idea of pleasure from that of generation. Furthermore, it is necessary to disregard one's unreasonable moral training. Sex, not marriage, is a sacrament. You admit it? Then why allow an ancient, inherited code to foist on you, a thinking being, the old, outmoded strictures? Sexual acts are not sins, errors, faults, weaknesses. The sexual acts give pleasure, and pleasure is desirable. So come, Mary, let us have some fun.

"And for the sake of Art, Mary. You desire to write, do you not, love? And you must admit that without knowing what all the shooting is about, a sincere artist is badly handicapped. How can you portray men if you have never known a man? How can you read and understand, see and understand, without ever having known the divine excitement? How can you hope to motivate a theft, a murder, a rape, a suicide, convincingly? And are you ever out of themes? In my bed, love, you will find new themes, new interpretations, new experiences. You will be able to judge for yourself whether love is only three minutes of rapture followed by a feeling of profound disgust, or the all-consuming fire, the divine principle, a foretaste of the joys of heaven? Come, Mary McGeeney, to bed and a new world.

"And now, finally, we come to the Time-argument. Do not confuse what I shall say under this head with the theories so much in vogue among the metaphysicians and physicists, those weavers of the wind. My 'Time' is that of the poets. In a little while, love, you will be dead; that is my burden. In a little while, we all will be dead. Golden lads and chimney-sweeps, all dead. And when dying, will you be able to say, I turn down an empty glass, having drunk to the full, lived to the full? Is it not madness to deny life? Hurry! Hurry! for all is soon over. Blown, O rose! in the morning, thou shalt fade ere noon. Do you realize the tune the clock is playing? The seconds, how they fly! All is soon over! All is soon over! Let us snatch, while yet we may, in this brief span, whose briefness merely gilds the bubble so soon destroyed, some few delights. Have you thought of the grave? O love! have you thought of the grave and of the change that shall come over your fair body? Your most beautiful bride—though now she be pleasant and sweet to the nose—will be damnably mouldy a hundred years hence. O how small a part of time they share, that are so wonderous sweet and fair. Ah, make the most of what we yet may spend before we too into the dust descend. Into the dust, Mary! Thy sweet plenty, in the dust. I tremble, I burn for thy sweet embrace. Be not miserly with thy white flesh. Give your gracious body, for such a short time lent you. Give, for in the giving you shall receive and still have what you give. Only time can rob you of your flesh, I cannot. And time will rob you—it will, it will! And those who husbanded the golden grain, and those who flung it to the wind like rain . . . "

Here Balso threw himself to the ground beside his beloved. How did she receive him? At first, by saying no.

No. No! Innocent, confused. Oh Balso! Oh Balso! with pictures of the old farm house, old pump, old folks at home, and the old oaken bucket—ivy over all.

Sir! Stamping her tiny foot—imperative, irate. Sir, how dare you, sir! Do you presume? Down, Rover, I say down! The prying thumbs of insolent chauffeurs. The queen chooses. Elizabeth of England, Catherine of Russia, Faustina of Rome.

These two noes graded into two yes-and-noes.

No . . . Oh . . . Oh, no. Eyes aswim with tears. Voice throaty, husky with repressed passion. Oh, how sweet, sweet-heart, sweetheart, sweetheart. Oh, I'm melting. My very bones are liquid. I'll swoon if you don't leave me alone. Leave me alone, I'm dizzy. No . . . No! You beast!

No: No, Balso, not tonight. No, not tonight. No! I'm sorry, Balso, but not tonight. Some other time, perhaps yes, but not tonight. Please be a dear, not tonight. Please!

But Balso would not take no for an answer, and he soon obtained the following yeses:

Allowing hot breath to escape from between moist, open lips: eyes upset, murmurs love. Tiger skin on divan. Spanish shawl on grand piano. Altar of Love. Church and Brothel. Odors of Ind and Afric. There's Egypt in your eyes. Rich, opulent love; beautiful, tapestried love; oriental, perfumed love.

Hard-bitten. Casual. Smart. Been there before. I've had policemen. No trace of a feminine whimper. Decidedly revisiting well-known, well-plowed ground. No new trees, wells, or even fences.

Desperate for life. Live! Experience! Live one's own. Your body is an instrument, an organ or a drum. Harmony. Order. Breasts. The apple of my eye, the pear of my abdomen. What is life without love? I burn! I ache! Hurrah!

Moooompitcher yaaaah. Oh I never hoped to know the passion, the sensuality hidden within you—yes, yes. Drag me down into the mire, drag. Yes! And with your hair the lust from my eyes brush. Yes . . . Yes . . . Ooh! Ah!

The miracle was made manifest. The Two became One. The

One that is all things and yet no one of them: the priest and the god, the immolation, the sacrificial rite, the libation offered to ancestors, the incantation, the sacrificial egg, the altar, the ego and the alter ego, as well as the father, the child, and the grandfather of the universe, the mystic doctrine, the purification, the syllable "Om", the path, the master, the witness, the receptacle, the Spirit of Public School 186, the last ferry that leaves for Weehawken at seven.

His body broke free of the bard. It took on a life of its own; a life that knew nothing of the poet Balso. Only to death can this release be likened—to the mechanics of decay. After death the body takes command; it performs the manual of disintegration with a marvelous certainty. So now, his body performed the evolutions of love with a like sureness.

In this activity, Home and Duty, Love and Art, were forgotten.

An army moved in his body, an eager army of hurrying sensations. These sensations marched at first methodically and then hysterically, but always with precision. The army of his body commenced a long intricate drill, a long involved ceremony. A ceremony whose ritual unwound and manoeuvred itself with the confidence and training of chemicals acting under the stimulus of a catalytic agent.

His body screamed and shouted as it marched and uncoiled; then, with one heaving shout of triumph, it fell back quiet.

The army that a moment before had been thundering in his body retreated slowly—victorious, relieved.

MISS LONELYHEARTS

TO MAX

Contents

Miss Lonelyhearts,
Help Me, Help Me

THE Miss Lonelyhearts of The New York *Post-Dispatch* (Are-you-in-trouble? — Do-you-need-advice? — Write-to-Miss-Lonelyhearts-and-she-will-help-you) sat at his desk and stared at a piece of white cardboard. On it a prayer had been printed by Shrike, the feature editor.

> *"Soul of Miss L, glorify me.*
> *Body of Miss L, nourish me.*
> *Blood of Miss L, intoxicate me.*
> *Tears of Miss L, wash me.*
> *Oh good Miss L, excuse my plea,*
> *And hide me in your heart,*
> *And defend me from mine enemies.*
> *Help me, Miss L, help me, help me.*
> *In sæcula sæculorum. Amen."*

Although the deadline was less than a quarter of an hour away, he was still working on his leader. He had gone as far as: "Life *is* worth while, for it is full of dreams and peace, gentleness and ecstasy, and faith that burns like a clear white flame on a grim dark altar." But he found it impossible to continue. The letters were no longer funny. He could not go on finding the same joke funny thirty times a day for months on end. And on most days he received more than thirty letters, all of them alike, stamped from the dough of suffering with a heart-shaped cookie knife.

On his desk were piled those he had received this morning. He started through them again, searching for some clew to a sincere answer.

Dear Miss Lonelyhearts—

I am in such pain I dont know what to do sometimes I think I will kill myself my kidneys hurt so much. My husband thinks no woman can be a good catholic and not have children irregardless of the pain. I was married honorable from our church but I never knew what married life meant as I never was told about man and wife. My grandmother never told me and she was the only mother I had but made a big mistake by not telling me as it dont pay to be inocent and is only a big disapointment. I have 7 children in 12 yrs and ever since the last 2 I have been so sick. I was operatored on twice and my husband promised no more children on the doctors advice as he said I might die but when I got back from the hospital he broke his promise and now I am going to have a baby and I dont think I can stand it my kidneys hurt so much. I am so sick and scared because I cant have an abortion on account of being a catholic and my husband so religious. I cry all the time it hurts so much and I dont know what to do.

Yours respectfully,
Sick-of-it-all

Miss Lonelyhearts threw the letter into an open drawer and lit a cigarette.

Dear Miss Lonelyhearts—
I am sixteen years old now and I dont know what to do and would appreciate it if you could tell me what to do. When I was a little girl it was not so bad because I got used to the kids on the block makeing fun of me, but now I would like to have boy friends like the other girls and go out on Saturday nites, but no boy will take me because I was born without a nose—although I am a good dancer and have a nice shape and my father buys me pretty clothes.
I sit and look at myself all day and cry. I have a big hole in the middle of my face that scares people even myself so I cant blame the boys for not wanting to take me out. My mother loves me, but she crys terrible when she looks at me.
What did I do to deserve such a terrible bad fate? Even if I did do some bad things I didnt do any before I was a year old and I was born this way. I asked Papa and he says he doesnt know, but that maybe I did something in the other world before I was born or that maybe I was being punished for his sins. I dont believe that because he is a very nice man. Ought I commit suicide?

Sincerely yours,
Desperate

The cigarette was imperfect and refused to draw. Miss Lonelyhearts took it out of his mouth and stared at it furiously. He fought himself quiet, then lit another one.

Dear Miss Lonelyhearts—

I am writing to you for my little sister Gracie because something awfull hapened to her and I am afraid to tell mother about it. I am 15 years old and Gracie is 13 and we live in Brooklyn. Gracie is deaf and dumb and biger than me but not very smart on account of being deaf and dumb. She plays on the roof of our house and dont go to school except to deaf and dumb school twice a week on tuesdays and thursdays. Mother makes her play on the roof because we dont want her to get run over as she aint very smart. Last week a man came on the roof and did something dirty to her. She told me about it and I dont know what to do as I am afraid to tell mother on account of her being lible to beat Gracie up. I am afraid that Gracie is going to have a baby and I listened to her stomack last night for a long time to see if I could hear the baby but I couldn't. If I tell mother she will beat Gracie up awfull because I am the only one who loves her and last time when she tore her dress they loked her in the closet for 2 days and if the boys on the blok hear about it they will say dirty things like they did on Peewee Conors sister the time she got caught in the lots. So please what would you do if the same hapened in your family.

Yours truly,
Harold S.

He stopped reading. Christ was the answer, but, if he did not want to get sick, he had to stay away from the Christ business. Besides, Christ was Shrike's particular joke. "Soul of Miss L, glorify me. Body of Miss L, save me. Blood of . . ." He turned to his typewriter.

Although his cheap clothes had too much style, he still looked like the son of a Baptist minister. A beard would become him, would accent his Old-Testament look. But even without a beard no one could fail to recognize the New England puritan. His forehead was high and narrow. His nose was long and fleshless. His bony chin was shaped and cleft like a hoof. On seeing him for the first time, Shrike had smiled and said, "The Susan Chesters, the Beatrice Fairfaxes and the Miss Lonelyhearts are the priests of twentieth-century America."

A copy boy came up to tell him that Shrike wanted to know if the stuff was ready. He bent over the typewriter and began pounding its keys.

But before he had written a dozen words, Shrike leaned over his shoulder. "The same old stuff," Shrike said. "Why don't you give them something new and hopeful? Tell them about art. Here, I'll dictate:

"Art Is a Way Out.

"Do not let life overwhelm you. When the old paths are choked with the débris of failure, look for newer and fresher paths. Art is just such a path. Art is distilled from suffering. As Mr. Polnikoff exclaimed through his fine Russian beard, when, at the age of eighty-six, he gave up his business to learn Chinese, 'We are, as yet, only at the beginning. . . .'

"Art Is One of Life's Richest Offerings.

"For those who have not the talent to create, there is appreciation. For those . . .

"Go on from there."

Miss Lonelyhearts
and the Dead Pan

WHEN Miss Lonelyhearts quit work, he found that the weather had turned warm and that the air smelt as though it had been artificially heated. He decided to walk to Delehanty's speakeasy for a drink. In order to get there, it was necessary to cross a little park.

He entered the park at the North Gate and swallowed mouthfuls of the heavy shade that curtained its arch. He walked into the shadow of a lamp-post that lay on the path like a spear. It pierced him like a spear.

As far as he could discover, there were no signs of spring. The decay that covered the surface of the mottled ground was not the kind in which life generates. Last year, he remembered, May had failed to quicken these soiled fields. It had taken all the brutality of July to torture a few green spikes through the exhausted dirt.

What the little park needed, even more than he did, was a drink. Neither alcohol nor rain would do. To-morrow, in his column, he would ask Broken-hearted, Sick-of-it-all, Desperate, Disillusioned-with-tubercular-husband and the rest of his correspondents to come here and water the soil with their tears. Flowers would then spring up, flowers that smelled of feet.

"Ah, humanity . . ." But he was heavy with shadow and the joke went into a dying fall. He tried to break its fall by laughing at himself.

Why laugh at himself, however, when Shrike was waiting at the speakeasy to do a much better job? "Miss Lonelyhearts, my friend, I advise you to give your readers stones. When they ask for bread don't give them crackers as does the Church, and don't, like the State, tell them to eat cake. Explain that man cannot live by bread alone and give them stones. Teach them to pray each morning: 'Give us this day our daily stone.'"

He had given his readers many stones; so many, in fact, that he had only one left—the stone that had formed in his gut.

Suddenly tired, he sat down on a bench. If he could only throw the stone. He searched the sky for a target. But the gray sky looked as if it had been rubbed with a soiled eraser. It held no angels, flaming crosses, olive-bearing doves, wheels within wheels. Only a newspaper struggled in the air like a kite with a broken spine. He got up and started again for the speakeasy.

Delehanty's was in the cellar of a brownstone house that differed from its more respectable neighbors by having an armored door. He pressed a concealed button and a little round window opened in its center. A blood-shot eye appeared, glowing like a ruby in an antique iron ring.

The bar was only half full. Miss Lonelyhearts looked around apprehensively for Shrike and was relieved at not finding him. However, after a third drink, just as he was settling into the warm mud of alcoholic gloom, Shrike caught his arm.

"Ah, my young friend!" he shouted. "How do I find you? Brooding again, I take it."

"For Christ's sake, shut up."

Shrike ignored the interruption. "You're morbid, my friend, morbid. Forget the crucifixion, remember the renaissance. There were no brooders then." He raised his glass, and the whole Borgia family was in his gesture. "I give you the renaissance. What a period! What pageantry! Drunken popes . . . Beautiful courtesans . . . Illegitimate children. . . ."

Although his gestures were elaborate, his face was blank. He practiced a trick used much by moving-picture comedians—the dead pan. No matter how fantastic or excited his speech, he never changed his expression. Under the shining white globe of his brow, his features huddled together in a dead, gray triangle.

"To the renaissance!" he kept shouting. "To the renaissance! To the brown Greek manuscripts and mistresses with the great smooth marbly limbs. . . . But that reminds me, I'm expecting one of my admirers—a cow-eyed girl of great intelligence." He illustrated the word *intelligence* by carving two enormous breasts in the air with his hands. "She works in a book store, but wait until you see her behind."

Miss Lonelyhearts made the mistake of showing his annoyance.

"Oh, so you don't care for women, eh? J. C. is your only sweetheart, eh? Jesus Christ, the King of Kings, the Miss Lonelyhearts of Miss Lonelyhearts. . . ."

At this moment, fortunately for Miss Lonelyhearts, the young woman expected by Shrike came up to the bar. She had long legs, thick ankles, big hands, a powerful body, a slender neck and a childish face made tiny by a man's haircut.

"Miss Farkis," Shrike said, making her bow as a ventriloquist does his doll, "Miss Farkis, I want you to meet Miss Lonelyhearts. Show him the same respect you show me. He, too, is a comforter of the poor in spirit and a lover of God."

She acknowledged the introduction with a masculine handshake.

"Miss Farkis," Shrike said, "Miss Farkis works in a book store and writes on the side." He patted her rump.

"What were you talking about so excitedly?" she asked.

"Religion."

"Get me a drink and please continue. I'm very much interested in the new thomistic synthesis."

This was just the kind of remark for which Shrike was waiting. "St. Thomas!" he shouted. "What do you take us for—stinking intellectuals? We're not fake Europeans. We were discussing Christ, the Miss Lonelyhearts of Miss Lonelyhearts. America has her own religions. If you need a synthesis, here is the kind of material to use." He took a clipping from his wallet and slapped it on the bar.

"ADDING MACHINE USED IN RITUAL OF WESTERN SECT . . . *Figures Will Be Used for Prayers for Condemned Slayer of Aged Recluse.* . . . DENVER, COLO., Feb. 2 (A. P.) Frank H. Rice, Supreme Pontiff of the Liberal Church of America has announced he will carry out his plan for a 'goat and adding machine' ritual for William Moya, condemned slayer, despite objection to his program by a Cardinal of the sect. Rice declared the goat would be used as part of a 'sack cloth and ashes' service shortly before and after Moya's execution, set for the week of June 20. Prayers for the condemned man's soul will be offered on an adding machine. Numbers, he explained, constitute the only universal language. Moya killed Joseph Zemp, an aged recluse, in an argument over a small amount of money."

Miss Farkis laughed and Shrike raised his fist as though to strike her. His actions shocked the bartender, who hurriedly asked them to go into the back room. Miss Lonelyhearts did not want to go along, but Shrike insisted and he was too tired to argue.

They seated themselves at a table inside one of the booths. Shrike again raised his fist, but when Miss Farkis drew back, he changed the gesture to a caress. The trick worked. She gave in to his hand until he became too daring, then pushed him away.

Shrike again began to shout and this time Miss Lonelyhearts understood that he was making a seduction speech.

"I am a great saint," Shrike cried, "I can walk on my own water. Haven't you ever heard of Shrike's Passion in the Luncheonette, or the Agony in the Soda Fountain? Then I compared the wounds in Christ's body to the mouths of a miraculous purse in which we deposit the small change of our sins. It is indeed an excellent conceit. But now let us consider the holes in our own bodies and into what these congenital wounds open. Under the skin of man is a wondrous jungle where veins like lush tropical growths hang along over-ripe organs and weed-like entrails writhe in squirming tangles of red and yellow. In this jungle, flitting from rock-gray lungs to golden intestines, from liver to lights and back to liver again, lives a bird called the soul. The Catholic hunts this bird with bread and wine, the Hebrew with a golden ruler, the Protestant on leaden feet with leaden words, the Buddhist with gestures, the Negro with blood. I spit on them all. Phooh! And I call upon you to spit. Phooh! Do you stuff birds? No, my dears, taxidermy is not religion. No! A thousand times no. Better, I say unto you, better a live bird in the jungle of the body than two stuffed birds on the library table."

His caresses kept pace with the sermon. When he had reached the end, he buried his triangular face like the blade of a hatchet in her neck.

Miss Lonelyhearts
and the Lamb

Miss Lonelyhearts went home in a taxi. He lived by himself in a room that was as full of shadows as an old steel engraving. It held a bed, a table and two chairs. The walls were bare except for an ivory Christ that hung opposite the foot of the bed. He had removed the figure from the cross to which it had been fastened and had nailed it to the wall with large spikes. But the desired effect had not been obtained. Instead of writhing, the Christ remained calmly decorative.

He got undressed immediately and took a cigarette and a copy of *The Brothers Karamazov* to bed. The marker was in a chapter devoted to Father Zossima.

"Love a man even in his sin, for that is the semblance of Divine Love and is the highest love on earth. Love all God's creation, the whole and every grain of sand in it. Love the animals, love the plants, love everything. If you love everything, you will perceive the divine mystery in things. Once you perceive it, you will begin to comprehend it better every day. And you will come at last to love the whole world with an all-embracing love."

It was excellent advice. If he followed it, he would be a big success. His column would be syndicated and the whole world would learn to love. The Kingdom of Heaven would arrive. He would sit on the right hand of the Lamb.

But seriously, he realized, even if Shrike had not made a sane view of this Christ business impossible, there would be little use in his fooling himself. His vocation was of a different sort. As a boy in his father's church, he had discovered that something stirred in him when he shouted the name of Christ, something secret and enormously powerful. He had played with this thing, but had never allowed it to come alive.

He knew now what this thing was—hysteria, a snake whose scales are tiny mirrors in which the dead world takes on a semblance of life. And how dead the world is . . . a world of doorknobs. He wondered if hysteria were really too steep a price to pay for bringing it to life.

For him, Christ was the most natural of excitements. Fixing his eyes on the image that hung on the wall, he began to chant: "Christ, Christ, Jesus Christ. Christ, Christ, Jesus Christ." But the moment the snake started to uncoil in his brain, he became frightened and closed his eyes.

With sleep, a dream came in which he found himself on the stage of a crowded theater. He was a magician who did tricks with doorknobs. At his command, they bled, flowered, spoke. After his act was finished, he tried to lead his audience in prayer. But no matter how hard he struggled, his prayer was one Shrike had taught him and his voice was that of a conductor calling stations.

"Oh, Lord, we are not of those who wash in wine, water, urine, vinegar, fire, oil, bay rum, milk, brandy, or boric acid. Oh, Lord, we are of those who wash solely in the Blood of the Lamb."

The scene of the dream changed. He found himself in his college dormitory. With him were Steve Garvey and Jud Hume. They had been arguing the existence of God from midnight until dawn, and now, having run out of whisky, they decided to go to the market for some applejack.

Their way led through the streets of the sleeping town into the open fields beyond. It was spring. The sun and the smell of vegetable birth renewed their drunkenness and they reeled between the loaded carts. The farmers took their horseplay good-naturedly. Boys from the college on a spree.

They found the bootlegger and bought a gallon jug of applejack, then wandered to the section where livestock was sold. They stopped to fool with some lambs. Jud suggested buying one to roast over a fire in the woods. Miss Lonelyhearts agreed, but on the condition that they sacrifice it to God before barbecuing it.

Steve was sent to the cutlery stand for a butcher knife, while the other two remained to bargain for a lamb. After a long, Armenian-like argument, during which Jud exhibited his farm training, the youngest was selected, a little, stiff-legged thing, all head.

They paraded the lamb through the market. Miss Lonelyhearts went first, carrying the knife, the others followed, Steve with the jug and Jud with the animal. As they marched, they sang an obscene version of "Mary Had a Little Lamb."

Between the market and the hill on which they intended to perform the sacrifice was a meadow. While going through it, they picked daisies and buttercups. Half way up the hill, they found a rock and covered it with the flowers. They laid the lamb among the flowers. Miss Lonelyhearts was elected priest, with Steve and Jud as his attendants. While they held the lamb, Miss Lonelyhearts crouched over it and began to chant.

"Christ, Christ, Jesus Christ. Christ, Christ, Jesus Christ."

When they had worked themselves into a frenzy, he brought the knife down hard. The blow was inaccurate and made a flesh wound. He raised the knife again and this time the lamb's violent struggles made him miss altogether. The knife broke on the altar. Steve and Jud pulled the animal's head back for him to saw at its throat, but only a small piece of blade remained in the handle and he was unable to cut through the matted wool.

Their hands were covered with slimy blood and the lamb slipped free. It crawled off into the underbrush.

As the bright sun outlined the altar rock with narrow shadows, the scene appeared to gather itself for some new violence. They bolted. Down the hill they fled until they reached the meadow, where they fell exhausted in the tall grass.

After some time had passed, Miss Lonelyhearts begged them to go back and put the lamb out of its misery. They refused to go. He went back alone and found it under a bush. He crushed its head with a stone and left the carcass to the flies that swarmed around the bloody altar flowers.

Miss Lonelyhearts
and the Fat Thumb

MISS LONELYHEARTS found himself developing an almost insane sensitiveness to order. Everything had to form a pattern: the shoes under the bed, the ties in the holder, the pencils on the table. When he looked out of a window, he composed the skyline by balancing one building against another. If a bird flew across this arrangement, he closed his eyes angrily until it was gone.

For a little while, he seemed to hold his own but one day he found himself with his back to the wall. On that day all the inanimate things over which he had tried to obtain control took the field against him. When he touched something, it spilled or rolled to the floor. The collar buttons disappeared under the bed, the point of the pencil broke, the handle of the razor fell off, the window shade refused to stay down. He fought back, but with too much violence, and was decisively defeated by the spring of the alarm clock.

He fled to the street, but there chaos was multiple. Broken groups of people hurried past, forming neither stars nor squares. The lamp-posts were badly spaced and the flagging was of different sizes. Nor could he do anything with the harsh clanging sound of street cars and the raw shouts of hucksters. No repeated group of words would fit their rhythm and no scale could give them meaning.

He stood quietly against a wall, trying not to see or hear. Then he remembered Betty. She had often made him feel that when she straightened his tie, she straightened much more. And he had once thought that if her world were larger, were *the* world, she might order it as finally as the objects on her dressing table.

He gave Betty's address to a cab driver and told him to hurry. But she lived on the other side of the city and by the time he got there, his panic had turned to irritation.

She came to the door of her apartment in a crisp, white linen dressing-robe that yellowed into brown at the edges. She held out both her hands to him and her arms showed round and smooth like wood that has been turned by the sea.

With the return of self-consciousness, he knew that only violence could make him supple. It was Betty, however, that he criticized. Her world was not the world and could never include the readers of his column. Her sureness was based on the power to limit experience arbitrarily. Moreover, his confusion was significant, while her order was not.

He tried to reply to her greeting and discovered that his tongue had become a fat thumb. To avoid talking, he awkwardly forced a kiss, then found it necessary to apologize.

"Too much lover's return business, I know, and I . . ." He stumbled purposely, so that she would take his confusion for honest feeling. But the trick failed and she waited for him to continue:

"Please eat dinner with me."

"I'm afraid I can't."

Her smile opened into a laugh.

She was laughing at him. On the defense, he examined her laugh for "bitterness," "sour-grapes," "a-broken-heart," "the devil-may-care." But to his confusion, he found nothing at which to laugh back. Her smile had opened naturally, not like an umbrella, and while he watched her laugh folded and became a smile again, a smile that was neither "wry," "ironical" nor "mysterious."

As they moved into the living-room, his irritation increased. She sat down on a studio couch with her bare legs under and her back straight. Behind her a silver tree flowered in the lemon wall-paper. He remained standing.

"Betty the Buddha," he said. "Betty the Buddha. You have the smug smile; all you need is the pot belly."

His voice was so full of hatred that he himself was surprised. He fidgeted for a while in silence and finally sat down beside her on the couch to take her hand.

More than two months had passed since he had sat with her on this same couch and had asked her to marry him. Then she had accepted him and they had planned their life after marriage, his job and her gingham apron, his slippers beside the fireplace and her ability to cook. He had avoided her since.

He did not feel guilty; he was merely annoyed at having been fooled into thinking that such a solution was possible.

He soon grew tired of holding hands and began to fidget again. He remembered that towards the end of his last visit he had put his hand inside her clothes. Unable to think of anything else to do, he now repeated the gesture. She was naked under her robe and he found her breast.

She made no sign to show that she was aware of his hand. He would have welcomed a slap, but even when he caught at her nipple, she remained silent.

"Let me pluck this rose," he said, giving a sharp tug. "I want to wear it in my buttonhole."

Betty reached for his brow. "What's the matter?" she asked. "Are you sick?"

He began to shout at her, accompanying his shouts with gestures that were too appropriate, like those of an old-fashioned actor.

"What a kind bitch you are. As soon as any one acts viciously, you say he's sick. Wife-torturers, rapers of small children, according to you they're all sick. No morality, only medicine. Well, I'm not sick. I don't need any of your damned aspirin. I've got a Christ complex. Humanity . . . I'm a humanity lover. All the broken bastards . . ." He finished with a short laugh that was like a bark.

She had left the couch for a red chair that was swollen with padding and tense with live springs. In the lap of this leather monster, all trace of the serene Buddha disappeared.

But his anger was not appeased. "What's the matter, sweetheart?" he asked, patting her shoulder threateningly. "Didn't you like the performance?"

Instead of answering, she raised her arm as though to ward off a blow. She was like a kitten whose soft helplessness makes one ache to hurt it.

"What's the matter?" he demanded over and over again. "What's the matter? What's the matter?"

Her face took on the expression of an inexperienced gambler about to venture all on a last throw. He was turning for his hat, when she spoke.

"I love you."

"You what?"

The need for repeating flustered her, yet she managed to keep her manner undramatic.

"I love you."

"And I love you," he said. "You and your damned smiling through tears."

"Why don't you let me alone?" She had begun to cry. "I felt swell before you came, and now I feel lousy. Go away. Please go away."

Miss Lonelyhearts
and the Clean Old Man

IN THE STREET again, Miss Lonelyhearts wondered what to do next. He was too excited to eat and afraid to go home. He felt as though his heart were a bomb, a complicated bomb that would result in a simple explosion, wrecking the world without rocking it.

He decided to go to Delehanty's for a drink. In the speakeasy, he discovered a group of his friends at the bar. They greeted him and went on talking. One of them was complaining about the number of female writers.

"And they've all got three names," he said. "Mary Roberts Wilcox, Ella Wheeler Catheter, Ford Mary Rinehart. . . ."

Then some one started a train of stories by suggesting that what they all needed was a good rape.

"I knew a gal who was regular until she fell in with a group and went literary. She began writing for the little magazines about how much Beauty hurt her and dished the boy friend who set up pins in a bowling alley. The guys on the block got sore and took her into the lots one night. About eight of them. They ganged her proper. . . ."

"That's like the one they tell about another female writer. When this hard-boiled stuff first came in, she dropped the trick English accent and went in for scram and lam. She got to hanging around with a lot of mugs in a speak, gathering material for a novel. Well, the mugs didn't know they were picturesque and thought she was regular until the barkeep put them wise. They got her into the back room to teach her a new word and put the boots to her. They didn't let her out for three days. On the last day they sold tickets to niggers. . . ."

Miss Lonelyhearts stopped listening. His friends would go on telling these stories until they were too drunk to talk. They were aware of their childishness, but did not know how else to revenge themselves. At college, and perhaps for a year afterwards, they had believed in literature, had believed in Beauty and in personal expression as an absolute end. When they lost this belief, they lost everything. Money and fame meant nothing to them. They were not worldly men.

Miss Lonelyhearts drank steadily. He was smiling an innocent, amused smile, the smile of an anarchist sitting in the movies with a bomb in his pocket. If the people around him only knew what was in his pocket. In a little while he would leave to kill the President.

Not until he heard his own name mentioned did he stop smiling and again begin to listen.

"He's a leper licker. Shrike says he wants to lick lepers. Barkeep, a leper for the gent."

"If you haven't got a leper, give him a Hungarian."

"Well, that's the trouble with his approach to God. It's too damn literary—plain song, Latin poetry, medieval painting, Huysmans, stained-glass windows and crap like that."

"Even if he were to have a genuine religious experience, it would be personal and so meaningless, except to a psychologist."

"The trouble with him, the trouble with all of us, is that we have no outer life, only an inner one, and that by necessity."

"He's an escapist. He wants to cultivate his interior garden. But you can't escape, and where is he going to find a market for the fruits of his personality? The Farm Board is a failure."

"What I say is, after all one has to earn a living. We can't all believe in Christ, and what does the farmer care about art? He takes his shoes off to get the warm feel of the rich earth between his toes. You can't take your shoes off in church."

Miss Lonelyhearts had again begun to smile. Like Shrike, the man they imitated, they were machines for making jokes. A button machine makes buttons, no matter what the power used, foot, steam or electricity. They, no matter what the motivating force, death, love or God, made jokes.

"Was their nonsense the only barrier?" he asked himself. "Had he been thwarted by such a low hurdle?"

The whisky was good and he felt warm and sure. Through the light-blue tobacco smoke, the mahogany bar shone like wet gold. The glasses and bottles, their high lights exploding, rang like a battery of little bells when the bartender touched them together. He forgot that his heart was a bomb to remember an incident of his childhood. One winter evening, he had been waiting with his little sister for their father to come home from church. She was eight years old then, and he was twelve. Made sad by the pause between playing and eating, he had gone to the piano and had begun a piece by Mozart. It was the first time he had ever voluntarily gone to the piano. His sister left her picture book to dance to his music. She had never danced before. She danced gravely and carefully, a simple dance yet formal. . . . As Miss Lonelyhearts stood at the bar, swaying slightly to the remembered music, he thought of children dancing. Square replacing oblong and being replaced by circle. Every child, everywhere; in the whole world there was not one child who was not gravely, sweetly dancing.

He stepped away from the bar and accidentally collided with a man holding a glass of beer. When he turned to beg the man's pardon, he received a punch in the mouth. Later he found himself at a table in the back room, playing with a loose tooth. He wondered why his hat did not fit and discovered a lump on the back of his head. He must have fallen. The hurdle was higher than he had thought.

His anger swung in large drunken circles. What in Christ's name was this Christ business? And children gravely dancing? He would ask Shrike to be transferred to the sports department.

Ned Gates came in to see how he was getting along and suggested the fresh air. Gates was also very drunk. When they left the speakeasy together, they found that it was snowing.

Miss Lonelyhearts' anger grew cold and sodden like the snow. He and his companion staggered along with their heads down, turning corners at random, until they found themselves in front of the little park. A light was burning in the comfort station and they went in to warm up.

An old man was sitting on one of the toilets. The door of his booth was propped open and he was sitting on the turned-down toilet cover.

Gates hailed him. "Well, well, smug as a bug in a rug, eh?"

The old man jumped with fright, but finally managed to speak. "What do you want? Please let me alone." His voice was like a flute; it did not vibrate.

"If you can't get a woman, get a clean old man," Gates sang.

The old man looked as if he were going to cry, but suddenly laughed instead. A terrible cough started under his laugh, and catching at the bottom of his lungs, it ripped into his throat. He turned away to wipe his mouth.

Miss Lonelyhearts tried to get Gates to leave, but he refused to go without the old man. They both grabbed him and pulled him out of the stall and through the door of the comfort station. He went soft in their arms and started to giggle. Miss Lonelyhearts fought off a desire to hit him.

The snow had stopped falling and it had grown very cold. The old man did not have an overcoat, but said that he found the cold exhilarating. He carried a cane and wore gloves because, as he said, he detested red hands.

Instead of going back to Delehanty's, they went to an Italian cellar close by the park. The old man tried to get them to drink coffee, but they told him to mind his own business and drank rye. The whisky burned Miss Lonelyhearts' cut lip.

Gates was annoyed by the old man's elaborate manners. "Listen, you," he said, "cut out the gentlemanly stuff and tell us the story of your life."

The old man drew himself up like a little girl making a muscle.

"Aw, come off," Gates said. "We're scientists. He's Havelock Ellis and I'm Krafft-Ebing. When did you first discover homosexualistic tendencies in yourself?"

"What do you mean, sir? I . . ."

"Yeh, I know, but how about your difference from other men?"

"How dare you . . ." He gave a little scream of indignation.

"Now, now," Miss Lonelyhearts said, "he didn't mean to insult you. Scientists have terribly bad manners. . . . But you are a pervert, aren't you?"

The old man raised his cane to strike him. Gates grabbed it from behind and wrenched it out of his hand. He began to cough violently and held his black satin tie to his mouth. Still coughing he dragged himself to a chair in the back of the room.

Miss Lonelyhearts felt as he had felt years before, when he had accidentally stepped on a small frog. Its spilled guts had

filled him with pity, but when its suffering had become real
to his senses, his pity had turned to rage and he had beaten
it frantically until it was dead.

"I'll get the bastard's life story," he shouted, and started
after him. Gates followed laughing.

At their approach, the old man jumped to his feet. Miss
Lonelyhearts caught him and forced him back into his chair.

"We're psychologists," he said. "We want to help you.
What's your name?"

"George B. Simpson."

"What does the B stand for?"

"Bramhall."

"Your age, please, and the nature of your quest?"

"By what right do you ask?"

"Science gives me the right."

"Let's drop it," Gates said. "The old fag is going to cry."

"No, Krafft-Ebing, sentiment must never be permitted to
interfere with the probings of science."

Miss Lonelyhearts put his arm around the old man. "Tell
us the story of your life," he said, loading his voice with
sympathy.

"I have no story."

"You must have. Every one has a life story."

The old man began to sob.

"Yes, I know, your tale is a sad one. Tell it, damn you, tell
it."

When the old man still remained silent, he took his arm and
twisted it. Gates tried to tear him away, but he refused to let
go. He was twisting the arm of all the sick and miserable,
broken and betrayed, inarticulate and impotent. He was twisting the arm of Desperate, Broken-hearted, Sick-of-it-all, Disillusioned-with-tubercular-husband.

The old man began to scream. Somebody hit Miss Lonelyhearts from behind with a chair.

Miss Lonelyhearts
and Mrs. Shrike

MISS LONELYHEARTS lay on his bed fully dressed, just as he had been dumped the night before. His head ached and his thoughts revolved inside the pain like a wheel within a wheel. When he opened his eyes, the room, like a third wheel, revolved around the pain in his head.

From where he lay he could see the alarm clock. It was half past three. When the telephone rang, he crawled out of the sour pile of bed clothes. Shrike wanted to know if he intended to show up at the office. He answered that he was drunk but would try to get there.

He undressed slowly and took a bath. The hot water made his body feel good, but his heart remained a congealed lump of icy fat. After drying himself, he found a little whisky in the medicine chest and drank it. The alcohol warmed only the lining of his stomach.

He shaved, put on a clean shirt and a freshly pressed suit and went out to get something to eat. When he had finished his second cup of scalding coffee, it was too late for him to go to work. But he had nothing to worry about, for Shrike would never fire him. He made too perfect a butt for Shrike's jokes. Once he had tried to get fired by recommending suicide in his column. All that Shrike had said was: "Remember, please, that your job is to increase the circulation of our paper. Suicide, it is only reasonable to think, must defeat this purpose."

He paid for his breakfast and left the cafeteria. Some exercise might warm him. He decided to take a brisk walk, but he soon grew tired and when he reached the little park, he slumped down on a bench opposite the Mexican War obelisk.

The stone shaft cast a long, rigid shadow on the walk in front of him. He sat staring at it without knowing why until he noticed that it was lengthening in rapid jerks, not as shadows usually lengthen. He grew frightened and looked up quickly at the monument. It seemed red and swollen in the dying sun, as though it were about to spout a load of granite seed.

He hurried away. When he had regained the street, he started to laugh. Although he had tried hot water, whisky, coffee, exercise, he had completely forgotten sex. What he really needed was a woman. He laughed again, remembering that at college all his friends had believed intercourse capable of steadying the nerves, relaxing the muscles and clearing the blood.

But he knew only two women who would tolerate him. He had spoiled his chances with Betty, so it would have to be Mary Shrike.

When he kissed Shrike's wife, he felt less like a joke. She returned his kisses because she hated Shrike. But even there Shrike had beaten him. No matter how hard he begged her to give Shrike horns, she refused to sleep with him.

Although Mary always grunted and upset her eyes, she would not associate what she felt with the sexual act. When he forced this association, she became very angry. He had been convinced that her grunts were genuine by the change that took place in her when he kissed her heavily. Then her body gave off an odor that enriched the synthetic flower scent she used behind her ears and in the hollows of her neck. No similar change ever took place in his own body, however. Like a dead man, only friction could make him warm or violence make him mobile.

He decided to get a few drinks and then call Mary from Delehanty's. It was quite early and the speakeasy was empty. The bartender served him and went back to his newspaper.

On the mirror behind the bar hung a poster advertising a mineral water. It showed a naked girl made modest by the mist that rose from the spring at her feet. The artist had taken a great deal of care in drawing her breasts and their nipples stuck out like tiny red hats.

He tried to excite himself into eagerness by thinking of the play Mary made with her breasts. She used them as the coquettes of long ago had used their fans. One of her tricks was to wear a medal low down on her chest. Whenever he asked to see it, instead of drawing it out she leaned over for him to look. Although he had often asked to see the medal, he had not yet found out what it represented.

But the excitement refused to come. If anything, he felt colder than before he had started to think of women. It was not his line. Nevertheless, he persisted in it, out of desperation, and went to the telephone to call Mary.

"Is that you?" she asked, then added before he could reply, "I must see you at once. I've quarreled with him. This time I'm through."

She always talked in headlines and her excitement forced him to be casual. "O.K.," he said. "When? Where?"

"Anywhere. I'm through with that skunk, I tell you, I'm through."

She had quarreled with Shrike before and he knew that in return for an ordinary number of kisses, he would have to listen to an extraordinary amount of complaining.

"Do you want to meet me here, in Delehanty's?" he asked.

"No, you come here. We'll be alone and anyway I have to bathe and get dressed."

When he arrived at her place, he would probably find Shrike there with her on his lap. They would both be glad to see him and all three of them would go to the movies where Mary would hold his hand under the seat.

He went back to the bar for another drink, then bought a quart of Scotch and took a cab. Shrike opened the door. Although he had expected to see him, he was embarrassed and tried to cover his confusion by making believe that he was extremely drunk.

"Come in, come in, homebreaker," Shrike said with a laugh. "The Mrs. will be out in a few minutes. She's in the tub."

Shrike took the bottle he was carrying and pulled its cork. Then he got some charged water and made two highballs.

"Well," Shrike said, lifting his drink, "so you're going in for this kind of stuff, eh? Whisky and the boss's wife."

Miss Lonelyhearts always found it impossible to reply to him. The answers he wanted to make were too general and began too far back in the history of their relationship.

"You're doing field work, I take it," Shrike said. "Well, don't put this whisky on your expense account. However, we like to see a young man with his heart in his work. You've been going around with yours in your mouth."

Miss Lonelyhearts made a desperate attempt to kid back. "And you," he said, "you're an old meanie who beats his wife."

Shrike laughed, but too long and too loudly, then broke off with an elaborate sigh. "Ah, my lad," he said, "you're wrong. It's Mary who does the beating."

He took a long pull at his highball and sighed again, still more elaborately. "My good friend, I want to have a heart-to-heart talk with you. I adore heart-to-heart talks and nowadays there are so few people with whom one can really talk. Everybody is so hard-boiled. I want to make a clean breast of matters, a nice clean breast. It's better to make a clean breast of matters than to let them fester in the depths of one's soul."

While talking, he kept his face alive with little nods and winks that were evidently supposed to inspire confidence and to prove him a very simple fellow.

"My good friend, your accusation hurts me to the quick. You spiritual lovers think that you alone suffer. But you are mistaken. Although my love is of the flesh flashy, I too suffer. It's suffering that drives me into the arms of the Miss Farkises of this world. Yes, I suffer."

Here the dead pan broke and pain actually crept into his voice. "She's selfish. She's a damned selfish bitch. She was a virgin when I married her and has been fighting ever since to remain one. Sleeping with her is like sleeping with a knife in one's groin."

It was Miss Lonelyhearts' turn to laugh. He put his face close to Shrike's and laughed as hard as he could.

Shrike tried to ignore him by finishing as though the whole thing were a joke.

"She claims that I raped her. Can you imagine Willie Shrike, wee Willie Shrike, raping any one? I'm like you, one of those grateful lovers."

Mary came into the room in her bathrobe. She leaned over Miss Lonelyhearts and said: "Don't talk to that pig. Come with me and bring the whisky."

As he followed her into the bedroom, he heard Shrike slam the front door. She went into a large closet to dress. He sat on the bed.

"What did that swine say to you?"

"He said you were selfish, Mary—sexually selfish."

"Of all the god-damned nerve. Do you know why he lets me go out with other men? To save money. He knows that I let them neck me and when I get home all hot and bothered, why he climbs into my bed and begs for it. The cheap bastard!"

She came out of the closet wearing a black lace slip and began to fix her hair in front of the dressing table. Miss Lonely-hearts bent down to kiss the back of her neck.

"Now, now," she said, acting kittenish, "you'll muss me."

He took a drink from the whisky bottle, then made her a highball. When he brought it to her, she gave him a kiss, a little peck of reward.

"Where'll we eat?" she asked. "Let's go where we can dance. I want to be gay."

They took a cab to a place called El Gaucho. When they entered, the orchestra was playing a Cuban rhumba. A waiter dressed as a South-American cowboy led them to a table. Mary immediately went Spanish and her movements became languorous and full of abandon.

But the romantic atmosphere only heightened his feeling of icy fatness. He tried to fight it by telling himself that it was childish. What had happened to his great understanding heart? Guitars, bright shawls, exotic foods, outlandish costumes—all these things were part of the business of dreams. He had learned not to laugh at the advertisements offering to teach writing, cartooning, engineering, to add inches to the biceps and to develop the bust. He should therefore realize that the people who came to El Gaucho were the same as those who wanted to write and live the life of an artist, wanted to be an engineer and wear leather puttees, wanted to develop a grip that would impress the boss, wanted to cushion Raoul's head on their swollen breasts. They were the same people as those who wrote to Miss Lonelyhearts for help.

But his irritation was too profound for him to soothe it in this way. For the time being, dreams left him cold, no matter how humble they were.

"I like this place," Mary said. "It's a little fakey, I know, but it's gay and I so want to be gay."

She thanked him by offering herself in a series of formal, impersonal gestures. She was wearing a tight, shiny dress that was like glass-covered steel and there was something cleanly mechanical in her pantomime.

"Why do you want to be gay?"

"Every one wants to be gay—unless they're sick."

Was he sick? In a great cold wave, the readers of his column crashed over the music, over the bright shawls and picturesque waiters, over her shining body. To save himself, he asked to see the medal. Like a little girl helping an old man to cross the street, she leaned over for him to look into the neck of her dress. But before he had a chance to see anything, a waiter came up to the table.

"The way to be gay is to make other people gay," Miss Lonelyhearts said. "Sleep with me and I'll be one gay dog."

The defeat in his voice made it easy for her to ignore his request and her mind sagged with his. "I've had a tough time," she said. "From the beginning, I've had a tough time. When I was a child, I saw my mother die. She had cancer of the breast and the pain was terrible. She died leaning over a table."

"Sleep with me," he said.

"No, let's dance."

"I don't want to. Tell me about your mother."

"She died leaning over a table. The pain was so terrible that she climbed out of bed to die."

Mary leaned over to show how her mother had died and he made another attempt to see the medal. He saw that there was a runner on it, but was unable to read the inscription.

"My father was very cruel to her," she continued. "He was a portrait painter, a man of genius, but . . ."

He stopped listening and tried to bring his great understanding heart into action again. Parents are also part of the business of dreams. My father was a Russian prince, my father was a Piute Indian chief, my father was an Australian sheep baron, my father lost all his money in Wall Street, my father was a portrait painter. People like Mary were unable to do without such tales. They told them because they wanted to talk about something besides clothing or business or the movies, because they wanted to talk about something poetic.

When she had finished her story, he said, "You poor kid," and leaned over for another look at the medal. She bent to help him and pulled out the neck of her dress with her fingers. This time he was able to read the inscription: "Awarded by the Boston Latin School for first place in the 100 yd. dash."

It was a small victory, yet it greatly increased his fatigue and he was glad when she suggested leaving. In the cab, he again begged her to sleep with him. She refused. He kneaded her body like a sculptor grown angry with his clay, but there was too much method in his caresses and they both remained cold.

At the door of her apartment, she turned for a kiss and pressed against him. A spark flared up in his groin. He refused to let go and tried to work this spark into a flame. She pushed his mouth away from a long wet kiss.

"Listen to me," she said. "We can't stop talking. We must talk. Willie probably heard the elevator and is listening behind the door. You don't know him. If he doesn't hear us talk, he'll know you're kissing me and open the door. It's an old trick of his."

He held her close and tried desperately to keep the spark alive.

"Don't kiss my lips," she begged. "I must talk."

He kissed her throat, then opened her dress and kissed her breasts. She was afraid to resist or to stop talking.

"My mother died of cancer of the breast," she said in a brave voice, like a little girl reciting at a party. "She died leaning over a table. My father was a portrait painter. He led a very gay life. He mistreated my mother. She had cancer of the breast. She . . ." He tore at her clothes and she began to mumble and repeat herself. Her dress fell to her feet and he tore away her underwear until she was naked under her fur coat. He tried to drag her to the floor.

"Please, please," she begged, "he'll come out and find us."

He stopped her mouth with a long kiss.

"Let me go, honey," she pleaded, "maybe he's not home. If he isn't, I'll let you in."

He released her. She opened the door and tiptoed in, carrying her rolled up clothes under her coat. He heard her switch on the light in the foyer and knew that Shrike had not been behind the door. Then he heard footsteps and limped behind a projection of the elevator shaft. The door opened and Shrike looked into the corridor. He had on only the top of his pajamas.

Miss Lonelyhearts
on a Field Trip

IT WAS cold and damp in the city room the next day, and Miss Lonelyhearts sat at his desk with his hands in his pockets and his legs pressed together. A desert, he was thinking, not of sand, but of rust and body dirt, surrounded by a back-yard fence on which are posters describing the events of the day. Mother slays five with ax, slays seven, slays nine. . . . Babe slams two, slams three. . . . Inside the fence Desperate, Broken-hearted, Disillusioned-with-tubercular-husband and the rest were gravely forming the letters MISS LONELYHEARTS out of white-washed clam shells, as if decorating the lawn of a rural depot.

He failed to notice Goldsmith's waddling approach until a heavy arm dropped on his neck like the arm of a deadfall. He freed himself with a grunt. His anger amused Goldsmith, who smiled, bunching his fat cheeks like twin rolls of smooth pink toilet paper.

"Well, how's the drunkard?" Goldsmith asked, imitating Shrike.

Miss Lonelyhearts knew that Goldsmith had written the column for him yesterday, so he hid his annoyance to be grateful.

"No trouble at all," Goldsmith said. "It was a pleasure to read your mail." He took a pink envelope out of his pocket and threw it on the desk. "From an admirer." He winked, letting a thick gray lid down slowly and luxuriously over a moist, rolling eye.

Miss Lonelyhearts picked up the letter.

Dear Miss Lonelyhearts—
I am not very good at writing so I wonder if I could have a talk with you. I am only 32 years old but have had a lot of trouble in my life and am unhappily married to a cripple. I need some good advice bad but cant state my case in a letter as I am not good at letters and it would take an expert to state my case. I know your a man and am glad as I dont trust women. You

86

were pointed out to me in Delehantys as the man who does the advice in the paper and the minute I saw you I said you can help me. You had on a blue suit and a gray hat when I came in with my husband who is a cripple.

I dont feel so bad about asking to see you personal because I feel almost like I knew you. So please call me up at Burgess 7-7323 which is my number as I need your advice bad about my married life.

An admirer,
Fay Doyle

He threw the letter into the waste-paper basket with a great show of distaste.

Goldsmith laughed at him. "How now, Dostoievski?" he said. "That's no way to act. Instead of pulling the Russian by recommending suicide, you ought to get the lady with child and increase the potential circulation of the paper."

To drive him away, Miss Lonelyhearts made believe that he was busy. He bent over his typewriter and started pounding out his column.

"Life, for most of us, seems a terrible struggle of pain and heartbreak, without hope or joy. Oh, my dear readers, it only seems so. Every man, no matter how poor or humble, can teach himself to use his senses. See the cloud-flecked sky, the foam-decked sea. . . . Smell the sweet pine and heady privet. . . . Feel of velvet and of satin. . . . As the popular song goes, 'The best things in life are free.' Life is . . .''

He could not go on with it and turned again to the imagined desert where Desperate, Broken-hearted and the others were still building his name. They had run out of sea shells and were using faded photographs, soiled fans, time-tables, playing cards, broken toys, imitation jewelry—junk that memory had made precious, far more precious than anything the sea might yield.

He killed his great understanding heart by laughing, then reached into the waste-paper basket for Mrs. Doyle's letter. Like a pink tent, he set it over the desert. Against the dark mahogany desk top, the cheap paper took on rich flesh tones. He thought of Mrs. Doyle as a tent, hair-covered and veined, and of himself as the skeleton in a water closet, the skull and crossbones on a scholar's bookplate. When he made the skeleton enter the flesh tent, it flowered at every joint.

But despite these thoughts, he remained as dry and cold as a polished bone and sat trying to discover a moral reason for not calling Mrs. Doyle. If he could only believe in Christ, then adultery would be a sin, then everything would be simple and the letters extremely easy to answer.

The completeness of his failure drove him to the telephone. He left the city room and went into the hall to use the pay station from which all private calls had to be made. The walls of the booth were covered with obscene drawings. He fastened his eyes on two disembodied genitals and gave the operator Burgess 7-7323.

"Is Mrs. Doyle in?"

"Hello, who is it?"

"I want to speak to Mrs. Doyle," he said. "Is this Mrs. Doyle?"

"Yes, that's me." Her voice was hard with fright.

"This is Miss Lonelyhearts."

"Miss who?"

"Miss Lonelyhearts, Miss Lonelyhearts, the man who does the column."

He was about to hang up, when she cooed, "Oh, hello. . . ."

"You said I should call."

"Oh, yes . . . what?"

He guessed that she wanted him to do the talking. "When can you see me?"

"Now." She was still cooing and he could almost feel her warm, moisture-laden breath through the earpiece.

"Where?"

"You say."

"I'll tell you what," he said. "Meet me in the park, near the obelisk, in about an hour."

He went back to his desk and finished his column, then started for the park. He sat down on a bench near the obelisk to wait for Mrs. Doyle. Still thinking of tents, he examined the sky and saw that it was canvas-colored and ill-stretched. He examined it like a stupid detective who is searching for a clew to his own exhaustion. When he found nothing, he turned his trained eye on the skyscrapers that menaced the little park from all sides. In their tons of forced rock and tortured steel, he discovered what he thought was a clew.

Americans have dissipated their racial energy in an orgy of stone breaking. In their few years they have broken more stones than did centuries of Egyptians. And they have done their work hysterically, desperately, almost as if they knew that the stones would some day break them.

The detective saw a big woman enter the park and start in his direction. He made a quick catalogue: legs like Indian clubs, breasts like balloons and a brow like a pigeon. Despite her short plaid skirt, red sweater, rabbit-skin jacket and knitted tam-o'-shanter, she looked like a police captain.

He waited for her to speak first.

"Miss Lonelyhearts? Oh, hello . . ."

"Mrs. Doyle?" He stood up and took her arm. It felt like a thigh.

"Where are we going?" she asked, as he began to lead her off.

"For a drink."

"I can't go to Delehanty's. They know me."

"We'll go to my place."

"Ought I?"

He did not have to answer, for she was already on her way. As he followed her up the stairs to his apartment, he watched the action of her massive hams; they were like two enormous grindstones.

He made some highballs and sat down beside her on the bed.

"You must know an awful lot about women from your job," she said with a sigh, putting her hand on his knee.

He had always been the pursuer, but now found a strange pleasure in having the rôles reversed. He drew back when she reached for a kiss. She caught his head and kissed him on his mouth. At first it ticked like a watch, then the tick softened and thickened into a heart throb. It beat louder and more rapidly each second, until he thought that it was going to explode and pulled away with a rude jerk.

"Don't," she begged.

"Don't what?"

"Oh, darling, turn out the light."

He smoked a cigarette, standing in the dark and listening to her undress. She made sea sounds; something flapped like a sail; there was the creak of ropes; then he heard the wave-against-a-wharf smack of rubber on flesh. Her call for him to hurry was a sea-moan, and when he lay beside her, she heaved, tidal, moon-driven.

Some fifteen minutes later, he crawled out of bed like an exhausted swimmer leaving the surf, and dropped down into a large armchair near the window. She went into the bathroom, then came back and sat in his lap.

"I'm ashamed of myself," she said. "You must think I'm a bad woman."

He shook his head no.

"My husband isn't much. He's a cripple like I wrote you, and much older than me." She laughed. "He's all dried up. He hasn't been a husband to me for years. You know, Lucy, my kid, isn't his."

He saw that she expected him to be astonished and did his best to lift his eyebrows.

"It's a long story," she said. "It was on account of Lucy that I had to marry him. I'll bet you must have wondered how it was I came to marry a cripple. It's a long story."

Her voice was as hypnotic as a tom-tom, and as monotonous. Already his mind and body were half asleep.

"It's a long, long story, and that's why I couldn't write it in a letter. I got into trouble when the Doyles lived above us on Center Street. I used to be kind to him and go to the movies with him because he was a cripple, although I was one of the most popular girls on the block. So when I got into trouble, I didn't know what to do and asked him for the money for an abortion. But he didn't have the money, so we got married instead. It all came through my trusting a dirty dago. I thought he was a gent, but when I asked him to marry me, why he spurned me from the door and wouldn't even give me money for an abortion. He said if he gave me the money that would mean it was his fault and I would have something on him. Did you ever hear of such a skunk?"

"No," he said. The life out of which she spoke was even

heavier than her body. It was as if a gigantic, living Miss Lonely-hearts letter in the shape of a paper weight had been placed on his brain.

"After the baby was born, I wrote the skunk, but he never wrote back, and about two years ago, I got to thinking how unfair it was for Lucy to have to depend on a cripple and not come into her rights. So I looked his name up in the tele-phone book and took Lucy to see him. As I told him then, not that I wanted anything for myself, but just that I wanted Lucy to get what was coming to her. Well, after keeping us waiting in the hall over an hour—I was boiling mad, I can tell you, thinking of the wrong he had done me and my child—we were taken into the parlor by the butler. Very quiet and lady-like, because money ain't everything and he's no more a gent than I'm a lady, the dirty wop—I told him he ought to do something for Lucy see'n' he's her father. Well, he had the nerve to say that he had never seen me before and that if I didn't stop bothering him, he'd have me run in. That got me riled and I lit into the bastard and gave him a piece of my mind. A woman came in while we were arguing that I figured was his wife, so I hollered, 'He's the father of my child, he's the father of my child.' When they went to the 'phone to call a cop, I picked up the kid and beat it.

"And now comes the funniest part of the whole thing. My husband is a queer guy and he always makes believe that he is the father of the kid and even talks to me about *our* child. Well, when we got home, Lucy kept asking me why I said a strange man was her papa. She wanted to know if Doyle wasn't really her papa. I must of been crazy because I told her that she should remember that her real papa was a man named Tony Benelli and that he had wronged me. I told her a lot of other crap like that—too much movies I guess. Well, when Doyle got home the first thing Lucy says to him is that he ain't her papa. That got him sore and he wanted to know what I had told her. I didn't like his high falutin' ways and said, 'The truth.' I guess too that I was kinda sick of see'n him moon over her. He went for me and hit me one on the cheek. I wouldn't let no man get away with that so I socked back and he swung at me with his stick but missed and fell on the floor and started to cry. The kid was on the floor crying too and that set me off because the next thing I know I'm on the floor bawling too."

She waited for him to comment, but he remained silent until she nudged him into speech with her elbow. "Your husband probably loves you and the kid," he said.

"Maybe so, but I was a pretty girl and could of had my pick. What girl wants to spend her life with a shrimp of a cripple?"

"You're still pretty," he said without knowing why, except that he was frightened.

She rewarded him with a kiss, then dragged him to the bed.

Miss Lonelyhearts
in the Dismal Swamp

SOON AFTER Mrs. Doyle left, Miss Lonelyhearts became physically sick and was unable to leave his room. The first two days of his illness were blotted out by sleep, but on the third day, his imagination began again to work.

He found himself in the window of a pawnshop full of fur coats, diamond rings, watches, shotguns, fishing tackle, mandolins. All these things were the paraphernalia of suffering. A tortured high light twisted on the blade of a gift knife, a battered horn grunted with pain.

He sat in the window thinking. Man has a tropism for order. Keys in one pocket, change in another. Mandolins are tuned G D A E. The physical world has a tropism for disorder, entropy. Man against Nature . . . the battle of the centuries. Keys yearn to mix with change. Mandolins strive to get out of tune. Every order has within it the germ of destruction. All order is doomed, yet the battle is worth while.

A trumpet, marked to sell for $2.49, gave the call to battle and Miss Lonelyhearts plunged into the fray. First he formed a phallus of old watches and rubber boots, then a heart of umbrellas and trout flies, then a diamond of musical instruments and derby hats, after these a circle, triangle, square, swastika. But nothing proved definitive and he began to make a gigantic cross. When the cross became too large for the pawnshop, he moved it to the shore of the ocean. There every wave added to his stock faster than he could lengthen its arms. His labors were enormous. He staggered from the last wave line to his work, loaded down with marine refuse—bottles, shells, chunks of cork, fish heads, pieces of net.

Drunk with exhaustion, he finally fell asleep. When he awoke, he felt very weak, yet calm.

There was a timid knock on the door. It was open and Betty tiptoed into the room with her arms full of bundles. He made believe that he was asleep.

"Hello," he said suddenly.

Startled, she turned to explain. "I heard you were sick, so I brought some hot soup and other stuff."

He was too tired to be annoyed by her wide-eyed little mother act and let her feed him with a spoon. When he had finished eating, she opened the window and freshened the bed. As soon as the room was in order, she started to leave, but he called her back.

"Don't go, Betty."

She pulled a chair to the side of his bed and sat there without speaking.

"I'm sorry about what happened the other day," he said. "I guess I was sick."

She showed that she accepted his apology by helping him to excuse himself. "It's the Miss Lonelyhearts job. Why don't you give it up?"

"And do what?"

"Work in an advertising agency, or something."

"You don't understand, Betty, I can't quit. And even if I were to quit, it wouldn't make any difference. I wouldn't be able to forget the letters, no matter what I did."

"Maybe I don't understand," she said, "but I think you're making a fool of yourself."

"Perhaps I can make you understand. Let's start from the beginning. A man is hired to give advice to the readers of a newspaper. The job is a circulation stunt and the whole staff considers it a joke. He welcomes the job, for it might lead to a gossip column, and anyway he's tired of being a leg man. He too considers the job a joke, but after several months at it, the joke begins to escape him. He sees that the majority of the letters are profoundly humble pleas for moral and spiritual advice, that they are inarticulate expressions of genuine suffering. He also discovers that his correspondents take him seriously. For the first time in his life, he is forced to examine the values by which he lives. This examination shows him that he is the victim of the joke and not its perpetrator."

Although he had spoken soberly, he saw that Betty still thought him a fool. He closed his eyes.

"You're tired," she said. "I'll go."

"No, I'm not tired. I'm just tired of talking, you talk a while."

She told him about her childhood on a farm and of her love for animals, about country sounds and country smells and of how fresh and clean everything in the country is. She said that he ought to live there and that if he did, he would find that all his troubles were city troubles.

While she was talking, Shrike burst into the room. He was drunk and immediately set up a great shout, as though he believed that Miss Lonelyhearts was too near death to hear distinctly. Betty left without saying good-by.

Shrike had evidently caught some of her farm talk, for he said: "My friend, I agree with Betty, you're an escapist. But I do not agree that the soil is the proper method for you to use."

Miss Lonelyhearts turned his face to the wall and pulled up the covers. But Shrike was unescapable. He raised his voice and talked through the blankets into the back of Miss Lonely-hearts' head.

"There are other methods, and for your edification I shall describe them. But first let us do the escape to the soil, as recommended by Betty:

"You are fed up with the city and its teeming millions. The ways and means of men, as getting and lending and spending, you lay waste your inner world, are too much with you. The bus takes too long, while the subway is always crowded. So what do you do? So you buy a farm and walk behind your horse's moist behind, no collar or tie, plowing your broad swift acres. As you turn up the rich black soil, the wind carries the smell of pine and dung across the fields and the rhythm of an old, old work enters your soul. To this rhythm, you sow and weep and chivy your kine, not kin or kind, between the pregnant rows of corn and taters. Your step becomes the heavy sexual step of a dance-drunk Indian and you tread the seed down into the female earth. You plant, not dragon's teeth, but beans and greens. . . .

"Well, what do you say, my friend, shall it be the soil?"

Miss Lonelyhearts did not answer. He was thinking of how Shrike had accelerated his sickness by teaching him to handle his one escape, Christ, with a thick glove of words.

"I take your silence to mean that you have decided against

the soil. I agree with you. Such a life is too dull and laborious. Let us now consider the South Seas:

"You live in a thatch hut with the daughter of the king, a slim young maiden in whose eyes is an ancient wisdom. Her breasts are golden speckled pears, her belly a melon, and her odor is like nothing so much as a jungle fern. In the evening, on the blue lagoon, under the silvery moon, to your love you croon in the soft sylabelew and vocabelew of her langorour tongorour. Your body is golden brown like hers, and tourists have need of the indignant finger of the missionary to point you out. They envy you your breech clout and carefree laugh and little brown bride and fingers instead of forks. But you don't return their envy, and when a beautiful society girl comes to your hut in the night, seeking to learn the secret of your happiness, you send her back to her yacht that hangs on the horizon like a nervous racehorse. And so you dream away the days, fishing, hunting, dancing, swimming, kissing, and picking flowers to twine in your hair. . . .

"Well, my friend, what do you think of the South Seas?"

Miss Lonelyhearts tried to stop him by making believe that he was asleep. But Shrike was not fooled.

"Again silence," he said, "and again you are right. The South Seas are played out and there's little use in imitating Gauguin. But don't be discouraged, we have only scratched the surface of our subject. Let us now examine Hedonism, or take the cash and let the credit go. . . .

"You dedicate your life to the pursuit of pleasure. No over-indulgence, mind you, but knowing that your body is a pleasure machine, you treat it carefully in order to get the most out of it. Golf as well as booze, Philadelphia Jack O'Brien and his chestweights as well as Spanish dancers. Nor do you neglect the pleasures of the mind. You fornicate under pictures by Matisse and Picasso, you drink from Renaissance glassware, and often you spend an evening beside the fireplace with Proust and an apple. Alas, after much good fun, the day comes when you realize that soon you must die. You keep a stiff upper lip and decide to give a last party. You invite all your old mistresses, trainers, artists and boon companions. The guests are dressed in black, the waiters are coons, the table is a coffin carved for you by Eric Gill. You serve caviar and blackberries and licorice candy and coffee without cream. After the dancing girls have finished, you get to your feet and call for silence in order to explain your philosophy of life. 'Life,' you say, 'is a club where they won't stand for squawks, where they deal you only one hand and you must sit in. So even if the cards are cold and marked by the hand of fate, play up, play up like a gentleman and a sport. Get tanked, grab what's on the buffet, use the girls upstairs, but remember, when you throw box cars, take the curtain like a dead game sport, don't squawk'. . . .

"I won't even ask you what you think of such an escape. You haven't the money, nor are you stupid enough to manage it. But we come now to one that should suit you much better. . . .

"Art! Be an artist or a writer. When you are cold, warm yourself before the flaming tints of Titian, when you are hungry, nourish yourself with great spiritual foods by listening to the noble periods of Bach, the harmonies of Brahms and the thunder of Beethoven. Do you think there is anything in the fact that their names all begin with B? But don't take a chance, smoke a 3 B pipe, and remember these immortal lines: *When to the suddenness of melody the echo parting falls the failing day.* What a rhythm! Tell them to keep their society whores and pressed duck with oranges. For you *l'art vivant*, the living art, as you call it. Tell them that you know that your shoes are broken and that there are pimples on your face, yes, and that you have buck teeth and a club foot, but that you don't care, for to-morrow they are playing Beethoven's last quartets in Carnegie Hall and at home you have Shakespeare's plays in one volume."

After art, Shrike described suicide and drugs. When he had finished with them, he came to what he said was the goal of his lecture.

"My friend, I know of course that neither the soil, nor the South Seas, nor Hedonism, nor art, nor suicide, nor drugs, can mean anything to us. We are not men who swallow camels only to strain at stools. God alone is our escape. The church is our only hope, the First Church of Christ Dentist, where He is worshiped as Preventer of Decay. The church whose symbol is the trinity new-style: Father, Son and Wire-haired

Fox Terrier. . . . And so, my good friend, let me dictate a letter to Christ for you:

Dear Miss Lonelyhearts of Miss Lonelyhearts—

I am twenty-six years old and in the newspaper game. Life for me is a desert empty of comfort. I cannot find pleasure in food, drink, or women—nor do the arts give me joy any longer. The Leopard of Discontent walks the streets of my city; the Lion of Discouragement crouches outside the walls of my citadel. All is desolation and a vexation of the spirit. I feel like hell. How can I believe, how can I have faith in this day and age? Is it true that the greatest scientists believe again in you?

I read your column and like it very much. There you once wrote: "When the salt has lost its savour, who shall savour it again?" Is the answer: "None but the Saviour?"

Thanking you very much for a quick reply, I remain yours truly,

A Regular Subscriber

Miss Lonelyhearts
in the Country

BETTY came to see Miss Lonelyhearts the next day and every day thereafter. With her she brought soup and boiled chicken for him to eat.

He knew that she believed he did not want to get well, yet he followed her instructions because he realized that his present sickness was unimportant. It was merely a trick by his body to relieve one more profound.

Whenever he mentioned the letters or Christ, she changed the subject to tell long stories about life on a farm. She seemed to think that if he never talked about these things, his body would get well, that if his body got well everything would be well. He began to realize that there was a definite plan behind her farm talk, but could not guess what it was.

When the first day of spring arrived, he felt better. He had already spent more than a week in bed and was anxious to get out. Betty took him for a walk in the zoo and he was amused by her evident belief in the curative power of animals. She seemed to think that it must steady him to look at a buffalo.

He wanted to go back to work, but she made him get Shrike to extend his sick leave a few days. He was grateful to her and did as she asked. She then told him her plan. Her aunt still owned the farm in Connecticut on which she had been born and they could go there and camp in the house.

She borrowed an old Ford touring car from a friend. They loaded it with food and equipment and started out early one morning. As soon as they reached the outskirts of the city, Betty began to act like an excited child, greeting the trees and grass with delight.

After they had passed through New Haven, they came to Bramford and turned off the State highway on a dirt road that led to Monkstown. The road went through a wild-looking stretch of woods and they saw some red squirrels and a partridge. He had to admit, even to himself that the pale new leaves, shaped and colored like candle flames, were beautiful and that the air smelt clean and alive.

There was a pond on the farm and they caught sight of it through the trees just before coming to the house. She did not have the key so they had to force the door open. The heavy, musty smell of old furniture and wood rot made them cough. He complained. Betty said that she did not mind because it was not a human smell. She put so much meaning into the word "human" that he laughed and kissed her.

They decided to camp in the kitchen because it was the largest room and the least crowded with old furniture. There were four windows and a door and they opened them all to air the place out.

While he unloaded the car, she swept up and made a fire in the stove out of a broken chair. The stove looked like a locomotive and was almost as large, but the chimney drew all right and she soon had a fire going. He got some water from the well and put it on the stove to boil. When the water was scalding hot, they used it to clean an old mattress that they had found in one of the bedrooms. Then they put the mattress out in the sun to dry.

It was almost sundown before Betty would let him stop working. He sat smoking a cigarette, while she prepared supper. They had beans, eggs, bread, fruit and drank two cups of coffee apiece.

After they had finished eating, there was still some light left and they went down to look at the pond. They sat close together with their backs against a big oak and watched a heron hunt frogs. Just as they were about to start back, two deer and a fawn came down to the water on the opposite side of the pond. The flies were bothering them and they went into the water and began to feed on the lily pads. Betty accidentally made a noise and the deer floundered back into the woods.

When they returned to the house, it was quite dark. They lit the kerosene lamp that they had brought with them, then dragged the mattress into the kitchen and made their bed on the floor next to the stove.

Before going to bed, they went out on the kitchen porch to smoke a last cigarette. It was very cold and he had to go back for a blanket. They sat close together with the blanket wrapped around them.

There were plenty of stars. A screech owl made a horrible

racket somewhere in the woods and when it quit, a loon began down on the pond. The crickets made almost as much
noise as the loon.

Even with the blanket around them it was cold. They went
inside and made a big fire in the stove, using pieces of a hard-
wood table to make the fire last. They each ate an apple, then
put on their pajamas and went to bed. He fondled her, but
when she said that she was a virgin, he let her alone and went
to sleep.

He woke up with the sun in his eyes. Betty was already busy
at the stove. She sent him down to the pond to wash and
when he got back, breakfast was ready. It consisted of eggs,
ham, potatoes, fried apples, bread and coffee.

After breakfast, she worked at making the place more comfortable and he drove to Monkstown for some fresh fruit and
the newspapers. He stopped for gas at the Aw-Kum-On Garage and told the attendant about the deer. The man said that
there was still plenty of deer at the pond because no yids ever
went there. He said it wasn't the hunters who drove out the
deer, but the yids.

He got back to the house in time for lunch and, after eating, they went for a walk in the woods. It was very sad under
the trees. Although spring was well advanced, in the deep
shade there was nothing but death—rotten leaves, gray and
white fungi, and over everything a funereal hush.

Later it grew very hot and they decided to go for a swim.
They went in naked. The water was so cold that they could
only stay in for a short time. They ran back to the house and
took a quick drink of gin, then sat in a sunny spot on the
kitchen porch.

Betty was unable to sit still for long. There was nothing to
do in the house, so she began to wash the underwear she had
worn on the trip up. After she had finished, she rigged a line
between two trees.

He sat on the porch and watched her work. She had her
hair tied up in a checked handkerchief, otherwise she was
completely naked. She looked a little fat, but when she lifted
something to the line, all the fat disappeared. Her raised arms
pulled her breasts up until they were like pink-tipped thumbs.

There was no wind to disturb the pull of the earth. The

new green leaves hung straight down and shone in the hot sun like an army of little metal shields. Somewhere in the woods a thrush was singing. Its sound was like that of a flute choked with saliva.

Betty stopped with her arms high to listen to the bird. When it was quiet, she turned towards him with a guilty laugh. He blew her a kiss. She caught it with a gesture that was childishly sexual. He vaulted the porch rail and ran to kiss her. As they went down, he smelled a mixture of sweat, soap and crushed grass.

Miss Lonelyhearts Returns

SEVERAL DAYS later, they started to drive back to the city. When they reached the Bronx slums, Miss Lonelyhearts knew that Betty had failed to cure him and that he had been right when he had said that he could never forget the letters. He felt better, knowing this, because he had begun to think himself a faker and a fool.

Crowds of people moved through the street with a dream-like violence. As he looked at their broken hands and torn mouths he was overwhelmed by the desire to help them, and because this desire was sincere, he was happy despite the feeling of guilt which accompanied it.

He saw a man who appeared to be on the verge of death stagger into a movie theater that was showing a picture called *Blonde Beauty.* He saw a ragged woman with an enormous goiter pick a love story magazine out of a garbage can and seem very excited by her find.

Prodded by his conscience, he began to generalize. Men have always fought their misery with dreams. Although dreams were once powerful, they have been made puerile by the movies, radio and newspapers. Among many betrayals, this one is the worst.

The thing that made his share in it particularly bad was that he was capable of dreaming the Christ dream. He felt that he had failed at it, not so much because of Shrike's jokes or his own self-doubt, but because of his lack of humility.

He finally got to bed. Before falling asleep, he vowed to make a sincere attempt to be humble. In the morning, when he started for his office, he renewed his vow.

Fortunately for him, Shrike was not in the city room and his humility was spared an immediate trial. He went straight to his desk and began to open letters. When he had opened about a dozen, he felt sick and decided to do his column for that day without reading any of them. He did not want to test himself too severely.

The typewriter was uncovered and he put a sheet of paper into the roller.

"Christ died for you.

"He died nailed to a tree for you. His gift to you is suffering and it is only through suffering that you can know Him. Cherish this gift, for . . ."

He snatched the paper out of the machine. With him, even the word Christ was a vanity. After staring at the pile of letters on his desk for a long time, he looked out the window. A slow spring rain was changing the dusty tar roofs below him to shiny patent leather. The water made everything slippery and he could find no support for either his eyes or his feelings.

Turning back to his desk, he picked up a bulky letter in a dirty envelope. He read it for the same reason that an animal tears at a wounded foot: to hurt the pain.

Dear Miss Lonelyhearts:—

Being an admirer of your column because you give such good advice to people in trouble as that is what I am in also I would appreciate very much your advising me what to do after I tell you my troubles.

During the war I was told if I wanted to do my bit I should marry the man I was engaged to as he was going away to help Uncle Sam and to make a long story short I was married to him. After the war was over he still had to remain in the army for one more year as he signed for it and naturaly I went to work as while doing this patriotic stunt he had only $18 dollars to his name. I worked for three years steady and then had to stay home because I became a mother and in the meantime of those years my husband would get a job and then would tire of it or want to roam. It was all right before the baby came because then I could work steady and then bills were paid but when I stopped everything went sliding backward. Then two years went by and a baby boy was added to our union. My girl will be eight and my boy six years of age.

I made up my mind after I had the second child that in spite of my health as I was hit by an auto while carrying the first I would get some work to do but debts collected so rapidly it almost took a derick to lift them let alone a sick woman. I went to work evenings when my husband would be home so as somebody could watch the baby and I did this until the baby was three years old when I thought of taking in a man who had been boarding with *his sister as she moved to Rochester and he had to look for a new place. Well my husband agreed as he figured the $15 dollars per he paid us would make it easier for him as this man was a widower with two children and as my husband knew him for twelve years being real pals then going out together etc. After the boarder was with us for about a year my husband didn't come home one night and then two nights etc. I listed him in the missing persons and after two and a half months I was told to go to Grove St. which I did and he was arrested because he refused to support me and my kids. When he served three months of the six the judge asked me to give him another chance which like a fool I did and when he got home he beat me up so I had to spend over $30 dollars in the dentist afterwards.*

He got a pension from the army and naturaly I was the one to take it to the store and cash it as he was so lazy I always had to sign his name and of course put per my name and through wanting to pay the landlord because he wanted to put us out I signed his check as usual but forgot to put per my name and for this to get even with me because he did three months time he sent to Washington for the copy of the check so I could be arrested for forgery but as the butcher knew about me signing the checks etc nothing was done to me.

He threatened my life many times saying no one solved the Mrs. Mills murder and the same will happen to you and many times when making beds I would find under his pillow a hammer, scissors, knife, stone lifter etc and when I asked him what the idea was he would make believe he knew nothing about it or say the children put them there and then a few months went buy and I was going to my work as usual as the boarder had to stay home that day due to the fact the material for his boss did not arrive and he could not go to work as he is a piece worker. I always made a habit of setting the breakfast and cooking the food the night before so I could stay in bed until seven as at that time my son was in the Kings County hospital with a disease which my husband gave me that he got while fighting for Uncle Sam and I had to be at the clinic for the needle to. So while I was in bed unbeknown to me my husband sent the boarder out for a paper and when he came back my husband was gone. So later when I came from my room I was told that my husband had gone out. I fixed the childs breakfast and ate my own then

*went to the washtub to do the weeks wash and while the boarder
was reading the paper at twelve o'clock noon my mother came
over to mind the baby as I had a chance to go out and make a
little money doing house work. Things were a little out of order
beds not dressed and things out of place and a little sweeping
had to be done as I was washing all morning and I didn't have
a chance to do it so I thought to do it then while my mother was
in the house with her to help me so that I could finish quickly.
Hurrying at break neck speed to get finished I swept through the
rooms to make sure everything was spick and span so when my
husband came home he couldn't have anything to say. We had
three beds and I was on the last which was a double bed when
stooping to put the broom under the bed to get at the lint and
the dust when lo and behold I saw a face like the mask of a devil
with only the whites of the eyes showing and hands clenched to
choke anyone and then I saw it move and I was so frighted that
almost till night I was hystirical and I was paralised from my
waist down. I thought I would never be able to walk again. A
doctor was called for me by my mother and he said the man
ought to be put in an asylum to do a thing like that. It was my
husband lieing under the bed from seven in the morning until
almost half past one o'clock lieing in his own dirt instead of
going to the bath room when he had to he dirtied himself waiting
to fright me.*

*So as I could not trust him I would not sleep with him and
as I told the boarder to find a new place because I thought maybe
he was jealous of something I slept in the boarders bed in an
other room. Some nights I would wake up and find him standing
by my bed laughing like a crazy man or walking around
stripped etc.*

*I bought a new sowing machine as I do some sowing for other
people to make both ends meet and one night while I was out
delivering my work I got back to find the house cleaned out and
he had pawned my sowing machine and also all the other pawn-
ables in the house. Ever since he frighted me I have been so nervous during the night when I get up for the children that he
would be standing behind a curtain and either jump out at me
or put his hand on me before I could light the light. Well as I
had to see that I could not make him work steady and that
I had to be mother and housekeeper and wage earner etc and I*

could not let my nerves get the best of me as I lost a good job once on account of having bad nerves I simply moved away from him and anyway there was nothing much left in the house. But he pleaded with me for another chance so I thought seeing he is the father of my children I will and then he did more crazy things to many to write and I left him again. Four times we got together and four times I left. Please Miss Lonelyhearts believe me just for the childrens sake is the bunk and pardon me because I dont know how you are fixed but all I know is that in over three years I got $200 dollars from him altogether.

About four months ago I handed him a warrant for his arrest for non support and he tore it up and left the house and I havent seen him since and as I had pneumonia and my little girl had the flu I was put in financial embarasment with the doctor and we had to go to the ward and when we came out of the hospital I had to ask the boarder to come to live with us again as he was a sure $15 dollars a week and if anything happened to me he would be there to take care of the children. But he tries to make me be bad and as there is nobody in the house when he comes home drunk on Saturday night I dont know what to do but so far I didnt let him. Where my husband is I dont know but I received a vile letter from him where he even accused his inocent children of things and sarcasticaly asked about the star boarder.

Dear Miss Lonelyhearts please dont be angry at me for writing such a long letter and taking up so much of your time in reading it but if I ever write all the things which happened to me living with him it would fill a book and please forgive me for saying some nasty things as I had to give you an idea of what is going on in my home. Every woman is intitiled to a home isnt she? So Miss Lonelyhearts please put a few lines in your column when you refer to this letter so I will know you are helping me. Shall I take my husband back? How can I support my children?

Thanking you for anything you can advise me in I remain yours truly—

Broad Shoulders

P.S. Dear Miss Lonelyhearts dont think I am broad shouldered but that is the way I feel about life and me I mean.

Miss Lonelyhearts
and the Cripple

M ISS LONELYHEARTS dodged Betty because she made
him feel ridiculous. He was still trying to cling to his
humility, and the farther he got below self-laughter, the easier
it was for him to practice it. When Betty telephoned, he refused to answer and after he had twice failed to call her back,
she left him alone.

One day, about a week after he had returned from the country, Goldsmith asked him out for a drink. When he accepted,
he made himself so humble that Goldsmith was frightened
and almost suggested a doctor.

They found Shrike in Delehanty's and joined him at the
bar. Goldsmith tried to whisper something to him about Miss
Lonelyhearts' condition, but he was drunk and refused to listen. He caught only part of what Goldsmith was trying to say.

"I must differ with you, my good Goldsmith," Shrike said.
"Don't call sick those who have faith. They are the well. It is
you who are sick."

Goldsmith did not reply and Shrike turned to Miss Lonelyhearts. "Come, tell us, brother, how it was that you first came
to believe. Was it music in a church, or the death of a loved
one, or, mayhap, some wise old priest?"

The familiar jokes no longer had any effect on Miss Lonelyhearts. He smiled at Shrike as the saints are supposed to have
smiled at those about to martyr them.

"Ah, but how stupid of me," Shrike continued. "It was the
letters, of course. Did I myself not say that the Miss Lonelyhearts are the priests of twentieth-century America?"

Goldsmith laughed, and Shrike, in order to keep him laughing, used an old trick; he appeared to be offended. "Goldsmith, you are the nasty product of this unbelieving age. You
cannot believe, you can only laugh. You take everything with
a bag of salt and forget that salt is the enemy of fire as well
as of ice. Be warned, the salt you use is not Attic salt, it is
coarse butcher's salt. It doesn't preserve; it kills."

The bartender who was standing close by, broke in to address Miss Lonelyhearts. "Pardon me, sir, but there's a gent here named Doyle who wants to meet you. He says you know his wife."

Before Miss Lonelyhearts could reply, he beckoned to someone standing at the other end of the bar. The signal was answered by a little cripple, who immediately started in their direction. He used a cane and dragged one of his feet behind him in a box-shaped shoe with a four-inch sole. As he hobbled along, he made many waste motions, like those of a partially destroyed insect.

The bartender introduced the cripple as Mr. Peter Doyle. Doyle was very excited and shook hands twice all around, then with a wave that was meant to be sporting, called for a round of drinks.

Before lifting his glass, Shrike carefully inspected the cripple. When he had finished, he winked at Miss Lonelyhearts and said, "Here's to humanity." He patted Doyle on the back. "Mankind, mankind . . ." he sighed, wagging his head sadly. "What is man that . . ."

The bartender broke in again on behalf of his friend and tried to change the conversation to familiar ground. "Mr. Doyle inspects meters for the gas company."

"And an excellent job it must be," Shrike said. "He should be able to give us the benefit of a different viewpoint. We newspapermen are limited in many ways and I like to hear both sides of a case."

Doyle had been staring at Miss Lonelyhearts as though searching for something, but he now turned to Shrike and tried to be agreeable. "You know what people say, Mr. Shrike?"

"No, my good man, what is it that people say?"

"Everybody's got a frigidaire nowadays, and they say that we meter inspectors take the place of the iceman in the stories." He tried, rather diffidently, to leer.

"What!" Shrike roared at him. "I can see, sir, that you are not the man for us. You can know nothing about humanity; you are humanity. I leave you to Miss Lonelyhearts." He called to Goldsmith and stalked away.

The cripple was confused and angry. "Your friend is a nut," he said. Miss Lonelyhearts was still smiling, but the character of his smile had changed. It had become full of sympathy and a little sad.

The new smile was for Doyle and he knew it. He smiled back gratefully.

"Oh, I forgot," Doyle said, "the wife asked me, if I bumped into you, to ask you to our house to eat. That's why I made Jake introduce us."

Miss Lonelyhearts was busy with his smile and accepted without thinking of the evening he had spent with Mrs. Doyle. The cripple felt honored and shook hands for a third time. It was evidently his only social gesture.

After a few more drinks, when Doyle said that he was tired, Miss Lonelyhearts suggested that they go into the back room. They found a table and sat opposite each other.

The cripple had a very strange face. His eyes failed to balance; his mouth was not under his nose; his forehead was square and bony; and his round chin was like a forehead in miniature. He looked like one of those composite photographs used by screen magazines in guessing contests.

They sat staring at each other until the strain of wordless communication began to excite them both. Doyle made vague, needless adjustments to his clothing. Miss Lonelyhearts found it very difficult to keep his smile steady.

When the cripple finally labored into speech, Miss Lonelyhearts was unable to understand him. He listened hard for a few minutes and realized that Doyle was making no attempt to be understood. He was giving birth to groups of words that lived inside of him as things, a jumble of the retorts he had meant to make when insulted and the private curses against fate that experience had taught him to swallow.

Like a priest, Miss Lonelyhearts turned his face slightly away. He watched the play of the cripple's hands. At first they conveyed nothing but excitement, then gradually they became pictorial. They lagged behind to illustrate a matter with which he was already finished, or ran ahead to illustrate something he had not yet begun to talk about. As he grew more articulate, his hands stopped trying to aid his speech and began to dart in and out of his clothing. One of them suddenly emerged from a pocket of his coat, dragging some sheets of letter paper. He forced these on Miss Lonelyhearts.

Dear Miss Lonelyhearts—

I am kind of ashamed to write you because a man like me dont take stock in things like that but my wife told me you were a man and not some dopey woman so I thought I would write to you after reading your answer to Disillusioned. I am a cripple 41 yrs of age which I have been all my life and I have never let myself get blue until lately when I have been feeling lousy all the time on account of not getting anywhere and asking myself what is it all for. You have a education so I figured may be you no. What I want to no is why I go around pulling my leg up and down stairs reading meters for the gas company for a stinking $22.50 per while the bosses ride around in swell cars living off the fat of the land. Dont think I am a greasy red. I read where they shoot cripples in Russia because they cant work but I can work better than any park bum and support a wife and child to. But thats not what I am writing you about. What I want to no is what is it all for my pulling my god damed leg along the streets and down in stinking cellars with it all the time hurting fit to burst so that near quitting time I am crazy with pain and when I get home all I hear is money money which aint no home for a man like me. What I want to no is what in hell is the use day after day with a foot like mine when you have to go around pulling and scrambling for a lousy three squares with a toothache in it that comes from useing the foot so much. The doctor told me I ought to rest it for six months but who will pay me when I am resting it. But that aint what I mean either because you might tell me to change my job and where could I get another one I am lucky to have one at all. It aint the job that I am complaining about but what I want to no is what is the whole stinking business for.

Please write me an answer not in the paper because my wife reads your stuff and I dont want her to no I wrote to you because I always said the papers is crap but I figured maybe you no something about it because you have read a lot of books and I never even finished high.

Yours truly,
Peter Doyle

While Miss Lonelyhearts was puzzling out the crabbed writing, Doyle's damp hand accidentally touched his under the table. He jerked away, but then drove his hand back and forced it to clasp the cripple's. After finishing the letter, he did not let go, but pressed it firmly with all the love he could manage. At first the cripple covered his embarrassment by disguising the meaning of the clasp with a handshake, but he soon gave in to it and they sat silently, hand in hand.

Miss Lonelyhearts
Pays a Visit

THEY LEFT the speakeasy together, both very drunk and very busy: Doyle with the wrongs he had suffered and Miss Lonelyhearts with the triumphant thing that his humility had become.

They took a cab. As they entered the street in which Doyle lived, he began to curse his wife and his crippled foot. He called on Christ to blast them both.

Miss Lonelyhearts was very happy and inside of his head he was also calling on Christ. But his call was not a curse, it was the shape of his joy.

When the cab drew up to the curb, Miss Lonelyhearts helped his companion out and led him into the house. They made a great deal of noise with the front door and Mrs. Doyle came into the hall. At the sight of her the cripple started to curse again.

She greeted Miss Lonelyhearts, then took hold of her husband and shook the breath out of him. When he was quiet, she dragged him into their apartment. Miss Lonelyhearts followed and as he passed her in the dark foyer, she goosed him and laughed.

After washing their hands, they sat down to eat. Mrs. Doyle had had her supper earlier in the evening and she waited on them. The first thing she put on the table was a quart bottle of guinea red.

When they had reached their coffee, she sat down next to Miss Lonelyhearts. He could feel her knee pressing his under the table, but he paid no attention to her and only broke his beatific smile to drink. The heavy food had dulled him and he was trying desperately to feel again what he had felt while holding hands with the cripple in the speakeasy.

She put her thigh under his, but when he still failed to respond, she got up abruptly and went into the parlor. They followed a few minutes later and found her mixing ginger-ale highballs.

They all drank silently. Doyle looked sleepy and his wife was just beginning to get drunk. Miss Lonelyhearts made no attempt to be sociable. He was busy trying to find a message. When he did speak it would have to be in the form of a message.

After the third highball, Mrs. Doyle began to wink quite openly at Miss Lonelyhearts, but he still refused to pay any attention to her. The cripple, however, was greatly disturbed by her signals. He began to fidget and mumble under his breath.

The vague noises he was making annoyed Mrs. Doyle. "What in hell are you talking about?" she demanded.

The cripple started a sigh that ended in a groan and then, as though ashamed of himself, said, "Ain't I the pimp, to bring home a guy for my wife?" He darted a quick look at Miss Lonelyhearts and laughed apologetically.

Mrs. Doyle was furious. She rolled a newspaper into a club and struck her husband on the mouth with it. He surprised her by playing the fool. He growled like a dog and caught the paper in his teeth. When she let go of her end, he dropped to his hands and knees and continued the imitation on the floor.

Miss Lonelyhearts tried to get the cripple to stand up and bent to lift him; but, as he did so, Doyle tore open Miss Lonelyhearts' fly, then rolled over on his back, laughing wildly.

His wife kicked him and turned away with a snort of contempt.

The cripple soon laughed himself out, and they all returned to their seats. Doyle and his wife sat staring at each other, while Miss Lonelyhearts again began to search for a message.

The silence bothered Mrs. Doyle. When she could stand it no longer, she went to the sideboard to make another round of drinks. But the bottle was empty. She asked her husband to go to the corner drug store for some gin. He refused with a single, curt nod of his head.

She tried to argue with him. He ignored her and she lost her temper. "Get some gin!" she yelled. "Get some gin, you bastard!"

Miss Lonelyhearts stood up. He had not yet found his message, but he had to say something. "Please don't fight," he pleaded. "He loves you, Mrs. Doyle; that's why he acts like that. Be kind to him."

She grunted with annoyance and left the room. They could hear her slamming things around in the kitchen.

Miss Lonelyhearts went over to the cripple and smiled at him with the same smile he had used in the speakeasy. The cripple returned the smile and stuck out his hand. Miss Lonelyhearts clasped it, and they stood this way, smiling and holding hands, until Mrs. Doyle reëntered the room.

"What a sweet pair of fairies you guys are," she said.

The cripple pulled his hand away and made as though to strike his wife. Miss Lonelyhearts realized that now was the time to give his message. It was now or never.

"You have a big, strong body, Mrs. Doyle. Holding your husband in your arms, you can warm him and give him life. You can take the chill out of his bones. He drags his days out in areaways and cellars, carrying a heavy load of weariness and pain. You can substitute a dream of yourself for this load. A buoyant dream that will be like a dynamo in him. You can do this by letting him conquer you in your bed. He will repay you by flowering and becoming ardent over you. . . ."

She was too astonished to laugh, and the cripple turned his face away as though embarrassed.

With the first few words Miss Lonelyhearts had known that he would be ridiculous. By avoiding God, he had failed to tap the force in his heart and had merely written a column for his paper.

He tried again by becoming hysterical. "Christ is love," he screamed at them. It was a stage scream, but he kept on. "Christ is the black fruit that hangs on the crosstree. Man was lost by eating of the forbidden fruit. He shall be saved by eating of the bidden fruit. The black Christ-fruit, the love fruit . . ."

This time he had failed still more miserably. He had substituted the rhetoric of Shrike for that of Miss Lonelyhearts. He felt like an empty bottle, shiny and sterile.

He closed his eyes. When he heard the cripple say, "I love you, I love you," he opened them and saw him kissing his wife. He knew that the cripple was doing this, not because of the things he had said, but out of loyalty.

"All right, you nut," she said, queening it over her husband. "I forgive you, but go to the drug store for some gin."

Without looking at Miss Lonelyhearts, the cripple took his hat and left. When he had gone Mrs. Doyle smiled. "You were a scream with your fly open," she said. "I thought I'd die laughing."

He did not answer.

"Boy, is he jealous," she went on. "All I have to do is point to some big guy and say, 'Gee, I'd love to have him love me up.' It drives him nuts."

Her voice was low and thick and it was plain that she was trying to excite him. When she went to the radio to tune in on a jazz orchestra, she waved her behind at him like a flag.

He said that he was too tired to dance. After doing a few obscene steps in front of him, she sat down in his lap. He tried to fend her off, but she kept pressing her open mouth against his and when he turned away, she nuzzled his cheek. He felt like an empty bottle that is being slowly filled with warm, dirty water.

When she opened the neck of her dress and tried to force his head between her breasts, he parted his knees with a quick jerk that spilled her to the floor. She tried to pull him down on top of her. He struck out blindly and hit her in the face. She screamed and he hit her again and again. He kept hitting her until she stopped trying to hold him, then he ran out of the house.

Miss Lonelyhearts
Attends a Party

MISS LONELYHEARTS had gone to bed again. This time his bed was surely taking him somewhere, and with great speed. He had only to ride it quietly. He had already been riding for three days.

Before climbing aboard, he had prepared for the journey by jamming the telephone bell and purchasing several enormous cans of crackers. He now lay on the bed, eating crackers, drinking water and smoking cigarettes.

He thought of how calm he was. His calm was so perfect that he could not destroy it even by being conscious of it. In three days he had gone very far. It grew dark in the room. He got out of bed, washed his teeth, urinated, then turned out the light and went to sleep. He fell asleep without even a sigh and slept the sleep of the wise and the innocent. Without dreaming, he was aware of fireflies and the slop of oceans.

Later a train rolled into a station where he was a reclining statue holding a stopped clock, a coach rumbled into the yard of an inn where he was sitting over a guitar, cap in hand, shedding the rain with his hump.

He awoke. The noise of both arrivals had combined to become a knocking on the door. He climbed out of bed. Although he was completely naked, he went to the door without covering himself. Five people rushed in, two of whom were women. The women shrieked when they saw him and jumped back into the hall.

The three men held their ground. Miss Lonelyhearts recognized Shrike among them and saw that he, as well as the others, was very drunk. Shrike said that one of the women was his wife and wanted to fight Miss Lonelyhearts for insulting her.

Miss Lonelyhearts stood quietly in the center of the room. Shrike dashed against him, but fell back, as a wave that dashes against an ancient rock, smooth with experience, falls back. There was no second wave.

Instead Shrike became jovial. He slapped Miss Lonelyhearts

on the back. "Put on a pair of pants, my friend," he said, "we're going to a party."

Miss Lonelyhearts picked up a can of crackers.

"Come on, my son," Shrike urged. "It's solitary drinking that makes drunkards."

Miss Lonelyhearts carefully examined each cracker before popping it into his mouth.

"Don't be a spoil-sport," Shrike said with a great deal of irritation. He was a gull trying to lay an egg in the smooth flank of a rock, a screaming, clumsy gull. "There's a game we want to play and we need you to play it.—'Everyman his own Miss Lonelyhearts.' I invented it, and we can't play without you."

Shrike pulled a large batch of letters out of his pockets and waved them in front of Miss Lonelyhearts. He recognized them; they were from his office file.

The rock remained calm and solid. Although Miss Lonelyhearts did not doubt that it could withstand any test, he was willing to have it tried. He began to dress.

They went downstairs, and all six of them piled into one cab. Mary Shrike sat on his lap, but despite her drunken wriggling the rock remained perfect.

The party was in Shrike's apartment. A roar went up when Miss Lonelyhearts entered and the crowd surged forward. He stood firm and they slipped back in a futile curl. He smiled. He had turned more than a dozen drunkards. He had turned them without effort or thought. As he stood smiling, a little wave crept up out of the general welter and splashed at his feet for attention. It was Betty.

"What's the matter with you?" she asked. "Are you sick again?"

He did not answer.

When every one was seated, Shrike prepared to start the game. He distributed paper and pencils, then led Miss Lonelyhearts to the center of the room and began his spiel.

"Ladies and gentlemen," he said, imitating the voice and gestures of a circus barker. "We have with us to-night a man whom you all know and admire. Miss Lonelyhearts, he of the singing heart—a still more swollen Mussolini of the soul.

"He has come here to-night to help you with your moral

and spiritual problems, to provide you with a slogan, a cause, an absolute value and a *raison d'être.*

"Some of you, perhaps, consider yourself too far gone for help. You are afraid that even Miss Lonelyhearts, no matter how fierce his torch, will be unable to set you on fire. You are afraid that even when exposed to his bright flame, you will only smolder and give off a bad smell. Be of good heart, for I know that you will burst into flame. Miss Lonelyhearts is sure to prevail."

Shrike pulled out the batch of letters and waved them above his head.

"We will proceed systematically," he said. "First, each of you will do his best to answer one of these letters, then, from your answers, Miss Lonelyhearts will diagnose your moral ills. Afterwards he will lead you in the way of attainment."

Shrike went among his guests and distributed the letters as a magician does cards. He talked continuously and read a part of each letter before giving it away.

"Here's one from an old woman whose son died last week. She is seventy years old and sells pencils for a living. She has no stockings and wears heavy boots on her torn and bleeding feet. She has rheum in her eyes. Have you room in your heart for her?

"This one is a jim-dandy. A young boy wants a violin. It looks simple; all you have to do is get the kid one. But then you discover that he has dictated the letter to his little sister. He is paralyzed and can't even feed himself. He has a toy violin and hugs it to his chest, imitating the sound of playing with his mouth. How pathetic! However, one can learn much from this parable. Label the boy Labor, the violin Capital, and so on . . ."

Miss Lonelyhearts stood it with the utmost serenity; he was not even interested. What goes on in the sea is of no interest to the rock.

When all the letters had been distributed, Shrike gave one to Miss Lonelyhearts. He took it, but after holding it for a while, he dropped it to the floor without reading it.

Shrike was not quiet for a second.

"You are plunging into a world of misery and suffering, peopled by creatures who are strangers to everything but disease and policemen. Harried by one, they are hurried by the other. . . .

"Pain, pain, pain, the dull, sordid, gnawing, chronic pain of heart and brain. The pain that only a great spiritual liniment can relieve. . . ."

When Miss Lonelyhearts saw Betty get up to go, he followed her out of the apartment. She too should see the rock he had become.

Shrike did not miss him until he discovered the letter on the floor. He picked it up, tried to find Miss Lonelyhearts, then addressed the gathering again.

"The master has disappeared," he announced, "but do not despair. I am still with you. I am his disciple and I shall lead you in the way of attainment. First let me read you this letter which is addressed directly to the master."

He took the letter out of its envelope, as though he had not read it previously, and began: " 'What kind of a dirty skunk are you? When I got home with the gin, I found my wife crying on the floor and the house full of neighbors. She said that you tried to rape her you dirty skunk and they wanted to get the police but I said that I'd do the job myself you . . .'

"My, oh my, I really can't bring myself to utter such vile language. I'll skip the swearing and go on. 'So that's what all your fine speeches come to, you bastard, you ought to have your brains blown out.' It's signed, 'Doyle.'

"Well, well, so the master is another Rasputin. How this shakes one's faith! But I can't believe it. I won't believe it. The master can do no wrong. My faith is unshaken. This is only one more attempt against him by the devil. He has spent his life struggling with the arch fiend for our sakes, and he shall triumph. I mean Miss Lonelyhearts, not the devil.

"The gospel according to Shrike. Let me tell you about his life. It unrolls before me like a scroll. First, in the dawn of childhood, radiant with pure innocence, like a rain-washed star, he wends his weary way to the University of Hard Knocks. Next, a youth, he dashes into the night from the bed of his first whore. And then, the man, the man Miss Lonely-hearts—struggling valiantly to realize a high ideal, his course shaped by a proud aim. But, alas! cold and scornful, the world heaps obstacle after obstacle in his path; deems he the goal at hand, a voice of thunder bids him 'Halt!' 'Let each hindrance be thy ladder,' thinks he. 'Higher, even higher, mount!' And so he climbs, rung by weary rung, and so he urges himself on, breathless with hallowed fire. And so . . ."

Miss Lonelyhearts
and the Party Dress

W HEN Miss Lonelyhearts left Shrike's apartment, he found Betty in the hall waiting for the elevator. She had on a light-blue dress that was very much a party dress. She dressed for things, he realized.

Even the rock was touched by this realization. No; it was not the rock that was touched. The rock was still perfect. It was his mind that was touched, the instrument with which he knew the rock.

He approached Betty with a smile, for his mind was free and clear. The things that muddied it had precipitated out into the rock.

But she did not smile back. "What are you grinning at?" she snapped.

"Oh, I'm sorry," he said. "I didn't mean anything."

They entered the elevator together. When they reached the street, he took her arm although she tried to jerk away.

"Won't you have a soda, please?" he begged. The party dress had given his simplified mind its cue and he delighted in the boy-and-girl argument that followed.

"No; I'm going home."

"Oh, come on," he said, pulling her towards a soda fountain. As she went, she unconsciously exaggerated her little-girl-in-a-party-dress air.

They both had strawberry sodas. They sucked the pink drops up through straws, she pouting at his smile, neither one of them conscious of being cute.

"Why are you mad at me, Betty? I didn't do anything. It was Shrike's idea and he did all the talking."

"Because you are a fool."

"I've quit the Miss Lonelyhearts job. I haven't been in the office for almost a week."

"What are you going to do?"

"I'm going to look for a job in an advertising agency."

He was not deliberately lying. He was only trying to say what she wanted to hear. The party dress was so gay and charming, light blue with a frothy lace collar flecked with pink, like the collar of her soda.

"You ought to see Bill Wheelright about a job. He owns an agency—he's a swell guy. . . . He's in love with me."

"I couldn't work for a rival."

She screwed up her nose and they both laughed.

He was still laughing when he noticed that something had gone wrong with her laugh. She was crying.

He felt for the rock. It was still there; neither laughter nor tears could affect the rock. It was oblivious to wind or rain.

"Oh . . ." she sobbed. "I'm a fool." She ran out of the store.

He followed and caught her. But her sobs grew worse and he hailed a taxi and forced her to get in.

She began to talk under her sobs. She was pregnant. She was going to have a baby.

He put the rock forward and waited with complete poise for her to stop crying. When she was quiet, he asked her to marry him.

"No," she said. "I'm going to have an abortion."

"Please marry me." He pleaded just as he had pleaded with her to have a soda.

He begged the party dress to marry him, saying all the things it expected to hear, all the things that went with strawberry sodas and farms in Connecticut. He was just what the party dress wanted him to be: simple and sweet, whimsical and poetic, a trifle collegiate yet very masculine.

By the time they arrived at her house, they were discussing their life after marriage. Where they would live and in how many rooms. Whether they could afford to have the child. How they would rehabilitate the farm in Connecticut. What kind of furniture they both liked.

She agreed to have the child. He won that point. In return, he agreed to see Bill Wheelright about a job. With a great deal of laughter, they decided to have three beds in their bedroom. Twin beds for sleep, very prim and puritanical, and between them a love bed, an ornate double bed with cupids, nymphs and Pans.

He did not feel guilty. He did not feel. The rock was a solidification of his feeling, his conscience, his sense of reality, his self-knowledge. He could have planned anything. A castle in Spain and love on a balcony or a pirate trip and love on a tropical island.

When her door closed behind him, he smiled. The rock had been thoroughly tested and had been found perfect. He had only to climb aboard the bed again.

Miss Lonelyhearts
Has a Religious Experience

AFTER a long night and morning, towards noon, Miss Lonelyhearts welcomed the arrival of fever. It promised heat and mentally unmotivated violence. The promise was soon fulfilled; the rock became a furnace.

He fastened his eyes on the Christ that hung on the wall opposite his bed. As he stared at it, it became a bright fly, spinning with quick grace on a background of blood velvet sprinkled with tiny nerve stars.

Everything else in the room was dead—chairs, table, pencils, clothes, books. He thought of this black world of things as a fish. And he was right, for it suddenly rose to the bright bait on the wall. It rose with a splash of music and he saw its shining silver belly.

Christ is life and light.

"Christ! Christ!" This shout echoed through the innermost cells of his body.

He moved his head to a cooler spot on the pillow and the vein in his forehead became less swollen. He felt clean and fresh. His heart was a rose and in his skull another rose bloomed.

The room was full of grace. A sweet, clean grace, not washed clean, but clean as the innersides of the inner petals of a newly forced rosebud.

Delight was also in the room. It was like a gentle wind, and his nerves rippled under it like small blue flowers in a pasture.

He was conscious of two rhythms that were slowly becoming one. When they became one, his identification with God was complete. His heart was the one heart, the heart of God. And his brain was likewise God's.

God said, "Will you accept it, now?"

And he replied, "I accept, I accept."

He immediately began to plan a new life and his future conduct as Miss Lonelyhearts. He submitted drafts of his column to God and God approved them. God approved his every thought.

Suddenly the door bell rang. He climbed out of bed and went into the hall to see who was coming. It was Doyle, the cripple, and he was slowly working his way up the stairs.

God had sent him so that Miss Lonelyhearts could perform a miracle and be certain of his conversion. It was a sign. He would embrace the cripple and the cripple would be made whole again, even as he, a spiritual cripple, had been made whole.

He rushed down the stairs to meet Doyle with his arms spread for the miracle.

Doyle was carrying something wrapped in a newspaper. When he saw Miss Lonelyhearts, he put his hand inside the package and stopped. He shouted some kind of a warning, but Miss Lonelyhearts continued his charge. He did not understand the cripple's shout and heard it as a cry for help from Desperate, Harold S., Catholic-mother, Broken-hearted, Broad-shoulders, Sick-of-it-all, Disillusioned-with-tubercular-husband. He was running to succor them with love.

The cripple turned to escape, but he was too slow and Miss Lonelyhearts caught him.

While they were struggling, Betty came in through the street door. She called to them to stop and started up the stairs. The cripple saw her cutting off his escape and tried to get rid of the package. He pulled his hand out. The gun inside the package exploded and Miss Lonelyhearts fell, dragging the cripple with him. They both rolled part of the way down the stairs.

A COOL MILLION

The Dismantling of Lemuel Pitkin

TO
S. J. PERELMAN

"John D. Rockefeller would give a cool million to have a stomach like yours."—OLD SAYING

I

T HE HOME of Mrs. Sarah Pitkin, a widow well on in years, was situated on an eminence overlooking the Rat River, near the town of Ottsville in the state of Vermont. It was a humble dwelling much the worse for wear, yet exceedingly dear to her and her only child, Lemuel.

While the house had not been painted for some time, owing to the straitened circumstances of the little family, it still had a great deal of charm. An antique collector, had one chanced to pass it by, would have been greatly interested in its architecture. Having been built about the time of General Stark's campaign against the British, its lines reflected the character of his army in whose ranks several Pitkins had marched.

One late fall evening, Mrs. Pitkin was sitting quietly in her parlor, when a knock was heard on her humble door.

She kept no servant, and, as usual, answered the knock in person.

"Mr. Slemp!" she said, as she recognized in her caller the wealthy village lawyer.

"Yes, Mrs. Pitkin, I come upon a little matter of business."

"Won't you come in?" said the widow, not forgetting her politeness in her surprise.

"I believe I will trespass on your hospitality for a brief space," said the lawyer blandly. "Are you quite well?"

"Thank you, sir—quite so," said Mrs. Pitkin as she led the way into the sitting room. "Take the rocking chair, Mr. Slemp," she said, pointing to the best chair which the simple room contained.

"You are very kind," said the lawyer, seating himself gingerly in the chair referred to.

"Where is your son, Lemuel?" continued the lawyer.

"He is in school. But it is nearly time for him to be home; he never loiters." And the mother's voice showed something of the pride she felt in her boy.

"Still in school!" exclaimed Mr. Slemp. "Shouldn't he be helping to support you?"

"No," said the widow proudly. "I set great store by learning, as does my son. But you came on business?"

"Ah, yes, Mrs. Pitkin. I fear that the business may be unpleasant for you, but you will remember, I am sure, that I act in this matter as agent for another."

"Unpleasant!" repeated Mrs. Pitkin apprehensively.

"Yes. Mr. Joshua Bird, Squire Bird, has placed in my hands for foreclosure the mortgage on your house. That is, he will foreclose," he added hastily, "if you fail to raise the necessary monies in three months from now when the obligation matures."

"How can I hope to pay?" said the widow brokenly. "I thought that Squire Bird would be glad to renew, as we pay him twelve per cent interest."

"I am sorry, Mrs. Pitkin, sincerely sorry, but he has decided not to renew. He wants either his money or the property."

The lawyer took his hat and bowed politely, leaving the widow alone with her tears.

(It might interest the reader to know that I was right in my surmise. An interior decorator, on passing the house, had been greatly struck by its appearance. He had seen Squire Bird about purchasing it, and that is why that worthy had decided to foreclose on Mrs. Pitkin. The name of the cause of this tragedy was Asa Goldstein, his business, "Colonial Exteriors and Interiors." Mr. Goldstein planned to take the house apart and set it up again in the window of his Fifth Avenue shop.)

As Lawyer Slemp was leaving the humble dwelling, he met the widow's son, Lemuel, on the threshold. Through the open door, the boy caught a glimpse of his mother in tears, and said to Mr. Slemp:

"What have you been saying to my mother to make her cry?"

"Stand aside, boy!" exclaimed the lawyer. He pushed Lem with such great force that the poor lad fell off the porch steps into the cellar, the door of which was unfortunately open. By the time Lem had extricated himself, Mr. Slemp was well on his way down the road.

Our hero, although only seventeen years old, was a strong, spirited lad and would have followed after the lawyer but for his mother. On hearing her voice, he dropped the ax which he had snatched up and ran into the house to comfort her.

The poor widow told her son all we have recounted and the two of them sat plunged in gloom. No matter how they racked their brains, they could not discover a way to keep the roof over their heads.

In desperation, Lem finally decided to go and see Mr. Nathan Whipple, who was the town's most prominent citizen. Mr. Whipple had once been President of the United States, and was known affectionately from Maine to California as "Shagpoke" Whipple. After four successful years in office, he had beaten his silk hat, so to speak, into a plowshare and had refused to run a second time, preferring to return to his natal Ottsville and there become a simple citizen again. He spent all his time between his den in the garage and the Rat River National Bank, of which he was president.

Mr. Whipple had often shown his interest in Lem, and the lad felt that he might be willing to help his mother save her home.

II

SHAGPOKE WHIPPLE lived on the main street of Ottsville in a two-story frame house with a narrow lawn in front and a garage that once had been a chicken house in the rear. Both buildings had a solid, sober look, and indeed, no one was ever allowed to create disorder within their precincts.

The house served as a place of business as well as a residence; the first floor being devoted to the offices of the bank and the second functioning as the home of the ex-president. On the porch, next to the front door, was a large bronze plate that read

RAT RIVER NATIONAL BANK
Nathan "Shagpoke" Whipple
PRES.

Some people might object to turning a part of their dwelling into a bank, especially if, like Mr. Whipple, they had hobnobbed with crowned heads. But Shagpoke was not proud, and he was of the saving kind. He had always saved: from the first time he received a penny at the age of five, when he had triumphed over the delusive pleasures of an investment in candy, right down to the time he was elected President of the United States. One of his favorite adages was "Don't teach your grandmother to suck eggs." By this he meant that the pleasures of the body are like grandmothers, once they begin to suck eggs they never stop until all the eggs (purse) are dry.

As Lem turned up the path to Mr. Whipple's house, the sun rapidly sank under the horizon. Every evening at this time, the ex-president lowered the flag that flew over his garage and made a speech to as many of the town's citizenry as had stopped to watch the ceremony. During the first year after the great man's return from Washington, there used to collect quite a crowd, but this had dwindled until now, as our hero approached the house, there was but a lone boy scout watching the ceremony. This lad was not present of his own free will, alas, but had been sent by his father, who was desirous of obtaining a loan from the bank.

Lem removed his hat and waited in reverence for Mr. Whipple to finish his speech.

"All hail Old Glory! May you be the joy and pride of the American heart, alike when your gorgeous folds shall wanton in the summer air and your tattered fragments be dimly seen through clouds of war! May you ever wave in honor, hope and profit, in unsullied glory and patriotic fervor, on the dome of the capitol, on the tented plain, on the wave-rocked topmast and on the roof of this garage!"

With these words, Shagpoke lowered the flag for which so many of our finest have bled and died, and tenderly gathered it up in his arms. The boy scout ran off hurriedly. Lem moved forward to greet the orator.

"I would like to have a few words with you, sir," said our hero.

"Certainly," replied Mr. Whipple with native kindness. "I am never too busy to discuss the problems of youth, for the youth of a nation is its only hope. Come into my den," he added.

The room into which Lem followed Mr. Whipple was situated in the back of the garage. It was furnished with extreme simplicity; some boxes, a cracker barrel, two brass spittoons, a hot stove and a picture of Lincoln were all it held.

When our hero had seated himself on one of the boxes, Shagpoke perched on the cracker barrel and put his congress gaiters near the hot stove. He lined up the distance to the nearest spittoon with a measuring gob of spittle and told the lad to begin.

As it will only delay my narrative and serve no good purpose to report how Lem told about his predicament, I will skip to his last sentence.

"And so," concluded our hero, "the only thing that can save my mother's home is for your bank to take over Squire Bird's mortgage."

"I would not help you by lending you money, even if it were possible for me to do so," was the surprising answer Mr. Whipple gave the boy.

"Why not, sir?" asked Lem, unable to hide his great disappointment.

"Because I believe it would be a mistake. You are too young to borrow."

"But what then shall I do?" asked Lem in desperation.

"There are still three months left to you before they can sell your house," said Mr. Whipple. "Don't be discouraged. This is the land of opportunity and the world is an oyster."

"But how am I to earn fifteen hundred dollars (for that was the face value of the mortgage) here in such a short time?" asked Lem, who was puzzled by the ex-president's rather cryptic utterances.

"That is for you to discover, but I never said that you should remain in Ottsville. Do as I did, when I was your age. Go out into the world and win your way."

Lem considered this advice for a while. When he spoke again, it was with courage and determination.

"You are right, sir. I'll go off to seek my fortune." Our hero's eyes shone with a light that bespoke a high heart.

"Good," said Mr. Whipple, and he was genuinely glad. "As I said before, the world is an oyster that but waits for hands to open it. Bare hands are best, but have you any money?"

"Something less than a dollar," said Lem sadly.

"It is very little, my young friend, but it might suffice, for you have an honest face and that is more than gold. But I had thirty-five dollars when I left home to make my way, and it would be nice if you had at least as much."

"Yes, it would be nice," agreed Lem.

"Have you any collateral?" asked Mr. Whipple.

"Collateral?" repeated Lem whose business education was so limited that he did not even know what the word meant.

"Security for a loan," said Mr. Whipple.

"No, sir, I'm afraid not."

"Your mother has a cow, I think?"

"Yes, Old Sue." The boy's face fell as he thought of parting with that faithful servitor.

"I believe that I could lend you twenty-five dollars on her, maybe thirty," said Mr. Whipple.

"But she cost more than a hundred, and besides she supplies us with milk, butter and cheese, the main part of our simple victuals."

"You do not understand," said Mr. Whipple patiently. "Your mother can keep the cow until the note that she will sign comes due in sixty days from now. This new obligation will be an added incentive to spur you on to success."

"But what if I fail?" asked Lem. Not that he was losing heart, be it said, but he was young and wanted encouragement.

Mr. Whipple understood how the lad felt and made an effort to reassure him.

"America," he said with great seriousness, "is the land of opportunity. She takes care of the honest and industrious and never fails them as long as they are both. This is not a matter of opinion, it is one of faith. On the day that Americans stop believing it, on that day will America be lost.

"Let me warn you that you will find in the world a certain few scoffers who will laugh at you and attempt to do you injury. They will tell you that John D. Rockefeller is a thief and that Henry Ford and other great men are also thieves. Do not believe them. The story of Rockefeller and of Ford is the story of every great American, and you should strive to make it your story. Like them you were born poor and on a farm. Like them, by honesty and industry, you cannot fail to succeed."

It is needless to say that the words of the ex-president encouraged our young hero, just as similar ones have heartened the youth of this country ever since it was freed from the irksome British yoke. He vowed then and there to go and do as Rockefeller and Ford had done.

Mr. Whipple drew up some papers for the lad's mother to sign and ushered him out of the den. When he had gone, the great man turned to the picture of Lincoln that hung on the wall and silently communed with it.

III

OUR HERO'S way home led through a path that ran along the Rat River. As he passed a wooded stretch, he cut a stout stick with a thick, gnarled top. He was twirling this club, as a bandmaster does his baton, when he was startled by a young girl's shriek. Turning his head, he saw a terrified figure pursued by a fierce dog. A moment's glance showed him that it was Betty Prail, a girl with whom he was in love in a boyish way.

Betty recognized him at the same moment.

"Oh, save me, Mr. Pitkin!" she exclaimed, clasping her hands.

"I will," said Lem resolutely.

Armed with the stick he had most fortunately cut, he rushed between the girl and her pursuer and brought the knob down with full force on the dog's back. The attention of the furious animal—a large bulldog—was diverted to his assailant, and with a fierce howl he rushed upon Lem. But our hero was wary and expected the attack. He jumped to one side and brought the stick down with great force on the dog's head. The animal fell, partly stunned, his quivering tongue protruding from his mouth.

"It won't do to leave him so," thought Lem; "when he revives he'll be as dangerous as ever."

He dealt the prostrate brute two more blows which settled its fate. The furious animal would do no more harm.

"Oh, thank you, Mr. Pitkin!" exclaimed Betty, a trace of color returning to her cheeks. "I was terribly frightened."

"I don't wonder," said Lem. "The brute was certainly ugly."

"How brave you are!" the young lady said in admiration.

"It doesn't take much courage to hit a dog on the head with a stick," said Lem modestly.

"Many boys would have run," she said.

"What, and left you unprotected?" Lem was indignant. "None but a coward would have done that."

"Tom Baxter was walking with me, and he ran away."

"Did he see the dog chasing you?"

"Yes."

"And what did he do?"

"He jumped over a stone wall."

"All I can say is that that isn't my style," said Lem. "Do you see how the dog froths at the mouth? I believe he's mad."

"How fearful!" exclaimed Betty with a shudder. "Did you suspect that before?"

"Yes, when I first saw him."

"And yet you dared to meet him?"

"It was safer than to run," said Lem, making little of the incident. "I wonder whose dog it was?"

"I'll tell you," said a brutal voice.

Turning his head, Lem beheld a stout fellow about three years older than himself, with a face in which the animal seemed to predominate. It was none other than Tom Baxter, the town bully.

"What have you been doing to my dog?" demanded Baxter with a snarl.

Addressed in this tone, Lem thought it unnecessary to throw away politeness on such a brutal customer.

"Killing him," he answered shortly.

"What business have you killing my dog?" demanded the bully with much anger.

"It was your business to keep the brute locked up, where he wouldn't do any harm," said Lem. "Besides, you saw him attack Miss Prail. Why didn't you interfere?"

"I'll flog you within an inch of your life," said Baxter with an oath.

"You'd better not try it," said Lem coolly. "I suppose you think I ought to have let the dog bite Miss Prail."

"He wouldn't have bitten her."

"He would too. He was chasing her with that intention."

"It was only in sport."

"I suppose he was frothing at the mouth only in sport," said Lem. "The dog was mad. You ought to thank me for killing him because he might have bitten you."

"That don't go down," said Baxter coarsely. "It's much too thin."

"It's true," said Betty Prail, speaking for the first time.

"Of course you'll stand up for him," said the butcher boy (for that was Baxter's business), "but that's neither here nor there. I paid five dollars for that dog, and if he don't pay me what I gave, I'll mash him."

"I shall do nothing of the sort," said Lem quietly. "A dog like that ought to be killed, and no one has any right to let him run loose, risking the lives of innocent people. The next time you get five dollars you ought to invest it better."

"Then you won't pay me the money?" cried the bully in a passion. "I'll break your head."

"Come on," said Lem, "I've got something to say about that," and he squared off scientifically.

"Oh, don't fight him, Mr. Pitkin," said Betty very much distressed. "He is much stronger than you."

"He'll find that out soon enough I'm thinking," growled Lem's opponent.

That Tom Baxter was not only larger, but stronger than our hero was no doubt true. On the other hand he did not know how to use his strength. It was merely undisciplined brute force. If he could have got Lem around the waist the latter would have been at his mercy, but our hero knew that well enough and didn't choose to allow it. He was a pretty fair boxer, and stood on his defense, calm and wary.

When Baxter rushed in, thinking to seize his smaller opponent, he was greeted by two rapid blows in the face, one of which struck him in the nose, the other in the eye, the effect of both being to make his head spin.

"I'll mash you for that," he yelled in a frenzy of rage, but as he rushed in again he never thought to guard his face. The result was a couple of more blows, the other eye and his mouth being assailed this time.

Baxter was astonished. He was expected to "chaw up" Lem at the first onset. Instead of that, there stood Lem cool and unhurt, while he could feel that his nose and mouth were bleeding and both of his eyes were rapidly closing.

He stopped short and regarded Lem as well as he could through his injured optics, then surprised our hero by smiling. "Well," he said shaking his head sheepishly, "you're the better man. I'm a rough customer, I expect, but I know when I'm bested. There's my hand to show that I don't bear malice."

Lem gave his hand in return without fear that there might be craft in the bully's offer of friendship. The former was a fair dealing lad himself and he thought that everyone was the same. However, no sooner did Baxter have a hold of his hand, than he jerked the poor boy into his embrace and squeezed him insensible.

Betty screamed and fainted, so great was her anxiety for Lem. Hearing her scream, Baxter dropped his victim to the ground and walked to where the young lady lay in a dead faint. He stood over her for a few minutes admiring her beauty. His little pig-like eyes shone with bestiality.

IV

I T IS with reluctance that I leave Miss Prail in the lecherous embrace of Tom Baxter to begin a new chapter, but I cannot with propriety continue my narrative beyond the point at which the bully undressed that unfortunate lady.

However, as Miss Prail is the heroine of this romance, I would like to use this opportunity to acquaint you with a little of her past history.

On her twelfth birthday, Betty became an orphan with the simultaneous death of her two parents in a fire which also destroyed what little property might have been left her. In this fire, or rather at it, she also lost something which, like her parents, could never be replaced.

The Prail farm was situated some three miles from Ottsville on a rough dirt road, and the amateur fire company, to whose ministrations all the fires in the district were left, was not very enthusiastic about dragging their apparatus to it. To tell the truth, the Ottsville Fire Company consisted of a set of young men who were more interested in dirty stories, checkers and apple-jack than they were in fire fighting. When the news of the catastrophe arrived at the fire house, the volunteer firemen were all inebriated, and their chief, Bill Baxter (father to the man in whose arms we left our heroine) was dead drunk.

After many delays, the fire company finally arrived at the Prail farm, but instead of trying to quench the flames they immediately set to work and looted the place.

Betty, although only twelve years old at the time, was a well-formed little girl with the soft, voluptuous lines of a beautiful woman. Dressed only in a cotton nightgown, she was wandering among the firemen begging them to save her parents, when Bill Baxter noticed her budding form and enticed her into the woodshed.

In the morning, she was found lying naked on the ground by some neighbors and taken into their house. She had a bad cold, but remembered nothing of what Bill Baxter had done to her. She mourned only the loss of her parents.

After a small collection had been taken up by the minister

to purchase an outfit, she was sent to the county orphan asylum. There she remained until her fourteenth year, when she was put out as a maid of all work to the Slemps, a prominent family of Ottsville, the head of which, Lawyer Slemp, we already know.

As one can well imagine, all was not beer and skittles in this household for the poor orphan. If she had been less beautiful, perhaps things would have gone better for her. As it was, however, Lawyer Slemp had two ugly daughters and a shrewish wife who were very jealous of their beautiful servant. They saw to it that she was badly dressed and that she wore her hair only in the ugliest possible manner. Yet despite these things, and although she had to wear men's shoes and coarse cotton stockings, our heroine was a great deal more attractive than the other women of the household.

Lawyer Slemp was a deacon in the church and a very stern man. Still one would think that as a male he would have less against the poor orphan than his women folks. But, unfortunately, it did not work out this way. Mr. Slemp beat Betty regularly and enthusiastically. He had started these beatings when she first came from the asylum as a little girl, and did not stop them when she became a splendid woman. He beat her twice a week on her bare behind with his bare hand.

It is a hard thing to say about a deacon, but Lawyer Slemp got little exercise and he seemed to take a great deal of pleasure in these bi-weekly workouts. As for Betty, she soon became inured to his blows and did not mind them as much as the subtler tortures inflicted on her by Mrs. Slemp and her daughters. Besides, Lawyer Slemp, although he was exceedingly penurious, always gave her a quarter when he had finished beating her.

It was with this weekly fifty cents that Betty hoped to effect her escape from Ottsville. She had already obtained part of an outfit, and was on her way home from town with the first store hat she had ever owned, when she met Tom Baxter and his dog.

The result of this unfortunate encounter we already know.

V

WHEN our hero regained consciousness, he found himself in a ditch alongside the path on which he had his set-to with Tom Baxter. It had grown quite dark, and he failed to notice Betty in some bushes on the other side of the path. He thought that she must have got safely away.

As he walked home his head cleared and he soon recovered his naturally high spirits. He forgot his unfortunate encounter with the bully and thought only of his coming departure for New York City.

He was greeted at the door of his humble home by his fond parent, who had been waiting anxiously for his return.

"Lem, Lem," said Mrs. Pitkin, "where have you been?"

Although our hero was loath to lie, he did not want to worry his mother unduly, so he said, "Mr. Whipple kept me."

The lad then told her what the ex-president had said. She was quite happy for her son and willingly signed the note for thirty dollars. Like all mothers, Mrs. Pitkin was certain that her child must succeed.

Bright and early the next morning, Lem took the note to Mr. Whipple and received thirty dollars minus twelve per cent interest in advance. He then bought a ticket for New York at the local depot, and waited there for the arrival of the steam cars.

Our hero was studying the fleeting scenery of New England, when he heard someone address him.

"Papers, magazines, all the popular novels! Something to read, mister?"

It was the news butcher, a young boy with an honest, open countenance.

Our hero was eager to talk, so he spoke to the newsboy.

"I'm not a great one for reading novels," he said. "My Aunt Nancy gave my ma one once but I didn't find much in it. I like facts and I like to study, though."

"I ain't much on story reading either," said the news butcher. "Where are you goin'?"

"To New York to make my fortune," said Lem candidly.

"Well, if you can't make money in New York, you can't make money anywhere." With this observation he began to hawk his reading matter further down the aisle.

Lem again took up his study of the fleeting scenery. This time he was interrupted by a stylishly dressed young man who came forward and accosted him.

"Is this seat engaged?" the stranger asked.

"Not as I know of," replied Lem with a friendly smile.

"Then with your kind permission I will occupy it," said the over-dressed stranger.

"Why, of course," said our hero.

"You are from the country, I presume," he continued affably as he sank into the seat alongside our hero.

"Yes, I am. I live near Bennington in the town of Ottsville. Were you ever there?"

"No. I suppose you are taking a vacation trip to the big city?"

"Oh, no; I'm leaving home to make my fortune."

"That's nice. I hope you are successful. By the way, the mayor of New York is my uncle."

"My, is that so?" said Lem with awe.

"Yes indeed, my name is Wellington Mape."

"Glad to make your acquaintance, Mr. Mape. I'm Lemuel Pitkin."

"Indeed! An aunt of mine married a Pitkin. Perhaps we're related."

Lem was quite elated at the thought that he might be kin to the mayor of New York without knowing it. He decided that his new acquaintance must be rich because of his clothing and his extreme politeness.

"Are you in business, Mr. Mape?" he asked.

"Well, ahem!" was that suave individual's rejoinder. "I'm afraid I'm rather an idler. My father left me a cool million, so I don't feel the need of working."

"A cool million!" ejaculated Lem. "Why, that's ten times a hundred thousand dollars."

"Just so," said Mr. Mape, smiling at the lad's enthusiasm.

"That's an awful pile of money! I'd be satisfied if I had five thousand right now."

"I'm afraid that five thousand wouldn't last me very long," said Mr. Mape with an amused smile.

"Gee! Where would anybody get such a pile of money unless they inherited it?"

"That's easy," said the stranger. "Why, I've made as much in one day in Wall Street."

"You don't say."

"Yes, I do say. You can take my word for it."

"I wish I could make some money," said Lem wistfully, as he thought of the mortgage on his home.

"A man must have money to make money. If now, you had some money. . . ."

"I've got a little under thirty dollars," said Lem.

"Is that all?"

"Yes, that's all. I had to give Mr. Whipple a note to borrow it."

"If that's all the money you have, you'd better take good care of it. I regret to say that despite the efforts of the mayor, my uncle, there are still many crooks in New York."

"I intend to be careful."

"Then you keep your money in a safe place?"

"I haven't hidden it because a secret pocket is the first place a thief would look. I keep it loose in my trousers where nobody would think I carried so much money."

"You are right. I can see that you are a man of the world."

"Oh, I can take care of myself, I guess," said Lem with the confidence of youth.

"That comes of being a Pitkin. I'm glad to know that we're related. You must call on me in New York."

"Where do you live?"

"At the Ritz. Just ask for Mr. Wellington Mape's suite of rooms."

"Is it a good place to live?"

"Why, yes. I pay three dollars a day for my board, and the incidentals carry my expenses up to as high as forty dollars a week."

"Gee," ejaculated Lem. "I could never afford it—that is, at first." And our hero laughed with the incurable optimism of youth.

"You of course should find a boarding house where they

give you plain but solid fare for a reasonable sum. . . . But I must bid you good morning, a friend is waiting for me in the next car."

After the affable Mr. Wellington Mape had taken his departure, Lem turned again to his vigil at the car window.

The news butcher had changed his cap. "Apples, bananas, oranges!" he shouted as he came down the aisle with a basket of fruit on his arm.

Lem stopped his rapid progress to ask him the price of an orange. It was two cents, and he decided to buy one to eat with the hard-boiled egg his mother had given him. But when our hero thrust his hand into his pocket, a wild spasm contracted his features. He explored further, with growing trepidation, and a sickly pallor began to spread over his face.

"What's the matter?" asked Steve, for that was the train boy's name.

"I've been robbed! My money's gone! All the money Mr. Whipple lent me has been stolen!"

VI

I WONDER who did it?" asked Steve.

"I can't imagine," answered Lem brokenly.

"Did they get much?"

"All I had in the world. . . . A little less than thirty dollars."

"Some smart leather must have gotten it."

"Leather?" queried our hero, not understanding the argot of the underworld with which the train boy was familiar.

"Yes, leather—pickpocket. Did anybody talk to you on the train?"

"Only Mr. Wellington Mape, a rich young man. He is kin to the mayor of New York."

"Who told you that?"

"He did himself."

"How was he dressed?" asked Steve, whose suspicions were aroused. (He had been "wire"—scout—to a "leather" when small and knew all about the dodge.) "Did he wear a pale blue hat?"

"Yes."

"And looked a great swell?"

"Yes."

"He got off at the last station and your dough-re-me went with him."

"You mean he got my money? Well, I never. He told me he was worth a cool million and boarded at the Ritz Hotel."

"That's the way they all talk—big. Did you tell him where you kept your money?"

"Yes, I did. But can't I get it back?"

"I don't see how. He got off the train."

"I'd like to catch hold of him," said Lem, who was very angry.

"Oh, he'd hit you with a piece of lead pipe. But look through your pockets, maybe he left you a dollar."

Lem put his hand into the pocket in which he had carried

148

his money and drew it out as though he had been bitten. Between his fingers he held a diamond ring.

"What's that?" asked Steve.

"I don't know," said Lem with surprise. "I don't think I ever saw it before. Yes, by gum, I did. It must have dropped off the crook's finger when he picked my pocket. I saw him wearing it."

"Boy!" exclaimed the train boy. "You're sure in luck. Talk about falling in a privy and coming up with a gold watch. You're certainly it. With a double t."

"What is it worth?" asked Lem eagerly.

"Permit me to look at it, my young friend, perhaps I can tell you," said a gentleman in a grey derby hat, who was sitting across the aisle. This stranger had been listening with great curiosity to the dialogue between our hero and the train boy.

"I am a pawnbroker," he said. "If you let me examine the ring, I can surely give you some idea of its value."

Lem handed the article in question to the stranger, who put a magnifying glass into his eye and looked at it carefully.

"My young friend, that ring is worth all of fifty dollars," he announced.

"I'm certainly in luck," said Lem. "The crook only stole twenty-eight dollars and sixty cents from me. But I'd rather have my money back. I don't want any of his."

"I'll tell you what I'll do," said the self-styled pawnbroker. "I'll advance you twenty-eight dollars and sixty cents against the ring, and agree to give it back for that sum and suitable interest if the owner should ever call for it."

"That's fair enough," said Lem gratefully, and he pocketed the money that the stranger tendered him.

Our hero paid for the piece of fruit that he had bought from the train boy and ate it with quiet contentment. In the meantime, the "pawnbroker" prepared to get off the train. When he had gathered together his meager luggage, he shook hands with Lem and gave him a receipt for the ring.

But no sooner had the stranger left, than a squad of policemen armed with sawed-off shotguns entered and started down the aisle. Lem watched their progress with great interest. His interest, however, changed to alarm, when they stopped at his seat and one of them caught him roughly by the throat. Handcuffs were then snapped around his wrists. Weapons pointed at his head.

VII

BEGORRA, we've got him," said Sergeant Clancy, who was in charge of the police squad.

"But I haven't done anything," expostulated Lem, turning pale.

"None of your lip, sweetheart," said the sergeant. "Will you go quietly or will you go quietly?" Before the poor lad had a chance to express his willingness to go, the police officer struck him an extremely hard blow on the head with his club.

Lem slumped down in his seat and Sergeant Clancy ordered his men to carry the boy off the train. A patrol wagon was waiting at the depot. Lem's unconscious form was dumped into the "Black Maria" and the police drove to the station house.

When our hero regained consciousness some hours later, he was lying on the stone floor of a cell. The little room was full of detectives and the air was foul with cigar smoke. Lem opened one eye, unwittingly giving the signal for the detectives to go into action.

" 'Fess up," said Detective Grogan, but before the boy could speak, he kicked him in the stomach with his heavy boot.

"Faith now," interfered Detective Reynolds, "give the lad a chance." He bent over Lem's prostrate form with a kind smile on his face and said, "Me lad, the jig is up."

"I'm innocent," protested Lem. "I didn't do anything."

"You stole a diamond ring and sold it," said another detective.

"I did not," replied Lem, with as much fire as he could muster under the circumstances. "A pickpocket dropped it in my pocket and I pawned it with a stranger for thirty dollars."

"Thirty dollars!" exclaimed Detective Reynolds, his voice giving great evidence of disbelief. "Thirty dollars for a ring that cost more than a thousand. Me lad, it won't wash." So saying the detective drew back his foot and kicked poor Lem behind the ear even harder than his colleague had done.

Our hero lost consciousness again, as was to be expected,

and the detectives left his cell, having first made sure that he was still alive.

A few days later, Lem was brought to trial, but neither judge nor jury would believe his story.

Unfortunately, Stamford, the town in which he had been arrested, was in the midst of a crime wave and both the police and judiciary were anxious to send people to jail. It also counted heavily against him that the man who had posed as a pawnbroker on the train was in reality Hiram Glazer alias "The Pinhead," a notorious underworld character. This criminal turned state's evidence and blamed the crime on our hero in return for a small fee from the district attorney who was shortly coming up for re-election.

Once the verdict of guilty had been brought in, Lem was treated with great kindness by everyone, even by the detectives who had been so brutal in the station house. It was through their recommendations, based on what they called his willingness to co-operate, that he received only fifteen years in the penitentiary.

Our hero was immediately transferred to prison, where he was incarcerated exactly five weeks after his departure from Ottsville. It would be hard to say from this that justice is not swift, although, knowing the truth, we must add that it is not always sure.

The warden of the state prison, Ezekiel Purdy, was a kind man if stern. He invariably made all newcomers a little speech of welcome and greeted Lem with the following words:

"My son, the way of the transgressor is hard, but at your age it is still possible to turn from it. However, do not squirm for you will get no sermon from me."

(Lem was not squirming. The warden's expression was purely rhetorical.)

"Sit down for a moment," added Mr. Purdy, indicating the chair in which he wanted Lem to sit. "Your new duties can wait yet awhile, as can the prison barber and tailor."

The warden leaned back in his chair and sucked meditatively on his enormous calabash pipe. When he began to talk again, it was with ardor and conviction.

"The first thing to do is to draw all your teeth," he said. "Teeth are often a source of infection and it pays to be on the safe side. At the same time we will begin a series of cold showers. Cold water is an excellent cure for morbidity."

"But I am innocent," cried Lem, when the full significance of what the warden had said dawned on him. "I am not morbid and I never had a toothache in my life."

Mr. Purdy dismissed the poor lad's protests with an airy wave of his hand. "In my eyes," he said, "the sick are never guilty. You are merely sick, as are all criminals. And as for your other argument; please remember that an ounce of prevention is worth a ton of cure. Because you have never had a toothache does not mean that you will never have one."

Lem could not help but groan.

"Be of good cheer, my son," said the warden brightly, as he pressed a button on his desk to summon a guard.

A few minutes later our hero was led off to the prison dentist where we will not follow him just yet.

VIII

Several chapters back I left our heroine, Betty Prail, lying naked under a bush. She was not quite so fortunate as Lem, and did not regain consciousness until after he had returned home.

When she recovered the full possession of her faculties, she found herself in what she thought was a large box that was being roughly shaken by some unknown agency. In a little while, however, she realized that she was in reality lying on the bottom of a wagon.

"Could it be that she was dead?" she asked herself. But no, she heard voices, and besides she was still naked. "No matter how poor a person is," she comforted herself, "they wrap him or her up in something before burial."

There were evidently two men on the driver's seat of the wagon. She tried to understand what they were saying, but could not because they spoke a foreign tongue. She was able to recognize their language as Italian, however, having had some few music lessons in the orphan asylum.

"Gli diede uno scudo, il che lo rese subito gentile," said one of her captors to the other in a guttural voice.

"Si, si," affirmed the other. "Questa vita terrena e quasi un prato, che'l serpente tra fiori giace." After this bit of homely philosophy, they both lapsed into silence.

But I do not want to mystify my readers any longer. The truth was that the poor girl had been found by white slavers, and was being taken to a house of ill-fame in New York City.

The trip was an exceedingly rough one for our heroine. The wagon in which she was conveyed had no springs to speak of, and her two captors made her serve a severe apprenticeship to the profession they planned for her to follow.

Late one night, the Italians halted their vehicle before the door of a Chinese laundry somewhere near Mott Street. After descending from their dilapidated conveyance, they scanned the street both up and down for a possible policeman. When they had made sure that it was deserted, they covered their captive with some old sacking and bundled her into the laundry.

There they were greeted by an ancient Chinaman, who was doing sums on an abacus. This son of the Celestial Empire was a graduate of the Yale University in Shanghai, and he spoke Italian perfectly.

"Qualche cosa de nuovo, signori?" he asked.

"Molto, molto," said the older and more villainous-looking of the two foreigners. "La vostra lettera l'abbiamo ricevuto, ma il danaro no," he added with a shrewd smile.

"Queste sette medaglie le trovero, compaesano," answered the Chinaman in the same language.

After this rather cryptic dialogue, the Chinaman led Betty through a secret door into a sort of reception room. This chamber was furnished in luxurious oriental splendor. The walls were sheathed in a pink satin that had been embroidered with herons in silver by some cunning workman. On the floor was a silk rug that must have cost more than a thousand dollars; the colors of which could well vie with the rainbow. Before a hideous idol, incense was burning, and its heady odor filled the air. It was evident that neither pains nor expense had been spared in the decoration of the room.

The old Chinaman struck a gong and ere its musical note died away an oriental woman with bound feet came to lead Betty off.

When she had gone, Wu Fong, for that was the Chinaman's name, began to haggle with the two Italians over her purchase price. The bargaining was done in Italian, and rather than attempt to make a word-for-word report of the transaction, I shall give only the result. Betty was knocked down to the Chinaman for six hundred dollars.

This was a big price, so far as prices went in the white slave market, but Wu Fong was set on having her. In fact it was he who had sent the two Italians to scour the New England countryside for a real American girl. Betty suited him down to the ground.

The reader may be curious to know why he wanted an American girl so badly. Let me say now that Wu Fong's establishment was no ordinary house of ill-fame. It was like that more famous one in the Rue Chabanis, Paris, France—a

"House of All Nations." In his institution he already had a girl from every country in the known world except ours, and now Betty rounded out the collection.

Wu Fong was confident that he would soon have his six hundred dollars back with interest, for many of his clients were from non-Aryan countries and would appreciate the services of a genuine American. Apropos of this, it is lamentable but a fact, nevertheless, that the inferior races greatly desire the women of their superiors. This is why the negroes rape so many white women in our southern states.

Each one of the female inmates of Wu Fong's establishment had a tiny two-room suite for her own use, furnished and decorated in the style of the country from which she came. Thus, Marie, the French girl, had an apartment that was Directoire. Celeste's rooms (there were two French girls because of their traditional popularity) were Louis the Fourteenth; she being the fatter of the two.

In her suite, the girl from Spain, Conchita, had a grand piano with a fancy shawl gracefully draped over it. Her armchair was upholstered in horsehide fastened by large buttons, and it had enormous steer-horns for arms. On one of her walls, a tiny balcony had been painted by a poor but consummate artist.

There is little use in my listing the equipment of the remaining some fifty-odd apartments. Suffice it to say that the same idea was carried out with excellent taste and real historical knowledge in all of them.

Still wearing the sacking into which the Italians had bundled her, our heroine was led to the apartment that had been prepared against her arrival.

The proprietor of the house had hired Asa Goldstein to decorate this suite and it was a perfect colonial interior. Antimacassars, ships in bottles, carved whalebone, hooked rugs—all were there. It was Mr. Goldstein's boast that even Governor Windsor himself could not have found anything wrong with the design or furnishings.

Betty was exhausted, and immediately fell asleep on the poster bed with its candlewick spread. When she awoke, she was given a hot bath which greatly refreshed her. She was then dressed by two skilful maids.

The costume that she was made to wear had been especially designed to go with her surroundings. While not exactly in period, it was very striking, and I will describe it as best I can for the benefit of my feminine readers.

The dress had a full waist made with a yoke and belt, a gored skirt, long, but not too long to afford a very distinct view of a well-turned ankle and a small, shapely foot encased in a snowy cotton stocking and a low heeled black slipper. The material of the dress was chintz—white ground with a tiny brown figure—finished at the neck with a wide white ruffle. On her hands she was made to wear black silk mitts with half-fingers. Her hair was worn in a little knot on the top of her head, and one thick short curl was kept in place by a puff-comb on each side of her face.

Breakfast, for so much time had elapsed, was served her by an old negro in livery. It consisted of buckwheat cakes with maple syrup, Rhode Island Johnny cakes, bacon biscuits, and a large slice of apple pie.

(Wu Fong was a great stickler for detail, and, like many another man, if he had expended as much energy and thought honestly, he would have made even more money without having to carry the stigma of being a brothel keeper. Alas!)

So resilient are the spirits of the young that Betty did the breakfast full justice. She even ordered a second helping of pie, which was brought to her at once by the darky.

After Betty had finished eating, she was given some embroidery to do. With the reader's kind permission we will leave her while she is still sewing, and before the arrival of her first client, a pockmarked Armenian rug merchant from Malta.

IX

JUSTICE will out. I am happy to acquaint my readers with the fact that the real criminal, Mr. Wellington Mape, was apprehended by the police some few weeks after Lem had been incarcerated in the state penitentiary.

But our hero was in a sorry state when the governor's pardon arrived, and for a while it looked as though the reprieve had come too late. The poor lad was in the prison infirmary with a bad case of pneumonia. Weakened greatly by the drawing of all his teeth, he had caught cold after the thirteenth icy shower and the fourteenth had damaged his lungs.

Due to his strong physique, however, and a constitution that had never been undermined by the use of either tobacco or alcohol, Lem succeeded in passing the crisis of the dread pulmonary disease.

On the first day that his vision was normal, he was surprised to see Shagpoke Whipple go through the prison infirmary carrying what was evidently a bed-pan and dressed in the uniform of a convict.

"Mr. Whipple," Lem called. "Mr. Whipple."

The ex-president turned and came towards the boy's bed.

"Hello, Lem," said Shagpoke, putting down the utensil he was carrying. "I'm glad to see that you're better."

"Thank you, sir. But what are you doing here?" asked Lem with bewildered surprise.

"I'm the trusty in charge of this ward. But what you really mean, I take it, is why am I here?"

The elderly statesman looked around. He saw that the guard was busy talking to a pretty nurse and drew up a chair.

"It's a long story," said Mr. Whipple with a sigh. "But the long and short of it is that the Rat River National failed and its depositors sent me here."

"That's too bad, sir," Lem said sympathetically. "And after all you had done for the town."

"Such is the gratitude of the mob, but in a way I can't blame them," Mr. Whipple said with all the horse sense for which he was famous. "Rather do I blame Wall Street and the Jewish International Bankers. They loaded me up with a lot of European and South American bonds, then they forced me to the wall. It was Wall Street working hand in hand with the Communists that caused my downfall. The bankers broke me, and the Communists circulated lying rumors about my bank in Doc Slack's barbershop. I was the victim of an un-American conspiracy."

Mr. Whipple sighed again, then said in a militant tone of voice: "My boy, when we get out of here, there are two evils undermining this country which we must fight with tooth and nail. These two arch-enemies of the American Spirit, the spirit of fair play and open competition, are Wall Street and the Communists."

"But how is my mother?" interrupted Lem, "and whatever became of our house? And the cow—did you have to sell her?" Our hero's voice trembled as he asked these questions for he feared the worst.

"Alas," sighed Mr. Whipple, "Squire Bird foreclosed his mortgage and Asa Goldstein took your home to his store in New York City. There is some talk of his selling it to the Metropolitan Museum. As for the cow, the creditors of my bank sheriffed her. Your mother disappeared. She wandered off during the foreclosure sale, and neither hair nor hide of her was seen again."

This terrible intelligence made our hero literally groan with anguish.

In an effort to cheer the boy up, Mr. Whipple kept on talking. "Your cow taught me a lesson," he said. "She was about the only collateral I had that paid one hundred cents on the dollar. The European bonds didn't bring ten cents on the dollar. The next bank I own will mortgage nothing but cows, good American cows."

"You expect to keep a bank again?" asked Lem, making a brave attempt not to think of his own troubles.

"Why, certainly," replied Shagpoke. "My friends will have me out of here shortly. Then I will run for political office, and after I have shown the American people that Shagpoke is still Shagpoke, I will retire from politics and open another bank. In fact, I am even considering opening the Rat River National a second time. I should be able to buy it in for a few cents on the dollar."

"Do you really think you can do it?" asked our hero with wonder and admiration.

"Why, of course I can," answered Mr. Whipple. "I am an American business man, and this place is just an incident in my career. My boy, I believe I once told you that you had an almost certain chance to succeed because you were born poor and on a farm. Let me now tell you that your chance is even better because you have been in prison."

"But what am I to do when I get out?" asked Lem with ill-concealed desperation.

"Be an inventor," Mr. Whipple replied without a moment's hesitation. "The American mind is noted for its ingenuity. All the devices of the modern world, from the safety pin to four-wheel brakes, were invented by us."

"But I don't know what to invent," said Lem.

"That's easy. Before you leave here I will give you several of my inventions to work on. If you perfect them we will split fifty-fifty."

"That'll be great!" exclaimed Lem with increased cheerfulness.

"My young friend, you don't want me to think that you were in any way discouraged by the misfortunes that befell you?" asked Mr. Whipple with simulated surprise.

"But I didn't even get to New York," apologized Lem.

"America is still a young country," Mr. Whipple said, assuming his public manner, "and like all young countries, it is rough and unsettled. Here a man is a millionaire one day and a pauper the next, but no one thinks the worse of him. The wheel will turn, for that is the nature of wheels. Don't believe the fools who tell you that the poor man hasn't got a chance to get rich any more because the country is full of chain stores. Office boys still marry their employer's daughters. Shipping clerks are still becoming presidents of railroads. Why, only the other day, I read where an elevator operator won a hundred thousand dollars in a sweepstake and was made a partner in a brokerage house. Despite the Communists and their vile propaganda against individualism, this is still the golden land of opportunity. Oil wells are still found in people's back yards. There are still gold mines hidden away in our mountain fastnesses. America is. . . ."

But while Shagpoke was still speaking, a prison guard came by and forced him hurriedly to resume his duties. He left with his bed-pan, before Lem had an opportunity to thank him properly for his inspiring little talk.

Helped not a little by the encouragement Mr. Whipple had given him, our hero mended rapidly. One day he was summoned to the office of Mr. Purdy, the warden. That official showed him the pardon from the governor.

As a parting gift, he presented Lem with a set of false teeth. He then conducted him to the prison gates, and stood there awhile with the boy, for he had grown fond of him.

Shaking Lem's hand in a hearty farewell, Mr. Purdy said:

"Suppose you had obtained a job in New York City that paid fifteen dollars a week. You were here with us in all twenty weeks, so you lost the use of three hundred dollars. However, you paid no board while you were here, which was a saving for you of about seven dollars a week or one hundred and forty dollars. This leaves you the loser by one hundred and sixty dollars. But it would have cost you at least two hundred dollars to have all your teeth extracted, so you're really ahead of the game forty dollars. Also, the set of false teeth I gave you cost twenty dollars new and is worth at least fifteen dollars in their present condition. This makes your profit about fifty-five dollars. Not at all a bad sum for a lad of your age to save in twenty weeks."

X

ALONG with his civilian clothes, the prison authorities turned back to Lem an envelope containing the thirty dollars he had had in his pockets on the day he was arrested.

He did not loiter in Stamford, but went immediately to the depot and bought a ticket for New York City. When the cars pulled into the station, he boarded them determined not to speak to any strangers. He was helped in this by the fact that he was not as yet used to his false teeth. Unless he exercised great care, they fell into his lap every time he opened his mouth.

He arrived in the Grand Central Station all intact. At first he was quite confused by the hustle and bustle of the great city, but when a Jehu standing by a broken-down Pierce Arrow hack accosted him, he had the presence of mind to shake his head in the negative.

The cabby was a persistent fellow. "Where do you want to go, young master?" he asked with sneering servility. "Is it the Ritz Hotel you're looking for?"

Lem took a firm purchase on his store teeth and asked, "That's one of those high-priced taverns, isn't it?"

"Yes, but I'll take you to a cheap one if you'll hire me."

"What's your charge?"

"Three dollars and a half, and half a dollar for your baggage."

"This is all the baggage I have," said Lem, indicating his few things tied in a red cotton handkerchief.

"I'll take you for three dollars, then," said the driver with a superior smile.

"No, thanks, I'll walk," said our hero. "I can't afford to pay your charge."

"You can't walk; it's over ten miles from this station to town," replied the Jehu without blushing, although it was evident that they were at that moment standing almost directly in the center of the city.

Without another word, Lem turned on his heel and walked away from the cab driver. As he made his way through the crowded streets, he congratulated himself on how he had handled his first encounter. By keeping his wits about him, he had saved over a tenth of his capital.

Lem saw a peanut stand, and as a matter of policy purchased a bag of the toothsome earth nuts.

"I'm from the country," he said to the honest-appearing merchant. "Can you direct me to a cheap hotel?"

"Yes," said the sidewalk vendor, smiling at the boy's candor. "I know of one where they charge only a dollar a day."

"Is that cheap?" asked our hero in surprise. "What then do they charge at the Ritz?"

"I have never stayed there, but I understand that it is as much as three dollars a day."

"Phew!" whistled Lem. "Think of that now. Twenty-one dollars a week. But I suppose they do you awfully well."

"Yes, I hear they set a very good table."

"Will you be so kind as to direct me to the cheap one of which you first spoke?"

"Certainly."

It was the Commercial House to which the peanut dealer advised Lem to go. This hostelry was located in a downtown street very near the Bowery and was not a stylish inn by any manner of means. However, it was held in good repute by many merchants in a small way of business. Our hero was well satisfied with the establishment when he found it. He had never before seen a fine hotel, and this structure being five stories above the offices seemed to him rather imposing than otherwise.

After being taken to his room, Lem went downstairs and found that dinner was ready, it being just noon. He ate with a country boy's appetite. It was not a luxurious meal, but compared with the table that Warden Purdy set it was a feast for the gods.

When he had finished eating, Lem asked the hotel clerk how to get to Asa Goldstein's store on Fifth Avenue. He was told to walk to Washington Square, then take the bus uptown.

After an exciting ride along the beautiful thoroughfare,

Lem descended from the bus before a store, across the front of which was a sign reading

ASA GOLDSTEIN, LTD.
Colonial Exteriors and Interiors

and in the window of which his old home actually stood.

At first the poor boy could not believe his eyes, but, yes, there it was exactly as in Vermont. One of the things that struck him was the seediness of the old house. When he and his mother had lived in it, they had kept it in a much better state of repair.

Our hero stood gazing at the exhibit for so long that he attracted the attention of one of the clerks. This suave individual came out to the street and addressed Lem.

"You admire the architecture of New England?" he said, feeling our hero out.

"No; it's that particular house that interests me, sir," replied Lem truthfully. "I used to live in it. In fact I was born in that very house."

"My, this is interesting," said the clerk politely. "Perhaps you would like to enter the shop and inspect it at first hand."

"Thank you," replied Lem gratefully. "It would give me a great deal of pleasure so to do."

Our hero followed after the affable clerk and was permitted to examine his old home at close range. To tell the truth, he saw it through a veil of tears, for he could think of nothing but his poor mother who had disappeared.

"I wonder if you would be so kind as to furnish me with a little information?" asked the clerk, pointing to a patched, old chest of drawers. "Where would your mother have put such a piece of furniture had she owned it?"

Lem's first thought on inspecting the article in question was to say that she would have kept it in the woodshed, but he thought better of this when he saw how highly the clerk valued it. After a little thought, he pointed to a space next to the fireplace and said, "I think she would have set it there."

"What did I tell you!" exclaimed the delighted clerk to his colleagues, who had gathered around to hear Lem's answer. "That's just the spot I picked for it."

The clerk then ushered Lem to the door, slipping a two

dollar note into the boy's hand as he shook it good-bye. Lem did not want to take the money because he felt that he had not earned it, but he was finally prevailed upon to accept it. The clerk told Lem that he had saved them the fee an expert would have demanded, since it was very important for them to know exactly where the chest of drawers belonged.

Our hero was considerably elated at his stroke of luck and marveled at the ease with which two dollars could be earned in York. At this rate of pay, he calculated, he would earn ninety-six dollars for an eight-hour day or five hundred and seventy-six dollars for a six-day week. If he could keep it up, he would have a million in no time.

From the store, Lem walked west to Central Park, where he sat down on a bench in the mall near the bridle path to watch the society people ride by on their beautiful horses. His attention was particularly attracted by a man driving a small spring wagon, underneath which ran two fine Dalmatians or coach dogs, as they are sometimes called. Although Lem was unaware of this fact, the man in the wagon was none other than Mr. Asa Goldstein, whose shop he had just visited.

The country-bred boy soon noticed that Mr. Goldstein was not much of a horseman. However, that individual was not driving his beautiful team of matched bays for pleasure, as one might be led to think, but for profit. He had accumulated a large collection of old wagons in his warehouse and by driving one of them in the mall he hoped to start a vogue for that type of equipage and thus sell off his stock.

While Lem was watching the storekeeper's awkward handling of the "leathers" or reins, the off horse, which was very skittish, took fright at a passing policeman and bolted. His panic soon spread to the other horse and the wagon went careening down the path wreaking havoc at every bound. Mr. Goldstein fell out when his vehicle turned over, and Lem had to laugh at the comical expression of mingled disgust and chagrin that appeared on his countenance.

But suddenly Lem's smile disappeared and his jaw became set, for he saw that a catastrophe was bound to occur unless something was immediately done to halt the maddened thoroughbreds.

XI

THE REASON for the sudden disappearance of the smile from our hero's face is easily explained. He had spied an old gentleman and his beautiful young daughter about to cross the bridle path, and saw that in a few more seconds they would be trampled under the iron hooves of the flying beasts.

Lem hesitated only long enough to take a firm purchase on his store teeth, then dashed into the path of the horses. With great strength and agility, he grasped their bridles and dragged them to a rearing halt, a few feet from the astounded and thoroughly frightened pair.

"That lad has saved your lives," said a bystander to the old gentleman, who was none other than Mr. Levi Underdown, president of the Underdown National Bank and Trust Company.

Unfortunately, however, Mr. Underdown was slightly deaf, and, although exceedingly kind, as his many large charities showed, he was very short tempered. He entirely misunderstood the nature of our hero's efforts and thought that the poor boy was a careless groom who had let his charges get out of hand. He became extremely angry.

"I've a mind to give you in charge, young man," said the banker, shaking his umbrella at our hero.

"Oh, don't, father!" interfered his daughter Alice, who also misunderstood the incident. "Don't have him arrested. He was probably paying court to some pretty nursemaid and forgot about his horses." From this we can readily see that the young lady was of a romantic turn of mind.

She smiled kindly at our hero, and led her irate parent from the scene.

Lem had been unable to utter one word in explanation because, during his tussle with the horses, his teeth had jarred loose and without them he was afraid to speak. All he could do was to gaze after their departing backs with mute but ineffectual anguish.

There being nothing else for it, Lem gave over the reins of the team to Mr. Goldstein's groom, who came running up at this juncture, and turned to search for his oral equipment in the mud of the bridle path. While he was thus occupied, a man representing the insurance company with which Mr. Goldstein carried a public liability policy approached him.

"Here is ten dollars, my lad," said the claim adjuster. "The gentleman whose horses you so bravely stopped wishes you to have this money as a reward."

Lem took it without thinking.

"Please sign this for me," added the insurance man, holding out a legal form which released his company from any and all claim to damages.

One of Lem's eyes had been so badly injured by a flying stone that he could not see out of it, but nevertheless he refused to sign.

The claim adjuster had recourse to a ruse. "I am an autograph collector," he said slyly. "Unfortunately, I have not my album with me, but if you will be so kind as to sign this piece of paper which I happened to have in my pocket, you will make me very happy. When I return home, I will immediately transfer your autograph to a distinguished place in my collection."

Befuddled by the pain in his injured eye, Lem signed in order to be rid of the importunate fellow, then bent again to the task of finding his store teeth. He finally discovered them deep in the mud of the bridle path. After carefully prying the set loose, he went to a public drinking fountain for the dual purpose of bathing both it and his hurt eye.

XII

WHILE he busied himself at the fountain, a young man approached. This stranger was distinguished from the usual run by his long black hair which tumbled in waves over the back of his collar and by an unusually high and broad forehead. On his head he wore a soft, black hat with an enormously wide brim. Both his tie, which was Windsor, and his gestures, which were Latin, floated with the same graceful freedom as his hair.

"Excuse me," said this odd-appearing individual, "but I witnessed your heroic act and I wish to take the liberty of congratulating you. In these effete times, it is rare indeed for one to witness a hero in action."

Lem was embarrassed. He hurriedly replaced his teeth and thanked the stranger for his praise. He continued, however, to bathe his wounded eye which was still giving him considerable pain.

"Let me introduce myself," the young man continued. "I am Sylvanus Snodgrasse, a poet both by vocation and avocation. May I ask your name?"

"Lemuel Pitkin," answered our hero, making no attempt to hide the fact that he was suspicious of this self-styled "poet." In fact there were many things about him that reminded Lem of Mr. Wellington Mape.

"Mr. Pitkin," he said grandly, "I intend to write an ode about the deed performed by you this day. You do not perhaps appreciate, having a true hero's modesty, the significance, the classicality—if I may be permitted a neologism—of your performance. Poor Boy, Flying Team, Banker's Daughter . . . it's in the real American tradition and perfectly fitted to my native lyre. Fie on your sickly Prousts, U.S. poets must write about the U.S."

Our hero did not venture to comment on these sentiments. For one thing, his eye hurt so much that even his sense of hearing was occupied with the pain.

Snodgrasse kept talking, and soon a crowd of curious people

gathered around him and poor Lemuel. The "poet" no longer addressed our hero, but the crowd in general.

"Gentlemen," said he in a voice that carried all the way to Central Park South, "and ladies, I am moved by this youth's heroism to venture a few remarks.

"There have been heroes before him—Leonidas, Quintus Maximus, Wolfe Tone, Deaf Smith, to mention only a few— but this should not prevent us from hailing L. Pitkin as the hero, if not of our time, at least of the immediate past.

"One of the most striking things about his heroism is the dominance of the horse motif, involving, as it does, not one but two horses. This is important because the depression has made all us Americans conscious of certain spiritual lacks, not the least of which is the symbolic horse.

"Every great nation has its symbolic horses. The grandeur that was Greece is made immortal by those marvelous equines, half god, half beast, still to be seen in the corners of the Parthenon pediment. Rome, the eternal city, how perfectly is her glory caught in those martial steeds that rear their fearful forms to Titus's triumph! And Venice, Queen of the Adriatic, has she not her winged sea horses, kindred to both air and water?

"Alas, only we are without. Do not point to General Sherman's horse or I will be angry, for that craven hack, that crow bait, is nothing. I repeat, nothing. What I want is for all my hearers to go home and immediately write to their congressmen demanding that a statue depicting Pitkin's heroic act be erected in every public park throughout our great country."

Although Sylvanus Snodgrasse kept on in this vein for quite some time, I will stop reporting his oration to acquaint you, dear reader, with his real purpose. As you have probably surmised, it was not so innocent as it seemed. The truth is that while he kept the crowd amused, his confederates circulated freely among its members and picked their pockets.

They had succeeded in robbing the whole crowd, including our hero, when a policeman made his appearance. Snodgrasse immediately discontinued his address and hurried off after his henchmen.

The officer dispersed the gathering and everyone moved away except Lem, who was lying on the ground in a dead faint. The bluecoat, thinking that the poor boy was drunk, kicked him a few times, but when several hard blows in the groin failed to budge him, he decided to call an ambulance.

XIII

ONE wintry morning, several weeks after the incident in the park, Lem was dismissed from the hospital minus his right eye. It had been so severely damaged that the physicians had thought best to remove it.

He had no money, for, as we have recounted, Snodgrasse's henchmen had robbed him. Even the teeth that Warden Purdy had given him were gone. They had been taken from him by the hospital authorities, who claimed that they did not fit properly and were therefore a menace to his health.

The poor lad was standing on a windy corner, not knowing which way to turn, when he saw a man in a coonskin hat. This remarkable headgear made Lem stare, and the more he looked the more the man seemed to resemble Shagpoke Whipple.

It was Mr. Whipple. Lem hastened to call out to him, and the ex-president stopped to shake hands with his young friend.

"About those inventions," Shagpoke said immediately after they had finished greeting each other. "It was too bad that you left the penitentiary before I could hand them over to you. Not knowing your whereabouts, I perfected them myself."

"But let us repair to a coffee place," he added, changing the subject, "where we can talk over your prospects together. I am still very much interested in your career. In fact, my young friend, America has never had a greater need for her youth than in these parlous times."

After our hero had thanked him for his interest and good wishes, Mr. Whipple continued to talk. "Speaking of coffee," he said, "did you know that the fate of our country was decided in the coffee shops of Boston during the hectic days preceding the late rebellion?"

As they paused at the door of a restaurant, Mr. Whipple asked Lem still another question. "By the way," he said, "I am temporarily without funds. Are you able to meet the obligation we will incur in this place?"

"No," replied Lem, sadly, "I am penniless."

"That's different," said Mr. Whipple with a profound sigh. "In that case we will go where I have credit."

Lem was conducted by his fellow townsman to an extremely poor section of the city. After standing on line for several hours, they each received a doughnut and a cup of coffee from the Salvation Army lassie in charge. They then sat down on the curb to eat their little snack.

"You are perhaps wondering," Shagpoke began, "how it is that I stand on line with these homeless vagrants to obtain bad coffee and soggy doughnuts. Be assured that I do it of my own free will and for the good of the state."

Here he paused long enough to skilfully "shoot a snipe" that was still burning. He puffed contentedly on his catch.

"When I left jail, it was my intention to run for office again. But I discovered to my great amazement and utter horror that my party, the Democratic Party, carried not a single plank in its platform that I could honestly endorse. Rank socialism was and is rampant. How could I, Shagpoke Whipple, ever bring myself to accept a program which promised to take from American citizens their inalienable birthright; the right to sell their labor and their children's labor without restrictions as to either price or hours?

"The time for a new party with the old American principles was, I realized, over-ripe. I decided to form it; and so the National Revolutionary Party, popularly known as the 'Leather Shirts,' was born. The uniform of our 'Storm Troops' is a coonskin cap like the one I am wearing, a deerskin shirt and a pair of moccasins. Our weapon is the squirrel rifle."

He pointed to the long queue of unemployed who stood waiting before the Salvation Army canteen. "These men," he said, "are the material from which I must fill the ranks of my party."

With all the formality of a priest, Shagpoke turned to our hero and laid his hand on his shoulder.

"My boy," he said, and his voice broke under the load of emotion it was forced to bear, "my boy, will you join me?"

"Certainly, sir," said Lem, a little unsurely.

"Excellent!" exclaimed Mr. Whipple. "Excellent! I herewith appoint you a commander attached to my general staff."

He drew himself up and saluted Lem, who was startled by the gesture.

"Commander Pitkin," he ordered briskly, "I desire to address these people. Please obtain a soap box."

Our hero went on the errand required of him, and soon returned with a large box, which Mr. Whipple immediately mounted. He then set about attracting the attention of the vagrants collected about the Salvation Army canteen by shouting:

"Remember the River Raisin!"

"Remember the Alamo!"

"Remember the Maine!"

and many other famous slogans.

When a large group had gathered, Shagpoke began his harangue.

"I'm a simple man," he said with great simplicity, "and I want to talk simply to you about simple things. You'll get no highfalutin' talk from me.

"First of all, you people want jobs. Isn't that so?"

An ominous rumble of assent came from the throats of the poorly dressed gathering.

"Well, that's the only and prime purpose of the National Revolutionary Party—to get jobs for everyone. There was enough work to go around in 1927, why isn't there enough now? I'll tell you; because of the Jewish international bankers and the Bolshevik labor unions, that's why. It was those two agents that did the most to hinder American business and to destroy its glorious expansion. The former because of their hatred of America and love for Europe and the latter because of their greed for higher and still higher wages.

"What is the rôle of the labor union today? It is a privileged club which controls all the best jobs for its members. When one of you applies for a job, even if the man who owns the plant wants to hire you, do you get it? Not if you haven't got a union card. Can any tyranny be greater? Has Liberty ever been more brazenly despised?"

These statements were received with cheers by his audience.

"Citizens, Americans," Mr. Whipple continued, when the noise had subsided, "we of the middle class are being crushed between two gigantic millstones. Capital is the upper stone and Labor the lower, and between them we suffer and die, ground out of existence.

"Capital is international; its home is in London and in Amsterdam. Labor is international; its home is in Moscow. We alone are American; and when we die, America dies.

"When I say that, I make no idle boast, for history bears me out. Who but the middle class left aristocratic Europe to settle on these shores? Who but the middle class, the small farmers and storekeepers, the clerks and petty officials, fought for freedom and died that America might escape from British tyranny?

"This is our country and we must fight to keep it so. If America is ever again to be great, it can only be through the triumph of the revolutionary middle class.

"We must drive the Jewish international bankers out of Wall Street! We must destroy the Bolshevik labor unions! We must purge our country of all the alien elements and ideas that now infest her!

"America for Americans! Back to the principles of Andy Jackson and Abe Lincoln!"

Here Shagpoke paused to let the cheers die down, then called for volunteers to join his "Storm Battalions."

A number of men came forward. In their lead was a very dark individual, who had extra-long black hair of an extremely coarse quality, and on whose head was a derby hat many sizes too small for him.

"Me American mans," he announced proudly. "Me got heap coon hat, two maybe six. Bye, bye catchum plenty more coon maybe." With this he grinned from ear to ear.

But Shagpoke was a little suspicious of his complexion, and looked at him with disfavor. In the South, where he expected to get considerable support for his movement, they would not stand for Negroes.

The good-natured stranger seemed to sense what was wrong, for he said, "Me Injun, mister, me chief along my people. Gotum gold mine, oil well. Name of Jake Raven. Ugh!"

Shagpoke grew cordial at once. "Chief Jake Raven," he said, holding out his hand, "I am happy to welcome you into our organization. We 'Leather Shirts' can learn much from your people, fortitude, courage and relentless purpose among other things."

After taking down his name, Shagpoke gave the Indian a card which read as follows:

EZRA SILVERBLATT

Official Tailor

to the

NATIONAL REVOLUTIONARY PARTY

Coonskin hats with extra long tails, deerskin shirts with or without fringes, blue jeans, moccasins, squirrel rifles, everything for the American Fascist at rock bottom prices. 30% off for Cash.

But let us leave Mr. Whipple and Lem busy with their recruiting to observe the actions of a certain member of the crowd.

The individual in question would have been remarkable in any gathering, and among the starved, ragged men that surrounded Shagpoke, he stuck out like the proverbial sore thumb. For one thing he was fat, enormously fat. There were other fat men present to be sure, but they were yellow, unhealthy, while this man's fat was pink and shone with health.

On his head was a magnificent bowler hat. It was a beautiful jet in color, and must have cost more than twelve dollars. He was snugly encased in a tight-fitting Chesterfield overcoat with a black velvet collar. His stiff-bosomed shirt had light grey bars, and his tie was of some rich but sober material in black and white pin-checks. Spats, rattan stick and yellow gloves completed his outfit.

This elaborate fat man tip-toed out of the crowd and made his way to a telephone booth in a nearby drugstore, where he called two numbers.

His conversation with the person answering his first call, a Wall Street Exchange, went something like this:

"Operative 6384XM, working out of the Bourse, Paris, France. Middle class organizers functioning on unemployed front, corner of Houston and Bleecker Streets."

"Thank you, 6384XM, what is your estimate?"

"Twenty men and a fire hose."

"At once, 6384XM, at once."

His second call was to an office near Union Square.

"Comrade R, please. . . . Comrade R?"

"Yes."

"Comrade R, this is Comrade Z speaking. Gay Pay Oo, Moscow, Russia. Middle class organizers recruiting on the corner of Houston and Bleecker Streets."

"Your estimate, comrade, for liquidation of said activities?"

"Ten men with lead pipes and brass knuckles to co-operate with Wall Street office of the I.J.B."

"No bombs required?"

"No, comrade."

"Der Tag!"

"Der Tag!"

Mr. Whipple had just enrolled his twenty-seventh recruit, when the forces of both the international Jewish bankers and the Communists converged on his meeting. They arrived in high-powered black limousines and deployed through the streets with a skill which showed long and careful training in that type of work. In fact their officers were all West Point graduates.

Mr. Whipple saw them coming, but like a good general his first thoughts were for his men.

"The National Revolutionary Party will now go underground!" he shouted.

Lem, made wary by his past experiences with the police, immediately took to his heels, followed by Chief Raven. Shagpoke, however, was late in getting started. He still had one foot on the soap box, when he was hit a terrific blow on the head with a piece of lead pipe.

XIV

MY MAN, if you can wear this glass eye, I have a job for you."

The speaker was an exceedingly dapper gentleman in a light grey fedora hat and a pince-nez with a black silk ribbon that fell to his coat opening in a graceful loop.

As he spoke, he held out at arm's length a beautiful glass eye.

But the object of his words did not reply; it did not even move. To anyone but a trained observer, he would have appeared to be addressing a bundle of old rags that someone had propped up on a park bench.

Turning the eye from side to side, so that it sparkled like a jewel in the winter sun, the man waited patiently for the bundle to reply. From time to time, he stirred it sharply with the Malacca walking stick he carried.

Suddenly a groan came from the rags and they shook slightly. The cane had evidently reached a sensitive spot. Encouraged, the man repeated his original proposition.

"Can you wear this eye? If so, I'll hire you."

At this, the bundle gave a few spasmodic quivers and a faint whimper. From somewhere below its peak a face appeared, then a greenish hand moved out and took the glittering eye, raising it to an empty socket in the upper part of the face.

"Here, let me help you," said the owner of the eye kindly. With a few deft motions he soon had it fixed in its proper receptacle.

"Perfect!" exclaimed the man, standing back and admiring his handiwork. "Perfect! You're hired!"

He then reached into his overcoat and brought forth a wallet from which he extracted a five dollar bill and a calling card. He laid both of these on the bench beside the one-eyed man, who by now had again become a quiescent bundle of greasy rags.

"Get yourself a haircut, a bath and a big meal, then go to my tailors, Ephraim Pierce and Sons, and they will fit you out with clothes. When you are presentable, call on me at the Ritz Hotel."

With these words, the man in the grey fedora turned sharply on his heel and left the park.

If you have not already guessed the truth, dear reader, let me acquaint you with the fact that the bundle of rags contained our hero, Lemuel Pitkin. Alas, to such a sorry pass had he come.

After the unfortunate termination of Shagpoke's attempt to recruit men for his "Leather Shirts," he had rapidly gone from bad to worse. Having no money and no way in which to obtain any, he had wandered from employment agency to employment agency without success. Reduced to eating from garbage pails and sleeping in empty lots, he had become progressively shabbier and weaker, until he had reached the condition we discovered him in at the beginning of this chapter.

But now things were looking up again, and just in time I must admit, for our hero had begun to doubt whether he would ever make his fortune.

Lem pocketed the five dollars that the stranger had left and examined the card.

ELMER HAINEY, ESQUIRE
RITZ HOTEL

This was all the bit of engraved pasteboard said. It gave no evidence of either the gentleman's business or profession. But this did not in any way bother Lem, for at last it looked as though he were going to have a job; and in the year of our Lord nineteen thirty-four that was indeed something.

Lem struggled to his feet and set out to follow Mr. Hainey's instructions. In fact he ate two large meals and took two baths. It was only his New England training that prevented him from getting two haircuts.

Having done as much as he could to rehabilitate his body, he next went to the shop of Ephraim Pierce and Sons, where he was fitted out with a splendid wardrobe complete in every detail. Several hours later, he walked up Park Avenue to wait on his new employer, looking every inch a prosperous young business man of the finest type.

When Lem asked for Mr. Hainey, the manager of the Ritz

bowed him into the elevator, which stopped to let him off at the fortieth floor. He rang the door bell of Mr. Hainey's suite and in a few minutes was ushered into that gentleman's presence by an English personal servant.

Mr. Hainey greeted the lad with great cordiality. "Excellent! Excellent!" he repeated three or four times in rapid succession as he inspected the transformed appearance of our hero.

Lem expressed his gratitude by a deep bow.

"If there is anything about your outfit that you dislike," he went on to say, "please tell me now before I give you your instructions."

Emboldened by his kind manner, Lem ventured an objection. "Pardon me, sir," he said, "but the eye, the glass eye you gave me is the wrong color. My good eye is blue-grey, while the one you provided me with is light green."

"Exactly," was Mr. Hainey's surprising answer. "The effect is, as I calculated, striking. When anyone sees you I want to make sure that they notice that one of your eyes is glass."

Lem was forced to agree to this strange idea and he did so with all the grace he could manage.

Mr. Hainey then got down to business. His whole manner changed, becoming as cold as a steel trap and twice as formal.

"My secretary," he said, "has typed a set of instructions which I will give you tonight. I want you to take them home and study them carefully, for you will be expected to do exactly as they order without the slightest deviation. One slip, please remember, and you will be immediately discharged."

"Thank you, sir," replied Lem. "I understand."

"Your salary," said Mr. Hainey, softening a bit, "will be thirty dollars a week and found. I have arranged room and board for you at the Warford House. Please go there tonight."

Mr. Hainey then took out his wallet and gave Lem three ten-dollar bills.

"You are very generous," said Lem, taking them. "I shall do my utmost to satisfy you."

"That's nice, but please don't show too much zeal, simply follow instructions."

Mr. Hainey next went to his desk and took from it several typewritten sheets of paper. He gave these to Lem.

"One more thing," he said, shaking hands at the door, "you may be a little mystified when you read your instructions, but that cannot be helped, for I am unable to give you a complete explanation at this time. However, I want you to know that I own a glass eye factory, and that your duties are part of a sales-promotion campaign."

XV

L EM restrained his curiosity. He waited until he was safely
ensconced in his new quarters in the Warford House
before opening the instructions Mr. Hainey had given him.

Here is what he read:

"Go to the jewelry store of Hazelton Frères and ask to see
their diamond stickpins. After looking at one tray, demand to
see another. While the clerk has his back turned, remove the
glass eye from your head and put it in your pocket. As soon
as the clerk turns around again, appear to be searching frantically on the floor for something.

"The following dialogue will then take place:

"*Clerk:* 'Have you lost something, sir?'

"*You:* 'Yes, my eye.' (Here indicate the opening in your
head with your index finger.)

"*Clerk:* 'That's unfortunate, sir. I'll help you look, sir.'

"*You:* 'Please do. (With much agitation.) I must find it.'

"A thorough search of the premises is then made, but of
course the missing eye cannot be found because it is safe in
your pocket.

"*You:* 'Please may I see one of the owners of this store; one
of the Hazelton Brothers?' (Note: Frères means brothers and
is not to be mistaken for the storekeeper's last name.)

"In a few minutes the clerk will bring Mr. Hazelton from
his office in the rear of the store.

"*You:* 'Mr. Hazelton, sir, I have had the misfortune to lose
my eye here in your shop.'

"*Mr. Hazelton:* 'Perhaps you left it at home.'

"*You:* 'Impossible! I would have felt the draft, for I walked
here from Mr. Hamilton Schuyler's house on Fifth Avenue.
No, I'm afraid that it was in its proper position when I entered
your place.'

"*Mr. Hazelton:* 'You can be certain, sir, that we will make
a thorough search.'

"*You:* 'Please do. I am, however, unable to wait the outcome of your efforts. I have to be in the Spanish embassy to

see the ambassador, Count Raymon de Guzman y Alfrache (the y is pronounced like the e in eat) within the hour.'

"Mr. Hazelton will bow profoundly on hearing with whom your appointment is.

"*You* (continuing): 'The eye I have lost is irreplaceable. It was made for me by a certain German expert, and cost a very large sum. I cannot get another because its maker was killed in the late war and the secret of its manufacture was buried with him. (Pause for a brief moment, bowing your head as though in sorrow for the departed expert.) However (you continue), please tell your clerks that I will pay one thousand dollars as a reward to anyone who recovers my eye.'

"*Mr. Hazelton:* 'That will be entirely unnecessary, sir. Rest assured that we will do everything in our power to discover it for you.'

"*You:* 'Very good. I am going to visit friends on Long Island tonight, but I will be in your shop tomorrow. If you have the eye, I will insist on paying the reward.'

"Mr. Hazelton will then bow you out of the shop.

"Until you receive further instructions from Mr. Hainey, you are to stay away from the near vicinity of Hazelton Frères.

"On the day following your visit to the shop call the Ritz Hotel and ask for Mr. Hainey's secretary. Tell him whether or not everything went off in accordance with these instructions. The slightest deviation on the part of Mr. Hazelton from the proscribed formula must be reported."

XVI

LEM'S job was a sinecure. He had merely to enact the same scene over one morning a week, each time in a different store. He soon had his part by heart, and once he had lost his embarrassment over having to say that he knew the Spanish Ambassador, he quite enjoyed his work. It reminded him of the amateur theatricals he had participated in at the Ottsville High School.

Then, too, his position permitted him a great deal of leisure. He used this spare time to good advantage by visiting the many interesting spots for which New York City is justly famous.

He also made an unsuccessful attempt to find Mr. Whipple. At the Salvation Army Post they told him that they had observed Mr. Whipple lying quietly in the gutter after the meeting of the "Leather Shirts," but that when they looked the next day to see if he were still there, they found only a large blood stain. Lem looked himself but failed even to find this stain, there being many cats in the neighborhood.

He was a sociable youth and quickly made friends with several of the other guests of the Warford House. None of them were his age, however, so that he was pleased when a young man named Samuel Perkins spoke to him.

Sam worked in a furnishing goods store on lower Broadway. He was very fond of dress and indulged in a variety of showy neckties, being able to get them at reduced rates.

"What line are you in?" he asked our hero in the lobby one evening while they were waiting for the supper bell to ring.

"I'm in the glass business," Lem answered cautiously, for he had been warned not to explain his duties to anyone.

"How much do you get?" was the forward youth's next question.

"Thirty dollars a week and found," said Lem, honestly.

"I get thirty-five without keep, but it's too little for me. A man can't live on that kind of money, what with the opera once a week and decent clothes. Why, my carfare alone comes to over a dollar, not counting taxi-cabs."

"Yes, it must be rather a tight squeeze for you," said Lem with a smile as he thought of all the large families who lived on smaller incomes than Mr. Perkins'.

"Of course," Sam went on, "the folks at home allow me another ten dollars a week. You see the old gent has money. But I tell you it sure melts away in this town."

"No doubt," said Lem. "There are a good many ways to spend money here."

"Suppose we go to the theatre tonight?"

"No," Lem replied, "I'm not as fortunate as you are. I have no wealthy father to fall back on and must save the little I earn."

"Well, then," said Sam, for that youth could not live without excitement of some sort, "what do you say we visit Chinatown? It'll only cost us carfare."

To this proposition Lem readily agreed. "I'd like very much to go," he said. "Perhaps Mr. Warren would like to join us."

Mr. Warren was another guest whose acquaintance Lem had made.

"What, that crank!" exclaimed Sam, who was by way of being somewhat of a snob. "He's soft in his upper story. Pretends that he's literary and writes for the magazines."

"He does, doesn't he?"

"Very likely, but did you ever see such shabby neckties as he wears?"

"He hasn't your advantages for getting them," said Lem with a smile, for he knew where the young man worked.

"How do you like the tie I have on? It's a stunner, isn't it?" asked Sam complacently.

"It's very striking," said Lem, whose tastes were much more sober.

"I get a new necktie every week. You see, I get them at half price. The girls always notice a fellow's necktie."

The supper bell sounded, and the two youths parted to go to their own tables. After eating, they met again in the lobby and proceeded to Chinatown.

XVII

L EM and his new friend wandered through Mott Street and
its environs, observing with considerable interest the curious customs and outlandish manners of that neighborhood's
large oriental population.

Early in the evening, however, an incident occurred which
made our hero feel sorry that he had ventured out with Sam
Perkins. When they came upon an ancient celestial, who was
quietly reading a newspaper under an arc lamp, Sam accosted
him before Lem could interfere.

"Hey, John," said the youth mockingly, "no tickee, no
washee." And he laughed foolishly in the manner of his kind.

The almond-eyed old man looked up from his newspaper
and stared coldly at him for a full minute, then said with great
dignity, "By the blessed beard of my grandfather, you're the
lousiest pimple-faced ape I ever did see."

At this Sam made as though to strike the aged oriental. But
that surprising individual was not in the least frightened. He
took a small hatchet out of his pocket and proceeded to shave
the hair from the back of his hand with its razor sharp edge.

Sam turned quite pale and began to bluster until Lem
thought it best to intervene.

But even this lesson in manners had no effect on the brash
youth. He so persisted in his unmannerly conduct that our
hero was tempted to part company with him.

Sam stopped in front of what was evidently an unlicensed
liquor parlor.

"Come on in," he said, "and have a whiskey."

"Thank you," said our hero, "but I don't care for whiskey."

"Perhaps you prefer beer?"

"I don't care to drink anything, thank you."

"You don't mean to say you're a temperance crank?"

"Yes, I think I am."

"Oh, go to the devil, you prude," said Sam, ringing a signal
button that was secreted in the door of the "blind pig."

To Lem's great relief, he at last found himself alone. It was still early, so he decided to continue his stroll.

He turned a corner not far from Pell Street, when, suddenly, a bottle smashed at his feet, missing his skull by inches.

Was it intentional or accidental?

Lem looked around carefully. The street was deserted and all the houses that faced on it had their blinds drawn. He noticed that the only store front on the block carried a sign reading, "Wu Fong, Wet Wash Laundry," but that meant nothing to him.

When he looked closer at the bottle, he was surprised to see a sheet of notepaper between the bits of shattered glass and stooped to pick it up.

At this the door of the laundry opened noiselessly to emit one of Wu Fong's followers, an enormous Chinaman. His felt slippers were silent on the pavement, and as he crept up on our hero, something glittered in his hand.

It was a knife.

XVIII

Many chapters earlier in this book, we left our heroine, Betty Prail, in the bad house of Wu Fong, awaiting the visit of a pock-marked Armenian from Malta.

Since then numbers of orientals, Slavs, Latins, Celts and Semites had visited her, sometimes as many as three in one night. However, so large a number was rare because Wu Fong held her at a price much above that of the other female inmates.

Naturally enough, Betty was not quite as happy in her situation as was Wu Fong. At first she struggled against the series of "husbands" that were forced on her, but when all her efforts proved futile, she adapted herself as best she could to her onerous duties. Nevertheless, she was continuously seeking a method of escape.

It was Betty, of course, who had authored the note in the bottle. She had been standing at her window, thinking with horror of the impending visit of a heavyweight wrestler called Selim Hammid Bey, who claimed to be in love with her, when she suddenly saw Lem Pitkin turn the corner and pass in front of the laundry. She had hastily written a note describing her predicament, and putting it into a bottle, had tossed it into the street.

But, unfortunately, her action had not gone unobserved. One of Wu Fong's many servants had been carefully watching her through the keyhole, and had immediately carried the intelligence to his master, who had sent the enormous Chinaman after Lem with a knife.

Before I take up where I left off in my last chapter, there are several changes in Wu Fong's establishment which I would like to report. These changes seem significant to me, and while their bearing on this history may not be obvious, still I believe it does exist.

The depression hit Wu Fong as hard as it did more respectable merchants, and like them he decided that he was overstocked. In order to cut down, he would have to specialize and could no longer run a "House of All Nations."

Wu Fong was a very shrewd man and a student of fashions. He saw that the trend was in the direction of home industry and home talent, and when the Hearst papers began their "Buy American" campaign he decided to get rid of all the foreigners in his employ and turn his establishment into an hundred percentum American place.

Although in 1928 it would have been exceedingly difficult for him to have obtained the necessary girls, by 1934 things were different. Many respectable families of genuine native stock had been reduced to extreme poverty and had thrown their female children on the open market.

He engaged Mr. Asa Goldstein to redecorate the house and that worthy designed a Pennsylvania Dutch, Old South, Log Cabin Pioneer, Victorian New York, Western Cattle Days, California Monterey, Indian, and Modern Girl series of interiors. In general the results were as follows:

Lena Haubengrauber from Perkiomen Creek, Bucks County, Pennsylvania. Her rooms were filled with painted pine furniture and decorated with slip ware, spatter ware, chalk ware and "Gaudy Dutch." Her simple farm dress was fashioned of bright gingham.

Alice Sweethorne from Paducah, Kentucky. Besides many fine pieces of old Sheraton from Savannah, in her suite there was a wonderful iron grill from Charleston whose beauty of workmanship made every visitor gasp with pleasure. She wore a ball gown of the Civil War period.

Mary Judkins from Jugtown Hill, Arkansas. Her walls were lined with oak puncheons chinked with mud. Her mattress was stuffed with field corn and covered by a buffalo robe. There was real dirt on her floors. She was dressed in homespun, butternut stained, and wore a pair of men's boots.

Patricia Van Riis from Gramercy Park, Manhattan, New York City. Her suite was done in the style known as Biedermeier. The windows were draped with thirty yards of white velvet apiece and the chandelier in her sitting room had over eight hundred crystal pendants attached to it. She was dressed like an early "Gibson Girl."

Powder River Rose from Carson's Store, Wyoming. Her apartment was the replica of a ranch bunk house. Strewn around it in well-calculated confusion were such miscellaneous articles as spurs, saddle blankets, straw, guitars, quirts, pearl-handled revolvers, hay forks and playing cards. She wore goat skin chaps, a silk blouse and a five-gallon hat with a rattlesnake band.

Dolores O'Riely from Alta Vista, California. In order to save money, Wu Fong had moved her into the suite that had been occupied by Conchita, the Spanish girl. He merely substituted a Mission chair for the horse-hide one with the steer horn arms and called it "Monterey." Asa Goldstein was very angry when he found out, but Wu Fong refused to do anything more about it, because he felt that she was bound to be a losing proposition. The style, he said, was not obviously enough American even in its most authentic forms.

Princess Roan Fawn from Two Forks, Oklahoma Indian Reservation, Oklahoma. Her walls were papered with birch bark to make it look like a wigwam and she did business on the floor. Except for a necklace of wolf's teeth, she was naked under her bull's eye blanket.

Miss Cobina Wiggs from Woodstock, Connecticut. She lived in one large room that was a combination of a locker in an athletic club and the office of a mechanical draughtsman. Strewn around were parts of an aeroplane, T-squares, calipers, golf clubs, books, gin bottles, hunting horns and paintings by modern masters. She had broad shoulders, no hips and very long legs. Her costume was an aviator's jumper complete with helmet attached. It was made of silver cloth and fitted very tightly.

Betty Prail from Ottsville, Vermont. Her furnishings and costume have already been described, and it should suffice to say here that they remained untouched.

These were not the only vital changes Wu Fong made in his establishment. He was as painstaking as a great artist and in order to be as consistent as one, he did away with the French cuisine and wines traditional to his business. Instead, he substituted an American kitchen and cellar.

When a client visited Lena Haubengrauber, it was possible for him to eat roast groundhog and drink Sam Thompson rye. While with Alice Sweethorne, he was served sow belly with grits and Bourbon. In Mary Judkins' rooms he received, if he so desired, fried squirrel and corn liquor. In the suite occupied by Patricia Van Riis, lobster and champagne wine were the rule. The patrons of Powder River Rose usually ordered mountain oysters and washed them down with forty-rod. And so on down the list: while with Dolores O'Riely, tortillas and prune brandy from the Imperial Valley; while with Princess Roan Fawn, baked dog and firewater; while with Betty Prail, fish chowder and Jamaica rum. Finally, those who sought the favors of the "Modern Girl," Miss Cobina Wiggs, were regaled with tomato and lettuce sandwiches and gin.

XIX

THE ENORMOUS Chinaman with the uplifted knife did not bring it down because he had been struck by a sudden thought. While he debated the pros and cons of his idea over in his mind, the unsuspecting youth picked up the note Betty had thrown at him.

> "*Dear Mr. Pitkin—*" he read.
> "*I am held captive. Please save me.*
> *Your grateful friend,*
> *Elizabeth Prail.*"

When our hero had thoroughly digested the contents of the little missive, he turned to look for a policeman. It was this that made the Chinaman decide on a course of action. He dropped the knife, and with a skilful oriental trick that took our hero entirely by surprise, pinned Lem's arms in such a way as to render him helpless.

He then whistled through his nose in coolie fashion. In obedience to this signal several more of Wu Fong's followers came running to his assistance. Although Lem struggled valiantly, he was overpowered and forced to enter the laundry.

Lem's captors dragged him into the presence of the sinister Wu Fong, who rubbed his hands gleefully as he inspected the poor lad.

"You have done well, Chin Lao Tse," he said, praising the man who had captured Lem.

"I demand to be set free!" expostulated our hero. "You have no right to keep me here."

But the crafty oriental ignored his protests and smiled inscrutably. He could well use a nice-looking American boy. That very night, he expected a visit from the Maharajah of Kanurani, whose tastes were notorious. Wu Fong congratulated himself; the gods were indeed good.

"Prepare him," said he in Chinese.

The poor lad was taken to a room that had been fitted out like a ship's cabin. The walls were paneled in teak, and there were sextants, compasses and other such gear in profusion.

His captors then forced him to don a tight-fitting sailor suit. After warning him in no uncertain terms not to try to escape, they left him to his own devices.

Lem sat on the edge of a bunk that was built into one corner of the room with his head buried in his hands. He wondered what new ordeal fate had in store for him, but being unable to guess, he thought of other things.

Would he lose his job if he failed to report to Mr. Hainey? Probably, yes. Where was his dear mother? Probably in the poorhouse, or begging from door to door, if she were not dead. Where was Mr. Whipple? Dead and buried in Potter's Field more than likely. And how could he get a message to Miss Prail?

Lem was still trying to solve this last problem, when Chin Lao Tse, the man who had captured him, entered the room, carrying a savage looking automatic in his hand.

"Listen, boy," he said menacingly, "see this gat? Well, if you don't behave I'll drill you clean."

Chin then proceeded to secrete himself in a closet. Before closing the door, he showed Lem that he intended to watch his every move through the keyhole.

The poor lad racked his brains, but could not imagine what was wanted of him. He was soon to find out, however.

There was a knock on the door and Wu Fong entered followed by a little dark man whose hands were covered with jewels. It was the Maharajah of Kanurani.

"My, wath a pithy thailer boy," lisped the Indian prince with unfeigned delight.

"I'm extremely happy that he finds favor in your august eyes, excellency," said Wu Fong with a servile bow, after which he backed out of the room.

The Maharajah minced up to our hero, who was conscious only of the man in the closet, and put his arm around the lad's waist.

"Thom on, pithy boy, giff me a kith," he said with a leer that transfigured his otherwise unremarkable visage into a thing of evil.

A wave of disgust made Lem's hair stand on end. "Does he think me a girl?" the poor lad wondered. "No, he called me a boy at least twice."

Lem looked towards the closet for instructions. The man in that receptacle opened its door and poked his head out. Puckering up his lips, he rolled his eyes amorously, at the same time pointing at the Indian prince.

When our hero realized what was expected of him, he turned pale with horror. He looked again at the Maharajah and what he saw of lust in that man's eyes made him almost swoon.

Fortunately for Lem, however, instead of swooning, he opened his mouth to scream. This was the only thing that could have saved him, for he spread his jaws too wide and his store teeth fell clattering to the carpet.

The Maharajah jumped away in disgust.

Then another lucky accident occurred. When Lem bent awkwardly to pick up his teeth, the glass eye that Mr. Hainey had given him popped from his head and smashed to smithereens on the floor.

This last was much too much for the Maharajah of Kanurani. He became enraged. Wu Fong had cheated him! What kind of a pretty boy was this that came apart so horribly?

Livid with anger, the Indian prince ran out of the room to demand his money back. After he had gotten it, he left the house, vowing never to return.

Wu Fong blamed the loss of the Maharajah's trade on Lem and was extremely vexed with the poor lad. He ordered his men to beat him roundly, strip him of his sailor suit, then throw him into the street with his clothes after him.

XX

LEM GATHERED together his clothing and crawled into the areaway of a deserted house, where he donned his things. His first thought was to find a policeman.

As is usual in such circumstances, a guardian of the law was not immediately forthcoming and he had to go several miles before he found a "peeler."

"Officer," said our hero as best he could minus his oral equipment, "I want to lodge a complaint."

"Yes," said Patrolman Riley shortly, for the poor lad's appearance was far from prepossessing. The Chinamen had torn his clothing and his eye was gone as well as his teeth.

"I want you to summon reinforcements, then immediately arrest Wu Fong who is running a disorderly house under the guise of a laundry."

"Wu Fong is it that you want me to arrest? Why, you drunken fool, he's the biggest man in the district. Take my advice and get yourself a cup of black coffee, then go home and sleep it off."

"But I have positive proof that he's keeping a girl in his house against her will, and he did me physical violence."

"One more word out of you about my great good friend," said the officer, "and off you go to jail."

"But . . ." began Lem indignantly.

Officer Riley was a man of his word. He did not let the poor lad finish, but struck him a smart blow on the head with his truncheon, then took him by the collar and dragged him to the station house.

When Lem regained consciousness several hours later, he found himself in a cell. He quickly remembered what had happened to him and tried to think of a way in which to extricate himself from his difficulties. The first thing was to tell his story to some superior police officer or magistrate. But no matter how loudly he called, he was unable to attract the attention of anyone.

Not until the next day was he fed, and then a small man of the Jewish persuasion entered his cell.

"Have you any money?" said this member of the chosen people.

"Who are you?" countered Lem with another question.

"Me? I'm your lawyer, Seth Abromovitz, Esquire. Please answer my first question or I won't be able to handle your case properly."

"My case?" queried Lem in astonishment. "I've done nothing."

"Ignorance of the law is no defense," said Lawyer Abromovitz pompously.

"Of what am I accused?" asked the poor lad in confusion.

"Of several things. Disorderly conduct and assaulting a police officer, for one; of conspiring to overthrow the government, for two; and last but not least, of using the glim racket to mulct storekeepers."

"But I didn't do any of these things," protested Lem.

"Listen, bud," said the lawyer, dropping all formality. "I'm not the judge, you don't have to lie to me. You're One-eyed Pitkin, the glim dropper, and you know it."

"It's true that I have but one eye but. . . ."

"But me no buts. This is a tough case. That is, unless you can grow an eye over night in that hole in your mug."

"I am innocent," repeated Lem sadly.

"If that's the line you intend to take, I wouldn't be surprised if you got life. But tell me, didn't you go to the store of Hazelton Frères and make believe you lost your eye?"

"Yes," said Lem, "but I didn't take anything or do anything."

"Didn't you offer a reward of one thousand dollars for the return of your eye?"

"Yes, but. . . ."

"Again, but. Please don't but me no buts. Your accomplice went around the next day and made believe he had found a glass eye on the floor of the store. Mr. Hazelton said that he knew who it belonged to and asked him for the eye. He refused to give it up, saying that it looked like a very valuable eye to him and that if Mr. Hazelton would give him the address of the man who owned it, he would return the eye himself. Mr. Hazelton thought that he was going to lose all chances of collecting the thousand dollar reward, so he of-

fered the man a hundred dollars for the eye. After some bargaining your accomplice went out with two hundred and fifty
dollars, and Mr. Hazelton is still waiting for you to come and
claim your eye."

"I didn't know about all that or I wouldn't have taken the
job even if I was starving," said Lem. "I was told that it was
a promotion idea for a glass eye company."

"O.K., son, but I'll have to think up a little better story.
Before I begin thinking, how much money have you?"

"I worked three weeks and was paid thirty dollars a week.
I have ninety dollars in a savings bank."

"That's not much. This conference is going to cost you one
hundred dollars with ten per cent off for cash or ninety dollars. Hand it over."

"I don't want you as my lawyer," said Lem.

"That's all right with me; but come through with the
dough for this conference."

"I don't owe you anything. I didn't hire you."

"Oh, yeh, you one-eyed rat," said the lawyer, showing his
true colors. "The courts appointed me and the courts will
decide how much you owe me. Give me the ninety and we'll
call it square. Otherwise I'll sue you."

"I'll give you nothing!" exclaimed Lem.

"Getting tough, eh? We'll soon see how tough you are. I'll
tell my friend the district attorney and you'll get life."

With this last as a parting shot, Lawyer Abromovitz left our
hero alone again in his cell.

XXI

SEVERAL DAYS later the prosecuting attorney paid the poor lad a visit. Elisha Barnes was that official's name, and he appeared to be a rather good-natured, indolent gentleman.

"Well, son," he said, "so you're about to discover that crime doesn't pay. But, tell me, have you any money?"

"Ninety dollars," said Lem truthfully.

"That's very little, so I guess you'd better plead guilty."

"But I'm innocent," protested Lem. "Wu Fong. . . ."

"Stop," interrupted Mr. Barnes, hurriedly. He had turned pale on hearing the Chinaman's name. "Take my advice and don't mention him around here."

"I'm innocent!" repeated Lem, a little desperately.

"So was Christ," said Mr. Barnes with a sigh, "and they nailed Him. However, I like you; I can see you're from New England and I'm a New Hampshire man myself. I want to help you. You've been indicted on three counts, suppose you plead guilty to one of the three and we forget the other two."

"But I'm innocent," repeated Lem again.

"Maybe, but you haven't got enough money to prove it, and besides you've got some very powerful enemies. Be sensible, plead guilty to the charge of disorderly conduct and take thirty days in the workhouse. I'll see that you don't get more. Well, what do you say?"

Our hero was silent.

"I'm giving you a fine break," Mr. Barnes went on. "If I wasn't too busy to prepare the state's case against you, I probably could get you sent away for at least fifteen years. But you see, elections are coming and I have to take part in the campaign. Besides I'm a busy man, what with this and what with that. . . . Do me a favor and maybe I can help you some time. If you make me prepare a case against you I'll get sore. I won't like you."

Lem finally agreed to do as the prosecuting attorney asked. Three days later he was sent to the workhouse for thirty days. The judge wanted to give him ninety, but Mr. Barnes lived up to his part of the bargain. He whispered something to the judge, who changed the term to the thirty days agreed upon.

A month later, when Lem was set free, he went directly to the savings bank for his ninety dollars. It was his intention to draw out the entire amount, so that he could get himself another set of false teeth and a glass eye. Without those things, he could not hope to get a job.

He presented his pass book at the paying teller's window. After a little wait, he was told that they could not give him his money because it had been attached by Seth Abromovitz. This was too much. It took all the manliness of our hero to suppress the tear that started to his good eye. With the faltering step of an old man, he stumbled out of the bank building.

Lem stood on the steps of the imposing edifice, and looked blankly at the swirling crowds that eddied past the great savings institution. Suddenly he felt a touch on his arm and a voice in his ear.

"Why so blue, duckie? How about a little fun?"

He turned mechanically and to his amazement saw that it was Betty Prail who had solicited him.

"You!" exclaimed both of the hometown friends together.

Anyone who had ever seen these two youngsters on their way home from church in Ottsville would have been struck by the great change that only a few years in the great world had made.

Miss Prail was rouged most obviously. She smelled of cheap perfume, and her dress revealed much too much of her figure. She was a woman of the streets, and an unsuccessful one at that.

As for our hero, Lemuel, minus an eye and all his teeth, he had acquired nothing but a pronounced stoop.

"How did you escape Wu Fong?" asked Lem.

"You helped me without knowing it," replied Betty. "He and his henchmen were so busy throwing you into the street that I was able to walk out of the house without anyone seeing me."

"I'm glad," said Lem.

The two young people were silent, and stood looking at

each other. They both wanted to ask the same question, but they were embarrassed. Finally, they spoke at the same time.

"Have you . . ."

That was as far as they got. They both stopped to let the other finish. There was a long silence, for neither wanted to complete the question. Finally, however, they spoke again.

". . . any money?"

"No," said Lem and Betty answering the question together as they had asked it.

"I'm hungry," said Betty sadly. "I just wondered."

"I'm hungry, too," said Lem.

A policeman now approached. He had been watching them since they met.

"Get along, you rats," he said gruffly.

"I resent your talking that way to a lady," said Lem indignantly.

"What's that?" asked the officer lifting his club.

"We are both citizens of this country and you have no right to treat us in this manner," went on Lem fearlessly.

The patrolman was just about to bring his truncheon down on the lad's skull, when Betty interfered and dragged him away.

The two youngsters walked along without talking. They felt a little better together because misery loves company. Soon they found themselves in Central Park, where they sat down on a bench.

Lem sighed.

"What's the matter?" asked Betty sympathetically.

"I'm a failure," answered Lem with still another sigh.

"Why, Lemuel Pitkin, how you talk!" exclaimed Betty indignantly. "You're only seventeen going on eighteen and. . . ."

"Well," interrupted Lem, a little ashamed of having admitted that he was discouraged. "I left Ottsville to make my fortune and so far I've been to jail twice and lost all my teeth and one eye."

"To make an omelette you have to break eggs," said Betty. "When you've lost both your eyes, you can talk. I read only the other day about a man who lost both of his eyes yet accumulated a fortune. I forget how, but he did. Then, too, think of Henry Ford. He was dead broke at forty and borrowed a thousand dollars from James Couzens; when he paid him back it had become thirty-eight million dollars. You're only seventeen and say you're a failure. Lem Pitkin, I'm surprised at you."

Betty continued to comfort and encourage Lem until it grew dark. With the departure of the sun, it also grew extremely cold.

From behind some shrubs that did not quite conceal him, a policeman began to eye the two young people suspiciously.

"I have nowhere to sleep," said Betty, shivering with cold.

"Nor have I," said Lem with a profound sigh.

"Let's go to the Grand Central Station," suggested Betty. "It's warm there, and I like to watch the people hurrying through. If we make believe we are waiting for a train, they won't chase us."

XXII

"It all seems like a dream to me, Mr. Whipple. This morning when I was set free from jail, I thought I would probably starve, and here I am on my way to California to dig gold."

Yes, it was Lem, our hero, talking. He was sitting in the dining room of the "Fifth Avenue Special" en route to Chicago, where he and the party he was traveling with were to change to "The Chief," crack train of the Atchison, Topeka and Santa Fe, and continue on to the high Sierras.

With him in the dining room were Betty, Mr. Whipple, and Jake Raven; and the four friends were in a cheerful mood as they ate the excellent food provided by the Pullman Company.

The explanation of how this had come about is quite simple. While Lem and Betty were warming themselves in the waiting room of the Grand Central Station, they had spied Mr. Whipple on line at one of the ticket booths. Lem had approached the ex-banker and had been greeted effusively by him, for he was indeed glad to see the boy. He was also glad to see Betty, whose father he had known before Mr. Prail's death in the fire.

After listening to Lem's account of the difficulties the two of them were in, he invited them to accompany him on his trip to California. It seemed that Mr. Whipple was going there with Jake Raven to dig gold from a mine that the redskin owned. With this money, he intended to finance the further activities of the National Revolutionary Party.

Lem was to help Mr. Whipple in the digging operations, while Betty was to keep house for the miners. The two young people jumped at this opportunity, as we can well imagine, and overwhelmed Mr. Whipple with their gratitude.

"In Chicago," said Shagpoke, when the dining car waiter had brought coffee, "we will have three hours and a half before 'The Chief' leaves for the Golden West. During that time, Lem, of course, will have to get himself a new set of store teeth and an eye, but I believe that the rest of us will still have time to pay a short visit to the World's Fair."

Mr. Whipple went on to describe the purpose of the fair,

until, on a courteous signal from the headwaiter, the little
party was forced to leave their table and retire to their berths.

In the morning, when the train pulled into the depot, they
disembarked. Lem was given some money to purchase the
things he needed, while the others started immediately for the
fair. He was to look for them on the grounds, if he got
through in time.

Lem hurried as much as he could and managed quickly to
select an eye and a set of teeth in a store devoted to that type
of equipment. He then set out for the fair grounds.

As he was walking down Eleventh Street towards the North
Entrance, he was accosted by a short, stout man, who wore a
soft, black felt hat, the brim of which was slouched over his
eyes. A full, brown beard concealed the lower part of his face.

"Excuse me," he said in a repressed tone of voice, "but I
think you are the young man I am looking for."

"How is that?" asked Lem, instantly on his guard, for he
did not intend to be snared by a sharper.

"Your name is Lemuel Pitkin, is it not?"

"It is, sir."

"I thought you answered the description given me."

"Given you by whom?" queried our hero.

"By Mr. Whipple, of course," was the surprising answer the
stranger made.

"Why should he have given you a description of me?"

"So I could find you at the fair."

"But why, when I am to meet him at the depot in two
hours from now?"

"An unfortunate accident has made it impossible for him
to be there."

"An accident?"

"Exactly."

"What kind of an accident?"

"A very serious one, I am afraid. He was struck by a sight-
seeing bus and. . . ."

"Killed!" cried Lem in dismay. "Tell me the truth, was he
killed?"

"No, not exactly, but he was seriously injured, perhaps
fatally. He was taken unconscious to a hospital. When he
regained his senses, he asked for you and I was sent to

fetch you to him. Miss Prail and Chief Raven are at his bedside."

Lem was so stunned by the dire news that it required some five minutes for him to recover sufficiently to gasp, "This is terrible!"

He asked the bearded stranger to take him to Mr. Whipple at once.

This was just what the man had counted on. "I have a car with me," he said with a bow. "Please enter it."

He then led our hero to a powerful limousine that was drawn up at the curb. Lem got in, and the chauffeur, who was wearing green goggles and a long linen duster, drove off at top speed.

All this seemed natural to the lad because of his agitated state of mind, and the rate at which the car traveled pleased him rather than otherwise for he was anxious to get to Mr. Whipple's bedside.

The limousine passed rapidly under one elevated structure and then another. There were fruit vendors on the street corners and merchants peddling neckties. People moved to and fro on the sidewalks; cabs, trucks and private vehicles flitted past. The roar of the great city rose on every side, but Lem saw and heard nothing.

"Where was Mr. Whipple taken?" he asked presently.

"To the Lake Shore Hospital."

"And is this the quickest way there?"

"Most certainly."

With this the stranger lapsed into moody silence again.

Lem looked from the window of the limousine and saw that the cars and trucks were growing less in number. Soon they disappeared from the streets altogether. The people also became fewer till no more than an occasional pedestrian was to be observed and then only of the lowest type.

As the car approached an extremely disreputable neighborhood, the bearded stranger drew the shade of one of its two windows.

"Why did you do that?" demanded Lem.

"Because the sun hurts my eyes," he said as he deliberately drew the other shade, throwing the interior into complete darkness.

These acts made Lem think that all was not quite as it should be.

"I must have one or both of these shades up," he said, reaching for the nearest one to raise it.

"And I say that they must both remain down," returned the man in a low harsh voice.

"What do you mean, sir?"

A strong hand suddenly fastened in a grip of iron on Lem's throat, and these words reached his ears:

"I mean, Lemuel Pitkin, that you are in the power of the Third International."

XXIII

ALTHOUGH thus suddenly attacked, Lem grappled with his assailant, determined to sell his life as dearly as possible. The lad had been one of the best athletes in the Ottsville High School, and when aroused he was no mean adversary, as the bearded man soon discovered. He tore at the hand which was strangling him and succeeded in removing it from his throat, but when he tried to cry out for help, he discovered that the terrible pressure had robbed him of his vocal powers.

Even if he had been able to cry out it would have been useless for him to do so because the chauffeur was in the plot. Without once looking behind, he stepped on his accelerator and turned sharply into a noisome, dark alley.

Lem struck out savagely and landed a stiff blow in his opponent's face. That worthy uttered a fierce imprecation but did not strike back. He was fumbling for something in his pocket.

Lem struck again, and this time his hand caught in the beard. It proved to be false and came away readily.

Although it was dark in the car, if you had been sitting in it, dear reader, you would have recognized our hero's assailant to be none other than the fat man in the Chesterfield overcoat. Lem, however, did not recognize him because he had never seen him before.

Suddenly, as he battled with the stranger, he felt something cold and hard against his forehead. It was a pistol.

"Now you fascist whelp, I have you! If you so much as move a finger, I'll blow you to hell!"

These words were not spoken; they were snarled.

"What do you want of me?" Lem managed to gasp.

"You were going to dig gold with Mr. Whipple. Where is the mine located?"

"I don't know," said Lem, speaking the truth, for Shagpoke had kept secret their final destination.

"You do know, you damned bourgeois. Tell me or. . . ."

He was interrupted by the wild scream of a siren. The car swerved and bucked wildly, then there was a terrific crash.

Lem felt as though he were being whirled rapidly through a dark tunnel full of clanging bells. Everything went black, and the last thing he was conscious of was a sharp, stabbing pain in his left hand.

When the poor lad recovered consciousness, he found himself stretched out upon a sort of a cot and he realized that he was still being carried somewhere. Near his head sat a man in a white suit, who was calmly smoking a cigar. Lem knew he was no longer in the limousine, for he saw that the rear end of the conveyance was wide open and admitted a great deal of light and air.

"What happened?" he asked naturally enough.

"So you are coming around, eh?" said the man in the white suit. "Well, I guess you will get well all right."

"But what happened?"

"You were in a bad smash-up."

"A smash-up? . . . Where are you taking me?"

"Don't get excited and I'll answer your questions. The limousine in which you were riding was struck by a fire engine and demolished. The driver must have run off, for you were the only one we found at the wreck. This is the ambulance of the Lake Shore Hospital and you are being taken there."

Lem now understood what he had been through, and thanked God that he was still alive.

"I hope you are not a violinist," the interne added mysteriously.

"No, I don't play, but why?"

"Because your left hand was badly mangled and I had to remove a part of it. The thumb, to be explicit."

Lem sighed deeply, but being a brave lad he forced himself to think of other things.

"What hospital is this ambulance from did you say?"

"The Lake Shore."

"Do you know how a patient called Nathan Whipple is getting on? He was run over on the fair grounds by a sight-seeing bus."

"We have no patient by that name."

"Are you certain?"

"Absolutely. I know every accident case in the hospital."

Of a sudden everything became clear to Lem. "Then he tricked me with a lie!" he cried.

"Who did?" asked the interne.

Lem ignored his question. "What time is it?" he demanded.

"One o'clock."

"I have still fifteen minutes to make the train. Stop and let me off, please."

The ambulance doctor stared at our hero and wondered if the lad had gone crazy.

"I must get off," repeated Lem frantically.

"As a private citizen you of course can do as you like, but I advise you to go to the hospital."

"No," said Lem, "please, I must get to the depot at once. I have to catch a train."

"Well, I certainly admire your pluck. By George, I have half a mind to help you."

"Do," begged Lem.

Without further argument, the interne told his driver to head for the depot at top speed and to ignore all traffic laws. After an exciting ride through the city, they arrived at their destination just as "The Chief" was about to pull out.

XXIV

As Lem had suspected, Mr. Whipple and his other friends were safe on the train. When they saw his bandaged hand, they demanded an explanation and the poor lad told the story of his adventure with the agent of the Third International. They were astounded and angered, as well they might be.

"One day," Mr. Whipple said ominously, "heads will roll in the sand, bearded and unbearded alike."

The rest of the trip proved uneventful. There happened to be an excellent doctor on board and he had our hero's hand in fair shape by the time the train reached southern California.

After several days of travel on horseback, the little party arrived at the Yuba River in the high Sierra Mountains. It was on one of the tributaries of this river that Jake Raven's gold mine was located.

Next to the diggings was a log cabin, which the men of the party soon had in a livable condition. Mr. Whipple and Betty occupied it, while Lem and the redskin made their bed under the stars.

One evening, after a hard day's work at the mine, the four friends were sitting around a fire drinking coffee, when a man appeared who might have sat for the photograph of a Western bad man without any alteration in his countenance or apparel.

He wore a red flannel shirt, pants of leather with the hair still on them, and a Mexican sombrero. He had a bowie knife in his boot and displayed two pearl-handled revolvers very ostentatiously.

When he was about two rods away from the group, he hailed it.

"How are you, strangers?" he asked.

"Pretty comfortable," said Shagpoke. "How fare you?"

"You're a Yank, ain't you?" he asked as he dismounted from his horse.

"Yes, from Vermont. Where might your home be?"

"I'm from Pike County, Missouri," was the answer. "You've heard of Pike, hain't you?"

"I've heard of Missouri," said Mr. Whipple with a smile, "but I can't say as I ever heard of your particular county."

The man with the leather pants frowned.

"You must have been born in the woods not to have heard of Pike County," he said. "The smartest fighters come from there. I kin whip my weight in wildcats, am a match for a dozen Injuns to oncet, and can tackle a lion without flinchin'."

"Won't you stop and rest with us?" said Mr. Whipple politely.

"I don't care if I do," was the uncouth Missourian's rejoinder. "You don't happen to have a bottle of whiskey with you, strangers?" he asked.

"No," said Lem.

The newcomer looked disappointed.

"I wish you had," he said. "I feel dry as a salt herring. What you doing here?"

"Mining," said Mr. Whipple.

"Grubbin' in the ground," said the stranger with disgust. "That's no job for a gentleman."

This last was uttered in such a magnificent tone of disdain that everyone smiled. In his red shirt, coarse leather breeches, and brown, not overclean skin, he certainly didn't look much like a gentleman in the conventional sense of the term.

"It's well enough to be a gentleman, if you've got money to fall back on," remarked Lem sensibly but not offensively.

"Is that personal?" demanded the Pike County man, scowling and half-rising from the ground.

"It's personal to me," said Lem quietly.

"I accept the apology," said the Missourian fiercely. "But you'd better not rile me, stranger, for I'm powerful bad. You don't know me, you don't. I'm a rip-tail roarer and a ring-tail squealer, I am. I always kills the man what riles me."

After this last bloodthirsty declaration, the man from Pike County temporarily subsided. He partook quietly of the coffee and cake which Betty served him. Suddenly he flared up again.

"Hain't that an Injun?" he shouted, pointing at Jake Raven and reaching for his gun.

Lem stepped hastily in front of the redskin, while Shagpoke grabbed the ruffian's wrist.

"He's a good friend of ours," said Betty.

"I don't give a darn," said the ring tail squealer. "Turn me loose and I'll massacree the danged aboriginee."

Jake Raven, however, could take care of himself. He pulled his own revolver and pointing it at the bad man said, "Rascal shut up or me kill um pronto quick."

At the sight of the Indian's drawn gun, the ruffian calmed down.

"All right," he said, "but it's my policy always to shoot an Injun on sight. The only good Injun is a dead one, is what I alluz say."

Mr. Whipple sent Jake Raven away from the fire and there was a long silence, during which everyone stared at the cheery flames. Finally the man from Pike County again broke into speech, this time addressing Lem.

"How about a game of cards, sport?" he asked. With these words he drew a greasy pack out of his pocket and shuffled them with great skill.

"I have never played cards in my life," said our hero.

"Where was you raised?" demanded the Missourian contemptuously.

"Ottsville, State of Vermont," said Lem. "I don't know one card from another, and don't want to know."

In no way abashed, the Pike man said, "I'll larn you. How about a game of poker?"

Mr. Whipple spoke up. "We do not permit gambling in this camp," he said firmly.

"That's durn foolishness," said the stranger, whose object it was to victimize his new friends, being an expert gambler.

"Perhaps it is," said Mr. Whipple. "But that's our business."

"Look here, hombre," blustered the bully. "I reckon you don't realize who you're a-talking to. 'Tarnal death and massacreeation, I'm the rip-tail roarer, I am."

"You told us that before," said Mr. Whipple quietly.

"Blood and massacreeation, if I don't mean it, too," exclaimed the Missourian with a fierce scowl. "Do you know how I treated a man last week?"

"No," said Mr. Whipple, truthfully.

"We was ridin' together over in Almeda County. We'd met

permiscuous, like we've met tonight. I was tellin' him how four b'ars attacked me to oncet, and how I fit 'em all single-handed, when he laughed and said he reckoned I'd been drinkin' and seed double. If he'd a-know'd me better he wouldn't have done it."

"What did you do?" asked Betty in horror.

"What did I do, madam?" echoed the Pike County man ferociously. "I told him he didn't realize who he'd insulted. I told him I was a ring-tail squealer and a rip-tail roarer. I told him that he had to fight, and asked him how it would be. Foot and fist, or tooth and nail, or claw and mudscraper, or knife, gun and tommyhawk."

"Did he fight?" asked Lem.

"He had to."

"How did it come out?"

"I shot him through the heart," said the Missourian coldly. "His bones are bleachin' in the canyon where he fell."

XXV

THE NEXT DAY, the Pike County man lay on his blankets until about eleven o'clock in the morning. He only got up when Lem, Jake and Shagpoke returned from their work on the creek to eat lunch. They were surprised to see him still in camp, but said nothing out of politeness.

Although they did not know it, the Missourian had not been sleeping. He had been lying under a tree, thinking dirty thoughts as he watched Betty go about her household chores.

"I'm hungry," he announced with great truculence. "When do we eat?"

"Won't you share our lunch?" asked Mr. Whipple with a sarcastic smile that was completely lost on the uncouth fellow.

"Thank ye, stranger, I don't mind if I do," the Pike County man said. "My fodder give out just before I made your camp, and I hain't found a place to stock up."

He displayed such an appetite that Mr. Whipple regarded him with anxiety. The camp was short of provisions, and if the stranger kept eating like that, he would have to take a trip into town that very afternoon for more food.

"You have a healthy appetite, my friend," Mr. Whipple said.

"I generally have," said the Pike man. "You'd orter keep some whiskey to wash these vittles down with."

"We prefer coffee," said Lem.

"Coffee is for children, whiskey for strong men," was the ring-tail squealer's rejoinder.

"I still prefer coffee," Lem said firmly.

"Bah!" said the other, disdainfully; "I'd as soon drink skim-milk. Good whiskey or cawn for me."

"The only thing I miss in this camp," said Mr. Whipple, "is baked beans and brown bread. Ever eat 'em, stranger?"

"No," said the Pike man, "none of your Yankee truck for me."

"What's your favorite food?" asked Lem with a smile.

"Sow teats and hominy, hoe-cakes and forty-rod."

"Well," said Lem, "it depends on how you've been

brought up. I like baked beans and brown bread and pumpkin pie. Ever eat pumpkin pie?"

"Yes."

"Like it?"

"I don't lay much on it."

Throughout this dialogue, the stranger ate enormous quantities of food and drank six or seven cups of coffee. Mr. Whipple realized that the damage was done and that he would have to go into the town of Yuba for a fresh supply of provisions.

Having finished three cans of pineapple, the Pike man became social over one of Mr. Whipple's cigars, which he had taken without so much as a "by-your-leave."

"Strangers," he said, "did you ever hear of the affair I had with Jack Scott?"

"No," said Mr. Whipple.

"Jack and me used to be a heap together. We went huntin' together, camped out for weeks together, and was like two brothers. One day we was a-ridin' out, when a deer started up about fifty yards ahead of us. We both raised our guns and shot at him. There was only one bullet into him, and I knowed it was mine."

"How did you know it?" asked Lem.

"Don't you get curious, stranger. I knowed it, and that was enough. But Jack said it was his. 'It's my deer,' he says, 'for you missed your shot.' 'Looka here, Jack,' says I, 'you're mistaken. You missed it. Don't you think I know my own bullet?' 'No, I don't,' says he. 'Jack,' says I calmly, 'don't talk that way. It's dangerous.' 'Do you think I'm afraid of you?' he says turnin' on me. 'Jack,' says I, 'don't provoke me. I kin whip my weight in wild cats.' 'You can't whip me,' he says. That was too much for me to stand. I'm the rip-tail roarer from Pike County, Missouri, and no man can insult me and live. 'Jack,' says I, 'we've been friends, but you've insulted me and you must pay with your life.' Then I up with my iron and shot him through the head."

"My, how cruel!" exclaimed Betty.

"I was sorry to do it, beautiful gal, for he was my best friend, but he disputed my word, and the man that does that has to make his will if he's got property."

No one said anything, so the Pike man continued to talk.

"You see," he said with a friendly smile, "I was brought up on fightin'. When I was a boy I could whip every boy in school."

"That's why they call you a rip-tail roarer," said Mr. Whipple jokingly.

"You're right, pardner," said the Pike man complacently.

"What did you do when the teacher gave you a licking?" asked Mr. Whipple.

"What did I do?" yelled the Missourian with a demoniac laugh.

"Yes, what?" asked Mr. Whipple.

"Why, I shot him dead," said the Pike man briefly.

"My," said Mr. Whipple with a smile. "How many teachers did you shoot when you were a boy?"

"Only one. The rest heard of it and never dared touch me."

After this last statement, the desperado lay down under a tree to finish in comfort the cigar he had snatched from Mr. Whipple.

Seeing that he did not intend to move just yet, the others proceeded to go about their business. Lem and Jake Raven went to the mine, which was about a mile from the cabin. Shagpoke saddled his horse for the ride into town after a fresh stock of provisions. Betty occupied herself over the washtub.

Some time had elapsed, when Lem and Jake Raven decided that they would need dynamite to continue their operations. Lem was down at the bottom of the shaft, so the Indian was the one to go to camp for the explosives.

When Jake did not return after several hours, Lem began to worry about him. He remembered what the Pike man had said about his Indian policy and was afraid that that ruffian might have done Jake an injury.

Our hero decided to go back and see if everything was all right. When he entered the clearing in which the cabin stood, he was surprised to find the place deserted.

"Hi, Jake!" Lem shouted bewilderedly. "Hi, Jake Raven!"

There was no answer. Only the woods sent his words back to him in an echo almost as loud as his shout.

Suddenly, a scream rent the silence. Lem recognized the voice of the screamer as Betty's, and ran quickly toward the cabin.

XXVI

T HE DOOR was locked. Lem hammered on it, but no one answered. He went to the wood pile to get an ax and there found Jake Raven lying on the ground. He had been shot through the chest. Hastily snatching up the ax, Lem ran to the cabin. A few hearty blows and the door tumbled in.

In the half gloom of the cabin, Lem was horrified to see the Pike man busily tearing off Betty's sole remaining piece of underwear. She was struggling as best she could, but the ruffian from Missouri was too strong for her.

Lem raised the ax high over his head and started forward to interfere. He did not get very far because the ruffian had prepared for just such a contingency by setting an enormous bear trap inside the door.

Our hero stepped on the pan of the trap and its saw-toothed jaws closed with great force on the calf of his leg, cutting through his trousers, skin, flesh and half-way into the bone besides. He dropped in a heap, as though he had been shot through the brain.

At the sight of poor Lem weltering in his own blood, Betty fainted. In no way disturbed, the Missourian went coolly about his nefarious business and soon accomplished his purpose.

With the hapless girl in his arms he then left the cabin. Throwing her behind his saddle, he pressed his cruel spurs into his horse's sides and galloped off in the general direction of Mexico.

Once more the deep hush of the primeval forest descended on the little clearing, making peaceful what had been a scene of wild torment and savage villainy. A squirrel began to chatter hysterically in a tree top and from somewhere along the brook came the plash of a rising trout. Birds sang.

Suddenly the birds were still. The squirrel fled from the tree in which he had been gathering pine cones. Something was moving behind the woodpile. Jake Raven was not dead after all.

With all the stoical disregard of pain for which his race is famous, the sorely wounded Indian crawled along on his hands and knees. His progress was slow but sure.

Some three miles away was the boundary line of the California Indian Reservation. Jake knew that there was an encampment of his people close by the line and it was to them that he was going for help.

After a long, tortuous struggle, he arrived at his destination, but his efforts had so weakened him that he fainted dead away in the arms of the first redskin to reach him. Not before, however, he had managed to mumble the following words:

"White man shoot. Go camp quick. . . ."

Leaving Jake to the tender ministrations of the village squaws, the warriors of the tribe assembled around the wigwam of their chief to plan a course of action. Somewhere a tom-tom began to throb.

The chief's name was Israel Satinpenny. He had been to Harvard and hated the white man with undying venom. For many years now, he had been trying to get the Indian nations to rise and drive the palefaces back to the countries from which they had come, but so far he had had little success. His people had grown soft and lost their war-like ways. Perhaps, with the wanton wounding of Jake Raven, his chance had come.

When the warriors had all gathered around his tent, he appeared in full war regalia and began a harangue.

"Red Men!" he thundered. "The time has come to protest in the name of the Indian Peoples and to cry out against that abomination of abominations, the paleface.

"In our father's memory this was a fair, sweet land, where a man could hear his heart beat without wondering if what he heard wasn't an alarm clock, where a man could fill his nose with pleasant flower odors without finding that they came from a bottle. Need I speak of springs that had never known the tyranny of iron pipes? Of deer that had never tasted hay? Of wild ducks that had never been banded by the U.S. Department of Conservation?

"In return for the loss of these things, we accepted the white man's civilization, syphilis and the radio, tuberculosis and the cinema. We accepted his civilization because he himself believed in it. But now that he has begun to doubt, why should we continue to accept? His final gift to us is doubt, a soul-corroding doubt. He rotted this land in the name of progress, and now it is he himself who is rotting. The stench of his fear stinks in the nostrils of the great god Manitou.

"In what way is the white man wiser than the red? We lived here from time immemorial and everything was sweet and fresh. The paleface came and in his wisdom filled the sky with smoke and the rivers with refuse. What, in his wisdom, was he doing? I'll tell you. He was making clever cigarette lighters. He was making superb fountain pens. He was making paper bags, door knobs, leatherette satchels. All the powers of water, air and earth he made to turn his wheels within wheels within wheels within wheels. They turned, sure enough, and the land was flooded with toilet paper, painted boxes to keep pins in, key rings, watch fobs, leatherette satchels.

"When the paleface controlled the things he manufactured, we red men could only wonder at and praise his ability to hide his vomit. But now all the secret places of the earth are full. Now even the Grand Canyon will no longer hold razor blades. Now the dam, O warriors, has broken and he is up to his neck in the articles of his manufacture.

"He has loused the continent up good. But is he trying to de-louse it? No, all his efforts go to keep on lousing up the joint. All that worries him is how he can go on making little painted boxes for pins, watch fobs, leatherette satchels.

"Don't mistake me, Indians. I'm no Rousseauistic philosopher. I know that you can't put the clock back. But there is one thing you can do. You can stop that clock. You can smash that clock.

"The time is ripe. Riot and profaneness, poverty and violence are everywhere. The gates of pandemonium are open and through the land stalk the gods Mapeeo and Suraniou.

"The day of vengeance is here. The star of the paleface is sinking and he knows it. Spengler has said so; Valery has said so; thousands of his wise men proclaim it.

"O, brothers, this is the time to run upon his neck and the bosses of his armor. While he is sick and fainting, while he is dying of a surfeit of shoddy."

Wild yells for vengeance broke from the throats of the warriors. Shouting their new war-cry of "Smash that clock!" they

smeared themselves with bright paint and mounted their ponies. In every brave's hand was a tomahawk and between his
teeth a scalping knife.

Before jumping on his own mustang, Chief Satinpenny ordered one of his lieutenants to the nearest telegraph office.
From there he was to send code messages to all the Indian
tribes in the United States, Canada and Mexico, ordering
them to rise and slay.

With Satinpenny leading them, the warriors galloped
through the forest over the trail that Jake Raven had come.
When they arrived at the cabin, they found Lem still fast in
the unrelenting jaws of the bear trap.

"Yeehoieee!" screamed the chief, as he stooped over the
recumbent form of the poor lad and tore the scalp from his
head. Then brandishing his reeking trophy on high, he sprang
on his pony and made for the nearest settlements, followed
by his horde of blood-crazed savages.

An Indian boy remained behind with instructions to fire
the cabin. Fortunately, he had no matches and tried to do it
with two sticks, but no matter how hard he rubbed them
together he alone grew warm.

With a curse unbecoming one of his few years, he left off
to go swimming in the creek, first looting Lem's bloody head
of its store teeth and glass eye.

XXVII

A FEW HOURS later, Mr. Whipple rode on the scene with his load of provisions. The moment he entered the clearing, he knew that something was wrong and hurried to the cabin. There he found Lem with his leg still in the bear trap.

He bent over the unconscious form of the poor, mutilated lad and was happy to discover that his heart still beat. He tried desperately to release the trap, but failed, and was forced to carry Lem out of the cabin with it dangling from his leg.

Placing our hero across the pommel of his saddle, he galloped all that night, arriving at the county hospital the next morning. Lem was immediately admitted to the ward, where the good doctors began their long fight to save the lad's life. They triumphed, but not before they had found it necessary to remove his leg at the knee.

With the disappearance of Jake Raven, there was no use in Mr. Whipple's returning to the mine, so he remained near Lem, visiting the poor boy every day. Once he brought him an orange to eat, another time some simple wild flowers which he himself had gathered.

Lem's convalescence was a long one. Before it was over all of Shagpoke's funds were spent, and the ex-president was forced to work in a livery stable in order to keep body and soul together. When our hero left the hospital, he joined him there.

At first Lem had some difficulty in using the wooden leg with which the hospital authorities had equipped him. Practice, however, makes perfect, and in time he was able to help Mr. Whipple clean the stalls and curry the horses.

It goes without saying that the two friends were not satisfied to remain hostlers. They both searched for more suitable employment, but there was none to be had.

Shagpoke's mind was quick and fertile. One day, as he watched Lem show his scalped skull for the twentieth time, he was struck by an idea. Why not get a tent and exhibit his young friend as the last man to have been scalped by the Indians and the sole survivor of the Yuba River massacre?

Our hero was not very enthusiastic about the plan, but Mr. Whipple finally managed to convince him that it was the only way in which they could hope to escape from their drudgery in the livery stable. He promised Lem that as soon as they had accumulated a little money, they would abandon the tent show and enter some other business.

Out of an old piece of tarpaulin they fashioned a rough tent. Mr. Whipple then obtained a crate of cheap kerosene lighters from a dealer in pedlar's supplies. With this meager equipment they took to the open road.

Their method of work was very simple. When they arrived at the outskirts of a likely town, they set up their tent. Lem hid himself inside it, while Mr. Whipple beat furiously on the bottom of a tin can with a stick.

In a short while, he was surrounded by a crowd eager to know what the noise was about. After describing the merits of his kerosene lighters, he made his audience a "dual" offer. For the same ten cents, they could both obtain a cigarette lighter and enter the tent where they would see the sole survivor of the Yuba River massacre, getting a close view of his freshly scalped skull.

Business was not as good as they had thought it would be. Although Mr. Whipple was an excellent salesman, the people they encountered had very little money to spend and could not afford to gratify their curiosity no matter how much it was aroused.

One day, after many weary months on the road, the two friends were about to set up their tent, when a small boy volunteered the information that there was a much bigger show being given free at the local opera house. Realizing that it would be futile for them to try to compete with this other attraction, they decided to visit it.

There were bills posted on every fence, and the two friends stopped to read one of them.

FREE   FREE   FREE

Chamber of American Horrors
Animate and Inanimate
Hideosities
also
Chief Jake Raven

COME ONE   COME ALL
S. Snodgrasse
Mgr.

FREE   FREE   FREE

Delighted to discover that their redskinned friend was still alive, they set out to find him. He was coming down the steps of the opera house just as they arrived there, and his joy on seeing them was very great. He insisted on their accompanying him to a restaurant.

Over his coffee, Jake explained that after being shot by the man from Pike County, he had crawled to the Indian encampment. There his wounds had been healed by the use of certain medicaments secret to the squaws of his tribe. It was this same elixir that he was now selling in conjunction with the "Chamber of American Horrors."

Lem in his turn told how he had been scalped and how Mr. Whipple had arrived just in time to carry him to the hospital. After listening sympathetically to the lad's story, Jake expressed his anger in no uncertain terms. He condemned Chief Satinpenny for being a hot-head, and assured Lem and Mr. Whipple that the respectable members of the tribe frowned on Satinpenny's activities.

Although Mr. Whipple believed Jake, he was not satisfied that the Indian rising was as simple as it seemed. "Where," he asked the friendly redskin, "had Satinpenny obtained the machine guns and whiskey needed to keep his warriors in the field?"

Jake was unable to answer this question, and Mr. Whipple smiled as though he knew a great deal more than he was prepared to divulge at this time.

XXVIII

I REMEMBER your administration very well," said Sylvanus Snodgrasse to Mr. Whipple. "It will be an honor to have you and your young friend, whom I also know and admire, in my employ."

"Thank you," said both Shagpoke and Lem together.

"You will spend today rehearsing your rôles and tomorrow you will appear in the pageant."

It was through the good offices of Jake Raven that the above interview was made possible. Realizing how poor they were, he had suggested that the two friends abandon their own little show and obtain positions in the one with which he was traveling.

As soon as Shagpoke and Lem left the manager's office, an inner door opened and through it entered a certain man. If they had seen him and had known who he was, they would have been greatly surprised. Moreover, they would not have been quite so happy over their new jobs.

This stranger was none other than the fat man in the Chesterfield overcoat, Operative 6384XM or Comrade Z as he was known at a different address. His presence in Snodgrasse's office is explained by the fact that the "Chamber of American Horrors, Animate and Inanimate Hideosities," although it appeared to be a museum, was in reality a bureau for disseminating propaganda of the most subversive nature. It had been created and financed to this end by the same groups that employed the fat man.

Snodgrasse had become one of their agents because of his inability to sell his "poems." Like many another "poet," he blamed his literary failure on the American public instead of on his own lack of talent and his desire for revolution was really a desire for revenge. Furthermore, having lost faith in himself, he thought it his duty to undermine the nation's faith in itself.

As its name promised, the show was divided into two parts, "animate" and "inanimate." Let us first briefly consider the latter, which consisted of innumerable objects culled from the popular art of the country and of an equally large number of manufactured articles of the kind detested so heartily by Chief Satinpenny.

("Can this be a coincidence?" Mr. Whipple was later to ask.)

The hall which led to the main room of the "inanimate" exhibit was lined with sculptures in plaster. Among the most striking of these was a Venus de Milo with a clock in her abdomen, a copy of Powers' "Greek Slave" with elastic bandages on all her joints, a Hercules wearing a small, compact truss.

In the center of the principal salon was a gigantic hemorrhoid that was lit from within by electric lights. To give the effect of throbbing pain, these lights went on and off.

All was not medical, however. Along the walls were tables on which were displayed collections of objects whose distinction lay in the great skill with which their materials had been disguised. Paper had been made to look like wood, wood like rubber, rubber like steel, steel like cheese, cheese like glass, and, finally, glass like paper.

Other tables carried instruments whose purposes were dual and sometimes triple or even sextuple. Among the most ingenious were pencil sharpeners that could also be used as earpicks, can openers as hair brushes. Then, too, there was a large variety of objects whose real uses had been cleverly camouflaged. The visitor saw flower pots that were really victrolas, revolvers that held candy, candy that held collar buttons and so forth.

The "animate" part of the show took place in the auditorium of the opera house. It was called "The Pageant of America or A Curse on Columbus," and consisted of a series of short sketches in which Quakers were shown being branded, Indians brutalized and cheated, negroes sold, children sweated to death. Snodgrasse tried to make obvious the relationship between these sketches and the "inanimate" exhibit by a little speech in which he claimed that the former had resulted in the latter. His arguments were not very convincing, however.

The "pageant" culminated in a small playlet which I will attempt to set down from memory. When the curtain rises, the audience sees the comfortable parlor of a typical American home. An old, white-haired grandmother is knitting near the fire while the three small sons of her dead daughter play together on the floor. From a radio in the corner comes a rich, melodic voice.

Radio: "The Indefatigable Investment Company of Wall Street wishes its unseen audience all happiness, health and wealth, especially the latter. Widows, orphans, cripples, are you getting a large enough return on your capital? Is the money left by your dear departed ones bringing you all that they desired you to have in the way of comforts? Write or telephone. . . ."

Here the stage becomes dark for a few seconds. When the lights are bright again, we hear the same voice, but see that this time it comes from a sleek, young salesman. He is talking to the old grandmother. The impression given is that of a snake and a bird. The old lady is the bird of course.

Sleek Salesman: "Dear Madam, in South America lies the fair, fertile land of Iguania. It is a marvelous country, rich in minerals and oil. For five thousand dollars—yes, Madam, I'm advising you to sell all your Liberty Bonds—you will get ten of our Gold Iguanians, which yield seventeen percentum per annum. These bonds are secured by a first mortgage on all the natural resources of Iguania."

Grandmother: "But I. . . ."

Sleek Salesman: "You will have to act fast, as we have only a limited number of Gold Iguanians left. The ones I am offering you are part of a series set aside by our company especially for widows and orphans. It was necessary for us to do this because otherwise the big banks and mortgage companies would have snatched up the entire issue."

Grandmother: "But I. . . ."

The Three Small Sons: "Goo, goo. . . ."

Sleek Salesman: "Think of these kiddies, Madam. Soon they will be ready for college. They will want Brooks suits and banjos and fur coats like the other boys. How will you feel when you have to refuse them these things because of your stubbornness?"

Here the curtain falls for a change of scene. It rises again on a busy street. The old grandmother is seen lying in the gutter with her head pillowed against the curb. Around her are arranged her three grandchildren, all very evidently dead of starvation.

Grandmother (feebly to the people who hurry past): "We are starving. Bread . . . Bread. . . ."

No one pays any attention to her and she dies.

An idle breeze plays mischievously with the rags draping the four corpses. Suddenly it whirls aloft several sheets of highly engraved paper; one of which is blown across the path of two gentlemen in silk hats, on whose vests huge dollar signs are embroidered. They are evidently millionaires.

First Millionaire (picking up engraved paper): "Hey, Bill, isn't this one of your Iguanian Gold Bonds?" (He laughs.)

Second Millionaire (echoing his companion's laughter): "Sure enough. That's from the special issue for widows and orphans. I got them out in 1928 and they sold like hot cakes. (He turns the bond over in his hands, admiring it.) "I'll tell you one thing, George, it certainly pays to do a good printing job."

Laughing heartily, the two millionaires move along the street. In their way lie the four dead bodies and they almost trip over them. They exit cursing the street cleaning department for its negligence.

XXIX

The "Chamber of American Horrors, Animate and Inanimate Hideosities," reached Detroit about a month after the two friends had joined it. It was while they were playing there that Lem questioned Mr. Whipple about the show. He was especially disturbed by the scene in which the millionaires stepped on the dead children.

"In the first place," Mr. Whipple said, in reply to Lem's questions, "the grandmother didn't have to buy the bonds unless she wanted to. Secondly, the whole piece is made ridiculous by the fact that no one can die in the streets. The authorities won't stand for it."

"But," said Lem, "I thought you were against the capitalists?"

"Not all capitalists," answered Shagpoke. "The distinction must be made between bad capitalists and good capitalists, between the parasites and the creators. I am against the parasitical international bankers, but not the creative American capitalists, like Henry Ford for example."

"Are not capitalists who step on the faces of dead children bad?"

"Even if they are," replied Shagpoke, "it is very wrong to show the public scenes of that sort. I object to them because they tend to foment bad feeling between the classes."

"I see," said Lem.

"What I am getting at," Mr. Whipple went on, "is that Capital and Labor must be taught to work together for the general good of the country. Both must be made to drop the materialistic struggle for higher wages on the one hand and bigger profits on the other. Both must be made to realize that the only struggle worthy of Americans is the idealistic one of their country against its enemies, England, Japan, Russia, Rome and Jerusalem. Always remember, my boy, that class war is civil war, and will destroy us."

"Shouldn't we then try to dissuade Mr. Snodgrasse from continuing with his show?" asked Lem innocently.

"No," replied Shagpoke. "If we try to he will merely get

rid of us. Rather must we bide our time until a good opportunity presents itself, then denounce him for what he is, and
his show likewise. Here, in Detroit, there are too many Jews,
Catholics and members of unions. Unless I am greatly mistaken, however, we will shortly turn south. When we get to
some really American town, we will act."

Mr. Whipple was right in his surmise. After playing a few
more mid-western cities, Snodgrasse headed his company
south along the Mississippi River, finally arriving in the town
of Beulah for a one-night stand.

"Now is the time for us to act," announced Mr. Whipple
in a hoarse whisper to Lem, when he had obtained a good
look at the inhabitants of Beulah. "Follow me."

Our hero accompanied Shagpoke to the town barber shop,
which was run by one Keely Jefferson, a fervent southerner
of the old school. Mr. Whipple took the master barber to one
side. After a whispered colloquy, he agreed to arrange a meeting of the town's citizens for Shagpoke to address.

By five o'clock that same evening, all the inhabitants of
Beulah, who were not colored, Jewish or Catholic, assembled
under a famous tree from whose every branch a negro had
dangled at one time or other. They stood together, almost a
thousand strong, drinking Coca-Colas and joking with their
friends. Although every third citizen carried either a rope or
a gun, their cheerful manner belied the seriousness of the
occasion.

Mr. Jefferson mounted a box to introduce Mr. Whipple.

"Fellow townsmen, Southerners, Protestants, Americans,"
he began. "You have been called here to listen to the words
of Shagpoke Whipple, one of the few Yanks whom we of the
South can trust and respect. He ain't no nigger-lover, he don't
give a damn for Jewish culture, and he knows the fine Italian
hand of the pope when he sees it. Mr. Whipple. . . ."

Shagpoke mounted the box which Mr. Jefferson vacated
and waited for the cheering to subside. He began by placing
his hand on his heart. "I love the South," he announced. "I
love her because her women are beautiful and chaste, her men
brave and gallant, and her fields warm and fruitful. But there
is one thing that I love more than the South . . . my country,
these United States."

The cheers which greeted this avowal were even wilder and hoarser than those that had gone before it. Mr. Whipple held up his hand for silence, but it was fully five minutes before his audience would let him continue.

"Thank you," he cried happily, much moved by the enthusiasm of his hearers. "I know that your shouts rise from the bottom of your honest, fearless hearts. And I am grateful because I also know that you are cheering, not me, but the land we love so well.

"However, this is not a time or place for flowery speeches, this is a time for action. There is an enemy in our midst, who, by boring from within, undermines our institutions and threatens our freedom. Neither hot lead nor cold steel are his weapons, but insidious propaganda. He strives by it to set brother against brother, those who have not against those who have.

"You stand here now, under this heroic tree, like the free men that you are, but tomorrow you will become the slaves of Socialists and Bolsheviks. Your sweethearts and wives will become the common property of foreigners to maul and mouth at their leisure. Your shops will be torn from you and you will be driven from your farms. In return you will be thrown a stinking, slave's crust with Russian labels.

"Is the spirit of Jubal Early and Francis Marion then so dead that you can only crouch and howl like hound dogs? Have you forgotten Jefferson Davis?

"No?

"Then let those of you who remember your ancestors strike down Sylvanus Snodgrasse, that foul conspirator, that viper in the bosom of the body politic. Let those. . . ."

Before Mr. Whipple had quite finished his little talk, the crowd ran off in all directions, shouting "Lynch him! Lynch him!" although a good three-quarters of its members did not know whom it was they were supposed to lynch. This fact did not bother them, however. They considered their lack of knowledge an advantage rather than a hindrance, for it gave them a great deal of leeway in their choice of a victim.

Those of the mob who were better informed made for the opera house where the "Chamber of American Horrors" was quartered. Snodgrasse, however, was nowhere to be found.

He had been warned and had taken to his heels. Feeling that they ought to hang somebody, the crowd put a rope around Jake Raven's neck because of his dark complexion. They then fired the building.

Another section of Shagpoke's audience, made up mostly of older men, had somehow gotten the impression that the South had again seceded from the Union. Perhaps this had come about through their hearing Shagpoke mention the names of Jubal Early, Francis Marion and Jefferson Davis. They ran up the Confederate flag on the courthouse pole, and prepared to die in its defense.

Other, more practical-minded citizens, proceeded to rob the bank and loot the principal stores, and to free all their relatives who had the misfortune to be in jail.

As time went on, the riot grew more general in character. Barricades were thrown up in the streets. The heads of negroes were paraded on poles. A Jewish drummer was nailed to the door of his hotel room. The housekeeper of the local Catholic priest was raped.

XXX

Lᴇᴍ lost track of Mr. Whipple when the meeting broke up, and was unable to find him again although he searched everywhere. As he wandered around, he was shot at several times, and it was only by the greatest of good luck that he succeeded in escaping with his life.

He managed this by walking to the nearest town that had a depot and there taking the first train bound northeast. Unfortunately, all his money had been lost in the opera house fire and he was unable to pay for a ticket. The conductor, however, was a good-natured man. Seeing that the lad had only one leg, he waited until the train slowed down at a curve before throwing him off.

It was only a matter of twenty miles or so to the nearest highway, and Lem contrived to hobble there before dawn. Once on the highway, he was able to beg rides all the way to New York City, arriving there some ten weeks later.

Times had grown exceedingly hard with the inhabitants of that once prosperous metropolis and Lem's ragged, emaciated appearance caused no adverse comment. He was able to submerge himself in the great army of unemployed.

Our hero differed from most of that army in several ways, however. For one thing, he bathed regularly. Each morning he took a cold plunge in the Central Park lake on whose shores he was living in a piano crate. Also, he visited daily all the employment agencies that were still open, refusing to be discouraged or grow bitter and become a carping critic of things as they are.

One day, when he timidly opened the door of the "Golden Gates Employment Bureau," he was greeted with a welcoming smile instead of the usual jeers and curses.

"My boy," exclaimed Mr. Gates, the proprietor, "we have obtained a position for you."

At this news, tears welled up in Lem's good eye and his throat was so choked with emotion that he could not speak.

Mr. Gates was surprised and nettled by the lad's silence, not realizing its cause. "It's the opportunity of a lifetime," he said chidingly. "You have heard of course of the great team of Riley and Robbins. They're billed wherever they play as 'Fifteen Minutes of Furious Fun with Belly Laffs Galore.' Well, Moe Riley is an old friend of mine. He came in here this morning and asked me to get him a 'stooge' for his act. He wanted a one-eyed man, and the minute he said that, I thought of you."

By now Lem had gained sufficient control over himself to thank Mr. Gates, and he did so profusely.

"You almost didn't get the job," Mr. Gates went on, when he had had enough of the mutilated boy's gratitude. "There was a guy in here who heard Moe Riley talking to me, and we had some time preventing him from poking out one of his eyes so that he could qualify for the job. We had to call a cop."

"Oh, that's too bad," said Lem sadly.

"But I told Riley that you also had a wooden leg, wore a toupee and store teeth, and he wouldn't think of hiring anybody but you."

When our hero reported to the Bijou Theatre, where Riley and Robbins were playing, he was stopped at the stage door by the watchman, who was suspicious of his tattered clothes. He insisted on getting in, and the watchman finally agreed to take a message to the comedians. Soon afterwards, he was shown to their dressing room.

Lem stood in the doorway, fumbling with the piece of soiled cloth that served him as a cap, until the gales of laughter with which Riley and Robbins had greeted him subsided. Fortunately, it never struck the poor lad that he was the object of their merriment or he might have fled.

To be perfectly just, from a certain point of view, not a very civilized one it must be admitted, there was much to laugh at in our hero's appearance. Instead of merely having no hair like a man prematurely bald, the grey bone of his skull showed plainly where he had been scalped by Chief Satinpenny. Then, too, his wooden leg had been carved with initials, twined hearts and other innocent insignia by mischievous boys.

"You're a wow!" exclaimed the two comics in the argot of their profession. "You're a riot! You'll blow them out of the back of the house. Boy, oh boy, wait till the pus-pockets and flea-pits get a load of you."

Although Lem did not understand their language, he was made exceedingly happy by the evident satisfaction he gave his employers. He thanked them effusively.

"Your salary will be twelve dollars a week," said Riley, who was the business man of the team. "We wish we could pay you more, for you're worth more, but these are hard times in the theatre."

Lem accepted without quibbling and they began at once to rehearse him. His rôle was a simple one, with no spoken lines, and he was soon perfect in it.

He made his début on the stage that same night. When the curtain went up, he was discovered standing between the two comics and facing the audience. He was dressed in an old Prince Albert, many times too large for him, and his expression was one of extreme sobriety and dignity. At his feet was a large box the contents of which could not be seen by the audience.

Riley and Robbins wore striped blue flannel suits of the latest cut, white linen spats and pale grey derby hats. To accent further the contrast between themselves and their "stooge," they were very gay and lively. In their hands they carried newspapers rolled up into clubs.

As soon as the laughter caused by their appearance had died down, they began their "breezy cross-fire of smart cracks."

Riley: "I say, my good man, who was that dame I saw you with last night?"

Robbins: "How could you see me last night? You were blind drunk."

Riley: "Hey, listen, you slob, that's not in the act and you know it."

Robbins: "Act? What act?"

Riley: "All right! All right! You're a great little kidder, but let's get down to business. I say to you: 'Who was that dame I saw you out with last night?' And you say: 'That was no dame, that was a damn.'"

Robbins: "So you're stealing my lines, eh?"

At this both actors turned on Lem and beat him violently over the head and body with their rolled-up newspapers. Their object was to knock off his toupee or to knock out his teeth and eye. When they had accomplished one or all of these goals, they stopped clubbing him. Then Lem, whose part it was not to move while he was being hit, bent over and with sober dignity took from the box at his feet, which contained a large assortment of false hair, teeth and eyes, whatever he needed to replace the things that had been knocked off or out.

The turn lasted about fifteen minutes and during this time Riley and Robbins told some twenty jokes, beating Lem ruthlessly at the end of each one. For a final curtain, they brought out an enormous wooden mallet labeled "The Works" and with it completely demolished our hero. His toupee flew off, his eye and teeth popped out, and his wooden leg was knocked into the audience.

At the sight of the wooden leg, the presence of which they had not even suspected, the spectators were convulsed with joy. They laughed heartily until the curtain came down, and for some time afterwards.

Our hero's employers congratulated him on his success, and although he had a headache from their blows, he was made quite happy by this. After all, he reasoned, with millions out of work he had no cause to complain.

One of Lem's duties was to purchase newspapers and out of them fashion the clubs used to beat him. When the performance was over, he was given the papers to read. They formed his only relaxation, for his meager salary made more complicated amusements impossible.

The mental reactions of the poor lad had been slowed up considerably by the hardships he had suffered, and it was a heart-rending sight to watch him as he bent over a paper to spell out the headlines. More than this he could not manage.

"PRESIDENT CLOSES BANKS FOR GOOD," he read one night. He sighed profoundly. Not because he had again lost the few dollars he had saved, which he had, but because it made him think of Mr. Whipple and the Rat River National Bank. He spent the rest of the night wondering what had become of his old friend.

Some weeks later he was to find out. "WHIPPLE DEMANDS DICTATORSHIP," he read. "LEATHER SHIRTS RIOT IN

SOUTH." Then, in rapid succession, came other headlines announcing victories for Mr. Whipple's National Revolutionary Party. The South and West, Lem learned, were solidly behind his movement and he was marching on Chicago.

XXXI

O NE DAY a stranger came to the theatre to see Lem. He addressed our hero as Commander Pitkin and said that he was Storm Trooper Zachary Coates.

Lem made him welcome and asked eagerly for news of Mr. Whipple. He was told that that very night Shagpoke would be in the city. Mr. Coates then went on to explain that because of its large foreign population New York was still holding out against the National Revolutionary Party.

"But tonight," he said, "this city will be filled with thousands of 'Leather Shirts' from upstate and an attempt will be made to take it over."

While talking he stared hard at our hero. Apparently satisfied with what he saw, he saluted briskly and said, "As one of the original members of the party, you are being asked to cooperate."

"I'll be glad to do anything I can to help," Lem replied.

"Good! Mr. Whipple will be happy to hear that, for he counted on you."

"I am something of a cripple," Lem added with a brave smile. "I may not be able to do much."

"We of the party know how your wounds were acquired. In fact one of our prime purposes is to prevent the youth of this country from being tortured as you were tortured. Let me add, Commander Pitkin, that in my humble opinion you are well on your way to being recognized as one of the martyrs of our cause." Here he saluted Lem once more.

Lem was embarrassed by the man's praise and hurriedly changed the subject. "What are Mr. Whipple's orders?" he asked.

"Tonight, wherever large crowds gather, in the parks, theatres, subways, a member of our party will make a speech. Scattered among his listeners will be numerous 'Leather Shirts' in plain clothes, who will aid the speaker stir up the patriotic fury of the crowd. When this fury reaches its proper height, a march on the City Hall will be ordered. There a monster mass meeting will be held which Mr. Whipple will address. He will demand and get control of the city."

"It sounds splendid," said Lem. "I suppose you want me to make a speech in this theatre?"

"Yes, exactly."

"I would if I could," replied Lem, "but I'm afraid I can't. I have never made a speech in my life. You see, I'm not a real actor but only a 'stooge.' And besides, Riley and Robbins wouldn't like it if I tried to interrupt their act."

"Don't worry about those gentlemen," Mr. Coates said with a smile. "They will be taken care of. As for your other reason, I have a speech in my pocket that was written expressly for you by Mr. Whipple. I have come here to rehearse you in it."

Zachary Coates reached into his pocket and brought out a sheaf of papers. "Read this through first," he said firmly, "then we will begin to study it."

That night Lem walked out on the stage alone. Although he was not wearing his stage costume, but the dress uniform of the "Leather Shirts," the audience knew from the program that he was a comedian and roared with laughter.

This unexpected reception destroyed what little self-assurance the poor lad had and for a minute it looked as though he were going to run. Fortunately, however, the orchestra leader, who was a member of Mr. Whipple's organization, had his wits about him and made his men play the national anthem. The audience stopped laughing and rose soberly to its feet.

In all that multitude one man alone failed to stand up. He was our old friend, the fat fellow in the Chesterfield overcoat. Secreted behind the curtains of a box, he crouched low in his chair and fondled an automatic pistol. He was again wearing a false beard.

When the orchestra had finished playing, the audience reseated itself and Lem prepared to make his speech.

"I am a clown," he began, "but there are times when even clowns must grow serious. This is such a time. I. . . ."

Lem got no further. A shot rang out and he fell dead, drilled through the heart by an assassin's bullet.

Little else remains to be told, but before closing this book there is one last scene which I must describe.

It is Pitkin's Birthday, a national holiday, and the youth of America is parading down Fifth Avenue in his honor. They are a hundred thousand strong. On every boy's head is a coonskin hat complete with jaunty tail, and on every shoulder rests a squirrel rifle.

Hear what they are singing. It is the "Lemuel Pitkin Song."

> " 'Who dares?'—this was L. Pitkin's cry,
> "As striding on the Bijou stage he came—
> " 'Surge out with me in Shagpoke's name,
> " 'For him to live, for him to die!'
> "A million hands flung up reply,
> "A million voices answered, 'I!' "

Chorus:

> "A million hearts for Pitkin, oh!
> "To do and die with Pitkin, oh!
> "To live and fight with Pitkin, oh!
> "Marching for Pitkin."

The youths pass the reviewing stand and from it Mr. Whipple proudly returns their salute. The years have dealt but lightly with him. His back is still as straight as ever and his grey eyes have not lost their keenness.

But who is the little lady in black next to the dictator? Can it be the Widow Pitkin? Yes, it is she. She is crying, for with a mother glory can never take the place of a beloved child. To her it seems like only yesterday that Lawyer Slemp threw Lem into the open cellar.

And next to the Widow Pitkin stands still another woman. This one is young and beautiful, yet her eyes too are full of tears. Let us look closer, for there is something vaguely familiar about her. It is Betty Prail. She seems to have some official position, and when we ask, a bystander tells us that she is Mr. Whipple's secretary.

The marchers have massed themselves in front of the reviewing stand and Mr. Whipple is going to address them.

"Why are we celebrating this day above other days?" he asks his hearers in a voice of thunder. "What made Lemuel Pitkin great? Let us examine his life.

"First we see him as a small boy, light of foot, fishing for bullheads in the Rat River of Vermont. Later, he attends the Ottsville High School, where he is captain of the nine and an excellent outfielder. Then, he leaves for the big city to make his fortune. All this is in the honorable tradition of his country and its people, and he has the right to expect certain rewards.

"Jail is his first reward. Poverty his second. Violence is his third. Death is his last.

"Simple was his pilgrimage and brief, yet a thousand years hence, no story, no tragedy, no epic poem will be filled with greater wonder, or be followed by mankind with deeper feeling, than that which tells of the life and death of Lemuel Pitkin.

"But I have not answered the question. Why is Lemuel Pitkin great? Why does the martyr move in triumph and the nation rise up at every stage of his coming? Why are cities and states his pallbearers?

"Because, although dead, yet he speaks.

"Of what is it that he speaks? Of the right of every American boy to go into the world and there receive fair play and a chance to make his fortune by industry and probity without being laughed at or conspired against by sophisticated aliens.

"Alas, Lemuel Pitkin himself did not have this chance, but instead was dismantled by the enemy. His teeth were pulled out. His eye was gouged from his head. His thumb was removed. His scalp was torn away. His leg was cut off. And, finally, he was shot through the heart.

"But he did not live or die in vain. Through his martyrdom the National Revolutionary Party triumphed, and by that triumph this country was delivered from sophistication, Marxism and International Capitalism. Through the National Revolution its people were purged of alien diseases and America became again American."

"Hail, the Martyrdom in the Bijou Theatre!" roar Shagpoke's youthful hearers when he is finished.

"Hail, Lemuel Pitkin!"

"All hail, the American Boy!"

THE DAY OF THE LOCUST

For Laura

I

Around quitting time, Tod Hackett heard a great din on the road outside his office. The groan of leather mingled with the jangle of iron and over all beat the tattoo of a thousand hooves. He hurried to the window.

An army of cavalry and foot was passing. It moved like a mob; its lines broken, as though fleeing from some terrible defeat. The dolmans of the hussars, the heavy shakos of the guards, Hanoverian light horse, with their flat leather caps and flowing red plumes, were all jumbled together in bobbing disorder. Behind the cavalry came the infantry, a wild sea of waving sabertaches, sloped muskets, crossed shoulder belts and swinging cartridge boxes. Tod recognized the scarlet infantry of England with their white shoulder pads, the black infantry of the Duke of Brunswick, the French grenadiers with their enormous white gaiters, the Scotch with bare knees under plaid skirts.

While he watched, a little fat man, wearing a cork sun-helmet, polo shirt and knickers, darted around the corner of the building in pursuit of the army.

"Stage Nine—you bastards—Stage Nine!" he screamed through a small megaphone.

The cavalry put spur to their horses and the infantry broke into a dogtrot. The little man in the cork hat ran after them, shaking his fist and cursing.

Tod watched until they had disappeared behind half a Mississippi steamboat, then put away his pencils and drawing board, and left the office. On the sidewalk outside the studio he stood for a moment trying to decide whether to walk home or take a streetcar. He had been in Hollywood less than three months and still found it a very exciting place, but he was lazy and didn't like to walk. He decided to take the streetcar as far as Vine Street and walk the rest of the way.

A talent scout for National Films had brought Tod to the Coast after seeing some of his drawings in an exhibit of undergraduate work at the Yale School of Fine Arts. He had been hired by telegram. If the scout had met Tod, he probably

wouldn't have sent him to Hollywood to learn set and costume designing. His large, sprawling body, his slow blue eyes
and sloppy grin made him seem completely without talent,
almost doltish in fact.

Yet, despite his appearance, he was really a very complicated
young man with a whole set of personalities, one inside the
other like a nest of Chinese boxes. And "The Burning of Los
Angeles," a picture he was soon to paint, definitely proved he
had talent.

He left the car at Vine Street. As he walked along, he examined the evening crowd. A great many of the people wore
sports clothes which were not really sports clothes. Their
sweaters, knickers, slacks, blue flannel jackets with brass buttons were fancy dress. The fat lady in the yachting cap was
going shopping, not boating; the man in the Norfolk jacket
and Tyrolean hat was returning, not from a mountain, but an
insurance office; and the girl in slacks and sneaks with a bandanna around her head had just left a switchboard, not a
tennis court.

Scattered among these masqueraders were people of a different type. Their clothing was somber and badly cut, bought
from mail-order houses. While the others moved rapidly, dart-
ing into stores and cocktail bars, they loitered on the corners
or stood with their backs to the shop windows and stared at
everyone who passed. When their stare was returned, their
eyes filled with hatred. At this time Tod knew very little about
them except that they had come to California to die.

He was determined to learn much more. They were the
people he felt he must paint. He would never again do a fat
red barn, old stone wall or sturdy Nantucket fisherman. From
the moment he had seen them, he had known that, despite
his race, training and heritage, neither Winslow Homer nor
Thomas Ryder could be his masters and he turned to Goya
and Daumier.

He had learned this just in time. During his last year in art
school, he had begun to think that he might give up painting
completely. The pleasures he received from the problems of
composition and color had decreased as his facility had increased and he had realized that he was going the way of all
his classmates, toward illustration or mere handsomeness.

When the Hollywood job had come along, he had grabbed it despite the arguments of his friends who were certain that he was selling out and would never paint again.

He reached the end of Vine Street and began the climb into Pinyon Canyon. Night had started to fall.

The edges of the trees burned with a pale violet light and their centers gradually turned from deep purple to black. The same violet piping, like a Neon tube, outlined the tops of the ugly, humpbacked hills and they were almost beautiful.

But not even the soft wash of dusk could help the houses. Only dynamite would be of any use against the Mexican ranch houses, Samoan huts, Mediterranean villas, Egyptian and Japanese temples, Swiss chalets, Tudor cottages, and every possible combination of these styles that lined the slopes of the canyon.

When he noticed that they were all of plaster, lath and paper, he was charitable and blamed their shape on the materials used. Steel, stone and brick curb a builder's fancy a little, forcing him to distribute his stresses and weights and to keep his corners plumb, but plaster and paper know no law, not even that of gravity.

On the corner of La Huerta Road was a miniature Rhine castle with tarpaper turrets pierced for archers. Next to it was a little highly colored shack with domes and minarets out of the *Arabian Nights*. Again he was charitable. Both houses were comic, but he didn't laugh. Their desire to startle was so eager and guileless.

It is hard to laugh at the need for beauty and romance, no matter how tasteless, even horrible, the results of that need are. But it is easy to sigh. Few things are sadder than the truly monstrous.

2

THE HOUSE he lived in was a nondescript affair called the San Bernardino Arms. It was an oblong three stories high, the back and sides of which were of plain, unpainted stucco, broken by even rows of unadorned windows. The façade was the color of diluted mustard and its windows, all double, were framed by pink Moorish columns which supported turnip-shaped lintels.

His room was on the third floor, but he paused for a moment on the landing of the second. It was on that floor that Faye Greener lived, in 208. When someone laughed in one of the apartments he started guiltily and continued upstairs.

As he opened his door a card fluttered to the floor. "Honest Abe Kusich," it said in large type, then underneath in smaller italics were several endorsements, printed to look like press notices.

' . . . *the Lloyds of Hollywood'* . . . *Stanley Rose.*

'*Abe's word is better than Morgan's bonds'*—*Gail Brenshaw.*

On the other side was a penciled message:

"Kingpin fourth, Solitair sixth. You can make some real dough on those nags."

After opening the window, he took off his jacket and lay down on the bed. Through the window he could see a square of enameled sky and a spray of eucalyptus. A light breeze stirred its long, narrow leaves, making them show first their green side, then their silver one.

He began to think of "Honest Abe Kusich" in order not to think of Faye Greener. He felt comfortable and wanted to remain that way.

Abe was an important figure in a set of lithographs called "The Dancers" on which Tod was working. He was one of the dancers. Faye Greener was another and her father, Harry, still another. They changed with each plate, but the group of uneasy people who formed their audience remained the same. They stood staring at the performers in just the way that they stared at the masqueraders on Vine Street. It was their stare that drove Abe and the others to spin crazily and leap into the air with twisted backs like hooked trout.

Despite the sincere indignation that Abe's grotesque depravity aroused in him, he welcomed his company. The little man excited him and in that way made him feel certain of his need to paint.

He had first met Abe when he was living on Ivar Street, in a hotel called the Chateau Mirabella. Another name for Ivar Street was "Lysol Alley," and the Chateau was mainly inhabited by hustlers, their managers, trainers and advance agents.

In the morning its halls reeked of antiseptic. Tod didn't like this odor. Moreover, the rent was high because it included police protection, a service for which he had no need. He wanted to move, but inertia and the fact that he didn't know where to go kept him in the Chateau until he met Abe. The meeting was accidental.

He was on the way to his room late one night when he saw what he supposed was a pile of soiled laundry lying in front of the door across the hall from his own. Just as he was passing it, the bundle moved and made a peculiar noise. He struck a match, thinking it might be a dog wrapped in a blanket. When the light flared up, he saw it was a tiny man.

The match went out and he hastily lit another. It was a male dwarf rolled up in a woman's flannel bathrobe. The round thing at the end was his slightly hydrocephalic head. A slow, choked snore bubbled from it.

The hall was cold and draughty. Tod decided to wake the man and stirred him with his toe. He groaned and opened his eyes.

"You oughn't to sleep there."

"The hell you say," said the dwarf, closing his eyes again.

"You'll catch cold."

This friendly observation angered the little man still more.

"I want my clothes!" he bellowed.

The bottom of the door next to which he was lying filled with light. Tod decided to take a chance and knock. A few seconds later a woman opened it part way.

"What the hell do you want?" she demanded.

"There's a friend of yours out here who . . ."

Neither of them let him finish.

"So what!" she barked, slamming the door.

"Give me my clothes, you bitch!" roared the dwarf.

She opened the door again and began to hurl things into the hall. A jacket and trousers, a shirt, socks, shoes and underwear, a tie and hat followed each other through the air in rapid succession. With each article went a special curse.

Tod whistled with amazement.

"Some gal!"

"You bet," said the dwarf. "A lollapalooza—all slut and a yard wide."

He laughed at his own joke, using a high-pitched cackle more dwarflike than anything that had come from him so far, then struggled to his feet and arranged the voluminous robe so that he could walk without tripping. Tod helped him gather his scattered clothing.

"Say, mister," he asked, "could I dress in your place?"

Tod let him into his bathroom. While waiting for him to reappear, he couldn't help imagining what had happened in the woman's apartment. He began to feel sorry for having interfered. But when the dwarf came out wearing his hat, Tod felt better.

The little man's hat fixed almost everything. That year Tyrolean hats were being worn a great deal along Hollywood Boulevard and the dwarf's was a fine specimen. It was the proper magic green color and had a high, conical crown. There should have been a brass buckle on the front, but otherwise it was quite perfect.

The rest of his outfit didn't go well with the hat. Instead of shoes with long points and a leather apron, he wore a blue, double-breasted suit and a black shirt with a yellow tie. Instead of a crooked thorn stick, he carried a rolled copy of the *Daily Running Horse*.

"That's what I get for fooling with four-bit broads," he said by way of greeting.

Tod nodded and tried to concentrate on the green hat. His ready acquiescence seemed to irritate the little man.

"No quiff can give Abe Kusich the fingeroo and get away with it," he said bitterly. "Not when I can get her leg broke for twenty bucks and I got twenty."

He took out a thick billfold and shook it at Tod.

"So she thinks she can give me the fingeroo, hah? Well, let me tell . . ."

Tod broke in hastily.

"You're right, Mr. Kusich."

The dwarf came over to where Tod was sitting and for a moment Tod thought he was going to climb into his lap, but he only asked his name and shook hands. The little man had a powerful grip.

"Let me tell you something, Hackett, if you hadn't come along, I'da broke in the door. That dame thinks she can give me the fingeroo, but she's got another thinkola coming. But thanks anyway."

"Forget it."

"I don't forget nothing. I remember. I remember those who do me dirt and those who do me favors."

He wrinkled his brow and was silent for a moment.

"Listen," he finally said, "seeing as you helped me, I got to return it. I don't want anybody going around saying Abe Kusich owes him anything. So I'll tell you what. I'll give you a good one for the fifth at Caliente. You put a fiver on its nose and it'll get you twenty smackeroos. What I'm telling you is strictly correct."

Tod didn't know how to answer and his hesitation offended the little man.

"Would I give you a bum steer?" he demanded, scowling. "Would I?"

Tod walked toward the door to get rid of him.

"No," he said.

"Then why won't you bet, hah?"

"What's the name of the horse?" Tod asked, hoping to calm him.

The dwarf had followed him to the door, pulling the bathrobe after him by one sleeve. Hat and all, he came to a foot below Tod's belt.

"Tragopan. He's a certain, sure winner. I know the guy who owns him and he gave me the office."

"Is he a Greek?" Tod asked.

He was being pleasant in order to hide the attempt he was making to maneuver the dwarf through the door.

"Yeh, he's a Greek. Do you know him?"

"No."

"No?"

"No," said Tod with finality.

"Keep your drawers on," ordered the dwarf, "all I want to know is how you know he's a Greek if you don't know him?"

His eyes narrowed with suspicion and he clenched his fists.

Tod smiled to placate him.

"I just guessed it."

"You did?"

The dwarf hunched his shoulders as though he were going to pull a gun or throw a punch. Tod backed off and tried to explain.

"I guessed he was a Greek because Tragopan is a Greek word that means pheasant."

The dwarf was far from satisfied.

"How do you know what it means? You ain't a Greek?"

"No, but I know a few Greek words."

"So you're a wise guy, hah, a know-it-all."

He took a short step forward, moving on his toes, and Tod got set to block a punch.

"A college man, hah? Well, let me tell . . ."

His foot caught in the wrapper and he fell forward on his hands. He forgot Tod and cursed the bathrobe, then got started on the woman again.

"So she thinks she can give me the fingeroo."

He kept poking himself in the chest with his thumbs.

"Who gave her forty bucks for an abortion? Who? And another ten to go to the country for a rest that time. To a ranch I sent her. And who got her fiddle out of hock that time in Santa Monica? Who?"

"That's right," Tod said, getting ready to give him a quick shove through the door.

But he didn't have to shove him. The little man suddenly darted out of the room and ran down the hall, dragging the bathrobe after him.

A few days later, Tod went into a stationery store on Vine Street to buy a magazine. While he was looking through the rack, he felt a tug at the bottom of his jacket. It was Abe Kusich, the dwarf, again.

"How's things?" he demanded.

Tod was surprised to find that he was just as truculent as he had been the other night. Later, when he got to know him better, he discovered that Abe's pugnacity was often a joke. When he used it on his friends, they played with him like one does with a growling puppy, staving off his mad rushes and then baiting him to rush again.

"Fair enough," Tod said, "but I think I'll move."

He had spent most of Sunday looking for a place to live and was full of the subject. The moment he mentioned it, however, he knew that he had made a mistake. He tried to end the matter by turning away, but the little man blocked him. He evidently considered himself an expert on the housing situation. After naming and discarding a dozen possibilities without a word from Tod, he finally hit on the San Bernardino Arms.

"That's the place for you, the San Berdoo. I live there, so I ought to know. The owner's strictly from hunger. Come on, I'll get you fixed up swell."

"I don't know, I . . ." Tod began.

The dwarf bridled instantly, and appeared to be mortally offended.

"I suppose it ain't good enough for you. Well, let me tell you something, you . . ."

Tod allowed himself to be bullied and went with the dwarf to Pinyon Canyon. The rooms in the San Berdoo were small and not very clean. He rented one without hesitation, however, when he saw Faye Greener in the hall.

3

TOD had fallen asleep. When he woke again, it was after eight o'clock. He took a bath and shaved, then dressed in front of the bureau mirror. He tried to watch his fingers as he fixed his collar and tie, but his eyes kept straying to the photograph that was pushed into the upper corner of the frame.

It was a picture of Faye Greener, a still from a two-reel farce in which she had worked as an extra. She had given him the photograph willingly enough, had even autographed it in a large, wild hand, "Affectionately yours, Faye Greener," but she refused his friendship, or, rather, insisted on keeping it impersonal. She had told him why. He had nothing to offer her, neither money nor looks, and she could only love a handsome man and would only let a wealthy man love her. Tod was a "good-hearted man," and she liked "good-hearted men," but only as friends. She wasn't hard-boiled. It was just that she put love on a special plane, where a man without money or looks couldn't move.

Tod grunted with annoyance as he turned to the photograph. In it she was wearing a harem costume, full Turkish trousers, breastplates and a monkey jacket, and lay stretched out on a silken divan. One hand held a beer bottle and the other a pewter stein.

He had gone all the way to Glendale to see her in that movie. It was about an American drummer who gets lost in the seraglio of a Damascus merchant and has a lot of fun with the female inmates. Faye played one of the dancing girls. She had only one line to speak, "Oh, Mr. Smith!" and spoke it badly.

She was a tall girl with wide, straight shoulders and long, swordlike legs. Her neck was long, too, and columnar. Her face was much fuller than the rest of her body would lead you to expect and much larger. It was a moon face, wide at the cheek bones and narrow at chin and brow. She wore her "platinum" hair long, letting it fall almost to her shoulders in back, but kept it away from her face and ears with a narrow blue ribbon that went under it and was tied on top of her head with a little bow.

She was supposed to look drunk and she did, but not with alcohol. She lay stretched out on the divan with her arms and legs spread, as though welcoming a lover, and her lips were parted in a heavy, sullen smile. She was supposed to look inviting, but the invitation wasn't to pleasure.

Tod lit a cigarette and inhaled with a nervous gasp. He started to fool with his tie again, but had to go back to the photograph.

Her invitation wasn't to pleasure, but to struggle, hard and sharp, closer to murder than to love. If you threw yourself on her, it would be like throwing yourself from the parapet of a skyscraper. You would do it with a scream. You couldn't expect to rise again. Your teeth would be driven into your skull like nails into a pine board and your back would be broken. You wouldn't even have time to sweat or close your eyes.

He managed to laugh at his language, but it wasn't a real laugh and nothing was destroyed by it.

If she would only let him, he would be glad to throw himself, no matter what the cost. But she wouldn't have him. She didn't love him and he couldn't further her career. She wasn't sentimental and she had no need for tenderness, even if he were capable of it.

When he had finished dressing, he hurried out of the room. He had promised to go to a party at Claude Estee's.

4

C LAUDE was a successful screen writer who lived in a big
house that was an exact reproduction of the old Dupuy
mansion near Biloxi, Mississippi. When Tod came up the walk
between the boxwood hedges, he greeted him from the enormous, two-story porch by doing the impersonation that went
with the Southern colonial architecture. He teetered back and
forth on his heels like a Civil War colonel and made believe
he had a large belly.

He had no belly at all. He was a dried-up little man with
the rubbed features and stooped shoulders of a postal clerk.
The shiny mohair coat and nondescript trousers of that official
would have become him, but he was dressed, as always, elaborately. In the buttonhole of his brown jacket was a lemon
flower. His trousers were of reddish Harris tweed with a
hound tooth check and on his feet were a pair of magnificent,
rust-colored blüchers. His shirt was ivory flannel and his
knitted tie a red that was almost black.

While Tod mounted the steps to reach his outstretched
hand, he shouted to the butler.

"Here, you black rascal! A mint julep."

A Chinese servant came running with a Scotch and soda.

After talking to Tod for a moment, Claude started him in
the direction of Alice, his wife, who was at the other end of
the porch.

"Don't run off," he whispered. "We're going to a sporting
house."

Alice was sitting in a wicker swing with a woman named
Mrs. Joan Schwartzen. When she asked him if he was playing
any tennis, Mrs. Schwartzen interrupted her.

"How silly, batting an inoffensive ball across something that
ought to be used to catch fish on account of millions are
starving for a bite of herring."

"Joan's a female tennis champ," Alice explained.

Mrs. Schwartzen was a big girl with large hands and feet
and square, bony shoulders. She had a pretty, eighteen-year-
old face and a thirty-five-year-old neck that was veined and

sinewy. Her deep sunburn, ruby colored with a slight blue tint, kept the contrast between her face and neck from being too startling.

"Well, I wish we were going to a brothel this minute," she said. "I adore them."

She turned to Tod and fluttered her eyelids.

"Don't you, Mr. Hackett?"

"That's right, Joan darling," Alice answered for him. "Nothing like a bagnio to set a fellow up. Hair of the dog that bit you."

"How dare you insult me!"

She stood up and took Tod's arm.

"Convoy me over there."

She pointed to the group of men with whom Claude was standing.

"For God's sake, convoy her," Alice said. "She thinks they're telling dirty stories."

Mrs. Schwartzen pushed right among them, dragging Tod after her.

"Are you talking smut?" she asked. "I adore smut."

They all laughed politely.

"No, shop," said someone.

"I don't believe it. I can tell from the beast in your voices. Go ahead, do say something obscene."

This time no one laughed.

Tod tried to disengage her arm, but she kept a firm grip on it. There was a moment of awkward silence, then the man she had interrupted tried to make a fresh start.

"The picture business is too humble," he said. "We ought to resent people like Coombes."

"That's right," said another man. "Guys like that come out here, make a lot of money, grouse all the time about the place, flop on their assignments, then go back East and tell dialect stories about producers they've never met."

"My God," Mrs. Schwartzen said to Tod in a loud, stagey whisper, "they *are* talking shop."

"Let's look for the man with the drinks," Tod said.

"No. Take me into the garden. Have you seen what's in the swimming pool?"

She pulled him along.

The air of the garden was heavy with the odor of mimosa and honeysuckle. Through a slit in the blue serge sky poked a grained moon that looked like an enormous bone button. A little flagstone path, made narrow by its border of oleander, led to the edge of the sunken pool. On the bottom, near the deep end, he could see a heavy, black mass of some kind.

"What is it?" he asked.

She kicked a switch that was hidden at the base of a shrub and a row of submerged floodlights illuminated the green water. The thing was a dead horse, or, rather, a life-size, realistic reproduction of one. Its legs stuck up stiff and straight and it had an enormous, distended belly. Its hammerhead lay twisted to one side and from its mouth, which was set in an agonized grin, hung a heavy, black tongue.

"Isn't it marvelous!" exclaimed Mrs. Schwartzen, clapping her hands and jumping up and down excitedly like a little girl.

"What's it made of?"

"Then you weren't fooled? How impolite! It's rubber, of course. It cost lots of money."

"But why?"

"To amuse. We were looking at the pool one day and somebody, Jerry Appis, I think, said that it needed a dead horse on the bottom, so Alice got one. Don't you think it looks cute?"

"Very."

"You're just an old meanie. Think how happy the Estees must feel, showing it to people and listening to their merriment and their oh's and ah's of unconfined delight."

She stood on the edge of the pool and "ohed and ahed" rapidly several times in succession.

"Is it still there?" someone called.

Tod turned and saw two women and a man coming down the path.

"I think its belly's going to burst," Mrs. Schwartzen shouted to them gleefully.

"Goody," said the man, hurrying to look.

"But it's only full of air," said one of the women.

Mrs. Schwartzen made believe she was going to cry.

"You're just like that mean Mr. Hackett. You just won't let me cherish my illusions."

Tod was half way to the house when she called after him. He waved but kept going.

The men with Claude were still talking shop.

"But how are you going to get rid of the illiterate mockies that run it? They've got a strangle hold on the industry. Maybe they're intellectual stumblebums, but they're damn good business men. Or at least they know how to go into receivership and come up with a gold watch in their teeth."

"They ought to put some of the millions they make back into the business again. Like Rockefeller does with his Foundation. People used to hate the Rockefellers, but now instead of hollering about their ill-gotten oil dough, everybody praises them for what the Foundation does. It's a swell stunt and pictures could do the same thing. Have a Cinema Foundation and make contributions to Science and Art. You know, give the racket a front."

Tod took Claude to one side to say good night, but he wouldn't let him go. He led him into the library and mixed two double Scotches. They sat down on the couch facing the fireplace.

"You haven't been to Audrey Jenning's place?" Claude asked.

"No, but I've heard tell of it."

"Then you've got to come along."

"I don't like pro-sport."

"We won't indulge in any. We're just going to see a movie."

"I get depressed."

"Not at Jenning's you won't. She makes vice attractive by skillful packaging. Her dive's a triumph of industrial design."

Tod liked to hear him talk. He was master of an involved comic rhetoric that permitted him to express his moral indignation and still keep his reputation for worldliness and wit.

Tod fed him another lead. "I don't care how much cellophane she wraps it in," he said—"nautch joints are depressing, like all places for deposit, banks, mail boxes, tombs, vending machines."

"Love is like a vending machine, eh? Not bad. You insert a coin and press home the lever. There's some mechanical activity inside the bowels of the device. You receive a small sweet, frown at yourself in the dirty mirror, adjust your hat, take a firm grip on your umbrella and walk away, trying to look as though nothing had happened. It's good, but it's not for pictures."

Tod played straight again.

"That's not it. I've been chasing a girl and it's like carrying something a little too large to conceal in your pocket, like a briefcase or a small valise. It's uncomfortable."

"I know, I know. It's always uncomfortable. First your right hand gets tired, then your left. You put the valise down and sit on it, but people are surprised and stop to stare at you, so you move on. You hide it behind a tree and hurry away, but someone finds it and runs after you to return it. It's a small valise when you leave home in the morning, cheap and with a bad handle, but by evening it's a trunk with brass corners and many foreign labels. I know. It's good, but it won't film. You've got to remember your audience. What about the barber in Purdue? He's been cutting hair all day and he's tired. He doesn't want to see some dope carrying a valise or fooling with a nickel machine. What the barber wants is armor and glamor."

The last part was for himself and he sighed heavily. He was about to begin again when the Chinese servant came in and said that the others were ready to leave for Mrs. Jenning's.

5

THEY started out in several cars. Tod rode in the front of the one Claude drove and as they went down Sunset Boulevard he described Mrs. Jenning for him. She had been a fairly prominent actress in the days of silent films, but sound made it impossible for her to get work. Instead of becoming an extra or a bit player like many other old stars, she had shown excellent business sense and had opened a callhouse. She wasn't vicious. Far from it. She ran her business just as other women run lending libraries, shrewdly and with taste.

None of the girls lived on the premises. You telephoned and she sent a girl over. The charge was thirty dollars for a single night of sport and Mrs. Jenning kept fifteen of it. Some people might think that fifty per cent is a high brokerage fee, but she really earned every cent of it. There was a big overhead. She maintained a beautiful house for the girls to wait in and a car and a chauffeur to deliver them to the clients.

Then, too, she had to move in the kind of society where she could make the right contacts. After all, not every man can afford thirty dollars. She permitted her girls to service only men of wealth and position, not to say taste and discretion. She was so particular that she insisted on meeting the prospective sportsman before servicing him. She had often said, and truthfully, that she would not let a girl of hers go to a man with whom she herself would not be willing to sleep.

And she was really cultured. All the most distinguished visitors considered it quite a lark to meet her. They were disappointed, however, when they discovered how refined she was. They wanted to talk about certain lively matters of universal interest, but she insisted on discussing Gertrude Stein and Juan Gris. No matter how hard the distinguished visitor tried, and some had been known to go to really great lengths, he could never find a flaw in her refinement or make a breach in her culture.

Claude was still using his peculiar rhetoric on Mrs. Jenning when she came to the door of her house to greet them.

"It's so nice to see you again," she said. "I was telling Mrs. Prince at tea only yesterday—the Estees are my favorite couple."

She was a handsome woman, smooth and buttery, with fair hair and a red complexion.

She led them into a small drawing room whose color scheme was violet, gray and rose. The Venetian blinds were rose, as was the ceiling, and the walls were covered with a pale gray paper that had a tiny, widely spaced flower design in violet. On one wall hung a silver screen, the kind that rolls up, and against the opposite wall, on each side of a cherry-wood table, was a row of chairs covered with rose and gray, glazed chintz bound in violet piping. There was a small projection machine on the table and a young man in evening dress was fumbling with it.

She waved them to their seats. A waiter then came in and asked what they wanted to drink. When their orders had been taken and filled, she flipped the light switch and the young man started his machine. It whirred merrily, but he had trouble in getting it focused.

"What are we going to see first?" Mrs. Schwartzen asked.

"*Le Predicament de Marie.*"

"That sounds ducky."

"It's charming, utterly charming," said Mrs. Jenning.

"Yes," said the cameraman, who was still having trouble. "I love *Le Predicament de Marie*. It has a marvelous quality that is too exciting."

There was a long delay, during which he fussed desperately with his machine. Mrs. Schwartzen started to whistle and stamp her feet and the others joined in. They imitated a rowdy audience in the days of the nickelodeon.

"Get a move on, slow poke."

"What's your hurry? Here's your hat."

"Get a horse!"

"Get out and get under!"

The young man finally found the screen with his light beam and the film began.

LE PREDICAMENT DE MARIE

ou

LA BONNE DISTRAIT

Marie, the "bonne," was a buxom young girl in a tight-fitting black silk uniform with very short skirts. On her head was a tiny lace cap. In the first scene, she was shown serving dinner to a middle-class family in an oak-paneled dining room full of heavy, carved furniture. The family was very respectable and consisted of a bearded, frock-coated father, a mother with a whalebone collar and a cameo brooch, a tall, thin son with a long mustache and almost no chin and a little girl wearing a large bow in her hair and a crucifix on a gold chain around her neck.

After some low comedy with father's beard and the soup, the actors settled down seriously to their theme. It was evident that while the whole family desired Marie, she only desired the young girl. Using his napkin to hide his activities, the old man pinched Marie, the son tried to look down the neck of her dress and the mother patted her knee. Marie, for her part, surreptitiously fondled the child.

The scene changed to Marie's room. She undressed and got into a chiffon negligee, leaving on only her black silk stockings and high-heeled shoes. She was making an elaborate night toilet when the child entered. Marie took her on her lap and started to kiss her. There was a knock on the door. Consternation. She hid the child in the closet and let in the bearded father. He was suspicious and she had to accept his advances. He was embracing her when there was another knock. Again consternation and tableau. This time it was the mustachioed son. Marie hid the father under the bed. No sooner had the son begun to grow warm than there was another knock. Marie made him climb into a large blanket chest. The new caller was the lady of the house. She, too, was just settling down to work when there was another knock.

Who could it be? A telegram? A policeman? Frantically Marie counted the different hiding places. The whole family was present. She tiptoed to the door and listened.

"Who can it be that wishes to enter now?" read the title card.

And there the machine stuck. The young man in evening dress became as frantic as Marie. When he got it running again, there was a flash of light and the film whizzed through the apparatus until it had all run out.

"I'm sorry, extremely," he said. "I'll have to rewind."

"It's a frameup," someone yelled.

"Fake!"

"Cheat!"

"The old teaser routine!"

They stamped their feet and whistled.

Under cover of the mock riot, Tod sneaked out. He wanted to get some fresh air. The waiter, whom he found loitering in the hall, showed him to the patio in back of the house.

On his return, he peeked into the different rooms. In one of them he found a large number of miniature dogs in a curio cabinet. There were glass pointers, silver beagles, porcelain schnauzers, stone dachshunds, aluminum bulldogs, onyx whippets, china bassets, wooden spaniels. Every recognized breed was represented and almost every material that could be sculptured, cast or carved.

While he was admiring the little figures, he heard a girl singing. He thought he recognized her voice and peeked into the hall. It was Mary Dove, one of Faye Greener's best friends.

Perhaps Faye also worked for Mrs. Jenning. If so, for thirty dollars . . .

He went back to see the rest of the film.

6

Tod's hope that he could end his trouble by paying a small fee didn't last long. When he got Claude to ask Mrs. Jenning about Faye, that lady said she had never heard of the girl. Claude then asked her to inquire through Mary Dove. A few days later she phoned him to say there was nothing doing. The girl wasn't available.

Tod wasn't really disappointed. He didn't want Faye that way, not at least while he still had a chance some other way. Lately, he had begun to think he had a good one. Harry, her father, was sick and that gave him an excuse for hanging around their apartment. He ran errands and kept the old man company. To repay his kindness, she permitted him the intimacies of a family friend. He hoped to deepen her gratitude and make it serious.

Apart from this purpose, he was interested in Harry and enjoyed visiting him. The old man was a clown and Tod had all the painter's usual love of clowns. But what was more important, he felt that his clownship was a clue to the people who stared (a painter's clue, that is—a clue in the form of a symbol), just as Faye's dreams were another.

He sat near Harry's bed and listened to his stories by the hour. Forty years in vaudeville and burlesque had provided him with an infinite number of them. As he put it, his life had consisted of a lightning series of "nip-ups," "high-gruesomes," "flying-W's" and "hundred-and-eights" done to escape a barrage of "exploding stoves." An "exploding stove" was any catastrophe, natural or human, from a flood in Medicine Hat, Wyoming, to an angry policeman in Moose Factory, Ontario.

When Harry had first begun his stage career, he had probably restricted his clowning to the boards, but now he clowned continuously. It was his sole method of defense. Most people, he had discovered, won't go out of their way to punish a clown.

He used a set of elegant gestures to accent the comedy of his bent, hopeless figure and wore a special costume, dressing like a banker, a cheap, unconvincing, imitation banker. The costume consisted of a greasy derby with an unusually high crown, a wing collar and polka dot four-in-hand, a shiny double-breasted jacket and gray-striped trousers. His outfit fooled no one, but then he didn't intend it to fool anyone. His slyness was of a different sort.

On the stage he was a complete failure and knew it. Yet he claimed to have once come very close to success. To prove how close, he made Tod read an old clipping from the theatrical section of the Sunday *Times.*

"BEDRAGGLED HARLEQUIN," it was headed.

"The commedia del' arte is not dead, but lives on in Brooklyn, or was living there last week on the stage of the Oglethorpe Theatre in the person of one Harry Greener. Mr. Greener is of a troupe called 'The Flying Lings,' who, by the time this reaches you, have probably moved on to Mystic, Connecticut, or some other place more fitting than the borough of large families. If you have the time and really love the theatre, by all means seek out the Lings wherever they may be.

"Mr. Greener, the bedraggled Harlequin of our caption, is not bedraggled but clean, neat and sweet when he first comes on. By the time the Lings, four muscular Orientals, finish with him, however, he is plenty bedraggled. He is tattered and bloody, but still sweet.

"When Mr. Greener enters the trumpets are properly silent. Mama Ling is spinning a plate on the end of a stick held in her mouth, Papa Ling is doing cartwheels, Sister Ling is juggling fans and Sonny Ling is hanging from the proscenium arch by his pigtail. As he inspects his strenuous colleagues, Mr. Greener tries to hide his confusion under some much too obvious worldliness. He ventures to tickle Sister and receives a powerful kick in the belly in return for this innocent attention. Having been kicked, he is on familiar ground and begins to tell a dull joke. Father Ling sneaks up behind him and tosses him to Brother, who looks the other way. Mr. Greener lands on the back of his neck. He shows his mettle by finishing his dull story from a recumbent position. When he stands up, the audience, which failed to laugh at his joke, laughs at his limp, so he continues lame for the rest of the act.

"Mr. Greener begins another story, even longer and duller than his first. Just before he arrives at the gag line, the orchestra blares loudly and drowns him out. He is very patient and very brave. He begins again, but the orchestra will not let him finish. The pain that almost, not quite, thank God, crumples his stiff little figure would be unbearable if it were not obviously make-believe. It is gloriously funny.

"The finale is superb. While the Ling Family flies through the air, Mr. Greener, held to the ground by his sense of reality and his knowledge of gravitation, tries hard to make the audience think that he is neither surprised nor worried by the rocketing Orientals. It's familiar stuff, his hands signal, but his face denies this. As time goes on and no one is hurt, he regains his assurance. The acrobats ignore him, so he ignores the acrobats. His is the final victory; the applause is for him.

"My first thought was that some producer should put Mr. Greener into a big revue against a background of beautiful girls and glittering curtains. But my second was that this would be a mistake. I am afraid that Mr. Greener, like certain humble field plants which die when transferred to richer soil, had better be left to bloom in vaudeville against a background of ventriloquists and lady bicycle riders."

Harry had more than a dozen copies of this article, several on rag paper. After trying to get a job by inserting a small advertisement in *Variety* (". . . 'some producer should put Mr. Greener into a big revue . . .' The *Times*"), he had come to Hollywood, thinking to earn a living playing comedy bits in films. There proved to be little demand for his talents, however. As he himself put it, he "stank from hunger." To supplement his meagre income from the studios, he peddled silver polish which he made in the bathroom of the apartment out of chalk, soap and yellow axle grease. When Faye wasn't at Central Casting, she took him around on his peddling trips in her Model T Ford. It was on their last expedition together that he had fallen sick.

It was on this trip that Faye acquired a new suitor by the name of Homer Simpson. About a week after Harry had taken to his bed, Tod met Homer for the first time. He was keeping the old man company when their conversation was interrupted by a light knock on the apartment door. Tod answered it and found a man standing in the hall with flowers for Faye and a bottle of port wine for her father.

Tod examined him eagerly. He didn't mean to be rude but at first glance this man seemed an exact model for the kind of person who comes to California to die, perfect in every detail down to fever eyes and unruly hands.

"My name is Homer Simpson," the man gasped, then shifted uneasily and patted his perfectly dry forehead with a folded handkerchief.

"Won't you come in?" Tod asked.

He shook his head heavily and thrust the wine and flowers at Tod. Before Tod could say anything, he had lumbered off.

Tod saw that he was mistaken. Homer Simpson was only physically the type. The men he meant were not shy.

He took the gifts in to Harry, who didn't seem at all surprised. He said Homer was one of his grateful customers.

"That Miracle Polish of mine sure does fetch 'em."

Later, when Faye came home and heard the story, she was very much amused. They both told Tod how they had happened to meet Homer, interrupting themselves and each other every few seconds to laugh.

The next night Tod saw Homer staring at the apartment house from the shadow of a date palm on the opposite side of the street. He watched him for a few minutes, then called out a friendly greeting. Without replying, Homer ran away. On the next day and the one after, Tod again saw him lurking near the palm tree. He finally caught him by approaching the tree silently from the rear.

"Hello, Mr. Simpson," Tod said softly. "The Greeners were very grateful for your gift."

This time Simpson didn't move, perhaps because Tod had him backed against the tree.

"That's fine," he blurted out. "I was passing . . . I live up the street."

Tod managed to keep their conversation going for several minutes before he escaped again.

The next time Tod was able to approach him without the stalk. From then on, he responded very quickly to his advances. Sympathy, even of the most obvious sort, made him articulate, almost garrulous.

7

Tod was right about one thing at least. Like most of the people he was interested in, Homer was a Middle-Westerner. He came from a little town near Des Moines, Iowa, called Wayneville, where he had worked for twenty years in a hotel.

One day, while sitting in the park in the rain, he had caught cold and his cold developed into pneumonia. When he came out of the hospital, he found that the hotel had hired a new bookkeeper. They offered to take him on again, but his doctor advised him to go to California for a rest. The doctor had an authoritative manner, so Homer left Wayneville for the Coast.

After living for a week in a railroad hotel in Los Angeles, he rented a cottage in Pinyon Canyon. It was only the second house the real estate agent showed him, but he took it because he was tired and because the agent was a bully.

He rather liked the way the cottage was located. It was the last house in the canyon and the hills rose directly behind the garage. They were covered with lupines, Canterbury bells, poppies, and several varieties of large yellow daisy. There were also some scrub pines, Joshua and eucalyptus trees. The agent told him that he would see doves and plumed quail, but during all the time he lived there, he saw only a few large, black velvet spiders and a lizard. He grew very fond of the lizard.

The house was cheap because it was hard to rent. Most of the people who took cottages in that neighborhood wanted them to be "Spanish" and this one, so the agent claimed, was "Irish." Homer thought that the place looked kind of queer, but the agent insisted that it was cute.

The house was queer. It had an enormous and very crooked stone chimney, little dormer windows with big hoods and a thatched roof that came down very low on both sides of the front door. This door was of gumwood painted like fumed oak and it hung on enormous hinges. Although made by machine, the hinges had been carefully stamped to appear hand-forged. The same kind of care and skill had been used to make the roof thatching, which was not really straw but heavy fire-proof paper colored and ribbed to look like straw.

The prevailing taste had been followed in the living room. It was "Spanish." The walls were pale orange flecked with pink and on them hung several silk armorial banners in red and gold. A big galleon stood on the mantelpiece. Its hull was plaster, its sails paper and its rigging wire. In the fireplace was a variety of cactus in gaily colored Mexican pots. Some of the plants were made of rubber and cork; others were real.

The room was lit by wall fixtures in the shape of galleons with pointed amber bulbs projecting from their decks. The table held a lamp with a paper shade, oiled to look like parchment, that had several more galleons painted on it. On each side of the windows red velvet draperies hung from black, double-headed spears.

The furniture consisted of a heavy couch that had fat monks for legs and was covered with faded red damask, and three swollen armchairs, also red. In the center of the room was a very long mahogany table. It was of the trestle type and studded with large-headed bronze nails. Beside each of the chairs was a small end table, the same color and design as the big one, but with a colored tile let into the top.

In the two small bedrooms still another style had been used. This the agent had called "New England." There was a spool bed made of iron grained like wood, a Windsor chair of the kind frequently seen in tea shops, and a Governor Winthrop dresser painted to look like unpainted pine. On the floor was a small hooked rug. On the wall facing the dresser was a colored etching of a snowbound Connecticut farmhouse, complete with wolf. Both of these rooms were exactly alike in every detail. Even the pictures were duplicates.

There was also a bathroom and a kitchen.

8

I⊤ TOOK Homer only a few minutes to get settled in his new home. He unpacked his trunk, hung his two suits, both dark gray, in the closet of one of his bedrooms and put his shirts and underclothes into the dresser drawers. He made no attempt to rearrange the furniture.

After an aimless tour of the house and the yard, he sat down on the couch in the living room. He sat as though waiting for someone in the lobby of a hotel. He remained that way for almost half an hour without moving anything but his hands, then got up and went into the bedroom and sat down on the edge of the bed.

Although it was still early in the afternoon, he felt very sleepy. He was afraid to stretch out and go to sleep. Not because he had bad dreams, but because it was so hard for him to wake again. When he fell asleep, he was always afraid that he would never get up.

But his fear wasn't as strong as his need. He got his alarm clock and set it for seven o'clock, then lay down with it next to his ear. Two hours later, it seemed like seconds to him, the alarm went off. The bell rang for a full minute before he began to work laboriously toward consciousness. The struggle was a hard one. He groaned. His head trembled and his feet shot out. Finally his eyes opened, then widened. Once more the victory was his.

He lay stretched out on the bed, collecting his senses and testing the different parts of his body. Every part was awake but his hands. They still slept. He was not surprised. They demanded special attention, had always demanded it. When he had been a child, he used to stick pins into them and once had even thrust them into a fire. Now he used only cold water.

He got out of bed in sections, like a poorly made automaton, and carried his hands into the bathroom. He turned on the cold water. When the basin was full, he plunged his hands in up to the wrists. They lay quietly on the bottom like a pair of strange aquatic animals. When they were thoroughly chilled and began to crawl about, he lifted them out and hid them in a towel.

He was cold. He ran hot water into the tub and began to undress, fumbling with the buttons of his clothing as though he were undressing a stranger. He was naked before the tub was full enough to get in and he sat down on a stool to wait. He kept his enormous hands folded quietly on his belly. Although absolutely still, they seemed curbed rather than resting.

Except for his hands, which belonged on a piece of monumental sculpture, and his small head, he was well proportioned. His muscles were large and round and he had a full, heavy chest. Yet there was something wrong. For all his size and shape, he looked neither strong nor fertile. He was like one of Picasso's great sterile athletes, who brood hopelessly on pink sand, staring at veined marble waves.

When the tub was full, he got in and sank down in the hot water. He grunted his comfort. But in another moment he would begin to remember, in just another moment. He tried to fool his memory by overwhelming it with tears and brought up the sobs that were always lurking uneasily in his chest. He cried softly at first, then harder. The sound he made was like that of a dog lapping gruel. He concentrated on how miserable and lonely he was, but it didn't work. The thing he was trying so desperately to avoid kept crowding into his mind.

One day when he was working in the hotel, a guest called Romola Martin had spoken to him in the elevator.

"Mr. Simpson, you're Mr. Simpson, the bookkeeper?"

"Yes."

"I'm in six-eleven."

She was small and childlike, with a quick, nervous manner. In her arms she coddled a package which obviously contained a square gin bottle.

"Yes," said Homer again, working against his natural instinct to be friendly. He knew that Miss Martin owed several weeks' rent and had heard the room clerk say she was a drunkard.

"Oh! . . ." the girl went on coquettishly, making obvious

their difference in size, "I'm sorry you're worried about your bill, I . . ."

The intimacy of her tone embarrassed Homer.

"You'll have to speak to the manager," he rapped out, turning away.

He was trembling when he reached his office.

How bold the creature was! She was drunk, of course, but not so drunk that she didn't know what she was doing. He hurriedly labeled his excitement disgust.

Soon afterwards the manager called and asked him to bring in Miss Martin's credit card. When he went into the manager's office, he found Miss Carlisle, the room clerk, there. Homer listened to what the manager was saying to her.

"You roomed six-eleven?"

"I did, yes, sir."

"Why? She's obvious enough, isn't she?"

"Not when she's sober."

"Never mind that. We don't want her kind in this hotel."

"I'm sorry."

The manager turned to Homer and took the credit card he was holding.

"She owes thirty-one dollars," Homer said.

"She'll have to pay up and get out. I don't want her kind around here." He smiled. "Especially when they run up bills. Get her on the phone for me."

Homer asked the telephone operator for six-eleven and after a short time was told that the room didn't answer.

"She's in the house," he said. "I saw her in the elevator."

"I'll have the housekeeper look."

Homer was working on his books some minutes later when his phone rang. It was the manager again. He said that six-eleven had been reported in by the housekeeper and asked Homer to take her a bill.

"Tell her to pay up or get out," he said.

His first thought was to ask that Miss Carlisle be sent because he was busy, but he didn't dare to suggest it. While making out the bill, he began to realize how excited he was. It was terrifying. Little waves of sensation moved along his nerves and the base of his tongue tingled.

When he got off at the sixth floor, he felt almost gay. His step was buoyant and he had completely forgotten his troublesome hands. He stopped at six-eleven and made as though to knock, then suddenly took fright and lowered his fist without touching the door.

He couldn't go through with it. They would have to send Miss Carlisle.

The housekeeper, who had been watching from the end of the hall, came up before he could escape.

"She doesn't answer," Homer said hurriedly.

"Did you knock hard enough? That slut is in there."

Before Homer could reply, she pounded on the door.

"Open up!" she shouted.

Homer heard someone move inside, then the door opened a few inches.

"Who is it, please?" a light voice asked.

"Mr. Simpson, the bookkeeper," he gasped.

"Come in, please."

The door opened a little wider and Homer went in without daring to look around at the housekeeper. He stumbled to the center of the room and stopped. At first he was conscious only of the heavy odor of alcohol and stale tobacco, but then underneath he smelled a metallic perfume. His eyes moved in a slow circle. On the floor was a litter of clothing, newspapers, magazines, and bottles. Miss Martin was huddled up on a corner of the bed. She was wearing a man's black silk dressing gown with light blue cuffs and lapel facings. Her close-cropped hair was the color and texture of straw and she looked like a little boy. Her youthfulness was heightened by her blue button eyes, pink button nose and red button mouth.

Homer was too busy with his growing excitement to speak or even think. He closed his eyes to tend it better, nursing carefully what he felt. He had to be careful, for if he went too fast, it might wither and then he would be cold again. It continued to grow.

"Go away, please, I'm drunk," Miss Martin said.

Homer neither moved nor spoke.

She suddenly began to sob. The coarse, broken sounds she made seemed to come from her stomach. She buried her face in her hands and pounded the floor with her feet.

Homer's feelings were so intense that his head bobbed
stiffly on his neck like that of a toy Chinese dragon.

"I'm broke. I haven't any money. I haven't a dime. I'm
broke, I tell you."

Homer pulled out his wallet and moved on the girl as
though to strike her with it.

She cowered away from him and her sobs grew stronger.

He dropped the wallet in her lap and stood over her, not
knowing what else to do. When she saw the wallet, she smiled,
but continued sobbing.

"Sit down," she said.

He sat down on the bed beside her.

"You strange man," she said coyly. "I could kiss you for
being so nice."

He caught her in his arms and hugged her. His suddenness
frightened her and she tried to pull away, but he held on and
began awkwardly to caress her. He was completely unconscious of what he was doing. He knew only that what he felt
was marvelously sweet and that he had to make the sweetness
carry through to the poor, sobbing woman.

Miss Martin's sobs grew less and soon stopped altogether.
He could feel her fidget and gather strength.

The telephone rang.

"Don't answer it," she said, beginning to sob once more.

He pushed her away gently and stumbled to the telephone.
It was Miss Carlisle.

"Are you all right?" she asked, "or shall we send for the
cops?"

"All right," he said, hanging up.

It was all over. He couldn't go back to the bed.

Miss Martin laughed at his look of acute distress.

"Bring the gin, you enormous cow," she shouted gaily.
"It's under the table."

He saw her stretch herself out in a way that couldn't be
mistaken. He ran out of the room.

Now in California, he was crying because he had never seen
Miss Martin again. The next day the manager had told him
that he had done a good job and that she had paid up and
checked out.

Homer tried to find her. There were two other hotels in

Wayneville, small run-down houses, and he inquired at both of them. He also asked in the few rooming places, but with no success. She had left town.

He settled back into his regular routine, working ten hours, eating two, sleeping the rest. Then he caught cold and had been advised to come to California. He could easily afford not to work for a while. His father had left him about six thousand dollars and during the twenty years he had kept books in the hotel, he had saved at least ten more.

9

H<small>E GOT OUT</small> of the tub, dried himself hurriedly with a rough towel, then went into the bedroom to dress. He felt even more stupid and washed out than usual. It was always like that. His emotions surged up in an enormous wave, curving and rearing, higher and higher, until it seemed as though the wave must carry everything before it. But the crash never came. Something always happened at the very top of the crest and the wave collapsed to run back like water down a drain, leaving, at the most, only the refuse of feeling.

It took him a long time to get all his clothing on. He stopped to rest after each garment with a desperation far out of proportion to the effort involved.

There was nothing to eat in the house and he had to go down to Hollywood Boulevard for food. He thought of waiting until morning, but then, although he was not hungry, decided against waiting. It was only eight o'clock and the trip would kill some time. If he just sat around, the temptation to go to sleep again would become irresistible.

The night was warm and very still. He started down hill, walking on the outer edge of the pavement. He hurried between lamp-posts, where the shadows were heaviest, and came to a full stop for a moment at every circle of light. By the time he reached the boulevard, he was fighting the desire to run. He stopped for several minutes on the corner to get his bearings. As he stood there, poised for flight, his fear made him seem almost graceful.

When several other people passed without paying any attention to him, he quieted down. He adjusted the collar of his coat and prepared to cross the street. Before he could take two steps someone called to him.

"Hey, you, mister."

It was a beggar who had spotted him from the shadow of a doorway. With the infallible instinct of his kind, he knew that Homer would be easy.

"Can you spare a nickel?"

"No," Homer said without conviction.

The beggar laughed and repeated his question, threateningly.

"A nickel, mister!"

He poked his hand into Homer's face.

Homer fumbled in his change pocket and dropped several coins on the sidewalk. While the man scrambled for them, he made his escape across the street.

The SunGold Market into which he turned was a large, brilliantly lit place. All the fixtures were chromium and the floor and walls were lined with white tile. Colored spotlights played on the showcases and counters, heightening the natural hues of the different foods. The oranges were bathed in red, the lemons in yellow, the fish in pale green, the steaks in rose and the eggs in ivory.

Homer went directly to the canned goods department and bought a can of mushroom soup and another of sardines. These and a half a pound of soda crackers would be enough for his supper.

Out on the street again with his parcel, he started to walk home. When he reached the corner that led to Pinyon Canyon and saw how steep and black the hill looked, he turned back along the lighted boulevard. He thought of waiting until someone else started up the hill, but finally took a taxicab.

10

ALTHOUGH Homer had nothing to do but prepare his scanty meals, he was not bored. Except for the Romola Martin incident and perhaps one or two other widely spaced events, the forty years of his life had been entirely without variety or excitement. As a bookkeeper, he had worked mechanically, totaling figures and making entries with the same impersonal detachment that he now opened cans of soup and made his bed.

Someone watching him go about his little cottage might have thought him sleep-walking or partially blind. His hands seemed to have a life and a will of their own. It was they who pulled the sheets tight and shaped the pillows.

One day, while opening a can of salmon for lunch, his thumb received a nasty cut. Although the wound must have hurt, the calm, slightly querulous expression he usually wore did not change. The wounded hand writhed about on the kitchen table until it was carried to the sink by its mate and bathed tenderly in hot water.

When not keeping house, he sat in the back yard, called the patio by the real estate agent, in an old broken deck chair. He went out to it immediately after breakfast to bake himself in the sun. In one of the closets he had found a tattered book and he held it in his lap without looking at it.

There was a much better view to be had in any direction other than the one he faced. By moving his chair in a quarter circle he could have seen a large part of the canyon twisting down to the city below. He never thought of making this shift. From where he sat, he saw the closed door of the garage and a patch of its shabby, tarpaper roof. In the foreground was a sooty, brick incinerator and a pile of rusty cans. A little to the right of them were the remains of a cactus garden in which a few ragged, tortured plants still survived.

One of these, a clump of thick, paddlelike blades, covered with ugly needles, was in bloom. From the tip of several of its topmost blades protruded a bright yellow flower, somewhat like a thistle blossom but coarser. No matter how hard the wind blew, its petals never trembled.

A lizard lived in a hole near the base of this plant. It was about five inches long and had a wedge-shaped head from which darted a fine, forked tongue. It earned a hard living catching the flies that strayed over to the cactus from the pile of cans.

The lizard was self-conscious and irritable, and Homer found it very amusing to watch. Whenever one of its elaborate stalks was foiled, it would shift about uneasily on its short legs and puff out its throat. Its coloring matched the cactus perfectly, but when it moved over to the cans where the flies were thick, it stood out very plainly. It would sit on the cactus by the hour without moving, then become impatient and start for the cans. The flies would spot it immediately and after several misses, it would sneak back sheepishly to its original post.

Homer was on the side of the flies. Whenever one of them, swinging too widely, would pass the cactus, he prayed silently for it to keep on going or turn back. If it lighted, he watched the lizard begin its stalk and held his breath until it had killed, hoping all the while that something would warn the fly. But no matter how much he wanted the fly to escape, he never thought of interfering, and was careful not to budge or make the slightest noise. Occasionally the lizard would miscalculate. When that happened Homer would laugh happily.

Between the sun, the lizard and the house, he was fairly well occupied. But whether he was happy or not is hard to say. Probably he was neither, just as a plant is neither. He had memories to disturb him and a plant hasn't, but after the first bad night his memories were quiet.

II

H<small>E HAD</small> been living this way for almost a month, when, one day, just as he was about to prepare his lunch, the door bell rang. He opened it and found a man standing on the step with a sample case in one hand and a derby hat in the other. Homer hurriedly shut the door again.

The bell continued to ring. He put his head out of the window nearest the door to order the fellow away, but the man bowed very politely and begged for a drink of water. Homer saw that he was old and tired and thought that he looked harmless. He got a bottle of water from the icebox, then opened the door and asked him in.

"The name, sir, is Harry Greener," the man announced in sing-song, stressing every other syllable.

Homer handed him a glass of water. He swallowed it quickly, then poured himself another.

"Much obliged," he said with an elaborate bow. "That was indeed refreshing."

Homer was astonished when he bowed again, did several quick jig steps, then let his derby hat roll down his arm. It fell to the floor. He stooped to retrieve it, straightening up with a jerk as though he had been kicked, then rubbed the seat of his trousers ruefully.

Homer understood that this was to amuse, so he laughed.

Harry thanked him by bowing again, but something went wrong. The exertion had been too much for him. His face blanched and he fumbled with his collar.

"A momentary indisposition," he murmured, wondering himself whether he was acting or sick.

"Sit down," Homer said.

But Harry wasn't through with his performance. He assumed a gallant smile and took a few unsteady steps toward the couch, then tripped himself. He examined the carpet indignantly, made believe he had found the object that had tripped him and kicked it away. He then limped to the couch and sat down with a whistling sigh like air escaping from a toy balloon.

Homer poured more water. Harry tried to stand up, but Homer pressed him back and made him drink sitting. He drank this glass as he had the other two, in quick gulps, then wiped his mouth with his handkerchief, imitating a man with a big mustache who had just drunk a glass of foamy beer.

"You are indeed kind, sir," he said. "Never fear, some day I'll repay you a thousandfold."

Homer clucked.

From his pocket Harry brought out a small can and held it out for him to take.

"Compliments of the house," he announced. " 'Tis a box of Miracle Solvent, the modern polish par excellence, the polish without peer or parallel, used by all the movie stars . . ."

He broke off his spiel with a trilling laugh.

Homer took the can.

"Thank you," he said, trying to appear grateful. "How much is it?"

"The ordinary price, the retail price, is fifty cents, but you can have it for the extraordinary price of a quarter, the wholesale price, the price I pay at the factory."

"A quarter?" asked Homer, habit for the moment having got the better of his timidity. "I can buy one twice that size for a quarter in the store."

Harry knew his man.

"Take it, take it for nothing," he said contemptuously.

Homer was tricked into protesting.

"I guess maybe this is a much better polish."

"No," said Harry, as though he were spurning a bribe. "Keep your money. I don't want it."

He laughed, this time bitterly.

Homer pulled out some change and offered it.

"Take it, please. You need it, I'm sure. I'll have two cans."

Harry had his man where he wanted him. He began to practice a variety of laughs, all of them theatrical, like a musician tuning up before a concert. He finally found the right one and let himself go. It was a victim's laugh.

"Please stop," Homer said.

But Harry couldn't stop. He was really sick. The last block

that held him poised over the runway of self-pity had been knocked away and he was sliding down the chute, gaining momentum all the time. He jumped to his feet and began doing Harry Greener, poor Harry, honest Harry, well-meaning, humble, deserving, a good husband, a model father, a faithful Christian, a loyal friend.

Homer didn't appreciate the performance in the least. He was terrified and wondered whether to phone the police. But he did nothing. He just held up his hand for Harry to stop.

At the end of his pantomime, Harry stood with his head thrown back, clutching his throat, as though waiting for the curtain to fall. Homer poured him still another glass of water. But Harry wasn't finished. He bowed, sweeping his hat to his heart, then began again. He didn't get very far this time and had to gasp painfully for breath. Suddenly, like a mechanical toy that had been overwound, something snapped inside of him and he began to spin through his entire repertoire. The effort was purely muscular, like the dance of a paralytic. He jigged, juggled his hat, made believe he had been kicked, tripped, and shook hands with himself. He went through it all in one dizzy spasm, then reeled to the couch and collapsed.

He lay on the couch with his eyes closed and his chest heaving. He was even more surprised than Homer. He had put on his performance four or five times already that day and nothing like this had happened. He was really sick.

"You've had a fit," Homer said when Harry opened his eyes.

As the minutes passed, Harry began to feel better and his confidence returned. He pushed all thought of sickness out of his mind and even went so far as to congratulate himself on having given the finest performance of his career. He should be able to get five dollars out of the big dope who was leaning over him.

"Have you any spirits in the house?" he asked weakly.

The grocer had sent Homer a bottle of port wine on approval and he went to get it. He filled a tumbler half full and handed it to Harry, who drank it in small sips, making the faces that usually go with medicine.

Speaking slowly, as though in great pain, he then asked Homer to bring in his sample case.

"It's on the doorstep. Somebody might steal it. The greater part of my small capital is invested in those cans of polish."

When Homer stepped outside to obey, he saw a girl near the curb. It was Faye Greener. She was looking at the house.

"Is my father in there?" she called out.

"Mr. Greener?"

She stamped her foot.

"Tell him to get a move on, damn it. I don't want to stay here all day."

"He's sick."

The girl turned away without giving any sign that she either heard or cared.

Homer took the sample case back into the house with him. He found Harry pouring himself another drink.

"Pretty fair stuff," he said, smacking his lips over it. "Pretty fair, all right, all right. Might I be so bold as to ask what you pay for a . . ."

Homer cut him short. He didn't approve of people who drank and wanted to get rid of him.

"Your daughter's outside," he said with as much firmness as he could muster. "She wants you."

Harry collapsed on the couch and began to breathe heavily. He was acting again.

"Don't tell her," he gasped. "Don't tell her how sick her old daddy is. She must never know."

Homer was shocked by his hypocrisy.

"You're better," he said as coldly as he could. "Why don't you go home?"

Harry smiled to show how offended and hurt he was by the heartless attitude of his host. When Homer said nothing, his smile became one expressing boundless courage. He got carefully to his feet, stood erect for a minute, then began to sway weakly and tumbled back on the couch.

"I'm faint," he groaned.

Once again he was surprised and frightened. He was faint.

"Get my daughter," he gasped.

Homer found her standing at the curb with her back to the house. When he called her, she whirled and came running toward him. He watched her for a second, then went in, leaving the door unlatched.

Faye burst into the room. She ignored Homer and went straight to the couch.

"Now what in hell's the matter?" she exploded.

"Darling daughter," he said. "I have been badly taken, and this gentleman has been kind enough to let me rest for a moment."

"He had a fit or something," Homer said.

She whirled around on him so suddenly that he was startled.

"How do you do?" she said, holding her hand forward and high up.

He shook it gingerly.

"Charmed," she said, when he mumbled something.

She spun around once more.

"It's my heart," Harry said. "I can't stand up."

The little performance he put on to sell polish was familiar to her and she knew that this wasn't part of it. When she turned to face Homer again, she looked quite tragic. Her head, instead of being held far back, now drooped forward.

"Please let him rest there," she said.

"Yes, of course."

Homer motioned her toward a chair, then got her a match for her cigarette. He tried not to stare at her, but his good manners were wasted. Faye enjoyed being stared at.

He thought her extremely beautiful, but what affected him still more was her vitality. She was taut and vibrant. She was as shiny as a new spoon.

Although she was seventeen, she was dressed like a child of twelve in a white cotton dress with a blue sailor collar. Her long legs were bare and she had blue sandals on her feet.

"I'm so sorry," she said when Homer looked at her father again.

He made a motion with his hand to show that it was nothing.

"He has a vile heart, poor dear," she went on. "I've begged and begged him to go to a specialist, but you men are all alike."

"Yes, he ought to go to a doctor," Homer said.

Her odd mannerisms and artificial voice puzzled him.

"What time is it?" she asked.

"About one o'clock."

She stood up suddenly and buried both her hands in her

hair at the sides of her head, making it bunch at the top in a shiny ball.

"Oh," she gasped prettily, "and I had a luncheon date."

Still holding her hair, she turned at the waist without moving her legs, so that her snug dress twisted even tighter and Homer could see her dainty, arched ribs and little, dimpled belly. This elaborate gesture, like all her others, was so completely meaningless, almost formal, that she seemed a dancer rather than an affected actress.

"Do you like salmon salad?" Homer ventured to ask.

"Salmon sal-ahde?"

She seemed to be repeating the question to her stomach. The answer was yes.

"With plenty of mayonnaise, huh? I adore it."

"I was going to have some for lunch. I'll finish making it."

"Let me help."

They looked at Harry, who appeared to be asleep, then went into the kitchen. While he opened a can of salmon, she climbed on a chair and straddled it with her arms folded across the top of its back and rested her chin on her arms. Whenever he looked at her, she smiled intimately and tossed her pale, glittering hair first forward, then back.

Homer was excited and his hands worked quickly. He soon had a large bowl of salad ready. He set the table with his best cloth and his best silver and china.

"It makes me hungry just to look," she said.

The way she said this seemed to mean that it was Homer who made her hungry and he beamed at her. But before he had a chance to sit down, she was already eating. She buttered a slice of bread, covered the butter with sugar and took a big bite. Then she quickly smeared a gob of mayonnaise on the salmon and went to work. Just as he was about to sit down, she asked for something to drink. He poured her a glass of milk and stood watching her like a waiter. He was unaware of her rudeness.

As soon as she had gobbled up her salad, he brought her a large red apple. She ate the fruit more slowly, nibbling daintily, her smallest finger curled away from the rest of her hand. When she had finished it, she went back to the living room and Homer followed her.

Harry still lay as they had left him, stretched out on the sofa. The heavy noon-day sun hit directly on his face, beating down on him like a club. He hardly felt its blows, however. He was busy with the stabbing pain in his chest. He was so busy with himself that he had even stopped trying to plan how to get money out of the big dope.

Homer drew the window curtain to shade his face. Harry didn't even notice. He was thinking about death. Faye bent over him. He saw, from under his partially closed eyelids, that she expected him to make a reassuring gesture. He refused. He examined the tragic expression that she had assumed and didn't like it. In a serious moment like this, her ham sorrow was insulting.

"Speak to me, Daddy," she begged.

She was baiting him without being aware of it.

"What the hell is this," he snarled, "a Tom show?"

His sudden fury scared her and she straightened up with a jerk. He didn't want to laugh, but a short bark escaped before he could stop it. He waited anxiously to see what would happen. When it didn't hurt he laughed again. He kept on, timidly at first, then with growing assurance. He laughed with his eyes closed and the sweat pouring down his brow. Faye knew only one way to stop him and that was to do something he hated as much as she hated his laughter. She began to sing.

> *"Jeepers Creepers!*
> *Where'd ya get those peepers? . . ."*

She trucked, jerking her buttocks and shaking her head from side to side.

Homer was amazed. He felt that the scene he was witnessing had been rehearsed. He was right. Their bitterest quarrels often took this form; he laughing, she singing.

> *"Jeepers Creepers!*
> *Where'd ya get those eyes?*
> *Gosh, all git up!*
> *How'd they get so lit up?*
> *Gosh all git . . ."*

When Harry stopped, she stopped and flung herself into a chair. But Harry was only gathering strength for a final effort.

He began again. This new laugh was not critical; it was horrible. When she was a child, he used to punish her with it. It was his masterpiece. There was a director who always called on him to give it when he was shooting a scene in an insane asylum or a haunted castle.

It began with a sharp, metallic crackle, like burning sticks, then gradually increased in volume until it became a rapid bark, then fell away again to an obscene chuckle. After a slight pause, it climbed until it was the nicker of a horse, then still higher to become a machinelike screech.

Faye listened helplessly with her head cocked on one side. Suddenly, she too laughed, not willingly, but fighting the sound.

"You bastard!" she yelled.

She leaped to the couch, grabbed him by the shoulders and tried to shake him quiet.

He kept laughing.

Homer moved as though he meant to pull her away, but he lost courage and was afraid to touch her. She was so naked under her skimpy dress.

"Miss Greener," he pleaded, making his big hands dance at the end of his arms. "Please, please . . ."

Harry couldn't stop laughing now. He pressed his belly with his hands, but the noise poured out of him. It had begun to hurt again.

Swinging her hand as though it held a hammer, she brought her fist down hard on his mouth. She hit him only once. He relaxed and was quiet.

"I had to do it," she said to Homer when he took her arm and led her away.

He guided her to a chair in the kitchen and shut the door. She continued to sob for a long time. He stood behind her chair, helplessly, watching the rhythmical heave of her shoulders. Several times his hands moved forward to comfort her, but he succeeded in curbing them.

When she was through crying, he handed her a napkin and she dried her face. The cloth was badly stained by her rouge and mascara.

"I've spoilt it," she said, keeping her face averted. "I'm very sorry."

"It was dirty," Homer said.

She took a compact from her pocket and looked at herself in its tiny mirror.

"I'm a fright."

She asked if she could use the bathroom and he showed her where it was. He then tiptoed into the living room to see Harry. The old man's breathing was noisy but regular and he seemed to be sleeping quietly. Homer put a cushion under his head without disturbing him and went back into the kitchen. He lit the stove and put the coffeepot on the flame, then sat down to wait for the girl to return. He heard her go into the living room. A few seconds later she came into the kitchen.

She hesitated apologetically in the doorway.

"Won't you have some coffee?"

Without waiting for her to reply, he poured a cup and moved the sugar and cream so that she could reach them.

"I had to do it," she said. "I just had to."

"That's all right."

To show her that it wasn't necessary to apologize, he busied himself at the sink.

"No, I had to," she insisted. "He laughs that way just to drive me wild. I can't stand it. I simply can't."

"Yes."

"He's crazy. We Greeners are all crazy."

She made this last statement as though there were merit in being crazy.

"He's pretty sick," Homer said, apologizing for her. "Maybe he had a sunstroke."

"No, he's crazy."

He put a plate of gingersnaps on the table and she ate them with her second cup of coffee. The dainty crunching sound she made chewing fascinated him.

When she remained quiet for several minutes, he turned from the sink to see if anything was wrong. She was smoking a cigarette and seemed lost in thought.

He tried to be gay.

"What are you thinking?" he said awkwardly, then felt foolish.

She sighed to show how dark and foreboding her thoughts were, but didn't reply.

"I'll bet you would like some candy," Homer said. "There isn't any in the house, but I could call the drugstore and they'd send it right over. Or some ice cream?"

"No, thanks, please."

"It's no trouble."

"My father isn't really a peddler," she said, abruptly. "He's an actor. I'm an actress. My mother was also an actress, a dancer. The theatre is in our blood."

"I haven't seen many shows. I . . ."

He broke off because he saw that she wasn't interested.

"I'm going to be a star some day," she announced as though daring him to contradict her.

"I'm sure you . . ."

"It's my life. It's the only thing in the whole world that I want."

"It's good to know what you want. I used to be a book-keeper in a hotel, but . . ."

"If I'm not, I'll commit suicide."

She stood up and put her hands to her hair, opened her eyes wide and frowned.

"I don't go to shows very often," he apologized, pushing the gingersnaps toward her. "The lights hurt my eyes."

She laughed and took a cracker.

"I'll get fat."

"Oh, no."

"They say fat women are going to be popular next year. Do you think so? I don't. It's just publicity for Mae West."

He agreed with her.

She talked on and on, endlessly, about herself and about the picture business. He watched her, but didn't listen, and whenever she repeated a question in order to get a reply, he nodded his head without saying anything.

His hands began to bother him. He rubbed them against the edge of the table to relieve their itch, but it only stimulated them. When he clasped them behind his back, the strain became intolerable. They were hot and swollen. Using the dishes as an excuse, he held them under the cold water tap of the sink.

Faye was still talking when Harry appeared in the doorway. He leaned weakly against the doorjamb. His nose was very

red, but the rest of his face was drained white and he seemed
to have grown too small for his clothing. He was smiling,
however.

To Homer's amazement, they greeted each other as though
nothing had happened.

"You okay now, Pop?"

"Fine and dandy, baby. Right as rain, fit as a fiddle and lively
as a flea, as the feller says."

The nasal twang he used in imitation of a country yokel
made Homer smile.

"Do you want something to eat?" he asked. "A glass of
milk, maybe?"

"I could do with a snack."

Faye helped him over to the table. He tried to disguise how
weak he was by doing an exaggerated Negro shuffle.

Homer opened a can of sardines and sliced some bread.
Harry smacked his lips over the food, but ate slowly and with
an effort.

"That hit the spot, all righty right," he said when he had
finished.

He leaned back and fished a crumpled cigar butt out of his
vest pocket. Faye lit it for him and he playfully blew a puff of
smoke in her face.

"We'd better go, Daddy," she said.

"In a jiffy, child."

He turned to Homer.

"Nice place you've got here. Married?"

Faye tried to interfere.

"Dad!"

He ignored her.

"Bachelor, eh?"

"Yes."

"Well, well, a young fellow like you."

"I'm here for my health," Homer found it necessary to say.

"Don't answer his questions," Faye broke in.

"Now, now, daughter, I'm just being friendly like. I don't
mean no harm."

He was still using exaggerated backwoods accent. He spat
dry into an imaginary spittoon and made believe he was shifting a cud of tobacco from cheek to cheek.

Homer thought his mimicry funny.

"I'd be lonesome and scared living alone in a big house like this," Harry went on. "Don't you ever get lonesome?"

Homer looked at Faye for his answer. She was frowning with annoyance.

"No," he said, to prevent Harry from repeating the uncomfortable question.

"No? Well, that's fine."

He blew several smoke rings at the ceiling and watched their behavior judiciously.

"Did you ever think of taking boarders?" he asked. "Some nice, sociable folks, I mean. It'll bring in a little extra money and make things more homey."

Homer was indignant, but underneath his indignation lurked another idea, a very exciting one. He didn't know what to say.

Faye misunderstood his agitation.

"Cut it out, Dad," she exclaimed before Homer could reply. "You've been a big enough nuisance already."

"Just chinning," he protested innocently. "Just chewing the fat."

"Well, then, let's get going," she snapped.

"There's plenty of time," Homer said.

He wanted to add something stronger, but didn't have the courage. His hands were braver. When Faye shook good-bye, they clutched and refused to let go.

Faye laughed at their warm insistence.

"Thanks a million, Mr. Simpson," she said. "You've been very kind. Thanks for the lunch and for helping Daddy."

"We're very grateful," Harry chimed in. "You've done a Christian deed this day. God will reward you."

He had suddenly become very pious.

"Please look us up," Faye said. "We live close-by in the San Berdoo Apartments, about five blocks down the canyon. It's the big yellow house."

When Harry stood, he had to lean against the table for support. Faye and Homer each took him by the arm and helped him into the street. Homer held him erect, while Faye went to get their Ford which was parked across the street.

"We're forgetting your order of Miracle Salve," Harry said, "the polish without peer or parallel."

Homer found a dollar and slipped it into his hand. He hid the money quickly and tried to become businesslike.

"I'll leave the goods tomorrow."

"Yes, that'll be fine," Homer said. "I really need some silver polish."

Harry was angry because it hurt him to be patronized by a sucker. He made an attempt to re-establish what he considered to be their proper relationship by bowing ironically, but didn't get very far with the gesture and began to fumble with his Adam's apple. Homer helped him into the car and he slumped down in the seat beside Faye.

They drove off. She turned to wave, but Harry didn't even look back.

12

HOMER spent the rest of the afternoon in the broken deck chair. The lizard was on the cactus, but he took little interest in its hunting. His hands kept his thoughts busy. They trembled and jerked, as though troubled by dreams. To hold them still, he clasped them together. Their fingers twined like a tangle of thighs in miniature. He snatched them apart and sat on them.

When the days passed and he couldn't forget Faye, he began to grow frightened. He somehow knew that his only defense was chastity, that it served him, like the shell of a tortoise, as both spine and armor. He couldn't shed it even in thought. If he did, he would be destroyed.

He was right. There are men who can lust with parts of themselves. Only their brain or their hearts burn and then not completely. There are others, still more fortunate, who are like the filaments of an incandescent lamp. They burn fiercely, yet nothing is destroyed. But in Homer's case it would be like dropping a spark into a barn full of hay. He had escaped in the Romola Martin incident, but he wouldn't escape again. Then, for one thing, he had had his job in the hotel, a daily all-day task that protected him by tiring him, but now he had nothing.

His thoughts frightened him and he bolted into the house, hoping to leave them behind like a hat. He ran into his bedroom and threw himself down on the bed. He was simple enough to believe that people don't think while asleep.

In his troubled state, even this delusion was denied him and he was unable to fall asleep. He closed his eyes and tried to make himself drowsy. The approach to sleep which had once been automatic had somehow become a long, shining tunnel. Sleep was at the far end of it, a soft bit of shadow in the hard glare. He couldn't run, only crawl toward the black patch. Just as he was about to give up, habit came to his rescue. It collapsed the shining tunnel and hurled him into the shadow.

When he awoke it was without a struggle. He tried to fall asleep once more, but this time couldn't even find the tunnel.

He was thoroughly awake. He tried to think of how very tired he was, but he wasn't tired. He felt more alive than he had at any time since Romola Martin.

Outside a few birds still sang intermittently, starting and breaking off, as though sorry to acknowledge the end of another day. He thought that he heard the lisp of silk against silk, but it was only the wind playing in the trees. How empty the house was! He tried to fill it by singing.

> *"Oh, say can you see,*
> *By the dawn's early light . . ."*

It was the only song he knew. He thought of buying a victrola or a radio. He knew, however, that he would buy neither. This fact made him very sad. It was a pleasant sadness, very sweet and calm.

But he couldn't let well enough alone. He was impatient and began to prod at his sadness, hoping to make it acute and so still more pleasant. He had been getting pamphlets in the mail from a travel bureau and he thought of the trips he would never take. Mexico was only a few hundred miles away. Boats left daily for Hawaii.

His sadness turned to anguish before he knew it and became sour. He was miserable again. He began to cry.

Only those who still have hope can benefit from tears. When they finish, they feel better. But to those without hope, like Homer, whose anguish is basic and permanent, no good comes from crying. Nothing changes for them. They usually know this, but still can't help crying.

Homer was lucky. He cried himself to sleep.

But he awoke again in the morning with Faye uppermost in his mind. He bathed, ate breakfast and sat in his deck chair. In the afternoon, he decided to go for a walk. There was only one way for him to go and that led past the San Bernardino Apartments.

Some time during his long sleep, he had given up the battle. When he came to the apartment house, he peered into the amber-lit hallway and read the Greener card on the letter box, then turned and went home. On the next night, he repeated the trip, carrying a gift of flowers and wine.

13

HARRY GREENER'S condition didn't improve. He remained in bed, staring at the ceiling with his hands
folded on his chest.

Tod went to see him almost every night. There were usually
other guests. Sometimes Abe Kusich, sometimes Anna and
Annabelle Lee, a sister act of the nineteen-tens, more often
the four Gingos, a family of performing Eskimos from Point
Barrow, Alaska.

If Harry were asleep or there were visitors, Faye usually
invited Tod into her room for a talk. His interest in her grew
despite the things she said and he continued to find her very
exciting. Had any other girl been so affected, he would have
thought her intolerable. Faye's affectations, however, were so
completely artificial that he found them charming.

Being with her was like being backstage during an ama-
teurish, ridiculous play. From in front, the stupid lines and
grotesque situations would have made him squirm with annoyance, but because he saw the perspiring stagehands and
the wires that held up the tawdry summerhouse with its tangle
of paper flowers, he accepted everything and was anxious for
it to succeed.

He found still another way to excuse her. He believed that
while she often recognized the falseness of an attitude, she
persisted in it because she didn't know how to be simpler or
more honest. She was an actress who had learned from bad
models in a bad school.

Yet Faye did have some critical ability, almost enough to
recognize the ridiculous. He had often seen her laugh at herself. What was more, he had even seen her laugh at her
dreams.

One evening they talked about what she did with herself
when she wasn't working as an extra. She told him that she
often spent the whole day making up stories. She laughed as
she said it. When he questioned her, she described her method
quite willingly.

She would get some music on the radio, then lie down on

her bed and shut her eyes. She had a large assortment of stories to choose from. After getting herself in the right mood,
she would go over them in her mind, as though they were a
pack of cards, discarding one after another until she found the
one that suited. On some days, she would run through the
whole pack without making a choice. When that happened,
she would either go to Vine Street for an ice cream soda or,
if she was broke, thumb over the pack again and force herself
to choose.

While she admitted that her method was too mechanical for
the best results and that it was better to slip into a dream
naturally, she said that any dream was better than no dream
and beggars couldn't be choosers. She hadn't exactly said this,
but he was able to understand it from what she did say. He
thought it important that she smiled while telling him, not
with embarrassment, but critically. However, her critical powers ended there. She only smiled at the mechanics.

The first time he had ever heard one of her dreams was late
at night in her bedroom. About half an hour earlier, she had
knocked on his door and had asked him to come and help her
with Harry because she thought he was dying. His noisy
breathing, which she had taken for the death rattle, had awak-
ened her and she was badly frightened. Tod put on his bathrobe and followed her downstairs. When he got to the
apartment, Harry had managed to clear his throat and his
breathing had become quiet again.

She invited him into her room for a smoke. She sat on the
bed and he sat beside her. She was wearing an old beach robe
of white toweling over her pajamas and it was very becoming.

He wanted to beg her for a kiss but was afraid, not because
she would refuse, but because she would insist on making it
meaningless. To flatter her, he commented on her appearance.
He did a bad job of it. He was incapable of direct flattery and
got bogged down in a much too roundabout observation. She
didn't listen and he broke off feeling like an idiot.

"I've got a swell idea," she said suddenly. "An idea how
we can make some real money."

He made another attempt to flatter her. This time by assuming an attitude of serious interest.

"You're educated," she said. "Well, I've got some swell

ideas for pictures. All you got to do is write them up and then we'll sell them to the studios."

He agreed and she described her plan. It was very vague until she came to what she considered would be its results, then she went into concrete details. As soon as they had sold one story, she would give him another. They would make loads and loads of money. Of course she wouldn't give up acting, even if she was a big success as a writer, because acting was her life.

He realized as she went on that she was manufacturing another dream to add to her already very thick pack. When she finally got through spending the money, he asked her to tell him the idea he was to "write up," keeping all trace of irony out of his voice.

On the wall of the room beyond the foot of her bed was a large photograph that must have once been used in the lobby of a theatre to advertise a Tarzan picture. It showed a beautiful young man with magnificent muscles, wearing only a narrow loin cloth, who was ardently squeezing a slim girl in a torn riding habit. They stood in a jungle clearing and all around the pair writhed great vines loaded with fat orchids. When she told her story, he knew that this photograph had a lot to do with inspiring it.

A young girl is cruising on her father's yacht in the South Seas. She is engaged to marry a Russian count, who is tall, thin and old, but with beautiful manners. He is on the yacht, too, and keeps begging her to name the day. But she is spoiled and won't do it. Maybe she became engaged to him in order to spite another man. She becomes interested in a young sailor who is far below her in station, but very handsome. She flirts with him because she is bored. The sailor refuses to be toyed with no matter how much money she's got and tells her that he only takes orders from the captain and to go back to her foreigner. She gets sore as hell and threatens to have him fired, but he only laughs at her. How can he be fired in the middle of the ocean? She falls in love with him, although maybe she doesn't realize it herself, because he is the first man who has ever said no to one of her whims and because he is so handsome. Then there is a big storm and the yacht is wrecked near an island. Everybody is drowned, but she manages to swim to shore. She makes herself a hut of boughs and lives on fish and fruit. It's the tropics. One morning, while she is bathing naked in a brook, a big snake grabs her. She struggles but the snake is too strong for her and it looks like curtains. But the sailor, who has been watching her from behind some bushes, leaps to her rescue. He fights the snake for her and wins.

Tod was to go on from there. He asked her how she thought the picture should end, but she seemed to have lost interest. He insisted on hearing, however.

"Well, he marries her, of course, and they're rescued. First they're rescued and then they're married, I mean. Maybe he turns out to be a rich boy who is being a sailor just for the adventure of it, or something like that. You can work it out easy enough."

"It's sure-fire," Tod said earnestly, staring at her wet lips and the tiny point of her tongue which she kept moving between them.

"I've got just hundreds and hundreds more."

He didn't say anything and her manner changed. While telling the story, she had been full of surface animation and her hands and face were alive with little illustrative grimaces and gestures. But now her excitement narrowed and became deeper and its play internal. He guessed that she must be thumbing over her pack and that she would soon select another card to show him.

He had often seen her like this, but had never before understood it. All these little stories, these little day-dreams of hers, were what gave such extraordinary color and mystery to her movements. She seemed always to be struggling in their soft grasp as though she were trying to run in a swamp. As he watched her, he felt sure that her lips must taste of blood and salt and that there must be a delicious weakness in her legs. His impulse wasn't to aid her to get free, but to throw her down in the soft, warm mud and to keep her there.

He expressed some of his desire by a grunt. If he only had the courage to throw himself on her. Nothing less violent than rape would do. The sensation he felt was like that he got when holding an egg in his hand. Not that she was fragile or even seemed fragile. It wasn't that. It was her completeness, her egglike self-sufficiency, that made him want to crush her.

But he did nothing and she began to talk again.

"I've got another swell idea that I want to tell you. Maybe you had better write this one up first. It's a backstage story and they're making a lot of them this year."

She told him about a young chorus girl who gets her big chance when the star of the show falls sick. It was a familiar version of the Cinderella theme, but her technique was much different from the one she had used for the South Sea tale. Although the events she described were miraculous, her description of them was realistic. The effect was similar to that obtained by the artists of the Middle Ages, who, when doing a subject like the raising of Lazarus from the dead or Christ walking on water, were careful to keep all the details intensely realistic. She, like them, seemed to think that fantasy could be made plausible by a humdrum technique.

"I like that one, too," he said when she had finished.

"Think them over and do the one that has the best chance."

She was dismissing him and if he didn't act at once the opportunity would be gone. He started to lean toward her, but she caught his meaning and stood up. She took his arm with affectionate brusqueness—they were now business partners—and guided him to the door.

In the hall, when she thanked him for coming down and apologized for having disturbed him, he tried again. She seemed to melt a little and he reached for her. She kissed him willingly enough, but when he tried to extend the caress, she tore free.

"Whoa there, palsy-walsy," she laughed. "Mama spank."

He started for the stairs.

"Good-bye now," she called after him, then laughed again.

He barely heard her. He was thinking of the drawings he had made of her and of the new one he would do as soon as he got to his room.

In "The Burning of Los Angeles" Faye is the naked girl in the left foreground being chased by the group of men and women who have separated from the main body of the mob. One of the women is about to hurl a rock at her to bring her down. She is running with her eyes closed and a strange half-smile on her lips. Despite the dreamy repose of her face, her body is straining to hurl her along at top speed. The only explanation for this contrast is that she is enjoying the release that wild flight gives in much the same way that a game bird must when, after hiding for several tense minutes, it bursts from cover in complete, unthinking panic.

14

Tod had other and more successful rivals than Homer Simpson. One of the most important was a young man called Earle Shoop.

Earle was a cowboy from a small town in Arizona. He worked occasionally in horse-operas and spent the rest of his time in front of a saddlery store on Sunset Boulevard. In the window of this store was an enormous Mexican saddle covered with carved silver, and around it was arranged a large collection of torture instruments. Among other things there were fancy, braided quirts, spurs with great spiked wheels, and double bits that looked as though they could break a horse's jaw without trouble. Across the back of the window ran a low shelf on which was a row of boots, some black, some red and some a pale yellow. All of the boots had scalloped tops and very high heels.

Earle always stood with his back to the window, his eyes fixed on a sign on the roof of a one-story building across the street that read: "Malted Milks Too Thick For A Straw." Regularly, twice every hour, he pulled a sack of tobacco and a sheaf of papers from his shirt pocket and rolled a cigarette. Then he tightened the cloth of his trousers by lifting his knee and struck a match along the underside of his thigh.

He was over six feet tall. The big Stetson hat he wore added five inches more to his height and the heels of his boots still another three. His polelike appearance was further exaggerated by the narrowness of his shoulders and by his lack of either hips or buttocks. The years he had spent in the saddle had not made him bowlegged. In fact, his legs were so straight that his dungarees, bleached a very light blue by the sun and much washing, hung down without a wrinkle, as though they were empty.

Tod could see why Faye thought him handsome. He had a two-dimensional face that a talented child might have drawn with a ruler and a compass. His chin was perfectly round and his eyes, which were wide apart, were also round. His thin mouth ran at right angles to his straight, perpendicular nose.

His reddish tan complexion was the same color from hairline
to throat, as though washed in by an expert, and it completed
his resemblance to a mechanical drawing.

Tod had told Faye that Earle was a dull fool. She agreed
laughing, but then said that he was "criminally handsome,"
an expression she had picked up in the chatter column of a
trade paper.

Meeting her on the stairs one night, Tod asked if she would
go to dinner with him.

"I can't. I've got a date. But you can come along."

"With Earle?"

"Yes, with Earle," she repeated, mimicking his annoyance.

"No, thanks."

She misunderstood, perhaps on purpose, and said, "He'll
treat this time."

Earle was always broke and whenever Tod went with them
he was the one who paid.

"That isn't it, and you damn well know it."

"Oh, isn't it?" she asked archly, then, absolutely sure of
herself, added, "Meet us at Hodge's around five."

Hodge's was the saddlery store. When Tod got there, he
found Earle Shoop at his usual post, just standing and just
looking at the sign across the street. He had on his ten-gallon
hat and his high-heeled boots. Neatly folded over his left arm
was a dark gray jacket. His shirt was navy-blue cotton with
large polka dots, each the size of a dime. The sleeves of his
shirt were not rolled, but pulled to the middle of his forearm
and held there by a pair of fancy, rose armbands. His hands
were the same clean reddish tan as his face.

"Lo, thar," was the way he returned Tod's salute.

Tod found his Western accent amusing. The first time he
had heard it, he had replied, "Lo, thar, stranger," and had
been surprised to discover that Earle didn't know he was being kidded. Even when Tod talked about "cayuses," "mean
hombres" and "rustlers," Earle took him seriously.

"Howdy, partner," Tod said.

Next to Earle was another Westerner in a big hat and boots,
sitting on his heels and chewing vigorously on a little twig.
Close behind him was a battered paper valise held together
by heavy rope tied with professional-looking knots.

Soon after Tod arrived a third man came along. He made a thorough examination of the merchandise in the window, then turned and began to stare across the street like the other two.

He was middle-aged and looked like an exercise boy from a racing stable. His face was completely covered with a fine mesh of wrinkles, as though he had been sleeping with it pressed against a roll of rabbit wire. He was very shabby and had probably sold his big hat, but he still had his boots.

"Lo, boys," he said.

"Lo, Hink," said the man with the paper valise.

Tod didn't know whether he was included in the greeting, but took a chance and replied.

"Howdy."

Hink prodded the valise with his toe.

"Goin' some place, Calvin?" he asked.

"Azusa, there's a rodeo."

"Who's running it?"

"A fellow calls himself 'Badlands Jack.' "

"That grifter! . . . You goin', Earle?"

"Nope."

"I gotta eat," said Calvin.

Hink carefully considered all the information he had received before speaking again.

"Mono's makin' a new Buck Stevens," he said. "Will Ferris told me they'd use more than forty riders."

Calvin turned and looked up at Earle.

"Still got the piebald vest?" he asked slyly.

"Why?"

"It'll cinch you a job as a road agent."

Tod understood that this was a joke of some sort because Calvin and Hink chuckled and slapped their thighs loudly while Earle frowned.

There was another long silence, then Calvin spoke again.

"Ain't your old man still got some cows?" he asked Earle.

But Earle was wary this time and refused to answer.

Calvin winked at Tod, slowly and elaborately, contorting one whole side of his face.

"That's right, Earle," Hink said. "Your old man's still got some stock. Why don't you go home?"

They couldn't get a rise out of Earle, so Calvin answered the question.

"He dassint. He got caught in a sheep car with a pair of rubber boots on."

It was another joke. Calvin and Hink slapped their thighs and laughed, but Tod could see that they were waiting for something else. Earle, suddenly, without even shifting his weight, shot his foot out and kicked Calvin solidly in the rump. This was the real point of the joke. They were delighted by Earle's fury. Tod also laughed. The way Earle had gone from apathy to action without the usual transition was funny. The seriousness of his violence was even funnier.

A little while later, Faye drove by in her battered Ford touring car and pulled into the curb some twenty feet away. Calvin and Hink waved, but Earle didn't budge. He took his time, as befitted his dignity. Not until she tooted her horn did he move. Tod followed a short distance behind him.

"Hi, cowboy," said Faye gaily.

"Lo, honey," he drawled, removing his hat carefully and replacing it with even greater care.

Faye smiled at Tod and motioned for them both to climb in. Tod got in the back. Earle unfolded the jacket he was carrying, slapped it a few times to remove the wrinkles, then put it on and adjusted its collar and shaped the roll of its lapels. He then climbed in beside Faye.

She started the car with a jerk. When she reached LaBrea, she turned right to Hollywood Boulevard and then left along it. Tod could see that she was watching Earle out of the corner of her eye and that he was preparing to speak.

"Get going," she said, trying to hurry him. "What is it?"

"Looka here, honey, I ain't got any dough for supper."

She was very much put out.

"But I told Tod we'd treat him. He's treated us enough times."

"That's all right," Tod interposed. "Next time'll do. I've got plenty of money."

"No, damn it," she said without looking around. "I'm sick of it."

She pulled into the curb and slammed on the brakes.

"It's always the same story," she said to Earle.

He adjusted his hat, his collar and his sleeves, then spoke.
"We've got some grub at camp."

"Beans, I suppose."

"Nope."

She prodded him.

"Well, what've you got?"

"Mig and me's set some traps."

Faye laughed.

"Rat traps, eh? We're going to eat rats."

Earle didn't say anything.

"Listen, you big, strong, silent dope," she said, "either make sense, or God damn it, get out of this car."

"They're quail traps," he said without the slightest change in his wooden, formal manner.

She ignored his explanation.

"Talking to you is like pulling teeth. You wear me out."

Tod knew that there was no hope for him in this quarrel. He had heard it all before.

"I didn't mean nothing," Earle said. "I was only funning. I wouldn't feed you rats."

She slammed off the emergency brake and started the car again. At Zacarias Street, she turned into the hills. After climbing steadily for a quarter of a mile, she reached a dirt road and followed it to its end. They all climbed out, Earle helping Faye.

"Give me a kiss," she said, smiling her forgiveness.

He took his hat off ceremoniously and placed it on the hood of the car, then wrapped his long arms around her. They paid no attention to Tod, who was standing off to one side watching them. He saw Earle close his eyes and pucker up his lips like a little boy. But there was nothing boyish about what he did to her. When she had had as much as she wanted, she pushed him away.

"You, too?" she called gaily to Tod, who had turned his back.

"Oh, some other time," he replied, imitating her casualness.

She laughed, then took out a compact and began to fix her mouth. When she was ready, they started along a little path that was a continuation of the dirt road. Earle led, Faye came next and Tod brought up the rear.

It was full spring. The path ran along the bottom of a narrow canyon and wherever weeds could get a purchase in its steep banks they flowered in purple, blue and yellow. Orange poppies bordered the path. Their petals were wrinkled like crepe and their leaves were heavy with talcumlike dust.

They climbed until they reached another canyon. This one was sterile, but its bare ground and jagged rocks were even more brilliantly colored than the flowers of the first. The path was silver, grained with streaks of rose-gray, and the walls of the canyon were turquoise, mauve, chocolate and lavender. The air itself was vibrant pink.

They stopped to watch a humming bird chase a blue jay. The jay flashed by squawking with its tiny enemy on its tail like a ruby bullet. The gaudy birds burst the colored air into a thousand glittering particles like metal confetti.

When they came out of this canyon, they saw below them a little green valley thick with trees, mostly eucalyptus, with here and there a poplar and one enormous black live-oak. Sliding and stumbling down a dry wash, they made for the valley.

Tod saw a man watching their approach from the edge of the wood. Faye also saw him and waved.

"Hi, Mig!" she shouted.

"Chinita!" he called back.

She ran the last ten yards of the slope and the man caught her in his arms.

He was toffee-colored with large Armenian eyes and pouting black lips. His head was a mass of tight, ordered curls. He wore a long-haired sweater, called a "gorilla" in and around Los Angeles, with nothing under it. His soiled duck trousers were held up by a red bandanna handkerchief. On his feet were a pair of tattered tennis sneakers.

They moved on to the camp which was located in a clearing in the center of the wood. It consisted of little more than a ramshackle hut patched with tin signs that had been stolen from the highway and a stove without legs or bottom set on some rocks. Near the hut was a row of chicken coops.

Earle started a fire under the stove while Faye sat down on a box and watched him. Tod went over to look at the chickens. There was one old hen and half a dozen game cocks. A great deal of pains had been taken in making the coops, which were of grooved boards, carefully matched and joined. Their floors were freshly spread with peat moss.

The Mexican came over and began to talk about the cocks. He was very proud of them.

"That's Hermano, five times winner. He's one of Street's Butcher Boys. Pepe and El Negro are still stags. I fight them next week in San Pedro. That's Villa, he's a blinker, but still good. And that one's Zapata, twice winner, a Tassel Dom he is. And that's Jujutla. My champ."

He opened the coop and lifted the bird out for Tod.

"A murderer is what the guy is. Speedy and how!"

The cock's plumage was green, bronze and copper. Its beak was lemon and its legs orange.

"He's beautiful," Tod said.

"I'll say."

Mig tossed the bird back into the coop and they went back to join the others at the fire.

"When do we eat?" Faye asked.

Miguel tested the stove by spitting on it. He next found a large iron skillet and began to scour it with sand. Earle gave Faye a knife and some potatoes to peel, then picked up a burlap sack.

"I'll get the birds," he said.

Tod went along with him. They followed a narrow path that looked as though it had been used by sheep until they came to a tiny field covered with high, tufted grass. Earle stopped behind a gum bush and held up his hand to warn Tod.

A mocking bird was singing near by. Its song was like pebbles being dropped one by one from a height into a pool of water. Then a quail began to call, using two soft guttural notes. Another quail answered and the birds talked back and forth. Their call was not like the cheerful whistle of the Eastern bobwhite. It was full of melancholy and weariness, yet marvelously sweet. Still another quail joined the duet. This one called from near the center of the field. It was a trapped bird, but the sound it made had no anxiety in it, only sadness, impersonal and without hope.

When Earle was satisfied that no one was there to spy on his poaching, he went to the trap. It was a wire basket about the size of a washtub with a small door in the top. He stooped over and began to fumble with the door. Five birds ran wildly along the inner edge and threw themselves at the wire. One of them, a cock, had a dainty plume on his head that curled forward almost to his beak.

Earle caught the birds one at a time and pulled their heads off before dropping them into his sack. Then he started back. As he walked along, he held the sack under his left arm. He lifted the birds out with his right hand and plucked them one at a time. Their feathers fell to the ground, point first, weighed down by the tiny drop of blood that trembled on the tips of their quills.

The sun went down before they reached the camp again. It grew chilly and Tod was glad of the fire. Faye shared her seat on the box with him and they both leaned forward into the heat.

Mig brought a jug of tequila from the hut. He filled a peanut butter jar for Faye and passed the jug to Tod. The liquor smelled like rotten fruit, but he liked the taste. When he had had enough, Earle took it and then Miguel. They continued to pass it from hand to hand.

Earle tried to show Faye how plump the game was, but she wouldn't look. He gutted the birds, then began cutting them into quarters with a pair of heavy tin shears. Faye held her hands over her ears in order not to hear the soft click made by the blades as they cut through flesh and bone. Earle wiped the pieces with a rag and dropped them into the skillet where a large piece of lard was already sputtering.

For all her squeamishness, Faye ate as heartily as the men did. There was no coffee and they finished with tequila. They smoked and kept the jug moving. Faye tossed away the peanut butter jar and drank like the others, throwing her head back and tilting the jug.

Tod could sense her growing excitement. The box on which they were sitting was so small that their backs touched and he could feel how hot she was and how restless. Her neck and face had turned from ivory to rose. She kept reaching for his cigarettes.

Earle's features were hidden in the shadow of his big hat, but the Mexican sat full in the light of the fire. His skin glowed and the oil in his black curls sparkled. He kept smiling at Faye in a manner that Tod didn't like. The more he drank, the less he liked it.

Faye kept crowding Tod, so he left the box to sit on the ground where he could watch her better. She was smiling back at the Mexican. She seemed to know what he was thinking and to be thinking the same thing. Earle, too, became aware of what was passing between them. Tod heard him curse softly and saw him lean forward into the light and pick up a thick piece of firewood.

Mig laughed guiltily and began to sing.

> "Las palmeras lloran por tu ausencia,
> Las laguna se seco—ay!
> La cerca de alambre que estaba en
> El patio tambien se cayo!"

His voice was a plaintive tenor and it turned the revolutionary song into a sentimental lament, sweet and cloying. Faye joined in when he began another stanza. She didn't know the words, but she was able to carry the melody and to harmonize.

> "Pues mi madre las cuidaba, ay!
> Toditito se acabo—ay!"

Their voices touched in the thin, still air to form a minor chord and it was as though their bodies had touched. The song was transformed again. The melody remained the same, but the rhythm broke and its beat became ragged. It was a rumba now.

Earle shifted uneasily and played with his stick. Tod saw her look at him and saw that she was afraid, but instead of becoming wary, she grew still more reckless. She took a long pull at the jug and stood up. She put one hand on each of her buttocks and began to dance.

Mig seemed to have completely forgotten Earle. He clapped his hands, cupping them to make a hollow, drumlike sound,

and put all he felt into his voice. He had changed to a more
fitting song.

> *"Tony's wife,*
> *The boys in Havana love Tony's wife . . ."*

Faye had her hands clasped behind her head now and she
rolled her hips to the broken beat. She was doing the
"bump."

> *"Tony's wife,*
> *They're fightin' their duels about Tony's wife . . ."*

Perhaps Tod had been mistaken about Earle. He was using
his club on the back of the skillet, using it to bang out the
rhythm.

The Mexican stood up, still singing, and joined her in the
dance. They approached each other with short mincing steps.
She held her skirt up and out with her thumbs and forefingers
and he did the same with his trousers. They met head on,
blue-black against pale-gold, and used their heads to pivot,
then danced back to back with their buttocks touching, their
knees bent and wide apart. While Faye shook her breasts and
her head, holding the rest of her body rigid, he struck the
soft ground heavily with his feet and circled her. They faced
each other again and made believe they were cradling their
behinds in a shawl.

Earle pounded the skillet harder and harder until it rang
like an anvil. Suddenly he, too, jumped up and began to
dance. He did a crude hoe-down. He leaped into the air and
knocked his heels together. He whooped. But he couldn't
become part of their dance. Its rhythm was like a smooth glass
wall between him and the dancers. No matter how loudly he
whooped or threw himself around, he was unable to disturb
the precision with which they retreated and advanced, separated and came together again.

Tod saw the blow before it fell. He saw Earle raise his stick
and bring it down on the Mexican's head. He heard the crack
and saw the Mexican go to his knees still dancing, his body
unwilling or unable to acknowledge the interruption.

Faye had her back to Mig when he fell, but she didn't turn
to look. She ran. She flashed by Tod. He reached for her ankle

to pull her down, but missed. He scrambled to his feet and ran after her.

If he caught her now, she wouldn't escape. He could hear her on the hill a little way ahead of him. He shouted to her, a deep, agonized bellow, like that a hound makes when it strikes a fresh line after hours of cold trailing. Already he could feel how it would be when he pulled her to the ground.

But the going was heavy and the stones and sand moved under his feet. He fell prone with his face in a clump of wild mustard that smelled of the rain and sun, clean, fresh and sharp. He rolled over on his back and stared up at the sky. The violent exercise had driven most of the heat out of his blood, but enough remained to make him tingle pleasantly. He felt comfortably relaxed, even happy.

Somewhere farther up the hill a bird began to sing. He listened. At first the low rich music sounded like water dripping on something hollow, the bottom of a silver pot perhaps, then like a stick dragged slowly over the strings of a harp. He lay quietly, listening.

When the bird grew silent, he made an effort to put Faye out of his mind and began to think about the series of cartoons he was making for his canvas of Los Angeles on fire. He was going to show the city burning at high noon, so that the flames would have to compete with the desert sun and thereby appear less fearful, more like bright flags flying from roofs and windows than a terrible holocaust. He wanted the city to have quite a gala air as it burned, to appear almost gay. And the people who set it on fire would be a holiday crowd.

The bird began to sing again. When it stopped, Faye was forgotten and he only wondered if he weren't exaggerating the importance of the people who come to California to die. Maybe they weren't really desperate enough to set a single city on fire, let alone the whole country. Maybe they were only the pick of America's madmen and not at all typical of the rest of the land.

He told himself that it didn't make any difference because he was an artist, not a prophet. His work would not be judged by the accuracy with which it foretold a future event but by its merit as painting. Nevertheless, he refused to give up the role of Jeremiah. He changed "pick of America's madmen" to "cream" and felt almost certain that the milk from which it had been skimmed was just as rich in violence. The Angelenos would be first, but their comrades all over the country would follow. There would be civil war.

He was amused by the strong feeling of satisfaction this dire conclusion gave him. Were all prophets of doom and destruction such happy men?

He stood up without trying to answer. When he reached the dirt road at the top of the canyon Faye and the car were gone.

15

S HE WENT to the pictures with that Simpson guy," Harry told him when he called to see her the next night.

He sat down to wait for her. The old man was very ill and lay on the bed with extreme care as though it were a narrow shelf from which he might fall if he moved.

"What are they making on your lot?" he asked slowly, rolling his eyes toward Tod without budging his head.

" 'Manifest Destiny,' 'Sweet and Low Down,' 'Waterloo,' 'The Great Divide,' 'Begging Your . . .' "

" 'The Great Divide'—" Harry said, interrupting eagerly. "I remember that vehicle."

Tod realized he shouldn't have got him started, but there was nothing he could do about it now. He had to let him run down like a clock.

"When it opened I was playing the Irving in a little number called 'Enter Two Gents,' a trifle, but entertainment, real entertainment. I played a Jew comic, a Ben Welch effect, derby and big pants— 'Pat, dey hoffered me a chob in de Heagle Laundreh' . . . 'Faith now, Ikey, and did you take it?' . . . 'No, who vants to vash heagles?' Joe Parvos played straight for me in a cop's suit. Well, the night 'The Great Divide' opened, Joe was laying up with a whisker in the old Fifth Avenue when the stove exploded. It was the broad's husband who blew the whistle. He was . . ."

He hadn't run down. He had stopped and was squeezing his left side with both hands.

Tod leaned over anxiously.

"Some water?"

Harry framed the word "no" with his lips, then groaned skillfully. It was a second-act curtain groan, so phony that Tod had to hide a smile. And yet, the old man's pallor hadn't come from a box.

Harry groaned again, modulating from pain to exhaustion, then closed his eyes. Tod saw how skillfully he got the maximum effect out of his agonized profile by using the pillow to set it off. He also noticed that Harry, like many actors, had very little back or top to his head. It was almost all face, like a mask, with deep furrows between the eyes, across the forehead and on either side of the nose and mouth, plowed there by years of broad grinning and heavy frowning. Because of them, he could never express anything either subtly or exactly. They wouldn't permit degrees of feeling, only the furthest degree.

Tod began to wonder if it might not be true that actors suffer less than other people. He thought about this for a while, then decided that he was wrong. Feeling is of the heart and nerves and the crudeness of its expression has nothing to do with its intensity. Harry suffered as keenly as anyone, despite the theatricality of his groans and grimaces.

He seemed to enjoy suffering. But not all kinds, certainly not sickness. Like many people, he only enjoyed the sort that was self-inflicted. His favorite method was to bare his soul to strangers in bar-rooms. He would make believe he was drunk, and stumble over to where some strangers were sitting. He usually began by reciting a poem.

> *"Let me sit down for a moment,*
> *I have a stone in my shoe.*
> *I was once blithe and happy,*
> *I was once young like you."*

If his audience shouted, "scram, bum!" he only smiled humbly and went on with his act.

> *"Have pity, folks, on my gray hair . . ."*

The bartender or someone else had to stop him by force, otherwise he would go on no matter what was said to him. Once he got started everyone in the bar usually listened, for he gave a great performance. He roared and whispered, commanded and cajoled. He imitated the whimper of a little girl crying for her vanished mother, as well as the different dialects of the many cruel managers he had known. He even did the off-stage noises, twittering like birds to herald the dawn of Love and yelping like a pack of bloodhounds when describing how an Evil Fate ever pursued him.

He made his audience see him start out in his youth to play Shakespeare in the auditorium of the Cambridge Latin

School, full of glorious dreams, burning with ambition. Follow him, as still a mere stripling, he starved in a Broadway rooming house, an idealist who desires only to share his art with the world. Stand with him, as, in the prime of manhood, he married a beautiful dancer, a headliner on the Gus Sun time. Be close behind him as, one night, he returned home unexpectedly to find her in the arms of a head usher. Forgive, as he forgave, out of the goodness of his heart and the greatness of his love. Then laugh, tasting the bitter gall, when the very next night he found her in the arms of a booking agent. Again he forgave her and again she sinned. Even then he didn't cast her out, no, though she jeered, mocked and even struck him repeatedly with an umbrella. But she ran off with a foreigner, a swarthy magician fellow. Behind she left memories and their baby daughter. He made his audience shadow him still as misfortune followed misfortune and, a middle-aged man, he haunted the booking offices, only a ghost of his former self. He who had hoped to play Hamlet, Lear, Othello, must needs become the Co. in an act called Nat Plumstone & Co., light quips and breezy patter. He made them dog his dragging feet as, an aged and trembling old man, he . . .

Faye came in quietly. Tod started to greet her, but she put her finger to her lips for him to be silent and motioned toward the bed.

The old man was asleep. Tod thought his worn, dry skin looked like eroded ground. The few beads of sweat that glistened on his forehead and temples carried no promise of relief. It might rot, like rain that comes too late to a field, but could never refresh.

They both tiptoed out of the room.

In the hall he asked if she had had a good time with Homer.

"That dope!" she exclaimed, making a wry face. "He's strictly home-cooking."

Tod started to ask some more questions, but she dismissed him with a curt, "I'm tired, honey."

16

THE NEXT AFTERNOON, Tod was on his way upstairs when he saw a crowd in front of the door to the Greeners' apartment. They were excited and talked in whispers.

"What's happened?" he asked.

"Harry's dead."

He tried the door of the apartment. It wasn't locked, so he went in. The corpse lay stretched out on the bed, completely covered with a blanket. From Faye's room came the sound of crying. He knocked softly on her door. She opened it for him, then turned without saying a word, and stumbled to her bed. She was sobbing into a face towel.

He stood in the doorway, without knowing what to do or say. Finally, he went over to the bed and tried to comfort her. He patted her shoulder.

"You poor kid."

She was wearing a tattered, black lace negligee that had large rents in it. When he leaned over her, he noticed that her skin gave off a warm, sweet odor, like that of buckwheat in flower.

He turned away and lit a cigarette. There was a knock on the door. When he opened it, Mary Dove rushed past him to take Faye in her arms.

Mary also told Faye to be brave. She phrased it differently than he had done, however, and made it sound a lot more convincing.

"Show some guts, kid. Come on now, show some guts."

Faye shoved her away and stood up. She took a few wild steps, then sat down on the bed again.

"I killed him," she groaned.

Mary and he both denied this emphatically.

"I killed him, I tell you! I did! I did!"

She began to call herself names. Mary wanted to stop her, but Tod told her not to. Faye had begun to act and he felt that if they didn't interfere she would manage an escape for herself.

"She'll talk herself quiet," he said.

In a voice heavy with self-accusation, she began to tell what had happened. She had come home from the studio and found Harry in bed. She asked him how he was, but didn't wait for an answer. Instead, she turned her back on him to examine herself in the wall mirror. While fixing her face, she told him that she had seen Ben Murphy and that Ben had said that if Harry were feeling better he might be able to use him in a Bowery sequence. She had been surprised when he didn't shout as he always did when Ben's name was mentioned. He was jealous of Ben and always shouted, "To hell with that bastard; I knew him when he cleaned spittoons in a nigger bar-room."

She realized that he must be pretty sick. She didn't turn around because she noticed what looked like the beginning of a pimple. It was only a speck of dirt and she wiped it off, but then she had to do her face all over again. While she was working at it, she told him that she could get a job as a dress extra if she had a new evening gown. Just to kid him, she looked tough and said, "If you can't buy me an evening gown, I'll find someone who can."

When he didn't say anything, she got sore and began to sing, "Jeepers Creepers." He didn't tell her to shut up, so she knew something must be wrong. She ran over to the couch. He was dead.

As soon as she had finished telling all this, she began to sob in a lower key, almost a coo, and rocked herself back and forth.

"Poor papa . . . Poor darling . . ."

The fun they used to have together when she was little. No matter how hard up he was, he always bought her dolls and candy, and no matter how tired, he always played with her. She used to ride piggy-back and they would roll on the floor and laugh and laugh.

Mary's sobs made Faye speed up her own and they both began to get out of hand.

There was a knock on the door. Tod answered it and found Mrs. Johnson, the janitress. Faye shook her head for him not to let her in.

"Come back later," Tod said.

He shut the door in her face. A minute later it opened

again and Mrs. Johnson entered boldly. She had used a pass-key.

"Get out," he said.

She tried to push past him, but he held her until Faye told him to let her go.

He disliked Mrs. Johnson intensely. She was an officious, bustling woman with a face like a baked apple, soft and blotched. Later he found out that her hobby was funerals. Her preoccupation with them wasn't morbid; it was formal. She was interested in the arrangement of the flowers, the order of the procession, the clothing and deportment of the mourners.

She went straight to Faye and stopped her sobs with a firm, "Now, Miss Greener."

There was so much authority in her voice and manner that she succeeded where Mary and Tod had failed.

Faye looked up at her respectfully.

"First, my dear," Mrs. Johnson said, counting one with the thumb of her right hand on the index finger of her left, "first, I want you to understand that my sole desire in this matter is to help you."

She looked hard at Mary, then at Tod.

"I don't get anything out of it, and it's just a lot of trouble."

"Yes," Faye said.

"All right. There are several things I have to know, if I'm to help you. Did the deceased leave any money or insurance?"

"No."

"Have you any money?"

"No."

"Can you borrow any?"

"I don't think so."

Mrs. Johnson sighed.

"Then the city will have to bury him."

Faye didn't comment.

"Don't you understand, child, the city will have to bury him in a pauper's grave?"

She put so much contempt into "city" and horror into "pauper" that Faye flushed and began to sob again.

Mrs. Johnson made as though to walk out, even took several steps in the direction of the door, then changed her mind and came back.

"How much does a funeral cost?" Faye asked.

"Two hundred dollars. But you can pay on the installment plan—fifty dollars down and twenty-five a month."

Mary and Tod both spoke together.

"I'll get the money."

"I've got some."

"That's fine," Mrs. Johnson said. "You'll need at least fifty more for incidental expenses. I'll go ahead and take care of everything. Mr. Holsepp will bury your father. He'll do it right."

She shook hands with Faye, as though she were congratulating her, and hurried out of the room.

Mrs. Johnson's little business talk had apparently done Faye some good. Her lips were set and her eyes dry.

"Don't worry," Tod said. "I can raise the money."

"No, thanks," she said.

Mary opened her purse and took out a roll of bills.

"Here's some."

"No," she said, pushing it away.

She sat thinking for a while, then went to the dressing table and began to fix her tear-stained face. She wore a hard smile as she worked. Suddenly she turned, lipstick in air, and spoke to Mary.

"Can you get me into Mrs. Jenning's?"

"What for?" Tod demanded. "I'll get the money."

Both girls ignored him.

"Sure," said Mary, "you ought to done that long ago. It's a soft touch."

Faye laughed.

"I was saving it."

The change that had come over both of them startled Tod. They had suddenly become very tough.

"For a punkola like that Earle. Get smart, girlie, and lay off the cheapies. Let him ride a horse, he's a cowboy, ain't he?"

They laughed shrilly and went into the bathroom with their arms around each other.

Tod thought he understood their sudden change to slang.

It made them feel worldly and realistic, and so more able to cope with serious things.

He knocked on the bathroom door.

"What do *you* want?" Faye called out.

"Listen, kid," he said, trying to imitate them. "Why go on the turf? I can get the dough."

"Oh, yeah! No, thanks," Faye said.

"But listen . . ." he began again.

"Go peddle your tripe!" Mary shouted.

17

O N THE DAY of Harry's funeral Tod was drunk. He hadn't seen Faye since she went off with Mary Dove, but he knew that he was certain to find her at the undertaking parlor and he wanted to have the courage to quarrel with her. He started drinking at lunch. When he got to Holsepp's in the late afternoon, he had passed the brave state and was well into the ugly one.

He found Harry in his box, waiting to be wheeled out for exhibition in the adjoining chapel. The casket was open and the old man looked quite snug. Drawn up to a little below his shoulders and folded back to show its fancy lining was an ivory satin coverlet. Under his head was a tiny lace cushion. He was wearing a Tuxedo, or at least had on a black bow tie with his stiff shirt and wing collar. His face had been newly shaved, his eyebrows shaped and plucked and his lips and cheeks rouged. He looked like the interlocutor in a minstrel show.

Tod bowed his head as though in silent prayer when he heard someone come in. He recognized Mrs. Johnson's voice and turned carefully to face her. He caught her eye and nodded, but she ignored him. She was busy with a man in a badly fitting frock coat.

"It's the principle of the thing," she scolded. "Your estimate said bronze. Those handles ain't bronze and you know it."

"But I asked Miss Greener," whined the man. "She okayed them."

"I don't care. I'm surprised at you, trying to save a few dollars by fobbing off a set of cheap gun-metal handles on the poor child."

Tod didn't wait for the undertaker to answer. He had seen Faye pass the door on the arm of one of the Lee sisters. When he caught up with her, he didn't know what to say. She misunderstood his agitation and was touched. She sobbed a little for him.

She had never looked more beautiful. She was wearing a

new, very tight black dress and her platinum hair was tucked up in a shining bun under a black straw sailor. Every so often, she carried a tiny lace handkerchief to her eyes and made it flutter there for a moment. But all he could think of was that she had earned the money for the outfit on her back.

She grew uneasy under his stare and started to edge away. He caught her arm.

"May I speak with you for a minute, alone?"

Miss Lee took the hint and left.

"What is it?" Faye asked.

"Not here," he whispered, making mystery out of his uncertainty.

He led her along the hall until he found an empty showroom. On the walls were framed photographs of important funerals and on little stands and tables were samples of coffin materials and models of tombstones and mausoleums.

Not knowing what to say, he accented his awkwardness, playing the inoffensive fool.

She smiled and became almost friendly.

"Give out, you big dope."

"A kiss . . ."

"Sure, baby," she laughed, "only don't muss me." They pecked at each other.

She tried to get away, but he held her. She became annoyed and demanded an explanation. He searched his head for one. It wasn't his head he should have searched, however.

She was leaning toward him, drooping slightly, but not from fatigue. He had seen young birches droop like that at midday when they are over-heavy with sun.

"You're drunk," she said, pushing him away.

"Please," he begged.

"Le'go, you bastard."

Raging at him, she was still beautiful. That was because her beauty was structural like a tree's, not a quality of her mind or heart. Perhaps even whoring couldn't damage it for that reason, only age or accident or disease.

In a minute she would scream for help. He had to say something. She wouldn't understand the aesthetic argument and with what values could he back up the moral one? The economic didn't make sense either. Whoring certainly paid. Half of the customer's thirty dollars. Say ten men a week.

She kicked at his shins, but he held on to her. Suddenly he began to talk. He had found an argument. Disease would destroy her beauty. He shouted at her like a Y.M.C.A. lecturer on sex hygiene.

She stopped struggling and held her head down, sobbing fitfully. When he was through, he let go of her arms and she bolted from the room. He groped his way to a carved, marble coffin.

He was still sitting there when a young man in a black jacket and gray striped trousers came in.

"Are you here for the Greener funeral?"

Tod stood up and nodded vaguely.

"The services are beginning," the man said, then opened a little casket covered with grosgrain satin and took out a dust cloth. Tod watched him go around the showroom wiping off the samples.

"Services have probably started," the man repeated with a wave at the door.

Tod understood this time and left. The only exit he could find led through the chapel. The moment he entered it, Mrs. Johnson caught him and directed him to a seat. He wanted badly to get away, but it was impossible to do so without making a scene.

Faye was sitting in the front row of benches, facing the pulpit. She had the Lee sisters on one side and Mary Dove and Abe Kusich on the other. Behind them sat the tenants of the San Berdoo, occupying about six rows. Tod was alone in the seventh. After him were several empty rows and then a scattering of men and women who looked very much out of place.

He turned in order not to see Faye's jerking shoulders and examined the people in the last rows. He knew their kind. While not torch-bearers themselves, they would run behind the fire and do a great deal of the shouting. They had come to see Harry buried, hoping for a dramatic incident of some sort, hoping at least for one of the mourners to be led weeping hysterically from the chapel. It seemed to Tod that they stared back at him with an expression of vicious, acrid boredom that trembled on the edge of violence. When they began to mutter among themselves, he half-turned and watched them out of the corner of his eyes.

An old woman with a face pulled out of shape by badly-fitting store teeth came in and whispered to a man sucking on the handle of a home-made walking stick. He passed her message along and they all stood up and went out hurriedly. Tod guessed that some star had been seen going into a restaurant by one of their scouts. If so, they would wait outside the place for hours until the star came out again or the police drove them away.

The Gingo family arrived soon after they had left. The Gingos were Eskimos who had been brought to Hollywood to make retakes for a picture about polar exploration. Although it had been released long ago, they refused to return to Alaska. They liked Hollywood.

Harry had been a good friend of theirs and had eaten with them quite regularly, sharing the smoked salmon, white fish, marinated and maatjes herrings they bought at Jewish delicatessen stores. He also shared the great quantities of cheap brandy they mixed with hot water and salt butter and drank out of tin cups.

Mama and Papa Gingo, trailed by their son, moved down the center aisle of the chapel, bowing and waving to everyone, until they reached the front row. Here they gathered around Faye and shook hands with her, each one in turn. Mrs. Johnson tried to make them go to one of the back rows, but they ignored her orders and sat down in front.

The overhead lights of the chapel were suddenly dimmed. Simultaneously other lights went on behind imitation stained-glass windows which hung on the fake oak-paneled walls. There was a moment of hushed silence, broken only by Faye's sobs, then an electric organ started to play a recording of one of Bach's chorales, "Come Redeemer, Our Saviour."

Tod recognized the music. His mother often played a piano adaptation of it on Sundays at home. It very politely asked Christ to come, in clear and honest tones with just the proper amount of supplication. The God it invited was not the King of Kings, but a shy and gentle Christ, a maiden surrounded by maidens, and the invitation was to a lawn fete, not to the home of some weary, suffering sinner. It didn't plead; it urged with infinite grace and delicacy, almost as though it were afraid of frightening the prospective guest.

So far as Tod could tell, no one was listening to the music. Faye was sobbing and the others seemed busy inside themselves. Bach politely serenading Christ was not for them.

The music would soon change its tone and grow exciting. He wondered if that would make any difference. Already the bass was beginning to throb. He noticed that it made the Eskimos uneasy. As the bass gained in power and began to dominate the treble, he heard Papa Gingo grunt with pleasure. Mama caught Mrs. Johnson eyeing him, and put her fat hand heavily on the back of his head to keep him quiet.

"Now come, O our Saviour," the music begged. Gone was its diffidence and no longer was it polite. Its struggle with the bass had changed it. Even a hint of a threat crept in and a little impatience. Of doubt, however, he could not detect the slightest trace.

If there was a hint of a threat, he thought, just a hint, and a tiny bit of impatience, could Bach be blamed? After all, when he wrote this music, the world had already been waiting for its lover more than seventeen hundred years. But the music changed again and both threat and impatience disappeared. The treble soared free and triumphant and the bass no longer struggled to keep it down. It had become a rich accompaniment. "Come or don't come," the music seemed to say, "I love you and my love is enough." It was a simple statement of fact, neither cry nor serenade, made without arrogance or humility.

Perhaps Christ heard. If He did, He gave no sign. The attendants heard, for it was their cue to trundle on Harry in his box. Mrs. Johnson followed close behind and saw to it that the casket was properly placed. She raised her hand and Bach was silenced in the middle of a phrase.

"Will those of you who wish to view the deceased before the sermon please step forward?" she called out.

Only the Gingos stood up immediately. They made for the coffin in a group. Mrs. Johnson held them back and motioned for Faye to look first. Supported by Mary Dove and the Lee girls, she took a quick peek, increased the tempo of her sobs for a moment, then hurried back to the bench.

The Gingos had their chance next. They leaned over the coffin and told each other something in a series of thick, explosive gutturals. When they tried to take another look, Mrs. Johnson herded them firmly to their seats.

The dwarf sidled up to the box, made a play with his handkerchief and retreated. When no one followed him, Mrs. Johnson lost patience, seeming to take what she understood as a lack of interest for a personal insult.

"Those who wish to view the remains of the late Mr. Greener must do so at once," she barked.

There was a little stir, but no one stood up.

"You, Mrs. Gail," she finally said, looking directly at the person named. "How about you? Don't you want a last look? Soon all that remains of your neighbor will be buried forever."

There was no getting out of it. Mrs. Gail moved down the aisle, trailed by several others.

Tod used them to cover his escape.

18

FAYE moved out of the San Berdoo the day after the funeral. Tod didn't know where she had gone and was getting up the courage to call Mrs. Jenning when he saw her from the window of his office. She was dressed in the costume of a Napoleonic vivandiere. By the time he got the window open, she had almost turned the corner of the building. He shouted for her to wait. She waved, but when he got downstairs she was gone.

From her dress, he was sure that she was working in the picture called "Waterloo." He asked a studio policeman where the company was shooting and was told on the back lot. He started toward it at once. A platoon of cuirassiers, big men mounted on gigantic horses, went by. He knew that they must be headed for the same set and followed them. They broke into a gallop and he was soon outdistanced.

The sun was very hot. His eyes and throat were choked with the dust thrown up by the horses' hooves and his head throbbed. The only bit of shade he could find was under an ocean liner made of painted canvas with real life boats hanging from its davits. He stood in its narrow shadow for a while, then went on toward a great forty-foot papier mache sphinx that loomed up in the distance. He had to cross a desert to reach it, a desert that was continually being made larger by a fleet of trucks dumping white sand. He had gone only a few feet when a man with a megaphone ordered him off.

He skirted the desert, making a wide turn to the right, and came to a Western street with a plank sidewalk. On the porch of the "Last Chance Saloon" was a rocking chair. He sat down on it and lit a cigarette.

From there he could see a jungle compound with a water buffalo tethered to the side of a conical grass hut. Every few seconds the animal groaned musically. Suddenly an Arab charged by on a white stallion. He shouted at the man, but got no answer. A little while later he saw a truck with a load of snow and several malamute dogs. He shouted again. The driver shouted something back, but didn't stop.

Throwing away his cigarette, he went through the swinging doors of the saloon. There was no back to the building and he found himself in a Paris street. He followed it to its end, coming out in a Romanesque courtyard. He heard voices a short distance away and went toward them. On a lawn of fiber, a group of men and women in riding costume were picnicking. They were eating cardboard food in front of a cellophane waterfall. He started toward them to ask his way, but was stopped by a man who scowled and held up a sign—"Quiet, Please, We're Shooting." When Tod took another step forward, the man shook his fist threateningly.

Next he came to a small pond with large celluloid swans floating on it. Across one end was a bridge with a sign that read, "To Kamp Komfit." He crossed the bridge and followed a little path that ended at a Greek temple dedicated to Eros. The god himself lay face downward in a pile of old newspapers and bottles.

From the steps of the temple, he could see in the distance a road lined with Lombardy poplars. It was the one on which he had lost the cuirassiers. He pushed his way through a tangle of briars, old flats and iron junk, skirting the skeleton of a Zeppelin, a bamboo stockade, an adobe fort, the wooden horse of Troy, a flight of baroque palace stairs that started in a bed of weeds and ended against the branches of an oak, part of the Fourteenth Street elevated station, a Dutch windmill, the bones of a dinosaur, the upper half of the Merrimac, a corner of a Mayan temple, until he finally reached the road.

He was out of breath. He sat down under one of the poplars on a rock made of brown plaster and took off his jacket. There was a cool breeze blowing and he soon felt more comfortable.

He had lately begun to think not only of Goya and Daumier but also of certain Italian artists of the seventeenth and eighteenth centuries, of Salvator Rosa, Francesco Guardi and Monsu Desiderio, the painters of Decay and Mystery. Looking down hill now, he could see compositions that might have actually been arranged from the Calabrian work of Rosa. There were partially demolished buildings and broken monuments half hidden by great, tortured trees, whose exposed roots writhed dramatically in the arid ground, and by shrubs that carried, not flowers or berries, but armories of spikes, hooks and swords.

For Guardi and Desiderio there were bridges which bridged nothing, sculpture in trees, palaces that seemed of marble until a whole stone portico began to flap in the light breeze. And there were figures as well. A hundred yards from where Tod was sitting a man in a derby hat leaned drowsily against the gilded poop of a Venetian barque and peeled an apple. Still farther on, a charwoman on a stepladder was scrubbing with soap and water the face of a Buddha thirty feet high.

He left the road and climbed across the spine of the hill to look down on the other side. From there he could see a ten-acre field of cockleburs spotted with clumps of sunflowers and wild gum. In the center of the field was a gigantic pile of sets, flats and props. While he watched, a ten-ton truck added another load to it. This was the final dumping ground. He thought of Janvier's "Sargasso Sea." Just as that imaginary body of water was a history of civilization in the form of a marine junkyard, the studio lot was one in the form of a dream dump. A Sargasso of the imagination! And the dump grew continually, for there wasn't a dream afloat somewhere which wouldn't sooner or later turn up on it, having first been made photographic by plaster, canvas, lath and paint. Many boats sink and never reach the Sargasso, but no dream ever entirely disappears. Somewhere it troubles some unfortunate person and some day, when that person has been sufficiently troubled, it will be reproduced on the lot.

When he saw a red glare in the sky and heard the rumble of cannon, he knew it must be Waterloo. From around a bend in the road trotted several cavalry regiments. They wore casques and chest armor of black cardboard and carried long horse pistols in their saddle holsters. They were Victor Hugo's soldiers. He had worked on some of the drawings for their uniforms himself, following carefully the descriptions in "Les Miserables."

He went in the direction they took. Before long he was passed by the men of Lefebvre-Desnouettes, followed by a regiment of gendarmes d'elite, several companies of chasseurs of the guard and a flying detachment of Rimbaud's lancers.

They must be moving up for the disastrous attack on La

Haite Santee. He hadn't read the scenario and wondered if it had rained yesterday. Would Grouchy or Blucher arrive? Grotenstein, the producer, might have changed it.

The sound of cannon was becoming louder all the time and the red fan in the sky more intense. He could smell the sweet, pungent odor of blank powder. It might be over before he could get there. He started to run. When he topped a rise after a sharp bend in the road, he found a great plain below him covered with early nineteenth-century troops, wearing all the gay and elaborate uniforms that used to please him so much when he was a child and spent long hours looking at the soldiers in an old dictionary. At the far end of the field, he could see an enormous hump around which the English and their allies were gathered. It was Mont St. Jean and they were getting ready to defend it gallantly. It wasn't quite finished, however, and swarmed with grips, property men, set dressers, carpenters and painters.

Tod stood near a eucalyptus tree to watch, concealing himself behind a sign that read, " 'Waterloo'—A Charles H. Grotenstein Production." Near by a youth in a carefully torn horse guard's uniform was being rehearsed in his lines by one of the assistant directors.

"Vive l'Empereur!" the young man shouted, then clutched his breast and fell forward dead. The assistant director was a hard man to please and made him do it over and over again.

In the center of the plain, the battle was going ahead briskly. Things looked tough for the British and their allies. The Prince of Orange commanding the center, Hill the right and Picton the left wing, were being pressed hard by the veteran French. The desperate and intrepid Prince was in an especially bad spot. Tod heard him cry hoarsely above the din of battle, shouting to the Hollande-Belgians, "Nassau! Brunswick! Never retreat!" Nevertheless, the retreat began. Hill, too, fell back. The French killed General Picton with a ball through the head and he returned to his dressing room. Alten was put to the sword and also retired. The colors of the Lunenberg battalion, borne by a prince of the family of Deux-Ponts, were captured by a famous child star in the uniform of a Parisian drummer boy. The Scotch Greys were destroyed and went to change into another uniform. Ponsonby's heavy dragoons were also cut to ribbons. Mr. Grotenstein would have a large bill to pay at the Western Costume Company.

Neither Napoleon nor Wellington was to be seen. In Wellington's absence, one of the assistant directors, a Mr. Crane, was in command of the allies. He reinforced his center with one of Chasse's brigades and one of Wincke's. He supported these with infantry from Brunswick, Welsh foot, Devon yeomanry and Hanoverian light horse with oblong leather caps and flowing plumes of horsehair.

For the French, a man in a checked cap ordered Milhaud's cuirassiers to carry Mont St. Jean. With their sabers in their teeth and their pistols in their hands, they charged. It was a fearful sight.

The man in the checked cap was making a fatal error. Mont St. Jean was unfinished. The paint was not yet dry and all the struts were not in place. Because of the thickness of the cannon smoke, he had failed to see that the hill was still being worked on by property men, grips and carpenters.

It was the classic mistake, Tod realized, the same one Napoleon had made. Then it had been wrong for a different reason. The Emperor had ordered the cuirassiers to charge Mont St. Jean not knowing that a deep ditch was hidden at its foot to trap his heavy cavalry. The result had been disaster for the French; the beginning of the end.

This time the same mistake had a different outcome. Waterloo, instead of being the end of the Grand Army, resulted in a draw. Neither side won, and it would have to be fought over again the next day. Big losses, however, were sustained by the insurance company in workmen's compensation. The man in the checked cap was sent to the dog house by Mr. Grotenstein just as Napoleon was sent to St. Helena.

When the front rank of Milhaud's heavy division started up the slope of Mont St. Jean, the hill collapsed. The noise was terrific. Nails screamed with agony as they pulled out of joists. The sound of ripping canvas was like that of little children whimpering. Lath and scantling snapped as though they were brittle bones. The whole hill folded like an enormous umbrella and covered Napoleon's army with painted cloth.

It turned into a rout. The victors of Bersina, Leipsic, Austerlitz, fled like schoolboys who had broken a pane of glass. "Sauve qui peut!" they cried, or, rather, "Scram!"

The armies of England and her allies were too deep in scenery to flee. They had to wait for the carpenters and ambulances to come up. The men of the gallant Seventy-Fifth Highlanders were lifted out of the wreck with block and tackle. They were carted off by the stretcher-bearers, still clinging bravely to their claymores.

19

Tod got a lift back to his office in a studio car. He had to ride on the running board because the seats were occupied by two Walloon grenadiers and four Swabian foot. One of the infantrymen had a broken leg, the other extras were only scratched and bruised. They were quite happy about their wounds. They were certain to receive several extra days' pay, and the man with the broken leg thought he might get as much as five hundred dollars.

When Tod arrived at his office, he found Faye waiting to see him. She hadn't been in the battle. At the last moment, the director had decided not to use any vivandieres.

To his surprise, she greeted him with warm friendliness. Nevertheless, he tried to apologize for his behavior in the funeral parlor. He had hardly started before she interrupted him. She wasn't angry, but grateful for his lecture on venereal disease. It had brought her to her senses.

She had still another surprise for him. She was living in Homer Simpson's house. The arrangement was a business one. Homer had agreed to board and dress her until she became a star. They were keeping a record of every cent he spent and as soon as she clicked in pictures, she would pay him back with six per cent interest. To make it absolutely legal, they were going to have a lawyer draw up a contract.

She pressed Tod for an opinion and he said it was a splendid idea. She thanked him and invited him to dinner for the next night.

After she had gone, he wondered what living with her would do to Homer. He thought it might straighten him out. He fooled himself into believing this with an image, as though a man were a piece of iron to be heated and then straightened with hammer blows. He should have known better, for if anyone ever lacked malleability Homer did.

He continued to make this mistake when he had dinner with them. Faye seemed very happy, talking about charge accounts and stupid sales clerks. Homer had a flower in his buttonhole, wore carpet slippers and beamed at her continually.

After they had eaten, while Homer was in the kitchen washing dishes, Tod got her to tell him what they did with themselves all day. She said that they lived quietly and that she was
glad because she was tired of excitement. All she wanted was
a career. Homer did the housework and she was getting a real
rest. Daddy's long sickness had tired her out completely. Homer liked to do housework and anyway he wouldn't let her
go into the kitchen because of her hands.

"Protecting his investment," Tod said.

"Yes," she replied seriously, "they have to be beautiful."

They had breakfast around ten, she went on. Homer
brought it to her in bed. He took a housekeeping magazine
and fixed the tray like the pictures in it. While she bathed and
dressed, he cleaned the house. Then they went downtown to
the stores and she bought all sorts of things, mostly clothes.
They didn't eat lunch on account of her figure, but usually
had dinner out and went to the movies.

"Then, ice cream sodas," Homer finished for her, as he
came out of the kitchen.

Faye laughed and excused herself. They were going to a
picture and she wanted to change her dress. When she had
left, Homer suggested that they get some air in the patio. He
made Tod take the deck chair while he sat on an upturned
orange crate.

If he had been careful and had acted decently, Tod couldn't
help thinking, she might be living with him. He was at least
better looking than Homer. But then there was her other pre-
requisite. Homer had an income and lived in a house, while
he earned thirty dollars a week and lived in a furnished room.

The happy grin on Homer's face made him feel ashamed
of himself. He was being unfair. Homer was a humble, grateful man who would never laugh at her, who was incapable of
laughing at anything. Because of this great quality, she could
live with him on what she considered a much higher plane.

"What's the matter?" Homer asked softly, laying one of his
heavy hands on Tod's knee.

"Nothing. Why?"

Tod moved so that the hand slipped off.

"You were making faces."

"I was thinking of something."

"Oh," Homer said sympathetically.

Tod couldn't resist asking an ugly question.

"When are you two getting married?"

Homer looked hurt.

"Didn't Faye tell about us?"

"Yes, sort of."

"It's a business arrangement."

"Yes?"

To make Tod believe it, he poured out a long, disjointed argument, the one he must have used on himself. He even went further than the business part and claimed that they were doing it for poor Harry's sake. Faye had nothing left in the world except her career and she must succeed for her daddy's sake. The reason she wasn't a star was because she didn't have the right clothes. He had money and believed in her talent, so it was only natural for them to enter into a business arrangement. Did Tod know a good lawyer?

It was a rhetorical question, but would become a real one, painfully insistent, if Tod smiled. He frowned. That was wrong, too.

"We must see a lawyer this week and have papers drawn up."

His eagerness was pathetic. Tod wanted to help him, but didn't know what to say. He was still fumbling for an answer when they heard a woman shouting from the hill behind the garage.

"Adore! Adore!"

She had a high soprano voice, very clear and pure.

"What a funny name," Tod said, glad to change the subject.

"Maybe it's a foreigner," Homer said.

The woman came into the yard from around the corner of the garage. She was eager and plump and very American.

"Have you seen my little boy?" she asked, making a gesture of helplessness. "Adore's such a wanderer."

Homer surprised Tod by standing up and smiling at the woman. Faye had certainly helped his timidity.

"Is your son lost?" Homer said.

"Oh, no—just hiding to tease me."

She held out her hand.

"We're neighbors. I'm Maybelle Loomis."

"Glad to know you, ma'am. I'm Homer Simpson and this is Mr. Hackett."

Tod also shook hands with her.

"Have you been living here long?" she asked.

"No. I've just come from the East," Homer said.

"Oh, have you? I've been here ever since Mr. Loomis passed on six years ago. I'm an old settler."

"You like it then?" Tod asked.

"Like California?" she laughed at the idea that anyone might not like it. "Why, it's a paradise on earth!"

"Yes," Homer agreed gravely.

"And anyway," she went on, "I have to live here on account of Adore."

"Is he sick?"

"Oh, no. On account of his career. His agent calls him the biggest little attraction in Hollywood."

She spoke so vehemently that Homer flinched.

"He's in the movies?" Tod asked.

"I'll say," she snapped.

Homer tried to placate her.

"That's very nice."

"If it weren't for favoritism," she said bitterly, "he'd be a star. It ain't talent. It's pull. What's Shirley Temple got that he ain't got?"

"Why, I don't know," Homer mumbled.

She ignored this and let out a fearful bellow.

"Adore! Adore!"

Tod had seen her kind around the studio. She was one of that army of women who drag their children from casting office to casting office and sit for hours, weeks, months, waiting for a chance to show what Junior can do. Some of them are very poor, but no matter how poor, they always manage to scrape together enough money, often by making great sacrifices, to send their children to one of the innumerable talent schools.

"Adore!" she yelled once more, then laughed and became a friendly housewife again, a chubby little person with dimples in her fat cheeks and fat elbows.

"Have you any children, Mr. Simpson?" she asked.

"No," he replied, blushing.

"You're lucky—they're a nuisance."

She laughed to show that she didn't really mean it and called her child again.

"Adore . . . Oh, Adore . . ."

Her next question surprised them both.

"Who do you follow?"

"What?" said Tod.

"I mean—in the Search for Health, along the Road of Life?"

They both gaped at her.

"I'm a raw-foodist, myself," she said. "Dr. Pierce is our leader. You must have seen his ads—'Know-All Pierce-All.' "

"Oh, yes," Tod said, "you're vegetarians."

She laughed at his ignorance.

"Far from it. We're much stricter. Vegetarians eat cooked vegetables. We eat only raw ones. Death comes from eating dead things."

Neither Tod nor Homer found anything to say.

"Adore," she began again. "Adore . . ."

This time there was an answer from around the corner of the garage.

"Here I am, mama."

A minute later, a little boy appeared dragging behind him a small sailboat on wheels. He was about eight years old, with a pale, peaked face and a large, troubled forehead. He had great staring eyes. His eyebrows had been plucked and shaped carefully. Except for his Buster Brown collar, he was dressed like a man, in long trousers, vest and jacket.

He tried to kiss his mother, but she fended him off and pulled at his clothes, straightening and arranging them with savage little tugs.

"Adore," she said sternly, "I want you to meet Mr. Simpson, our neighbor."

Turning like a soldier at the command of a drill sergeant, he walked up to Homer and grasped his hand.

"A pleasure, sir," he said, bowing stiffly with his heels together.

"That's the way they do it in Europe," Mrs. Loomis beamed. "Isn't he cute?"

"What a pretty sailboat!" Homer said, trying to be friendly.

Both mother and son ignored his comment. She pointed to Tod, and the child repeated his bow and heel-click.

"Well, we've got to go," she said.

Tod watched the child, who was standing a little to one side of his mother and making faces at Homer. He rolled his eyes back in his head so that only the whites showed and twisted his lips in a snarl.

Mrs. Loomis noticed Tod's glance and turned sharply. When she saw what Adore was doing, she yanked him by the arm, jerking him clear off the ground.

"Adore!" she yelled.

To Tod she said apologetically, "He thinks he's the Frankenstein monster."

She picked the boy up, hugging and kissing him ardently. Then she set him down again and fixed his rumpled clothing.

"Won't Adore sing something for us?" Tod asked.

"No," the little boy said sharply.

"Adore," his mother scolded, "sing at once."

"That's all right, if he doesn't feel like it," Homer said.

But Mrs. Loomis was determined to have him sing. She could never permit him to refuse an audience.

"Sing, Adore," she repeated with quiet menace. "Sing 'Mama Doan Wan' No Peas.'"

His shoulders twitched as though they already felt the strap. He tilted his straw sailor over one eye, buttoned up his jacket and did a little strut, then began:

> *"Mama doan wan' no peas,*
> *An' rice, an' cocoanut oil,*
> *Just a bottle of brandy handy all the day.*
> *Mama doan wan' no peas,*
> *Mama doan wan' no cocoanut oil."*

His singing voice was deep and rough and he used the broken groan of the blues singer quite expertly. He moved his body only a little, against rather than in time with the music. The gestures he made with his hands were extremely suggestive.

> *"Mama doan wan' no gin,*
> *Because gin do make her sin,*

Mama doan wan' no glass of gin,
Because it boun' to make her sin,
An' keep her hot and bothered all the day."

He seemed to know what the words meant, or at least his body and his voice seemed to know. When he came to the final chorus, his buttocks writhed and his voice carried a top-heavy load of sexual pain.

Tod and Homer applauded. Adore grabbed the string of his sailboat and circled the yard. He was imitating a tugboat. He tooted several times, then ran off.

"He's just a baby," Mrs. Loomis said proudly, "but he's got loads of talent."

Tod and Homer agreed.

She saw that he was gone again and left hurriedly. They could hear her calling in the brush back of the garage.

"Adore! Adore . . ."

"That's a funny woman," Tod said.

Homer sighed.

"I guess it's hard to get a start in pictures. But Faye is awfully pretty."

Tod agreed. She appeared a moment later in a new flower print dress and picture hat and it was his turn to sigh. She was much more than pretty. She posed, quivering and balanced, on the doorstep and looked down at the two men in the patio. She was smiling, a subtle half-smile uncontaminated by thought. She looked just born, everything moist and fresh, volatile and perfumed. Tod suddenly became very conscious of his dull, insensitive feet bound in dead skin and of his hands, sticky and thick, holding a heavy, rough felt hat.

He tried to get out of going to the pictures with them, but couldn't. Sitting next to her in the dark proved the ordeal he expected it to be. Her self-sufficiency made him squirm and the desire to break its smooth surface with a blow, or at least a sudden obscene gesture, became irresistible.

He began to wonder if he himself didn't suffer from the ingrained, morbid apathy he liked to draw in others. Maybe he could only be galvanized into sensibility and that was why he was chasing Faye.

He left hurriedly, without saying good-bye. He had decided

to stop running after her. It was an easy decision to make, but a hard one to carry out. In order to manage it, he fell back on one of the oldest tricks in the very full bag of the intellectual. After all, he told himself, he had drawn her enough times. He shut the portfolio that held the drawings he had made of her, tied it with a string, and put it away in his trunk.

It was a childish trick, hardly worthy of a primitive witch doctor, yet it worked. He was able to avoid her for several months. During this time, he took his pad and pencils on a continuous hunt for other models. He spent his nights at the different Hollywood churches, drawing the worshipers. He visited the "Church of Christ, Physical" where holiness was attained through the constant use of chest-weights and spring grips; the "Church Invisible" where fortunes were told and the dead made to find lost objects; the "Tabernacle of the Third Coming" where a woman in male clothing preached the "Crusade Against Salt"; and the "Temple Moderne" under whose glass and chromium roof "Brain-Breathing, the Secret of the Aztecs" was taught.

As he watched these people writhe on the hard seats of their churches, he thought of how well Alessandro Magnasco would dramatize the contrast between their drained-out, feeble bodies and their wild, disordered minds. He would not satirize them as Hogarth or Daumier might, nor would he pity them. He would paint their fury with respect, appreciating its awful, anarchic power and aware that they had it in them to destroy civilization.

One Friday night in the "Tabernacle of the Third Coming," a man near Tod stood up to speak. Although his name most likely was Thompson or Johnson and his home town Sioux City, he had the same counter-sunk eyes, like the heads of burnished spikes, that a monk by Magnasco might have. He was probably just in from one of the colonies in the desert near Soboba Hot Springs where he had been conning over his soul on a diet of raw fruit and nuts. He was very angry. The message he had brought to the city was one that an illiterate anchorite might have given decadent Rome. It was a crazy jumble of dietary rules, economics and Biblical threats. He claimed to have seen the Tiger of Wrath stalking the walls of the citadel and the Jackal of Lust skulking in the shrubbery, and he connected these omens with "thirty dollars every Thursday and meat eating."

Tod didn't laugh at the man's rhetoric. He knew it was unimportant. What mattered were his messianic rage and the emotional response of his hearers. They sprang to their feet, shaking their fists and shouting. On the altar someone began to beat a bass drum and soon the entire congregation was singing "Onward Christian Soldiers."

20

As TIME went on, the relationship between Faye and Homer began to change. She became bored with the life they were leading together and as her boredom deepened, she began to persecute him. At first she did it unconsciously, later maliciously.

Homer realized that the end was in sight even before she did. All he could do to prevent its coming was to increase his servility and his generosity. He waited on her hand and foot. He bought her a coat of summer ermine and a light blue Buick runabout.

His servility was like that of a cringing, clumsy dog, who is always anticipating a blow, welcoming it even, and in a way that makes overwhelming the desire to strike him. His generosity was still more irritating. It was so helpless and unselfish that it made her feel mean and cruel, no matter how hard she tried to be kind. And it was so bulky that she was unable to ignore it. She had to resent it. He was destroying himself, and although he didn't mean it that way, forcing her to accept the blame.

They had almost reached a final crisis when Tod saw them again. Late one night, just as he was preparing for bed, Homer knocked on his door and said that Faye was downstairs in the car and that they wanted him to go to a night club with them.

The outfit Homer wore was very funny. He had on loose blue linen slacks and a chocolate flannel jacket over a yellow polo shirt. Only a Negro could have worn it without looking ridiculous, and no one was ever less a Negro than Homer.

Tod drove with them to the "Cinderella Bar," a little stucco building in the shape of a lady's slipper, on Western Avenue. Its floor show consisted of female impersonators.

Faye was in a nasty mood. When the waiter took their order, she insisted on a champagne cocktail for Homer. He wanted coffee. The waiter brought both, but she made him take the coffee back.

Homer explained painstakingly, as he must have done many times, that he could not drink alcohol because it made him sick. Faye listened with mock patience. When he finished, she laughed and lifted the cocktail to his mouth.

"Drink it, damn you," she said.

She tilted the glass, but he didn't open his mouth and the liquor ran down his chin. He wiped himself, using the napkin without unfolding it.

Faye called the waiter again.

"He doesn't like champagne cocktails," she said. "Bring him brandy."

Homer shook his head.

"Please, Faye," he whimpered.

She held the brandy to his lips, moving the glass when he turned away.

"Come on, sport—bottoms up."

"Let him alone," Tod finally said.

She ignored him as though she hadn't even heard his protest. She was both furious and ashamed of herself. Her shame strengthened her fury and gave it a target.

"Come on, sport," she said savagely, "or mama'll spank."

She turned to Tod.

"I don't like people who won't drink. It isn't sociable. They feel superior and I don't like people who feel superior."

"I don't feel superior," Homer said.

"Oh, yes, you do. I'm drunk and you're sober and so you feel superior. Goddamned, stinking superior."

He opened his mouth to reply and she poured the brandy into it, then clapped her hand over his lips so that he couldn't spit it back. Some of it came out of his nose.

Still without unfolding the napkin, he wiped himself. Faye ordered another brandy. When it came, she held it to his lips again, but this time he took it and drank it himself, fighting the stuff down.

"That's the boy," Faye laughed. "Well done, sloppy-boppy."

Tod asked her to dance in order to give Homer a moment alone. When they reached the floor, she made an attempt to defend herself.

"That guy's superiority is driving me crazy."

"He loves you," Tod said.

"Yeah, I know, but he's such a slob."

She started to cry on his shoulder and he held her very tight. He took a long chance.

"Sleep with me."

"No, baby," she said sympathetically.

"Please, please . . . just once."

"I can't, honey. I don't love you."

"You worked for Mrs. Jenning. Make believe you're still working for her."

She didn't get angry.

"That was a mistake. And anyway, that was different. I only went on call enough times to pay for the funeral and besides those men were complete strangers. You know what I mean?"

"Yes. But please, darling. I'll never bother you again. I'll go east right after. Be kind."

"I can't."

"Why . . . ?"

"I just can't. I'm sorry, darling. I'm not a tease, but I can't like that."

"I love you."

"No, sweetheart, I can't."

They danced until the number finished without saying anything else. He was grateful to her for having behaved so well, for not having made him feel too ridiculous.

When they returned to the table, Homer was sitting exactly as they had left him. He held the folded napkin in one hand and the empty brandy glass in the other. His helplessness was extremely irritating.

"You're right about the brandy, Faye," Homer said. "It's swell! Whoopee!"

He made a little circular gesture with the hand that held the glass.

"I'd like a Scotch," Tod said.

"Me, too," Faye said.

Homer made another gallant attempt to get into the spirit of the evening.

"Garsoon," he called to the waiter, "more drinks."

He grinned at them anxiously. Faye burst out laughing and Homer did his best to laugh with her. When she stopped suddenly, he found himself laughing alone and turned his laugh into a cough, then hid the cough in his napkin.

She turned to Tod.

"What the devil can you do with a slob like that?"

The orchestra started and Tod was able to ignore her question. All three of them turned to watch a young man in a tight evening gown of red silk sing a lullaby.

> *"Little man, you're crying,*
> *I know why you're blue,*
> *Someone took your kiddycar away;*
> *Better go to sleep now,*
> *Little man, you've had a busy day . . ."*

He had a soft, throbbing voice and his gestures were matronly, tender and aborted, a series of unconscious caresses. What he was doing was in no sense parody; it was too simple and too restrained. It wasn't even theatrical. This dark young man with his thin, hairless arms and soft, rounded shoulders, who rocked an imaginary cradle as he crooned, was really a woman.

When he had finished, there was a great deal of applause. The young man shook himself and became an actor again. He tripped on his train, as though he weren't used to it, lifted his skirts to show he was wearing Paris garters, then strode off swinging his shoulders. His imitation of a man was awkward and obscene.

Homer and Tod applauded him.

"I hate fairies," Faye said.

"All women do."

Tod meant it as a joke, but Faye was angry.

"They're dirty," she said.

He started to say something else, but Faye had turned to Homer again. She seemed unable to resist nagging him. This time she pinched his arm until he gave a little squeak.

"Do you know what a fairy is?" she demanded.

"Yes," he said hesitatingly.

"All right, then," she barked. "Give out! What's a fairy?"

Homer twisted uneasily, as though he already felt the ruler on his behind, and looked imploring at Tod, who tried to help him by forming the word "homo" with his lips.

"Momo," Homer said.

Faye burst out laughing. But his hurt look made it impossible not to relent, so she patted his shoulder.

"What a hick," she said.

He grinned gratefully and signaled the waiter to bring another round of drinks.

The orchestra began to play and a man came over to ask Faye to dance. Without saying a word to Homer, she followed him to the floor.

"Who's that?" Homer asked, chasing them with his eyes.

Tod made believe he knew and said that he had often seen him around the San Berdoo. His explanation satisfied Homer, but at the same time set him to thinking of something else. Tod could almost see him shaping a question in his head.

"Do you know Earle Shoop?" Homer finally asked.

"Yes."

Homer then poured out a long, confused story about a dirty black hen. He kept referring to the hen again and again, as though it were the one thing he couldn't stand about Earle and the Mexican. For a man who was incapable of hatred, he managed to draw a pretty horrible picture of the bird.

"You never saw such a disgusting thing, the way it squats and turns its head. The roosters have torn all the feathers off its neck and made its comb all bloody and it has scabby feet covered with warts and it cackles so nasty when they drop it into the pen."

"Who drops it into what pen?"

"The Mexican."

"Miguel?"

"Yes. He's almost as bad as his hen."

"You've been to their camp?"

"Camp?"

"In the mountains?"

"No. They're living in the garage. Faye asked me if I minded if a friend of hers lived in the garage for a while because he was broke. But I didn't know about the chickens or the Mexican. . . . Lots of people are out of work nowadays."

"Why don't you throw them out?"

"They're broke and they have no place to go. It isn't very comfortable living in a garage."

"But if they don't behave?"

"It's just that hen. I don't mind the roosters, they're pretty, but that dirty hen. She shakes her dirty feathers each time and clucks so nasty."

"You don't have to look at it."

"They do it every afternoon at the same time when I'm usually sitting in the chair in the sun having got back from shopping with Faye and just before dinner. The Mexican knows I don't like to see it so he tries to make me look just for spite. I go into the house, but he taps on the windows and calls me to come out and watch. I don't call that fun. Some people have funny ideas of what's fun."

"What's Faye say?"

"She doesn't mind the hen. She says it's only natural."

Then, in case Tod should mistake this for criticism, he told him what a fine, wholesome child she was. Tod agreed, but brought him back to the subject.

"If I were you," he said, "I'd report the chickens to the police. You have to have a permit to keep chickens in the city. I'd do something and damned quick."

Homer avoided a direct answer.

"I wouldn't touch that thing for all the money in the world. She's all over scabs and almost naked. She looks like a buzzard. She eats meat. I saw her one time eating some meat that the Mexican got out of the garbage can. He feeds the roosters grain but the hen eats garbage and he keeps her in a dirty box."

"If I were you, I'd throw those bastards out and their birds with them."

"No, they're nice enough young fellows, just down on their luck, like a lot of people these days, you know. It's just that hen . . ."

He shook his head wearily, as though he could smell and taste her.

Faye was coming back. Homer saw that Tod was going to speak to her about Earle and the Mexican and signaled desperately for him not to do it. She, however, caught him at it and was curious.

"What have you guys been chinning about?"

"You, darling," Tod said. "Homer has a t.l. for you."

"Tell me, Homer."

"No, first you tell me one."

"Well, the man I just danced with asked me if you were a movie big shot."

Tod saw that Homer was unable to think of a return compliment so he spoke for him.

"I said you were the most beautiful girl in the place."

"Yes," Homer agreed. "That's what Tod said."

"I don't believe it. Tod hates me. And anyway, I caught you telling him to keep quiet. You were shushing him."

She laughed.

"I bet I know what you were talking about." She mimicked Homer's excited disgust. " 'That dirty black hen, she's all over scabs and almost naked.' "

Homer laughed apologetically, but Tod was angry.

"What's the idea of keeping those guys in the garage?" he demanded.

"What the hell is it your business?" she replied, but not with real anger. She was amused.

"Homer enjoys their company. Don't you, sloppy-boppy?"

"I told Tod they were nice fellows just down on their luck like a lot of people these days. There's an awful lot of unemployment going around."

"That's right," she said. "If they go, I go."

Tod had guessed as much. He realized there was no use in saying anything. Homer was again signaling for him to keep quiet.

For some reason or other, Faye suddenly became ashamed of herself. She apologized to Tod by offering to dance with him again, flirting as she suggested it. Tod refused.

She broke the silence that followed by a eulogy of Miguel's game chickens, which was really meant to be an excuse for herself. She described what marvelous fighters the birds were, how much Miguel loved them and what good care he took of them.

Homer agreed enthusiastically. Tod remained silent. She asked him if he had ever seen a cock fight and invited him to the garage for the next night. A man from San Diego was coming North with his birds to pit them against Miguel's.

When she turned to Homer again, he leaned away as

though she were going to hit him. She flushed with shame at this and looked at Tod to see if he had noticed. The rest of the evening, she tried to be nice to Homer. She even touched him a little, straightening his collar and patting his hair smooth. He beamed happily.

21

W HEN Tod told Claude Estee about the cock fight, he wanted to go with him. They drove to Homer's place together.

It was one of those blue and lavender nights when the luminous color seems to have been blown over the scene with an air brush. Even the darkest shadows held some purple.

A car stood in the driveway of the garage with its headlights on. They could see several men in the corner of the building and could hear their voices. Someone laughed, using only two notes, ha-ha and ha-ha, over and over again.

Tod stepped ahead to make himself known, in case they were taking precautions against the police. When he entered the light, Abe Kusich and Miguel greeted him, but Earle didn't.

"The fights are off," Abe said. "That stinkola from Diego didn't get here."

Claude came up and Tod introduced him to the three men. The dwarf was arrogant, Miguel gracious and Earle his usual wooden, surly self.

Most of the garage floor had been converted into a pit, an oval space about nine feet long and seven or eight wide. It was floored with an old carpet and walled by a low, ragged fence made of odd pieces of lath and wire. Faye's coupe stood in the driveway, placed so that its headlights flooded the arena.

Claude and Tod followed Abe out of the glare and sat down with him on an old trunk in the back of the garage. Earle and Miguel came in and squatted on their heels facing them. They were both wearing blue denims, polka-dot shirts, big hats and high-heeled boots. They looked very handsome and picturesque.

They sat smoking silently, all of them calm except the dwarf, who was fidgety. Although he had plenty of room, he suddenly gave Tod a shove.

"Get over, lard-ass," he snarled.

Tod moved, crowding against Claude, without saying anything. Earle laughed at Tod rather than the dwarf, but the dwarf turned on him anyway.

"Why, you punkola! Who you laughing at?"

"You," Earle said.

"That so, hah? Well, listen to me, you pee-hole bandit, for two cents I'd knock you out of them prop boots."

Earle reached into his shirt pocket and threw a coin on the ground.

"There's a nickel," he said.

The dwarf started to get off the trunk, but Tod caught him by the collar. He didn't try to get loose, but leaned forward against his coat, like a terrier in a harness, and wagged his great head from side to side.

"Go on," he sputtered, "you fugitive from the Western Costume Company, you . . . you louse in a fright-wig, you."

Earle would have been much less angry if he could have thought of a snappy comeback. He mumbled something about a half-pint bastard, then spat. He hit the instep of the dwarf's shoe with a big gob of spittle.

"Nice shot," Miguel said.

This was apparently enough for Earle to consider himself the winner, for he smiled and became quiet. The dwarf slapped Tod's hand away from his collar with a curse and settled down on the trunk again.

"He ought to wear gaffs," Miguel said.

"I don't need them for a punk like that."

They all laughed and everything was fine again.

Abe leaned across Tod to speak to Claude.

"It would have been a swell main," he said. "There was more than a dozen guys here before you come and some of them with real dough. I was going to make book."

He took out his wallet and gave him one of his business cards.

"It was in the bag," Miguel said. "I got five birds that would of won easy and two sure losers. We would of made a killing."

"I've never seen a chicken fight," Claude said. "In fact, I've never even seen a game chicken."

Miguel offered to show him one of his birds and left to get

it. Tod went down to the car for the bottle of whiskey they had left in a side pocket. When he got back, Miguel was holding Jujutla in the light. They all examined the bird.

Miguel held the cock firmly with both hands, somewhat in the manner that a basketball is held for an underhand toss. The bird had short, oval wings and a heart-shaped tail that stood at right angles to its body. It had a triangular head, like a snake's, terminating in a slightly curved beak, thick at the base and fine at the point. All its feathers were so tight and hard that they looked as though they had been varnished. They had been thinned out for fighting and the lines of its body, which was like a truncated wedge, stood out plainly. From between Miguel's fingers dangled its long, bright orange legs and its slightly darker feet with their horn nails.

"Juju was bred by John R. Bowes of Lindale, Texas," Miguel said proudly. "He's a six times winner. I give fifty dollars and a shotgun for him."

"He's a nice bird," the dwarf said grudgingly, "but looks ain't everything."

Claude took out his wallet.

"I'd like to see him fight," he said. "Suppose you sell me one of your other birds and I put it against him."

Miguel thought a while and looked at Earle, who told him to go ahead.

"I've got a bird I'll sell you for fifteen bucks," he said.

The dwarf interfered.

"Let me pick the bird."

"Oh, I don't care," Claude said, "I just want to see a fight. Here's your fifteen."

Earle took the money and Miguel told him to get Hermano, the big red.

"That red'll go over eight pounds," he said, "while Juju won't go more than six."

Earle came back carrying a large rooster that had a silver shawl. He looked like an ordinary barnyard fowl.

When the dwarf saw him, he became indignant.

"What do you call that, a goose?"

"That's one of Street's Butcher Boys," Miguel said.

"I wouldn't bait a hook with him," the dwarf said.

"You don't have to bet," Earle mumbled.

The dwarf eyed the bird and the bird eyed him. He turned to Claude.

"Let me handle him for you, mister," he said.

Miguel spoke quickly.

"Earle'll do it. He knows the cock."

The dwarf exploded at this.

"It's a frame-up!" he yelled.

He tried to take the red, but Earle held the bird high in the air out of the little man's reach.

Miguel opened the trunk and took out a small wooden box, the kind chessmen are kept in. It was full of curved gaffs, small squares of chamois with holes in their centers and bits of waxed string like that used by a shoemaker.

They crowded around to watch him arm Juju. First he wiped the short stubs on the cock's legs to make sure they were clean and then placed a leather square over one of them so that the stub came through the hole. He then fitted a gaff over it and fastened it with a bit of the soft string, wrapping very carefully. He did the same to the other leg.

When he had finished, Earle started on the big red.

"That's a bird with lots of cojones," Miguel said. "He's won plenty fights. He don't look fast maybe, but he's fast all right and he packs an awful wallop."

"Strictly for the cook stove, if you ask me," the dwarf said.

Earle took out a pair of shears and started to lighten the red's plumage. The dwarf watched him cut away most of the bird's tail, but when he began to work on the breast, he caught his hand.

"Leave him be!" he barked. "You'll kill him fast that way. He needs that stuff for protection."

He turned to Claude again.

"Please, mister, let me handle him."

"Make him buy a share in the bird," Miguel said.

Claude laughed and motioned for Earle to give Abe the bird. Earle didn't want to and looked meaningly at Miguel.

The dwarf began to dance with rage.

"You're trying to cold-deck us!" he screamed.

"Aw, give it to him," Miguel said.

The little man tucked the bird under his left arm so that his hands were free and began to look over the gaffs in the box. They were all the same length, three inches, but some had more pronounced curves than the others. He selected a pair and explained his strategy to Claude.

"He's going to do most of his fighting on his back. This pair'll hit right that way. If he could get over the other bird, I wouldn't use them."

He got down on his knees and honed the gaffs on the cement floor until they were like needles.

"Have we a chance?" Tod asked.

"You can't ever tell," he said, shaking his extra large head. "He feels almost like a dead bird."

After adjusting the gaffs with great care, he looked the bird over, stretching its wings and blowing its feathers in order to see its skin.

"The comb ain't bright enough for fighting condition," he said, pinching it, "but he looks strong. He may have been a good one once."

He held the bird in the light and looked at its head. When Miguel saw him examining its beak, he told him anxiously to quit stalling. But the dwarf paid no attention and went on muttering to himself. He motioned for Tod and Claude to look.

"What'd I tell you!" he said, puffing with indignation. "We've been cold-decked."

He pointed to a hair line running across the top of the bird's beak.

"That's not a crack," Miguel protested, "it's just a mark."

He reached for the bird as though to rub its beak and the bird pecked savagely at him. This pleased the dwarf.

"We'll fight," he said, "but we won't bet."

Earle was to referee. He took a piece of chalk and drew three lines in the center of the pit, a long one in the middle and two shorter ones parallel to it and about three feet away.

"Pit your cocks," he called.

"No, bill them first," the dwarf protested.

He and Miguel stood at arm's length and thrust their birds together to anger them. Juju caught the big red by the comb and held on viciously until Miguel jerked him away. The red, who had been rather apathetic, came to life and the dwarf had trouble holding him. The two men thrust their birds together again, and again Juju caught the red's comb. The big cock became frantic with rage and struggled to get at the smaller bird.

"We're ready," the dwarf said.

He and Miguel climbed into the pit and set their birds down on the short lines so that they faced each other. They held them by the tails and waited for Earle to give the signal to let go.

"Pit them," he ordered.

The dwarf had been watching Earle's lips and he had his bird off first, but Juju rose straight in the air and sank one spur in the red's breast. It went through the feathers into the flesh. The red turned with the gaff still stuck in him and pecked twice at his opponent's head.

They separated the birds and held them to the lines again.

"Pit 'em!" Earle shouted.

Again Juju got above the other bird, but this time he missed with his spurs. The red tried to get above him, but couldn't. He was too clumsy and heavy to fight in the air. Juju climbed again, cutting and hitting so rapidly that his legs were a golden blur. The red met him by going back on his tail and hooking upward like a cat. Juju landed again and again. He broke one of the red's wings, then practically severed a leg.

"Handle them," Earle called.

When the dwarf gathered the red up, its neck had begun to droop and it was a mass of blood and matted feathers. The little man moaned over the bird, then set to work. He spit into its gaping beak and took the comb between his lips and sucked the blood back into it. The red began to regain its fury, but not its strength. Its beak closed and its neck straightened. The dwarf smoothed and shaped its plumage. He could do nothing to help the broken wing or the dangling leg.

"Pit 'em," Earle said.

The dwarf insisted that the birds be put down beak to beak on the center line, so that the red would not have to move to get at his opponent. Miguel agreed.

The red was very gallant. When Abe let go of its tail, it made a great effort to get off the ground and meet Juju in the air, but it could only thrust with one leg and fell over on its side. Juju sailed above it, half turned and came down on its back, driving in both spurs. The red twisted free, throwing Juju, and made a terrific effort to hook with its good leg, but fell sideways again.

Before Juju could get into the air, the red managed to drive a hard blow with its beak to Juju's head. This slowed the smaller bird down and he fought on the ground. In the pecking match, the red's greater weight and strength evened up for his lack of a leg and a wing. He managed to give as good as he got. But suddenly his cracked beak broke off, leaving only the lower half. A large bubble of blood rose where the beak had been. The red didn't retreat an inch, but made a great effort to get into the air once more. Using its one leg skillfully, it managed to rise six or seven inches from the ground, not enough, however, to get its spurs into play. Juju went up with him and got well above, then drove both gaffs into the red's breast. Again one of the steel needles stuck.

"Handle them," Earle shouted.

Miguel freed his bird and gave the other back to the dwarf. Abe, moaning softly, smoothed its feathers and licked its eyes clean, then took its whole head in his mouth. The red was finished, however. It couldn't even hold its neck straight. The dwarf blew away the feathers from under its tail and pressed the lips of its vent together hard. When that didn't seem to help, he inserted his little finger and scratched the bird's testicles. It fluttered and made a gallant effort to straighten its neck.

"Pit birds."

Once more the red tried to rise with Juju, pushing hard with its remaining leg, but it only spun crazily. Juju rose, but missed. The red thrust weakly with its broken bill. Juju went into the air again and this time drove a gaff through one of the red's eyes into its brain. The red fell over stone dead.

The dwarf groaned with anguish, but no one else said anything. Juju pecked at the dead bird's remaining eye.

"Take off that stinking cannibal!" the dwarf screamed.

Miguel laughed, then caught Juju and removed its gaffs. Earle did the same for the red. He handled the dead cock gently and with respect.

Tod passed the whiskey.

22

T HEY were well on their way to getting drunk when Homer came out to the garage. He gave a little start when he saw the dead chicken sprawled on the carpet. He shook hands with Claude after Tod had introduced him, and with Abe Kusich, then made a little set speech about everybody coming in for a drink. They trooped after him.

Faye greeted them at the door. She was wearing a pair of green silk lounging pajamas and green mules with large pompons and very high heels. The top three buttons of her jacket were open and a good deal of her chest was exposed but nothing of her breasts; not because they were small, but because they were placed wide apart and their thrust was upward and outward.

She gave Tod her hand and patted the dwarf on the top of the head. They were old friends. In acknowledging Homer's awkward introduction of Claude, she was very much the lady. It was her favorite role and she assumed it whenever she met a new man, especially if he were someone whose affluence was obvious.

"Charmed to have you," she trilled.

The dwarf laughed at her.

In a voice stiff with hauteur, she then ordered Homer into the kitchen for soda, ice and glasses.

"A swell layout," announced the dwarf, putting on the hat he had taken off in the doorway.

He climbed into one of the big Spanish chairs, using his knees and hands to do it, and sat on the edge with his feet dangling. He looked like a ventriloquist's dummy.

Earle and Miguel had remained behind to wash up. When they came in, Faye welcomed them with stilted condescension.

"How do you do, boys? The refreshments will be along in a jiffy. But perhaps you prefer a liqueur, Miguel?"

"No, mum," he said, a little startled. "I'll have what the others have."

He followed Earle across the room to the couch. Both of

them took long, wooden steps, as though they weren't used to being in a house. They sat down gingerly with their backs straight, their big hats on their knees and their hands under their hats. They had combed their hair before leaving the garage and their small round heads glistened prettily.

Homer took the drinks around on a small tray.

They all made a show of manners, all but the dwarf, that is, who remained as arrogant as ever. He even commented on the quality of the whiskey. As soon as everyone had been served, Homer sat down.

Faye alone remained standing. She was completely self-possessed despite their stares. She stood with one hip thrown out and her hand on it. From where Claude was sitting he could follow the charming line of her spine as it swooped into her buttocks, which were like a heart upside down.

He gave a low whistle of admiration and everyone agreed by moving uneasily or laughing.

"My dear," she said to Homer, "perhaps some of the men would like cigars?"

He was surprised and mumbled something about there being no cigars in the house but that he would go to the store for them if . . . Having to say all this made him unhappy and he took the whiskey around again. He poured very generous shots.

"That's a becoming shade of green," Tod said.

Faye peacocked for them all.

"I thought maybe it was a little gaudy . . . vulgar, you know."

"No," Claude said enthusiastically, "it's stunning."

She repaid him for his compliment by smiling in a peculiar, secret way and running her tongue over her lips. It was one of her most characteristic gestures and very effective. It seemed to promise all sorts of undefined intimacies, yet it was really as simple and automatic as the word thanks. She used it to reward anyone for anything, no matter how unimportant.

Claude made the same mistake Tod had often made and jumped to his feet.

"Won't you sit here?" he said, waving gallantly at his chair.

She accepted by repeating the secret smile and the tongue caress. Claude bowed, but then, realizing that everyone was watching him, added a little mock flourish to make himself less ridiculous. Tod joined them, then Earle and Miguel came over. Claude did the courting while the others stood by and stared at her.

"Do you work in pictures, Mr. Estee?" she asked.

"Yes. You're in pictures, of course?"

Everyone was aware of the begging note in his voice, but no one smiled. They didn't blame him. It was almost impossible to keep that note out when talking to her. Men used it just to say good morning.

"Not exactly, but I hope to be," she said. "I've worked as an extra, but I haven't had a real chance yet. I expect to get one soon. All I ask is a chance. Acting is in my blood. We Greeners, you know, were all theatre people from away back."

"Yes. I . . ."

She didn't let Claude finish, but he didn't care.

"Not musicals, but real dramas. Of course, maybe light comedies at first. All I ask is a chance. I've been buying a lot of clothes lately to make myself one. I don't believe in luck. Luck is just hard work, they say, and I'm willing to work as hard as anybody."

"You have a delightful voice and you handle it well," he said.

He couldn't help it. Having once seen her secret smile and the things that accompanied it, he wanted to make her repeat it again and again.

"I'd like to do a show on Broadway," she continued. "That's the way to get a start nowadays. They won't talk to you unless you've had stage experience."

She went on and on, telling him how careers are made in the movies and how she intended to make hers. It was all nonsense. She mixed bits of badly understood advice from the trade papers with other bits out of the fan magazines and compared these with the legends that surround the activities of screen stars and executives. Without any noticeable transition, possibilities became probabilities and wound up as inevitabilities. At first she occasionally stopped and waited for Claude to chorus a hearty agreement, but when she had a good start, all her questions were rhetorical and the stream of words rippled on without a break.

None of them really heard her. They were all too busy watching her smile, laugh, shiver, whisper, grow indignant, cross and uncross her legs, stick out her tongue, widen and narrow her eyes, toss her head so that her platinum hair splashed against the red plush of the chair back. The strange thing about her gestures and expressions was that they didn't really illustrate what she was saying. They were almost pure. It was as though her body recognized how foolish her words were and tried to excite her hearers into being uncritical. It worked that night; no one even thought of laughing at her. The only move they made was to narrow their circle about her.

Tod stood on the outer edge, watching her through the opening between Earle and the Mexican. When he felt a light tap on his shoulder, he knew it was Homer, but didn't turn. When the tap was repeated, he shrugged the hand away. A few minutes later, he heard a shoe squeak behind him and turned to see Homer tiptoeing off. He reached a chair safely and sank into it with a sigh. He put his heavy hands on the knees, one on each, and stared for a while at their backs. He felt Tod's eyes on him and looked up and smiled.

His smile annoyed Tod. It was one of those irritating smiles that seem to say: "My friend, what can you know of suffering?" There was something very patronizing and superior about it, and intolerably snobbish.

He felt hot and a little sick. He turned his back on Homer and went out the front door. His indignant exit wasn't very successful. He wobbled quite badly and when he reached the sidewalk, he had to sit down on the curb with his back against a date palm.

From where he was sitting, he couldn't see the city in the valley below the canyon, but he could see the reflection of its lights, which hung in the sky above it like a batik parasol. The unlighted part of the sky at the edge of the parasol was a deep black with hardly a trace of blue.

Homer followed him out of the house and stood standing behind him, afraid to approach. He might have sneaked away without Tod's knowing it, if he had not suddenly looked down and seen his shadow.

"Hello," he said.

He motioned for Homer to join him on the curb.

"You'll catch cold," Homer said.

Tod understood his protest. He made it because he wanted to be certain that his company was really welcome. Nevertheless, Tod refused to repeat the invitation. He didn't even turn to look at him again. He was sure he was wearing his long-suffering smile and didn't want to see it.

He wondered why all his sympathy had turned to malice. Because of Faye? It was impossible for him to admit it. Because he was unable to do anything to help him? This reason was a more comfortable one, but he dismissed it with even less consideration. He had never set himself up as a healer.

Homer was looking the other way, at the house, watching the parlor window. He cocked his head to one side when someone laughed. The four short sounds, ha-ha and again ha-ha, distinct musical notes, were made by the dwarf.

"You could learn from him," Tod said.

"What?" Homer asked, turning to look at him.

"Let it go."

His impatience both hurt and puzzled Homer. He saw that and motioned for him to sit down, this time emphatically.

Homer obeyed. He did a poor job of squatting and hurt himself. He sat nursing his knee.

"What is it?" Tod finally said, making an attempt to be kind.

"Nothing, Tod, nothing."

He was grateful and increased his smile. Tod couldn't help seeing all its annoying attributes, resignation, kindliness, and humility.

They sat quietly, Homer with his heavy shoulders hunched and the sweet grin on his face, Tod frowning, his back pressed hard against the palm tree. In the house the radio was playing and its blare filled the street.

They sat for a long time without speaking. Several times Homer started to tell Tod something but he didn't seem able to get the words out. Tod refused to help him with a question.

His big hands left his lap, where they had been playing "here's the church and here the steeple," and hid in his armpits. They remained there for a moment, then slid under his thighs. A moment later they were back in his lap. The right hand cracked the joints of the left, one by one, then the left did the same service for the right. They seemed easier for a moment, but not for long. They started "here's the church" again, going through the entire performance and ending with the joint manipulation as before. He started a third time, but catching Tod's eyes, he stopped and trapped his hands between his knees.

It was the most complicated tic Tod had ever seen. What made it particularly horrible was its precision. It wasn't pantomime, as he had first thought, but manual ballet.

When Tod saw the hands start to crawl out again, he exploded.

"For Christ's sake!"

The hands struggled to get free, but Homer clamped his knees shut and held them.

"I'm sorry," he said.

"Oh, all right."

"But I can't help it, Tod. I have to do it three times."

"Okay with me."

He turned his back on him.

Faye started to sing and her voice poured into the street.

> *"Dreamed about a reefer five feet long*
> *Not too mild and not too strong,*
> *You'll be high, but not for long,*
> *If you're a viper—a vi-paah."*

Instead of her usual swing delivery, she was using a lugubrious one, wailing the tune as though it were a dirge. At the end of every stanza, she shifted to an added minor.

> *"I'm the queen of everything,*
> *Gotta be high before I can swing,*
> *Light a tea and let it be,*
> *If you're a viper—a vi-paah."*

"She sings very pretty," Homer said.

"She's drunk."

"I don't know what to do, Tod," Homer complained. "She's drinking an awful lot lately. It's that Earle. We used to have a lot of fun before he came, but now we don't have any fun any more since he started to hang around."

"Why don't you get rid of him?"

"I was thinking about what you said about the license to keep chickens."

Tod understood what he wanted.

"I'll report them to the Board of Health tomorrow."

Homer thanked him, then insisted on explaining in detail why he couldn't do it himself.

"But that'll only get rid of the Mexican," Tod said. "You'll have to throw Earle out yourself."

"Maybe he'll go with his friend?"

Tod knew that Homer was begging him to agree so that he could go on hoping, but he refused.

"Not a chance. You'll have to throw him out."

Homer accepted this with his brave, sweet smile.

"Maybe . . ."

"Tell Faye to do it," Tod said.

"Oh, I can't."

"Why the hell not? It's your house."

"Don't be mad at me, Toddie."

"All right, Homie, I'm not mad at you."

Faye's voice came through the open window.

> *"And when your throat gets dry,*
> *You know you're high,*
> *If you're a viper."*

The others harmonized on the last word, repeating it.

"Vi-paah . . ."

"Toddie," Homer began, "if . . ."

"Stop calling me Toddie, for Christ's sake!"

Homer didn't understand. He took Tod's hand.

"I didn't mean nothing. Back home we call . . ."

Tod couldn't stand his trembling signals of affection. He tore free with a jerk.

"Oh, but, Toddie, I . . ."

"She's a whore!"

He heard Homer grunt, then heard his knees creak as he struggled to his feet.

Faye's voice came pouring through the window, a reedy wail that broke in the middle with a husky catch.

"High, high, high, high, when you're high,
Everything is dandy,
Truck on down to the candy store,
Bust your conk on peppermint candy!
Then you know your body's sent,
Don't care if you don't pay rent,
Sky is high and so am I,
If you're a viper—a vi-paah."

23

WHEN Tod went back into the house, he found Earle, Abe Kusich and Claude standing together in a tight group, watching Faye dance with Miguel. She and the Mexican were doing a slow tango to music from the phonograph. He held her very tight, one of his legs thrust between hers, and they swayed together in long spirals that broke rhythmically at the top of each curve into a dip. All the buttons on her lounging pajamas were open and the arm he had around her waist was inside her clothes.

Tod stood watching the dancers from the doorway for a moment, then went to a little table on which the whiskey bottle was. He poured himself a quarter of a tumblerful, tossed it off, then poured another drink. Carrying the glass, he went over to Claude and the others. They paid no attention to him; their heads moved only to follow the dancers, like the gallery at a tennis match.

"Did you see Homer?" Tod asked, touching Claude's arm.

Claude didn't turn, but the dwarf did. He spoke as though hypnotized.

"What a quiff! What a quiff!"

Tod left them and went to look for Homer. He wasn't in the kitchen, so he tried the bedrooms. One of them was locked. He knocked lightly, waited, then repeated the knock. There was no answer, but he thought he heard someone move. He looked through the keyhole. The room was pitch dark.

"Homer," he called softly.

He heard the bed creak, then Homer replied.

"Who is it?"

"It's me—Toddie."

He used the diminutive with perfect seriousness.

"Go away, please," Homer said.

"Let me in for a minute. I want to explain something."

"No," Homer said, "go away, please."

Tod went back to the living room. The phonograph record had been changed to a fox-trot and Earle was now dancing with Faye. He had both his arms around her in a bear hug and they were stumbling all over the room, bumping into the walls and furniture. Faye, her head thrown back, was laughing wildly. Earle had both eyes shut tight.

Miguel and Claude were also laughing, but not the dwarf. He stood with his fists clenched and his chin stuck out. When he couldn't stand any more of it, he ran after the dancers to cut in. He caught Earle by the seat of his trousers.

"Le'me dance," he barked.

Earle turned his head, looking down at the dwarf from over his shoulder.

"Git! G'wan, git!"

Faye and Earle had come to a halt with their arms around each other. When the dwarf lowered his head like a goat and tried to push between them, she reached down and tweaked his nose.

"Le'me dance," he bellowed.

They tried to start again, but Abe wouldn't let them. He had his hands between them and was trying frantically to pull them apart. When that wouldn't work, he kicked Earle sharply in the shins. Earle kicked back and his boot landed in the little man's stomach, knocking him flat on his back. Everyone laughed.

The dwarf struggled to his feet and stood with his head lowered like a tiny ram. Just as Faye and Earle started to dance again, he charged between Earle's legs and dug upward with both hands. Earle screamed with pain, and tried to get at him. He screamed again, then groaned and started to sink to the floor, tearing Faye's silk pajamas on his way down.

Miguel grabbed Abe by the throat. The dwarf let go his hold and Earle sank to the floor. Lifting the little man free, Miguel shifted his grip to his ankles and dashed him against the wall, like a man killing a rabbit against a tree. He swung the dwarf back to slam him again, but Tod caught his arm. Then Claude grabbed the dwarf and together they pulled him away from the Mexican.

He was unconscious. They carried him into the kitchen and held him under the cold water. He came to quickly, and began to curse. When they saw he was all right, they went back to the living room.

Miguel was helping Earle over to the couch. All the tan had drained from his face and it was covered with sweat. Miguel loosened his trousers while Claude took off his necktie and opened his collar.

Faye and Tod watched from the side.

"Look," she said, "my new pajamas are ruined."

One of the sleeves had been pulled almost off and her shoulder stuck through it. The trousers were also torn. While he stared at her, she undid the top of the trousers and stepped out of them. She was wearing tight black lace drawers. Tod took a step toward her and hesitated. She threw the pajama bottoms over her arm, turned slowly and walked toward the door.

"Faye," Tod gasped.

She stopped and smiled at him.

"I'm going to bed," she said. "Get that little guy out of here."

Claude came over and took Tod by the arm.

"Let's blow," he said.

Tod nodded.

"We'd better take the homunculus with us or he's liable to murder the whole household."

Tod nodded again and followed him into the kitchen. They found the dwarf holding a big piece of ice to the side of his head.

"There's some lump where that greaser slammed me."

He made them finger and admire it.

"Let's go home," Claude said.

"No," said the dwarf, "let's go see some girls. I'm just getting started."

"To hell with that," snapped Tod. "Come on."

He pushed the dwarf toward the door.

"Take your hands off, punk!" roared the little man.

Claude stepped between them.

"Easy there, citizen," he said.

"All right, but no shoving."

He strutted out and they followed.

Earle still lay stretched on the couch. He had his eyes closed and was holding himself below the stomach with both hands. Miguel wasn't there.

Abe chuckled, wagging his big head gleefully.

"I fixed that buckeroo."

Out on the sidewalk he tried again to get them to go with him.

"Come on, you guys—we'll have some fun."

"I'm going home," Claude said.

They went with the dwarf to his car and watched him climb in behind the wheel. He had special extensions on the clutch and brake so that he could reach them with his tiny feet.

"Come to town?"

"No, thanks," Claude said politely.

"Then to hell with you!"

That was his farewell. He let out the brake and the car rolled away.

24

Tod woke up the next morning with a splitting headache. He called the studio to say he wouldn't be in and remained in bed until noon, then went downtown for breakfast. After several cups of hot tea, he felt a little better and decided to visit Homer. He still wanted to apologize.

Climbing the hill to Pinyon Canyon made his head throb and he was relieved when no one answered his repeated knocks. As he started away, he saw one of the curtains move and went back to knock once more. There was still no answer.

He went around to the garage. Faye's car was gone and so were the game chickens. He went to the back of the house and knocked on the kitchen door. Somehow the silence seemed too complete. He tried the handle and found that the door wasn't locked. He shouted hello a few times, as a warning, then went through the kitchen into the living room.

The red velvet curtains were all drawn tight, but he could see Homer sitting on the couch and staring at the backs of his hands which were cupped over his knees. He wore an old-fashioned cotton nightgown and his feet were bare.

"Just get up?"

Homer neither moved nor replied.

Tod tried again.

"Some party!"

He knew it was stupid to be hearty, but he didn't know what else to be.

"Boy, have I got a hang-over," he went on, even going so far as to attempt a chuckle.

Homer paid absolutely no attention to him.

The room was just as they had left it the night before. Tables and chairs were overturned and the smashed picture lay where it had fallen. To give himself a reason for staying, he began to tidy up. He righted the chairs, straightened the carpet and picked up the cigarette butts that littered the floor. He also threw aside the curtains and opened a window.

"There, that's better, isn't it?" he asked cheerfully.

366

Homer looked up for a second, then down at his hands again. Tod saw that he was coming out of his stupor.

"Want some coffee?" he asked.

He lifted his hands from his knees and hid them in his armpits, clamping them tight, but didn't answer.

"Some hot coffee—what do you say?"

He took his hands from under his arms and sat on them. After waiting a little while he shook his head no, slowly, heavily, like a dog with a foxtail in its ear.

"I'll make some."

Tod went to the kitchen and put the pot on the stove. While it was boiling, he took a peek into Faye's room. It had been stripped. All the dresser drawers were pulled out and there were empty boxes all over the floor. A broken flask of perfume lay in the middle of the carpet and the place reeked of gardenia.

When the coffee was ready, he poured two cups and carried them into the living room on a tray. He found Homer just as he had left him, sitting on his hands. He moved a small table close to him and put the tray on it.

"I brought a cup for myself, too," he said. "Come on— drink it while it's hot."

Tod lifted a cup and held it out, but when he saw that he was going to speak, he put it down and waited.

"I'm going back to Wayneville," Homer said.

"A swell idea—great!"

He pushed the coffee at him again. Homer ignored it. He gulped several times, trying to swallow something that was stuck in his throat, then began to sob. He cried without covering his face or bending his head. The sound was like an ax chopping pine, a heavy, hollow, chunking noise. It was repeated rhythmically but without accent. There was no progress in it. Each chunk was exactly like the one that proceeded. It would never reach a climax.

Tod realized that there was no use trying to stop him. Only a very stupid man would have the courage to try to do it. He went to the farthest corner of the room and waited.

Just as he was about to light a second cigarette, Homer called him.

"Tod!"

"I'm here, Homer."

He hurried over to the couch again.

Homer was still crying, but he suddenly stopped even more abruptly than he had started.

"Yes, Homer?" Tod asked encouragingly.

"She's left."

"Yes, I know. Drink some coffee."

"She's left."

Tod knew that he put a great deal of faith in sayings, so he tried one.

"Good riddance to bad rubbish."

"She left before I got up," he said.

"What the hell do you care? You're going back to Wayneville."

"You shouldn't curse," Homer said with the same lunatic calm.

"I'm sorry," Tod mumbled.

The word "sorry" was like dynamite set off under a dam. Language leaped out of Homer in a muddy, twisting torrent. At first, Tod thought it would do him a lot of good to pour out in this way. But he was wrong. The lake behind the dam replenished itself too fast. The more he talked the greater the pressure grew because the flood was circular and ran back behind the dam again.

After going on continuously for about twenty minutes, he stopped in the middle of a sentence. He leaned back, closed his eyes and seemed to fall asleep. Tod put a cushion under his head. After watching him for a while, he went back to the kitchen.

He sat down and tried to make sense out of what Homer had told him. A great deal of it was gibberish. Some of it, however, wasn't. He hit on a key that helped when he realized that a lot of it wasn't jumbled so much as timeless. The words went behind each other instead of after. What he had taken for long strings were really one thick word and not a sentence. In the same way several sentences were simultaneous and not a paragraph. Using this key, he was able to arrange a part of what he had heard so that it made the usual kind of sense.

After Tod had hurt him by saying that nasty thing about

Faye, Homer ran around to the back of the house and let himself in through the kitchen, then went to peek into the parlor. He wasn't angry with Tod, just surprised and upset because Tod was a nice boy. From the hall that led into the parlor he could see everybody having a good time and he was glad because it was kind of dull for Faye living with an old man like him. It made her restless. No one noticed him peeking there and he was glad because he didn't feel much like joining the fun, although he liked to watch people enjoy themselves. Faye was dancing with Mr. Estee and they made a nice pair. She seemed happy. Her face shone like always when she was happy. Next she danced with Earle. He didn't like that because of the way he held her. He couldn't see what she saw in that fellow. He just wasn't nice, that's all. He had mean eyes. In the hotel business they used to watch out for fellows like that and never gave them credit because they would jump their bills. Maybe he couldn't get a job because nobody would trust him, although it was true as Faye said that a lot of people were out of work nowadays. Standing there peeking at the party, enjoying the laughing and singing, he saw Earle catch Faye and bend her back and kiss her and everybody laughed although you could see Faye didn't like it because she slapped his face. Earle didn't care, he just kissed her again, a long nasty one. She got away from him and ran toward the door where he was standing. He tried to hide, but she caught him. Although he didn't say anything, she said he was nasty spying on her and wouldn't listen when he tried to explain. She went into her room and he followed to tell about the peeking, but she carried on awful and cursed him some more as she put red on her lips. Then she knocked over the perfume. That made her twice as mad. He tried to explain but she wouldn't listen and just went on calling him all sorts of dirty things. So he went to his room and got undressed and tried to go to sleep. Then Tod woke him up and wanted to come in and talk. He wasn't angry, but didn't feel like talking just then, all he wanted to do was go to sleep. Tod went away and no sooner had he climbed back into bed when there was some awful screaming and banging. He was afraid to go out and see and he thought of calling the police, but he was scared to go in the hall where the phone was so he started to get dressed to climb out of the window and go for help because it sounded like murder but before he finished putting his shoes on, he heard Tod talking to Faye and he figured that it must be all right or she wouldn't be laughing so he got undressed and went back to bed again. He couldn't fall asleep wondering what had happened, so when the house was quiet, he took a chance and knocked on Faye's door to find out. Faye let him in. She was curled up in bed like a little girl. She called him daddy and kissed him and said that she wasn't angry at him at all. She said there had been a fight but nobody got hurt much and for him to go back to bed and that they would talk more in the morning. He went back like she said and fell asleep, but he woke up again as it was just breaking daylight. At first he wondered why he was up because when he once fell asleep, usually he didn't get up before the alarm clock rang. He knew that something had happened, but he didn't know what until he heard a noise in Faye's room. It was a moan and he thought he was dreaming, but he heard it again. Sure enough, Faye was moaning all right. He thought she must be sick. She moaned again like in pain. He got out of bed and went to her door and knocked and asked if she was sick. She didn't answer and the moaning stopped so he went back to bed. A little later, she moaned again so he got out of bed, thinking she might want the hot water bottle or some aspirin and a drink of water or something and knocked on her door again, only meaning to help her. She heard him and said something. He didn't understand what but he thought she meant for him to go in. Lots of times when she had a headache he brought her an aspirin and a glass of water in the middle of the night. The door wasn't locked. You'd have thought she would have locked the door because the Mexican was in bed with her, both of them naked and she had her arms around him. Faye saw him and pulled the sheets over her head without saying anything. He didn't know what to do, so he backed out of the room and closed the door. He was standing in the hall, trying to figure out what to do, feeling so ashamed, when Earle appeared with his boots in his hand. He must have been sleeping in the parlor. He wanted to know what the trouble was. "Faye's sick," he said, "and I'm getting her a glass of water." But then Faye moaned again and Earle heard it. He pushed open the door. Faye screamed. He could hear Earle and Miguel cursing each other and fighting. He was afraid to call the police on account of Faye and didn't know what to do. Faye kept on screaming. When he opened the door again, Miguel fell out with Earle on top of him and both of them tearing at each other. He ran inside the room and locked the door. She had the sheets over her head, screaming. He could hear Earle and Miguel fighting in the hall and then he couldn't hear them any more. She kept the sheets over her head. He tried to talk to her but she wouldn't answer. He sat down on a chair to guard her in case Earle and Miguel came back, but they didn't and after a while she pulled the sheets away from her face and told him to get out. She pulled the sheets over her face again when he answered, so then he waited a little longer and again she told him to get out without letting him see her face. He couldn't hear either Miguel or Earle. He opened the door and looked out. They were gone. He locked the doors and windows and went to his room and lay down on his bed. Before he knew it he fell asleep and when he woke up she was gone. All he could find was Earle's boots in the hall. He threw them out the back and this morning they were gone.

25

Tod went into the living room to see how Homer was getting on. He was still on the couch, but had changed his position. He had curled his big body into a ball. His knees were drawn up almost to his chin, his elbows were tucked in close and his hands were against his chest. But he wasn't relaxed. Some inner force of nerve and muscle was straining to make the ball tighter and still tighter. He was like a steel spring which has been freed of its function in a machine and allowed to use all its strength centripetally. While part of a machine the pull of the spring had been used against other and stronger forces, but now, free at last, it was striving to attain the shape of its original coil.

Original coil . . . In a book of abnormal psychology borrowed from the college library, he had once seen a picture of a woman sleeping in a net hammock whose posture was much like Homer's. "Uterine Flight," or something like that, had been the caption under the photograph. The woman had been sleeping in the hammock without changing her position, that of the foetus in the womb, for a great many years. The doctors of the insane asylum had been able to awaken her for only short periods of time and those months apart.

He sat down to smoke a cigarette and wondered what he ought to do. Call a doctor? But after all Homer had been awake most of the night and was exhausted. The doctor would shake him a few times and he would yawn and ask what the matter was. He could try to wake him up himself. But hadn't he been enough of a pest already? He was so much better off asleep, even if it was a case of "Uterine Flight."

What a perfect escape the return to the womb was. Better by far than Religion or Art or the South Sea Islands. It was so snug and warm there, and the feeding was automatic. Everything perfect in that hotel. No wonder the memory of those accommodations lingered in the blood and nerves of everyone. It was dark, yes, but what a warm, rich darkness. The grave wasn't in it. No wonder one fought so desperately against being evicted when the nine months' lease was up.

Tod crushed his cigarette. He was hungry and wanted his dinner, also a double Scotch and soda. After he had eaten, he would come back and see how Homer was. If he was still asleep, he would try to wake him. If he couldn't, he might call a doctor.

He took another look at him, then tiptoed out of the cottage, shutting the door carefully.

26

Tod didn't go directly to dinner. He went first to Hodge's saddlery store thinking he might be able to find out something about Earle and through him about Faye. Calvin was standing there with a wrinkled Indian who had long hair held by a bead strap around his forehead. Hanging over the Indian's chest was a sandwich board that read—

TUTTLE'S TRADING POST
for
GENUINE RELICS OF THE OLD WEST
Beads, Silver, Jewelry, Moccasins,
Dolls, Toys, Rare Books, Postcards.
TAKE BACK A SOUVENIR
from
TUTTLE'S TRADING POST

Calvin was always friendly.

"'Lo, thar," he called out, when Tod came up.

"Meet the chief," he added, grinning. "Chief Kiss-My-Towkus."

The Indian laughed heartily at the joke.

"You gotta live," he said.

"Earle been around today?" Tod asked.

"Yop. Went by an hour ago."

"We were at a party last night and I . . ."

Calvin broke in by hitting his thigh a wallop with the flat of his palm.

"That must've been some shindig to hear Earle tell it. Eh, Skookum?"

"Vas you dere, Sharley?" the Indian agreed, showing the black inside of his mouth, purple tongue and broken orange teeth.

"I heard there was a fight after I left."

Calvin smacked his thigh again.

"Sure musta been. Earle get himself two black eyes, lulus."

"That's what comes of palling up with a dirty greaser," said the Indian excitedly.

He and Calvin got into a long argument about Mexicans. The Indian said that they were all bad. Calvin claimed he had known quite a few good ones in his time. When the Indian cited the case of the Hermanos brothers who had killed a lonely prospector for half a dollar, Calvin countered with a long tale about a man called Tomas Lopez who shared his last pint of water with a stranger when they both were lost in the desert.

Tod tried to get the conversation back to what interested him.

"Mexicans are very good with women," he said.

"Better with horses," said the Indian. "I remember one time along the Brazos, I . . . ."

Tod tried again.

"They fought over Earle's girl, didn't they?"

"Not to hear him tell it," Calvin said. "He claims it was dough—claims the Mex robbed him while he was sleeping."

"The dirty, thievin' rat," said the Indian, spitting.

"He claims he's all washed up with that bitch," Calvin went on. "Yes, siree, that's his story, to hear him tell it."

Tod had enough.

"So long," he said.

"Glad to meet you," said the Indian.

"Don't take any wooden nickels," Calvin shouted after him.

Tod wondered if she had gone with Miguel. He thought it more likely that she would go back to work for Mrs. Jenning. But either way she would come out all right. Nothing could hurt her. She was like a cork. No matter how rough the sea got, she would go dancing over the same waves that sank iron ships and tore away piers of reinforced concrete. He pictured her riding a tremendous sea. Wave after wave reared its ton on ton of solid water and crashed down only to have her spin gaily away.

When he arrived at Musso Frank's restaurant, he ordered a steak and a double Scotch. The drink came first and he sipped it with his inner eye still on the spinning cork.

It was a very pretty cork, gilt with a glittering fragment of mirror set in its top. The sea in which it danced was beautiful, green in the trough of the waves and silver at their tips. But for all their moon-driven power, they could do no more than net the bright cork for a moment in a spume of intricate lace. Finally it was set down on a strange shore where a savage with pork-sausage fingers and a pimpled butt picked it up and hugged it to his sagging belly. Tod recognized the fortunate man; he was one of Mrs. Jenning's customers.

The waiter brought his order and paused with bent back for him to comment. In vain. Tod was far too busy to inspect the steak.

"Satisfactory, sir?" asked the waiter.

Tod waved him away with a gesture more often used on flies. The waiter disappeared. Tod tried the same gesture on what he felt, but the driving itch refused to go. If only he had the courage to wait for her some night and hit her with a bottle and rape her.

He knew what it would be like, lurking in the dark in a vacant lot, waiting for her. Whatever that bird was that sang at night in California would be bursting its heart in theatrical runs and quavers and the chill night air would smell of spice pink. She would drive up, turn the motor off, look up at the stars, so that her breasts reared, then toss her head and sigh. She would throw the ignition keys into her purse and snap it shut, then get out of the car. The long step she took would make her tight dress pull up so that an inch of glowing flesh would show above her black stocking. As he approached carefully, she would be pulling her dress down, smoothing it nicely over her hips.

"Faye, Faye, just a minute," he would call.

"Why, Tod, hello."

She would hold her hand out to him at the end of her long arm that swooped so gracefully to join her curving shoulder.

"You scared me!"

She would look like a deer on the edge of the road when a truck comes unexpectedly around a bend.

He could feel the cold bottle he held behind his back and the forward step he would take to bring . . .

"Is there anything wrong with it, sir?"

The fly-like waiter had come back. Tod waved at him, but this time the man continued to hover.

"Perhaps you would like me to take it back, sir?"

"No, no."

"Thank you, sir."

But he didn't leave. He waited to make sure that the customer was really going to eat. Tod picked up his knife and cut a piece. Not until he had also put some boiled potato in his mouth did the man leave.

Tod tried to start the rape going again, but he couldn't feel the bottle as he raised it to strike. He had to give it up.

The waiter came back. Tod looked at the steak. It was a very good one, but he wasn't hungry any more.

"A check, please."

"No dessert, sir?"

"No, thank you, just a check."

"Check it is, sir," the man said brightly as he fumbled for his pad and pencil.

27

W HEN Tod reached the street, he saw a dozen great violet shafts of light moving across the evening sky in wide crazy sweeps. Whenever one of the fiery columns reached the lowest point of its arc, it lit for a moment rose-colored domes and delicate minarets of Kahn's Persian Palace Theatre. The purpose of this display was to signal the world premiere of a new picture.

Turning his back on the searchlights, he started in the opposite direction, toward Homer's place. Before he had gone very far, he saw a clock that read a quarter past six and changed his mind about going back just yet. He might as well let the poor fellow sleep for another hour and kill some time by looking at the crowds.

When still a block from the theatre, he saw an enormous electric sign that hung over the middle of the street. In letters ten feet high he read that—

"MR. KAHN A PLEASURE DOME DECREED"

Although it was still several hours before the celebrities would arrive, thousands of people had already gathered. They stood facing the theatre with their backs toward the gutter in a thick line hundreds of feet long. A big squad of policemen was trying to keep a lane open between the front rank of the crowd and the façade of the theatre.

Tod entered the lane while the policeman guarding it was busy with a woman whose parcel had torn open, dropping oranges all over the place. Another policeman shouted for him to get the hell across the street, but he took a chance and kept going. They had enough to do without chasing him. He noticed how worried they looked and how careful they tried to be. If they had to arrest someone, they joked good-naturedly with the culprit, making light of it until they got him around the corner, then they whaled him with their clubs. Only so long as the man was actually part of the crowd did they have to be gentle.

Tod had walked only a short distance along the narrow lane

when he began to get frightened. People shouted, commenting on his hat, his carriage, and his clothing. There was a continuous roar of catcalls, laughter and yells, pierced occasionally by a scream. The scream was usually followed by a sudden movement in the dense mass and part of it would surge forward wherever the police line was weakest. As soon as that part was rammed back, the bulge would pop out somewhere else.

The police force would have to be doubled when the stars started to arrive. At the sight of their heroes and heroines, the crowd would turn demoniac. Some little gesture, either too pleasing or too offensive, would start it moving and then nothing but machine guns would stop it. Individually the purpose of its members might simply be to get a souvenir, but collectively it would grab and rend.

A young man with a portable microphone was describing the scene. His rapid, hysterical voice was like that of a revivalist preacher whipping his congregation toward the ecstasy of fits.

"What a crowd, folks! What a crowd! There must be ten thousand excited, screaming fans outside Kahn's Persian tonight. The police can't hold them. Here, listen to them roar."

He held the microphone out and those near it obligingly roared for him.

"Did you hear it? It's a bedlam, folks. A veritable bedlam! What excitement! Of all the premieres I've attended, this is the most . . . the most . . . stupendous, folks. Can the police hold them? Can they? It doesn't look so, folks . . ."

Another squad of police came charging up. The sergeant pleaded with the announcer to stand further back so the people couldn't hear him. His men threw themselves at the crowd. It allowed itself to be hustled and shoved out of habit and because it lacked an objective. It tolerated the police, just as a bull elephant does when he allows a small boy to drive him with a light stick.

Tod could see very few people who looked tough, nor could he see any working men. The crowd was made up of the lower middle classes, every other person one of his torchbearers.

Just as he came near the end of the lane, it closed in front of him with a heave, and he had to fight his way through.

Someone knocked his hat off and when he stooped to pick it up, someone kicked him. He whirled around angrily and found himself surrounded by people who were laughing at him. He knew enough to laugh with them. The crowd became sympathetic. A stout woman slapped him on the back, while a man handed him his hat, first brushing it carefully with his sleeve. Still another man shouted for a way to be cleared.

By a great deal of pushing and squirming, always trying to look as though he were enjoying himself, Tod finally managed to break into the open. After rearranging his clothes, he went over to a parking lot and sat down on the low retaining wall that ran along the front of it.

New groups, whole families, kept arriving. He could see a change come over them as soon as they had become part of the crowd. Until they reached the line, they looked diffident, almost furtive, but the moment they had become part of it, they turned arrogant and pugnacious. It was a mistake to think them harmless curiosity seekers. They were savage and bitter, especially the middle-aged and the old, and had been made so by boredom and disappointment.

All their lives they had slaved at some kind of dull, heavy labor, behind desks and counters, in the fields and at tedious machines of all sorts, saving their pennies and dreaming of the leisure that would be theirs when they had enough. Finally that day came. They could draw a weekly income of ten or fifteen dollars. Where else should they go but California, the land of sunshine and oranges?

Once there, they discover that sunshine isn't enough. They get tired of oranges, even of avocado pears and passion fruit. Nothing happens. They don't know what to do with their time. They haven't the mental equipment for leisure, the money nor the physical equipment for pleasure. Did they slave so long just to go to an occasional Iowa picnic? What else is there? They watch the waves come in at Venice. There wasn't any ocean where most of them came from, but after you've seen one wave, you've seen them all. The same is true of the airplanes at Glendale. If only a plane would crash once in a while so that they could watch the passengers being consumed in a "holocaust of flame," as the newspapers put it. But the planes never crash.

Their boredom becomes more and more terrible. They realize that they've been tricked and burn with resentment. Every day of their lives they read the newspapers and went to the movies. Both fed them on lynchings, murder, sex crimes, explosions, wrecks, love nests, fires, miracles, revolutions, wars. This daily diet made sophisticates of them. The sun is a joke. Oranges can't titillate their jaded palates. Nothing can ever be violent enough to make taut their slack minds and bodies. They have been cheated and betrayed. They have slaved and saved for nothing.

Tod stood up. During the ten minutes he had been sitting on the wall, the crowd had grown thirty feet and he was afraid that his escape might be cut off if he loitered much longer. He crossed to the other side of the street and started back.

He was trying to figure what to do if he were unable to wake Homer when, suddenly, he saw his head bobbing above the crowd. He hurried toward him. From his appearance, it was evident that there was something definitely wrong.

Homer walked more than ever like a badly made automaton and his features were set in a rigid, mechanical grin. He had his trousers on over his nightgown and part of it hung out of his open fly. In both of his hands were suitcases. With each step, he lurched to one side then the other, using the suitcases for balance weights.

Tod stopped directly in front of him, blocking his way.

"Where're you going?"

"Wayneville," he replied, using an extraordinary amount of jaw movement to get out this single word.

"That's fine. But you can't walk to the station from here. It's in Los Angeles."

Homer tried to get around him, but he caught his arm.

"We'll get a taxi. I'll go with you."

The cabs were all being routed around the block because of the preview. He explained this to Homer and tried to get him to walk to the corner.

"Come on, we're sure to get one on the next street."

Once Tod got him into a cab, he intended to tell the driver to go to the nearest hospital. But Homer wouldn't budge, no matter how hard he yanked and pleaded. People stopped to watch them, others turned their heads curiously. He decided to leave him and get a cab.

"I'll come right back," he said.

He couldn't tell from either Homer's eyes or expression whether he heard, for they both were empty of everything, even annoyance. At the corner he looked around and saw that Homer had started to cross the street, moving blindly. Brakes screeched and twice he was almost run over, but he didn't swerve or hurry. He moved in a straight diagonal. When he reached the other curb, he tried to get on the sidewalk at a point where the crowd was very thick and was shoved violently back. He made another attempt and this time a policeman grabbed him by the back of the neck and hustled him to the end of the line. When the policeman let go of him, he kept on walking as though nothing had happened.

Tod tried to get over to him, but was unable to cross until the traffic lights changed. When he reached the other side, he found Homer sitting on a bench, fifty or sixty feet from the outskirts of the crowd.

He put his arm around Homer's shoulder and suggested that they walk a few blocks further. When Homer didn't answer, he reached over to pick up one of the valises. Homer held on to it.

"I'll carry it for you," he said, tugging gently.

"Thief!"

Before Homer could repeat the shout, he jumped away. It would be extremely embarrassing if Homer shouted thief in front of a cop. He thought of phoning for an ambulance. But then, after all, how could he be sure that Homer was crazy? He was sitting quietly on the bench, minding his own business.

Tod decided to wait, then try again to get him into a cab. The crowd was growing in size all the time, but it would be at least half an hour before it over-ran the bench. Before that happened, he would think of some plan. He moved a short distance away and stood with his back to a store window so that he could watch Homer without attracting attention.

About ten feet from where Homer was sitting grew a large eucalyptus tree and behind the trunk of the tree was a little boy. Tod saw him peer around it with great caution, then suddenly jerk his head back. A minute later he repeated the maneuver. At first Tod thought he was playing hide and seek, then noticed that he had a string in his hand which was attached to an old purse that lay in front of Homer's bench. Every once in a while the child would jerk the string, making the purse hop like a sluggish toad. Its torn lining hung from its iron mouth like a furry tongue and a few uncertain flies hovered over it.

Tod knew the game the child was playing. He used to play it himself when he was small. If Homer reached to pick up the purse, thinking there was money in it, he would yank it away and scream with laughter.

When Tod went over to the tree, he was surprised to discover that it was Adore Loomis, the kid who lived across the street from Homer. Tod tried to chase him, but he dodged around the tree, thumbing his nose. He gave up and went back to his original position. The moment he left, Adore got busy with his purse again. Homer wasn't paying any attention to the child, so Tod decided to let him alone.

Mrs. Loomis must be somewhere in the crowd, he thought. Tonight when she found Adore, she would give him a hiding. He had torn the pocket of his jacket and his Buster Brown collar was smeared with grease.

Adore had a nasty temper. The completeness with which Homer ignored both him and his pocketbook made him frantic. He gave up dancing it at the end of the string and approached the bench on tiptoes, making ferocious faces, yet ready to run at Homer's first move. He stopped when about four feet away and stuck his tongue out. Homer ignored him. He took another step forward and ran through a series of insulting gestures.

If Tod had known that the boy held a stone in his hand, he would have interfered. But he felt sure that Homer wouldn't hurt the child and was waiting to see if he wouldn't move because of his pestering. When Adore raised his arm, it was too late. The stone hit Homer in the face. The boy turned to flee, but tripped and fell. Before he could scramble away, Homer landed on his back with both feet, then jumped again.

Tod yelled for him to stop and tried to yank him away. He

shoved Tod and went on using his heels. Tod hit him as hard as he could, first in the belly, then in the face. He ignored the blows and continued to stamp on the boy. Tod hit him again and again, then threw both arms around him and tried to pull him off. He couldn't budge him. He was like a stone column.

The next thing Tod knew, he was torn loose from Homer and sent to his knees by a blow in the back of the head that spun him sideways. The crowd in front of the theatre had charged. He was surrounded by churning legs and feet. He pulled himself erect by grabbing a man's coat, then let himself be carried along backwards in a long, curving swoop. He saw Homer rise above the mass for a moment, shoved against the sky, his jaw hanging as though he wanted to scream but couldn't. A hand reached up and caught him by his open mouth and pulled him forward and down.

There was another dizzy rush. Tod closed his eyes and fought to keep upright. He was jostled about in a hacking cross surf of shoulders and backs, carried rapidly in one direction and then in the opposite. He kept pushing and hitting out at the people around him, trying to face in the direction he was going. Being carried backwards terrified him.

Using the eucalyptus tree as a landmark, he tried to work toward it by slipping sideways against the tide, pushing hard when carried away from it and riding the current when it moved toward his objective. He was within only a few feet of the tree when a sudden, driving rush carried him far past it. He struggled desperately for a moment, then gave up and let himself be swept along. He was the spearhead of a flying wedge when it collided with a mass going in the opposite direction. The impact turned him around. As the two forces ground against each other, he was turned again and again, like a grain between millstones. This didn't stop until he became part of the opposing force. The pressure continued to increase until he thought he must collapse. He was slowly being pushed into the air. Although relief for his cracking ribs could be gotten by continuing to rise, he fought to keep his feet on the ground. Not being able to touch was an even more dreadful sensation than being carried backwards.

There was another rush, shorter this time, and he found himself in a dead spot where the pressure was less and equal.

He became conscious of a terrible pain in his left leg, just above the ankle, and tried to work it into a more comfortable position. He couldn't turn his body, but managed to get his head around. A very skinny boy, wearing a Western Union cap, had his back wedged against his shoulder. The pain continued to grow and his whole leg as high as the groin throbbed. He finally got his left arm free and took the back of the boy's neck in his fingers. He twisted as hard as he could. The boy began to jump up and down in his clothes. He managed to straighten his elbow, by pushing at the back of the boy's head, and so turn half way around and free his leg. The pain didn't grow less.

There was another wild surge forward that ended in another dead spot. He now faced a young girl who was sobbing steadily. Her silk print dress had been torn down the front and her tiny brassiere hung from one strap. He tried by pressing back to give her room, but she moved with him every time he moved. Now and then, she would jerk violently and he wondered if she was going to have a fit. One of her thighs was between his legs. He struggled to get free of her, but she clung to him, moving with him and pressing against him.

She turned her head and said, "Stop, stop," to someone behind her.

He saw what the trouble was. An old man, wearing a Panama hat and horn-rimmed glasses, was hugging her. He had one of his hands inside her dress and was biting her neck.

Tod freed his right arm with a heave, reached over the girl and brought his fist down on the man's head. He couldn't hit very hard but managed to knock the man's hat off, also his glasses. The man tried to bury his face in the girl's shoulder, but Tod grabbed one of his ears and yanked. They started to move again. Tod held on to the ear as long as he could, hoping that it would come away in his hand. The girl managed to twist under his arm. A piece of her dress tore, but she was free of her attacker.

Another spasm passed through the mob and he was carried toward the curb. He fought toward a lamp-post, but he was swept by before he could grasp it. He saw another man catch the girl with the torn dress. She screamed for help. He tried to get to her, but was carried in the opposite direction. This rush also ended in a dead spot. Here his neighbors were all shorter than he was. He turned his head upward toward the sky and tried to pull some fresh air into his aching lungs, but it was all heavily tainted with sweat.

In this part of the mob no one was hysterical. In fact, most of the people seemed to be enjoying themselves. Near him was a stout woman with a man pressing hard against her from in front. His chin was on her shoulder, and his arms were around her. She paid no attention to him and went on talking to the woman at her side.

"The first thing I knew," Tod heard her say, "there was a rush and I was in the middle."

"Yeah. Somebody hollered, 'Here comes Gary Cooper,' and then wham!"

"That ain't it," said a little man wearing a cloth cap and pullover sweater. "This is a riot you're in."

"Yeah," said a third woman, whose snaky gray hair was hanging over her face and shoulders. "A pervert attacked a child."

"He ought to be lynched."

Everybody agreed vehemently.

"I come from St. Louis," announced the stout woman, "and we had one of them pervert fellers in our neighborhood once. He ripped up a girl with a pair of scissors."

"He must have been crazy," said the man in the cap. "What kind of fun is that?"

Everybody laughed. The stout woman spoke to the man who was hugging her.

"Hey, you," she said. "I ain't no pillow."

The man smiled beatifically but didn't move. She laughed, making no effort to get out of his embrace.

"A fresh guy," she said.

The other woman laughed.

"Yeah," she said, "this is a regular free-for-all."

The man in the cap and sweater thought there was another laugh in his comment about the pervert.

"Ripping up a girl with scissors. That's the wrong tool."

He was right. They laughed even louder than the first time.

"You'd a done it different, eh, kid?" said a young man with a kidney-shaped head and waxed mustaches.

The two women laughed. This encouraged the man in the cap and he reached over and pinched the stout woman's friend. She squealed.

"Lay off that," she said good-naturedly.

"I was shoved," he said.

An ambulance siren screamed in the street. Its wailing moan started the crowd moving again and Tod was carried along in a slow, steady push. He closed his eyes and tried to protect his throbbing leg. This time, when the movement ended, he found himself with his back to the theatre wall. He kept his eyes closed and stood on his good leg. After what seemed like hours, the pack began to loosen and move again with a churning motion. It gathered momentum and rushed. He rode it until he was slammed against the base of an iron rail which fenced the driveway of the theatre from the street. He had the wind knocked out of him by the impact, but managed to cling to the rail. He held on desperately, fighting to keep from being sucked back. A woman caught him around the waist and tried to hang on. She was sobbing rhythmically. Tod felt his fingers slipping from the rail and kicked backwards as hard as he could. The woman let go.

Despite the agony in his leg, he was able to think clearly about his picture, "The Burning of Los Angeles." After his quarrel with Faye, he had worked on it continually to escape tormenting himself, and the way to it in his mind had become almost automatic.

As he stood on his good leg, clinging desperately to the iron rail, he could see all the rough charcoal strokes with which he had blocked it out on the big canvas. Across the top, parallel with the frame, he had drawn the burning city, a great bonfire of architectural styles, ranging from Egyptian to Cape Cod colonial. Through the center, winding from left to right, was a long hill street and down it, spilling into the middle foreground, came the mob carrying baseball bats and torches. For the faces of its members, he was using the innumerable sketches he had made of the people who come to California to die; the cultists of all sorts, economic as well as religious, the wave, airplane, funeral and preview watchers—all those poor devils who can only be stirred by the promise of miracles and then only to violence. A super "Dr. Know-All

Pierce-All" had made the necessary promise and they were marching behind his banner in a great united front of screwballs and screwboxes to purify the land. No longer bored, they sang and danced joyously in the red light of the flames.

In the lower foreground, men and women fled wildly before the vanguard of the crusading mob. Among them were Faye, Harry, Homer, Claude and himself. Faye ran proudly, throwing her knees high. Harry stumbled along behind her, holding on to his beloved derby hat with both hands. Homer seemed to be falling out of the canvas, his face half-asleep, his big hands clawing the air in anguished pantomime. Claude turned his head as he ran to thumb his nose at his pursuers. Tod himself picked up a small stone to throw before continuing his flight.

He had almost forgotten both his leg and his predicament, and to make his escape still more complete he stood on a chair and worked at the flames in an upper corner of the canvas, modeling the tongues of fire so that they licked even more avidly at a corinthian column that held up the palmleaf roof of a nutburger stand.

He had finished one flame and was starting on another when he was brought back by someone shouting in his ear. He opened his eyes and saw a policeman trying to reach him from behind the rail to which he was clinging. He let go with his left hand and raised his arm. The policeman caught him by the wrist, but couldn't lift him. Tod was afraid to let go until another man came to aid the policeman and caught him by the back of his jacket. He let go of the rail and they hauled him up and over it.

When they saw that he couldn't stand, they let him down easily to the ground. He was in the theatre driveway. On the curb next to him sat a woman crying into her skirt. Along the wall were groups of other disheveled people. At the end of the driveway was an ambulance. A policeman asked him if he wanted to go to the hospital. He shook his head no. He then offered him a lift home. Tod had the presence of mind to give Claude's address.

He was carried through the exit to the back street and lifted into a police car. The siren began to scream and at first he thought he was making the noise himself. He felt his lips with his hands. They were clamped tight. He knew then it was the siren. For some reason this made him laugh and he began to imitate the siren as loud as he could.

OTHER WRITINGS

Euripides—A Playwright

THE tawdry melodrama of "Uncle Tom's Cabin." The dirt of a Restoration play by Wycherly. The sex alarums by the propagandist Brieux. The bloody sensationalism of the Old Testament. The box-office symbolisms of Carl Capek. The waving of his country's flag as George M. Cohan never waved it. The stretching of the long arm of coincidence as Thomas Hardy never dared stretch it. The eternal triangle. In short, the art of that great Greek dramatist, Euripides.

Euripides is a perambulating source-book and a consistent fount of inspiration for the genius of all subsequent civilizations. Seneca, Dante, Racine, Corneille, Goethe, Grilplatzer, Milton, Keats, Shelley, Browning (their names are as the Egyptian Gods in number) all are in deep debt to him. Even Shakespeare has the master player in Hamlet do a poor version of Hecuba to prove his merit. Being able to quote Euripides has saved not alone the first-nighters, who were in the Sicilian expedition, but also many a latter-day intellectual has good cause to burn offerings of thanks at his shrine. The peculiar fact about this wholesale borrowing and rewriting of Euripides is, that no matter how great the genius of the subsequent writer, he invariably fails. Euripides, to explain this, might paraphrase Shakespeare and say, "He who steals my ideas steals something as cheap as potatoes in Ireland, while he who steals my style steals my very essence." This seems rational and adequate explanation of Seneca's magnificent failures and Henri Bernstein's cheap plagiarisms.

To turn to a more particular criticism of Euripides' plays in the "Alcestis," Euripides wrote one of the best of plays, full of true pathos and keen humor, both of which sometimes verge upon burlesque. The happy ending is understood from the start and none of the grief is sentimental. This is the play which J. J. Chapman says, "The bourgeoisie takes his half-grown family to see."

Heracles struts, waves his club and shows his biceps; the women wail, Admetus whines; there is grace, there is spice—there are laughs and there are tears. And there is a happy ending that everybody knows is coming but in which he delights, nevertheless. Alcestis returns and is accepted mid speeches which God might quote. No painting by Vermeer has half its happy loveliness or one by Gaugin its color. It is a play that Lewis Carroll's Alice must see in her looking glass.

To Milton and to Swinburne a Greek play is a symphony of beautiful, solemn declamation and ceremony. To me, however, it is more—it is exciting, varied, and moving life, in which every word sparkles with action and every action with wit. "In seeking to understand Greek plays we must forget Milton and think rather of Moliere," says James Huneker. This is what we must keep in mind when we read the "Bacchae." Most of the students of this play make it out to be a mystical allegory or a sort of Oberammergau play. Apropos of this, I. T. Beckwith, in preface to the "Bacchae" says, "A play in which faith celebrates its rights, and unbelief is put to shame, must, by reason of the seriousness of its import and the lofty religious inspiration pervading the whole and manifesting itself in many brilliant and profound utterances, have attained great fame in antiquity." It was much read, as the frequent citations and reminiscences of the Greek and Roman writers show, and was often cited.

"The choral odes follow the progress of the action more closely, perhaps, than in any other play of Euripides, expressing the emotions that accompany a devout faith as it passes from the most buoyant hopefulness through a gradual darkening struggle out again into complete triumph."

Let us now examine the text of the "Bacchae." According to the legend, the Bacchantes, followers of Dionysus, tore Pentheus to pieces for his refusal to worship the new god. Both Pentheus and Dionysus are the grandsons of Cadmus, one of the Argonauts. At the time the story begins, Cadmus had resigned the government of Thebes, and turned it over to his grandson, Pentheus.

At the opening of the play Dionysus enters as prologue and explains that he has come disguised as a mortal with the Bacchantes in his train. He says that he has come back to his birthplace in order to punish his mother's two sisters, who have never taken seriously the story of his divine birth. Thebes soon discovers that Dionysus is a god.

Next comes a vaudeville act that is one of the finest things ever done on the stage. The team is Tiresias, the mythical sooth-sayer, and Cadmus, the great mythic Hellene. James Huneker calls these old men Moses and Aaron. They come in, dressed for Bacchic rites, each with a small thyrsus in his hands, and garlands of flowers on their heads, "beribboned for the fray"—Chapman has a good description of their "act" in his "Greek Genius," in which he says, "They exhibit the characters of the gay old bourgeoisie, delighted at their own temerity, knowing they will be laughed at, yet resolved to enjoy themselves." . . . . The audience must have gripped its umbrellas with joy! . . . . The old darlings enter, meeting as by appointment, clap each other on the shoulder, admire each other's dresses, swear they will dance like good ones—they alone of the city. But they alone are wise! "They will not be ashamed of their old age, not they! The god never distinguishes between old and young, but demands worship from both: they clasp hands in rapture (Tiresias being blind) and are about to leave when enters the gloomy and boorish Pentheus. As a foil to the old gentlemen, Pentheus is perfect." This scene of the two old men belongs among the greatest things in drama.

The chorus, after their departure, celebrates in a hymn to Bacchus and Venus. This hymn is in a manner that P. Descharme thinks sublimely religious, and A. W. Verral a ribald drinking song. But it is not a drinking song, Chapman thinks, or a religious hymnal. It is as refined as Praxitiles' statuary and as conventional. All I will venture is that it is very good poetry.

There is hardly a page in this play where the Greek fear of being laughed at does not come up. When Dionysus tells of his triumph over Pentheus in the stable, the punishment of Pentheus is made drastic because of the ridicule to which it makes him subject. (Even Medea kills her children out of the fear that she will be ridiculed for her lack of success in life.) I cannot continue to tell in detail the rest of the play, but you cannot touch it anywhere without having the desire, when once started, to write and never stop writing. There is not a moment in the whole play where it is not dynamic and stimulating.

In summing up, I feel the desire to express the unexpressible praise, but I realize that I am incapable. The most I can accomplish is to throw a few soiled flowers on a Parnassus of laurel and bay, heaped up by his more capable admirers.

In reading Euripides, we find ourself ready to classify him at moments as a satirist and at other moments as a man of feeling. Of course he was both. Sometimes he seems like a religious man and again like a charlatan. Of course he was neither. He was a great playwright.

—Nathaniel v. W. Weinstein

Casements (Brown University), July 1923

"Through the Hole in
the Mundane Millstone"

THREE MEN read *The Dream Life of Balso Snell* and, having
in mind perhaps an older story involving Picasso, exclaimed in rapid succession:

"Almost as funny as the Venus de Milo!"

"As funny as the Venus de Milo!"

"Funnier than the Venus de Milo!"

We quote this incident not only because the book is extremely funny, but also because the hero of it, Balso Snell, a
lyric poet by trade, often indulges in violent exclamations. The
examples that follow have been chosen at random from the
text:

"O Anon! O Onan!"

"O Beer! O Meyerbeer! O Bach! O Offenbach!"

"O Constipation of Desire! O Diarrhoea of Love!"

English humor has always prided itself on being good na-
tured and in the best of taste. This fact makes it difficult to
compare N. W. West with other comic writers, as he is vicious,
mean, ugly, obscene and insane. We feel with good cause. For
much too long has the whimsical, family-joke (tongue in
cheek, hand over heart, good-fellows all) dominated our
literature. With the French, however, West can well be
compared. In his use of the violently disassociated, the
dehumanized marvelous, the deliberately criminal and imbe-
cilic, he is much like Guillaume Apollinaire, Jarry, Ribemont-
Dessaignes, Raymond Roussel, and certain of the surrealistes.

Nevertheless, the mechanism used—an "anywhere out of
the world" device—makes a formal comparison with Lewis
Carroll possible. Just as Alice escapes through the looking
glass, Balso Snell escapes the real world by entering the
Wooden Horse of the Greeks which he finds in the tall grass
surrounding the walls of Troy. Inside he hires a philosophic
guide who insists on discussing the nature of art. After a violent argument, Balso eludes him only to run into Maloney
the Areopagite who is attempting to crucify himself with
thumb tacks. Maloney tells Balso that he is writing a life of

Saint Puce. This saint is a flea who built a church in the armpit of our Lord; a church "whose walls are the flesh of Christ, whose windows are rose with the blood of Christ." After Maloney, he meets John Raskolnikov Gilson, the twelve year old murderer of an idiot, and Miss McGeeney, a school teacher who is writing the life of Samuel Perkins, a man who can smell the strength of iron or even the principles involved in an isosceles triangle.

It becomes apparent to Balso that the intestine of the horse is inhabited solely by authors in search of an audience. Disgusted, he attempts to get out but is tricked into listening to other tales. All of these tales are elephantine close-ups of various literary positions and their technical methods; close-ups that make Kurt Schwitters' definition, "Tout ce'que l'artiste crache, c'est l'art" seem like an understatement.

Advertisement for
The Dream Life of Balso Snell, 1931

Some Notes on Violence

Is THERE any meaning in the fact that almost every manuscript we receive has violence for its core? They come to us from every state in the Union, from every type of environment, yet their highest common denominator is violence. It does not necessarily follow that such stories are the easiest to write or that they are the first subjects that young writers attempt. Did not sweetness and light fill the manuscripts rejected, as well as accepted, by the magazines before the war, and Art those immediately after it? We did not start with the ideas of printing tales of violence. We now believe that we would be doing violence by suppressing them.

———

In America violence is idiomatic. Read our newspapers. To make the front page a murderer has to use his imagination, he also has to use a particularly hideous instrument. Take this morning's paper: FATHER CUTS SON'S THROAT IN BASEBALL ARGUMENT. It appears on an inside page. To make the first page, he should have killed three sons and with a baseball bat instead of a knife. Only liberality and symmetry could have made this daily occurrence interesting.

———

And how must the American writer handle violence? In the July "Criterion," H.S.D. says of a story in our first number that ". . . the thing is incredible, as an event, in spite of its careful detail, simply because such things cannot happen without arousing the strongest emotions in the spectator. (Does not H.S.D. mean, "in the *breast* of the spectator?") Accordingly (the reviewer continues), only an emotional description of the scene will be credible . . ." Credible to an Englishman, yes, perhaps, or to a European, but not to an American. In America violence is daily. If an "emotional description" in the European sense is given an act of violence, the American should say, "What's all the excitement about," or, "By God, that's a mighty fine piece of writing, that's art."

———

What is melodramatic in European writing is not necessarily

399

so in American writing. For a European writer to make violence real, he has to do a great deal of careful psychology and
sociology. He often needs three hundred pages to motivate
one little murder. But not so the American writer. His audience has been prepared and is neither surprised nor shocked
if he omits artistic excuses for familiar events. When he reads
a little book with eight or ten murders in it, he does not
necessarily condemn the book as melodramatic. He is far from
the ancient Greeks, and still further from those people who
need the naturalism of Zola or the realism of Flaubert to make
writing seem "artistically true."

N. West

Contact, October 1932

Some Notes on Miss L.

I CAN'T do a review of *Miss Lonelyhearts*, but here, at random, are some of the things I thought when writing it:

As subtitle: "A novel in the form of a comic strip." The chapters to be squares in which many things happen through one action. The speeches contained in the conventional balloons. I abandoned this idea, but retained some of the comic strip technique: Each chapter instead of going forward in time, also goes backward, forward, up and down in space like a picture. Violent images are used to illustrate commonplace events. Violent acts are left almost bald.

Lyric novels can be written according to Poe's definition of a lyric poem. The short novel is a distinct form especially fitted for use in this country. France, Spain, Italy have a literature as well as the Scandinavian countries. For a hasty people we are too patient with the Bucks, Dreisers and Lewises. Thank God we are not all Scandinavians.

Forget the epic, the master work. In America fortunes do not accumulate, the soil does not grow, families have no history. Leave slow growth to the book reviewers, you only have time to explode. Remember William Carlos Williams' description of the pioneer women who shot their children against the wilderness like cannonballs. Do the same with your novels.

Psychology has nothing to do with reality nor should it be used as motivation. The novelist is no longer a psychologist. Psychology can become something much more important. The great body of case histories can be used in the way the ancient writers used their myths. Freud is your Bullfinch; you can not learn from him.

With this last idea in mind, Miss Lonelyhearts became the portrait of a priest of our time who has a religious experience. His case is classical and is built on all the cases in James' *Varieties of Religious Experience* and Starbuck's *Psychology of Religion*. The psychology is theirs not mine. The imagery is

mine. Chapt. I—maladjustment. Chapt. III—the need for taking symbols literally is described through a dream in which a
symbol is actually fleshed. Chapt. IV—deadness and disorder;
see Lives of Bunyan and Tolstoy. Chapt. VI—self-torture by
conscious sinning: see life of any saint. And so on.

I was serious therefore I could not be obscene.
I was honest therefore I could not be sordid.
A novelist can afford to be everything but dull.

Contempo, May 15, 1933

Business Deal

FOR AN HOUR after his barber left him, Mr. Eugene Kling-spiel, West Coast head of Gargantual Pictures, worked ceaselessly. First he read *The Hollywood Reporter*, *Variety*, and *The Film Daily*. Then he measured out two spoonfuls of bicarbonate and lay down on the couch to make decisions. Before long Mr. Klingspiel had fallen into what he called a gentle reverie. He saw Gargantual Pictures swallowing its competitors like a boa-constrictor, engulfing whole amusement chains. In a delicious half-doze, he found himself wondering whether to absorb Balaban & Katz; but finding no use for Katz, he absorbed only Balaban, and turned next to Spyros Skouras and his seven brothers. Perhaps at the outset he ought to absorb only three of them. But which three? The three in the middle or two on one end and one on the other? Finally he arranged the eight Skourases into a squad of tin soldiers and executed five at random. The repeated buzz of the dictograph cut short his delicious sport. He flipped the switch irritably.

"Who is it?"

"Hwonh hwonh hwonh hwonh hwonh."

"I'll see them later," said Mr. Klingspiel. "Send in Charlie Baer."

"Hwonh-hwonh."

He lit a cigar, turned his back on the door, and set his features into a scowl which would have done credit to a Japanese print. No punk kid two years out of Columbia College could hold *him* up for money, no matter how many hit pictures he'd written. After a dignified interval, he swung around. Charlie Baer, moon-faced and unconcerned, was staring out of another window with his back to Mr. Klingspiel.

"Well, Charlie." Mr. Klingspiel controlled his irritation at this breach of respect and essayed a kindly smile. "I sent for you yesterday."

"Aha." Charlie stared placidly at Mr. Klingspiel. His dewy innocence was positively revolting.

"My girl phoned you at the Writers' Building, but they said you were working with Roy Zinsser in Malibu." Mr. Klingspiel cleared his throat. Maybe a good joke would clear the atmosphere. "Vas you dere, Sharlie?" He regretted it immediately; Charlie's frigid stare made his remark almost indelicate. So this weasel thinks he can hijack me, Mr. Klingspiel reflected angrily.

"Charlie," he began, screwing his face into an expression of deep disapproval, "I dint like that last script. It lacked guts. It dint have the most important thing a good comedy script should have."

"What's that?" asked Charlie without curiosity.

"Spontinuity," replied Mr. Klingspiel gravely. "Now if I were you, Charlie, I'd take that idea home and maul it around in your mind over-night."

"Oke," said Charlie, reaching for his hat.

"Oh, just one more thing." Mr. Klingspiel made believe he was consulting some papers. "You expire on the fifteenth, am I right?"

"Yep."

"Well, Charlie, I'm gonna lay it on the line. You did some great pictures. I'm gonna extend you another year, but this time at two-fifty a week." Charlie's eyes remained fixed on his. Mr. Klingspiel was radiant. "In other words, double what you're getting now. How's that?"

"No good," said Charlie. "Five hundred a week or I don't work."

"Listen to me," said Klingspiel. "Answer me one thing. How many fellers do you know twenty-three years old that make two-fifty a week?"

"I've got to think about my old age," said Charlie.

"When I was twenty-three," went on Mr. Klingspiel, well into his Plowboy-to-President mood, "what was I? A green kid working for buttons. All I could afford was a bowl of milk and crackers. You don't know how lucky you are."

"Yes, I do," said Charlie. "I once tried a bowl of milk and crackers."

"Now, look here, Charlie," said Mr. Klingspiel patiently, "why don't you get wise to yourself? A single man like you in no time could bank——"

"Five hundred," interrupted Charlie bovinely. Mr. Klingspiel drummed softly on his desk.

"Listen, Charlie," he said after a moment, "let me tell you a story. It's a story about Adolph Rubens, the man who founded this great organization." Charlie's eyes drooped slightly. "Just picture to yourself that there ain't no Hollywood, no film business, nothing. It's twenty-eight years ago. A poor little furrier named Adolph Rubens is walking down a windy street in St. Louis. He's a little man, Charlie, but he's a fighter. He's cold and hungry, but in that man's brain is a dream. Everybody laughs at him and calls it Rubens' Folly, but he don't care. Why? Because in his brain he sees a picture of a mighty amusement ennaprise bringing entertainment and education to millions of people from coast to coast. And today that dream has come true. This ain't a business, Charlie; it's a monument created by the public to Adolph Rubens' ideals, and we're building all the time."

"Five hundred dollars or I stop building," said Charlie in the same metallic tone.

"Charlie," said Mr. Klingspiel after a moment, "I want you to do something. Come here. Not there—come around this side of the desk." He arose. "Now you sit down in my chair. That's right." He encircled the desk, then turned and faced Charlie. "Now put yourself in my place. You're Eugene Klingspiel, the head of Gargantual Pictures. You got a payroll of three hundred and forty-six thousand dollars a week. You got stars that are draining you dry. Nobody goes to pictures any more, they stay home and listen to the radio. You got a lot of dead-wood writers drawing their check like clockwork every Wednesday. Now, in walks a fella named Charlie Baer. He don't want much, only the shirt off your back. And what do you say to him?" He gripped the edges of the desk and stared into Charlie's face.

"Five hundred dollars or I turn in my badge," droned Charlie. Mr. Klingspiel's eyes glittered. The mongoose sat comfortably and waited for the cobra to strike again.

"Now let's be sensible," said Mr. Klingspiel. "I could buy four gagmen for what I'm paying you." Charles stood up. "But I'll tell you what I'm gonna do. Three hundred——"

"Mr. Klingspiel," said Charlie, "there's something I ought to tell you. Metro——"

"What?" Mr. Klingspiel quivered like a stag.

"Metro offered me four-fifty yesterday."

"So that's it," said Mr. Klingspiel. "That's how much loyalty you got. We pick you up from the gutter—four-twenty-five!"

"Listen," said Charlie coldly, "I'm a scenario-writer, not a peddler." He put on his hat.

"Just a minute," said Mr. Klingspiel. His face cleared suddenly. "I'm gonna teach that Metro crowd a lesson. Beginning the fifteenth Charlie Baer gets five hundred dollars a week from Gargantual—and Eugene Klingspiel *personally* guarantees that! And any time you got any problems I want you to come—— Where you going?"

"Lunch," said Charlie, and smiled briefly. "You know, just a bowl of milk and crackers."

Mr. Klingspiel belched and grabbed for the bicarbonate.

Americana, October 1933

Soft Soap for the Barber

Father Goose: The Story of Mack Sennett, by Gene Fowler. New York: Covici, Friede. 407 pages. $3.

F ROM Shirtsleeves to Shirtsleeves in one generation is just as true an American legend as from Ploughboy to President or from Poland to Polo. Moreover, we, who are without ambition, prefer it.

Mack Sennett went from boilermaker to president of the Keystone Company. The Keystone Company is finished and so is Mack Sennett. This fact should make everyone but Gilbert Seldes feel a little better. Perhaps one day a final chapter will be written to Drinkwater's biography of Carl Laemmle and to Will Irwin's biography of Adolph Zukor. Perhaps they too will go the way of Mack Sennett. Hope springs eternal, etc.

And yet, maybe the men who make the pictures are not to blame. Perhaps we should blame the man for whom the pictures are made—"the barber in Peoria." As Fowler says, "The history of the cinema indicates that a man will pay a dollar to get a dime's worth of entertainment, but will not part with a dime to get a dollar's worth of ideals"—or ideas. Fowler is right. Whenever somebody forgets this fact, forgets to ask what "the barber in Peoria" will think, a great deal of money is lost.

It is strange, but the movies are always trying to forget "the barber." Even Mack Sennett tried *once* to forget him. He lost several hundred thousand dollars, then took another look at the sign hanging on the wall of his scenario department. "Remember: The extent of intelligence of the average public mind is eleven years. Moving pictures should be made accordingly." Sennett never forgot again.

Other Hollywood directors and supervisors never seem to learn this lesson. Every year some one of them gets a little punch-drunk, goes highbrow and forgets "the barber." A picture like "The Crowd" is the result. "The barber" remains in his barbershop and the theatres are empty. It takes two or three films like "Dames" to get him to the Bijoux again.

Of course many things can be said in defense of "the bar-ber." Gene Fowler wisely leaves that to Gilbert Seldes; we prefer to leave it to Mike Gold, and no offense meant.

The New Republic, November 14, 1934

UNPUBLISHED WRITINGS
AND FRAGMENTS

The Impostor

IN ORDER to be an artist one has to live like one." We know now that this is nonsense, but in Paris, in those days, we didn't know it. "Artists are all crazy." This is another statement from the same credo. Of course these ideas and others like them were foisted on us by the non-artist, but we didn't realize it then. We came to the business of being an artist with the definitions of the non-artist and took libels for the truth. In order to be recognized as artists, we were everything our enemies said we were.

"All artists are crazy." Well, one of the easiest things to be is "crazy," that is if you are satisfied with the uninformed layman's definition of craziness. To be really crazy is quite a job. You have to have a great deal of mental and physical control and do a great deal of scientific reading. We didn't have the control or want to do the reading; nor were these things necessary. Tourists and the folks back home, not doctors, were on our jury.

As time went on, being "crazy" became more difficult. The jury gradually changed. Fellow artists began to sit on it. This wasn't quite as bad as doctors would have been, but it was pretty bad. Long hair and a rapt look wouldn't get you to first base anymore. Even dirt, sandals and "nightmindness" wasn't enough. You had to be original.

By the time I got to Montparnasse, the second stage was well advanced. All the more obvious roles had been dropped and the less obvious ones were being played by experts. There were still a few gents with long hair, but no one took them seriously and they were never invited to the important parties. What was I to do? But how was I to make the grade?

After hiding in my hotel for about a week, not daring to show myself at the *Dome* for fear of making a bad impression, I hit on a great idea. I had come to Paris from a runner's job in Wall Street and still had the clothes I had worn there. Instead of buying a strange outfit and trying to cultivate some new idiosyncrasies, I decided to go in the other direction. "Craziness" through the exaggeration of normality was to be my method. In this land of soft shirts, worn open to the navel, and corduroy trousers, I would wear hard collars and carefully pressed suits of formal, stylish cut, and carry clean gloves and a tightly rolled umbrella. I would have precise, elaborate manners and exhibit pronounced horror at the slightest, *public* breach of the conventions.

I was a big success right from the start. When I entered the *Dome*, beer was spilled at many of the tables. More important, I was asked to all the parties.

It was at a party that I first met Beano Walsh. We were attracted to each other immediately because we both realized that the other made him a perfect background. We were the absolute maximum in contrast—you know the rule, black against white surrounded by grey. Even our conversation was entirely different. I talked technically about field trials, the use of the 'scope in rifle shooting and game cycles, while Beano talked lyrically about ancient Egypt, the Elgin marbles and our mother the sea. When I lifted my glass, it was with a cheery " 'Ware all!" Beano's toast was "A dead whale or a stove boat!" or, sometimes, simply "Beauty!"

Beano was a stocky, young man, short but very heavily muscled. He had arms as thick as thighs, a cedar post neck and on his head a great, living fan of red hair that was like some strange, monster sea-urchin in erection. Summer and winter, he caged his hair in a derby. It was worth watching him do it. The struggle was terrific. He always won, but the victories were costly. No matter how strongly built his derby in less than a month the pressure of his hair ruined its shape. The rest of his costume consisted of a basket ball shirt with the insignia of the *Celtic A. C.* on the front, a pair of army, riding trousers, leather puttees and sneakers.

He was supposed to be a sculptor. In those days, if not in these, art critics, like Hollywood directors, insisted on type-casting. As a sculptor, Beano was cast perfectly. One look at his marvelous hands proved that; Rodin might have modeled them.

Oscar Hahn's art-scouts had discovered him on a coal barge in the East River and had arranged for him to be sent to Paris to study. When they discovered him, he hadn't as yet made any sculpture, but according to the standards in vogue then—

based, perhaps, on Cellini's autobiography and Van Gogh's letters—he certainly looked and talked as though he might produce some wonderful stuff.

I had known Beano about a month when I was locked out of my hotel room for not paying the rent. My mother refused to send me any more money. She wanted me to come home and had sent me a return steamship ticket which I was trying to sell. When Beano heard of my troubles, he invited me to move into his studio.

His studio was one of a row of car-barns, back of the *Gare Montparnasse* in a street called the *Impasse Galliard*. It was sixty feet long, forty high and forty wide. Whoever had converted the place into a studio had spent very little money on the job. A skylight had been cut in the domed ceiling and the car tracks had been covered with cheap, pine flooring. That was all. Only our kind of artist would have lived in such a place.

The winter of 25 was a very cold one. Beano had an old, pot-bellied stove that we kept white hot, but of course it couldn't begin to heat that enormous room. It had a hard time taking the chill off the corner in which it stood. The tenant who had lived in the place before Beano had left behind a Belgian girl. She was a gross, blousy creature, shaped like the stove. She gave off a lot of animal heat, but neither of us wanted to go near her. There was still a third heating agent—alcohol. We drank it continuously and so managed to stay alive.

Beano worked, but the girl and I only hugged the stove. She found it too cold in the streets for her profession. I couldn't punch the typewriter without taking off my gloves and I didn't dare take them off. I might have lost a finger. But Beano worked, or, at least, tried to.

I watched him and saw at once that something was wrong. He never finished anything. He spent hours on a head, using sheet after sheet of expensive drawing paper, without making a single sketch that satisfied him. He blocked in the features, then with a sudden curse, he ripped the paper from the board and crumpled it viciously. Ten minutes later, he tacked up another sheet and began again. A few lines this time, and again the curses and the frantic destruction.

I watched this go on for days. It was pathetic. Here was a man who could talk a whole gallery full of art works and who looked like a genius yet couldn't draw worth a damn.

When I asked him why he didn't go to art school, the very idea seemed to make him frantic. He swore at me for five minutes. He was against all schools. He was a genius; the equal of Michael Angelo. He had examined the drawings produced in the schools and they stank. . . . Beano really had a great deal of taste and knew a bad drawing when he saw one. Maybe that's why he never finished any of his own.

One day he came home with a crate of chisels, a dozen mauls and a truck load of marble blocks. He had a new idea. All spontaneity was lost when a sculptor worked from a drawing. He should work directly in stone. He must see the living thing in the stone and strive to chop it free.

Whatever it was he saw in the stone he couldn't chop it free. He stared at a piece of marble for a long time, then suddenly began to hack at it. The chisel always slipped or the marble cracked before he had taken twenty strokes. He then would go berserk and attack the block directly with the maul until he had shattered it or driven it right through the flooring. He certainly could hit a terrific wallop. A little later, he would take a fresh stone and begin again. But the end was always the same.

When he had destroyed the whole carload of marble, he went on a big drunk. I tagged along to keep him out of trouble. One night, although he had a very big load on, he stepped out of character and talked sense. It was the first time he had ever stepped out of character with me. He said that he was worried because one of Mr. Oscar Hahn's scouts intended to visit his studio soon and would want to see what progress he had made. He had nothing to show for the past year, not a single drawing. His scholarship would surely be cancelled. He was a great sculptor all right, but he needed time to develop, to find himself. If they took away his scholarship, he would have to go back to the coal barges.

There was so much pathos and real, quivering fear in his manner that I started to put my arm around his shoulders, but before I could finish the gesture he stepped back into character. He became the old Beano again, the mad genius, a carver of heroes, a stark, earthy elemental force. "Michael Angelo," he roared, as though he were calling a hog of that name on the Kansas prairies. "Michael Angelo . . ."

Then he collapsed. Several of the more friendly waiters helped me get him into a cab. When we arrived at the studio, the Belgian helped me put him to bed. As she said herself, often, it was her *metier*.

The next few days Beano stayed fairly sober, drinking only enough to keep warm. He was busy buying books, anatomy books. When he had accumulated about fifty volumes, he began to study them. Then he set up his board and started to draw once more. He tried to copy the illustrations. He spent almost a week on a drawing which showed how a head is built up in layers from a skull and another week on one which showed the bone, tendons and muscles of an arm. But it was no use. He just couldn't draw worth a damn. I was lucky to be out when he finally had his frenzy. I came home to find the floor littered with pages and big holes in the wall plaster where the books had struck. The Belgian had a black eye. She had stopped a flying book.

A few days later, Beano received a note from Mr. Simonsohn, Mr. Oscar Hahn's agent, saying that he would be in the following month to examine what Beano had produced in the way of art. I was surprised to see that Beano was not as disturbed as he had been. In lieu of work, he told me, he would overwhelm the man with a brilliant idea. After all they had given him the scholarship originally because of an idea and without seeing any work.

I was dozing near the stove one afternoon, when Beano knocked me to the floor with a wallop between the shoulder blades. He stood over me, yelling, "I've got it! I've got it!" "You've got what?" I asked. "The idea!" he bellowed.

Without letting me get up from the floor, he explained the "idea." While he talked, I kept wondering whether Mr. Simonsohn would swallow his nonsense. I knew it wasn't entirely impossible. Beano put so much passion into his exposition and used so many brilliant gestures that he almost convinced me. He would have made a great actor.

Minus the passion and the rest of the fireworks, his "idea" went something like this: He had discovered—or decided—

that all the anatomy books were wrong because they used a man only five feet ten inches tall for their charts. Some used a man even shorter. They should have used a man six feet tall because the perfect, modern man is six feet tall. Since the anatomy of all modern sculpture is based on these books, all modern sculpture is wrong. Merely increasing the charts two inches would not correct the error because a six foot man is not only taller but different. A new anatomy book had to be written, and not until he had written it could he even think of drawing or sculpture.

I thought of a lot of objections but I didn't word any of them. He was in no mood for argument. I hoped Mr. Simonsohn would swallow the "idea," but I didn't worry about it. I had my own troubles. I was very busy trying to swindle my mother out of some money.

During the next few weeks, I saw very little of Beano. He left the car-barn very early in the morning, before I got up, and returned late at night. His clothes began to smell strongly of formaldehyde. Later I found out about the smell. He was spending all his time in the morgue on the lookout for a perfect, six foot man. With a tape and a pair of calipers, he measured all the likely bodies that were brought in. Some influential friends of his had obtained permission for him to buy a corpse.

That winter enormous crowds of Americans used to gather before dinner at the *Dome* every evening for drinks. Although the cafe was very large, it was hard to get a table inside and the late arrivals were forced to sit out on the terrace, huddled over a noxious salamander. The night that Beano found his man, I was sitting there trying to keep warm without being asphyxiated by the coke fumes. With me at the table were three other expatriates, artists all.

While we were sitting there, hawking and cusping over our drinks, a cab pulled into the curb close by us. In it was Beano. He stuck his head out of the window and shouted.

"Eureka!"

"What?" one of us called back.

"Eureka! I've got him!"

"You've got what?"

"The six foot man."

"Come over and have a drink," I said without much enthusiasm.

Beano refused. He had to go home and build an icebox in which to hang the stiff. When no one urged him, however, he changed his mind about the drink and came over to the table. The cab remained at the curb.

We greeted him apathetically. He had been shouting his "idea" at us for weeks and we were sick of it. After all, it is only natural for a man's own poses to interest him more than they do his friends. Our mistake was that we took his madness for the same kind as our own.

Beano showed that he was hurt by our lack of interest. He sulked. In order to cheer him up, I asked where the stiff was.

"Out in the cab," he answered.

"What?"

He laughed happily at our amazement, and went on to explain. About an hour ago, he had been standing near the door of the morgue embalming room when a corpse was wheeled out. It was that of a dead sailor who had been fished from the Seine. The stiff had already been put aside for some medical school, but he insisted on measuring it. When he found that it fitted his requirements perfectly, he persuaded the official in charge to sell it to him. The morgue people wanted to send it to his studio in an ambulance. The cost was too high, so he said he would take it home in a cab. They were horrified, but he kicked up so much fuss that they finally agreed, just to get rid of him. He had them rope its head between its knees to make the bundle compact, then wrap it in heavy paper.

Beano produced a bill of sale and made us all examine it. The document was on the stationery of the city morgue, and covered with tax stamps. Then he invited us out to the cab to see for ourselves. We went. On the back seat lay an enormous bundle wrapped in heavy brown paper. Beano tore a large hole in the paper and we looked through it. I saw a bare, muscular shoulder and part of a sunburned neck. A pale blue color was just beginning to come through the tan.

We returned to our table. We all felt kind of queasy and subdued, but not Beano. He was in great form. He gestured and roared—the "man of the renaissance." He demanded that the waiter bring him a fresh bottle of brandy and a tumbler. He pushed the tumbler aside and drank out of the bottle, wiping his mouth with a gesture that Titian might have envied. He pounded on the table and talked, not to us, but the cafe in general. He made a speech about his new anatomy book and his six foot man. A crowd gathered to listen to him. All those who understood what he was talking about went out to the cab to inspect the stiff. In their eagerness, they tore at the wrapping paper until the body was completely naked.

Suddenly a woman screamed. The sound came from near the cab and I turned to look. I saw a middle-aged lady in a mink coat. She stood on the curb near the cab and swayed as though she were going to faint while from her mouth came a series of short, gasping screams. She sounded a lot like the steam whistle of a factory.

I knew what had happened. Thinking the cab free, she had opened the door and had started to get in.

Two cops came running across the street from the *Select*. The fat lady pointed—she didn't want to stop screaming—to the corpse. When the cops saw it, they got excited and started to argue with each other like a pair of stage Italians. Then Beano turned and saw what was happening. He ran into the street with us after him.

He acknowledged ownership of the stiff and said that the lady who was still screaming was a damned hypocrite who probably knew a lot worse looking and deader men intimately. The cops called him a murderer and a necrophile among other things. They wouldn't look at the bill of sale. He began to get sore. When one of the cops made a grab for him, he hauled off and knocked the man into the gutter.

That was very bad. The other cop got out his whistle and blew it and more cops came running from all sides. They piled all over Beano and soon had him trussed up. One of them went into the cafe to call a patrol wagon. I tried to argue with the sergeant, but he shoved me away.

The police wrapped the stiff in a table cloth and put it into the wagon, then hustled Beano in after it. We could hear him hollering that if they so much as damaged a single hair on the head of his property, he would sue the city, have them broken, have them walking a beat in Passy, etc., etc. We piled into a taxi and followed the wagon to the station house.

When we got there, Beano was standing in front of the bench with a cop on either side of him and the corpse was stretched out on the floor under the table cloth. Behind the bench was a police captain. He wasn't the usual run of police official, but a jovial, smiling little man, smoking a pipe with a silver top. He looked very intelligent and I thought he might give Beano a break. As it turned out, however, Beano would have been a great deal better off if the captain had been stupid.

The sergeant made the charges; they were murder and assaulting and injuring an officer. The captain grinned and said he would hear the more serious charge first, that of injuring a policeman; the murder charge could wait. He laughed at his own joke and looked at us. We smiled back to get in with him, but we all knew it was no joke. As a foreigner, the best Beano could hope for was deportation without a jail sentence. The deportation was certain, and he stood a fine chance of going to jail for a few months into the bargain. There goes his scholarship, I thought; he'll be back on the barges in no time now.

All the cops, there was about ten of them, swore they had witnessed the assault, even the one who had driven the patrol wagon swore to it. Then the captain let Beano talk. His defense was a very lame one, but he didn't seem to know it. He admitted that he had punched the cop, but claimed that he had done it in defense of his lawful possessions. The cop had tried to steal his corpse. He had been only defending his property, an inalienable right respected in all civilized countries. Beano then brought out his bill of sale.

The captain was delighted with Beano's argument. He kept grinning and wiping the top of his bald head. When Beano had finished, he called the morgue and checked the purchase. He dismissed the murder charge, but said that he had to hold Beano for assault. I stepped forward and asked him to set bail. He refused. Beano turned on me and told me to mind my own business. Going to jail didn't seem to bother him in the least. All that worried him was what they were going to do with his stiff.

The magistrate answered that he would have it sent back to the morgue. This made Beano frantic, and he began to plead.

He made a speech. He told the magistrate about his new anatomy book and begged him not to take the stiff away. If he did, the magistrate's name would go down in history as the man who put back the clock of art, the man who frustrated the genius of Beano Walsh.

The magistrate listened to all this with a broad grin on his face. He was very much amused and having one hell of a time. When Beano had finished, he made a speech. First he talked about Lafayette and Pershing, then about how much the French love art. Paris, he said, was the only city in the world where even the cops loved art. He, himself, although only a police magistrate liked nothing better than to stroll through the Louvre. He was a true art-lover. Under no circumstance did he want to risk becoming notorious as the man who had hindered the progress of art. He wound up by saying that Beano would not be separated from his beloved corpse, not for a second, no, he would have it put in the same cell with him.

Beano thanked him and said that he would remember the magistrate all his life because he had acted like a true Frenchman. Then he asked if he could speak to me alone for a few seconds. The magistrate gave him permission.

"For Christ's sake," I whispered to him, "let him send that stiff back to the morgue."

He grinned at me. "No," he said, "listen to me, and do what I say. I'll beat the rap, just you watch, and I'll get that scholarship renewed into the bargain. Call Simonsohn, Mr. Hahn's man, at the Hotel Royale, and tell him what happened. Have him here in the morning. Then get me a large block of drawing paper and have it sent into my cell. I've got pencils."

I tried to argue with him, but it was no use. He just grinned. The last thing he said was "A stove boat, my friend, or a dead whale." When the jailor led him off he winked at me. Two cops put the stiff on a sort of wheelbarrow and trundled it after him.

We said goodbye to the magistrate, who was still laughing, and went outside to a cafe that had a telephone. One of the other guys went to buy drawing paper, while I called up Mr. Simonsohn. I told him that Beano was in jail and explained what had happened. He seemed very cold, but promised to be at the station house with a French lawyer in time for the trial.

When I arrived at the station house, early the next morning, no one was there except a sergeant and the turnkey. I asked to see Beano, but the officer in charge refused to give me permission. The magistrate had left orders that absolutely no one was to go into his cell, not even the police. The officer was called away and I approached the turnkey. I gave him a twenty-five franc note and he was very friendly. He had seen Beano when he went to the cell to give him the drawing paper we had bought, but not since then. After some hesitation, he told me that my friend had made a lot of noise around three o'clock that morning, but that he had not investigated because of the magistrate's orders. The orders were unusual, he admitted, but he guessed that the idea was to give Beano a good scare by making him spend a night in a cell with a corpse.

When the magistrate came in, I had to stop questioning the turnkey. Soon afterwards, a group of our friends arrived, then Mr. Simonsohn came in with a French lawyer. The lawyer was an ex-judge and knew the magistrate well. They went off together to the magistrate's private office. I went over to speak to Mr. Simonsohn. He asked me to explain what had happened. I did my best to make the theory of the six foot man sound as reasonable and as impressive as possible by telling it in Beano's words, but I couldn't get his passion into it. I was worrying about the scholarship. Although I made a hash of it, Mr. Simonsohn seemed impressed and was quite sympathetic. He even sighed with pleasure when I had finished: "Ah, you artists!"

When he started to talk I found out why his manner had changed so much since last night when I had talked to him over the phone. Soon after I called, a squad of reporters had arrived at his hotel and had demanded to know all about Beano and the Oscar Hahn Foundation. As secretary of the Foundation he had been quoted extensively and in some of this morning's papers they had run his picture. He showed me the pictures with a great deal of pride. I realized that Beano had put it over and that he was a cinch for a renewal of the scholarship.

I asked Mr. Simonsohn what the lawyer intended to do about the assault charge. He said that if it couldn't be fixed with the magistrate for a suspended sentence, they would plead temporary insanity and send Beano to the country for a week.

While we talked, the little police court filled with people—reporters, photographers, Americans and the merely curious. The magistrate was very much impressed. When the turnkey left to bring in the prisoner, he permitted Mr. Simonsohn, the lawyer, several reporters and myself to go along. I walked in front of the procession—it was almost a triumphal one—with the turnkey. We moved fast and soon got some distance ahead of the others. The turnkey told me that Beano was in a special cell reserved for drunks and other violent folks that was separated from the main block by a long corridor. When we came in sight of it, I called out, "We're here, Beano!" My idea was to warn him, but when he didn't answer, I again had a premonition that something was wrong. I broke into a run with the turnkey after me.

I got there first and peered through the bars. The cell was full of deep shadow and I couldn't see anything. All I got was a strong whiff of formaldehyde and another smell, an acid, which I didn't recognize. The turnkey opened the door and I popped in ahead of him while he was taking the key out of the lock. I took a quick glance around but didn't see the prisoner. "He's gone," I blurted out. The turnkey took a look and acted fast. He forced back the others, who had just come up, and slammed the door with me inside, then ran to turn in the alarm.

Along one wall of the cell was a wooden bench with a mattress and pillow and on it lay the stiff. He was in terrible condition, broken and torn. One of his arms had been skinned out and the muscles, bone and sinew exposed. A penknife was sticking in his chest and there were great wounds in his belly from which stained wads of cotton protruded. The floor was covered with drawing paper. I picked up a sheet and examined it. I saw that Beano had been trying to draw the skinned arm. It was an anatomical drawing, but very crude. A child might have done better.

Then I spotted Beano. He was under the bench and partially hidden by the legs of the stiff which hung down. He lay
huddled up in one corner with his face to the wall.

"Beano," I hollered at him, "for Christ's sake come out of
there." He didn't move, so I prodded him with my foot.
"That's enough," I said, getting sore. "Snap out of it. You've
beaten the rap and Simonsohn told me he would renew the
scholarship." I pleaded with him, "Please Beano, please." But
he neither moved nor spoke.

When the turnkey and the cops burst into the cell, I pointed
him out to them. They reached under the bench and hauled
him into the middle of the room. His eyes were open and he
was wearing his derby hat, but he couldn't, or wouldn't, stand
on his feet. He didn't say a word. As they dragged him by
me, I thought at the time that he winked but I'm not sure
now.

He beat the rap, all right. They didn't even arraign him on
the charges. And he got the scholarship renewed, too, at least
the Hahn Foundation still supported him.

Mr. Simonsohn sent him to the country and after he had
been there a week I went to visit him. It was a hospital disguised as a model [   ]. I saw the doctor in charge and got
permission to visit him. An orderly showed me to his room.
It was a tiny place, a cell in fact, much like the one in the
station house. Beano was still wearing his derby but the rest
of his clothes had been changed for a bathrobe and carpet
slippers.

"Hello, Beano," I said.

He didn't answer.

I laughed awkwardly. "Cut it out," I said. "You've gotten
everything you wanted. Snap out of it. What the hell more
do you want?"

He gave no sign that he had heard me. I went on talking
but nothing I said seemed to make any impression on him.
He just sat on the bed and stared at me. When I found myself
shouting hysterically at him, I got out and left. I turned back
for a last time, and said, "All right, Beano, if you won't say
anything, at least wink at me." He didn't move.

I went back to see the doctor. I was determined to give the

game away. "He's a fake," I blurted out as soon as I got to the doctor's office. "The whole thing is a swindle. He's not crazy. He's putting it on to fool the police."

The doctor heard me out, and when I had finished, he said quite calmly, "That's what we thought when he arrived. The board of this hospital now feels certain that he is crazy. He's insane and will never leave an asylum again in his life."

I tried to argue.

"Listen," the doctor said, losing patience, "your friend simulated insanity in order to get by as a sane man. The insane are sometimes very clever you know. He's an insane man who knows he's insane. I'm almost certain he must have been in a hospital before. Instead of hiding his disease, which would be the obvious thing to do, he hid only part of it, the more serious part, and used the part he exposed to hide the rest. But he's really crazy, and he went too far with it."

All the way back to Paris in the train, I kept wondering about the doctor and almost came to the conclusion that it was he that was crazy. But he must have been right because Beano is still in an asylum.

Western Union Boy

Iғ you're not very busy, a grown man in the uniform of a Western Union boy should make you feel a little sick. He is a touching sight and unless you've got something else to do you should be touched. I often am.

All Western Union boys do not deliver messages. Some of them are lawyers, writers and so forth. But all of them are busy doing something under their regular occupations, and it is this something that makes them "Western Union boys." What they are doing is failing, mechanically, yet desperately and seriously, they are failing. The mechanical part of it is very important.

"Western Union boys" are eager. They try hard to please. They permit themselves dreams—I have proof. They have adventures. But what they are really always doing is failing. You know it and they know you know it. They even laugh at themselves! Not often, I admit, but the thing is that they do laugh. It is a peculiar sort of laughter. It can be dismissed with something about a breaking heart and a jester's motley, but it shouldn't be. And, anyway, the Kingdom of Heaven is paved with "Western Union boys," at least I hope so.

My favorite "Western Union boy" is F. Winslow. At college he was known simply as F. He was of fair size and not bad looking, but he had very few friends. You instinctively spotted the uniform and avoided him.

He went out for the freshman baseball team, but the coach took one look at him and never even gave him a suit. The coach was superstitious. He was a very good coach.

In his senior year F became famous. It happened this way. F was a grind. He wanted badly to make good and worked like hell to get Phi Beta Kappa. He missed it by a few points in his junior year, but was almost sure to get it as a senior. He worried about the key a great deal and decided to take no chances, so he went into his English 43 exam with a crib sheet in his pocket. The exam was easy and he didn't have to use the crib sheet, but in some way or other he got it mixed in

with his exam paper and he handed the two of them in together.

The dean made an example of him and threw him out of
college before graduation. When the story got out, he was a
campus figure for a few days.

I didn't see F again until he came into my office one day.
I was in the construction business then, and my secretary told
me that there was a man who wanted to see me who refused
to tell his business. I don't know why, but I said show him
in. It was F.

I wasn't very busy and I felt a little sick when I saw him.
We shook hands. He said are you an officer of this company.
It sounded like boasting, but I nodded yes. Then he said, I'm
sorry, Harry, but I have to serve a paper on you. He was really
sorry. I smiled and took the summons. It was an accident case,
and I tried to make him feel better by telling him that we
were completely covered by insurance.

I asked him to sit down. He was heavy with his story—he
had been carrying it for more than the usual nine months—
and I was to deliver him. So . . . I said. The labor pains began
immediately.

It seems—the inevitable beginning—that after busting out
of college he had come to New York and had entered a law
school. He had about a thousand dollars and by working in
the summers he hoped to make it do. During the second se-
mester, he was run over by an automobile that didn't stop.
The hospital took the thousand dollars and the nearest he
could get to the law business—he is a sticker—was serving
papers.

Foolishly, I asked him how he liked his job. I guess I was
nervous or something.

It seems that he did well the first few months and saved
almost enough money to go back to law school. But one day
he had to serve a summons in a tough neighborhood. His
man was a very big guy and very drunk. When F handed him
the paper, he tore it up and threw F down a flight of stairs.
The man went to jail, but F had to go back to the hospital.

I bowed him out of the office.

Well, I didn't see F again for a few years. One day, however, I ran into him in a speakeasy. He was drunk. He came up and put his arm around me—college chums. He looked as though he were going to cry, he was so glad to see me. The old familiar faces sort of thing. Well, how are you, I asked. Well, it seems . . . but I'll spare you.

The booze was doing something to him. He began to analyze himself. I was surprised. Not that "Western Union boys" do not indulge in self-analysis, but they rarely do it well. F was rather good at it.

I am a sun field player, he said; I'm always in right field.

Now this isn't a bad definition of a "Western Union boy." If you have ever played ball, you'll know what he meant. In the big league the right fielder is usually as good as the other fielders, but not in the lots. There he is the last man chosen; no one wants him on his side. A right fielder always has the sun in his eyes; he always gets a bad bounce; it is the short field and he is always running into the fence.

The liquor made F poetic, but I'll try to give you what he said as best I can. It seems that he suffers from nightmares, or rather one recurring nightmare. It is about a ball game he once played in.

He has a cousin who had been captain of baseball at Princeton. Every summer, this cousin, as was usual in those days, organized a semi-pro team to play for some town or other. One season his team was to represent Mineville in the Adirondack League. He gave F a job as right fielder. F showed up pretty good in practice, but then the first game came along. It was Mineville vs. Pottersville on the Pottersville fair grounds. To show that they were real pros, all the players took a chew of tobacco before the game started. F had never chewed before, but he took one too because he was anxious to make good.

The sun was very hot in right field as it always is. What with the heat and the tobacco, F felt like going home. So far he had been lucky; he had gotten to the fifth inning without having a ball hit to him. But in the fifth, with a man on second and third, a pop fly was hit to right field. F didn't move except to swallow the plug of tobacco. The ball hit him in the chest.

He fell to his feet and fumbled for it in the grass, but his eyes were closed and he couldn't find it. The first baseman had to come out and field it for him. When he opened his eyes, he saw his cousin running towards him with a bat in his hands. F ran off the field and hid in the woods behind third base. His cousin thrashed around in the bushes looking for him until the umpire called play ball.

When the game was over, F came out of the woods and went to the bus that was getting ready to take the team back to Mineville. But his cousin picked up a bat and wouldn't let him get near the bus. He had to hitch hike back in his spiked shoes. That night he packed up and went home.

F still dreams of that fifth inning and of his cousin with the bat. He has this dream regularly about once a week.

If I remember correctly, he was very drunk when he finished telling me about it and he tried to tell me that the story was symbolic. His cousin represents Life, the ball is Fate, and the bus I think he calls The Traction Interests or maybe it is The Public Weal.

Mr. Potts of Pottstown

POTTSTOWN is a sleepy, sun-drenched village on the Whip-sauki River in southern Tennessee. Mr. Potts was the town's principal citizen and owner of the Potts Pot Works, makers of cooking utensils.

He lived in a plantation on the edge of the town and in the shadow of his factory. His house, from the outside, was the ordinary, dilapidated mansion of the 'befo de woh' type; but inside it was something else. It was the abode of a fearful and fearless man—a soldier, hunter and explorer, no less.

The walls of the parlor were covered from top to bottom with firearms and steel blades; all the weapons of all the countries in the wide world—carbines, rifles, shotguns, blunderbusses, swords, daggers, bayonets, Malay krisses. In one corner, even, there stood a small cannon. Everything in the place was polished and labelled, as in a museum, with obliging little cards reading: "Poisoned Arrows! Do not touch!" or, "Loaded! Take care, please!"

In the middle of this room was a table on which stood a jug of corn liquor and a litter of books—stories of hunting the bear, the lion, the eagle, the tiger and so on. Beside the table sat a man around forty, very stout and ruddy, wearing Simon Legree's wide black planter's hat. In one hand he held a book and in the other a Sharpe's buffalo rifle. While he read God knows what fearful tale of bloodshed and heroic deeds, his honest kindly face was twisted in a bad imitation of ferociousness.

This man was Potts himself, the Potts of Pottstown, the great, the dreadnought, the incomparable Potts of Pottstown; expert with all weapons and afraid of no man.

Afraid of no man, yes, but of one woman, alas, not a little. That woman was Nancy Larkin, his housekeeper. When Potts heard her in the hall, his feet came down off the table with a bang, he hid the jug and hung up the rifle. Nancy's tongue was her weapon, and against it his whole armory was of no avail. He, too, had a gifted tongue and was fluent, but while he laid down a rhetorical barrage, Nancy would pierce him with her dagger tongue. He dreaded these encounters.

The truth is, however, these two were very fond of each other despite their great differences of character and aspect. The lanky, sharp, practical Nancy coddled the heroic dreamer Potts and kept him out of trouble. Potts, alas, like many great men of action was susceptible to colds in the head and Nancy protected him from draughts. Potts, also, while he talked of pemmican and bear steak liked very much to eat things like fried chicken, black-eyed peas, hoe cake, mustard greens and chitterlings. Nancy was a great Southern cook in the old style.

From this it might seem that Potts was only a blowhard, a fireside adventurer. But that was not entirely true. The truth is that two entirely different men occupied his stout body. At one and the same time, he was Quixote-Potts and Sancho-Potts. Quixote-Potts shouted "Up and at 'em" while Sancho-Potts, thinking of his frequent colds, murmured, "Stay home, my friend."

The duet went something like this:

Quixote-Potts	*Sancho-Potts*
(highly excited)	(quite calmly)
Cover yourself with glory, Potts.	Potts, cover yourself with flannel.
(Still more excited)	(Still more calmly)
O for the terrible double-barrelled rifle! O for bowie-knives, lassoes and moccasins!	O for knitted waistcoats! O for the welcome padded caps with ear-flaps!
(Above all self-control)	(Ringing for Nancy)
A battle-axe! fetch me a battle-axe!	Now, then, do bring me a bowl of chicken broth and shut that window.

Whereupon Nancy would appear with the bowl of steaming soup. She would set it before him, then shut the window. Thus it came about that Potts of Pottstown never had left Pottstown, and, seemingly, never would, despite his great love of adventure.

2

Pottstown was a town of sportsmen. All its citizens were shooting mad, from the greatest to the least. Potts, our hero, was president of the Hunt Club and had much to do with the enthusiasm of the inhabitants. He it was who led them into the field and laid down the rules of the chase.

Every Sunday morning the male half of Pottstown flew to arms, let loose its hounds and bird-dogs and rushed into the fields and woods, with game-bag and rifle or fowling-piece on shoulder. From every side, rang the yelp of dogs, the blowing of horns and whistles and the cracking of whips. In equipment, at least, and in costume, these hunters were second to none.

But, unfortunately, there was a lack of game in the neighborhood, an absolute dearth. For five miles around Pottstown, forms, lairs, burrows were empty and nesting places abandoned. Nothing covered with fur, hair or feathers, absolutely nothing, was to be found.

This sad fact did not bother the members of the Pottstown Hunt as much as it would have less resourceful men. The country was beautiful, if empty, and their wives, whom they had left behind, were not beautiful. Moreover, their game bags were stuffed with food and corn liquor. The huntsmen gathered together under a large tree and spent the day eating enormously, drinking copiously and listening to Potts tell of hairbreadth escapes from the fangs of wolves and the talons of bears. Then, drunkenly, they helped each other stand, called their dogs and started home, singing such songs as "Frankie and Johnnie," and "The Eagles, They Fly High."

Although their wives complained and called Potts an old fool and a fake, they did not complain too bitterly about these Sunday excursions. After all, they reasoned, it is better for the men to get drunk in the open air than in some foul saloon where they might be exposed to the wiles of a painted hussy. They didn't object to the Sunday hunt, but they did very much to the Thursday night meetings of the club. If it wasn't for these meetings, Potts would not have had to go to Switzerland.

The Pottstown Hunt met in Potts' parlor, among other reasons because he was the only bachelor. Because of the women's objections, many a man had to sneak out of his house to get to it, but only rarely was one of the members absent. Everyone came. Mr. Bascom the druggist, Doc Margate, Mr. Ridley the hardware merchant, Mr. Soames the lumber dealer, everyone. The meetings were much like the hunts. The members drank and ate a great deal, listened to Potts' stories, sang songs and played cards. Under the influence of Potts, the weapons on the walls and the fiery corn, these meek and mild merchants became a tough, wild gang, but they broke up quietly enough when Nancy, the housekeeper, gave the order.

Only one member of the club, Mr. Sayles, the town lawyer, was unhappy and disgruntled. This Mr. Sayles was a teetotaler and had a bad liver which prevented him from enjoying his food. Then, too, firearms made him nervous. But, more than anything else, he was jealous of Potts' leadership and authority in matters of venery.

This lean, embittered creature did not have the courage to challenge the great Potts in the open, nor yet could he stay away from the meetings. He attended all of them, drank milk, jumped when a gun went off and refused to gamble or sing. Worse, he carped at and doubted the stories Potts told. He was a thorn in the side of that great man.

Lawyer Sayles plotted the downfall of his honest, generous, stout rival. No one in the club would aid him so he turned to the women of the town for help. He described the orgies that went on in Potts' house and had them up in arms. They forbid their husbands to attend, dragged them to church on Sunday and locked them in on Thursday night.

Potts was heartbroken. He tried to rally the members to fight against this tyranny, but without success. Even his crony, Jeb Hawks the town printer and publisher, was unable to get out on Thursday night. Potts was desolate.

He was to be still more desolate. One night, Jeb Hawks came to his house, bringing news. Lawyer Sayles had formed a new club, an alpine club, the Pottstown Mountaineers. All the men of the Hunt Club were joining it because their wives said that if they wanted a club it had to be the new one. The club was to meet in Sayles' house and Sayles was to be president.

Potts hid his chagrin under a hearty laugh. There were no mountains near Pottstown. Yes, Jeb said, but the women claimed that there was no game either.

The next Sunday, the great Potts peered from behind the curtains of his parlor while the new club went past. Instead of hunting clothes, they wore mountain climbing costumes, instead of guns they carried alpenstocks, instead of game-bags they had stuffed rucksacks. Lawyer Sayles marched proudly in front, and near the Potts residence had the temerity to yodel. Potts grabbed up a rifle and drew a bead on his perfidious rival, but thought better of it and put the gun down. He was miserable.

Nancy hated to see him suffer and asked him why he did not join the new club. He laughed bitterly at this, but then reconsidered. He sent a telegram to Abercrombie and Fitch ordering a complete climbing outfit in the latest mode down to ice glasses and spiked shoes. From a bookstore, he ordered a library of mountain climbing books. In a few days, he knew everything there was to know about that sport. He could talk glibly to Nancy of crevasses, avalanches, *couloirs*, etc. He was ready to attend the next meeting of the Pottstown Mountaineers.

Alas for Potts' hopes, however. He was not to regain his lost leadership so easily. When he stalked into the room, dressed in his new outfit, with a strong rope around his middle and a cock feather in his hat, his erstwhile admirers burst out laughing. When he tried to tell them about the last British attempt to climb Nagana-Pat in Tibet, they just hooted at him. Lawyer Sayles' cackle irritated him more than anything else. Quixote-Potts almost brained Sayles with an ice axe, but Sancho-Potts let the weapon fall from his hand. He stalked out of the place with as much dignity as he could manage.

Such is the way of the world. In this manner are great men often treated by those who were once glad to fawn on them. It was in this vein that Potts talked to his faithful friend Jeb, who had followed him out of the meeting. But Philosophy could never console a man of action like Potts. He would show those fools. "An eagle does not hunt flies," he thundered. "I will show them that Potts is still Potts. Let them play at mountain climbing. I will climb mountains. Tomorrow, I leave for the Alps."

Jeb did not try to dissuade his rash friend. He felt sure that Potts would not go. But he was wrong. Sancho-Potts was almost obliterated by the chagrin and anguish of Quixote-Potts.

The great Potts went home and drank a great deal of corn liquor. By the time the sun rose, he was sufficiently fortified for the trip. But he had to sneak out without wakening Nancy. She would not let him go. He carried his shoes in his hands as he passed the door of her bedroom. Accidentally(?) he dropped them with a great clatter. But she did not call out. His last hope was gone. The die was cast. Go he must. He took another long pull at the jug, then dressed in his mountain climbing outfit, carrying rope, ice axe and alpenstock, he left Pottstown before anyone was awake.

3

Switzerland—The Palace-Ritz Hotel

When the Swiss train pulled into the station, a formidable personage moved down the aisle, an Alpinist weighed down with ropes, folding tent, axes, etc. He stabbed people with his alpenstock, cut the toes of their shoes with his climbing spikes, harpooned others with the handle of his ice-pick. His passage, as it had been everywhere he went, was marked by yelps of astonishment, curses, elbowing, screams of pain and angry looks.

But the traveller had eyes only for the mountain that loomed up in back of the station. Ignoring the excited crowds of porters and hotel runners, who tried to relieve him of his tent and paraphernalia, he made a bee-line for the mountain. It was to be his first ascent.

He went through an orchard, climbed a few fences, was chased by a dog, stampeded some dairy cows, and finally reached the slope. The last human he saw was an old woman hanging up some washing. When she had taken a long look at him, she burst into laughter; the sight of Potts of Pottstown and his equipment made her almost die with mirth.

"All foreigners are crazy." With this consoling observation, Potts continued his ardous ascent.

Soon there were no more paths, no more trees nor pastures. It began to snow. Take care of your eyes! Immediately he drew his glasses from their case and adjusted the great goggles firmly. The moment was a solemn one. He had reached the snow-line!

He advanced with great precaution, thinking of the crevasses and avalanches of which he had read. Night would surprise him on the mountain. With super-human effort, using rope and alpenstock, he mounted a small rock to get a better view. Eureka! In the distance he saw lights. Was it the hut of some lone mountaineer? He made for it.

Mr. Potts did not know it, but if he had wandered just a few paces to the right of his course, he would have come to a broad highway over which many cars were streaming up the mountain. Or, if he had wandered to the left, he would have come across a busy street car track that also took passengers up the mountain. In fact, the light he had spied came, not from a lonely hut, but from the many windows of the elaborate Palace-Ritz Hotel.

O Baedeker! O Cooks Tour!

Idle tourists with their noses flattened against the hotel windows watched with wonder his approach. The porters, bell boys, doormen, room clerks and assistant managers also watched with wonder. Nothing like this had ever before been seen on the lawn of the Palace-Ritz.

For a moment, Mr. Potts of Pottstown gazed at the many-storied hotel and its uniformed attendants, its glass galleries and colonnades and red velvet carpet. But however greatly surprised he was, the guests seemed much more so; and when he entered the magnificent lobby, a curious, gaping, pushing crowd filled the place; gentlemen in evening clothes, holding billiard cues or books, ladies with lorgnettes, others with children; while the heads of maids and footmen protruded over the banisters. Dogs barked; children wailed.

Mr. Potts was not perturbed. He was used to creating a sensation wherever he went and took it as a tribute. He threw the snow off his head and back with a grandiloquent gesture and spoke to the company in general.

"Phew, what weather! Fit for neither man nor beast!"

When no one moved, he thundered again:

"A room! A room for the weary wayfarer!"

The timid manager approached warily and guided Mr. Potts to the register. After Potts had signed, the manager started to bow him to the lift. But not for Potts. No elevators for him.

"An elevator! An elevator for Potts, the climber!" His exclamations and the fearful gestures with which he accompanied them, caused his paraphernalia to rattle like a junk wagon. "Never! Up and at 'em!"

He made for the stairs.

4

The hotel was full of guests, but they were a very stiff, formal bunch—cold noodles all. There was Astier-Rhehu of the French Academy; the Baron de Stoltz, an old Austrian diplomat; Lord Chippendale, a member of the Jockey Club and Parliament; Professor Schwanthaler of Bonn University and others of like caliber: dead, dull and dry. In the dining room, they ate sparingly and coldly, speaking only to the waiters and to them only in whispers. It was funereal.

When Potts had washed and had rid himself of his climbing tools, he burst into the dining room with a cheery, "Howdy, folks! 'Evening all!" Necks were craned, but their owners soon turned back to their food with a grimace of distaste. They were shocked by what they thought was vulgarity, but what was really vitality.

There were only a few vacant chairs. The head waiter tried to lead Potts to one between two old crones, but he had spotted a vacant place next to a very pretty girl and he made for it.

While eating, he tried to strike up a conversation but his neighbors refused to utter a word. The pretty girl at his left only smiled into her napkin. At his right was an Italian, a handsome young fellow, who twisted his mustaches with indignation. This young man was sore because Potts had gotten between himself and the girl.

Potts announced that he was from Pottstown, but no one was interested. No one even asked where Pottstown was. He was almost miserable. The pretty girl took pity on him. She told him that she was from Bulgaria and that her name was Sonia Maniloff. She was staying in the hotel with her sick brother and some friends from home.

Potts asked her about the wolf hunting in her country; he had heard that it was good. She didn't know anything about hunting, but asked him if he was a sportsman, and what he hunted. He told her about the grizzlies in the Rockies and the alligators in the swamps of Florida. He talked not alone to her but to the whole table, the whole dining room in fact. No one, however, commented. They got up and left while he was still talking and left him to wrestle alone with the French menu. Even the pretty Sonia Maniloff, she had told him her name, on the arm of a bearded Bulgarian with the young Italian dancing after her. It was impossible for him to get any fried chicken and corn bread although he offered a fabulous sum. He thought of Nancy.

In the *salon* of the Palace-Ritz, the guests sat around in frozen silence. They sat in groups, even on isolated chairs, bored stiff. It was like a morgue. The entrance of Potts the Alpinist did not wake them, and he crept into a chair, overcome, for once, by the glacial atmosphere and the icy formality.

But not for long was he overwhelmed. Some musicians came in and began to play. At the very first notes, Potts jumped to his feet as if galvanized.

"That's the stuff," he shouted. "Get hot, boys."

Then he went into action. He treated the musicians to champagne, imitated the cornet, imitated the drums, snapped his fingers, rolled his eyes, cut a few capers, all to the profound astonishment of the other guests who came rushing into the *salon* from all sides. Suddenly, as the musicians attacked the tune with the fury of gypsies, Potts sprang across the floor and caught Sonia in his arms and whirled around in a frenzied gallop.

The impetus was given; the entire hotel, thawed and tumultuous now, was carried away by it. Everyone began to dance round and round. It was that devil of a fellow Potts who had set them going. Resistance was impossible. This terrible Alpinist was like the whirlwind. The madness quickly spread. The musicians went crazy, and the staid guests likewise. Everyone danced. Professor Schwanthaler, Monsieur Astier-Rhehu, Baron de Stoltz, even the ancient Lord Chippendale spun giddily.

Sonia soon tired and Potts led her to a corner of the room. They were talking animatedly about Tennessee, when a group of Bulgarians descended on them in a body and carried Sonia off. For some reason or other, they acted, did these bearded giants, as though they were very suspicious of him. Potts did not know it, but the jealous Italian had been whispering to them about him and making unkind gestures.

Potts started off to bed, with a farewell glance at the spinning, jigging guests, but then remembered that he had failed to say good night to the beautiful Sonia. He found her with the bearded Bulgarians and the young Italian.

"You are a hunter," said one of the Bulgarians, a truly ferocious fellow. He was not laughing.

"I am," said Potts.

"And what do you hunt?"

"The large carnivore and the great deer. I . . ."

The Bulgarian cut him short. "And do you find any of them in Switzerland?"

Potts turned to Sonia and bowed gallantly. "Only gazelles," he said with a smile, but a pleasant one.

Sonia's whole manner towards him had changed. "You are engaged in a dangerous pursuit," she said sternly. "Take care that you do not lose your life."

Potts was stupefied. He did not know what to make of it. Who did they mistake him for?

He went to his room full of wonder, and not a little trepidation.

5

The next morning, when Potts was preparing to go downstairs to breakfast, he found a note under his door with the following words on it:

"Spy, we see through your ridiculous disguise. We have spared you this time, but if you follow us, beware!"

Potts smiled, but wryly. Could it be that that villain, Lawyer Sayles was trying to turn him aside by threats because he was afraid of what they would say in Pottstown when they had heard that he had climbed the Jungfrau.

He was still puzzling over the note, when the breakfast bell sounded. Food drove all other thoughts out of his head and he hurried down to the dining room. When he took his place at the table, he was surprised to see that neither Sonia or her Bulgarian friends were there. In their places sat an English family. While he was asking the waiter where the Bulgarians were the young Italian came up. He, too, was surprised to hear that Sonia had left. He swore in Italian and ran out of the dining room in a big hurry. Potts sighed, but didn't get up, and busied himself in a futile attempt to get hot cakes and sausage. He had to be satisfied with oatmeal. Again he sighed for Nancy.

There was no train leaving for the Jungfrau until the next day, so he decided to go on an excursion to the birthplace of William Tell. If he couldn't be Potts of Pottstown, there was no hero he would rather be than William Tell.

In the bus were the well known, frozen faces of Astier-Rhehu, Professor Schwanthaler, Lord Chippendale and the aged Baron de Stoltz. They too were going on the excursion to the birthplace of William Tell, and with them was their wives.

The bus stopped in front of a little town hall and the party entered. A painter on a tall ladder was busy doing a mural, representing the principal episodes in the life of William Tell. He was working on a picture of the shooting of the apple. One model, a young boy, stood posing with an apple on his head, while an older man with a long beard posed as Tell himself with the crossbow.

"I call that most characteristic," said the pontifical Astier-Rhehu.

And Professor Schwanthaler, a camp stool under his arm, announced, "Superb! Magnificent!"

The ladies marveled in turn, while the painter bowed from his ladder—"Shön! Ach, shön!" and "Equis! Delicieux!"

Suddenly a voice rang out like a trumpet blast.

"Ridiculous!"

It was Mr. Potts of Pottstown, a little the worse for liquor, and everyone turned to stare at him. The mural painter almost tumbled from his ladder.

"That man does not know how to hold a crossbow," said Potts the expert, gratified by the disturbance he had made. "And I know what I am talking about."

"Who are you?" asked the artist.

"Who am I," exclaimed Potts, a little puzzled, perhaps for the moment he had forgotten. "Go and ask my name of the panthers of Arizona, ask the bears of Nebraska. *They* perhaps will inform you!"

There was a simultaneous recoil, a general alarm, at these words.

"But," asked the model with the beard, "in what way am I wrong?"

Potts snatched the crossbow from the man. "Look at me— you!" he thundered. He put the crossbow to his shoulder and fell into the proper heroic position.

"Splendid," exclaimed the artist. "He is right. Don't stir."

Feverishly he began to paint Potts as he stood there, a dumpy, round-backed man, wrapped in a muffler to the chin and fixing the terrified tourists with his flaming eye.

"William Tell to the T," said the artist.

"Really!" said Potts. "You see the resemblance, then?"

Potts preened himself and the crossbow began to go off. Something began to unwind near his chin and make a noise; the weapon came alive in his hands. It had turned into an infernal machine and was preparing to shoot with God knows what dreadful results. Potts didn't know what to do. He was afraid to move. It looked as though the bolt would surely shatter either the skull or the apple on the top of the skull of the boy model. The tourists clung to each other panicstricken.

The painter dove from his ladder in the nick of time. A magnificent flying tackle! He brought Potts to the floor with a crash. The crossbolt went into the ceiling with a thud.

Pandemonium reigned. The ladies screamed and fainted; the gentlemen swore.

The two models jumped to the aid of the painter. They

picked up the groaning Potts and threw him out the door where he landed in a snow bank. He lay quietly for a few seconds, but he was not dead. One of his hands began to move and soon produced a bottle from one of the pockets of his Norfolk jacket. He sneezed and took several long drinks, then got to his feet and staggered to a bench.

From somewhere nearby a man began to yodel. Potts listened with annoyance. He looked for a rock to throw, but couldn't find one. Suddenly, he realized that the tune was a familiar one. Yes, by God, as sure as God made little green apples, the tune was "Oh, the Eagles, They Fly High in Mobile." There was no mistaking it.

Potts went eagerly to investigate. He saw a young fellow in the picturesque costume of a Swiss peasant, surrounded by picturesque goats and yodeling at the top of his voice. The fellow couldn't possibly be an American. Potts was about to turn away, when the yodeler saw him.

"Mr. Potts, suh," he called out, "is it you, suh?"

There could be no mistaking that accent, the man, whoever he was, didn't come from far North of Pottstown.

"It's me, Jimmy Larkin," the Swiss peasant went on. With these words, he removed the large, luxuriant mustache he was wearing.

"Sure enough," exclaimed Potts. "But what the devil are you doing here, Jimmy?"

"I'm local color; I'm atmosphere. I work for the company."

"Herding goats?"

"Oh, these goats are props, too; local color. The company owns them. . . . But how is Aunt Nancy?"

"You shiftless pole-cat! What do you mean, running off from home . . ." Mr. Potts' guilty conscience stopped him and he changed the subject. "What is this company you're telling me about? Are you an actor?"

"In a way, and all Switzerland is my stage."

Jimmy explained to the amazed Potts.

"Switzerland," he said, "is nothing but a fake, an amusement park owned by a very wealthy company. The whole show is put on for the tourist trade—lakes, forests, glaciers, yodelers, peasants, goats, milkmaids, mountains and the rest of it. It's all scenery."

"I suspected as much," said Potts.

"It's like the opera," went on Jimmy.

"The mountains, too, eh?" asked Potts, beginning to regain the confidence he had lost during the William Tell episode. "But how about the avalanches and crevasses?"

"All fake," said Jimmy airily. "If you tumble into a crevasse you fall on soft snow, and there is a Porter at the bottom of every one of them to brush your clothes and ask for your baggage."

"My," said Potts.

"Yes, suh, the keeping up of the crevasses is one of the Company's biggest expenses."

"Well, but how do you explain those accidents—that on the Matterhorn, when a party was buried with their guides."

"Just bait for the Alpine Clubs. To keep them coming. The Matterhorn was going down as an attraction; but after the accident the receipts went up immediately."

"But how about the people who were lost?"

"The Company hid them for six months. It was a big expense; but they got it back in new business."

"Well, well," said Potts, gleefully. "I'm off to climb the Jungfrau tomorrow."

"Certainly," said Jimmy; "the Company'll take care of you. I've been up it twenty times myself."

"Suppose I get dizzy."

"Just shut your eyes."

"If I slip?"

"Let yourself slip. It's like the theatre. You run no risk."

6

Potts, accompanied by Nancy's neer-do-well nephew, Jimmy, was on his way to the Jungfrau. The two of them were riding comfortably in a compartment of an express train. Potts was surrounded by his Alpine equipment. They were eating and drinking heartily, and enjoying the different frauds they were able to point out to each other in the Swiss landscape.

Suddenly, Potts remembered the threatening note he had received and took it out of his pocket.

"Talking of frauds," he said, "here's a joke your company played on me." He handed over the note.

A puzzled frown appeared on Jimmy's face. "The company never sent that," he said.

"No?"

"No. It wouldn't be good business." Jimmy thought hard. "Tell me, Mr. Potts, did anyone speak to you at the hotel?"

"They weren't a very sociable bunch, kind of fish-like if you ask me, but there was some Bulgarians who . . ."

"Ah, Bulgarians," said Jimmy wisely.

"One was a very pretty girl, called Sonia Maniloff."

"Sonia Maniloff," exclaimed Jimmy, hitting the ceiling. "Phew . . . The notorious Red Sonia!"

"Why, she had black hair and beautiful . . ."

"Mr. Potts, say no more. Do you know who those Bulgarians are?"

"Just Bulgarians, I suppose . . ."

"Well, Red Sonia is the woman who shot General Feliannine through the heart at the opera. They're anarchists."

"That child an assassin! You're drunk."

Jimmy gave him the horrid details.

"Sonia and the three bearded men, her friends, are a notorious group of dynamiters and regicides. The leader is a guy named Bobiline, who only last year blew up the Winter Palace of the King of Bulgaria."

"My . . ."

Jimmy didn't let him finish. "They're the ones who sent you the note."

"Me," said Potts with a shudder. "Why me?"

"They think you're a spy."

"A spy! . . ."

"Yes," said Jimmy with smug certainty. "You. They're followed by detectives where ever they go and they thought you were one because of your disguise."

"My disguise. What disguise?"

"Your Alpine costume and snow glasses."

Potts thought a moment. "I know who the spy is," he said. "It's that Italian that was following them around. I have to warn poor Sonia."

"Don't go near them. They'll kill you on sight."

"Bah," said Potts, taking a pistol out of his pocket. "The first one that tries to harm me gets this."

"No," said Jimmy sadly. "They'll poison you, or blow you up. They're clever; they work in the dark."

Potts put his gun away with a shaking hand. "What'll I do?"

"Go home," said Jimmy.

"Never, I couldn't face the club."

"Well, then go straight to the Jungfrau, climb it and then take the first boat back to Pottstown."

7

The Adventurer

THE TITLE is of course comic. How else since I am the adventurer. But there's some truth in it. Once I was a colonist bound for a faraway island in the South Pacific. Once I lived with a beautiful girl, robbed for her and fought over her. Once I cooked my food on a deserted beach over a driftwood fire in the bay of San Miguel Torres while the trim Swallow, a fifty foot ketch, rode serenely at anchor close by.

Out of little scraps a life, a character. Buttons, string, bits of leather, a great deal of soiled paper, a few shouts, a way of clasping the hands, of going up steps, of smoothing a lapel, some prejudices, a reoccurring dream, a distaste for bananas, a few key words repeated endlessly. With time the neck thickens, a vein appears on the edge of the forehead, a few grey hairs, some fat accumulates and innumerable scars. More buttons, more string, more soiled paper, a few more gestures appear and a few more prejudices, figs are added to bananas and the number of key words increases. Memories pile up, hindering action, covering everything, making everything second-hand, rubbed, frayed, soiled. The gestures and the prejudices, the dislikes, all become one and that one not itself but once removed, a dull echo. The trail becomes hard to follow, not grown over, but circular, winding back into itself, without direction, without goal. Moving not in space, but only in time. The neck grows still thicker, another vein swells, more fat, the scars lose even the memory of the original wound. It is only later. Never further, never nearer.

But did you struggle? Were you heroic?

Only once, and then out of innocence. I have always taken the comic view except for that one time on the beach at San Miguel Torres.

The comic view, quietly. No derision. No farce. No laughter.

I wanted something else. I had a reoccurring dream.

A meadow. A meadow with small white flowers and a few blue ones and a few yellow. An acre of sweet grass, all straight and stiff like tiny swords, with here and there a taller clump tufted with seed pods. The meadow at the edge of a quiet wood. And a house nearby, and someone to love. I almost forgot the deer. There must be deer, too. But above all dignity.

My father was an extremely undignified man. He was a janitor in an old apartment house on Lexington Avenue in New York City. Being a janitor was of course a tremendous handicap. He was completely without grace or calm.

He was tall and skinny and moved in jerks. He wore overalls with all the store and manufacturer's tags still on them and a stained derby hat. Although his salary was almost enough, he spent a great deal of time picking over the rubbish sent down in the dumbwaiters. There might be one or two chocolates in a discarded candy box. He would put them aside for me, pointing out that they were untouched, in perfect condition. I was ashamed and wouldn't eat them. However, I always took them and threw them away when he wasn't looking because I knew he would be hurt. I didn't want to make him more ashamed than he already was.

But he didn't pick over the refuse to find something to eat. What he searched for were momentoes of pleasure. Fans, perfume bottles, an embroidered slipper, a gilt dance card, theatre programs, elaborate menus, things of that sort. He collected them in barrels. When he died, he had almost filled the fifth barrel with his collection. Once put away, I never saw him look at them again, but when making a discovery, he would fondle it and grunt over it.

Did he imagine the owner of this or that fan flirting with him? Did he back up the vague scent still left in an old bottle with a mental picture of a beautiful woman at her toilet? I doubt it. He was far too humble. His emotions were much more generalized. These things were symbols of pleasure, impersonal, abstract, in some strange, perverted way, pure.

And now, twenty years later, I am a great deal like him. I do my picking over in the library, the concert hall and the art gallery. I fill no barrels, but have collected a few records, a few books and a few reproductions of famous paintings.

I wear a derby hat in the winter (my father wore his in the

summer as well) and a neat blue suit with all the tags carefully removed. I am an order clerk in a wholesale grocery house.

"Two hundred cases of Rosedale Superb Peas, one hundred ditto of Rosedale A. I. Superb peas."

"Good morning, Mr. Pearce."

"Good morning, Joe."

"Nice day, Miss Reily."

"Good morning, Mr. Rucker."

I am Joe Rucker. Even Mr. Pearce and Miss Reily have more dignity. They are less nervous and don't fight so bitterly for respect.

In the subway I read Aristotle's "Ars Poetica," in translation of course, or Gibbon's "Decline and Fall of the Roman Empire," hoping that people will notice the title and realize that they have to do with a superior man, a college man or even a professor of some sort. Could anything be more humble or undignified? Or unreal? Or soiled and second-hand?

Twenty years ago, when I was seventeen, it was very different. The gesture was almost the same, but bright and clean and new. I always had a book under my arm then, too, but my ears were full of the clang of brass and the snap of silk banners in a stiff breeze. Even the smells were different. Acrid and sharp and hot.

Then, as now, I spent a great deal of time in the public libraries, but the debris had only started to pile up. I had yet to cover the bottom of my first barrel. The scars were only scabs then. No, they were open wounds still.

I lived in a cellar, but as a conspirator. Something lurked around the corner behind the coal bin. Any minute it would happen. I dodged down the damp stone corridors, slipped past the rows of ash cans to the sanctuary of my little cell under the sidewalk. It was lit by a window in the ceiling that had glass six inches thick to support the people walking above it. The light that came through even when the sun shone directly on it was pale green and full of silver motes like that at the bottom of the sea. I got rid of my messenger boy's uniform as fast as I could. It wasn't degrading or ridiculous. It was a disguise I wore to fool my enemies.

In those days I fooled them completely. Today they have found me out. A skinny clerk with cultural pretensions, living in a small room in a walkup in Brooklyn, surrounded by books on how to think. A little queer. He says he likes serious music and pictures. A secret drunkard, arguing with strangers about life, boring even the whores.

Still playing games of course. Or rather, after drinking a few beers too many or listening to Eroica, fighting a disastrous rear-guard action.

Take the fortysecond street branch of the Public Library. When I was seventeen and lived in my father's cellar it was a continuous delight. A storehouse of high adventure. Far places. Trackless deserts. Picturesque uniforms. Austere codes. Walled cities to be stormed. Ferocious natives to be outwitted. Heaving decks on which to swing a cutlass. All for a cause— science, sometimes, or comradeship, or country, or fortune, or revenge, or even simply a gallant gesture.

Now the library to me is a monstrous place. I have become one of those poor people who farm books. One of that twitching crowd that searches old issues of the medical journals for pornography and facts about strange diseases; or one of the furtive cartoonists without talent who exhume jokes from old magazines and try to resell them; or one of the employees of an insurance company gathering statistics on death; or a contest enterer working out some involved puzzle in order to win an automobile or ten thousand dollars. One of a shabby, busy, innumerable horde. Again my father and his ash barrels.

Or take the philosophy reading room where I usually hang out these days. It is full of alchemists, astrologers, cabalists, demonologists, magicians, atheists and the founders of new religious systems.

I find it hard to sit there surrounded by these monomanias, these reflections of myself, and yet I do, night after night. Habit is stronger than fear. Decay is a fine narcotic, warm and reassuring.

I hide among the books, burrowing under them, stuffing my eyes, ears and mouth with them. Only at home, at night, am I amazed at the bandage. A hundred million words, one after another, put down at great expense, at the cost of much suffering, gathered in ten thousand deliriums.

The apocalypse of the Second Hand!

My father's barrels multiplied by ten million!

Sometimes it seems to me that I can smell the books. They have a terrible odor. They smell like the breaths of their readers. They smell like a closet full of old shoes through which a steam pipe passes. The smell of decay and death.

I have often thought of burning the library down. But it would take an acetylene torch of tremendous power to even char it. Besides the gesture would be misunderstood. Hitler did it first. I don't mean what he means. I mean something entirely different of course.

The meadow again and the quiet wood. So gay, so fresh, so full of light and grace. The books were once like that, too, some grave as swans, some bright and clean and new as a mountain brook.

After my kind of fire, the young grass pushes through the black ash and the deer come to browse in the early morning. It is very still. A buck tosses his horns as though they were garlanded with tiny crystal bells. The does move out of the quiet wood and lower their heads sedately to crop. A leaf whirls by and a fawn shys at it, then dances with mock fright, bounding on four stiff legs, making a pattern of his little rushes and spins, an intricate figure whose design is joy.

Once, I felt something like that dancer. I skipped up the steps of the library by the stone lions, wearing my green uniform with the faded orange trimmings, the sleeves too short and the collar too tight. I took off my cap with its embroidered "Am. Del. Ser." as I ran through the marble corridors without a glance at Lawrence refusing to surrender to the British, Erasmus in his study with a copy of the Dance of Life on his lap, the dreaming spires of Oxford.

Nor did I see the people I passed with their rubbed, soiled faces, each one intent on his private hysteria, each one seeking the proof of the truth and reality of their own monomania. I failed to recognize either the ravelers or unravelers, busy behind their eyes untangling and tangling, some with a firm hold on a strand that must surely lead somewhere, others fumbling for such a strand.

If anyone can be snug in the main reading room I was.

A hot sun shown over the Aegean, the wine-dark sea. I was with Jason and his crew of heroes, Orestes, who was to die so tragically at Thebes, Clymnos, the straight-backed one, shield-bearer to King Agamemnon, and the others. I wore a helmet with a horse-hair plume. My oar was behind that of Hercules and I watched the muscles of his back round and flatten as he swung the heavy sweep to the rhythm of young Hyacinth's song. Hyacinth, he of the round neck and golden curls, sang of ancient Kings, of their loves and of their deaths. How full my heart was and how gladly I pulled to the beat of his clear, treble voice.

But all the while, Ganymede, cup-bearer to Zeus, was also listening and watching. He was jealous of Hyacinth's music and of how much we all loved him. He became furious when he saw how quick and light Hercules' thick fingers became as he scooped up a floating lily to make a garland for the youth.

We stopped our argosy to stretch and drink wine, pulling our great boat up on the white sand. We fell to playing with a discus in a meadow. Like a little deer, Hyacinth bounded here and there to retrieve the heavy disc for us.

The sun shown down as we lay about in the cool grass, shouting taunts and boisterous jokes at one another. Hercules rose and approached the line to throw. The saucer was like a scallop shell in his giant hand. Once around he spun, twisting tight the great muscles, then he unwound and hurled the disc far into the heavens. With a gay shout, Hyacinth ran to retrieve it. Watching from Olympus, Ganymede saw his chance. He made the sun shine full into the running boy's eyes so that he lost the discus in flight and stopped to rub his eyes. The metal swooped from the sky like a hawk and bit deep into his round neck, striking him to the ground where he rolled once in the sweet grass, then was still.

We hurried to him where he lay in the little meadow at the edge of the still wood.

We leaned on our shovels and listened to Hercules' lamentation, as he shouted his sorrow at the unrelenting sun.

But the sun relented.

I was first to see the miracle and called the others to witness. From the new-turned earth a flower had thrust, a flower much like the dead boy in grace and beauty. And on its petals was the word of mourning, "IO." We called this flower Hyacinth, as have all men since.

Time meant nothing to me then, nor did space. From ancient Greece to nineteenth century Africa was just a quick thumbing through the card index, a scrawled request blank and a few minutes wait for my number to be flashed on the electric call board.

Back to my table again. Before I had read a paragraph I was surrounded by curled giant ferns. The smell of my own damp, soiled clothing was that of the rank soil on which I sat, clutching a Holland and Holland magnum.

Someone, somewhere dropped a book, shattering the heavy silence and stilling the shrill wing-rubbing of a far away beetle. I didn't lift my eyes from Du Chaillu's "Gorilla Hunting in Africa." The crash was that of the beast I was hunting. My thin fingers tightened around the smooth, cold, double-barreled rifle, and my thumb reached for the hammer.

It was quite a trick, but I managed it easily. In one part of my mind, I was conscious of the package on the table in front of me and of the minute hand of the large clock on the wall. I had to deliver the package uptown by four o'clock and in order to do that I had to be out of the library by three-thirty at the latest.

As the hour approached, the two problems became one. Would the gorilla get to me before the second hand reached six. Would I shoot one that chapter and receive a medal from King Albert of Belgium in whose forest I was hunting. To-morrow was Sunday and the library was closed. I might not get uptown Monday. I read faster, not skipping, but without pausing to thicken and embroider the drab, matter-of-fact prose.

The end of the chapter came without my firing the magnum. The crash I had heard proved to have been made by a deer, almost a gazelle in daintiness, with tiny spiral horns that needed only strings to be a lute. It stopped close to where I was hiding and lifted its head to test the air, dilating its velvet nostrils to catch the taint it suspected but could not quite locate. It stood rigidly, all its sinews vibrating, framed in giant ferns and great fan-like leaves.

In my pocket was a light shot load that fitted the magnum, put there for just such chance. Fresh meat was needed badly in camp. I did not fire or even think to do so. My men would have to eat beans again tonight or go to bed hungry.

Stealthily, watching to make sure no librarian saw me, I broke off a piece of sticky candy bar and put it in my mouth, never for a moment losing sight of the deer. I had managed this so quietly that the creature stopped trembling and stretched its neck to eat the bell-like flowers on a nearby vine. It looked directly at me as it chewed, its large eyes quiet with satisfaction and peace.

The second hand reached six. I left the deer among the ferns and flowers, and reached for the parcel.

After the last errand was run, I would go home for supper, then hurry to Central Park. I spent even more time there than I did in the library.

I loved that jagged green tear in the corset of concrete that covers Manhattan Island. I still love it, but I rarely visit it anymore. I find it hard to breathe there with everyone you see gasping so avidly for breath.

Lately, the park seems filled with cripples of many kinds. On weekdays especially, they congregate on the benches that line the walks. Some with pencils for sale and others with gum. Do they live by selling to each other? Still more terrible is the concentration with which they read last week's newspapers.

The cripples are there, too, on Saturdays and Sundays of course, but on those days they are blurred by the violence of gangs of children who roam the walks, trampling the flowers, chasing birds and stoning squirrels. I have often wondered why the great trees and serene fields seem to multiply the viciousness of the poor brats. Can it be that an unconscious memory of an older way of life torments them. It certainly isn't true that they lack a sense of beauty or that their spirits are innately ugly. No one who has ever seen them dancing gravely in some dark alley to the tinkle of a hand organ can believe that of them.

When I was seventeen neither the cripples nor the children, nor even the prostitutes whose beat it was, nor the homosexualists on their ever pressing search for romance, bothered me. I was almost completely unaware of them. My sole interest in them was to make sure that they did not discover the secret hiding place I had on the brush covered hill back of the lake.

The park is full of such little secret nests, a good many of them unknown even to the park police and gardeners. For the most part, the background gardening in the park is in the "natural style" and the bushes have been allowed to grow up in a dense cover that becomes almost impenetrable the further back from the walks one goes. Here and there, a break in the green wall can be found which, if followed, will lead to a tiny, hardly perceptible path. Although used by humans, they seem like the runs of some very small and furtive animal. To travel over it, one has to stoop far over and move very slowly. In some places it is even necessary to go on hand and knee.

Certain sections of the park are honeycombed with them and they carry an almost continuous stream of traffic. It is strange to watch them at their jumping off places. Most of them make for the brush abruptly. They are strolling down a walk apparently just out for an airing when they reach a point opposite one of the paths. They pause for a second, as though to admire some tree, but really to see if anyone is watching, then vault the rail and dash for the bushes. Once hidden, they usually wait, watching the path for some time before penetrating deeper into the undergrowth.

The little nests at the end of the trails are of many kinds. Some are merely holes in the brush, just large enough to sit in without being seen and from which nothing can be seen. Others are located near spots used by lovers and from these the whole progress of an affair can be watched, usually with envy by the lonely spy. A few are larger, almost like a hut, and the occupant can lie down at full length and play at being in the forest. The most elaborate are in two sections, one for complete concealment, and another, a look out on the top of a rock or in the lower branches of a tree from which a bird's eye view of the park can be obtained.

I first learned about these places when I was a child and used to play Indian scout in the park with a little gang of other boys. We fished for goldfish in the lake with a bent pin for a hook and balls of dough for bait. We also had a trap line of mice traps, a few rat traps, and several badly made snares after a design in the boyscout manual. We caught squirrels and an occasional rabbit. We skinned everything with old razor blades, stretched and salted the skins, also according to the instructions in the manual, and tried to cook and eat the carcasses. All of which, of course, was against the law and we used the trails to avoid the police and park attendants.

As we grew older the trapping and fishing became less exciting. We started to go to the park at night. We used the trails then to spy on the grown people who hid in the brush. We would sit by the hour watching two men kiss or a woman masturbate. We would wait until they were at the height of their excitement, then suddenly shout foul names and run, yelling wildly.

It is a strange thing, but we were untouched in any serious way by the things we saw. We were playing a game that involved certain virtues (also found in the Scout Manual) such as knowing the signs and habits of our quarry, stalking, trailing, observing carefully, remaining absolutely still and so forth. We would no more think of imitating the people we hunted than Daniel Boone would imitate a bear he had seen grubbing in a rotten tree. The climax of our hunt was savagely cruel and yet it was the only climax we could manage. We had neither rifles nor cameras, nor were we sufficiently civilized to merely move off as quietly as we had come satisfied with the chase alone. We had to have our moment of triumph.

Our little gang broke up as its members grew older and went to work. I became a messenger boy and went to the park very rarely. About this time, I discovered the library, and almost forgot it entirely.

One evening, however, on my way home from work, I passed the edge of it and hesitated. A flock of wild ducks were wheeling above the lake in the dying light of the red sun. They seemed above me on Fifth Avenue, then with a wild last swoop banked sharply and came down on the water fast, churning it rosy for a second in the stained light.

I followed the ducks into the park and stood for a while on the shores of the lake, watching the restless play which for them was a prelude to sleep. I loitered there even after it was too dark to make out anything of them but the black raft they made far out on the water.

Although remnants of light clothed the great hotels along Central Park South with beauty, I turned my back on them and stared off at the black hill behind the lake with its fringe of gaunt trees. They had a greater beauty still.

Where the excitement came from I don't know and yet I trembled. I felt a great inward rush of emotion as I looked at the little lake with the dingy pergola on its far shore and beyond that the great black hill.

How quick I was to name it all. Lake Elsinore, the Chapel perilous and the Singing Wood. A swan boat was anchored by the boat dock at the pergola. Its faded white paint a rosy silver in the magic light. Within I knew a king lay sorely wounded in the groin, and it was his loss of manhood through this grievous wound that had made a desert of the once rich meadow land.

I didn't tell myself this story. In those days I never had to. A story is—and then something happened and then something else happened. This was simultaneous, like a great picture. My head and heart were full of one, great timeless image in which a white arm proffered a sword from the water, garlanded maidens danced in the dark wood and a dying king in stained armor groaned a prayer for his virility. And I, inside the same dark picture, knelt beside a wayside crucifix, clasping the spear of Joseph of Arimathea in my arms.

From that night on the park shared my time with the library and often got the most of it. I rediscovered the little trails and hiding places and became one of those furtive people who lurk in the brush, hiding and dreaming. I made a nest for myself near the top of the hill that lay beyond the lake, a little hollow in the midst of a tangle of Spanish Broom that had been allowed to run wild.

Three Eskimos

You may not remember the picture I mean, but we billed it as Raw Forces of Man and Nature in Heroic Struggle Amid Scenic Wonders of the Frozen North. In the sweep of all show ages, our talk went, there has never been an attraction like this one. From humble obscurity, came these great Eskimo actors, to seduce a world steeled to sentiment and steeped in cold sophistication. It is a conquest so amazing, so without precedent, so frenzied and so devastating that only cosmic vision can grasp its import . . . the world must be content to give itself in spellbound rapture.

That's the way we billed it. We were surprised at the studio, but it flopped. I guess it was too beautiful for the dopes. As I've often said, you can't make money with arty pictures.

The picture was directed by Sam Oldersween, the great German master. You remember what we said about him in our distributor's book. Sam Oldersween is the mightiest creative power in the field of drama! His devotion to reality remains as uncompromising as ever . . . but box-office is his goal, first, last and down to the final dollar.

And yet the picture was a flop. It was about Eskimos, and who cares about Eskimos, I guess. We found that out.

But box-office trouble wasn't the only headache those Eskimos gave us. We made the picture up in the Frozen North, as billed, but we cut it in the studios in Hollywood. Well, Sam Oldersween insisted on bringing back with him, in case of retakes, an Eskimo family. Japs or Jews wouldn't do for retakes, not even Armenians, no he had to have Eskimos. The others aren't greasy enough, I guess. So we brought back a papa Eskimo named Joe, a mama Eskimo named Anne, a young buck named Eddie, and a young bitch named Mary.

And were they a headache. I don't know who picked me, but I was supposed to ride herd on those four pus-pockets. Well, I dumped them in a cheap hotel and let it go at that. Catch me feeding them raw fish, or even watching them eat it.

Then the trouble started. Joe, the papa, went to house and got everything. He started to rot on me. He gave all he had to mama and she began to stink.

Burn the Cities

The Eastern star calls with its hundred knives
Burn the cities
Burn the cities

Burn Jerusalem
It is easy
City of birth a star
A rose in color a daisy in shape
Calls with its hundred knives
Calls three kings
Club diamond heart
Burn Jerusalem and bring
The spade king to the Babe
Nailed to his six-branched tree
Upon the sideboard of a Jew
Marx
Performs the miracle of loaves and fishes

II

Burn the cities
Burn Paris
City of light
Twice-burned city
Warehouse of the arts
The spread hand is a star with points
The fist a torch
Burn the cities
Burn Paris
City of light
Twice-burned city
Warehouse of the arts

The spread hand is a star
The fist a torch
Workers of the World

Unite
Burn Paris

Paris will burn easily
Paris is fat
Only an Eskimo could eat her
Only a Turk could love her
The Seine is her bidet
She will not hold urine
She squats upon the waters and they are oil
A placid slop
Only the sick can walk on it
Fire alone can make it roar
Not like a burning barn but muted
Muted by a derby hat
So also my sorrow
City of my youth
Is muted by a derby hat

The flames of Paris are sure to be well-shaped
Some will be like springs
Some like practiced tongues
Some like gay flags
Others like dressed hair
Many will dance
Only the smells will be without order

The spread hand is a star with points
The fist a torch
Workers of the World
Unite
Burn Paris

III

Burn the cities
Burn London
Slow cold city
Do not despair
London will burn
It will burn

In the heat of tired eyes
In the grease of fish and chips
The English worker will burn it
With coal from Wales
With oil from Persia
The Indian will give him fire
There is sun in Egypt
The Negro will give him fire
Africa is the land of fire
London is cold
It will nurse the flame
London is tired
It will welcome the flame
London is lecherous
It will embrace the flame
London will burn

Tibetan Night

IN KASKAZ, the principal city of Tibet, the evening is lemon, the night purple, the dawn violet, and the day acrid with the odor of dogs. Moreover, almost it alone, of the many cities of the world, knows not the dictatorship of the proletariat. Perhaps because the Comintern has never heard of the place, perhaps because that august body does not give a darn about it. However it might be, despite the success of the world revolution, Kaskaz is still free.

I was told that the American restaurants were the best places to dine. There are about half a dozen of these from which to choose, all quite recently opened by refugees from the Soviet of North America. If I desired hog and hominy, my informant said, I should go to a place called "The Blue and the Grey," if it was fish chowder that I wanted, he recommended "Pardee's Tea Shop." I chose the "Restaurant Banjo" for fried chicken with yams, Maryland style.

When I entered the company was engaged in eating and drinking; a few Tibetans in overcoats an inch thick and a few Tartars with butter on their hair, but mostly Americans. The manager, an old Dartmouth athlete of good family, welcomed me at the door. Across the front of his varsity sweater several decorations were pinned; I made out an elk's tooth, a DKE pin, a Wanamaker Mile medal and an honorary police badge.

I looked around. A famous jazz band, "The Fruit Jar Drinkers," was playing the "Beale Street Blues," and very well, too. The waitresses all looked exactly like Katharine Hepburn and wore gingham dresses, sunbonnets and high button shoes. My attention was attracted by a lady with broad shoulders, small hips and long legs in a soiled and patched gown that must have been designed by Elizabeth Hawes. She had her back to me and was saying: "Gee, that's a swell tune. Bud Drake sang it the night the reds burnt Boston. Alas!" Then she turned around.

"Cobina Sawyer," I cried, "you here!"

"Why, hello Paul," she said. "Yes, I am an exile, a refugee from the red terror, to coin a phrase."

It was an old joke, loaded with memories of other times and places. I felt suddenly sad and very tired. I picked up a bit, however, when I saw that she was still beautiful and still had that fresh-from-the-showers look.

"But tell me about yourself," I said, remembering my manners.

"There is little to tell. My sort are through, I suppose."

I pretended, in order to cheer her up, to foresee the end of the Bolshevik regime.

"Yes," she agreed, "some day perhaps, we shall return to America . . . perhaps . . ."

"But what about Hamilton Fish? I understand that he still has an army in the field. And there is Grover Whalen and his men, hiding in the Everglades."

"My brother is serving in Whalen's army. He has no shoes and lives on raw onions. Ned Ballou, the man I was speaking to when you came in was with Hamilton Fish. He almost died of exposure. Now he washes dishes in this restaurant. You remember Ned, don't you? He was with us in Placid the winter you said you loved me."

I began to cry softly. Alas, my heart is as chipped as a tramp's knife.

"Is there nothing I can do?"

"Yes, Paul, you can help me get my sable coat out of pawn. In its lining is enough money to take me to New York."

"Let us do so at once."

First we had to go to Cobina's lodgings for the pawn ticket. She lived in a damp cellar. We went in and found three elderly people partaking of their evening meal. They were Mr. E. Stevens Birdsall and his sisters, Sophina and Pauline, aunts of Cobina's. The two Daughters of the first American Revolution were eating out of one broken dish, while the aged investment broker, Mr. Birdsall, ate out of another.

"I want to go to Beacon Hill," cried Sophina.

I realized immediately that the poor old thing was cracked and crazed. Beacon Hill was no more. The communists had leveled it as flat as Jamaica Plains.

"You can't go back there," taunted her sister. "If you do the bolshys will shoot you." And she imitated the sound of a shot quite cleverly with her mouth.

Mr. Birdsall said to me: "Didn't I meet you once at the Union League?"

I shook my head no, and examined this famous director of corporations. He was quite naked under his Prince Albert, and there was oat straw in his beard.

"I hope, Mr. Morand," he said, "that you will excuse our inability to entertain you properly. Soon, however, we will return to our Connecticut estates. You must visit us there next spring. We will go in my yacht to the crew races at New London. . . ."

He was interrupted by his sister, Sophina. "I want to go back to Beacon Hill," she cried again. "I miss the Boston Symphony concerts so much."

Hurriedly we escaped from the cellar, leaving the three old people alone with their meagre devices. On our way to the pawnshop, we passed the American Press Bureau. "There's a diagram of the Fish-Whalen front," Cobina said.

I saw a large map of the United States with a thread running across the southern tip of Florida; all north of the line was red, all south of it white.

While we watched a bulletin was posted which announced that for strategical reasons the White Army had withdrawn in good order to the Dry Tortugas.

"We must have confidence," Cobina said without confidence. "Look at all these people; they are kept alive only by their belief in Fish and Whalen."

I looked around at the crowd and listened for their comment on the dispatch. It was just such a gathering as one used to see at the Spaniel field trials on Fisher's Island. Intellectuals in rags remembered for each other that Ernest Hemingway used to fish off the Dry Tortugas. A banker with a frock coat over his canvas trousers described a stay he had made in the Casa Marina Hotel in Key West. A dowager in a torn riding habit and carpet slippers said that she had never liked Florida. The president of a famous university, wearing a bathrobe and with burlap wound around his feet, told of an expedition he had once sent to Long Pine Key.

From the Press Bureau we went directly to the shop that had Cobina's sable coat in pawn. The lining had not been touched; her money was safe.

She prepared to leave me.

"I'll see you in New York," I said.

"No, by the time you get there all my money will be gone and . . ."

I did not let her finish. "Be brave," I pleaded. "As an expert veterinarian, you can always get a job from the soviet. They'll be glad to have you."

"No, I shall go at once to the Ritz Hotel, then dine in Central Park at the Casino. That will leave me with just enough money for a last drunk at Tony's. In the morning, I shall hang myself. Good-bye."

Before I could summon up the courage to tell her that the Ritz was a museum, Tony's a workingman's chess club and the Central Park Casino a place for "Quiet and Noisy Fun," she was gone.

Proposal to the Guggenheim Foundation

PROJECT

A GENERAL IDEA of the type of novel I mean to write can be obtained from the models I have in mind. They are: *A Portrait of the Artist as a Young Man,* by James Joyce; *The Education of Henry Adams,* by Henry Adams; *Le Jeune Européen,* by Drieu La Rochelle.

I intend to tell the story of a young man of my generation; that which graduated from college just before the boom and became thirty years old during the Depression. I want to show the difference between it and the one that came before; the famous "lost generation."

Chapter One
Elementary school in New York City. First ideas of American history, the world, or what is worthwhile.

Chapter Two
High School during the war. Introduction to sex. Ideas about conduct. The morals of sport.

Chapter Three
College in New England. The post-flapper period. A first attempt at definitions, including that of Beauty. Arguments over whether anything is really worth while. A discussion of values. The necessity for laughing at everything, love, death, ambition, etc.

Chapter Four
Business and the objectives involved. An attempt to love, and the difficulties encountered. The impossibility of experiencing a genuine emotion.

Chapter Five
Europe in 1927. The ideas of Spengler and Valery. The ne-

cessity for violence. The composition of a suicide note as an exercise in rhetoric.

Chapter Six

The return to America. A discussion of values and objectives at a class reunion. The discovery of economics.

This is a very brief synopsis. I hope, however, that it suggests something of what I mean to do.

No attempt has been made to describe what actually happens to my protagonist because I think that an outline of adventures is meaningless. Nevertheless, the ideas I have briefly described will be hidden as carefully as possible in the body of my narrative.

Good Hunting

A Play in Three Acts
(with Joseph Schrank)

Cast of Characters

BRIGADIER GENERAL HARGREAVES	Commanding Brigade
COLONEL JARVIS	General Staff I.
MAJOR FITZSIMMONS.	General Staff II.
CAPTAIN STUART STEWARD THE LAIRD OF KILBRECHT . .	General Staff III
CAPTAIN RAM SINGH, THE NIZAM OF LADORE . . .	Indian Colonial
LIEUTENANT FRENIQUE.	French Liaison Officer
LIEUTENANT GERALD FORSYTE . .	Aide de Camp
PRIVATE BOWKER	Batman to General
MAJOR GENERAL SIR ARTHUR REYNOLDS	Commander of Division
WILLIAM LEWIS.	Journalist
HANK RUSSO	Reporter
MARIE (GRETCHEN VON TREITHOFF)	German Spy
LIZETTE	French Peasant Woman
GRACE HARGREAVES	General's Wife
MONSIEUR JERVAIS	French Art Commissioner

Soldiers and non-commissioned officers, two French workmen, German General and staff.

The Scene is the EGLISE DES VINGT PUCELLES in the town of Millefleurs, France, early in the World War, when it was occupied by a brigade headquarters staff of the British Expeditionary Forces.

Act One
Just Before Breakfast

Act Two
Just After Luncheon, the Next Day

Act Three
Dawn, the Following Day.

———

NOTE:
None of the characters in this play is entirely imaginary, nor are any of the incidents completely fictitious.

———

Act One

Scene: The *Church of the Twenty Virgins* was built about the time of that great soldier-heroine, Jean of Arc, who was executed for, among other things, defeating the *British Expeditionary Force* of that day. Times have changed, however, and the British are now defending France.

MAJOR GENERAL HARGREAVES, D.S.O., M.M., D.S.C. etc., etc., is in charge of activities on a portion of the French front, commanding a brigade of British Infantry. He and his staff are the brains of this force while the troops (at present, much closer to the German line and not nearly so comfortable) are the brawn.

At Rise: When the curtain rises, it reveals the main part of the church and the audience finds itself sitting where it would if it had come to worship instead of applaud. The brigade staff has added to but not changed any of the furnishings. Across the front of the pulpit is fastened a very large colored map stuck full of English and German flags which show

the position of the troops. There are several pieces
of office furniture; desks and tables, filing cabinets,
a field telephone switchboard, a wireless set, telegraph equipment, and two large crates containing
carrier pigeons. Standing in front of the map is
COLONEL JARVIS, roast beef to the heel. He has a
habitual air of deference and seems very anxious
to avoid offending anybody. At the moment, he is
busy changing the flags in accordance with a communique he is holding in his hand. SERGEANT
BOWKER, the General's batman, is polishing a
beautiful pair of riding boots with all the love that
good servants have for inanimate objects. He is a
solid citizen of about fifty who knows his job and
his place. At the field telephone sits SIGNALMAN
SAM THOMPSON (he never takes off his earphones
nor leaves the switchboard, and when he isn't
working, he is sound asleep) and WILLIAM LEWIS,
a journalist, who is speaking to his Paris office.
LEWIS is neat and respectable. He represents a paper of the calibre of the MANCHESTER GUARDIAN,
and is most certainly *not* in the line of war correspondents that starts with Richard Harding Davis
and ends, pray God, with Floyd Gibbons. The
other correspondent, HANK RUSSO, sloppy and disreputable, who enters some moments after the curtain has risen, most definitely is.

LEWIS
(Into phone)
Hello . . . Simpson . . . This is Lewis . . . While I think of
it . . . you got some of those French names wrong in yesterday's story. Lieutenant Frenique, the French liaison officer
here, called it to my attention . . . he's most sensitive about
it . . . Thank you . . . Not much new today. The position of
our front lines is the same . . . about ten miles east of this
church. Our barrage has been going on for the past seven
hours . . . probable routine offensive with the same objective
. . . the Pepper Mill.

(While he is talking, HANK RUSSO enters, carrying a heavy cane and hurries to the switchboard. Everyone ignores him)

RUSSO

Get my office, Sam.

THOMPSON

Mr. Lewis has the Paris wire.

LEWIS

(into phone)
Two new battalions have moved up . . . Both Irish Guard Contingents . . . probably form the spearhead of attack . . . Yes, of course . . . I'll phone again if the situation warrants . . . Right! Oh, er—and I'm grateful for the chocolate and cigars . . . Thank you.
(Hangs up. THOMPSON gets busy with his wires, talking quietly into transmitter)

RUSSO

(Turning on Lewis with bitter indignation)
Hoarding the goodies, hah?
(LEWIS ignores this completely. He leaves the switchboard. Shifting suddenly to a whine)
Gimme some . . . I'm supposed to be your colleague . . . your buddy . . .
(Hurt)
And you expect us Yankees to forget the Revolution of '76 and come in on your side . . .
(To silence him, LEWIS tosses him a cigar and a caramel. RUSSO catches them with the skill of an organ-grinder's monkey and pops both into his mouth at once)

RUSSO

(To Thompson)
Well? How about it, Sam?

THOMPSON

I'm trying to get them, Mr. Russo.

(A courier enters, goes up to Jarvis and salutes)

COURIER

Despatches from Divisional Headquarters, sir.

(JARVIS takes them. COURIER salutes again and exits)

JARVIS

(Handing despatches to Bowker)

For General Hargreaves.

(BOWKER takes despatches)

BOWKER

Thank you, sir. I'll put them with the rest of his letters.

(Exits)

(MAJOR FITZSIMMONS enters. He is a Canadian, about thirty-five years old, with an alert, keen manner and a caustic tongue. He is the only one of the officers who is not completely spruce and natty. As he is not the professional military type, he is continually exasperated by the stupidities of the military mind and method around him. However, his sense of humor helps him keep his exasperation under control; usually the furthest he goes in expressing it is a slow burn)

FITZSIMMONS

'Morning, Jarvis.

JARVIS

(Cheerfully)

Oh, good morning! Nasty day, what? Poisonous fog.

FITZSIMMONS

General Hargreaves still asleep?

JARVIS

Yes.

(FITZSIMMONS shakes his head worried)

FITZSIMMONS

(Turning to Lewis politely)

Will you wait outside please, Bill?

LEWIS

Certainly.

(Exits)

RUSSO

Got something for me, Fitzie?

FITZSIMMONS

No. Get out.

RUSSO

(Arrogantly)
Listen, Fitzie, I got a story to file right away with my Paris office.

FITZSIMMONS

(Snapping)
We're busy now—get out of here.

JARVIS

You can use the phone later.

RUSSO

(Crumbling)
The way you push me around, I don't know why I keep calling your guys heroes . . .
(Exits)

JARVIS

That foreigner has an unfortunate manner.

FITZSIMMONS

I wish Hargreaves would get up. I've got to talk to him.

JARVIS

What about, Fitzsimmons?

FITZSIMMONS

The fog. I believe that—
(He is interrupted by the entrance of three men wearing raincoats—LIEUTENANT MARCEL FRENIQUE, during peace time an employee of the French Government's Travel Bureau, now liaison officer with the British, CAPTAIN STEWARD, THE LAIRD OF KILBRECHT, in kilts and bonnet, and the NIZAM OF LADORE, CAPTAIN RAM SINGH, in the blue and scarlet of the Rhajputur Rifles, complete with jade green turban)

JARVIS

Good morning, gentlemen!

FRENIQUE

(Gaily)

Ah, mon Colonel . . . ah, mon Major . . . Exquisite French morning.

KILBRECHT

(Dourly, with heavy, almost incomprehensible Scotch accent)

Terrible weather.

NIZAM OF LADORE

(In Babu, completely incomprehensible)

Aroo——shatazi.

JARVIS

Have a good gallop?

FRENIQUE

(Exclaiming)

It was beautiful! We rode through the French scene!

FITZSIMMONS

Hard not to—in France.

FRENIQUE

(Enthusiastically)

The exquisite fog makes of everything mother of pearl, tinted rose and silver . . . Before the war, when I was head of the government tourist bureau, the fogs of this part of France were known for their medicinal qualities. People came from as far as Chicago to cure asthma and other pulmonary ailments by breathing it.

JARVIS

I say! My mother has asthma.

FRENIQUE

There was a project to bottle it for use in less fortunate lands.

FITZSIMMONS

(Impatiently)

It's a lovely fog! An exquisite fog! But we haven't got asthma—we've got a war.

KILBRECHT

(Surprised)
Why, what's wrong?

FITZSIMMONS

This is the first real fog we've had in weeks. We've got to take advantage of it.

JARVIS

(Consulting watch)
Our attack is set to begin in an hour and a half.

FITZSIMMONS

The fog won't last that long. We've got to change the plan.

JARVIS

(A little hurt)
It was most carefully prepared, Fitzsimmons.
(Moves to map and points to it)
We attack with the first, second and third battalions in the assault wave. The fourth, fifth and sixth will form the support and mop up. When the objective has been taken, the support will pass through the first wave and pursue the enemy, so that the assault can dig in and consolidate the positions won. They will pass through the tip of the salient here, rolling back the flanks and . . .

FITZSIMMONS

(Interrupting)
Williamson's . . . "The Art of War"—page sixty-three.

JARVIS

We used it in practice maneuvers before the war with great success.

KILBRECHT

Excellent tactics.

FRENIQUE

(Nodding)
Very neat plan—Joffre employs it regularly.

FITZSIMMONS

But the Germans have the same text book!

JARVIS

Williamson is the accepted authority on trench tactics involving limited objectives.

KILBRECHT

Williamson's mother, by the way, was a Scot—a McLean.

FITZSIMMONS

We've been trying to take the Pepper Mill for months with that plan. We've held up the advance on the whole front. We've been hurled back again and again . . . routed . . . destroyed!

KILBRECHT

An attack is never entirely wasted. Experience under fire, you know, has moral value.

FRENIQUE

Marvelous training.

JARVIS

After all, we *are* turning a rabble of bookkeepers and farmers into an army of battle-tried soldiers.

FITZSIMMONS

What's left of them.

FRENIQUE
(As though they should be glad)
They died for France!

FITZSIMMONS

Sure—only one live recruit is better than a dozen dead veterans.

KILBRECHT

I shouldn't jump to conclusions that way, Fitzsimmons.

JARVIS

What would you substitute?

FITZSIMMONS

Stop the barrage and attack under cover of the fog.

JARVIS

You know how strongly General Hargreaves is opposed to innovations.

KILBRECHT

Besides, the Ordnance would be hellish mad.

JARVIS

They're a highly organized unit—to ask them to cease firing prematurely would be an imposition.

KILBRECHT

We'd never hear the end of it.

JARVIS

It doesn't pay to get into the bad books of the gunners—they can make a lot of trouble.

FRENIQUE

The French Army is using an eight hour barrage in all attacks of this nature. C'est comme il faut on the whole front.

FITZSIMMONS

It's like a time-table! When it starts, the Germans look at their watches and go to sleep. Eight hours later their officers yell: "Fix bayonets, here come the British!"—and a few minutes later—sure enough, here we are!

JARVIS

Really, Fitzsimmons, you exaggerate.

FITZSIMMONS

A surprise attack is our only chance of taking the Pepper Mill. This fog is a perfect opportunity.

JARVIS

(To Nizam)
What do you think, sir?

FITZSIMMONS

Why ask him? None of us can understand what he says.

JARVIS

It would be rude not to—he's attached to this staff.
(Turns to Nizam)

NIZAM

Benishelenskays.

FITZSIMMONS

Thank you.

(The NIZAM turns on his heels and stalks over to the cages of pigeons, takes a bag of corn from a pocket of his magnificent uniform and proceeds to feed them, paying no more attention to the others. JARVIS follows him with his eye)

JARVIS

He seems to be really fond of those carrier pigeons . . .

FITZSIMMONS

We're wasting time.

KILBRECHT

In any case, we'd have to wait until Hargreaves gets up.

FITZSIMMONS

But the fog won't wait. We must *wake* him.

JARVIS

(Doubtfully)
I don't know whether we dare risk doing that . . .

FITZSIMMONS

(Sharply)
Why not?

JARVIS

He played cribbage until three this morning.

FRENIQUE

Besides, what would Bowker say?

JARVIS

Yes, of course, there's Bowker to consider.

FITZSIMMONS

I forgot about Bowker.
(Calls out)
Bowker! Oh, Bowker!
(BOWKER enters, carrying a pair of trousers in one hand
and a pressing iron in the other. He comes to attention
before FITZSIMMONS—more like a trained servant than a
trained soldier)
Bowker, wake the General.

BOWKER

Pardon me, sir—but it is not eleven o'clock.

FITZSIMMONS

That's an order!

BOWKER

(With a worried look at Jarvis)
Yes, sir, I know, sir, but—

FITZSIMMONS

Well?

JARVIS

(Intervening hastily)
Er—let me speak to him.
(To Bowker)
There is an emergency, Bowker . . . er . . .

BOWKER

Yes, sir—pardon my presumption, sir; but I have been in General Hargreaves' service for thirty-two years . . .

FITZSIMMONS

Just now you're a non-commissioned officer on active duty—
I'm ordering you to wake the General.

BOWKER

Begging your pardon, sir, but the General, when I undressed
him for bed, said "Bowker, I'll rise at eleven." Those were
his orders, sir.

FITZSIMMONS

Do you realize you're laying yourself open to court martial?

JARVIS

Leave off, Fitzsimmons—One doesn't order another man's servants around. It simply isn't done.

FITZSIMMONS

(Suddenly changing his tactics.

Very earnestly)

Bowker, I wouldn't for the world have you violate your duty to your master. But the whole British Army has been held up by our failure to take the Pepper Mill. Today's fog provides us with a great opportunity. By eleven o'clock, it will have lifted. I appeal to you, Bowker, not as a soldier, not as a servant, but as an Englishman. If you love your country as I know you do, wake the General.

BOWKER

(Bowing and backing away)

I do love England, sir . . . but I would love her less if I disobeyed my master.

(He turns and exits hastily)

KILBRECHT

(Looking after him with profound admiration)

A valuable man that!

JARVIS

Not many of his breed left!

FRENIQUE

In France we have servants with more finesse . . . none of greater character.

KILBRECHT

Character is an admirable trait in a servant.

(Removing raincoat)

I could do with a spot of whisky.

FITZSIMMONS

So could I.

KILBRECHT

(Going to door, followed by FITZSIMMONS and FRENIQUE)

Come along then. My uncle, the McMurrough of Castle
Rosskirk, sent me some of his own distilling.

FRENIQUE

(As they exit)
I prefer cognac.

(JARVIS returns to his work at map as RUSSO peeps in,
sees the coast is clear, enters and hurries to switchboard)

RUSSO

(To Thompson)
My office! And step on it!
(THOMPSON gets busy. RUSSO turns to JARVIS)
What does that fellow Fitzsimmons think I am? My stuff is
syndicated in over two hundred American papers.

JARVIS

We appreciate that, Mr. Russo. But please remember that
we've extended you a very special privilege in the use of our
wires.

RUSSO

Yeah—but look what I'm doing for you fellows—I'm keeping
this brigade in the headlines.

THOMPSON

(Into phone)
American News?
(To Russo)
You're through to Paris.
(Goes to sleep)

RUSSO

(Into phone)
Hell, Jake . . . this is Hank Russo . . . listen!
(His voice becomes tense with excitement)
I'm at a field telephone in the front line trenches . . . a stone's
throw from the vicious Hun . . . waiting for the zero hour
to go over the top. If I come back alive, I'll send you a story
of how it feels to be in action . . . for the Sunday Supple-
ments . . . That's worth a few bucks extra, ain't it? . . . I
know, but I'm taking my life in my hands . . .

(He suddenly wallops the side of the switchboard with his cane, making a terrific bang. SAM sleeps on)

JARVIS

Mr. Russo! You'll wake General Hargreaves!

RUSSO

(Into phone)

Jake . . . Jake . . . can you hear me? Phew! That was close . . . High explosive shell . . . wiped out a whole platoon about ten yards from me . . . I guess my number ain't up yet though . . .

(Laughs artificially)

They'll have to use a silver bullet to get old Hank Russo . . . The men in the trench with me are Irish . . . wild Irish . . . red hair and laughing blue eyes . . . cool as cucumbers, these lads from the banks of the Shannon . . . sure and they're fighting fools, every man jack of 'em . . . We're crouched in the trench ready to spring at the throats of the Huns, the nun-rapers . . . In every man's veins beats the blood of . . .

(Suddenly slams side of desk again)

JARVIS

That switchboard is the property of the army . . . You will be held responsible for any and all damage . . .

(RUSSO begins again to pour his excitement into the phone)

RUSSO

A hand grenade . . . Jake! Can you hear me? . . . Sure, I'll be careful . . . only a few seconds now . . . the Captain is raising his arm . . . the men are crossing themselves . . . They're spitting on their hands to get a firm grip on their rifles . . . The Captain is about to put his whistle to his lips . . .

(He takes a whistle out of his pocket)

What a moment! Of this gallant band, how many will live to enjoy victory! Are they thinking of their sweethearts and wives in far off Erin with the kiddies playing around on that little old front lawn, the missus rocking on the porch and a good old-fashioned Irish stew cooking on the kitchen stove . . . ?

(He suddenly blows the whistle)

We're off! Into the teeth of the enemies' fire! For God, King and Country! Call you back!
> (He slams up the receiver, then pulls out a handkerchief and mops his brow. To Thompson)

Boston'll eat up that Irish stuff. I wish they'd use some Jewish troops for my New York readers.

> (FITZSIMMONS enters, followed by KILBRECHT and FRE-NIQUE)

FITZSIMMONS
> (To Russo)

You here again!

RUSSO
Now don't get tough. You gotta play ball with me if you want good notices.

FITZSIMMONS
> (Shouting)

Sentry!
> (SOLDIER at door with rifle presents arms)

Throw this polecat out bodily.

RUSSO
> (Shrugging)

What can an unarmed man do?
> (Exits quickly)

KILBRECHT
> (Looking after Russo, and shaking his head sadly)

Shocking bad form . . .

FRENIQUE
He's proved rather helpful.

FITZSIMMONS
His article about finding a bishop nailed to a church door created quite some anti-German feeling.

JARVIS
Just so. He helps to keep the Yankees interested.

FITZSIMMONS
Yes . . . in case we might need them.

KILBRECHT

Heaven forbid!

JARVIS

Of course, the American army would be—er—very questionable assistance.

(Two ORDERLIES enter, carrying a set of very expensive Peel's luggage, all brand new; also shotgun cases, rod cases and a set of golf sticks)

Ah! The new aide most likely. . . .

FITZSIMMONS

(Dryly)

Equipped for a bit of sport.

JARVIS

Wellington said the battle of Waterloo was won on the playing fields of Eton.

(After the ORDERLIES, comes a handsome young man in a smart, new uniform. LIEUTENANT GERALD FORSYTE of the Coldstream Guards. He carries a new trench coat folded over his arm. He has an eager smile and charmingly disingenuous manner)

GERALD

(Drawing to attention in front of Jarvis)

Lieutenant Forsyte, sir, reporting.

JARVIS

Welcome, Mr. Forsyte. Glad to have you here.

(They shake hands)

GERALD

Thank you, sir.

JARVIS

(Turns and introduces the other officers)

Er—Lieutenant Frenique of the French Army . . . liaison . . . Captain Stuart Steward, the Laird of Kilbrecht.

(The NIZAM has left the pigeons)

The Nizam of Ladore, Captain Ram Singh . . .

(FITZSIMMONS has approached)

Major Fitzsimmons . . .
 (They shake hands in turn)

AD LIBS

How'dydo.
Charmed.
A pleasure, Mr. Forsyte.

NIZAM

Gro-ajuzack.

 (To the astonishment of all, GERALD answers the Nizam)

GERALD

Gro . . .

JARVIS

You speak his language?

GERALD

My father was in the Indian Service. I was raised there.

NIZAM

 (Excitedly)
Minala alida le ityo nyrani shatzi binook, etc.

JARVIS

 (Excitedly)
That's what he's been saying for months! What does it mean?

GERALD

He says the next time the enemy attacks, we should do what
his ancestors did at the siege of Kapurthala.

JARVIS

 (Eagerly)
What was that?

GERALD

 (To Nizam)
Bowk aroo asti?

NIZAM

Bashi . . . bashi snoot ra!

GERALD

They turned loose a herd of hungry lions.

JARVIS

Oh . . . hardly practicable.

KILBRECHT

Where would we get the beasts?
(Profoundly)
It won't work.

FITZSIMMONS

(Smiling)
It's not in Williamson!

FRENIQUE

In any case, permission would have to be obtained from the French Government . . . But, tell me, Mr. Forsyte, how did you come . . . by way of Amiens?

GERALD

No, Arles.

FRENIQUE

(The travel official)
This time of year, it would have been better to have gone by Amiens . . . a hundred miles further . . .
(Exalted)
But a hundred miles of France! How did you travel!

GERALD

By staff car.

FRENIQUE

(Sadly)
Too bad . . . You would have enjoyed the beauty of the countryside more if you had come on a bicycle.

FITZSIMMONS

It would only have taken three months.

FRENIQUE

Ah, yes! The quaint inns, the picturesque peasants . . . the stop beside the road for an apple and a glass of wine. To know France is to love her.

> (Turns to KILBRECHT, as though this reminds him of something)

Kilbrecht, let us find Lizette.

KILBRECHT
> (To others, apologetically)

She has a lamb for sale. Quite cheap, I understand.

FRENIQUE
> (Rhapsodically)

We shall have a gigot for dinner . . . tender, succulent . . . I shall cook it. Foyot himself showed me how. Twenty shades of brown, from gold through tan to rust.

KILBRECHT
I could do with a bit of mutton.

FRENIQUE
> (Taking his arm, as they go out)

With it, we shall drink a Chateau du Mouton, 1903 . . .

JARVIS
Excuse me, gentlemen—I must finish a letter to my mother.
> (To Gerald)

I hope you'll enjoy your stay with us, Mr. Forsyte.

GERALD
> (Gratefully)

Oh, thank you, sir. I'm sure I shall.

JARVIS
We're quite comfortable here in this church. It used to be a hospital before we took over.

GERALD
I noticed the red cross painted on the roof.

JARVIS
I must remember to have it removed.
> (He exits. The NIZAM remains, sticking to Gerald with pathetic eagerness)

GERALD
(Looking after Jarvis)
Nice chap. Seems a bit worried.

FITZSIMMONS
Lots of debts back home.

GERALD
Too bad. You've got a splendid crowd here. I hope they won't find me too dull. This is my first campaign.

FITZSIMMONS
Do you play cribbage?

GERALD
Rather!

FITZSIMMONS
Then there's no reason why you shouldn't be popular. Only don't talk shop.

GERALD
Shop?

FITZSIMMONS
The war.

GERALD
(Puzzled frown)
Really, I don't understand.

FITZSIMMONS
(Smiling wryly)
Good. You'll be very well liked. My trouble is that I don't like cribbage.

GERALD
(Quite innocently)
Then why did you choose the army as a career?

FITZSIMMONS
I didn't. I'm in the soap business. I supplied all the army posts. Years ago I joined up—out of *sheer* . . . patriotism.

GERALD

(The snob shows slightly)
Oh, I see . . . you're a reserve officer.

FITZSIMMONS

And a Colonial from a very unfashionable colony—Canada.

GERALD

(Throwing a dog a bone)
I've heard some reserve officers make excellent soldiers.

FITZSIMMONS

Very few. They haven't the proper military slant.

GERALD

Yes—of course—tradition and training are extremely important.

FITZSIMMONS

Much more than intelligence!
(Before GERALD can think of the answer, FITZSIMMONS turns and shouts)
Orderly!
(To Gerald)
You want to unpack, I suppose.

GERALD

Yes, thanks.

(A SOLDIER comes in)

FITZSIMMONS

Take Mr. Forsyte's kit into eight.
(To Gerald as Orderly picks up luggage)
Nice quarters, you'll find . . . though the windows are stained glass.

(The Orderly moves off with luggage)

GERALD

Oh, I expect to rough it.
(He starts after the Orderly, followed by the NIZAM. FITZSIMMONS goes to a desk. Before Gerald reaches the door, he has to pass a confession box that stands to one side. As he does so, a girl pops her head out mysteriously,

sees him and pops back in again. GERALD is astounded and doesn't know what to do. With a puzzled frown, he goes back to Fitzsimmons, who is working over some papers and maps)

GERALD

Excuse me, sir . . . but is this place still used for religious purposes?

FITZSIMMONS

No, of course not.

GERALD

(A little excited)
There's someone in the confession box . . . a girl.

FITZSIMMONS

(Carelessly)
Oh—that's Marie.
(Goes back to papers)

GERALD

But isn't that highly irregular?

FITZSIMMONS

She cleans up around here. Don't pay any attention to her.

GERALD

But . . . er . . . she was peeping.

FITZSIMMONS

(Flatly)
Let her peep.

(GERALD is still puzzled. He starts off again, eyeing the box suspiciously. As he passes it, the door, which is slightly ajar, closes mysteriously again. As he exits, followed by the Nizam, Jarvis enters, carrying some letters)

JARVIS

(Very military)
Sentry!
(The GUARD presents arms and comes forward. JARVIS hands him letters)

See that these are posted.
>   (GUARD goes back to door)

> GUARD
>   (Shouting)
Orderly!

> FITZSIMMONS
>   (Loudly)
Oh, Jarvis—here are the completed plans for Thursday's attack. (Nods significantly toward the confession box and moves downstage, carrying papers and long blue envelope. JARVIS moves with him)

> JARVIS
>   (Taking papers and looking significantly toward confession box. In a whisper)
The plans for Marie?

> FITZSIMMONS
>   (In a low voice)
Yes.

> JARVIS
>   (Examining plans with a smile)
Hmmm . . . amusing, aren't they?

> FITZSIMMONS
They're based on the principles of Lewis Carroll . . . everything backward, like Alice in Wonderland.

> JARVIS
>   (Still examining plan)
So I see . . . Barrage *after* attack . . . entire brigade advances without support battalions . . . not in rank, but crawling . . . no rifles . . . only hand grenades . . . only to be used under blanket of fog . . .
>   (Guffaws)
Preposterous!
>   (Returns plans to Fitzsimmons)

> FITZSIMMONS
I'd sooner use this insane tactic than the one you fellows cribbed from the text book!

JARVIS
(Patronising)
But my dear Fitzsimmons—leading the men with hand grenades—they'd be walking mines.

FITZSIMMONS
Rifles just get in their way out there. If we had a few tanks
. . .

JARVIS
(Laughs)
Those rattletraps! Hargreaves said the man who invented them must be mad!

FITZSIMMONS
They'd take the Mill for us.

JARVIS
(Taking his arm in a fatherly way)
Listen, Fitzsimmons, don't advocate tanks. Every man who has is blacklisted by the higher command. Sir Arthur has a fit when they're mentioned! To us cavalry men, they're anathema.

FITZSIMMONS
To us soap men, they're the answer to trench warfare!
    (JARVIS shakes his head sadly as they start toward confession box)

FITZSIMMONS
(Loudly)
I'll put the *plans* in the usual place 'til we need them.

JARVIS
[   ] envelope in the top drawer and locks it)

FITZSIMMONS
(Loudly, turning to Jarvis)
Care to take a turn about the grounds, Jarvis?

JARVIS
(Loudly)
Delighted . . .
    (They exit)

(The door of the confession box opens and MARIE peeks out, looking around the room. She is a strikingly pretty young girl of about seventeen, dressed like a charwoman in an opera. She comes out of the box with a bucket and wash rag, puts them down and hurries over to the desk into which Fitzsimmons had just deposited the envelope. She extracts a key from her dress and is about to open the top drawer, when General Hargreaves' voice is heard from offstage, in a hoarse, angry shout)

HARGREAVES
(Offstage)
Bowker! Where the devil are you? Bowker . . . Bowker!

(MARIE quickly replaces the key in her dress, hurries over to her bucket, drops down on her knees and starts to mop up the floor as Bowker hurries in, carrying a whiskey bottle on a tray)

BOWKER
(Hurrying across to General's room)
Coming, sir, coming!
(He exits into the General's room just as the General again shouts "Bowker!" The voices of Fitzsimmons and Jarvis are heard offstage)

JARVIS
(Offstage)
Frightful fog—worse than London!
(As Fitzsimmons and Jarvis enter, Marie picks up the bucket and hurries out, the two men watching her. The minute she's gone, FITZSIMMONS goes to the desk, unlocks the top drawer and looks into it. He shakes his head negatively to Jarvis and closes the drawer. BOWKER comes out of the General's room)
The General awake, Bowker?

BOWKER
Yes, sir. He's dressing now, sir.
(He hurries out)

FITZSIMMONS

Good. Now if we can get him to act promptly.

JARVIS

(Hastily)

Oh, I wouldn't discuss it 'til after breakfast! He's awfully un-reasonable until he's had his tea and toast.

FITZSIMMONS

I'll risk it.

(To Sam, dozing at the switchboard)

Thompson! Thompson!

THOMPSON

(Turning)

Yes, sir.

FITZSIMMONS

Keep wires open to all battalion commanders!

THOMPSON

Yes, sir.

(BOWKER comes in with an Orderly. They carry a table-cloth, silverware, etc. They go to one of the tables and start spreading it for breakfast)

JARVIS

Er—how is the General this morning, Bowker?

BOWKER

On the moody side, sir. He was disappointed by the mist. He would have much preferred to breakfast in the garden.

JARVIS

(Shaking his head)

That's bad . . .

(FRENIQUE enters, followed by KILBRECHT and LIZETTE, leading a lamb on a ribbon-decorated halter. She is a vo-luptuous charmer, full blown, a little on the blousy side, in fact, the French peasant girl of song and story—with a streak of hard common sense thrown in for reality's sake. From here up to the entrance of the General, BOWKER and ORDERLY come and go, setting the break-fast on the table)

LIZETTE

(Gaily as she enters)
Bonjour, messieurs!

JARVIS

(Staring at the lamb)
Hello! What's this?

LIZETTE

She is Georgette—a little gigot for the General. Tres tendre, n'est-ce-pas?

KILBRECHT

Not another bit of mutton left in the countryside.

FRENIQUE

The peasant who owned her—he would not part with her until Lizette told him she was for the table of our beloved General Hargreaves!

KILBRECHT

Damn decent of him! Only wants ten quid for her.

FITZSIMMONS

That's fifty dollars!

FRENIQUE

(Smiling proudly)
Yes—we are a gracious people—we love our allies!

FITZSIMMONS

(Half to himself, turning away)
With a love that passeth misunderstanding . . .

(RUSSO and LEWIS, the two newspapermen, come in, RUSSO pushing forward arrogantly)

RUSSO

Well, boys . . . get something for me?

FITZSIMMONS

I told you to stay out.

RUSSO

(Pointing to Lizette)

If that dame can come in with a load of live chops . . .

(FITZSIMMONS gives him a look, turns away and goes to desk, busying himself with papers. To Jarvis)

Wait'll you see the notices I give that guy . . . !

(LEWIS goes to the big map and studies it. JARVIS goes to FITZSIMMONS and looks over a plan with him. RUSSO joins FRENIQUE, KILBRECHT and LIZETTE around the lamb)

RUSSO

What's that—the new mascot?

(LIZETTE and KILBRECHT ignore him. LIZETTE is busy making a conquest of Kilbrecht. He is responding in his stiff Scotch way)

LIZETTE

Your uniform . . . it is droll . . . but chic, very chic.

KILBRECHT

We Scots have always worn the kilt.

LIZETTE

A man in skirts . . .

(Shivers delightedly)

It gives me a frisson . . . thrill. . . . How do you say—

KILBRECHT

Naughty!

LIZETTE

(Coquettishly)

I would like it . . . a kilt.

KILBRECHT

A trifle too short for you.

LIZETTE

(Pulling up her skirts)

Oh—I have pretty legs.

RUSSO

She sells a lot more than lamb.

FRENIQUE

The women of France are known the world over for their charms . . . from the lowliest peasant to the debutante of the Faubourg St. Germain.

RUSSO

(Mockingly)
Yeah . . . men of less fortunate lands pay monee . . .
(To Lizette)
If the war only lasts, you'll buy that goose farm, ha, baby?

LIZETTE

(Chidingly, to Russo)
You are bad, my monkey!

KILBRECHT

(To Lizette)
I've got an old pair of kilts you could have . . .

RUSSO

(Contemptuously)
Trying to swap for it, hah?

LIZETTE

Oh, I would be so happy!

FRENIQUE

(Buttonholing Russo)
In your despatches, my dear Russo, don't you think a little more local color would help . . . some mention of the scene, of the glamour of France and of things French.

RUSSO

Pay for your ads.

GENERAL HARGREAVES

(Offstage, impatiently)
Bowker . . . ! Bowker . . . !

(Everybody looks around at the door, BOWKER, who has just put the finishing touches to the breakfast table, hurries to the General's room)

BOWKER

(Calling out)
Yes, sir—coming, sir!

JARVIS

(Shaking his head)
He's in a beastly temper . . .

(BOWKER opens the door and looks into the room)

HARGREAVES

(Offstage)
Bowker, is my breakfast ready?

BOWKER

Yes, sir.
(Closes door. To Lewis and Russo)
Pardon me, gentlemen, would you mind leaving, please?
(LEWIS nods and exits. RUSSO remains, however)

RUSSO

Why? What's the matter? Why're you chasing me?

BOWKER

General Hargreaves is about to breakfast.

FITZSIMMONS

And he has a sensitive stomach.
(Turns toward door)
Sentry!
(The GUARD appears in the door. Nodding toward
Russo)
Throw him out.
(RUSSO shrugs his shoulders and steps quickly toward
door, muttering under his breath)

RUSSO

Yah—tin soldiers!
(Exits)

HARGREAVES

(Offstage)
Bowker!

BOWKER

Yes, sir.
(He opens the door with a flourish and GENERAL HAR-
GREAVES enters. He is a gray-haired, portly gentleman of
about fifty, ruddy with health and high blood pressure.
British—BUT British)

HARGREAVES

Good morning.

(The officers come to attention. LIZETTE and the lamb,
behind the group of officers, are unnoticed by the General. He makes for the table Bowker has set)

AD LIBS

'Morning, sir.
Good morning.
Bowka-ru.
Bonjour.

HARGREAVES

(To Bowker, sitting)
What's for breakfast, Bowker?

BOWKER

(Bowing)
Strawberries, sir . . . porridge and cream . . . grilled kidneys . . .

HARGREAVES

Excellent . . .

BOWKER

(Bowing)
Thank you, sir.

FITZSIMMONS

I have a very important suggestion to make.

HARGREAVES

(Eating)
After breakfast, Fitzsimmons.

FITZSIMMONS

It's important . . . the fog—

HARGREAVES

Beastly. Bad for my rheumatism. I miss my annual cure at the mineral baths. If we don't win this war soon so I can take the waters, I don't know *what* I'll do.

FRENIQUE

General Hargreaves, I assure you the French waters—at Vichy or Aix-le-Bains are much superior to the German.

HARGREAVES

I've tried them. No good. Nieubad's the place—helps me no end.

FITZSIMMONS

General Hargreaves, our attack is scheduled to start in forty-five minutes. If we're to make any changes . . .

HARGREAVES

(Hurt)

Really, Fitzsimmons . . . you know my rule—no shop talk at meals.

FITZSIMMONS

But an emergency—

HARGREAVES

(With an air of uttering an epigram)

War is a succession of emergencies. I have served in more than ten campaigns and only by leading an orderly, well-regulated life—no matter what the conditions—can I boast the best stomach in the higher command.

FITZSIMMONS

(With heroic patience)

If I may explain . . .

HARGREAVES

My dear Fitzsimmons, you'll give yourself nervous indigestion.

(FITZSIMMONS turns away with a shrug)

JARVIS

(Shaking his head)

Bad for a soldier . . . nervous bowels.

KILBRECHT

An army travels on its stomach.

FITZSIMMONS
(Over his shoulder)
We're not going anywhere!

HARGREAVES

All the more reason for not hurrying. Bowker, where *did* you find these kidneys?

BOWKER
(Pleased)
You like them, sir?

HARGREAVES

Excellent! Excellent!

BOWKER

Thank you, sir.
(HARGREAVES eats with gusto as BOWKER waits on him attentively)

JARVIS

The new aide is here—Mr. Forsyte.

HARGREAVES

Ah yes! One of the Norfolk Forsytes . . . an old county family. Have him join us.

JARVIS
(To man helping Bowker)
Orderly—please ask Mr. Forsyte to step in.
(ORDERLY comes to attention and exits)

HARGREAVES
(Pointedly to Fitzsimmons)
The Forsytes are all soldiers . . . I served with his uncle, Sir William, at Ladysmith and again at Akabir. Excellent stock.

JARVIS
(Sighing)
Those were decent campaigns . . . none of this living in burrows like muskrats.

HARGREAVES

(Firmly)
No shop, Jarvis.

JARVIS

(Emotionally for him)
Beg pardon, sir . . . but I miss cavalry action badly.

HARGREAVES

So do I, so do I! Sometimes I think it was a mistake to dis-mount. One glorious, sweeping charge—that was the way, eh, Jarvis!

FITZSIMMONS

(Sarcastically)
Might as well use bows and arrows.

HARGREAVES

Don't scoff at the English bowman . . . the gray goose feather . . . They beat the French at Crecy and Agincourt, eh, Frenique?

FRENIQUE

At Poitiers it was different. We destroyed you.

HARGREAVES

Overpowered by a greatly superior force, let's say . . . We drew back strategically to consolidate our positions. But I'm forgetting my own rule. No shop, gentlemen, no shop.

FRENIQUE

(Waving toward Lizette)
What do you think of that lamb, sir?

HARGREAVES

Bring it here, my good woman.
        (LIZETTE comes forward with beast . . . HARGREAVES
        looks at her with interest)

FRENIQUE

Nice—no? She is so young, so tender, so fat . . .

LIZETTE

(To Frenique, with a curtesy)
Merci, mon Lieutenant!

HARGREAVES

Hmm . . . what do you think, Bowker?
(BOWKER bends to feel, Military joke)
Mind you, Bowker—not *her* leg.

BOWKER

Certainly not, sir.
(HARGREAVES roars with laughter—the others joining—
all but Fitzsimmons)

LIZETTE

(Ogling Hargreaves)
Ah, mon General . . . I don't mind—I am grateful to the
saviours of my beloved France.

FRENIQUE

(Smiling)
We love our allies . . .

BOWKER

(His inspection completed)
Seems to be a very satisfactory beast, sir.
(Exits)

KILBRECHT

I like mutton boiled plain.

FRENIQUE

(Indignantly)
You would boil this . . . this baby?! Barbarian! Have you no
civilization?

HARGREAVES

(To Kilbrecht)
You carry your Calvinism too far, really.

LIZETTE

(Softly, to Kilbrecht)
The plain fashion . . . a la mode ancienne . . . I like it, too.

HARGREAVES

Take it around to the kitchen.
(She starts off)

KILBRECHT
(Quickly)
I'll see that she gets her money from the Quartermaster.
(He goes quickly after LIZETTE. GERALD enters followed by the NIZAM and goes to the General, drawing to attention. The NIZAM goes over to the pigeons and feeds them)

GERALD
Leftenant Forsyte, sir.

HARGREAVES
Glad to have you with us, young Forsyte.
(He shakes hands with Gerald)
Bowker, a chair.
(GERALD sits near him)

GERALD
Thank you.
(During this scene, MARIE comes in with her pail and rag and after a moment, disappears, unnoticed, into a pew)

HARGREAVES
How's your uncle, Sir William?

GERALD
Very well, sir. He sent his regards.

HARGREAVES
Still keeps the Norfolk hounds, I take it?

GERALD
Yes, sir . . . hunts them regularly.

HARGREAVES
Excellent idea!

FITZSIMMONS
Bolsters the home morale.

(BOWKER enters with a coffee pot and two letters and goes to the General)

BOWKER
(Placing coffee pot on table and holding letters in his hand)
Your mail, sir.

HARGREAVES
Anything I *must* read, Bowker?

BOWKER
There's one from Mr. Stimpson, the veterinary . . . another from your wife, sir.

HARGREAVES
(Grunting)
Give me the one from Stimpson.

BOWKER
(Handing him the letter)
There is also a despatch from Division Headquarters, Sir Arthur Reynolds, marked urgent.

HARGREAVES
(Glancing at the letter he has opened)
Later.
(To Gerald)
I bought a bay gelding at Tatt's . . . one from Lord Clavershap's . . .

FITZSIMMONS
(Going to Hargreaves)
Now that you have finished breakfast, if I may be permitted to . . .

HARGREAVES
In a minute, Fitzsimmons . . . I want to digest what I've eaten. You're like my wife . . . all you Americans are so impatient.

FITZSIMMONS
I'm a Canadian.

HARGREAVES
Yes, of course . . . I'm sorry if I offended you.
(To Gerald)

My wife is an American. I married her when I was a military attache in Washington. Daughter of a Senator.
(Frowning)
One of my most difficult and arduous campaigns.

GERALD

I met Mrs. Hargreaves in London at the Sedgows—before leaving.

HARGREAVES

Oh. How is she?

GERALD

Very well, sir.

HARGREAVES

(Sentimentally)
I rather miss Grace . . .

GERALD

She's coming out, sir.

HARGREAVES

(Exploding)
What?!

GERALD

Yes. She left England before I did.

(HARGREAVES snatches the letter from Bowker and tears it open. His jaw sags)

HARGREAVES

It's true. This is no place for a woman. We must stop her.

FITZSIMMONS

(Sarcastically)
Double the guard!

FRENIQUE

(Smiling)
A cordon sanitaire!

HARGREAVES

(Taking it seriously)

Grace would get through a rolling barrage of high explosive.
Jarvis! Suggest something, man!

JARVIS

Have her stopped at the railroad!

HARGREAVES

That's it! Have her arrested!

JARVIS

On what charge?

HARGREAVES

Arson, mayhem—anything. Only stop her!
    (JARVIS hurries to switchboard, wakes THOMPSON, who
    gets busy with wires. To Bowker)
Clear it away . . . Leave the whiskey.
    (He reaches for bottle and pours some)

JARVIS
    (Returning to Hargreaves)
Won't you open the despatch from Sir Arthur, sir? It looks
extremely important.

FITZSIMMONS

That's shop, Jarvis.

    (BOWKER hands despatch to Hargreaves)

HARGREAVES
    (Not noticing the sarcasm. Opening despatch)
Well, we may as well get down to business. Let me see . . .
    (He starts reading, then breaks off suddenly, his jaw sag-
    ging)
My God! . . . Sir Arthur is congratulating us!

FITZSIMMONS

What for?

HARGREAVES
    (Looking at communique with puzzled frown)
On our "splendid victory."
    (Everyone is puzzled by this except Frenique)

FRENIQUE
(Suddenly excited)
Victory! Another piece of France snatched from the jaws of the blonde beast!

FITZSIMMONS
What victory?

HARGREAVES
(Reading)
"I personally congratulate you, your gallant staff and your heroic men for the victorious assault on Position S-438 yesterday . . ."

JARVIS
That's the Pepper Mill!

KILBRECHT
Could the troops have taken it without our knowing?

FITZSIMMONS
(Wryly)
That would be insubordination.

HARGREAVES
(Reading with deeper and deeper gloom)
"I am surprised not to have received a formal report in last night's despatches. In the future, my dear Hargreaves, do not let your modesty interfere with the sending of detailed communiques. So far, my information is confined entirely to newspaper accounts . . ."

FITZSIMMONS
Oh, *that's* it!

(JARVIS picks up a bundle of newspapers from the desk and rips off cover)

HARGREAVES
(Sadly)
All London is ringing with our acclaim.

JARVIS
(Staring at paper, as KILBRECHT and FRENIQUE crowd
around him)
Headlines clear across the page!
(Reads mournfully)
"Hargreaves Brigade Takes Pepper Hill . . . Thorn Removed
From Path of British Lion . . . Victory Assures Vote of Con-
fidence for Cabinet . . ."

HARGREAVES
(Groaning)
This is terrible . . . terrible!

KILBRECHT
(Trying to top him)
Most embarrassing.

FRENIQUE
(Hastily)
It's not in the French papers.

JARVIS
What a horrible mistake.

FITZSIMMONS
We've lost thousands of men trying to take that cranberry
bog, and now it's been taken—by the newspapers!

HARGREAVES
(Looking at them)
Who's responsible for this?

KILBRECHT
It looks like the work of spies.

FITZSIMMONS
Spies, nothing!
(Shouts)
Orderly! Send in that American journalist.

GUARD
Yes, sir.
(Salutes and exits)

FITZSIMMONS

He's capable of anything.

(RUSSO hurries in)

RUSSO

Got something for me?

FITZSIMMONS

(Coldly)
You sent out a story yesterday?

RUSSO

(Scenting trouble)
Yeah . . . sure. Why?

FITZSIMMONS

What was it?

RUSSO

Well, I kind of made a mistake.
(Whines)
I sent it out before the attack.

FITZSIMMONS

You reported the Pepper Mill taken!

RUSSO

(Hedging)
Well—I—it looked like it was *gonna* be taken yesterday . . .
And anyway, defeat isn't news on *this* front. It's about time
my readers got a break!

FITZSIMMONS

You think we're fighting this war for your readers?

RUSSO

Who else?

FITZSIMMONS

Well—that's as good a reason as any.

HARGREAVES

(Sputtering)
Sir? How dare you send out a premature report?

RUSSO

Well, I—I had to if I was going to make the cheap cable rates to America.

JARVIS

Unheard of!

RUSSO

(Slyly)

I'll send out a denial if you want me to—but I was only trying to give you guys a break. You can't expect us Americans to come in on the losing side.

FITZSIMMONS

Get out! And stay out of here! If you send another word on the Pepper Mill, I'll have you run off the whole front!

RUSSO

(Whining)

You can't do that. You guys are my bread and butter.

FITZSIMMONS

Sentry!

(RUSSO ducks out)

KILBRECHT

We ought to ship that foreigner back to North America.

HARGREAVES

I'd like nothing better. Unfortunately, my hands are tied—special instructions from the War Office.

KILBRECHT

They insist on saddling us with those bounders.

JARVIS

Hadn't we better inform Sir Arthur Reynolds of the error at once, sir?

HARGREAVES

(Very worried)

Well, er . . . no . . . not just yet. Perhaps we can . . . er . . . think of something.

FITZSIMMONS

There is nothing else.

JARVIS

I'm afraid not, sir.

HARGREAVES

(Thinking very hard)
You see, we've disappointed Sir Arthur so many times . . .
when he gets the denial he'll be furious! We'll probably all be
broken in rank.

FITZSIMMONS

But he's bound to discover it sooner or later.

HARGREAVES

(Ignoring this)
You know, gentlemen, I'm not trying to save our own skins,
but . . .
(Hitting on something)
er . . . Sir Arthur's not a well man—he has a bad heart.

JARVIS

(Helping Hargreaves)
Yes, that's true—Colonel Grosbeak, his aide, told me that
when Sir Arthur left England for the war his doctors warned
him that he *must* avoid excitement.

HARGREAVES

Exactly. The truth might infuriate him so that he'd—er . . .
drop dead! A desperate situation such as this demands heroic
measures.

JARVIS

We've got to save Sir Arthur.

KILBRECHT

The Empire can't afford to lose him.

JARVIS

We're doing it for England!

FITZSIMMONS

(Teasing a little)
But, *gentlemen*—!

HARGREAVES

He won't be here for at least another month—not until the

Spring Offensive starts . . . In the meantime, we'll *take* the
Pepper Mill!

JARVIS

(Doubtfully)
That would solve it . . .

HARGREAVES

Of course! We'll make good that report! We'll attack!

FITZSIMMONS

We've been attacking for months.

HARGREAVES

Not for nothing am I known as Bulldog Hargreaves. We'll
hammer the enemy and keep hammering!

FITZSIMMONS

There's no reason to expect victory unless the plan is changed.

HARGREAVES

(Glaring at him)
What are you talking about?

FITZSIMMONS

I've been trying to suggest all morning that we use this fog
for a surprise attack.

HARGREAVES

Another one of your confounded novelties! Novelties may sell
soap—but this is an emergency!
(Waves despatch)

FITZSIMMONS

All the more reason for trying something new.

HARGREAVES

Stop nagging, Fitzsimmons. We're in enough trouble as it is.
Have you no faith in the superior courage of our men? You
forget it is the British who are attacking.

FITZSIMMONS

We're using Irish in the assault wave.

NIZAM

Joras nu animi severa Ranthala.

JARVIS

(To Gerald)
Won't you translate?

HARGREAVES

(Astounded)
Do you understand him, Forsyte?

GERALD

Yes, sir—he says that we should do what his ancestors did at
the battle of Ranthala.

FITZSIMMONS

Lions, again?

GERALD

No, boiling oil—he says we should pour it on the enemy.

HARGREAVES

(This reminds him)
My wife! What'd you do to stop her, Jarvis?

JARVIS

(To Thompson)
Any news from the railhead?

THOMPSON

Yes, sir—Mrs. Hargreaves has been arrested. They'll send her
back to Paris on the next train.

HARGREAVES

Good.

GERALD

(Looking out of door)
The mist's beginning to lift.

FITZSIMMONS

There goes our chance.

FRENIQUE

In France the sun never hides his glory for long!

HARGREAVES
(Staring at despatch and shaking his head despondently)
Come along, gentlemen. Let's take our usual stroll—although
I doubt that I'll enjoy it this morning.

JARVIS
(Sympathetically, as they start for door)
I'm sure we'll take the Pepper Mill, sir.

HARGREAVES
We *must* take it; I'll dictate a stirring statement to the troops
calling for victory!
(HARGREAVES, followed by the others, exits. GERALD,
who has lingered a moment, looking at the map, starts
to follow. When he is half-way to the door, MARIE slowly
rises from a pew and looks after him. She takes a step
or two to leave the pew. In squeezing through a rather
narrow space, her eyes glued on Gerald, she drops her
pail with a clatter. She is startled as GERALD whirls
around)

GERALD
Oh!
(Taking in the situation, he hurries over to her)
Here, let me help you.
(GERALD and MARIE both bend down to reach for the
pail and take hold of the handle simultaneously. They rise
together, both still holding the pail and look at each
other—obviously interested)

MARIE
(Softly, after a pause)
Thank you so much . . .

GERALD
(A little confused as he looks down into her eyes)
Er—not at all—it's quite all right . . . Er—you're not hurt,
are you?

MARIE
(Her eyes glued on his)
No . . . thank you . . . you are very nice—to help me . . .

GERALD

Why—er—it's nothing at all—really.

MARIE

(Softly)
Oh, yes . . . it is . . . nobody else would pick up my pail for me.

GERALD

(Hardly aware of what he's saying)
I—er—don't see why not . . .
(Suddenly aware he is still holding the pail, he lets go of it hastily. With an effort at sternness to overcome his embarrassment)
I say—what were you doing in that pew?

MARIE

I was asleep.
(Looking at her pail and rag)
I work so hard . . .

GERALD

Oh, I'm sorry. May I—er—
(Taking pail and rag from her and sets them down on the floor. Suddenly remembers something)
But—look here, weren't you peeping out of that confession box before?

MARIE

Yes.

GERALD

What were you doing in there?

MARIE

I was looking at you . . . General . . .

GERALD

(Taken aback)
Oh—I see—Er—
(With a little laugh)
I'm not a general, you know.

MARIE

No . . . ? You will be—soon—you are so brave.

GERALD

Why—thank you . . .
    (Looking at her curiously)
You're an odd sort of charwoman . . .
    (Notices her hands)
Why, your hands aren't at all—

MARIE

    (Holding out her hands)
They are beautiful, aren't they . . . ! See what long, slender fingers I've got . . . that's the sign of an artist . . . I am a bayadere—a temple dancer.

GERALD

    (Amazed)
Are you really?

MARIE

Yes—I know the twenty-one dances of love and the seventeen dances of death. What kind of fingers have you?
    (She catches his hand and examines it)
They're nice and strong . . . I like nice, strong hands on a man.

GERALD

    (Withdrawing his hand)
Really . . . er . . . this is . . .

MARIE

You've got the nicest fingers of any of the officers. Colonel Jarvis' are like little pork sausages . . . he has a coarse nature.

GERALD

    (Astounded)
What?

MARIE

    (Unheeding)
General Hargreaves' are ugly with blunt ends . . . a sign that he gives in to his lower self . . . in secret, I think. Do you like poetry?

GERALD

Yes . . . I suppose so . . .

MARIE

I don't like men who don't like poetry . . . Major Fitzsimmons is nice, but he detests Omar Khayyam . . . and anyway, he's too old for me . . . Colonel Jarvis is fat . . . The General is always eating . . . Frenique is a flirt . . . Mr. Russo is vulgar . . . Do you like dogs, too?

GERALD

(Relieved at the change)
Yes . . . I raise them.

MARIE

What kind?

GERALD

(Safer ground now)
Fox hounds. I own the Imperial Champion . . . Music of Folkstone. Won at Gruft's last year.

MARIE

Do you love him?

GERALD

(Uncomfortable)
Well, he's a good hound . . . has a very keen nose.

MARIE

Noses show character . . . I like nice noses . . .

GERALD

(Smiling)
A long, tapering nose means an artist, I suppose . . .

MARIE

(Very serious)
No . . . but if the nostrils flare out, it means a passionate nature . . . Mine flare . . . see . . . Do you like passion?

GERALD

(Embarrassed again)
Er—I suppose so. Yes.

MARIE

I do. It keeps things from being dull. That's why I went to war.

GERALD

Isn't this village your home?

MARIE

Oh, no. I'm an Oriental.

GERALD

You're a what?

MARIE

An Oriental . . . Javanese.

GERALD

But you have—blue eyes . . . a rather—deep blue . . .

MARIE

Only half of me is Javanese—the other half is Dutch. My mother was a priestess in the Temple Nasputi—my father—a sea Captain, seduced her. She loved him as only a Javanese can love . . . I'm the fruit of their union . . .

GERALD

But you don't look like a half-caste.

MARIE

Some night I'll wear my dancing robes for you—you'll see.

GERALD

I say—that'll be fascinating.

MARIE

(Mysteriously)
I'll dance the temple dances . . . let you drown in the perfume of my hair . . .

GERALD

It *is* nice—your hair . . .

MARIE

Men have destroyed themselves to touch it . . .

GERALD

(Astounded)
Have they really?

MARIE

Bah . . . their jewels and flowers weary me . . . Beauty carries a curse! Men are vile! That's why I came here to do a servant's work . . . to expiate.

GERALD

Really!

MARIE

My Javanese name is Kanda Swany—"The Eye of the Jewel"—here, I'm plain Marie . . . So be it. Scrubbing the floors helps me to forget.

(FITZSIMMONS enters)

MARIE

(Quickly picking up her pail and rag)
Good byc!
(She hurries out, GERALD starting after her)

FITZSIMMONS

(Coming up to Gerald)
Getting acquainted with the help?

GERALD

Why—er—she's—

FITZSIMMONS

Pretty!

GERALD

Well, yes—but . . . rather odd—a Javanese temple dancer doing char work . . . It's a bit thick, what?

FITZSIMMONS

There aren't any Javanese temples around here to dance in—so I wouldn't worry about her.
(Goes to his desk)

GERALD

Yes, of course . . . but . . . er . . .
(Still in a reverie, he starts slowly after Marie. HAR-GREAVES, JARVIS, KILBRECHT and the NIZAM enter)

JARVIS

(Consulting watch)
It's eleven-fifty.
    (Stopping Gerald)
Mr. Forsyte, will you stand by—the attack is about ready to start.

GERALD

Certainly, sir.

JARVIS

(Going to switchboard, followed by FITZSIMMONS, who puts on earphones)
All wires clear?

THOMPSON

Yes, sir.
    (Handing him message)
This is for General Hargreaves, sir.
    (JARVIS gives message to HARGREAVES)

HARGREAVES

(Groaning)
Good heavens! It's Grace. She's escaped!

JARVIS

(Amused)
Did she overpower the guard?

HARGREAVES

No—no—they put her through to Sir Arthur and he gave her safe conduct to the front. The old fool.

JARVIS

(Sympathetically)
Too bad . . .

FITZSIMMONS

The attack's starting.

HARGREAVES

She'll soon be here . . .
    (Groans)
I'd rather it were the Germans.

JARVIS

(To Thompson)
Give us all reports immediately. Orderly—help Thompson.

(ORDERLY takes seat at switchboard next to Thompson.
A second Orderly takes down stenographic notes of every
move in the attack. KILBRECHT and FRENIQUE go to wall
map and move flags in accordance with reports, repeating
half aloud each move as they do so)

THOMPSON

Major Strahe reports lines moving forward.

JARVIS

We're off!

THOMPSON

Second Battalion—third and fourth companies engaging enemy gun on left flank.

ORDERLY

First Battalion—difficulty leaving trench because of enemy
fire—but now attacking.

FITZSIMMONS

(To Jarvis)
That's their wood battery—it should be silenced!

JARVIS

(To Orderly)
Get me Ordnance.
(Hurries to phone, followed by FITZSIMMONS. ORDERLY
hands him receiver)
Hello . . . Haskins . . . this is Jarvis . . . Their cannon in
Gervaise wood are making it deuced difficult . . . be a good
fellow and see if you can't silence them. Thanks, old chap . . .
good hunting.
(Returns receiver to Orderly. To Hargreaves, cheerfully)
Haskins will silence that wood battery, sir.

HARGREAVES

(Distractedly)
Fine!

(Calling Gerald)
Young Forsyte!

GERALD
(Stepping to Hargreaves' side)
Yes, sir?

HARGREAVES
Did my wife give any particular reason for wanting to come out here?

GERALD
No, sir. But I gathered she felt the need of a little change.

HARGREAVES
(Shaking his head)
She's at her worst at such times.

THOMPSON
Major Strahe reports battery partially silenced . . .

JARVIS
Good—if those gunner chaps only keep hammering.

ORDERLY
Third and Fourth companies, second battalion, still engaged with enemy machine gun. Signaled for aid.

FITZSIMMONS
Tell Major Stevens to keep advancing the third and fourth— let his support mop up—that's what they're for, damn it!

JARVIS
(To Hargreaves, enthusiastically)
Wood battery silenced!

HARGREAVES
Splendid!
(To Gerald)
Grace is a good old girl—but she's so *confounded* cheerful.

THOMPSON
Fourth Battalion says our shells are falling short . . .

JARVIS
Get Ordnance again.

FITZSIMMONS
(Snatching phone)
Hello . . . Ordnance . . .
(Bursts with rage)
God damn you gunners! Keep those shells ahead of us . . . !
(Slams up phone. GERALD goes to switchboard)

JARVIS
(Apprehensively)
You'll antagonize Haskins.

THOMPSON
Machine gun silenced . . . Fifth Battalion on schedule, sir . . .

FITZSIMMONS
Where's the Sixth? Why don't we hear from Albright? Get
Albright.

GERALD
(To Jarvis)
This *is* exciting—my first experience under fire!

JARVIS
We're going splendidly!

FITZSIMMONS
(Snapping)
We always get this far!

GERALD
It gives you a queer sensation not to hear the firing . . .

FITZSIMMONS
Cup your hand over your ear . . .
(GERALD does so)
That humming noise . . . like a swarm of bees.

GERALD
(Excited)
Yes . . . I hear it!

FITZSIMMONS
That's the war.

THOMPSON

Albright lost two platoons in a mined culvert—but they've rallied and continue to advance.

FITZSIMMONS

Damn the patrols! They should have spotted those mines last night!

THOMPSON

Second and Third Battalion have reached wire. Much wire remains uncut. First also stalled at wire.

FITZSIMMONS

(Annoyed)
What's the use of a barrage if it doesn't even cut wire!

JARVIS

(Very excited—to Hargreaves)
General Hargreaves! We're in the enemy's front line! Second Battalion!

HARGREAVES

Magnificent! We'll make good that despatch.
(Suddenly deflated)
Now if there were only some way of stopping Grace . . .

ORDERLY

Sixth Battalion advancing toward enemy's second line! Second Battalion mopping up! Left arm of salient still occupied by enemy!

FITZSIMMONS

Where's the Third? They should be in there!

ORDERLY

Third Battalion progress impeded by machine guns . . . in area of right arm of salient . . . encircling movement begun by A and C companies.

THOMPSON

Fourth Battalion still unable to clean out machine gun nest . . . still attempt frontal attack . . .

FITZSIMMONS
Why don't they use grenades?

ORDERLY
Fifth Battalion stopped by fire from second enemy line . . .
Sixth also unable to advance.

THOMPSON
Fourth Battalion under heavy fire. Attempting to maintain position.

FITZSIMMONS
(To Thompson)
Get me Haskins—quick!

JARVIS
Be careful with him.

FITZSIMMONS
(Into phone)
Lift the barrage on enemy second line—hammer their guns.
No—we're no longer attacking. Hammer their guns!

JARVIS
(Apprehensively)
They'll counter-attack soon.

FITZSIMMONS
They won't have to—their artillery'll blow us out.

THOMPSON
Albright is calling for more guns, sir.

FITZSIMMONS
Albright—Fitzsimmons! They're giving us all the guns they've
got—try to hang on.

JARVIS
We're being hammered pretty bad.

FITZSIMMONS
(Deeply disturbed, calling out to Hargreaves)
Second Battalion reports position untenable—facing annihi-
lation.

JARVIS

(Thinking aloud)
We always break down at this same point.

FITZSIMMONS

(To Hargreaves)
What are your instructions, sir?

HARGREAVES

Tell 'em to withdraw.

(FITZSIMMONS turns to phone. Suddenly shouts are heard offstage)

GUARD

(At door)
You can't pass, ma'am.

HARGREAVES

(Apprehensively—rising)
She's here!

(GRACE HARGREAVES enters, pushing guard with bayonet ahead of her. She is a woman of about thirty-eight, still attractive. She is wearing a dress that is in the style of a military uniform with a hat to match. She is full of energy—extremely cheerful, determined to understand everything and to "help")

GRACE

(Shoving bayonet aside)
Young man—stop sticking that thing in my face!

HARGREAVES

(Hopelessly)
No use—let her by.
(GRACE rushes to Hargreaves)

GRACE

Blinkey, darling!
(They embrace. Holding him at arm's length)
You've been drinking whiskey at breakfast!
(Dropping it)
How's the war going?

HARGREAVES

Well enough. You shouldn't have come out. The front's no
place for you.

GRACE

But it is darling. This is where things are happening.
(Looking around at the others with interest. GERALD
comes forward to greet her, as does Frenique. To Gerald)
Oh, hello, Mr. Forsyte.

GERALD

Howdy do, Mrs. Hargreaves . . . this is Lieutenant Frenique
of the French Army . . .

GRACE

Hello, Lieutenant.
(FRENIQUE, extremely gallant, bows, kissing her hand)

FRENIQUE

Charmed, madam—may I compliment you on your dress.

GRACE

(Delighted)
Thank you! Just a little thing for the front.
(To Hargreaves)
Aren't you going to introduce me to the rest of the staff?

HARGREAVES

(Reluctantly)
Yes, of course.
(To staff)
Gentlemen—
(They all turn)
This is my wife.

(Ad lib greetings from officers)

GRACE

I do hope you'll be patient and explain everything to me—I
so want to help.

HARGREAVES

Please, Grace . . . We're busy.

GRACE

(To Frenique)

Lieutenant—and you, Gerald, won't you be my guides? I don't like to bother the General when he's working.

(She pats Hargreaves' cheek, puts her arm through Gerald's and Frenique's arms and starts in the direction of the map. HARGREAVES follows helplessly)

FRENIQUE

Certainly, Madame.

GRACE

What a decorative map . . . and those charming little flags . . . what are they for?

FRENIQUE

They show the position of the troops, Madame.

GRACE

How very imaginative.

(Turning to Hargreaves)

Your idea, Blinkey?

(GRACE and her guides move to the switchboard where Thompson and the Orderly are busy with the wires. FITZSIMMONS and JARVIS are hovering anxiously around them)

Really, this is fascinating! Who are they calling?

HARGREAVES

(Helplessly)

Please, Grace . . .

GRACE

But I must know all about it . . . I've promised to lecture when I return. Several women's clubs have invited me to. I want to tell them everything . . .

FITZSIMMONS

That'll be the end of recruiting.

GRACE

Oh no—it should help.

THOMPSON

Major Strahe reports all battalions are withdrawing to original positions.

GRACE

How are we doing?

JARVIS

(Tragically)
We've failed.

HARGREAVES

(Fiercely)
We'll attack again tomorrow!

GRACE

(Cheerfully)
Of course! You can't always win. Sir Arthur told me about your wonderful victory yesterday.
(HARGREAVES groans)
What was it you captured, Blinkey—a pepper grinder or something?

HARGREAVES

(Very uncomfortable)
Nothing, Grace—nothing at all.

GRACE

Don't be so modest, darling. Sir Arthur let me come out to see you as a reward for what you did.

HARGREAVES

(Groaning)
Oh . . .

GRACE

(Looking around)
Isn't it *weird*—living in a church. Must make every day feel like Sunday . . . I don't like the way the furniture is arranged.
(Reflectively)
What the place needs is splashes of color—and just loads and loads of flowers . . . a woman's touch!

(She pauses suddenly as she and everyone else listen
to the sound of an airplane motor overhead, a swelling
hum)

FITZSIMMONS

Sounds like a German . . . a Taub bomber . . .

GRACE

(Not frightened)
Oh, will he drop something on us?

HARGREAVES

No—certainly not—we have an unwritten agreement with the
enemy—we don't bomb each other's staffs.

(During the following, the sound of the airplane grows
steadily louder)

GRACE

Oh!
(Returns to her original idea)
Let's see . . . haven't you some more of those delightful maps
we could hang up? We should have the place all fixed before
Sir Arthur comes.

HARGREAVES

(Shocked)
What?

JARVIS

(Hardly able to speak)
Sir Arthur—coming here?

GRACE

(Surprised)
Yes, of course! He'll be here tomorrow.

FITZSIMMONS

There goes tomorrow's attack.

GRACE

(Noticing their consternation)
Why, what's the matter, boys?

HARGREAVES
(Brokenly)
Did—did he say why he's coming?

GRACE
It's because of your victory, darling. He wants to congratulate
you personally.

FITZSIMMONS
How's his heart?

(Suddenly there is a tremendous explosion—a part of the
ceiling falls with a crash)

HARGREAVES
(Great indignation)
The barbarians!

AD LIBS FROM OFFICERS
The dirty Bosches!
Scoundrels!
Bombing staff headquarters!
Unheard of!
What treachery!
The blackguards!

(FITZSIMMONS rushes to door and shouts outside as
others mill around)

AD LIBS
The dirty dogs!
Ill-mannered louts!
What's the war coming to!

HARGREAVES
Are they mad—bombing the staff!

(FITZSIMMONS appears at door again)

FITZSIMMONS
It's not their fault!

HARGREAVES
What!

FITZSIMMONS

We forgot to take the red cross off the roof! They thought this place was still a hospital!

CURTAIN

Act Two

Scene: The next day. About 4:30 P.M.

The room has been decorated with a profusion of flowers, gay peasant pottery, bits of bright cloth, etc.

As the curtain rises, JARVIS is discovered at the campaign map with Fitzsimmons and Gerald. JARVIS is reluctantly pulling little flags from the map and replacing them according to instructions Fitzsimmons gives him from the paper he is holding. GERALD follows their conversation with interest. The NIZAM is feeding the pigeons.

FITZSIMMONS

(Reading from paper)

A and B companies, third battalion . . . forced to retreat at eight minutes past twelve . . . New position identical with that held before attack.

GERALD

(Cheerfully)

Well, we didn't lose any ground.

FITZSIMMONS

No.

(From paper)

D company, same battalion, retired in good order . . .

GERALD

You've forgotten C company.

JARVIS

C company has been joined with D, making D full strength again.

(Moves flags)

FITZSIMMONS

(Ironically)

They'll get two dinners per man tonight and double tobacco ration.

JARVIS

(Philosophically)

Wellington said, "You've got to break eggs to make an omelette."

FITZSIMMONS

We're not using eggs.

JARVIS

We must take the long view—every defeat is a victory in a war of attrition.

FITZSIMMONS

What would the men in the front lines think of that?

JARVIS

They know nothing of military science.

FITZSIMMONS

I think I could explain your war of attrition so they'd understand it. It's like checkers. We have so many more men on the board than they have that we can afford to lose three of ours for every one of theirs and still win.

JARVIS

(Shocked)

The censors would never permit such an explanation.

FITZSIMMONS

Of course not. You couldn't make war without the censors.

(GRACE enters, followed by Marie, Kilbrecht and Frenique. The women are carrying more flowers, wrapped in paper)

GRACE

We bought some more flowers. Before I'm through with this gloomy old place you won't *know* it's a church!

FRENIQUE

But madame, it has been one of France's crowning glories for seven hundred years!

GRACE

That's long enough. Marie! unwrap those.

MARIE

Yes, ma'am.
        (She unties strings)

GERALD

Mrs. Hargreaves, I want to thank you for putting those flowers in my room.
        (MARIE looks up at this)

GRACE

In your room? Marie and I put some in the General's room—But not yours.
        (She starts fussing with the string around the package)

MARIE

        (Softly, to Gerald, as she opens a package)
Did you like the flowers in your room . . . ?

GERALD

Yes, they—
        (Suddenly)
You put them there?
        (MARIE looks up at him and nods shyly)
Really now—you shouldn't have . . .

MARIE

Do you understand the language of flowers?

GERALD

        (Confused)
Why—er—no, I can't say I do—precisely . . .

MARIE

It is the language of the heart . . .

GERALD

(Slowly, as he looks into her eyes)
I say—that's—frightfully interesting . . .

GRACE

(Having difficulty with a string)
Haven't any of you a dagger . . . or even a knife? What kind
of soldiers are you?
(Pointing to Nizam)
Get his sword.
(They stare at her, so she does it herself, pulling it out of
the scabbard with a flourish)

NIZAM

(Cursing and reaching for revolver)
Adamya—no—phuti!

GERALD

(Hastily)
Menushi—sobot—

NIZAM

(Returning pistol sullenly)
Baxeno shta rubanyas me asha.

GRACE

(Opening parcels with sword)
What's he making those sounds for?

GERALD

(Apologetic)
Why—er—He says the sword's been spoiled by a woman
touching it.

GRACE

Isn't that just like a man! The thing's dull anyway.

NIZAM

Shteno—surkaya . . .

GERALD

He says his grandfather cut a hundred throats with it.

GRACE

Well, the old man spoiled the edge . . .

(The NIZAM recovers his sword. BOWKER comes in on his way to the garden, carrying some silver)

(Stopping him and examining the silver)
What beautiful Chinese silver, Bowker. Does the government issue it?

BOWKER

No, ma'am. We captured it in the Boxer rebellion.

GRACE

Looting!

BOWKER

(Smiling)
Spoils of war, rather, ma'am.

GRACE

The General should bring things like that home. What's the use of being a soldier's wife if one doesn't get souvenirs?
(BOWKER bows and exits. GRACE places some flowers, and looks around appraisingly, her eyes falling on the pigeons. The NIZAM watches her, on the alert. Pointing to the pigeons)
Of course, those pigeons will have to go.

JARVIS

They are carrier pigeons, Mrs. Hargreaves.

GRACE

We can find some other place for them, I'm sure. I don't mind a canary or two, but it's silly trying to live with pigeons!

NIZAM

(Who has been watching her intently. Bursts out)
Nudi bayada meni oko bosh! Oko bosh!

GRACE

(To Nizam)
What?

(To Gerald)
What's the matter with him now?

GERALD

He says he's taken the birds under his royal protection.

GRACE

That's perfectly ridiculous!
(With a shrug)
Oh, well, I'll have them removed when he's out. I don't want to encourage the Indian Nationalist movement.
(RUSSO and LEWIS enter)

RUSSO

What are you going to do—tell fortunes in here?

FITZSIMMONS

I told you to stay out!

RUSSO

I wanna use the phone . . . I got a hot human interest story from a guy who eye-witnessed the rapings of a dozen nuns by a blonde beast!

GRACE

A dozen!

RUSSO

Well—maybe ten. Say . . . you wanna give me a story for America?

GRACE

I'd love to!

LEWIS

I'm from the London Daily Press, Mrs. Hargreaves.

RUSSO

Okay—you can listen, too.
(To Grace)
What I want is a woman's slant on the war.

GRACE

I think we're deliberately being kept out of it. It's all very well to knit socks and run street cars, but we women can do more—much more!

RUSSO

What do you want to do—get into the trenches?

GRACE

If necessary! Woman is just as brave as man. Is it nothing to bear children?

RUSSO

That's terrific!

(HARGREAVES enters from his room, holding some papers and looking very worried. He stops short and looks around with indignant amusement at the decorations)

HARGREAVES

What is this? . . . a bazaar?

GRACE

Why, Blinkey, darling, we're making it more cheerful and homey.

HARGREAVES

(Roaring doubtfully)

This is a Brigade Staff Headquarters of His Majesty's Forces in France—not a Bloomsbury tea shop!

GRACE

Blinkey—don't shout—you're not on parade.

HARGREAVES

(To Sentry at door)

Guard! . . . Clear this room of everyone without official business!

(GUARD moves forward and starts herding the two journalists, Grace and Marie out)

GRACE

(Indignantly)

But, Blinkey! We haven't finished.

HARGREAVES

Please leave, Grace.

RUSSO

(Arrogantly)

Now wait a minute—

GUARD

(To Russo)
Get out!
(LEWIS and MARIE exit)

GRACE

(To Russo)
I'll give you the rest of the interview outside . . .

HARGREAVES

(Calling after her, apprehensively)
Grace, please be careful of that fellow!

(GRACE and RUSSO exit. BOWKER sticks his head cautiously out of the General's room, looks around and enters burdened down with a large vase filled with flowers, three or four fancy cushions, a peasant shawl and a lamp with a gaudy fringed shade. Everybody turns to watch him as he walks quickly and quietly across the room and exits through another door)

(HARGREAVES looks at the despatch in his hand, his face full of worry)

HARGREAVES

(Looking at them solemnly)
Gentlemen—I have official notification of Sir Arthur's visit. He'll be here shortly.

KILBRECHT

(Shaking his head)
Frightful mess . . .

HARGREAVES

To make matters worse, he's already recommended all of you for promotions—and mentioned me in a special communique to the King.
(Wistfully)
If it were only true . . .

FITZSIMMONS

Well, it isn't.

KILBRECHT

You'll be the laughing stock of the service.

JARVIS

We might be retired in half pay—and I'm frightfully hard up.

KILBRECHT

The Lairds of Kilbrecht hold their rank by inheritance. I can't
be demoted.
   (History lesson)
At the Battle of Glenliveret, the Duke of Monmouth, then
Baron McBornmooth, issued a ukase making my great-great-
great grandfather a . . .

FITZSIMMONS

We've heard the story.

JARVIS

   (Equally tragic)
My mother will be heartbroken . . . she starved herself to put
me through Sandhurst and a commission . . . I still owe her
money.

FRENIQUE

   (With a shrug)
I'm sorry for you gentlemen.

JARVIS

Thanks, old man . . .

NIZAM

   (Gravely)
Rojo seeanopsom.

FITZSIMMONS

   (To Nizam)
Thank you.

JARVIS

We should have sent out that denial immediately.

HARGREAVES

I was certain Sir Arthur wouldn't come for at least another
month.

JARVIS

If we could only have kept it from him a little longer . . .

FITZSIMMONS

One look at that map is all he'll need.

(HARGREAVES slowly goes over to the map and stares at it silently)

JARVIS

Of course he won't visit the front line.

FITZSIMMONS

Naturally not. It's very muddy out there.

HARGREAVES
(Slowly, still looking at the map)
This is the only way he'll find out . . .
(He turns, a thought growing stronger and stronger)
Our careers hang on a few little pins . . .
(He looks at the others as though they too must have gotten the same thought. And they have! JARVIS has an expression of desperate hope on his face, KILBRECHT looks shocked, FITZSIMMONS and FRENIQUE surprised and GERALD a little puzzled)

KILBRECHT
(With a note of horror)
General Hargreaves . . . really . . .

HARGREAVES

I assure you, gentlemen, I'm not thinking of myself. It's for the good of the entire service that we—prevent this disgrace . . . Otherwise, I wouldn't stoop to such—a— er—

FITZSIMMONS
(Helping him)
Subterfuge.

(ORDERLY enters and goes to FRENIQUE)

JARVIS

We appreciate that, sir.

FITZSIMMONS

And then there's always Sir Arthur's bad heart.

ORDERLY

(To Frenique)
Monsieur Jervais, from Paris, to see you, sir.

FRENIQUE

(To the officers)
I am of the French Army. The responsibility is not mine.
(Exits with Orderly)

HARGREAVES

We need only a little more time to take that position.

FITZSIMMONS

We've had five months and failed.

HARGREAVES

(Working himself up)
We'll attack again! We'll hammer them to bits—tomorrow.

FITZSIMMONS

Or the next day.

KILBRECHT

But suppose—

HARGREAVES

We won't fail!

JARVIS

(Catching fire)
We can do it!

GERALD

(Enthusiastically)
I'm sure of it!

FITZSIMMONS

That settles it!

HARGREAVES

(Self-intoxicated)
Tomorrow's thrust will be irresistible! Victory must be ours!

NIZAM

(Infected with excitement)
Scroos ha bajewls!

GERALD
(Translating)
Poison the bayonets!

JARVIS
(On fire, as far as phlegm can burn)
Victory!

KILBRECHT
Victory! Up, St. Andrew!

HARGREAVES
(Taking Jarvis' arm)
Come along—we'll go over every detail of tomorrow's plan.

FITZSIMMONS
Why do that? It's the same plan.

JARVIS
(On surer ground now)
Napoleon said details are more important than troops or cannon.

HARGREAVES
(Turning to Fitzsimmons, taking the plunge)
Fitzsimmons—move those flags forward!

JARVIS
(Excitedly, as Fitzsimmons goes to map)
The die is cast! Victory follows the flag!
(HARGREAVES and JARVIS, followed by KILBRECHT exit to General's room)

FITZSIMMONS
I thought it was trade.

GERALD
(Enthusiastically)
Good old Bulldog Hargreaves! He'll do it.

FITZSIMMONS
(Moving flag on map with a flourish)
It's done!

(FRENIQUE enters with Monsieur Jervais, who is a little man, in a frock coat, derby hat, an extremely high stiff collar. He carries a brief case and wears pince-nez. His manner is pedantic)

JERVAIS

(As they enter)
Bonjours, Messieurs. . . .

FRENIQUE

Gentlemen, this is Monsieur Jervais of the Academic Française . . . Major Fitzsimmons, Leftenant Forsyte . . .
(FITZSIMMONS and GERALD bow, as does Jervais)

JERVAIS

Gallant defenders! In the name of French culture and of Western civilization, I greet you gratefully.

FITZSIMMONS

(Dryly)
Thanks.

FRENIQUE

Ever mindful of the artistic heritage which France holds in keeping for the world—even in these times of dire distress—the Republic has—

FITZSIMMONS

(Impatiently)
What does he want?

FRENIQUE

(Not at all perturbed)
Monsieur Jervais is here to make an inventory of the art treasures and to remove the most valuable for safe keeping to Paris.

JERVAIS

(Bows)
The Germans are thieves. I understand that a professor of aesthetics is attached to every one of their Armies to make sure they steal only the most authentic objects of art!

FRENIQUE

We captured one of them at the Somme.

(Very indignantly)
His pockets were stuffed with catalogues of the museums.
Next to each item he wanted was a check.

FITZSIMMONS

That's how Napoleon filled the Louvre with Italian and Egyptian art.

FRENIQUE

But that was different!

JERVAIS

(Indignant)
Certainment!

FITZSIMMONS

Go ahead! Take what you want!

FRENIQUE

It is necessary to have a representative of the British staff with us to counter-check the inventory.

FITZSIMMONS

Mr. Forsyte will go with you.

JERVAIS

Monsieur, in the name of the Republic Français, I thank you for your assistance. By defending France you defend civilization! Liberte! Egalite! Fraternite!
     (He bows and exits with Gerald and Frenique. As they leave, RUSSO appears at door held back by Guard)

RUSSO

(Shouting)
I gotta use the phone!

FITZSIMMONS

Throw him out.
     (GUARD pulls Russo out. FITZSIMMONS exits to Hargreaves' room. The stage is empty for a minute, then a panel in the lower part of the altar opens and MARIE peeks out. She comes into the room and starts for desk. At the same time, RUSSO climbs in through a window near telephone, unseen by Marie. He starts toward

phone, then sees her and watches as she goes to desk, takes key out of pocket, unlocks drawer, takes out blue envelope and thrusts it into her bosom. She turns to leave. RUSSO darts quickly across the room and catches her from behind)

RUSSO

(Struggling with her)

Spy!

(Tries to reach into her blouse)

I saw you steal 'em. Give me those papers!

MARIE

Let me go!

(GERALD enters and misunderstands the scene completely. He rushes to Marie's rescue)

GERALD

(Catching Russo by shoulder)

Take your hand out of there!

RUSSO

(Frightened squeal)

I . . . I caught her . . .

(GERALD delivers a stiff right sock to Russo's jaw)

GERALD

You beast!

(MARIE runs for shelter to Gerald's enveloping arms and lifts her lips toward his)

MARIE

(Innocently)

He tried to rape me.

GERALD

(Bending toward her)

The rotter!

(They kiss)

RUSSO

(From floor)

She's a spy! I caught her stealing papers!

(GERALD is too busy kissing her to hear, and RUSSO gets frantic)
You're in the plot! You're a spy, too! I'll have you shot!

(GRACE enters)

GRACE

Oh! Oh . . . Really, Lieutenant . . . ! During business hours?
(GERALD and MARIE disentangle)

GERALD

(Embarrassed)
I . . . er . . .

GRACE

(To Russo, who is getting to his feet)
And you, Mr. Russo . . . playing on the floor like a child.

RUSSO

He knocked me down—the dirty spy!

GRACE

Why, Mr. Russo! What language! I believe you're drunk.

RUSSO

He *is* a spy! She, too.

GRACE

Nonsense!—I know his family. Splendid people.

GERALD

He tried to kiss Marie.

MARIE

Rape, Madam!

GRACE

Oh, dear!

RUSSO

I didn't. I saw her steal papers from that desk.
(At this, GERALD steps toward him, truculently while MARIE starts to hurry off)
She's escaping!
(He grabs her again)

GERALD

Keep your hands off her!

RUSSO

(To Grace)
Look in her blouse—see what you find.

GRACE

What do you expect me to find?
(MARIE has her back to the others. She hastily snatches
the envelope from the neck of her dress and starts to jam
it into her mouth)

RUSSO

She's eating them!

(GRACE snatches the envelope from Marie's mouth)

GRACE

My dear! They'll give you indigestion!
(Looks at envelope. Reads)
"Plans for Attack." Why, she *is* a spy!

RUSSO

(Triumphant)
Sure she is! What a story!
(Shakes his head in awe)
What a story!

GERALD

I simply can't believe it . . .
(Turning to Marie, with shocked sorrow)
It's terrible!

MARIE

(Proud bravery)
War is terrible!

GERALD

(Hurt)
But a girl like you . . .

RUSSO

(The Accuser)
She's a femme fatale!

GRACE

(Shaking her head)
Such an honest face, too!

MARIE

It's a mask . . .

GERALD

But, Marie . . . I . . . How horrible! You're likely to be
shot!

RUSSO

Likely?! She's gotta be shot!

MARIE

I will not falter even at the grave.

GRACE

Nonsense! You ought to be spanked.

GERALD

(Sorrow—not anger)
And all the time you—you were making me feel sorry for
you.

MARIE

(Femme fatale)
I toy with all men. It is my career . . .

RUSSO

What a story!
(FITZSIMMONS enters—takes in scene at a glance)
Fitzie—she's a spy. I caught her at it.

FITZSIMMONS

(Carelessly)
Yes, I know.

RUSSO

(Dumbfounded)
You know what?

FITZSIMMONS

(Impatiently)
I know she's a spy. Now get out of here!

RUSSO
(Horrified)
Then you're in league with her! You're all spies! It's a conspiracy!

(As GUARD starts rushing RUSSO off, the GENERAL, JARVIS and KILBRECHT enter in time to hear his next line)

HARGREAVES
Here! What's all this?
(GUARD stops short. RUSSO breaks away from him and goes to Hargreaves)

RUSSO
I just caught a spy—her! She was stealing papers—tried to swallow them like a goat—
(Pointing at Fitzsimmons, accusingly)
—and *this* guy says he knows all about it!

HARGREAVES
(Astonished)
What! Fitzsimmons—are you harboring a female spy?

FITZSIMMONS
Yes,—but—

HARGREAVES
(To Guard)
Put her under arrest!

(GUARD signals outside. Two other guards enter and lead Marie off)

RUSSO
(While this is happening)
He's one, too! So's that young guy. Benedict Arnolds, both of 'em!

FITZSIMMONS
(Formally, to Hargreaves)
I must ask, sir, to have this civilian removed—if there is to be an inquiry.
(HARGREAVES nods)

RUSSO

You can't pull the wool over my eyes.

FITZSIMMONS

Guard!
    (Man at door comes forward)

RUSSO

How about the freedom of the Press?

GUARD

    (Taking Russo by collar)
Outside, you!

RUSSO

Guys a lot tougher than you tried to gag Hank Russo, and never got away with it.
    (He is dragged off)

HARGREAVES

Now, then, Fitzsimmons, what does all this mean. Is this girl a spy or not?

FITZSIMMONS

She is, but—

HARGREAVES

    (Judiciously)
Well, then, we'll have to shoot her.

GERALD

    (Horrified)
General Hargreaves . . .

GRACE

Blinkey—how brutal! So all those atrocity stories are true!

HARGREAVES

    (Hurt protest)
But we always shoot spies!

KILBRECHT

    (Nodding)
Regulations.

FITZSIMMONS

In this case an exception should be made. She was working for us.

HARGREAVES

(Puzzled)

Not for the Germans?

FITZSIMMONS

She thought she was—however, Jarvis and I—

HARGREAVES

Jarvis!

(Turning on him, hurt)

Are you involved in this, too?

(JARVIS sorrowfully hangs his head)

FITZSIMMONS

I'm willing to take sole responsibility. We've been using her to send *false* information to the Germans.

HARGREAVES

(Shaking his head)

Very irregular . . .

GERALD

How could you trick her that way? It's not at all sporting.

FITZSIMMONS

No. But we've thrown the enemy's calculations off several times. She steals only what we *want* her to steal.

GRACE

Oh, I think that's a *lovely* arrangement!

FITZSIMMONS

(Taking plans from Grace and handing them to Hargreaves)

They aren't real plans—they're fantastic nonsense.

GRACE

Now, do you see, Blinky?

HARGREAVES

(Examining plans)

Hmmm!

FITZSIMMONS

Everything Williamson tells you not to do—I compiled it from the list of DON'TS in the back of the book.

HARGREAVES

Hmmm. . . .

(Slowly puts papers back in envelope)

FITZSIMMONS

If we expose her, the Germans will send another who might prove difficult. We might even get a spy we can't depend on.

GERALD

(Amazed and shocked still)

But—she's such a nice girl—spying!

(Reflectively)

It might be her Oriental blood. . . .

FITZSIMMONS

She's been thoroughly investigated by the Intelligence. Her real name's Gretchen von Treithoff.

GERALD

(Trying to restrain his eagerness)

You mean she's—er—all *white*?

FITZSIMMONS

Certainly. She comes from an excellent Alsatian family . . . ran away from boarding school to be a spy.

GERALD

Oh, that's wonderful. . . !

(Catching himself)

I mean—er—wonderfully—interesting. . . .

FITZSIMMONS

(Dryly)

I see what you mean.

GERALD

But—all those things she told me—about being a temple dancer . . .

FITZSIMMONS

She got it out of a book.

HARGREAVES

Well, I don't know . . . regulations call for all spies to be executed.

GRACE

(Losing patience)
Don't be stubborn.

(THOMPSON, at phone, stands up at attention)

THOMPSON

Beg pardon, General Hargreaves, guard at Boissy Bridge reports the passing of cars—Sir Arthur Reynolds and staff.

GRACE

Oh! Sir Arthur! Nice!

HARGREAVES

(To Fitzsimmons, nervously)
He's almost here—parade the guard.
(Tosses fake plans on desk and starts for his room. FITZSIMMONS exits, followed by Kilbrecht)

GERALD

(Worried)
What have you decided about Marie, sir?

HARGREAVES

Later!
(Exits to his room with Jarvis)

GERALD

(Worried)
I don't want to seem unpatriotic, but Marie . . .

GRACE

Don't worry—I'll get Sir Arthur to let her off.

GERALD

(Hopefully)
Mrs. Hargreaves! Do you think you can?

GRACE

Of course. I know *just* how to approach him.

(Looks around the room)

I'm glad I got the place looking a little more cheerful—he's *such* a dear man!

(Going to desk)

What a mess . . .

(She sweeps papers from it, including fake plans, hesitates for a moment, looking for a place to throw them)

I saw some cute trash baskets in the village . . . all over flowers.

(She sees leather courier's pouch hanging from desk, picks it up, sees it is empty and thrusts desk papers, including the blue envelope, into it, closing it)

GERALD

(Sorrowfully)

She could be talked to . . . reformed . . .

GRACE

Of course. Why don't you send for her and have a long heart to heart talk? Every woman likes that.

GERALD

(Doubtfully)

Perhaps I'd better ask General Hargreaves' permission.

GRACE

Oh, he won't mind. Tell him I suggested it.

(Looking pocket mirror, fussing with hair)

I've got to tidy up before Sir Arthur arrives.

(She exits. GERALD takes a step or two toward Hargreaves' door and pauses. A Courier enters from the street)

COURIER

(To Gerald, saluting)

Despatches for the line, sir?

GERALD

Just a moment—I'll inform Captain Steward.

(GERALD exits. RUSSO appears at window near telephone and climbs in, unnoticed by Courier)

RUSSO
(Waking Thompson)
My Paris office—right away!
(THOMPSON gets busy with wires while Russo sits at telephone desk, back to the room, keeping an alert eye on the door)

THOMPSON
(Into transmitter—ad libs)
'Lo, Crecy . . . Paris, please . . . Grenoble . . . Paris . . . American Press.

RUSSO
(Slipping Thompson a bill)
Here's your five.

THOMPSON
You said ten.

RUSSO
You'll take five—or I'll charge you with accepting a bribe.

THOMPSON
But you're giving it to me!

RUSSO
I'm a war correspondent—I'm immune.
(They separate quickly as Kilbrecht and Gerald enter. Russo ducks behind switchboard)

COURIER
(Saluting)
Courier for the line despatches, sir.

(KILBRECHT goes to the courier's pouch which Grace has just stuffed with paper and hands it to him)

KILBRECHT
There you are.

(COURIER salutes and exits with pouch. KILBRECHT after him. GERALD again turns to Hargreaves' door and pauses.

Finally, making up his mind he knocks and in response
to Hargreaves' muffled "come in" exits into Hargreaves'
room)

THOMPSON

(Into phone)
Hello . . . American Press, Paris . . .
(To Russo)
You're through.
(Goes to sleep)

RUSSO

(Very excited)
Jake? . . . Give me Jake . . . Russo . . . Yeah . . . I survived
. . . without a scratch . . . Yeah, listen . . . I, personally,
myself, your correspondent, caught a spy stealing papers right
in headquarters. A beautiful young woman with a form like
Venus, but with evil eyes . . . Yeah, probably Mata Hari, herself . . . Got it? . . . Well . . . here's the payoff . . . the
whole staff is in love with her . . . from second louie to General, himself . . . She's got them all in her toils . . . When I
turned her in with the evidence, I got a bust in the jaw . . .
They won't shoot her . . . Naw . . . They don't care what
she steals . . . They'll barter honor, country, everything, for
one of her smiles . . . the dirty traitors . . . Yeah . . . One
look at her and I was ready to sell out myself . . . Yeah, she's
that hot . . . a swell number . . .
  How about a bonus?
  (There are voices at the door and finishes quickly)
So long . . .
  (He darts to window and exits through it as GERALD
  enters)

GERALD

(Calling)
Sentry! Have the prisoner, Miss von Treithoff, brought in.

GUARD

(Saluting)
Yes, sir.
  (He goes back to station at door and shouts offstage)
Orderly!

(GERALD sinks into a chair, face in his hands, LIZETTE enters, carrying a tiny pig in her arms. GERALD doesn't look up. LIZETTE goes over to him. She is wearing a pair of Kilbrecht's kilts for a skirt and open work black silk stockings with rosette garters that show under the kilt. A very exciting get-up)

LIZETTE

(Coquetting)
Pardon, monsieur . . .

GERALD

(Sighing)
Take it around to the kitchen.

LIZETTE

But he is for le General . . . Little Victor . . .

GERALD

General Hargreaves is busy.

LIZETTE

(Ignoring this)
Look how pink and white and tender he is . . . my Victor
. . .
(Holds out pig)

GERALD

Yes, of course . . . see the quartermaster, please.

LIZETTE

(Working hard at her ancient trade)
Hold baby . . .
(Puts Victor in Gerald's arms before he can resist, then bends down and reaches under her kilt for one of her garters and takes it off)

GERALD

But really . . .

LIZETTE

(Putting garter around pig's neck)
Chic, no? . . . Et drolle . . . Who can resist? . . .

GERALD
(Thrusting pig back into her arms)
Please go away.

LIZETTE
(Hurt)
You English have no joie de vivre . . .

GERALD
(Sighs)
In the morning she may be dead.

LIZETTE
Victor? But for that he was born. He don't mind.
(Pantomimes illustration of butchering with imaginary
knife)
Gently, across the throat, so . . . In a second it is over. He is
a hero, mon petit Victor . . . He dies bravely, like a soldier.

(GERALD has his head in his hands through this and when
LIZETTE sees she can't get a rise out of him, she leaves
with a shrug and little Victor. As she exits past the guard,
MARIE is brought in by a corporal and squad. Two soldiers with rifles in front of her, two behind and a corporal
in charge with one hand on his pistol, all looking very
determined and ready for any emergency)

GERALD
(Rises, excited)
Marie . . .
(He gazes raptly at her, then suddenly comes to and ad-
dresses the guard)
Attention!
(GUARD stands rigid, presenting arms)
Fall out!
(Squad breaks ranks and relaxes)
Dismissed!
(Squad exits. GERALD and MARIE look at each other, a
second, GERALD somewhat embarrassed, MARIE smiling
bravely at him. They draw together and GERALD takes
her hands tenderly in his)

GERALD

(Chokingly)
Marie—they may shoot you at dawn tomorrow.

MARIE

(Smiling enigmatically)
Yes, I know.

GERALD

(His distress growing)
Darling, how could you do it? Spying is—er—such rotten bad form.

MARIE

(The mysterious smile again)
Have you forgotten what I told you about my past—my Oriental blood?

GERALD

(Pained)
But you come from an excellent family.

MARIE

(Hurt)
That's insulting.

GERALD

Please . . . This may be the last time we'll ever be alone together.
(She leans towards him and he embraces her)
I can't lose you this way—it's too awful.

MARIE

(Acting again)
C'est l'guerre!

GERALD

Marie . . .

MARIE

I have a request to make of General Hargreaves. He must not refuse me.

GERALD

What is it?

MARIE

I want to spend tonight—my last on earth—in your arms.

GERALD

(Shocked)
Oh, but, Marie . . .

MARIE

In the morning their rifles can have my spent body.

GERALD

Can we get a parson on such short notice?

MARIE

Love will be our sacrament.

GERALD

But that's impossible!

MARIE

Why?

GERALD

(Looking for a way out)
Er—er—Hargreaves would never permit it.

MARIE

Those condemned to death are always granted a last request.

GERALD

(Innocently)
You're supposed to ask for a good meal.

(The sounds of automobiles arriving are heard offstage.
BOWKER hurries in, goes to Hargreaves' door and
knocks. Hargreaves' voice off: "Yes?")

BOWKER

Sir Arthur Reynolds has arrived, sir.
(The door opens and HARGREAVES, pulling on his white
gloves, enters with Jarvis. BOWKER hurries off)

HARGREAVES

(To Gerald, with a glance at Marie)
Forsyte, clear the room, please.

GERALD

Yes, sir.
(HARGREAVES exits)
Guard!
(The squad enters, falls in about Marie, and marches her out)

(SIR ARTHUR enters, with HARGREAVES and entire staff dancing attendance on him. SIR ARTHUR is a gray-haired little old man, very dapper and smart despite his seventy years)

SIR ARTHUR

(Beaming at them)
Well, gentlemen, I'm proud of you. Not I alone, but the King and all England join me in your praise.
(HARGREAVES and the others shuffle their feet guiltily and stare at the ground)
Promotions and honors will follow, of course, but nothing that a grateful nation can give will ever be adequate recompense for your victory. History alone can give that. And history will, gentlemen, history assuredly will.
(He pauses, staring at them fondly)
In those annals reserved for immortal battles, the Pepper Mill . . .
(Waves toward map)
. . . will be inscribed in letters of gold!

HARGREAVES

(Feebly)
Ah . . . er . . . thank you, Sir Arthur.

SIR ARTHUR

Not at all. By the way, Hargreaves—I haven't received written confirmation from you as yet.

(HARGREAVES and the others turn rigid with apprehension)

HARGREAVES

(Mumbling)
Why—er—er—

SIR ARTHUR

(Not noticing anything)
But it's probably arrived during my absence.
(The strain eases for a minute—but only for a minute as
SIR ARTHUR goes to map and looks at it, very pleased)
Excellent! Excellent!
(Turns to officers)
And now, gentlemen, I have important news for you. Your
victory is doubly significant because it smashed the lock that
held back our Spring Offensive. With the Mill in our hands
we will be able to launch it immediately!

(HARGREAVES and the others are dumbstruck)

HARGREAVES

(Tragically)
Did—did you say—immediately, sir . . . ?

SIR ARTHUR

Tomorrow!

HARGREAVES

But I—I thought it was a month off . . .

SIR ARTHUR

(Suddenly Olympian)
Sir Arthur Reynolds strikes while the iron is hot! It is my way!

HARGREAVES

(Half crazy with worry)
Er . . . Sir Arthur . . . we . . . we . . .

SIR ARTHUR

(Going right on—waving stick at map as he piles on the
tragedy)
The entire sector will take part in the offensive. I have already
issued orders to all Brigade Commanders.

HARGREAVES

But, Sir Arthur—

SIR ARTHUR

(Sternly)

I know your troops are tired . . . But I will brook no delay.
I demand superhuman effort. Attack!

(Sinks into a chair)

HARGREAVES

Yes, sir . . . but . . . but . . .

SIR ARTHUR

Damn it, man! stop mumbling! We attack tomorrow, that's
final! Lloyd George and his committee were with us all week.
They're having plenty of trouble with the Colonies and the
draft. An election is approaching—victories mean votes! This
has to be kept a popular war.

HARGREAVES

I don't underestimate the importance of victories—but—

SIR ARTHUR

(Cutting him short again)

A decisive one right now will encourage America. Their bankers are beginning to worry about the money they're lending
us.

(HARGREAVES looks around at his staff for support but
they are unable to give any. They mop their brows and
look miserable)

HARGREAVES

(Heaving a deep breath)

Sir Arthur—I must tell you—

(GRACE enters at this moment wearing a stunning gown)

GRACE

(Bubbling over)

Why, Sir Arthur! Hello!

(SIR ARTHUR rises)

SIR ARTHUR

(Very gallantly)

Dear lady . . .

(He takes her hand, kisses it—very much the old buck)
How very stunning you look!

GRACE

Oh! Sir Arthur, do you really think so! Do you like this frock?

SIR ARTHUR

Charming, my dear . . . charming.

GRACE

Oh, thank you! I think there's no excuse for a woman looking dowdy—even in the trenches!

SIR ARTHUR

Exactly! Hargreaves is a lucky dog to have you here.

GRACE

He has you to thank, Sir Arthur.

SIR ARTHUR

Against regulations—but his victory and *your charms* . . . !

GRACE

Oh, Sir Arthur, you *are* a flatterer! Will you take tea with us?

SIR ARTHUR

Happy to. But is it time for tea?

GRACE

In half an hour.

SIR ARTHUR

And I haven't had my afternoon nap.
(To HARGREAVES)
Is there a cot I might stretch out on for a bit?

HARGREAVES

There's one in my quarters.

SIR ARTHUR

Doctor's orders.
(To Grace)
Forty winks help me think . . . or thinks . . . That's it . . . forty winks help me thinks!

(Every one laughs politely and with some strain)
In my youth I wrote limericks.

GRACE

(Coyly)
No love poems? . . .

SIR ARTHUR

(Very pleased with himself)
On occasion, dear lady, on occasion!

HARGREAVES

(Showing way to his door)
This way, Sir Arthur.

SIR ARTHUR

Thank you.
(SIR ARTHUR exits. HARGREAVES closes door and turns
to the others. They look like a group of condemned men)

HARGREAVES

(With a groan)
Good Lord . . .

KILBRECHT

Sir Arthur will have to be told the truth.

JARVIS

Every minute we delay makes it worse.

HARGREAVES

(Shaking his head)
It's frightful . . . frightful . . . His bad heart— He's apt to
fall dead.

FITZSIMMONS

We'll have to risk that.

HARGREAVES

(Drawing another deep breath)
Yes—I'm afraid—we must . . .

GRACE

(Going to Hargreaves)
Blinkey—what on earth *is* the matter?

KILBRECHT

(Literal)

Mrs. Hargreaves . . . we didn't take the Pepper Mill!

GRACE

Oh, Blinkey—and I was counting on your promotion and larger salary . . . I'd spent it already.

HARGREAVES

I might even be retired!

GRACE

On half-pay! Heavens! Your salary's too small now.

JARVIS

If you'd like me to go in with you, sir . . .

GRACE

I'm sure I can help you. *I'll* speak to Sir Arthur.

HARGREAVES

(Tempted)

Well, Grace, . . . I . . .

KILBRECHT

We can't hide behind a woman's skirts.

FITZSIMMONS

Maybe we can.

GRACE

I won't tell him a thing. I'll just put him in a good mood.

(Goes to Hargreaves' door)

Oh, Blinkey, dear, will you please have Bowker send in some champagne.

(She exits)

HARGREAVES

(Astonished)

Champagne!

(Calls)

Bowker!

FRENIQUE

French champagne is excellent for the heart.

(BOWKER hurries in)

BOWKER

Yes, sir.

HARGREAVES

A bottle of champagne for Sir Arthur.

BOWKER

Yes, sir.

FRENIQUE

Mum's extra dry, 1908, if possible, Bowker.

BOWKER

Yes, sir.
(Turns to go)

JARVIS

(To Hargreaves)
That champagne may put him in a good humor.

HARGREAVES

(Calling to Bowker)
Bowker! Make that two bottles.

BOWKER

Yes, sir.
(Exits)

HARGREAVES

I think perhaps I'd better wait until he's had several glasses.
It's bound to change his outlook.

FITZSIMMONS

Maybe we'd better have some, too.

(LEWIS enters and goes up to Hargreaves)

LEWIS

(Indignantly)
General Hargreaves—I'm being discriminated against.

JARVIS

(Hastily)
Not now, please.

LEWIS

This is important. Yesterday Russo received the Pepper Mill story and I didn't. Today the spy story is being withheld from me.

(RUSSO enters)

RUSSO

How'd you know about that?

LEWIS

My office gave me hell for not sending it in.

RUSSO

How'd they know?

LEWIS

They've got a spy in your office.

(Everybody turns as Bowker reenters and hurries by carrying champagne in bucket and exits into General's room)

RUSSO

(Scenting a story)
Spy! Who's getting the booze?

LEWIS

General Hargreaves, I must insist upon my rights.

RUSSO

G'wan—if you're a reporter, dig up your own stuff.

LEWIS

(Indignantly)
I've abided by all the regulations unlike this—this *American.* I want that spy story.

RUSSO

I'll give it to you—for a ten spot—write it for you for twenty-five.

LEWIS

General Hargreaves—

HARGREAVES

Get out—both of you!

FITZSIMMONS

Sentry!

(SENTRY grabs Russo and hustles him out, LEWIS following)

(In the meantime THOMPSON has handed Jarvis a message)

JARVIS

(Reading message to Hargreaves)

Major Strahe reports heavy blanket of fog settling over front line area.

HARGREAVES

What's wrong with Strahe? Does he think we're interested in weather reports just now?

(HARGREAVES and the others turn and look at his door in amazement as loud laughter from Grace and Sir Arthur is heard. The door opens and BOWKER comes in)

(Anxiously)

What are they doing, Bowker?

BOWKER

Mrs. Hargreaves is amusing Sir Arthur, sir.

(He hurries out)

(Grace's voice comes over singing "Hello, Central—Give Me No-Man's Land")

FITZSIMMONS

(To Hargreaves)

I believe this is as good a moment as any to—er—face Sir Arthur.

HARGREAVES

(Heroically, at door)

I faced the Zulus in Tanganyka, the Bolos in Malay—

(SIR ARTHUR'S voice is heard raised in a note or two of song)

FITZSIMMONS
(Listening)
There's a bit of the Bolo in Sir Arthur.

HARGREAVES
Well—here goes . . .

JARVIS
Let's hope for the best.

KILBRECHT
Steady on!

HARGREAVES
(Feebly)
Well—here goes.
(He is about to exit into his room when there is a commotion at the switchboard. THOMPSON wakes up and talks into phone)

THOMPSON
Yes . . . yes . . .
(Turning, addresses Hargreaves)
Pardon me, sir. The attack has started.
(HARGREAVES takes his hand from the door knob, turns and stares from Thompson to the officers. They are all astonished)

HARGREAVES
Attack? What attack?

JARVIS
No attack was ordered.

KILBRECHT
Seems to be an error of some sort.

FRENIQUE
(Shrugging)
I know nothing.
(Exits)

FITZSIMMONS

It might be a good idea to look at a copy of the orders of the day.

HARGREAVES

Where are they? Get them!

JARVIS

Right here.
(Unlocks drawer in desk, pulls out case of papers and leafs through them hurriedly)

KILBRECHT

The orders called for the men to rest today.

JARVIS

(Looking at them dumbfounded, papers in hand)
I say!

HARGREAVES

Well?

JARVIS

(Amazed)
All the copies are here. The brigade never received any orders.

(HARGREAVES snatches papers from him, looks through them)

HARGREAVES

(Puzzled and angry)
They're here all right . . .

JARVIS

Where's the despatch case?

KILBRECHT

I gave it to the courier a little while ago.

JARVIS

It must have been empty.

KILBRECHT

(Weightily)
My belief is that there's been an error of some sort.

FITZSIMMONS

Suppose we find out.
(To Thompson)
Get me Major Strahe.
(Clamps on head receiver, JARVIS putting on another set)

THOMPSON

Major Strahe—Major Fitzsimmons calling, sir.

FITZSIMMONS

(In phone)
Say, Strahe—what's going on out there?
(FITZSIMMONS and JARVIS listen intently)

HARGREAVES

(Very impatiently)
Well—well, damn it—

FITZSIMMONS

They received orders to attack . . . headquarters' courier . . .

JARVIS

(Taking off earphones)
He says everything in regular form . . . a detailed plan . . .

FITZSIMMONS

(Taking off earphones)
They've left their positions . . .
(To Thompson)
What's the line say?

THOMPSON

Sir, Colonel Ames reports everything going according to schedule. The enemy has no suspicion we are attacking.

HARGREAVES

Nobody seems to know anything.

FITZSIMMONS

For once, not even the Germans.

HARGREAVES

What? Get Ordnance.

KILBRECHT

Damned peculiar, isn't it!

> (JERVAIS and two working men in overalls come in. The working men, under Jervais' anxious supervision, start to remove a small pulpit)

JARVIS

(Into phone)
Haskins? What are your cannon doing? What? . . . Nothing!
(To Hargreaves)
They've gone over without artillery—under a blanket of fog.

HARGREAVES

Preposterous!

FITZSIMMONS

(Slowly)
I think I know what's happened . . .
(To Hargreaves)
What did you do with those fake plans we prepared for the spy, sir?

HARGREAVES

Why, I—let me see . . . I threw them on that desk when Sir Arthur arrived.

KILBRECHT

(Looking at desk)
They're not there now.

GERALD

Mrs. Hargreaves cleared up a bit.

HARGREAVES

Grace is always putting things away—but what has that to do with it?

THOMPSON

Colonel Ames reports our advance patrol has crawled through the cranberry bog disguised as bushes and captured the German outposts.

HARGREAVES

(Flabbergasted)
Disguised as bushes!

FITZSIMMONS

That's from Macbeth!

THOMPSON

Yes, sir—they had small bushes tied on their backs.

FITZSIMMONS

That settles it!

HARGREAVES

Grace!!! Good Lord . . .
(To Jarvis, frantically)
Get the co-ordinating officer—see if we can withdraw.

JARVIS

(To Thompson)
Major Strahe—quick!

FITZSIMMONS

Withdraw! We've just captured their outposts!

THOMPSON

(To Jarvis)
They're through, sir.

HARGREAVES

(To Jarvis, anxiously)
Don't let him know what happened . . . it'll sound bad . . .
just see if we can call it off.

JARVIS

(Into phone)
Strahe, about that attack . . .
(Stops and listens)

HARGREAVES

Well, well?

JARVIS

(Turning)
It's too late. Four battalions have already reached the enemy's
barbed wire.

HARGREAVES
(Collapsing in chair)
This is disastrous!

FITZSIMMONS
Maybe not. The Germans still don't know we're attacking.

JARVIS
How are we going to get through their wire? There was no
barrage.

FITZSIMMONS
The plan called for them to carry shears.

JARVIS
Attack with scissors?

FITZSIMMONS
With nail files—if it'll work.

HARGREAVES
(Groaning, his head in his hands)
Good Lord . . .

FITZSIMMONS
(Going to Jarvis at switchboard)
Well?

JARVIS
(Tearing off his headpiece, excitedly)
Albright and McGrevy are starting a pincer movement—looks
as though it may work!

THOMPSON
(Excitedly)
Major Strahe, co-ordinating, says two battalions in enemy first
line trench!

FITZSIMMONS
Great! But we've got to blast hell out of their second line
before they can get their counter-attack going.
(To Thompson)
Get Ordnance.

KILBRECHT

Be awfully embarrassing if we take the Mill. We won't be able to explain it.

FITZSIMMONS

We'll act as though we *meant* it.

(The working men, followed by JERVAIS, who is urging them in French to be careful, brush by the Officers, carrying out the pulpit and exit)

THOMPSON

(Handing phone to Fitzsimmons)
Ordnance, sir.

FITZSIMMONS

(Into phone, with mounting anger)
Ordnance . . . Fitzsimmons . . . we're in enemy trench . . . No . . . No! . . . We didn't have time to send out a barrage schedule . . . it's a surprise attack . . . We need cannon now . . . all you've got. What . . . ? But we must have it—you've got to give it to us.
(Aside to Jarvis)
That nit-wit Haskins says he hasn't had sufficient notice for a barrage—his men are cleaning the cannon.

JARVIS

(Taking phone)
Let me speak to him—he's very touchy.
(Into phone)
Hello, old man! This is Jarvis . . . Pretty well, thank you—a slight catarrah . . . Yes, I will . . . Look, Haskins, be a good fellow—help us out with some cannon . . . I know—it's frightfully embarrassing . . . We didn't mean to slight you . . . Of course we value your cooperation! But we've been having a bit of spy trouble and tried to keep the attack secret . . . yes . . . Really we'd appreciate it awfully if you could get that second line barrage going . . . Yes, that'll be fine . . . as soon as you can . . . Thanks, old man—good hunting!
(Puts down phone)

FITZSIMMONS
(Impatiently)
Well?

JARVIS
He'll do the best he can, but he doesn't promise much . . .
his shells were ordered for tomorrow. Besides, he's offended
at not being notified.

FITZSIMMONS
We'll send him an engraved card next time.

THOMPSON
(To Jarvis)
Colonel Ames reporting, sir.

(JARVIS puts on his headpiece again. LIZETTE enters with
the little pig in her arms, followed by Frenique)

LIZETTE
(Coming up to Hargreaves, coquettishly)
Oh, mon General . . . I have brought Victor for you.

FRENIQUE
The only pig left in the village.

HARGREAVES
(Touching mustache, smiling)
Thank you. You're being very helpful.

LIZETTE
Oh, I have done nothing for you yet, mon General . . . I
wish to do more.

HARGREAVES
(More mustache work)
Errumph!

(There is a commotion at the switchboard. JARVIS takes
off his headpiece and throws it up in the air)

JARVIS
(Shouting)
We've done it! We've done it!
(Rushes over to Hargreaves)

We've broken through! We've pinched off their salient!

> HARGREAVES
>
> (Astonished)

What?

> JARVIS

Yes, sir! Enemy completely surprised! Third battalion got through disguised as sheep!

> HARGREAVES

As what?

> JARVIS

They wore sheepskins and advanced on all fours.

> (Everybody turns and looks questioningly at Fitzsimmons)

> FITZSIMMONS
>
> (Nodding slowly)

It was in the plan . . .

> JARVIS

The enemy is withdrawing to their reserve position at Beaucassis. The Pepper Mill is ours!

> HARGREAVES
>
> (Catching fire)

Victory!

> (Shaking hands with everybody in sight)

We've done it! Victory!

> (Shouting to Guard)

Get my Orderly!

> GUARD

Yes, sir.

> (KILBRECHT bursts into a few bars of "Scots Wha Hae Wi Wallace Bled")

> HARGREAVES

This'll revolutionize trench warfare!

> FITZSIMMONS

We'll issue bushes and sheepskins over the whole front!

JARVIS

Superb tactic! Congratulations, General Hargreaves!

HARGREAVES

Thank you!

    (ORDERLY enters, goes to Hargreaves, salutes)

HARGREAVES

Dictation!

ORDERLY

    (Taking out stenographic pad and pencil)

Yes, sir.

HARGREAVES

Divisional Headquarters!

    (Thinks for a moment)

We have met the enemy and they are ours—Hargreaves.

    (Adds)

Put yesterday's date on it.

    (ORDERLY salutes and exits)

LIZETTE

    (Admiringly, to Hargreaves)

You are the saviour of my beloved France! You shall have
Victor for nothing—only what he cost.

    (Advances as though to kiss him when Grace's voice is
    heard offstage and the door-knob turns)

HARGREAVES

    (Pushing Lizette away in a panic)

Later.

LIZETTE

    (She hurries to door, and turns)

For France!

    (LIZETTE exits as SIR ARTHUR and GRACE enter arm in
    arm, with the over-sober dignity of the drunk)

GRACE

    (To Hargreaves)

Sir Arthur is *such* an understanding man, Blinkey—you can
tell him *all* your troubles.

HARGREAVES
(With dignity)
We *have* no troubles, my dear.
(Triumphantly, as Grace stares at him astonished)
Sir Arthur, shall we go over tomorrow's plan? The map is
completely prepared.
(LEWIS enters)

SIR ARTHUR
(Disregarding this)
Your wife has very kindly offered to show me the town.
(To Grace)
Come along, my dear.
(He leads her to the door and hands her out. LEWIS stops
him as he is about to follow)

LEWIS
Pardon me, Sir Arthur. I'm Lewis, a journalist—in Lord
Leverhold's employ.

SIR ARTHUR
(Respectful at Lord Leverhold's name)
Lord Leverhold, eh? What is it, my man?

LEWIS
I've been discriminated in favor of an American journalist.

SIR ARTHUR
In what way?

LEWIS
A German spy was captured, and I've been refused the story.

SIR ARTHUR
Hargreaves, has a German spy been captured?

HARGREAVES
(Meekly)
Yes, Sir Arthur.

SIR ARTHUR
Has she been shot?

HARGREAVES
No, Sir Arthur.

SIR ARTHUR

Then shoot her—at once. And let this man have exclusive
photographs of the execution.
    (To Lewis)
How's that?

LEWIS

Thank you, sir—thank you. Er—I beg your pardon, but could
you make that execution tomorrow morning instead?

SIR ARTHUR

Why?

LEWIS

The light's a bit too dim at present—and I have no flashlight
equipment.

SIR ARTHUR

Very well. Tomorrow.

LEWIS

Thank you, sir.
    (Exits)

    (During this scene, THOMPSON suddenly becomes very
    busy at switchboard. He hands Jarvis a message. JARVIS
    stares at it dumbfounded, turns anxiously to FITZSIM-
    MONS, gets his attention and hands him the message.
    Fitzsimmons registers consternation and immediately
    starts towards Hargreaves to get his attention, but is un-
    able to do so as Sir Arthur is speaking)

GRACE

    (Offstage)
Artie—are you coming?

SIR ARTHUR

In a moment, dear lady.
    (To Hargreaves)
Hargreaves! Tomorrow the eyes of all England will be on you
and your gallant brigade. As a reward for taking the Pepper
Mill, you will have the honor of leading the Spring Offensive.

HARGREAVES

We're deeply grateful for the honor, Sir Arthur and we're fully prepared.

SIR ARTHUR

The Spring offensive must sweep everything before it. I give you for your battle cry the immortal words of our warrior forefathers—
(Fiercely triumphant)
St. George for England!

GRACE

(Offstage)
Artie—Artie,—you old bastard!

(SIR ARTHUR exits hastily)

FITZSIMMONS

(Holding up message)
General Hargreaves—

HARGREAVES

(Waving him aside. Turning to officers, greatly pleased)
Gentlemen, this has been a red-letter day—one that will go echoing down the—

FITZSIMMONS

(Again stepping up to Hargreaves)
Pardon me, General Hargreaves, this is very important.

HARGREAVES

Please let me finish what I started to say.
(Starts his speech again)
Gentlemen,—this has been a red-letter day—one that will go echoing down the—
(He stops short, his mouth open as his eye falls on the message which Fitzsimmons is holding in front of his face)
Good Lord!

KILBRECHT

What is it?

HARGREAVES
(Shaking his head)
I don't understand it.

KILBRECHT
Read it, man!

FRENIQUE
Have they lost the Mill?

FITZSIMMONS
No . . .
(Reads)
"Entire brigade has crossed Vesey Brook and is advancing on Beaucassis!"

(The OFFICERS look at one another dumbfounded)

JARVIS
They've left the Pepper Mill . . .

KILBRECHT
It's foolhardy! Nothing but short grass for cover.

HARGREAVES
Get Strahe!

JARVIS
Yes, sir.
(To Thompson)
Major Strahe—quick!

THOMPSON
Yes, sir.

HARGREAVES
Both flanks exposed. It's suicide!

FITZSIMMONS
I didn't know our troops were going to get those plans.

THOMPSON
Major Strahe, sir.

(JARVIS puts on earphones—as all rush to switchboard)

HARGREAVES

(Springs to phone himself and shouts into Thompson's
mouthpiece)

For God's sake! They've advanced too far. Stop them! Withdraw!

(He is unable to hear Strahe's reply because Jarvis has on
phones)

What is he saying, Jarvis? Well? Well? Damn it!

JARVIS

(Who has the receiver)

He says they're only following orders.

HARGREAVES

(Frantic)

What orders? For God's sake, Fitzsimmons, after they took
the Mill what did that crazy plan call for?

FITZSIMMONS

(Slowly, as he finally recalls it)

To keep right on going!

(They all stare at him, astonished and dismayed, as the
curtain falls)

CURTAIN

Act Three

Scene: Just before the curtain rises, a volley of shots is
heard offstage. This is repeated at intervals several
times up to Grace's entrance.

At rise, the first rays of day have begun to break
through the windows, showing everything in a
chilly, gray light. This grows gradually stronger
through the scene.

FITZSIMMONS, FRENIQUE, and KILBRECHT in various stages of undress stand at switchboard, tense.
THOMPSON is busy, plugging in wires and pulling

them out again, and frantically clicking the telegraph instrument. GERALD is slumped in a chair,
in the depths of depression.

THOMPSON
(Into transmitter, anxiously)
Hello, hello . . .
(Pulls plug, presses buttons)
Hello, hello, hello . . .
(Again plug and buttons)
Hello, hello . . .

FITZSIMMONS
(Nervously)
Anything, Thompson?

(The others look up to catch his answer)

THOMPSON
Nothing, sir.

FITZSIMMONS
Keep trying.

THOMPSON
(Into phone)
Hello, hello. . . . .

(JARVIS enters hastily, buttoning his tunic)

JARVIS
Well?

FITZSIMMONS
Not a thing. The field wire to the front lines is still dead—
the runners haven't returned,—

KILBRECHT
The men we sent to look for them haven't come back either.

JARVIS
Anything from Strahe?

KILBRECHT
Not since last night.

FRENIQUE

Perhaps he has gone to look for the troops himself.

FITZSIMMONS

Gentlemen,—I'm afraid we must face it—we've lost the brigade.

KILBRECHT

Impossible!

FITZSIMMONS

We've managed it.

JARVIS

This comes of your innovations, Fitzsimmons.

FITZSIMMONS

I guess we should have stuck to Williamson. He makes a big point of always knowing where the troops are.

KILBRECHT

(To Fitzsimmons)

Look here,—if that crazy plan of yours called for them to keep right on going, they might be on their way to Berlin!

FITZSIMMONS

Or Paris.

KILBRECHT

They'd have to pass here to get to Paris.

FITZSIMMONS

You're right,—and we'd hear them. Nine thousand men couldn't tiptoe by.

KILBRECHT

Certainly not.

FITZSIMMONS

The dogs in the village would bark.

THOMPSON

(Handing message to Fitzsimmons)

From Sir Arthur, sir.

FITZSIMMONS

(Reading)
"General orders for Spring offensive. Your brigade will begin
the stretch at exactly 7:15 A.M. The hour of victory is at hand.
England expects——"
(Looks up)
And so forth.

KILBRECHT

That gives us less than a half-hour.

JARVIS

What'll we do?

FITZSIMMONS

Gentlemen, I hesitate to suggest this, but I'm afraid we'll have
to take an extremely drastic step—
(Solemnly)
We'll have to wake General Hargreaves.

JARVIS

(Trying to be helpful)
Er—shall I call Bowker?

FITZSIMMONS

Not this time.
(As everyone watches, he goes to Hargreaves' door and
knocks loudly)
General Hargreaves! General Hargreaves!

HARGREAVES

(Offstage—sleepily)
What's the matter?

FITZSIMMONS

The hour of attack has come.

(There are some mumbled, discontented sounds from
Hargreaves, and then the door opens, and he comes
out,—very stern and military, despite the fact that he
is wearing a purple dressing gown, slippers and an old-
fashioned sleeping cap)

HARGREAVES
(Barking loudly)
Attention!
(They are startled by this strange command and look at him in amazement. He roars)
Attention!
(Several of them snap to attention. FITZSIMMONS takes a step forward to protest)

FITZSIMMONS
This is no time for military capers.

HARGREAVES
(Bellowing)
Am I in command here? Attention!
(This time they all obey and stand rigidly. HARGREAVES passes along the front of their line, as though he were on parade, snorting grumpily)
About, turn!
(They turn, facing the wall)
Very sloppy. If a soldier can't take orders, he's not fit to give them.
(With this, he motions through the open door to someone inside. LIZETTE tiptoes out, carrying Victor, the pig. She crosses quickly and exits, blowing Hargreaves a kiss which he gallantly catches)
About *turn*!
(They all turn)
At ease!
(They all relax. FITZSIMMONS and JARVIS step forward to speak, but HARGREAVES goes to his door)
I'll speak to you gentlemen as soon as I've had my bath.
(Exits)

FITZSIMMONS
Is there anything in regulations about having a General declared incompetent?

KILBRECHT
There would have to be a commission of inquiry.

FITZSIMMONS

Let's form one.

(GRACE enters, looking sleepy and wearing a stunning negligee)

GRACE

Good morning. I thought I heard shots. Is anything wrong?

GERALD

(Pitifully, rising)
Mrs. Hargreaves,—that's the firing squad. For Marie . . .

FRENIQUE

They're just practising, Madame.

KILBRECHT

Sergeant Parks wants to make a nice clean job of it.

GRACE

(Shocked)
Clean job!

KILBRECHT

Yes, madam. Headquarters troops don't use a rifle much.

GERALD

(Brokenly)
Mrs. Hargreaves,—she didn't realize what she was doing.

GRACE

(Very sympathetically)
Dear boy . . . I know just how you feel. I was in love with a handsome South American once who borrowed a horse and was hung.

FRENIQUE

Ah, madame . . . we all have our memories . . .

GERALD

I'd rather they shot me.

GRACE

I couldn't do a thing with Sir Arthur yesterday. He was drunk.

GERALD

General Hargreaves is our only hope now.

GRACE

Blinkey wouldn't hurt a fly himself. He's simply terrified of Sir Arthur.
(Another volley of shots offstage)
For Heaven's sake! Tell them to stop!
(She goes to Hargreaves' door and knocks. FRENIQUE joins the other officers)
Blinkey, darling!
(Muffled sounds from Hargreaves offstage. He throws open the door and enters, only partly dressed, and irritated)
(Brightly)
Good morning.

HARGREAVES

(Grouchily)
Grace, what are you doing up before noon?

GRACE

How can I sleep with all that shooting?
(The officers, worried, approach Hargreaves in a group)

FITZSIMMONS

Pardon me, sir—

HARGREAVES

Well, what's wrong now?

FITZSIMMONS

We've received orders to attack in twenty-five minutes.

JARVIS

We're still unable to locate the troops.

HARGREAVES

What about Strahe?

KILBRECHT

There's been no word from him.

GRACE

Excuse me, gentlemen. I'll let you have the General in a moment.

FITZSIMMONS

Mrs. Hargreaves, this is very important.

HARGREAVES

We're fighting a war, Grace.

GRACE

(Determinedly)
A human life is important, too,—and look what you're doing to Gerald.

(HARGREAVES turns to Gerald who looks the picture of despair. The OFFICERS go to the switchboard where THOMPSON has become busy with his lines again)

HARGREAVES

(Very soldierly, to Gerald)
Show some grit, man!

GRACE

But he loves her.

GERALD

I want to marry her.

HARGREAVES

(With shocked indignation)
Absurd! Who are her people? What set does she move in? How does she look on a horse?

GRACE

You didn't see me ride before you married me.

HARGREAVES

I was infatuated.

GRACE

So is he.

HARGREAVES

Six months from now he'll be glad we shot her.

GRACE

Blinkey,—you're just showing off.

GERALD

I looked the family up in the Almanac de Gotha. She's the daughter of Baron Hans von Treithoff, and heir to Schloss Treithoff, the family seat in Swabia.
(Taking a deep breath)
But I'd marry her if she really were only a charwoman.

GRACE

(To Hargreaves)
That's how you felt about me, darling,—remember?

(Everybody gets excited as sounds come from the telegraph apparatus at the switchboard)

JARVIS

That's the field wire!

(THOMPSON works the instrument excitedly. The Officers crowd around him)

FITZSIMMONS

Anything, Thompson?

THOMPSON

No message, sir. Sounds as though they're trying to repair it.

HARGREAVES

That must be Strahe trying to get through to us now. Fitzsimmons, stand by.
(To Jarvis and Kilbrecht)
Come along, gentlemen, while I finish dressing.
(Turns to go)

GRACE

(Catching his arm)
Blinkey! Let Gerald have that poor girl in to breakfast at least.

HARGREAVES

All right, Grace,—but stop nagging. We're in trouble.
(Exits, followed by Jarvis and Kilbrecht)

GRACE

(To Gerald)
Cheer up! I'll keep after him. Send for Marie,—she can have anything she wants for breakfast.

GERALD

(Trying to be brave)
Thank you very much.
(He tries to smile bravely and calls to the Orderly)
Sentry, have the prisoner, Miss von Treithoff, brought in.

GUARD

Yes, sir.
(Exits, as MONSIEUR JERVAIS enters with two French working men)

JERVAIS

(Bowing)
Bonjours, Messieurs, 'dame.

FRENIQUE

Bonjour, Monsieur Jervais. Ça marche?

JERVAIS

Bien.
(To Fitzsimmons)
Alors,—we will finish removing the valuables this morning.
(Volley of shots offstage)
(Panicked)
The Germans!

FRENIQUE

(Smiling)
One German—a spy—to be shot.

(JERVAIS draws himself up to his full five feet four and becomes very brave and military)

JERVAIS

(Ferociously)
The enemy must be exterminated,—man, woman and child!
(With mounting hysteria, surprising in such a mild looking gent)
Torn out, root and branch. Slaughtered! Annihilated! Their

cities must run with blood. Their brains must be dashed out! Their hearts plucked quivering from their bodies!

(He shoots his cuffs and subsides into the academician again. To working men, indicating a heavy, carved chair)

Prenez ce fauteuil.

GRACE

(Upset)
My, my . . .

FITZSIMMONS

(Ironically)
He's a patriot!

JERVAIS

Merci, monsieur!

(The working men go to the chair and start to carry it out)

GRACE

You'll have this place bare as a car barn.

JERVAIS

(With a bow)
Next week experts will come to remove the stained glass windows.

GRACE

It's too draughty now! General Hargreaves has rheumatism.

(JERVAIS shrugs, and follows the working men out, FRE-NIQUE going with him)

THOMPSON

(Handing Fitzsimmons message)
G. H., sir.

FITZSIMMONS

(Reading)
"All brigades in your sector ready for attack, and will move forward in support as soon as you reach position between Hills 68 H. L. and 69 N. M. at 7:25."

(To Thompson)
How about Strahe?

THOMPSON

Trying, sir.

(The GUARD brings in Marie. GUARD exits. GERALD stares
at her in surprise, a second. She is wearing a beautiful
black, low-cut tea gown, slinky and svelte—the kind of
gown a female spy would wear in a magazine illustration.
MARIE and GERALD go into each other's arms)

GERALD

(Brokenly)
They're going to kill you.

MARIE

Be brave, my soldier.

GRACE

(To Marie)
What a stunning dress!

MARIE

It's my execution dress.

GRACE

You poor child . . .

GERALD

(Heart-brokenly)
She mustn't die.

GRACE

Don't be morbid, dear. You'll only depress her.

MARIE

(Gallantly)
I'm not afraid . . .

GERALD

It's horrible.

GRACE

(To Gerald)
There, there,—everyone says it's quite painless. A blinding
flash, and it's all over.

GERALD

(Brokenly)
My God!

MARIE

Gerald, darling—bear up!

(JERVAIS enters again with his man)

JERVAIS

Apres l'autre fauteuil—la boite . . .
(Pointing to confession box)
et c'est tout. Nous sommes finis.
(They take chair and exit, FITZSIMMONS watching them.
He looks around the room thoughtfully, his eyes lighting
on the confession box)

FITZSIMMONS

(Suddenly)
Marie!
(Points to box)
Get in there—hurry!

GRACE

(Admiringly, as she gets the idea)
Why, Major!

MARIE

(To Gerald)
Goodbye, darling . . .

GERALD

Darling . . .
(They start to embrace)

FITZSIMMONS

(Interrupting them)
Hurry in that box.
(To Gerald and Grace)
You two come over here.

(FITZSIMMONS, GRACE and GERALD form a little circle in
front of the sentry at the door, so that his view of the
room is blocked. From this position the three are unable

to see the front of the confession box. MARIE glides to confession box. She opens the door carefully. Suddenly, a hand
reaches out from inside the box and pulls the door shut.
She stands there, astonished, not knowing what to do)

FITZSIMMONS
(Whispering)
She should be safely in Paris in a few hours.

GERALD
(Anxiously)
Will she be all right in there?

GRACE
Of course! I've spent *hours* in telephone booths.

(JERVAIS and the two working men enter. FITZSIMMONS,
GRACE and GERALD delay them, for a moment to give
Marie plenty of time)

FITZSIMMONS
Ah, Monsieur Jervais,—the confession box is next?

JERVAIS
Yes, thank you, Major.

GRACE
Be very careful with it,—it's beautiful.

JERVAIS
Rest tranquil, madame. I am an expert.

(They can't hold Jervais any longer. He and his workmen
pass them into room. They turn to follow and see MARIE
standing helplessly. They are astonished)

GERALD
Marie . . . !

GRACE
But, darling . . . !

FITZSIMMONS
What the devil!

(Before she can answer, the two workmen lift the confession box horizontally. Suddenly a noise is heard inside

it, and it sways wildly. The workmen drop it with a crash.
GRACE shrieks. FITZSIMMONS yanks door open. RUSSO
sits up like a jack-in-the-pulpit. Ad libs from Workmen,
JERVAIS, GERALD and FITZSIMMONS. "Mon Dieu! In-
croyable! Good Lord! That stinker!" RUSSO smiles sheepishly. FITZSIMMONS grabs him by the collar and yanks
him out)

JERVAIS
(Hastily)
Alphonse! Guy! La boite! Allez—vite! Allons-y!
(The Workmen rush the box out, followed by Jervais)

FITZSIMMONS
(Shaking Russo)
What were you doing in there?

RUSSO
Nothing,—I—

FITZSIMMONS
(Incredulously)
Nothing!
(Notices papers sticking out of Russo's pocket)
What's this?
(Pulling papers from Russo's pocket)
Papers!
(Looks thoughtfully a second, glances at Marie, then
back at Russo, and is struck by an inspiration)
You're a *spy*!

RUSSO
(Indignantly)
Who—*me*?

FITZSIMMONS
(The inspiration growing)
We caught you red-handed.

RUSSO
It's a lie. You wouldn't give me any news, so I had to do this.

FITZSIMMONS
You've probably been doing it right along—stealing military
secrets.

(Looks at papers. Reads)
"Sex triangle in staff headquarters . . . rivalry for love of
beautiful spy between cynical major and love-lorn lieutenant . . ."

RUSSO

It's a Sunday feature.

FITZSIMMONS

Obviously in code. Sentry!
(SOLDIER runs in and grabs him)
Arrest him!

RUSSO

You can't do this to me!

FITZSIMMONS

(To Sentry)
Just hold him 'til I see General Hargreaves.

(The SENTRY takes Russo to a corner of the room. LEWIS
enters loaded down with photographic equipment, camera, tripod, etc.)

LEWIS

(Cheerfully)
Good morning! I'm ready, Major Fitzsimmons!

FITZSIMMONS

For what?

LEWIS

The execution.

FITZSIMMONS

(Looking him over thoughtfully)
I see . . .

LEWIS

I've tested the light,—it's perfect. I can get just the dramatic
shadow I want.

GRACE

Don't be so bloodthirsty.

LEWIS
(Hurt)
But—Sir Arthur promised me that photograph. I wired my paper yesterday to expect it. I'll lose my position if I don't get it.

FITZSIMMONS
There's a new development. We've discovered that Marie is just a poor, helpless tool in the hands of a sinister master mind, who hypnotized her into working for him.
(RUSSO stares at Fitzsimmons with growing alarm)
There's the real spy—Russo!

LEWIS
(Astounded)
Russo!

RUSSO
(Simultaneously)
Hey! You're framing me!

GRACE
Don't look in his eyes—he'll hypnotize you.

RUSSO
(Trying to break loose again)
I never hypnotized nobody. I'm a reporter!

FITZSIMMONS
(To Sentry)
Keep that man quiet!

(RUSSO subsides as SENTRY raises gun butt threateningly)

LEWIS
(Whistles)
I always was suspicious of that American, sir. He's so secretive—and peculiar.

RUSSO
Why—you Judas!

LEWIS

(Enthusiastically)
I'd be glad to appear against him.

RUSSO

(Yelling)
I'll cripple you for this, Lewis!

FITZSIMMONS

Thank you—we'll use you as a material witness.

LEWIS

And now, about my photograph, sir?

FITZSIMMONS

I suppose you won't mind photographing Russo's execution
instead of Marie's?

RUSSO

(Getting violent again)
Why, you dirty limeys—you can't get away with this!

LEWIS

(Fervently)
Oh, no, sir! It will be a pleasure.
(Holding up his equipment)
I'm ready now.

FITZSIMMONS

You'll have to restrain yourself a bit.

LEWIS

But I *can't* wait. My paper expects the photograph today.
They've set aside the space.

FITZSIMMONS

Let 'em run some poetry.

LEWIS

(Getting angry)
I was afraid of this! I demand to see General Hargreaves.
(Shouts)
General Hargreaves! General Hargreaves!

(HARGREAVES throws open the door and enters, followed
by the other OFFICERS)

HARGREAVES

(Very angry)

What is this confounded rumpus?

RUSSO

(Going to Hargreaves, dragging the Sentry with him)

They're trying to cold deck me, chief.

GERALD

He was concealed in the confession box taking notes in code.

KILBRECHT

He probably cut our field wire.

JARVIS

He sent out that false report yesterday.

FITZSIMMONS

Let's shoot him!

HARGREAVES

He should be shot,—of course,—but Americans are so touchy. . . .

FITZSIMMONS

I don't think he's an American—I've heard him talk German.

GRACE

So've I.

RUSSO

I don't know a word of it! I was born in Brooklyn! I went to Boys' High!

KILBRECHT

I never did like his confounded accent.

RUSSO

(Pulling out watch fob)

Here's a medal I got for running! It says Boys' High on it.

FITZSIMMONS

Probably killed an American and stole his watch.

HARGREAVES

A miserable specimen.

(An ORDERLY comes in and salutes. He is holding a carrier pigeon. With him is the NIZAM, very much interested in the pigeon)

ORDERLY

This pigeon was just caught, sir.

(FITZSIMMONS hastily removes message from its leg. The NIZAM, with cooing noises, takes bird lovingly, and carries it to cage. ORDERLY exits)

FITZSIMMONS

(Holding tiny scroll to light)
It's from Major Strahe . . .

OFFICERS

(Ad lib)
Thank God!
At last!
What does it say, man?
Read it?

FITZSIMMONS

(Reading)
"No trace of brigade . . . running out of pigeons."

RUSSO

What a story. . . . !
(They all turn and stare at him, apprehensively)

FITZSIMMONS

(To Hargreaves)
Now, you've *got* to shoot him.

HARGREAVES

Unquestionably!

RUSSO

(Panicky)
No! No! I won't send the story out. I won't tell anybody you lost your army.

FITZSIMMONS

You'll never get a chance to.
(To Sentry)
Take him away.

RUSSO

(As he is being hustled out)
Lemme use that phone! You can't do this to me! I'm innocent!

FITZSIMMONS

Be a man—die bravely.

RUSSO

(Screaming)
I'm on your side! I love the Allies . . . I was just . . .
(Tries to break from Sentry)
Help! Help!
(He is dragged out. LEWIS goes right after him with his camera)

LEWIS

(Turning at door. To Hargreaves)
Thank you, sir!
(Exits)

GRACE

(To Hargreaves)
Now, you'll let Marie go, won't you?

GERALD

General Hargreaves,—let me take her away. I'll resign my commission . . . we'll go to a neutral country . . . We'll . . .

HARGREAVES

(Waving him away impatiently)
Impossible!

GRACE

I've got a *wonderful* idea! Shoot her with blank cartridges, and smuggle her out in a coffin. . . .

HARGREAVES

(His patience at an end)
Enough of this nonsense! I've got important things to think about. Kilbrecht! See that the formalities are observed. Shoot them and have done.

KILBRECHT

Yes, sir.

(To Sentry)
Take her away.

(The SENTRY moves forward to take Marie from Gerald's arms)

MARIE

(Bravely)
Goodbye, darling.

GERALD

(Brokenly)
I'll come with you.

MARIE

No. It's better this way. Gerald, be brave!
(They embrace. She separates from him and goes off with Sentry)

GRACE

Blinkey, I'll never forgive you for this.
(She goes toward door)

HARGREAVES

But, Grace,—Sir Arthur ordered it.

KILBRECHT

Ours not to reason why, Mrs. Hargreaves.
(Exits. GRACE exits to her room)

HARGREAVES

(To Officers)
Quite frankly, gentlemen,—I'm worried.

NIZAM

(Suddenly, excited pointing to pigeons)
Bleni bayada nemoo bik!
(They all turn and stare at him)

JARVIS

Perhaps he's found another message. Please translate, Forsyte.

GERALD

(To Nizam)
Ocha?

NIZAM

(Again pointing towards pigeons)
Necham bayada paka admya bik!

GERALD

One of the pigeons laid an egg.
(The NIZAM nods repeatedly, and smiles engagingly as
GERALD translates)

JARVIS

Oh!

FITZSIMMONS

(To Hargreaves)
Shall I get Sir Arthur on the phone, sir?

JARVIS

We can't delay any longer, sir.

HARGREAVES

(Heavily)
Yes, gentlemen,—I'm afraid there's nothing else for it,—we
must report to Sir Arthur.

JARVIS

Without the brigade,—we'll be drummed out of service.

HARGREAVES

(Collapsing into a chair)
Court martial and disgrace . . . it would have been better if
we had been lost with the troops.

FRENIQUE

In the French Army that would be considered the proper
thing.

HARGREAVES

After thirty years in the army . . . I worked hard for my
stars . . .
(Touches sleeve)
Thirsty in Arabia, typhoid in China—a spear in my back in
Africa,—fell from my horse and broke my leg in India . . .

JARVIS

I looked forward to my pension . . .

FITZSIMMONS

I might be able to use you in my soap business.

(The telegraph instrument suddenly begins to click.
Everybody looks up hopefully)

What is it, Thompson?

THOMPSON

(Writing)

The field wire just came alive, sir.

(Everybody rushes over to the switchboard, THOMPSON
finishes writing and hands Fitzsimmons slip of paper.
FITZSIMMONS looks at it)

HARGREAVES

(Impatiently)

Well?

FITZSIMMONS

(Reading)

"Gott strafe England. Gott strafe England. Gott strafe England."

(Looks up)

"God destroy England"—repeated three times.

HARGREAVES

(Puzzled)

What's that?

THOMPSON

Pardon me, sir. The Germans always use that phrase when
testing their apparatus.

HARGREAVES

(Alarmed)

They've captured our field telegraph.

FRENIQUE

That means they're between us and the brigade.

JARVIS

The brigade's been cut off.

FRENIQUE

They're on top of us!

FITZSIMMONS

That settles it. We've *got* to get out of here.

HARGREAVES

(Rising slowly, and calling)
Bowker! Bowker!

JARVIS

(To Sentry)
Order the staff cars.

SENTRY

Yes, sir.

BOWKER

(Hurrying in)
Yes, sir?

HARGREAVES

Pack my luggage. We're withdrawing.

BOWKER

Yes, sir. I have it almost all packed.
(Hurries into Hargreaves' room)

JARVIS

He must have been eavesdropping.
(Starts collecting papers from the desk, emptying drawers, etc., with FRENIQUE and FITZSIMMONS)

FRENIQUE

What a pity to abandon this cathedral to the barbarians. They'll steal the windows.
(He exits with some papers)

(GRACE enters as a volley of shots rings out offstage)

GRACE

Oh, they've done it! You heartless brutes!
(She hurries to Gerald and puts her hand consolingly on his shoulder)

GERALD

I'll ask to be sent to the trenches.

HARGREAVES

Grace, we've no time for that now. Hurry, and pack your things. We're leaving.

GRACE

(Surprised)
Why?

HARGREAVES

It's highly technical,—you wouldn't understand.

GRACE

(Meaningly)
I hope Sir Arthur does.

(More sounds come from the telegraph instrument)

FITZSIMMONS

What is it, Thompson?

THOMPSON

The Germans are still testing, sir. The same words,—only they've added Lloyd George.

(GRACE exits)

FITZSIMMONS

They shouldn't mix sentiment with business.

(BOWKER comes in with a pair of old boots)

BOWKER

(To Hargreaves)
Shall I pack these, sir? They're quite worn.

HARGREAVES

(Distracted)
Don't bother me.

BOWKER

Thank you, sir.
(Exits)

(GRACE enters)

GRACE

Blinkey, can I borrow one of your bags? I can't . . .
(She pauses as KILBRECHT comes running in)

GERALD

(Brokenly)
Captain Steward—how did she—what were her last words?

KILBRECHT

(Very excited)
We didn't shoot her!

GERALD

Thank God!
(Hurries out)

GRACE

Oh! *Nice!*

HARGREAVES

Why not?

FITZSIMMONS

What were those shots?

KILBRECHT

The Germans! They fired a volley at us!

HARGREAVES

Good Lord!

GRACE

(Pats her hair)
I look a sight!
(SOLDIER with trunks on barrow comes out of her room)
Take them back.
(He obeys, and she goes after him. KILBRECHT reaches for his pistol. The NIZAM draws his sword)

FITZSIMMONS

What are you going to do?

KILBRECHT

(Fiercely)
Fight! To the death!

NIZAM

Blini oka poo!

FITZSIMMONS

Don't be childish!

(The two Warriors subside)

HARGREAVES

(Calling impatiently)
Bowker! Bowker!

(BOWKER hurries in, carrying luggage)

BOWKER

Yes, sir.

HARGREAVES

The enemy has us surrounded.

BOWKER

(Complete equanimity)
Very good, sir.
(HARGREAVES exits to his room, followed by Bowker)

JARVIS

Too bad we couldn't notify Sir Arthur we're unable to attack.

FITZSIMMONS

(Consulting watch)
He knows it now,—it's 7:15.

(JARVIS, KILBRECHT, and FITZSIMMONS button up their tunics, and prepare to surrender. They put on their hats. A guard of German soldiers commanded by a SERGEANT marches in)

(All British guards are ceremoniously relieved of their rifles, and marched out, the English officers watching. A German guard remains)

JARVIS

(Critically to Kilbrecht)
Rather sloppy!

KILBRECHT

Rather!

(A group of officers enters. There is a Prussian General
somewhat like Hargreaves with a mustache that turns up
instead of down, and a Bavarian Jarvis. There is also a
German Colonial officer from the Cameroon Islands, the
color of the Nizam, wearing a turban. They are very stern
and military, bowing sharply and saluting with precision
and castinet heels. The British likewise)

JARVIS

(Stepping forward and saluting)
May I present myself, gentlemen, Colonel Jarvis, of the
Queen's Own Stiffkey Lancers.

(The German Colonel, VON SHIMMELPFENIG, steps forward)

VON SHIMMELPFENIG

Colonel von Shimmelpfenig Kaiserlicher Muensterberg Uhl-
anen.
(The English bow. The German General steps forward
and the Colonel introduces him)
General Landknecht Balthur von Hertzen zu Liebfrau, of His
Imperial Highness' Death Head Hussars!

(The General bows. The English officers bow)

(Indicating Cameroon Islander)
Captain Ras Mahamoud of the Cameroon Bush.

(The RAS MAHAMOUD steps forward and performs a mysterious Oriental gesture)

RAS

Oro aborijak.

JARVIS

May I introduce the rest of our staff? Captain Stuart Steward,
the Laird of Kilbrecht, King's Own Cuttykilt Highlanders.

(KILBRECHT bows—the Germans bow)
Captain Ram Singh, the Nizam of Ladore of the Royal Rhaj-
put Lancers.
    (The NIZAM steps forward and performs the identical
    gesture as the Ras)

NIZAM

Oro aborijak.

JARVIS

Major Fitzsimmons, Canadian Militia.
    (FITZSIMMONS nods—Germans bow)

FITZSIMMONS

No name,—just a number.

    (BOWKER appears at Hargreaves' door)

BOWKER

    (With a flourish)
Brigadier General Francis Hargreaves of the Queen's Own
Batherskin Buffs!
    (Everyone stiffens to attention as HARGREAVES enters,
    dressed to the nines, wearing sword, medals, etc. The two
    Generals salute formally, and then a smile of recognition
    breaks over their faces)

HARGREAVES

Lieby!

LIEBFRAU

Blinkey!
    (They shake hands enthusiastically)

HARGREAVES

Haven't seen you since the 1912 maneuvers.

LIEBFRAU

    (As they shake hands)
A bit awkward,—meeting this way, old man. Hard lines.

HARGREAVES

    (Like a tennis loser)
There's no one I'd rather lose to.

LIEBFRAU

Breaks of the game—you put up a good show.

HARGREAVES

Thanks, old fellow.

(During the above, BOWKER goes off to the garden, the NIZAM and the RAS go to inspect the pigeons, both talking happily in whatever it is they talk. The two generals talk quietly together. The other officers have gathered in a little knot by themselves)

JARVIS

(To Shimmelpfenig)
I didn't know the Uhlans had dismounted.

SHIMMELPFENIG

We hope to be mounted again soon.

KILBRECHT

War doesn't seem the same without horses.

(GRACE comes in like a charming hostess greeting unexpected guests)

GRACE

General Liebfrau! this *is* a surprise!

(LIEBFRAU bows over her hand, kissing it)

LIEBFRAU

Dear lady! I'm delighted to see you again.

GRACE

(Smiling)
Are you going to put us behind bars?

LIEBFRAU

Certainly not. I shall arrange for you and General Hargreaves to be interned at my country place—Schloss Birnbauch.

GRACE

Isn't that near the mineral baths?

LIEBFRAU

Yes. Nieubad is just a short drive away.

GRACE

Oh, how convenient! Blinkey, you'll be able to cure your rheumatism.

(RUSSO, GERALD, and MARIE enter. GERALD and MARIE beaming with happiness. RUSSO stands to one side looking the situation over while MARIE runs to Liebfrau, followed by Gerald)

MARIE

General Liebfrau!

LIEBFRAU

Lieber maedchen!
(They embrace)
Your mama has been bombarding me with letters. What are you doing here, naughty?

MARIE

Spying . . . But I'm giving it up to get married.

LIEBFRAU

(Shaking his head)
One escapade after another . . .

RUSSO

(Going up to Shimmelpfenig)
Say, chief, I'm from the American News Service. When are you gonna get that switchboard hooked up? I wanna talk to my Berlin Office.

SHIMMELPFENIG

(Curtly)
We have no time for you now.
(Turns away from him)

(The switchboard buzzer sounds)

THOMPSON

(To Fitzsimmons who is standing near him)
Sir Arthur, sir . . .

(SIR ARTHUR's voice bellowing curses comes over the

wire, everybody listening in amazement. FITZSIMMONS
picks up the phone)

FITZSIMMONS
(Calmly in phone)
Gott strafe England! Gott strafe England! Gott strafe England!
(Throws the phone down and turns to the others. Amid
a dead silence, they are all staring at him astounded and
dumbfounded)

HARGREAVES
(Red in the face)
Really, Fitzsimmons,—what are you doing?

LIEBFRAU
(Puzzled)
What's the meaning of it?

SHIMMELPFENIG
(Puzzled)
We always say that when testing our apparatus.

FITZSIMMONS
(Trying to laugh it off)
For a moment, I forgot which side I was on.
(The ENGLISH OFFICERS look embarrassed. The GER-
MANS look at Fitzsimmons very suspiciously)

LIEBFRAU
(Indicating Thompson)
Replace that man.

SHIMMELPFENIG
Guard!
(GERMAN SENTRY enters. Having at Thompson)
Take him out. Send in Signalman Shultz.

(SENTRY exits with Thompson. BOWKER appears at the
door)

BOWKER
Breakfast is served in the garden.

GRACE

You'll all stay to breakfast.

LIEBFRAU

It will be an imposition.

GRACE

Oh, no—I insist.

(SIGNALMAN SHULTZ enters and salutes)

SHIMMELPFENIG

Take over that switchboard. Check the connections to Berlin.

SHULTZ

(Salutes)
Yes, sir—we have one connection completed already.
(Sits down at switchboard)

(The NIZAM and the RAS, who have been chattering in undertones, at the pigeon cage, come over to Hargreaves)

NIZAM

(To Hargreaves)
Ledi maraka forad lochum.

HARGREAVES

(To Ras)
What is he saying?

RAS

(Bows)
Your Excellency, he is saying, now that the pigeons are of no use, he would like to have them.

HARGREAVES

What for?

RAS

Your Excellency, he wants to eat them.

HARGREAVES

Oh— Yes—of course.

(The NIZAM and RAS both bow and return to the cages. They signal to a guard who joins them)

GRACE

Come along, everybody!

(Everybody starts to file out to the garden laughing and chattering, FITZSIMMONS and RUSSO looking after them. The NIZAM and the RAS are followed out by a GUARD carrying the pigeon cases)

RUSSO

(Buttonholing Shimmelpfenig, who is on his way out with Liebfrau)

Say, chief, how about it? Do I talk to my Berlin office?

SHIMMELPFENIG

(To Liebfrau)

What shall I do about this American journalist, sir?

LIEBFRAU

(Looking Russo over)

American journalist? Hm . . . Show him every courtesy. We must keep America's friendship.

RUSSO

Thanks. Give Hank Russo a break and he'll give you a break—every time!

(He goes to switchboard)

LIEBFRAU

(Under his breath to Shimmelpfenig, as they exit)

Schweinhund!

RUSSO

(To German signalman)

Hey! get me the American News Service in Berlin.

(The Signalman gets busy. RUSSO turns to FITZSIMMONS)

Well Fitzie, you're off the payroll now, hah?

FITZSIMMONS

I never liked this way of making a living.

RUSSO

Aw—you're always crabbin'—war sells newspapers.

SIGNALMAN

(To Russo)
American News, sir.

(RUSSO grabs phone, FITZSIMMONS watching him)

RUSSO

(In phone)
Hello—American News? . . . Oh! hello Mac! This is Hank
Russo . . . Yeah—I'm covering the Germans now . . . Listen—I gotta talk fast—
(His voice becomes tense with excitement)
I'm at a field telephone in the front line trenches . . . a stone's
throw from the vicious redcoats . . . waiting for the zero hour
. . . The men in the trenches with me are Bavarians—no
longer beer drinking, song singing burghers, but fierce warriors eager to spring at the frog eaters and limeys . . . What
a moment! . . . In another second they'll risk death so that
their country may have a place in the sun . . .
(Suddenly pulls whistle out of pocket and blows it)
There goes the whistle! We're off! Into the teeth of the enemy's fire! For Gott, Kaiser and Vaterland!

FITZSIMMONS

For God, King and Country!

CURTAIN

Before the Fact

Screen Play by
Boris Ingster and Nathanael West

FADE IN

INT. CENTRAL CRIMINAL COURT—LONDON—
AFTERNOON

1   MED. SHOT—Court clerk. The clerk, dressed in a medieval mantle and wearing a wig, raps with his gavel and announces in a typical sing-song the opening of the case:

> COURT CLERK
> All persons who have anything to do before my Lords the King's Justices of Oyer and Terminer, and general gaol delivery . . .

2   LONG SHOT—Ellen is seated in the dock. She is wearing black and is heavily veiled. There is a warder on either side of her, placed there for her custody, but seemingly indifferent to and unconscious of her presence. Opposite and above Ellen are the seats of the learned Judges. The court is crowded with barristers, solicitors, reporters and jurymen. A dull October light falls from the lofty leaded windows. Everyone is on his feet as the robed Judges file in and take their seats.

> COURT CLERK
> . . . for the jurisdiction of the Central Criminal Court, draw near and give your attendance . . . God save the King, and my Lords the King's Justices . . .

> PRESIDING JUDGE
> (sonorously)
> The counsel may proceed.

As everyone sits down,

DISSOLVE OUT

DISSOLVE IN

INT. CENTRAL CRIMINAL COURT—LONDON—
AFTERNOON

3   MED. SHOT—of the Counsel for the Crown coming
to his peroration, and as he does so, his voice rising and
ringing out clearly.

> COUNSEL FOR CROWN
>
> . . . and because this woman has admitted her
> crime, I demand in the name of the Crown and
> before God that she be found guilty of having wil-
> fully murdered her husband.

CAMERA PANS with him, as he comes toward Ellen.

4   CLOSE SHOT—of Ellen. She swallows, barely resisting
the desire to touch her throat with her hands.

5   FULL SHOT—As Counsel for Crown passes the Counsel for Defense, he gestures gracefully toward dock indicating the witness is his. Counsel for Defense rises and
half bows to his colleague. CAMERA PANS with him,
as he walks over to Ellen.

> COUNSEL FOR DEFENSE
>
> If Your Lordship please, we do not wish to dispute
> or deny the facts as presented by the Crown. We
> only ask the Court and the Jury to listen to this
> woman's story.

He bows to Judge, including Jury in gesture, and turns to
Ellen in witness box.

6   MED. SHOT—Counsel for Defense and Ellen.

> COUNSEL FOR DEFENSE
>
> Now, Lady Aysgarth, would you please tell the
> Court all the events and circumstances leading up
> to that tragic night when you picked up a gun and
> shot your husband.

                                    ELLEN
I—

                              (she halts)

                        COUNSEL FOR DEFENSE
Go on, please.

                                    ELLEN
                (she hesitates, still unable to begin, then:)
Everything starts quite far back—when I first met
Sir Anthony. I . . .
                          (she breaks off suddenly)

                        COUNSEL FOR DEFENSE
                              (friendly)
You can go as far back as necessary.

As Ellen begins her testimony, CAMERA MOVES IN to a
CLOSE SHOT of Ellen.

                                    ELLEN
                (launching herself with an effort)
It may sound strange—but it always seems to have
started with a dream . . .
                        (smiles a little bitterly)
I had lots of them in those days—the kind all
young girls have, I imagine. Maybe because time
moves so slowly in the country—maybe because I
read too much bad poetry . . .
                  (she pauses a second and pulls herself
                      back to the more concrete)
It was late in May . . .
(gradually the quality of her voice changes as she
remembers and takes on a younger, happier note)
I remember, we were having what the farmers call
"growing weather"—when days are bright and
sunny and everything is straining to burst into
flower . . .

As Ellen talks, a light, airy melody begins in a musical accompaniment to her voice.

                                              FADE OUT

FADE IN

INT. ABBOT MONCKFORD—ELLEN'S BEDROOM—
MORNING

7   Five years before, coming to Ellen, lying in a bed, a girl
of twenty-three, very attractive, with a delicate mouth,
beautiful eyes and a lovely figure. Spring and sunshine
stream through the latticed shutters. As we come into
the scene we hear knocking on the bedroom door, and
Ellen turns over in bed.

> ELLEN'S VOICE
> (narrating)
> *. . . It was Sunday morning. I was still in bed—*
> *asleep and in the midst of a dream . . . I woke up*
> *at the sound of someone knocking at my door . . .*

Harriet enters the room. She is eighteen, blond, excitable. She
crosses the room quickly and opens the shutters out, letting
in even more light.

> ELLEN'S VOICE
> (cont'd)
> *. . . It was Harriet, my maid . . .*

> HARRIET
> (cheery)
> Good morning, Miss Ellen.

> ELLEN
> (pulling the covers over her head)
> Go away—I'm sleepy.

> HARRIET
> (persisting)
> But, Miss Ellen, the first church bells have rung.
> Better get up.

Harriet brings Ellen's robe and mules to the side of the bed,
bustling. Ellen turns over lazily, luxuriating, then smiles sleepily.

> ELLEN
> (yawning)
> You know, Harriet—you've a definite talent for
> spoiling my best dreams.

HARRIET

Oh, I'm sorry, Miss Ellen. I didn't know you were dreaming.

(then eagerly)

What was it about?

ELLEN

(with a sigh)

A man . . .

HARRIET

A man? What was he like? Did he say anything?

ELLEN

I'm not sure whether he did or not—but I remember I kept on hearing bells ringing.

Harriet stops laying out Ellen's things at this and gets terribly excited.

HARRIET

Why, Miss Ellen—that means a wedding!

ELLEN

(laughs)

Don't be silly. It means simply that I must've heard the church bell in my sleep.

HARRIET

(absolute faith)

Oh, no! Bells in a dream's a wedding for sure! Now, if you'd dreamed of a fork, it would have meant guests, or a salt shaker would have meant money—but *bells 's a wedding*.

ELLEN

(laughs again)

And if you don't get my bath ready soon it'll mean I'll be late for church.

She rises and puts on her robe.

HARRIET

Yes, Miss Ellen.

(goes to bathroom, pausing at door)
What did he look like? Was he very handsome?

ELLEN
(half-closing her eyes and trying to
recapture the dream)
I don't know— He didn't have a face.

This stops Harriet.

HARRIET
(puzzled)
No face? I wonder what that means?

ELLEN
Nothing . . . The tub, please, Harriet.

As Harriet reluctantly enters bathroom, Ellen goes to her mirror. She starts brushing her hair up for bath cap.

8   CLOSER SHOT—Ellen. She frowns at herself as she works.

ELLEN'S VOICE
(narrating; over low sound of running water)
. . . I looked at myself—the way every woman does from time to time—studying my hair, eyes, mouth, complexion—they all seemed good . . . Then why wasn't I married? I was old-fashioned enough to take it for granted that happiness for a woman lay only in marriage. I wanted desperately to be happy. And yet I had turned down two offers. Both from men I liked but didn't love . . . I wanted love even more than happiness . . . But maybe I had made a mistake. Perhaps I wouldn't get another chance. The English countryside is full of spinsters—bitter, hard, unfulfilled . . .

9   MED. SHOT—the bedroom. Harriet returns from the bathroom. The water has stopped running.

HARRIET
It's ready, Miss Ellen.

> ELLEN
> (a little startled)

Oh—thank you.

Ellen finishes brushing her hair, ties it up with a little ribbon.
Harriet gets a bath cap for her.

> HARRIET
> (gossipy)
> There's a new gentleman staying at the Frasers'—
> Sir Anthony Aysgarth. I got a peek at him—hand-
> some as can be.
> (then primly)
> But handsome is as handsome does, I always say.

> ELLEN
> (smiling)

What does that mean?
> (starts toward bathroom)

> HARRIET
> I don't think he's the marrying kind. They say he's
> been in and out of a dozen engagements.

> ELLEN
> (going into bathroom)

Perhaps he's choosy.

As Ellen closes the bathroom door,

> WIPE OUT

WIPE IN

EXT. GARDEN TERRACE—ABBOT MONCKFORD—
MORNING

10   FULL SHOT. The open, flagstone-paved terrace leads
     down into the garden—a riot of flowers enclosed by a
     high brick wall. Ellen enters terrace from the house. She
     is dressed simply and not very smartly. As Ellen comes
     onto the terrace she is greeted by a leaping, barking dog.
     CAMERA PANS with her as she crosses to where her
     father is having breakfast on the terrace, reading the
     Sunday *London Times*. Commander McLaidlaw is sixty,

iron-gray hair, an erect carriage; he is a retired naval officer, V.C. He is severe in his general censure of the world, indulgent with his daughter.

> ELLEN
> (patting dog as she walks toward her father)
> Don't talk so much, Gilmore.
>> (kissing her father)
> 'Morning, Admiral.

11   MED. SHOT—Ellen and the Commander.

> COMMANDER
> 'Morning, Ellen.

Ellen picks up a piece of toast, not bothering to sit at the place that has been set for her at the table.

> COMMANDER
> (cont'd)
> Aren't you going to sit down?

> ELLEN
> Haven't got time.
>> (pours herself a cup of tea)
> Late already.

> COMMANDER
> (grunts)
> Always late. You're getting slack, my dear.

> ELLEN
> (laughs)
> Anything in the paper, Father?

> COMMANDER
> (grumpily, with rising indignation)
> Same tommyrot from one day to the next! Full of politics, scandal and fires, but not a word about the Fleet. Don't they even know His Majesty's ships are on manoeuvers in the North Sea?

Ellen merely grins affectionately at his outburst and drinks her tea.

ELLEN
(after a pause; casually)
Father, do you know a Sir Anthony Aysgarth?

COMMANDER
(grumpily)
No. Never heard of him.

ELLEN
He's staying with the Frasers. I think he's a cousin
of the Middletons in Devon.

COMMANDER
(barking)
Who?

ELLEN
Sir Anthony.

COMMANDER
What's that name again?

ELLEN
Aysgarth.

COMMANDER
Oh . . . Must be the son of old Tom Aysgarth.
Tom married a Middleton. Pity the boy turned out
so badly. Tom may have been a fool, but he was a
decent sort.

ELLEN
(casually)
What's the matter with Sir Anthony?

COMMANDER
A bad lot. Turned out of a club—or ought to have
been turned out. Something unpleasant, anyway.
Staying at the Frasers', hmm?

ELLEN
Yes. But surely Mrs. Fraser wouldn't have him
down if it had been anything like that?

COMMANDER

Well, it may have been a woman—or a horse—or
something.

(he dives back into his paper)

ELLEN

(she smiles at him and bends down to kiss him)

'Bye, darling. I'll be back right after church.

The Commander grunts and goes back to his paper. As Ellen
runs toward the garden gate, she starts humming again the
old ballad.

ELLEN

(cont'd)

(singing)

When I was one and twenty . . .

DISSOLVE

EXT. COUNTRY ROAD—DAY

12   FULL SHOT—Ellen on bicycle. On both sides of the
road is a stone wall; beyond the walls, woods of low-
flung birch and maple. It is a beautiful day, the country
full with voices of birds. The score carries the melody
Ellen started to hum in previous scene.

ELLEN'S VOICE

(narrating)

*. . . I kept humming to myself as I pedalled along
just as I did on any other Sunday. There was nothing
to warn me . . .*

13   CLOSE SHOT—Ellen on the bicycle. Her humming is
abruptly punctured by a wild explosion. As she looks
down, startled, CAMERA MOVES DOWN to reveal
the cause of the explosion: a flat tire.

ELLEN'S VOICE

*. . . that on this day I was to meet the man I was
to marry. No ring around the sun—nothing in the
sky but a few fleecy little clouds—It was all so usual
. . . I had an ordinary little accident . . .*

14   FULL SHOT—Ellen examining her bicycle. She is no
      longer humming. Several cars pass her, then an open one
      slows down and comes to a halt beside her.

                          ELLEN'S VOICE
          *. . . and he didn't come on a white horse, but in the
          Frasers' little sport car . . .*

In the car are the Fraser girls: Alice, Jane, and Mrs. Fraser.
They are very British and roast beef to the heel. At the driver's
seat is Tony Aysgarth.

                          TONY
          Anything we can do?

As Ellen turns around, the girls recognize her.

                          AD LIBS
          Hello, Ellen . . .
          Hello, Alice . . .
          Etc.

                          ALICE
                    (not too cordially)
          Can we help?

                          JANE
                    (nor her)
          How about a lift?

Ellen looks irresolutely at those in the car, her attention drawn
to Tony, who is staring quite frankly at her.

                          ALICE
              (catching the mutual interest)
          Oh, I say, I'm sorry, Ellen. This is Tony Aysgarth.
          Tony, this is Miss McLaidlaw.

                          TONY
                    (grinning at her)
          Hello.

                          ELLEN
                    (a little stiffly)
          How do you do, Sir Anthony?

Tony smiles. It is an infectious, intimate smile that immediately puts Ellen off her guard. Alice catches the exchange.

> ALICE
> (breaking it up)
> Come on—climb in, Ellen.
> (pointedly)
> You can sit in back with Mother.

> ELLEN
> No. Thanks just the same.

> JANE
> Nonsense. Come along.

> ELLEN
> Really, I'd just as soon walk.

> MRS. FRASER
> (impatiently)
> Don't be stubborn, child—you'll make us all late for church.

> ALICE
> Maybe she really does want to walk. Start her up, Tony . . .

> TONY
> But this is silly . . .

To everybody's surprise, he jumps out of the car.

> TONY
> (cont'd)
> Tell you what—you drive and I'll stay and fix the tire.

> ELLEN
> No, no, really—

> TONY
> Oh, it's quite all right. I like doing things like this. In fact, there's nothing I like better than patching tires.

ELLEN

But—

ALICE

Funny, I never knew you were a frustrated garage mechanic.

TONY

Haven't I ever told you? It's sort of a leftover from my childhood when I used to take apart clocks.

ELLEN

But, really—

ALICE
(starting car; nastily)
D'you think you'll make it home by dinner?

TONY
(equally sarcastic)
I'll try . . .

ALICE
(to Ellen)
'Bye, darling—and better stay on the main highway.

With this Alice steps on the accelerator, and the Frasers bound forward in a cloud of dust.

15   MED. SHOT—Tony and Ellen. He waits until the car drives off, then stands up slowly. Ellen, covertly, has been watching him. Tony is tall, good-looking, with one of the merriest faces Ellen has ever seen.

ELLEN

It's very kind of you, but you really shouldn't've.

TONY
(candidly)
Why?

ELLEN

Well, for one thing, the Frasers—

TONY

Oh, that. Well, you can't expect them to be too kind to the local opposition.

ELLEN

Opposition?

TONY

Yes, you know—the other pretty girl in the neighborhood.

ELLEN

Oh . . .
                    (changes subject)
Don't you think we'd better do something about the tire.

TONY

Oh, yes . . . Didn't I see a garage somewhere around here?

ELLEN

Garage?

TONY
                    (one of his smiles)
I'm afraid I should've told you I never did manage to put those clocks together again.

ELLEN

Oh—I see . . .
          (she frowns slightly, picks up her bike, and
          moves toward road; a touch of the formal)
I think I'd better get along. Good-bye, Sir Anthony.

Ellen starts off, Tony following.

TONY
          (taking complete command of the situation)
Well, at least let me help you wheel your bike.
               (they start walking)
Were you going to the village?

ELLEN

Yes, to church.

TONY
(with mock despair)

You, too!
(then lightly)
Isn't there anything else to do here—and on a
lovely day like this!

ELLEN

I'm afraid not.

TONY
(stopping suddenly)

Look, I've a wonderful idea. What do you say we
leave the bike at the garage—buy ourselves some
fruit and cheese, then go some place and have a
picnic?

ELLEN
(coldly)

Sounds very tempting, but I'm afraid I can't—

TONY

Oh, come, be a sportsman. It's *such* a lovely day.
Tell you what—we'll flip a coin on it. How's that?

ELLEN

No!

But Tony already has a shilling piece out of his trouser pocket,
and flips it in the air.

TONY
(the coin on the back of his palm)

Call it!

ELLEN
(in spite of herself)

Heads.

TONY

Heads—

(looks at coin, but shields it with his
hand from Ellen)
—it's *not*. We picnic.

ELLEN
(laughing)
Oh, no, we don't!

TONY
(mock horror)
What!—You're not going to welsh on a gambling
debt, are you?

ELLEN
(laughing)
But I never agreed to the bet.

TONY
A lame excuse—
(taking bicycle and pushing it forward)
Come along, Miss McLaidlaw.
DISSOLVE OUT

DISSOLVE IN

EXT. COUNTRY PATH—DAY

16　MED. SHOT—Ellen and Tony walking along a path
through a wood. Tony carries a picnic basket, covered
with a napkin.

ELLEN'S VOICE
(narrating)
*. . . It is hard for me even now to explain why I
went with him. I suppose I was curious. I'd often
heard of men with his kind of reputation, but I'd
never met one . . .*

17　FULL SHOT—Ellen and Tony. They pause in front of
a sign: "NO TRESPASSING." For a moment they argue,
then Tony wins by peremptorily picking Ellen up and
swinging her over the wall.

ELLEN'S VOICE
. . . or perhaps I did it to spite Alice Fraser. I'm afraid I never did like her . . . But whatever the reason, I found that I thoroughly enjoyed being with him . . .

DISSOLVE

EXT. COUNTRY—DAY

18   FULL SHOT—Ellen and Tony, sitting under a lonely huge oak tree standing on top of a knoll. It is later in the day and the shadows have lengthened. They have finished their picnic and Tony has his jacket off.

ELLEN'S VOICE
. . . He was so charming and gay, and so disarmingly frank . . .

19   MED. SHOT—Ellen and Tony, at oak tree.

TONY
. . . She was bored with her husband, and I—I was just bored . . . Does it shock you?

ELLEN
(smiling)
Should it?
(then instinctively jealous)
Was she beautiful?

TONY
Oh, yes—quite . . . And then one day her husband walked in and made a scene . . . Poor chap, he felt even more ridiculous than I did . . . Naturally, after that everybody expected us to marry. And when we didn't everyone decided I was a cad . . .

ELLEN
Well, why didn't you marry her?

TONY
What on earth for? And she certainly didn't want

to marry *me*. She had to have someone with a great deal more money than I had . . . But that's enough of that . . . Why don't you tell me something about yourself?

ELLEN

There isn't very much to tell. I'm afraid I'm just an ordinary country girl.

TONY

Or you'd like me to think you are.

ELLEN

Why should I?

TONY

I haven't quite decided . . .
(suddenly, point blank)
But you've got the warmest skin I've ever seen— it simply glows. You must be tremendously alive inside.

Ellen is startled by the suddenness of this compliment and tries to turn it away.

ELLEN
(rather feebly)
Tell me, do you really enjoy saying things you don't mean?

TONY
(grinning at her)
I can be critical, too.
(shrewdly)
Why do you try to hide how pretty you are?

ELLEN
(startled again)
Hide? . . .

TONY

That tweed get-up of yours, and that woolen sweater. You can't possibly like having scratchy stuff next to your skin.

ELLEN
(she is uncomfortable, but can't help
being interested)
I've always worn things like this . . .

TONY
Of course you have—but why? Are you afraid to
be attractive?

Before she can answer, he leans over and pulls at the high
neck of her sweater—a gesture that is no more familiar than
one a dressmaker might make. But his voice and his look are
the opposite.

TONY
(cont'd)
And why do you hide your shoulders? They're
beautiful.

Ellen, with an effort, tries to make a joke of it.

ELLEN
Do you want me to go to church in a bathing
suit?—that's where I was going, you know.

TONY
(ignoring her remark)
—you're not prim, you're not rugged, you're not
dull—You just make believe you're all those things.

ELLEN
That's silly. Why should I go to all that trouble?

TONY
Because you want to play safe—a bad mistake!
There's no fun in being safe . . .

ELLEN
(a little frightened)
I think I'd better go home.

TONY
(smiling)
I haven't frightened you, have I?

ELLEN
(too vehemently)

No.

    (anxiously looking for some definite way out)
But I have to give my father his medicine.

TONY
(he becomes quite gentlemanly; jumping up)
In that case, perhaps we'd better . . .
    (as she starts to get up, he holds out his hand)
Let me help you.

ELLEN

Thank you.

He pulls her up, then abruptly, before she can even suspect what he is going to do, he holds her tightly and kisses her. She struggles to free herself.

ELLEN
(cont'd)
No! Stop it! Please . . .

Her struggles grow less and he pulls her to him a second time and soon she isn't struggling at all.

DISSOLVE

EXT. GATE OF ABBOT MONCKFORD—DAY

20   FULL SHOT. Ellen and Tony come along, wheeling the bicycle. She turns in at the gate and faces him across it.

ELLEN'S VOICE
(narrating)
. . . He was quite gay all the way home. I didn't laugh very much, and yet I was strangely happy. Then he said something which didn't seem very important at the time . . .

21   MED. SHOT—Ellen and Tony. Before Ellen's voice has finished, Tony has taken a coin out of his pocket and is tossing it in the air.

> TONY
> (lightly)
> Isn't it funny, but sometimes it's better to lose a bet than to win one?

> ELLEN
> What?

> TONY
> Remember when we tossed—church or picnic—you called heads. Well, you won, it *was* heads.

> ELLEN
> (laughing)
> But that's cheating!

> TONY
> Aren't you glad I did?

> ELLEN
> (admitting that he's right by avoiding the question)
> I have to go in now . . .

> TONY
> I'll ring you tomorrow.

She smiles shyly at him, then hurries toward the house.

DISSOLVE

INT. ELLEN'S BEDROOM—ABBOT MONCKFORD—NIGHT

22   CLOSE SHOT—Ellen, looking at herself in the mirror. As she studies her reflection, she lowers the shoulder straps of her nightgown to better see the line of her shoulders.

> ELLEN'S VOICE
> (narrating)
> *. . . I don't know how I managed to live through the rest of the day. There was only one thought in my mind . . . he liked me. He said I had beautiful*

*shoulders. He kissed me! . . . And tomorrow he was
going to call me! . . .*

As she turns the switch and plunges the room into darkness,

DISSOLVE

INT. HALLWAY—ABBOT MONCKFORD—
AFTERNOON

23   CLOSE SHOT—telephone on a small table. CAMERA
PANS over to Ellen standing nearby re-arranging the
flowers in a vase. During the scene she glances at the
large grandfather's clock standing in a corner and indicating 6:13.

ELLEN'S VOICE

*. . . The next day nothing could drag me out of
earshot of the telephone. I was sure he would call, but
I didn't know when. Before lunch? Lunch passed and
he hadn't. Tea went by, too . . .*

Suddenly the phone rings. Ellen rushes over to it and picks
up the receiver. Her face falls as she discovers that it isn't
Tony, and passes the receiver to Harriet, who also came out
to answer the phone.

ELLEN'S VOICE
(cont'd)

*. . . He would certainly call in the evening. But he
didn't . . .*

DISSOLVE

INT. ELLEN'S BEDROOM—ABBOT MONCKFORD—
NIGHT

24   Ellen is in bed. She pulls the switch of the lamp on the
night table and closes her eyes, ready to fall asleep.

ELLEN'S VOICE

*. . . I went to bed, and that night my dream had a
face—Tony's . . .*

DISSOLVE

INT. HALLWAY—ABBOT MONCKFORD—DAY

25   CLOSE SHOT—Ellen at the phone. She picks up receiver, hesitates, then places it back.

ELLEN'S VOICE

. . . The next day I even thought of calling him at the Frasers'. But my pride wouldn't let me . . .

DISSOLVE

INT. LIVING ROOM—ABBOT MONCKFORD—AFTERNOON

26 MED. SHOT. Ellen, standing at the window looking out into the garden. It is raining.

ELLEN'S VOICE

. . . The day after that I started making excuses for him. Perhaps he'd been called back to London . . . perhaps he'd been in an accident . . .
(turns abruptly from window and goes to piano)
. . . Finally I knew the phone wasn't going to ring. He wasn't going to call. All he had been doing was spending an afternoon under a tree . . .

DISSOLVE OUT

DISSOLVE IN

INT. ELLEN'S BEDROOM—ABBOT MONCKFORD—NIGHT

27 MED. SHOT—Ellen. She is quietly crying in her bed with her head buried in the pillow. Bright moonlight falls in a square across the quilt. Gilmore, her spaniel, looks up sadly from his basket at his sobbing mistress.

ELLEN'S VOICE

. . . But I didn't hate him for it. I hated myself . . . It was my own fault that he didn't call. Maybe I wasn't forward enough. Maybe I should've shown more plainly what he made me feel . . . By then I was ready to crawl on my knees to meet him . . .
(her voice breaks; then a touch of bitter irony creeps into it)
. . . How silly of me. Sooner or later someone was sure to tell him that when my father died I would come into a hundred thousand pounds . . .

Suddenly there is the sound of some pebbles striking the

window. Gilmore pricks up his ears and lets out a short bark. Ellen turns her head toward him.

> **ELLEN**
> Shush, Gil—quiet! What's the matter with you?

But Gilmore continues to bark. She gets out of bed and goes to window.

EXT. ELLEN'S BEDROOM—NIGHT

28   FULL SHOT—Tony, standing on the lawn under Ellen's window.

INT. ELLEN'S BEDROOM—NIGHT

29   CLOSE SHOT.—Ellen. She recognizes Tony—opens window.

> **ELLEN**
> (it's almost a sob)
> Tony!

EXT. ELLEN'S BEDROOM—NIGHT

30   FULL SHOT—Tony.

> **TONY**
> (a loud whisper)
> Hello, Ellen.

INT. ELLEN'S BEDROOM—NIGHT

31   CLOSE SHOT—Ellen.

> **ELLEN**
> What—what're you doing there?

EXT. ELLEN'S BEDROOM—NIGHT

32   CLOSE SHOT—Tony.

> **TONY**
> (grinning at her and sweeping his hat off)
> I tried to borrow a guitar and a Spanish cape, but the Frasers aren't equipped for serenading. Come on down.

INT. ELLEN'S BEDROOM—NIGHT

33   CLOSE SHOT—Ellen.

ELLEN
(leaning out of window)
But it's so terribly late.

EXT. ELLEN'S BEDROOM—NIGHT
34   CLOSE SHOT—Tony.

TONY
I'm sorry— But I couldn't sneak away earlier. You have to earn your keep when you're a guest of the Frasers . . . Come on out.

INT. ELLEN'S BEDROOM—NIGHT
35   MED. SHOT—Ellen at window. Suddenly she remembers that she has only her nightgown on and pulls the neck together self-consciously.

ELLEN
But . . . I'm not dressed.

EXT. ELLEN'S BEDROOM—NIGHT
36   MED. SHOT—Tony.

TONY
Then at least let me in—I *must* see you.

INT. ELLEN'S BEDROOM—NIGHT
37   CLOSE SHOT—Ellen.

ELLEN
(undecided)
But . . .

EXT. ELLEN'S BEDROOM—NIGHT
38   CLOSE SHOT—Tony.

TONY
Please!

INT. ELLEN'S BEDROOM—NIGHT
39   CLOSE SHOT—Ellen.

ELLEN
(smiling, too)
All right—but only for a few minutes.

WIPE OUT

WIPE IN

INT. HALLWAY—ABBOT MONCKFORD—NIGHT

40   FULL SHOT. Ellen, in a hastily thrown on negligee, opens the door to Tony.

> TONY
>
> Hello. . . .

> ELLEN
> (nervously)
> We've got to be awfully quiet—the whole house is asleep.

> TONY
>
> Good.

> ELLEN
>
> Let's go in there—it's furthest from the bedrooms.

As they go along the hall—

> TONY
> (sincerely contrite)
> I've been wanting to see you for days. But the Frasers had "plans" every night, and I couldn't get out of them.

> ELLEN
>
> You might've called up.

> TONY
>
> Can't stand phones—they're so deadly impersonal. Impossible to say anything over them.

INT. DRAWING ROOM—ABBOT MONCKFORD—NIGHT

41   FULL SHOT. Georgian. It's lit by great shafts of moonlight, pouring in through the windows on one side. Ellen goes to switch on light, but Tony stops her.

> TONY
>
> Don't!
> (gestures at the lighting effect)

Look at it—that silver light. You don't want to spoil it.

> ELLEN
> (protesting)

But . . .

> TONY
> (interrupts her gently)

Come over to the window seat where I can look at you.

Ellen goes. Tony follows her.

> ELLEN
> (nervously)

We really shouldn't be here this way.

> TONY
> (he makes her sit down)

Must you always play safe?

42   MED. SHOT—Ellen and Tony.

> ELLEN

It isn't that. It's . . .

> TONY
> (looking at her)

You *are* lovely.

> ELLEN
> (with a soft laugh)

It's the light.

There is a slight pause, then Tony notices the piano.

> TONY

Who plays?

> ELLEN

I do—a little.

Tony sits and plays very softly, improvising, with his eyes on her.

TONY

I've been thinking of you a lot, since that picnic.

ELLEN
(after a pause)
What's that you're playing?

TONY
(very seriously)
It's you—but not in a tweed suit . . . It's like you
are now.

ELLEN

It's beautiful . . .

TONY

It has to be.

ELLEN

I didn't know you were a musician . . .

TONY
(bitter against himself)
I might've been, if I were a Pole, or a Bohemian,
or something— But I'm Tony Aysgarth—a spend-
thrift, a gentleman—nothing really but a society
tramp.

ELLEN

That sounds so bitter.

TONY

But it's true. And for the first time in my life, I'm
sorry it is.

ELLEN

Why?

He stands up suddenly and goes toward her—his voice throbs.

TONY

Because I've fallen in love with you.

ELLEN
(she is bewildered by this outburst)
I don't believe it. Why, we've barely met!

TONY

Please—*you must!* It's not a wild idea. I've known it ever since we sat together under that tree . . . You're the only woman who can help me make something of my life. You're good. You have strength . . . I know I haven't much to offer, but I do know that I *can* make you happy.

Ellen is overwhelmed by this torrent that pours from Tony. The best she can do is stammer haphazardly.

ELLEN

But, Tony . . . This is all . . .

TONY

You don't have to turn me down now. There'll be a chance to do it when I ask you to marry me . . .

He takes her in his arms and kisses her. Ellen returns his kiss.

FADE OUT

FADE IN

EXT. ANCIENT STONE CHURCH BELFRY—DAY

43   The bells are moving and their ringing weaves into the accompanying score.

ELLEN'S VOICE
(narrating)

. . . *A few short weeks later he asked me and I said yes. Of course, Father was completely against it . . .*

EXT. CHURCH—DAY

44   FULL SHOT. The entrance is decorated with garlands of fresh greenery. A few curious villagers crowd around it. A village constable is keeping them back, importantly.

ELLEN'S VOICE

. . . *Poor darling . . . He saw through Tony from the first. But I was in love and blind. He stormed, sulked, pleaded with me. I cried, and that was one thing he couldn't face . . .*

INT. VESTRYROOM—CHURCH—DAY

45 FULL SHOT—small mirror and bureau. Lit by stained glass window. Harriet, Ellen's maid, is putting some last touches to Ellen's gown. Her father is standing watching, his face grim.

> ELLEN'S VOICE
> *. . . Oddly enough we were to be married in the same church I was on my way to that day we'd first met . . .*

A Warden sticks his head in the door.

> WARDEN
> (breathless)
> Miss McLaidlaw—one chorus of the wedding march, then you enter with your father. One chorus—remember.

> ELLEN
> (smiling at her father)
> We'll remember, Mr. Granby.

The Warden pops his head back. Commander McLaidlaw takes a step toward his daughter, then speaks to the maid.

> COMMANDER
> Aren't you through, yet, Harriet? I want to speak to my daughter.

> HARRIET
> Yes, sir . . .
> (she takes a few quick, final pats)
> I'm just going.
> (to Ellen)
> You look just beautiful, Miss Ellen.

The sound of the organ playing the wedding march comes over softly and continues throughout scene.

> ELLEN
> Thank you, Harriet.

As Harriet opens her mouth to say something else, the Com-

mander arrumphs and Harriet flees. Ellen goes over to him
and straightens his tie. The Commander speaks with an effort.

> COMMANDER
> There's still time, Ellen—
> (the smile leaves Ellen's face; he takes her hands)
> Let's postpone it— We'll get to know him a little
> better . . .

> ELLEN
> (interrupting him gently)
> Please, Father . . . We've been over all that . . .
> This is my wedding day.

> COMMANDER
> I know, child . . . Please forgive me. I guess I'm
> just a stubborn old fool.

> ELLEN
> (gently)
> No, darling—you just want me to be happy . . .

As the old man tries to think of something else to dissuade
her, the vestryman pops his foolish face in again.

> WARDEN
> (excited)
> Now! Now!!

> COMMANDER
> We're coming.

He draws himself up and offers Ellen his arm.

> ELLEN
> Your tie, Father . . .
> (she starts fixing it)

> COMMANDER
> Ellen . . . darling . . . If anything goes wrong,
> come home. Promise me that.

> ELLEN
> (nods and smiles)
> I promise—but nothing will.

The Commander opens the door, and the music swells.

FADE OUT

FADE IN

INT. TRAIN COMPARTMENT—NIGHT

46   Ellen and Tony, in traveling clothes. The porter puts up the last bag. Tony tips him. The porter exits, closing the door. Tony turns to Ellen, takes her hat off, tosses it aside and, taking her in his arms, kisses her passionately.

ELLEN'S VOICE
(narrating)

. . . I had read about love, dreamed about it, discussed it in endless schoolgirl conversations, but I never knew how much overpowering happiness it could bring . . .

WIPE

EXT. TRAIN—NIGHT—(STOCK SHOT)

47   CLOSE SHOT—of driving wheels of a locomotive moving at a great rate of speed.

ELLEN'S VOICE

. . . I was so happy that it seemed almost sinful . . .

WIPE

EXT. RAILROAD TRACKS—NIGHT—(STOCK SHOT)

48   SHOT of railroad tracks swiftly moving past camera.

ELLEN'S VOICE

. . . as if I had snatched all the happiness there was in the world, leaving none over for anyone else . . .

DISSOLVE

EXT. PARIS—DAY—(STOCK SHOT)

49   RAPIDLY MOVING SHOT of the Champs-Elysées in Paris with the Arc de Triomphe in the b.g.

ELLEN'S VOICE

. . . It seems incredible now that during all those

weeks of being so close to each other, I never got the slightest inkling of what Tony was really like . . .

DISSOLVE OUT

DISSOLVE IN

EXT. COUNTRYSIDE—DAY—(STOCK SHOT)

50 MOVING SHOT of the Mediterranean from a car driving along the Grand Corniche—the rock of Monaco in b.g.

ELLEN'S VOICE

. . . He was so perfect—attentive, affectionate, patient, gentle . . . only in Monte Carlo . . . I was a little tired . . .

DISSOLVE

INT. BEDROOM SUITE—MONTE CARLO—NIGHT

51 FULL SHOT. Ellen stirs uneasily in the large double bed, throwing her arm over the empty part.

ELLEN'S VOICE

. . . and I wanted to go to bed. Tony said he would go down for a last cigarette. I woke up in the middle of the night . . .

ELLEN
(cont'd)
(only half awake)

Tony . . . Tony!

Suddenly she realizes that Tony isn't there. She sits up, fully awake now, and snaps on the bed light. She takes an anxious look at the small traveling clock on the night table.

INSERT   CLOCK: It reads 3:05

52 MED. SHOT. Ellen lifts receiver of telephone.

ELLEN

Desk, please . . . This is Lady Aysgarth . . . I wonder if you've seen my husband? . . .

(listens)

Oh . . . The Casino . . .
                    (frowns a second)
    Thank you.

She puts down the receiver and thinks; then determinedly gets out of bed and starts to dress.

DISSOLVE OUT

DISSOLVE IN

INT. GAMING ROOM—CASINO—NIGHT

53   FULL SHOT. Ellen enters shyly, looks about at the several tables. Several men and women in evening dress are playing in that hushed funereal formality so typical of vice. She sees Tony off-scene and goes quickly toward him.

54   MED. SHOT—Tony at roulette table, as the Croupier calls: "Fait vos jeu, m'sieurs, 'dames." Tony moves his last stack of chips forward on the black, grim and unsmiling.

CROUPIER
(spins the ball)
    Rien ne vas plus! . . .

ELLEN
(coming up behind him)
    Tony . . .

As he turns to her, his expression changes to one of affectionate joy at seeing her.

TONY
(easily)
    Hello, darling . . . What're you doing up at this hour?

ELLEN
(sweetly)
    I got lonesome . . .

He takes her hand in a caress, but his eyes remain glued to the wheel.

> CROUPIER
> (calling result of spin)
> Rouge, vingt-un, impaire . . .
> (pulling away Tony's stack with hoe)

> TONY
> (rising)
> Well, that's that.

Nonchalantly he turns from the table and puts his arm through Ellen's, giving it a little hug at the same time. CAMERA PANS with them as they go towards supper room.

> TONY
> (cont'd)
> You came in the nick of time. I'm famished and I haven't a sou left. Do you think you've enough in that bag to stand your poor husband a spot of food?

> ELLEN
> (laughing)
> I don't know if I should. Perhaps if I let you go hungry, it'll teach you not to gamble.

> TONY
> It's been tried before—but I'm afraid I'm hopeless.
> (he laughs open-heartedly)

> DISSOLVE

INT. SUPPER ROOM—CASINO—NIGHT

55   MED. SHOT. Ellen and Tony at a corner table finishing their meal. Ellen is laughing at some joke of Tony's.

> TONY
> (looking about for waiter)
> Garçon . . .

A little old waiter with a typical droop, sad eyes and humble manner, comes to the table.

TONY
(cont'd)

Check, please.

WAITER
(putting check down)

Oui, Monsieur.

Tony takes Ellen's pocketbook lying between them on the table, reaches into it, takes out a folded bill, and tosses it in grand manner to the waiter.

WAITER
(cont'd)

Merci, Monsieur.

He exits.

TONY

Thanks . . . monkeyface.

ELLEN

Monkeyface? I'm not sure I like that.

TONY

But you are!—if you could only see yourself eating. First, your little jaws pounce on every mouthful— then snap . . .
(he illustrates, clicking his jaws)
. . . just like a monkey.
(he bends over to kiss her)

ELLEN
(pleased, but horrified)

Not in front of all these people. Tony—you can't!

TONY

You're forgetting we're not in England. Here it's just like shaking hands.

He leans over and kisses her ardently. They break as the waiter returns. Ellen starts powdering her nose.

> WAITER
>
> Your change, Monsieur.

Tony glances at it, realizes the waiter made a mistake, then hurriedly pockets it and gets up.

> TONY
>
> Let's go.

They start out.

> ELLEN
>
> Where're you going, Tony? The exit is this way.

> TONY
>
> I want to make one last little bet.

> ELLEN
>
> But you haven't any money.

> TONY
>
> I just found some . . .

DISSOLVE

INT. GAMING ROOM—CASINO—NIGHT

56   MED. SHOT. Tony and Ellen standing at roulette table.

> TONY
>
> Now let's see—we were married on the eigh-teenth— Perhaps that's my lucky number.

> ELLEN
>
> Where'd you get all that money?

> TONY
> (scanning table)
>
> That fool waiter brought me change for five hun-dred francs instead of a hundred.

> ELLEN
> (shocked)
>
> And you took it?

> TONY
>
> Of course, Monkeyface— It's lucky money.

ELLEN

Give it to me—I'll take it back to him.

CROUPIER

Rien ne vas plus! . . .

Tony hurriedly drops the bills on number 18. The wheel spins. Again a look of desperation comes into Tony's face.

ELLEN

How could you! They'll take it out of his wages. And he looked so pathetic. I'm sure he has a wife and a lot of children.

TONY

I'll bet everything I win that he isn't even married. They all look like that. It makes the tips bigger.

ELLEN

Tony . . .

CROUPIER

Dix-huit—rouge—paire.

TONY
(exulting)

Darling—we won! Fourteen thousand francs! Let's find a horse and choke him.

The banker pays Tony.

ELLEN

Let's find that waiter and give him back his money.

Tony was about to bet again, but he stops.

TONY

But, of course!—Where is he?

DISSOLVE OUT

DISSOLVE IN

INT. SUPPER ROOM—CASINO—NIGHT

57   MED. SHOT. Tony and Ellen enter just as the little old waiter shuffles by carrying a drink.

TONY

Hey, you, there!

(waiter stops)

Come here.

(waiter comes over)

You gave me the wrong change.—There it is—
with a little interest.

Tony thrusts a few hundred franc notes into his hand, laughing at the old man's overwhelming surprise and sudden joy.

WAITER

Oh, merci, monsieur—I can't thank you enough.

TONY

Oh, by the way, Madame thought—you're not
married, are you?

WAITER

But, oui, monsieur.

TONY

But you haven't any children?

WAITER

But, oui, monsieur—

(modestly)

—eleven!

Ellen holds out her hand, and Tony laughs and gives her the
rest of the money.

FADE OUT

FADE IN

INT. LIVING ROOM—TONY'S APARTMENT—DAY

58   FULL SHOT . . . SHOOTING towards door. It is def-
      initely the home of a bachelor whose sole interest is
      horses. The walls are covered by scores of prints and
      photographs of race horses. Every Derby winner is there,
      with the weights they carried, the jockeys, the owners,
      and the price they paid. Tony enters carrying Ellen
      across the threshold.

TONY

Herc we are!

ELLEN

Home at last!

They laugh, and he puts her down gently, holding her and kissing her.

ELLEN
(cont'd)
(looking about)
I didn't know you were so fond of horses, Tony.

TONY
(purposely misinterpreting)
You're right, Monkeyface—we'll have to do it over. I'm afraid a London bachelor's flat is hardly the background for you.

ELLEN
(notices package on nearby trunk)
Look! What's that?
(goes to it)
It's from Abbot Monckford—
(starts opening it)
Must be from Father.

TONY
(helping her)
Probably a lot of preserves to keep us from starving.

The package is open, and Ellen takes out a magnificent pair of silver candlesticks.

ELLEN
Oh, the darling! . . . . What did you say?

TONY
(takes candlestick and looks at it)
You might as well know it, Monkeyface—we're broke.

(he looks at the silversmith's mark on bottom)
Hmm, the real thing . . .
     (he puts candlestick back on table)

ELLEN
(horrified)
Broke? But, darling, why did we spend all that money in France?

TONY
That wasn't my money. I borrowed a thousand to marry you on. I thought we did rather well to make it last seven weeks—with enough left for taxi fare home from the station . . .

During the above he crosses over to piano and starts playing.

ELLEN
(following after him)
But—what are we going to do?

TONY
Oh, I expect something'll turn up— Maybe I can even borrow another thousand to tide us over.

ELLEN
(horrified)
But, Tony, we can't live like that!

TONY
Are you sorry I decided to make sure of you first, and see about keeping you later?

ELLEN
No, of course not! But . . .

TONY
Well, then why get so upset about it?

ELLEN
But what're we going to live on?

TONY
Couldn't perhaps your father increase your allowance a bit—now that you have a husband?

ELLEN
(shocked)

Tony!

TONY

You don't think I'm particularly fond of the idea?
. . . But what else is there?
(he runs a particularly brilliant passage
on the piano)

ELLEN
(bursting into tears)
Tony—you frighten me— What's going to happen
to us?

TONY

(interrupts her by taking her in his arms)
Nothing . . .
(he kisses her)

ELLEN
(struggling)
Tony, don't—I don't want you to kiss me.
(he continues to kiss her. Ellen, weakly)
Please, Tony . . .
(as he kisses her behind ear)
What are you doing . . . ?

TONY

I love you . . .

FADE OUT

FADE IN

INT. KITCHEN—TONY'S APARTMENT—NIGHT

59   FULL SHOT. Ellen, in a dinner dress, is standing beside
the stove and tasting the soup from the big ladle and
smiling approvingly at the cook, who beams back at her.

ELLEN'S VOICE
(narrating)
. . . *Tony was right . . . things did work out after*
all—and quite simply, too . . .

She goes over to a table in the middle of the kitchen on which stands a tray of hors d'oeuvres. She adds a final touch to the arrangement and steals one for herself.

ELLEN'S VOICE
(cont'd)
. . . Through a friend of my father's he got a job with an insurance company. He seemed to be working quite hard. Even Father had begun to think that perhaps he was wrong about Tony. . . .

DISSOLVE

INT. SMALL DINING ROOM—TONY'S APARTMENT— NIGHT

60   FULL SHOT. Refurnished in a sound modern fashion. Harriet is working at setting the table. Ellen enters from the kitchen and walks over to the table to inspect Harriet's work.

ELLEN'S VOICE
. . . I asked Father for an advance on my allowance to re-do the flat, and he was quite glad to give it to me. It turned out rather nicely . . .

ELLEN
(turning to Harriet)
Harriet, where are those little ash trays I bought the other day?

HARRIET
(picking them up from sideboard)
Here they are, ma'am . . .

ELLEN
(taking ash trays)
And don't forget to put on the candlesticks.

HARRIET
I couldn't find them, ma'am . . .

ELLEN
Perhaps Cook took them to polish.

> HARRIET
>
> I shouldn't think so—but I'll ask her.

Harriet goes. Ellen starts distributing ash trays around table.

> ELLEN'S VOICE
> (narrating)
> *. . . I was quite happy during that time . . . A good part of it was, I believe, that I felt I was being a good wife—that I was really helping him make something of himself . . .*

Harriet returns.

> HARRIET
>
> No, ma'am—Cook hasn't seen the candlesticks.

> ELLEN
> (puzzled)
> That's strange. I . . .
> (the buzzer interrupts)
> That must be Sir Anthony . . . I'll answer it. See if you can find them somewhere.

Ellen goes toward door.

WIPE OUT

WIPE IN

INT. FOYER—TONY'S APARTMENT—NIGHT

61   MED. SHOT. Ellen enters and goes to door, opening it with a smile. It isn't Tony, however, but Beaky Thwaite. Mr. Thwaite is very tall with broad, stooped shoulders, and a red, fleshy eagle beak. Anywhere but in England he would be a caricature—there, he is a rich public school boy who could do with a few lessons in grammar and diction.

> BEAKY
> (looking around)
> Hello! Hello . . .

> ELLEN
> (laughing)

Hello.

> BEAKY

Looks like the wrong kennel, what? 'T's Tony Aysgarth's, I want.

Ellen immediately sees that this big slob means no insult.

> ELLEN
> (smiling)

You must be Mr. Thwaite— I'm Lady Aysgarth— Won't you come in?

Harriet has come into the foyer and takes Beaky's hat and umbrella.

> BEAKY
> (grinning at Ellen, as though he had come
> to a tremendous conclusion)

Old Tony's wife, eh? Well—
> (shaking her hand)

Congratulations, and all that sort of thing.

> ELLEN

Thank you.

She leads him towards living room.

INT. LIVING ROOM—TONY'S APARTMENT—NIGHT

62 FULL SHOT. It has all been done over in good sound modern taste. Beaky stops on the threshold, astonished.

> BEAKY

The woman's touch, eh?—Oh, I say, jolly sort of show . . . Where are all the horses?

> ELLEN

Stored in a closet, thank heavens.

> BEAKY
> (admiringly)

Hmm— Firm touch on the reins, eh?

Harriet enters with cocktails and hors d'oeuvres, serving Ellen and Beaky.

                    ELLEN
Have one, won't you?

                    BEAKY
                 (taking one)
Thanks. Where is the old boy?

                    ELLEN
He should be along any minute . . . You were in
school with him, weren't you, Mr. Thwaite?

                    BEAKY
Rather. Shared a study. Bosom friends and all that
sort of nonsense. How is he? Last time I ran into
him was at Ascot. He dropped quite a packet. Still
playing the ponies, I expect, eh?

                    ELLEN
                  (uneasily)
N-No, I don't think he does much of that now.

                    BEAKY
What? Must've changed a bit. Double harness, I
suppose. Told me he was married last time I saw
him. "Oh, come," I said, "not down to that, old
boy, are you?"

                    ELLEN
Will you have another cocktail, Mr. Thwaite?

                    BEAKY
         (conscious of ice in Ellen's voice)
No, thanks. Perhaps I oughtn't to have said that,
what?

From off scene comes the sound of a buzzer.

                    ELLEN
That must be Tony. Will you excuse me?
                (she goes to open door)

63   MED. SHOT. Ellen opens door. Tony enters and hur-
      riedly kisses Ellen on the forehead. CAMERA PANS
      with them as they rejoin Beaky.

TONY
(to Ellen)
Hello, darling . . .
(shaking hands with Beaky)
Well, Beaky— How are you? Great to see you
again. You look fit.

BEAKY
Hello. . . .

TONY
Sorry I'm late, Monkeyface— Got held up at the
office . . . Have I time to change?

ELLEN
Afraid not, darling. I'm sure Mr. Thwaite'll forgive
you.

BEAKY
Certainly, I've seen him come in to dinner in
shorts— Ho-ho!

As all three laugh, and start towards dining room—

DISSOLVE OUT

DISSOLVE IN

INT. DINING ROOM—TONY'S FLAT—NIGHT
64   FULL SHOT. They are all at the table.

BEAKY
(between bites)
. . . Come to think of it, this is the first meal
you've ever stood me, old boy.

TONY
Don't worry—you're going to pay for this one,
too. Got enough insurance on that place of yours
in Yorkshire?

BEAKY
(roars with laughter)
Now, now! None of that! I'm a guest!

TONY

Sorry, old chap, but you've just got too much money for one man.

BEAKY
(to Ellen)

Hasn't changed a bit. That's what he used to say at school when I got my allowance from home— Good old school days, what?
(pauses thoughtfully and absently twists
ash tray in front of him)

ELLEN
(to Tony)

By the way, darling—something strange happened today. The candlesticks Father gave us seem to've vanished.

TONY
(smiling at her)

Oh, I took them. I was hoping I'd have them back before you missed them.

ELLEN

Where are they?

TONY

At the silversmith's. I knocked one over and bent its branch. I took the other one so he could fix it just right.

ELLEN

Oh . . .
(she turns to Beaky, as Harriet passes with plate)
How about another slice?

BEAKY

No, thanks. I'm running to fat as it is. Got a bad ticker. Was told to knock off my oats a bit by the vet— Ho-ho! . . .

DISSOLVE

EXT. LONDON STREET—DAY

65   MED. SHOT. Ellen, carrying a couple of small pack-
      ages, is shopping around in the windows as she walks
      along.

> ELLEN'S VOICE
> (narrating)
> *. . . The candlesticks never came back. Whenever I
> asked Tony about them, he put me off with some ex-
> cuse or other. It seemed rather strange that the silver-
> smith should take so much time to repair them, but
> I still didn't suspect anything . . .*

Ellen passes a window of an antique shop. Among a few paintings and precious china prominently displayed, stand the candlesticks. Ellen stops and, as though not believing her eyes,
approaches the window.

> ELLEN'S VOICE
> (cont'd)
> *. . . Then one day, as I was shopping in Jeremy
> Street, there in the window of an antique shop were
> the candlesticks marked for sale. . . .*

Determinedly she goes into the shop.

INT. ANTIQUE SHOP—DAY

66   FULL SHOT. Full of all sorts of rare curios and objets
      d'art. A gracious little white-haired man comes forward.

> ANTIQUE DEALER
> (cheerfully)
> Good day, Madam— Can I help you?

> ELLEN
> (hesitantly)
> Those candlesticks in the window—are they for
> sale?

> DEALER
> Everything here is for sale, Madam—
> (he goes to window and takes out one)

If I could afford to collect for pleasure, I would
never part with these.

> ELLEN
> (weakly)

Have you had them long?

> DEALER

Oh, no—just a few weeks . . . Aren't they beautiful, Madam?

> ELLEN
> (afraid of the answer)

Do you . . . Do you know where they came from?

> DEALER

Naturally— Of course, I can't divulge their source
unless you're seriously interested . . .

> ELLEN
> (desperately)

I am.

> DEALER

They have quite an important history. Originally,
they belonged to Lord Nelson—who gave them to
a Lieutenant McLaidlaw who served under him
as his flag officer and in whose family they remained ever since. I bought them from a certain
Sir Anthony Aysgarth—who married into the family. . . .

As the dealer chats on pleasantly, Ellen feels dizzy and
grasps the counter in order not to fall. The dealer finally notices it.

> DEALER
> (cont'd)

What's the matter? Are you ill, Madam? Can I get
you a glass of water?

> ELLEN
> (forcing herself to sound natural)

No, thank you—I'm all right.

(she fumbles with her pocket book)
How much are they? . . .

DISSOLVE

EXT. ANTIQUE SHOP—DAY

67   Ellen walks out of the shop dazed. She stops for a min-
      ute, as though not knowing where to go, then hails a
      cab.

ELLEN'S VOICE
(narrating)
. . . *It was such a nasty thing to do—no matter how*
much he needed the money . . . I took a cab and
went straight to his office . . .

A cab drives up to the curb, and as Ellen enters it,

DISSOLVE OUT

DISSOLVE IN

INT. RECEPTION ROOM—LARGE INSURANCE
OFFICE—DAY

68   FULL SHOT. Heavy oak wainscoting, etc. An old clerk
      is behind the information desk as Ellen comes up to it.

ELLEN
I would like to see Sir Anthony Aysgarth, please.

CLERK
(answers slowly, with a friendly smile)
I'm sorry, madam—but he is no longer with us.

ELLEN
(stunned for a moment)
You must be mistaken. I'm sure . . .
(trails off weakly)

CLERK
He left the firm some weeks ago.

ELLEN
(hesitates and half turns to go, then:)
May I see Lord Melbeck, then?

> CLERK

What name shall I say?

> ELLEN

Lady Aysgarth.

> CLERK
> (raises his eyebrows)

Thank you.

The clerk busies himself with announcer, as Ellen watches him nervously.

WIPE OUT

WIPE IN

INT. LORD MELBECK'S OFFICE—INSURANCE OFFICE—DAY

69   FULL SHOT. Elaborate, sombre. Lord Melbeck, grey-haired, dignified executive, stands up as Ellen comes in. He smiles and greets her self-consciously.

> LORD MELBECK

Hello, Ellen . . . er . . . How's your father?

> ELLEN

Thank you, Lord Melbeck— Not too well, but he never complains—you know him.

> LORD MELBECK

Yes . . . er . . . Afraid he and I are getting on in years . . .

For a moment there is a pause. Now Ellen is even more conscious that something is wrong.

> ELLEN

I . . . I came in to see you about my husband.

> LORD MELBECK
> (becoming a little rattled; hastily)

Oh . . . er . . . there's nothing to worry about, Ellen. I told him I . . . er . . . wouldn't prosecute.

ELLEN
(goes white and rigid; weakly)
What?

LORD MELBECK
(extremely uncomfortable)
That I wouldn't prosecute . . . er . . . He'll pay
me back some time . . .

ELLEN
(fighting to keep calm)
What did he do?

LORD MELBECK
Oh, er . . . I'm sorry. I thought you knew . . . er
. . . It wasn't . . . Well, a little irregularity in the
accounts . . . I couldn't keep him on, of course,
but I . . . er . . .
(trails off)

ELLEN
I see . . . Thank you, Lord Melbeck.

She turns towards the door. He accompanies her to it, holding
her arm.

LORD MELBECK
Er . . . Terribly sorry, my dear . . .
(changes subject)
Er . . . Best regards to your father.

ELLEN
(mechanically)
Thank you, Lord Melbeck . . .

DISSOLVE

INT. LIVING ROOM—TONY'S FLAT—DAY
70   FULL SHOT. Harriet, who is pulling the curtains together, turns as Ellen enters. Ellen's face is drawn with
strain and anxiety. She hesitates a moment, then starts
towards bedroom.

> HARRIET
> (noticing)
> Can I get you some tea, ma'am?

> ELLEN
> No, thanks.
> (grimly; making a decision)
> Bring my luggage up right away.

Ellen goes upstairs. Harriet stares after her a moment, then obeys.

INT. ELLEN'S BEDROOM—TONY'S FLAT—DAY

71   FULL SHOT. Ellen enters, takes her hat off and drops her gloves. She sits wearily on the edge of the bed, exhausted by the emotional strain. She stands up when Harriet enters carrying several suitcases.

> HARRIET
> Shall I put them on the bed, ma'am?

> ELLEN
> (with a lump in her throat)
> Any place . . .

> HARRIET
> Something wrong, ma'am?

> ELLEN
> (mastering herself)
> I'm going home to Abbot Monckford. You're coming with me.

> HARRIET
> (reacting to it)
> Yes, ma'am.

As they start taking things out of the bureau, Tony's voice is heard bellowing cheerfully:

> TONY'S VOICE
> Yoo-hoo! Monkeyface! . . . Where are you?

Sound of Tony coming up steps two at a time. Ellen stops

and looks toward door, her face grim. Tony bounds into the room, waving a set of keys.

> TONY
> (cont'd)
> (laughing)
>
> Look—you're getting careless. You left your keys in the door. Suppose someone came in—he could've stolen everything!

Ellen turns and he sees her white, strained face and speaks in sober tone.

> TONY
> (cont'd)
>
> What's going on?

> ELLEN
> (to Harriet)
>
> Harriet, will you call the porter, please, and have my trunks brought up . . .

> HARRIET
> (glancing from Ellen to Tony)
>
> Yes, ma'am.
>> (she goes)

> TONY
> (acting very lightly)
>
> Going somewhere?

> ELLEN
> (quietly)
>
> Home.
>> (turns back to bureau for more things)

> TONY
> (easily)
>
> Why? What's wrong?
>> (she doesn't answer; merely takes out
>> some more clothes from bureau)
>
> Oh . . . So the cat's out . . .

> (sitting down and lighting cigarette—not
> at all put out)
> Well, I tried to keep it from you as long as I
> could . . .
>> (Ellen still refuses to answer; goes on
>> with her packing)
> I was in a tight spot. I needed some money in a
> hurry, and I certainly couldn't get it from you . . .
> So I took a chance— I thought it was a sure thing.
>> (a short bitter laugh)
> It was—until the jockey fell off after leading all the
> way by eight lengths . . .

Ellen stops with some things in her hands and turns to Tony
as though to speak, but instead she makes an effort and keeps
silent, turning again to the suitcase on her bed.

> ELLEN'S VOICE
> (narrating)
> *. . . I didn't say anything—what was there to say?*
> *Tell him that he was a thief? That he stole to gamble?*
> *. . . It wouldn't've meant anything to him. I sud-*
> *denly realized that he was a moral cripple. He simply*
> *had no conscience—no sense of right or wrong. It*
> *meant as little to him as color to a blind man . . .*

Tony is annoyed and flips his cigarette abruptly into the fireplace. Then he rises, talking as he goes to the fireplace and
picks up a poker, holding it in his hand.

> TONY
> So you won't even talk to me?—Very well, let's say
> I *am* a thief. What did you expect when you made
> me take that dull little job peddling insurance—
> that I'd live on it? Why do you think I married
> you?

He puts the poker back in its place with extreme gentleness
that stands out in sharp contrast to the violence of his feeling.

> TONY
> (cont'd)
> What an idiot I was! I might've just as well married

one of my creditors! . . . All right—go home! Put
on those dowdy tweeds. Get your bike out of the
garage and go pedalling over the countryside . . .
Perhaps that'll make you happy again . . .

He walks out. Without looking after him, she sits down
weakly on the edge of the bed, then buries her face in the
pillow with a sob.

> ELLEN

Tony . . . Oh, Tony . . .

After a little pause, from the drawing room below comes the
sound of the piano, at first a few violent chords, then the
melody we have come to know, continuing through the rest
of the scene. Harriet enters scene.

> HARRIET
> (as she notices Ellen crying)
> Beg pardon, ma'am—the porter.

The porter brings in a trunk, sets it down and exits.

> ELLEN
> (sits up, wiping her eyes)
> Thank you . . .

She stands up and starts snapping valise together.

DISSOLVE

INT. HALLWAY—ABBOT MONCKFORD—NIGHT

72   FULL SHOT. Ellen enters, followed by Harriet carrying
some luggage. The maid who opens the door takes the
bag Ellen is carrying.

> MAID

How d'do, ma'am.

> ELLEN

Hello, Mary. Is my father in?

> MAID
> (uneasily)
> Yes, ma'am.

> ELLEN
>
> Where is he?

> MAID
>
> In his room, ma'am. The doctor's been here all day.

> ELLEN
>
> The doctor? He isn't sick, is he?

As she goes toward the drawing room and the two maids continue on with the luggage, a little old country doctor with a gentle old-fashioned face enters.

> DOCTOR SOAMES
> (taking her hands)
>
> How do you do, my dear. I'm so glad to see you. I was a little worried my telegram wouldn't get there in time for you to make the six-thirty.

> ELLEN
>
> Telegram? . . . Is it—Is he very bad, Doctor Soames?

> DOCTOR SOAMES
> (he hesitates for the right words)
>
> Well . . . er . . . not *too* bad. He's had another stroke, of course. I thought it would be best to wire you.

> ELLEN
>
> Can I see him?

> DOCTOR SOAMES
>
> Not now, I'm afraid, Ellen. He's asleep.

DISSOLVE

INT. DRAWING ROOM—ABBOT MONCKFORD—NIGHT

73   FULL SHOT—Ellen and Doctor Soames. Fire in the grate. Ellen is standing at a window staring out, her back eloquent of unhappiness and tension. Soames is playing

preoccupied solitaire at a small table, looking up at her sympathetically.

ELLEN

Has he any chance at all, Doctor Soames?

DOCTOR SOAMES

Hard to say, my dear. If he pulls through this one, he may go on for years.

ELLEN

(almost a prayer)

He must live. He's all I've got left.

Doctor Soames looks at her in surprise and is about to say something when the nurse enters.

NURSE

He's awake now.

Ellen turns and looks inquiringly at Doctor Soames.

DOCTOR SOAMES

You can go in, child. But please don't let him talk too much— The slightest excitement might be very dangerous.

ELLEN

I understand.

Ellen follows the nurse out.

WIPE

INT. COMMANDER'S BEDROOM—ABBOT MONCKFORD—NIGHT

74   FULL SHOT. The old man is lying in his very large bed. He looks shrunken and worn, but his voice booms out as he makes a gallant effort.

ELLEN

Hello, Father . . .

COMMANDER

Hello, there, darling.

Ellen goes to his bed.

> ELLEN
> How do you feel?

> COMMANDER
> (a little indignant)
> All right. Just . . . er . . . a little . . . er . . .
> something. That Soames is a worrier. No need to
> send for you.
> (laughs)
> Plenty of fight in the old hulk yet.

> ELLEN
> (patting his hand solicitously)
> That's the spirit, darling. But you've got to take
> real care.

> COMMANDER
> (he has been examining her face carefully)
> You don't look well, Ellen— Hope that old saw-
> bones didn't scare you . . .

> ELLEN
> (forces a smile; trying to be casual)
> Oh, no—just a little tired from the train ride.

> COMMANDER
> (frowning)
> How's . . . er . . . your husband?

Ellen hesitates, deciding to lie, and the old man notices it.

> ELLEN
> Oh, he's all right.
> (too enthusiastic)
> He's fine!

> COMMANDER
> (suspicious)
> Are you telling me the truth?

> ELLEN
> Of course, darling.

> COMMANDER
> (not satisfied)
> All right. But remember—if anything goes wrong,
> this is your home.

> ELLEN
> I know, darling. But everything *is* all right. As a
> matter of fact, he would have come with me, but
> something came up in the office . . . But we
> mustn't talk so much. The main thing's for you to
> get well.

The door has opened, and the nurse speaks to Ellen.

> NURSE
> Lady Aysgarth—Doctor Soames asked me to tell
> you that your husband's arrived.

Luckily Ellen has her face away from the Commander so that
he can't see her thunderstruck astonishment.

> ELLEN
> (with an effort)
> Thank you, nurse.

> COMMANDER
> (pleased)
> Rot! He shouldn't have come . . . Really—every-
> body's making too much fuss.

> ELLEN
> Good night, Admiral. See you in the morning.

As the nurse puts a thermometer in the Commander's mouth,
Ellen goes towards door.

> WIPE OUT

WIPE IN

INT. DRAWING ROOM—ABBOT MONCKFORD—
NIGHT

75   FULL SHOT. Tony and a tall, dignified man with a
      beard, are talking to Soames. Ellen hesitates at the door,

looking at Tony. He goes to her immediately, his face sympathetic and contrite.

> TONY
> (acting the considerate husband)
> Hello, darling . . . I came as fast as I could.

> ELLEN
> But . . .

> TONY
> This is Sir William Bentley. I thought it would be a good idea to have a specialist . . .

> SIR WILLIAM
> How do you do, Lady Aysgarth?

> ELLEN
> How do you do?

> TONY
> (to Soames)
> I thought you wouldn't mind, Doctor Soames . . .

> SOAMES
> (burbles eagerly)
> I'm delighted. There's no one in the entire pro-fession I'd rather have for a consultant than Sir William.

> SIR WILLIAM
> Very kind of you, Soames . . . Should we see the patient now?

> SOAMES
> By all means.

Sir William bows to Ellen and follows Soames.

76   TWO SHOT—Ellen and Tony.

> TONY
> I must apologize for my intrusion, darling—

(his voice drops and becomes warm
with feeling—intimate)
But when the telegram arrived, I felt I had to come
. . . I know how much he means to you, and I
thought you might want to have someone besides
old Soames.

ELLEN
(trying to be impersonal)
It was very kind of you to bring Sir William.

TONY
And I also wanted to tell you how sorry I am. I
behaved like a beast. I swear to you, darling, I
didn't mean a word of it. I felt so miserable inside—I just lashed out. I really wanted to hurt myself—and I hurt you instead . . . I know it's
unforgivable—but I just wanted you to know—
(he waits for reaction from Ellen, and
when there is none:)
Well, goodbye, darling. Do let me know in the
morning how Father is, will you?
(he starts towards door)

ELLEN
(matter-of-fact)
There's no train till morning.

TONY
(turning)
Oh . . .
(pause)
Well, I'll stay at the inn.

ELLEN
That isn't necessary. There are plenty of spare
rooms in the house.

TONY
Very well— If you think it's better.

DISSOLVE

EXT. BELFRY—DAY

77   FULL SHOT. The sky is leaden and rain is drizzling down on the old tower. The bells are pealing sorrowfully announcing a funeral . . .

> ELLEN'S VOICE
> (narrating)
> . . . *But Tony didn't take the train the next morning, nor the one after. He remained at Abbot Monckford through all those long, miserable days of my father's illness . . .*

DISSOLVE

EXT. VILLAGE CEMETERY—DAY—
(DRIZZLING RAIN)

78   LONG SHOT. The vicar, standing under an umbrella held by the church warden, is reading the internment ceremony. A few friends and neighbors stand around in a small tight group—all under umbrellas.

> ELLEN'S VOICE
> . . . *I couldn't help but feel very grateful. He was so considerate, so understanding, and he so delicately avoided the mention of anything personal— He was like an old and dear friend . . .*

DISSOLVE OUT

DISSOLVE IN

EXT. VILLAGE CEMETERY—DAY—
(DRIZZLING RAIN)

79   MED. SHOT—Ellen, dressed in black, quietly sobbing into her handkerchief. Harriet stands beside her, holding her arm. A little behind them, Tony stands discreetly, watching Ellen out of the corner of his eye.

> ELLEN'S VOICE
> . . . *And not until it was all over did I realize that all I had left in the world was Tony . . .*

FADE OUT

FADE IN

(NOTE: The following shots must be visualized as a series of typical English sporting prints.)

EXT. ORCHARD—DAY—(STOCK)
80   FULL SHOT—Apple tree in bloom.

>   ELLEN'S VOICE
>   (narrating)
> . . . *During the next two years or so we were quite
> happy together. True, it wasn't the reckless, giddy
> happiness of the first months of our married life* . . .

DISSOLVE

EXT. FIELD—DAY—(SPRING)—(STOCK??)
81   FULL SHOT—Farmer walking behind plow drawn by
      an enormous gray Percheron.

>   ELLEN'S VOICE
> . . . *But for that very reason, I felt secure. It seemed
> more real, more solid, more enduring* . . .

DISSOLVE

EXT. FIELD—DAY—(FALL)—(STOCK)
82   FULL SHOT—a harvest scene.

>   ELLEN'S VOICE
> . . . *By the terms of my father's will I was assured
> of a modest but comfortable income. Poor darling,
> he didn't trust Tony to the last, and made sure that
> I couldn't touch the principal unless I left Tony or
> became a widow* . . .

DISSOLVE OUT

DISSOLVE IN

EXT. FIELD—DAY—(FALL)
83   CLOSE SHOT—Huntsman raising his horn to give sig-
      nal for beginning of the hunt.

ELLEN'S VOICE

. . . We remained at Abbot Monckford, and Tony took to country life as though he had never known any other . . .

DISSOLVE

EXT. FIELD—DAY—(FALL)—(STOCK)

84 FULL SHOT—Hounds racing after the fox.

85 LONG SHOT—(STOCK)—The hunt. Riders spread all over the field follow the hounds over fences, etc.

ELLEN'S VOICE

. . . I was amazed at the change in him. It seemed as though there wasn't even a trace left of the old Tony in this hearty country squire . . .

DISSOLVE

INT. DRAWING ROOM—ABBOT MONCKFORD—
EARLY EVENING

86 FULL SHOT. A group of members of the local hunt have gathered in the drawing room to have some hot punch before dispersing to their homes. They are all in hunt dress and riding clothes.

ELLEN'S VOICE

. . . And Abbot Monckford became one of the most popular houses in the shire . . .

Tony is the center of a group of men at the fireplace and is telling a story. Beaky, close beside him, hangs on every word.

TONY

. . . So they brought the poor Cockney before the magistrate. "Simpkins," said the magistrate, "I can understand that a man might want to kill his wife, but why did you cut her into five thousand little pieces?"—"Beggin' your Lordship's pardon," said Simpkins, "I did it in a moment of h'anger . . ."

It is greeted by roars of appreciative laughter, none heartier than Beaky's.

BEAKY
(slapping his thigh)
Ho-ho! In a moment of h'anger! That's the best
one yet, Tony.

87   MED. SHOT—Ellen, in riding clothes, comes over to
an old battle-axe dowager drinking hot cup, sitting beside a quiet-looking, open-faced and middle-aged man.
He is Richard Kirby.

ELLEN
Some more, Lady Heaslip?

LADY HEASLIP
(roaring)
Heavens no! . . . What do you want me to do—
fall on my face? I did nothing all day but fall on
everything else.

Ellen laughs.

LADY HEASLIP
(cont'd)
(nodding at Richard)
Give him some. Maybe it'll make him talk about
something else besides the weather.

Richard smiles and holds out his, which Ellen fills.

RICHARD
Thank you.

ELLEN
(the gracious hostess)
I hope you've enjoyed the run, Mr. Kirby. I don't
suppose you do much fox-hunting in Canada?

RICHARD
Oh, yes, we do—some. Only we trap them and sell
the skins.

Ellen smiles.

LADY HEASLIP
What did I tell you? If it isn't the car he makes or

the weather, it's business. Why don't you learn a few jokes from Tony?

From off scene comes another roar of laughter.

> LADY HEASLIP
> (cont'd)
>
> He's such fun!
> (to Ellen)
> We should all be very grateful to you, my dear, for snaring him. He's brought the old graveyard to life.
> (she spies Tony who is crossing over towards them)
> Oh, there you are—you blackguard. Are your ears burning?

> TONY
>
> Saw you sitting in the middle of Wilkins' Brook . . . What were you doing—cooling off?

> LADY HEASLIP
> (she almost splits a gut)
>
> Go on! . . .

> TONY
> (taking Ellen's arm)
> Will you forgive us?
> (to Ellen, moving her away)
> I want to speak to you for a moment, darling.

CAMERA PANS with them as he leads her across hall toward library.

INT. LIBRARY—ABBOT MONCKFORD—
EARLY EVENING

88   MED. SHOT. A small, book-lined room. Tony and Ellen enter. Ellen stares at him in amazement as Tony's manner becomes grim, and he carefully closes the door.

> ELLEN
>
> What's wrong?

TONY

Everything! I'm in a frightful jam. There's a man outside who came down from London . . . I've simply got to give him money.

ELLEN

Why? . . . What's happened? . . .
(suddenly terrified)
Tony, you haven't been gambling again?

TONY

No, of course not. It's an old note of mine. From years ago. I'd completely forgotten about it.

ELLEN

How much is it?

TONY

Twenty-six hundred pounds.

ELLEN

(surprised and shocked by the sum)
But . . . How're we going to pay it? You know we haven't got that kind of money.

TONY

(bitterly)
Thanks to that fool will of your father's . . . Darling, we've got to raise it. You don't understand—I'll go to prison. Can't you borrow it somewhere?

ELLEN

Not twenty-six hundred pounds! The most I can get is an advance on the rest of the year's income.

TONY

(impatiently)
How much is that?

ELLEN

There's only one quarter left—it'll be about six hundred . . . I suppose I could manage to run the house on credit for a few months.

> TONY
>
> No—that won't do any good. It's all—or nothing.

> ELLEN
> (very upset)
>
> But, Tony, what'll you do?

> TONY
>
> Never mind. I'll get it from Beaky.

He stalks out angrily. Ellen slumps into a chair, staring after him.

> ELLEN'S VOICE
> (narrating)
>
> *. . . It was the same old thing all over again—he was gambling . . . From that moment on, the feeling of impending disaster never left me . . .*

Ellen shudders, and, as though seeing something terrible, hides her face with her hands.

> DISSOLVE

INT. DINING ROOM—ABBOT MONCKFORD—DAY
89   FULL SHOT. Tony, Ellen and Beaky at breakfast, helping themselves from the silver containers on the sideboard. Harriet enters with a letter for Beaky.

> ELLEN'S VOICE
>
> *. . . A few days later we were having breakfast. Harriet came in with some mail for Beaky, who was staying with us . . .*

> BEAKY
> (taking letter)
>
> For me? Why the devil would they write me here, what? Mind if I look at it?

> ELLEN
>
> Certainly not.

> TONY
> (helping himself at the sideboard)

If it's from that barmaid you were telling about,
you'd better read it aloud.

> BEAKY

Haw-haw . . . It's from the bank.

> TONY
> (he reacts nervously, then attempts lamely to
> joke; coming over to the table)

Don't tell me *you* overdraw your account, too.

> BEAKY

I say, here's a rum show. Fancy! Some bloke forged
my name to a check!

90   CLOSE SHOT—Ellen, as she notices Tony's nervous-
ness.

> ELLEN
> (looking at Tony)

Was it for much?

91   THREE SHOT—Ellen, Tony and Beaky.

> BEAKY
> (grinning with delight)

Quite. Those fool bankers— First they pay it. Then
they ask if it's my signature, haw!

> TONY
> (forced lightness)

Maybe it is—perhaps you were drunk when you
wrote it.

> BEAKY

Drunk? Not with this wheezy pump of mine . . .
Besides, drunk or sober, I never cross my t's like
that . . . But I must say the rest of it is pretty
close.

> TONY
> (taking check)

Let me see . . . Nasty charge—forgery.

                    BEAKY
Suppose I'd better ring the bank and tell them,
what?

                    ELLEN
May I see it, too?

Tony pretends he hasn't heard her.

                    TONY
                (casually, to Beaky)
There's no hurry. They're insured. Besides, you
can't settle a thing like that by phone.

                    BEAKY
I guess you're right. It'll take affidavits and all that
sort of truck. Perhaps I'd better drive down to
London.

                    TONY
There's no rush— They can't do anything over the
weekend, anyway. Wait till Monday, and I'll drive
with you.

                    BEAKY
All right—but you drive.
                (to Ellen)
Nothing I hate like dodging through city traffic.

                    ELLEN
Tony?

                    TONY
Yes?

                    ELLEN
Please show me the check.

Tony hesitates, looking up at her, his face stony. Then, with
a sudden gesture, he flips it over to her. She picks it up.

INSERT   CHECK for twenty-six hundred pounds, drawn
          on a private British bank.

ELLEN'S VOICE
(narrating)
. . . *My hands shook as I held the check. When I saw the sum I knew I was right—Tony had forged it. That's what he meant when he said he would get it from Beaky . . . There was nothing I could do except wonder how it would all end . . .*

DISSOLVE

INT. ABBOT MONCKFORD—DRAWING ROOM—NIGHT

92   MED. CLOSE SHOT—Ellen, sitting in a chair doing some embroidery on a frame.

ELLEN'S VOICE
. . . *And then it occurred to me that Tony and Beaky were old and intimate friends. Perhaps if he talked to him—told him the truth—Beaky would understand . . .*

93   FULL SHOT. Tony is sitting at the piano pounding away at a great rate, while Beaky stands beside him, one arm around his shoulder, and singing at the top of their voices. Like a pair of overgrown kids, they are harmonizing on all the old songs they sang in their school days.

ELLEN'S VOICE
(a touch of irony creeps into her voice)
. . . *After all, they went to school together . . . They wore the same tie . . .*

Their heads close together, Tony and Beaky combine atrociously on the last chord of the song, and then turn to Ellen for applause.

BEAKY
Good as a music hall turn, what?

ELLEN
(smiles at them)
Perhaps. But I didn't go to Harrow with you, so I don't have to listen to this.

(rises)
Good night.

Beaky and Tony laugh as she turns to go up.

> BEAKY
> Cheerio, old girl!

> ELLEN
> Don't drink too much, Beaky.

> BEAKY
> Don't worry—I won't.

> TONY
> Good night, darling.

As she walks across the room, Tony plays softly the melody we heard in the early part of the picture.

INT. STAIRCASE—ABBOT MONCKFORD—NIGHT

94   FULL SHOT. Ellen goes up the stairs. The orchestra picks up the theme that Tony is playing, introducing sinister overtones into it.

DISSOLVE

INT. ELLEN'S BEDROOM—ABBOT MONCKFORD—NIGHT

95   FULL SHOT. Ellen is preparing for bed.

> ELLEN'S VOICE
> (narrating)
> . . . *I went to bed feeling sure that Tony must've settled the problem of the check, because they were both so happy and gay . . .*

DISSOLVE OUT

DISSOLVE IN

INT. ELLEN'S BEDROOM—ABBOT MONCKFORD—NIGHT

96   MED. SHOT—Ellen in bed. The lights are out. She is tossing and turning in her sleep. CAMERA gradually MOVES to a CLOSE SHOT of Ellen.

ELLEN'S VOICE

. . . I was tired and fell asleep very quickly . . . But even in my sleep, I was uneasy. I had a nightmare . . .

Suddenly off scene the light goes on, illuminating Ellen's face. She wakes up with a start.

TONY'S VOICE
(o.s.)

Ellen, wake up!

97   MED. SHOT. Tony is leaning over the bed, shaking Ellen's shoulder. He is disheveled and in his shirt sleeves.

TONY

Wake up! Ellen! Ellen!

ELLEN
(tearing loose from her sleep)

Tony! What's happened?

TONY

Something awful . . . Poor Beaky, he . . .

ELLEN
(sitting up with an hysterical impulse and grabbing his arm; fighting the thought)

No! Oh, no! . . .

TONY

Poor devil . . . He shouldn't have had all that brandy.

ELLEN
(almost to herself)

He's dead . . .
(a sudden scream)
You murdered him!

Tony claps his hand over her lips, holding her jaw shut. While Tony is talking, she claws at him and beats him with her clenched fists, hysterically.

TONY

Quiet! What's the matter with you? Are you crazy?
The house is full of people—
(quickly)
He had a heart attack. You know he had a bad
heart— Everybody knows that! Dr. Soames says it
must've been the brandy.
(he lets go of her mouth as she starts sobbing)

ELLEN

Oh, go away, please . . .
(she turns and buries her face in pillow, sobbing)

TONY
(brokenly)
He was such a decent sort . . . Poor devil . . .

He turns and goes.

DISSOLVE OUT

DISSOLVE IN

INT. TRAIN COMPARTMENT—MORNING—(RAIN)—
(PROCESS B.G.)

98   MED. SHOT. Ellen is sitting very stiffly, staring out of
the rain-drenched window at the grey landscape. On the
seat opposite her is Harriet. She is quite upset and is
sniffling into a handkerchief. All through the narrative,
as an accompaniment to it, we hear the clicking of the
wheels on the rails and an occasional low whistle.

ELLEN'S VOICE
(narrating)
*. . . I ran away . . . Perhaps I should've gone to
the police, but what could I've told them? I tried to
talk to Doctor Soames . . . he told me to take a sed-
ative . . . I realized that I could never prove that
Tony had somehow forced Beaky to take those extra
drinks. Not by violence—he was too subtle for that.
But how could poor Beaky refuse a toast to the dear
old school?—and another to their dear old alma
mater? . . .*

The conductor enters the compartment.

> CONDUCTOR
> London in five minutes, ma'am—

Ellen looks up, startled.

> ELLEN
> (almost inaudibly)
> Thank you . . .

FADE OUT

99　CAMERA is on bow-shaped window in which can be read, in reverse lettering:
"FARQUHAR AND SMITH, LTD.
BANKERS"

As the CAMERA TILTS DOWN, we see Ellen sitting in front of the manager's desk. The manager is a grey-haired executive.

> MANAGER
> Very good, Lady Aysgarth— You can depend on it. As for Abbot Monckford—would you want us to let it for you, or would you rather we closed it?

> ELLEN
> Close it is best, I think.

> MANAGER
> Very well

Ellen rises. The Manager follows suit.

> ELLEN
> And I hope you'll make absolutely certain that *no one* gets my new address.

> MANAGER
> (tentatively)
> Sir Anthony has phoned several times . . .

> ELLEN
> (interrupting)
> No one, please.

> MANAGER
> (bowing)

As you wish.

INT. MAIN ROOM OF BANK—DAY

100   FULL SHOT. Teller's cages on one side. (This is a private English bank and is small and quite simple compared to what we have in America.)

CAMERA TRUCKS with Ellen as she crosses toward the street door. On her way she passes close to one of the high writing desks at which a man is standing writing a check. He looks up. He is Richard Kirby.

> RICHARD

How do you do, Lady Aysgarth?

> ELLEN
> (stops, smiling unsurely)

How do you do?

> RICHARD

I guess you don't remember me?—I'm Richard Kirby— We met in your house in Dorsetshire—I was with Lady Heaslip.

> ELLEN

Oh, yes, of course. You're the Canadian who talks about the weather and makes the Kirby car . . .

> RICHARD

That's right. I even have one outside.—Can I give you a lift somewhere?

> ELLEN

No, thanks—
> (she grins)

To tell you the truth, I wouldn't know where to tell you to drop me. I'm not quite sure I know where to go . . .

> RICHARD
> (laughing)

Well, looks like we're in the same boat—I don't know what to do with myself, either.

(he looks up at clock)
Say, it's almost one o'clock. How about some lunch?

ELLEN
(not knowing which to say)
Well . . .

RICHARD
Please do. I'm so tired of having my lunches alone.

ELLEN
Very well . . .
(they start toward the street)
Where shall we go?

RICHARD
You'll have to say—I'm afraid I'm only a poor Canadian lost in the wilds of London.

DISSOLVE

INT. CHERINO'S RESTAURANT—DAY
101   MED. SHOT. A small but extremely smart restaurant in the neighborhood of New Bond Street. Ellen and Richard are seated at a table in front of a large Palladium window, through which can be seen a typical London street. They are having coffee.

ELLEN
Are you going to be in England long, Mr. Kirby?

RICHARD
I really don't know. You see, this is my first vacation, and I don't quite know what to do with it—
(grins down at her)
—or with myself . . . Does a pipe bother you?

ELLEN
No.
(he lights it)
Perhaps it's just that you're not used to the idea of having nothing to do.

RICHARD

Maybe. Or else I'm one of those men who slave
for years to make their pile—and then discover that
it's too late to start having fun when you're forty-
five.

ELLEN

Nonsense. It's simply that you've worked so long
you've forgotten how to play— Or perhaps you
just have no one to play with.

RICHARD

I guess that's it. But for *that*, I'm afraid it is too
late.

ELLEN

What has age got to do with it?
(bitterly)
As a matter of fact, it's better to meet the right
person when you're forty-five than the wrong one
when you're twenty-three.

RICHARD
(with a laugh)
I hope you're right.

He knocks his pipe out against the heel of his hand. Ellen
smiles watching it.

RICHARD
(cont'd)
I guess a pipe is out of place in a restaurant.

ELLEN
(smiling)
Oh, it isn't that. But you knock it out just the way
my father used to.

RICHARD
(laughs)
So I remind you of your father—I told you it was
too late!

They laugh. The waiter comes in with the check and Richard puts down a note and gestures for the waiter to keep the change. As the waiter bows and goes off, Richard pulls Ellen's chair back, and they leave the table.

> ELLEN'S VOICE
> (narrating)
> . . . *It's funny what makes you like people. A tiny little gesture, like knocking out a pipe, made me suddenly feel at ease with Richard. It was as though I had known him for a long, long time . . .*

DISSOLVE

INT. OPERA HOUSE—NIGHT

102   MED. SHOT—of a small segment of the audience. Richard and Ellen, in evening dress, are watching the stage as from off scene we hear a few bars of some opera. (Stock)

> ELLEN'S VOICE
> . . . *It was such a pleasure to be with someone again. I hadn't talked to anyone since I came to London . . .*

DISSOLVE

EXT. STREET—A RAINY DAY—(PROCESS B.G.)

103   FULL SHOT. A policeman has just halted the traffic. Among the group of pedestrians hurrying across are Ellen and Richard. She is hugging close to him as he holds an umbrella over her.

> ELLEN'S VOICE
> . . . *I was afraid that if I saw people who knew Tony and me I'd be reminded that we were once happy together and I might weaken. And I wanted to make my escape complete . . .*

DISSOLVE OUT

DISSOLVE IN

INT. LIVING ROOM—ELLEN'S LONDON FLAT—
NIGHT

104   FULL SHOT. Ellen is curled up in a big chair, wearing
a dinner dress, with a gay plaid over her knees. Richard
is stretched out comfortably on the fireplace sofa, puffing his pipe and talking in a relaxed way.

> ELLEN'S VOICE
> *. . . Richard and I saw a great deal of each other
> and became very, very good friends . . .*

> RICHARD
> The first thing I invented was a mouse trap . . . I
> was about eleven . . . It worked! My father almost
> lost a toe in it.
>> (he laughs)
> And when he got through with me, I'd almost lost
> the skin off my back.

> ELLEN
> I'm trying to imagine you as a little boy, but for
> some reason I can't. You look as though you'd
> never been anything but Mr. Kirby, the automobile
> man.

> RICHARD
> It's funny, but I can't think of myself as a kid ei-
> ther. I guess it's because I wasn't a child very long.
> I wasn't quite thirteen when I went to work.

> ELLEN
>> (sympathetically)
> The poor boy . . . It must've been awful.

> RICHARD
> It was pretty awful. But not so much the going
> cold and hungry as . . . being alone, never hearing
> a kind word . . . never knowing anyone decent
> . . . never even dreaming that there were people
> who were gentle, lovely . . .

(he hesitates, then ventures to say it)
—like you.

They are both silent for a moment. Richard breaks it.

> RICHARD
> (cont'd)
> Ellen, do you mind if I ask you something very
> personal?

> ELLEN
> No—of course not.

> RICHARD
> I know you've separated from your husband— Is
> it permanent?

> ELLEN
> (firmly)
> Yes. It is.

> RICHARD
> (quietly)
> Do you think you'd want to marry me? You must
> know that I'm in love with you.

> ELLEN
> (troubled)
> I know, Richard. And I think I want to marry you.
> But . . .

> RICHARD
> You still love him?

> ELLEN
> No. It's something else. It's hard to explain, Rich-
> ard, particularly to a man. When I'm with you, I'm
> completely free of him and very happy, but . . .
> I'm afraid. There's something in me that still be-
> longs to him. I hate myself for it.

> RICHARD
> I believe I understand . . .
> (he holds her)
> But you'll forget him in Canada.

ELLEN

I wish we were there already.

(they kiss)

DISSOLVE OUT

DISSOLVE IN

INSERT   SERIES OF TELEPHONE MESSAGE FORMS
of the Devon House—Ellen's apartment house—
all stating that Sir Anthony Aysgarth has called.

ELLEN'S VOICE

(narrating)

*. . . At first Tony refused even to listen to the sug-
gestion of a divorce. Somehow he managed to get my
address. When I wouldn't see him, he kept calling
me on the telephone . . .*

DISSOLVE

INT. FOYER—ELLEN'S FLAT—LONDON—DAY

105   CLOSE SHOT. Ellen at the phone impatiently listening
to Tony's pleas.

ELLEN'S VOICE

*. . . He pleaded with me frantically, swearing that
he loved me, that he couldn't live without me, and
threatened to kill himself . . . Not that I believed a
word of it . . .*

DISSOLVE

EXT. DEVON HOUSE—NIGHT

106   FULL SHOT. Ellen comes out of the apartment house.
The doorman hails a cab. Suddenly Tony steps out of
the shadow and accosts her as she is about to climb into
the cab. She ignores him and drives off.

ELLEN'S VOICE

*. . . But it upset me. Finally, I told Richard that I
would go away with him without the divorce. Per-*

*haps I could get one later in Canada or the States
. . . But he didn't like the idea and said he would
talk to Tony himself . . . A few days later he told
me that everything was settled . . .*

DISSOLVE OUT

DISSOLVE IN

INSERT   LARGE ENVELOPE addressed to Lady Aysgarth. The envelope, held by Ellen's hands, has
the return address of the law firm of BEACHAM
AND NEWGATE, Solicitors. HOLD for a moment, then the hands tear the envelope and un-
fold the message. It is Ellen's divorce decree.

ELLEN'S VOICE
*. . . It seemed too good to be true. But there were no
further difficulties and our divorce finally went
through the courts. . . . At the same time I came into
full possession of my father's estate . . .*

DISSOLVE

INT. RICHARD'S CAR—DAY—(PROCESS)
107   MED. SHOT—Ellen and Richard. The car is driving
along a residential street in the West End of London.

RICHARD
D'you think you'll miss England very much?

ELLEN
I imagine I will some day—but not for a long
while.

RICHARD
Anyway, it's not really so far—we can always hop
over for a visit . . .
          (suddenly remembering something)
Wait a minute . . .
          (he starts going through his pockets)
I spend a week looking for it, and then forget to
give it to you . . .

> (he finally finds it—a small jewel box, and flips it
>   open, showing a diamond ring)
> There!

                    ELLEN
>   (taking the box)
> Oh . . . Thank you . . .
>   (she kisses him, then puts on the ring)

                    RICHARD
> You know, I've got a hunch that maybe you're be-
> ginning to really like me.

                    ELLEN
>   (tenderly)
> Only a hunch? . . .

                    RICHARD
> No—I know you do. But you warned me yourself
> not to expect too much.

                    ELLEN
> That's all gone now. And I'm so grateful to you
> for it.

The car comes to a halt. Richard takes her hand and silently
squeezes it, then starts out.

EXT. STREET—DEVON HOUSE—DAY
108–110 MED. SHOT. Richard gets out and helps Ellen out.

                    RICHARD
> See you for lunch?

                    ELLEN
> Right. Where?

                    RICHARD
>   (smiles at her)
> Cherino's—

She nods, smiling, and starts to go. He shouts after her

                    RICHARD
>   (cont'd)
> One o'clock—sharp.

He climbs into the car, which pulls off. Ellen continues toward the house.

DISSOLVE OUT

DISSOLVE IN

INT. SMALL FOYER—ELLEN'S FLAT—
DEVON HOUSE—DAY

III   FULL SHOT. Harriet has opened door for Ellen and shuts it behind her.

ELLEN
(joyfully)
Better start packing again— We sail next Monday.

HARRIET
(her first reaction is a happy one; delighted)
Oh, ma'am—isn't that just wonderful?—You'll be so happy with Mr. Kirby—
(suddenly starts to sniffle)
I just know you will.

ELLEN
Thank you, Harriet . . . What's the matter?

HARRIET
I'm sorry, ma'am. But Canada is so far from Dorsetshire. I've never been to a foreign land before.

ELLEN
It's all right, Harriet—they understand English there.

Harriet sniffles some more.

ELLEN
(cont'd)
(sympathetically)
Of course, if you'd rather not go? . . .

HARRIET
(stops sniffling at once)
Oh, no, ma'am. It was just the idea.

(then suddenly remembers)

Goodness me—I forgot. There's a Doctor Jarvis
been calling all morning.

ELLEN

Doctor Jarvis? Did he leave a message?

HARRIET

No, ma'am—excepting he said it was important,
and to please have you call him up soon's you came
home. The number's on the pad, ma'am. . . .

Ellen goes to the phone.

ELLEN
(into phone)

West End 1783, please . . .
(pause)

Dr. Jarvis, please . . . Dr. Jarvis? This is Lady Aysgarth—you called me?

MAN'S VOICE
(over phone; very matter-of-factly)

Yes. I've been attending your husband, Sir Anthony. He's very ill.

ELLEN
(calmly)

What's the matter with him?

MAN'S VOICE
(over phone)

He took an overdose of sleeping draught—vero-
nal. Intentionally, I'm afraid.

ELLEN

But . . . what can I do?

MAN'S VOICE
(over phone)

Well, someone must assume the responsibility, and
unless the family takes charge, I'll have to call in
the authorities.

ELLEN

But . . . Sir Anthony and I are no longer married
. . . I'm afraid there's nothing I can do. However,
if it's a matter of money . . .

MAN'S VOICE
(with complete disinterest)
That's up to you, Lady Aysgarth. I merely felt it
my duty to let you know. His address is—83 Lad-
brook Center. Good day.
(hangs up)

As Ellen hangs up, an ironic smile crosses her face. She shrugs
and goes towards drawing room.

ELLEN'S VOICE
(narrating)
*. . . It was obviously a trick and I tried to dismiss
it as such. But then it occurred to me that he
might've very well done it . . .*

INT. DRAWING ROOM—ELLEN'S FLAT—DAY
112   FULL SHOT. Ellen goes to the window. She remains
there for a few moments, with her back to the camera,
thinking.

ELLEN'S VOICE
*. . . He was a gambler and it would be just like
him to bet his life against my coming to see him . . .*

She turns abruptly away from the window, crosses over to
the coffee table on which are her hat and gloves, and picks
them up.

ELLEN'S VOICE
(cont'd)
*. . . Of course, it's very easy now to say I was a fool
for having gone. But, after all, what had I to be
afraid of? . . .*

DISSOLVE OUT

DISSOLVE IN

INT. TAXICAB—DAY—(PROCESS)

113   MED. SHOT—Ellen sitting thoughtfully in the corner of the cab.

> ELLEN'S VOICE
> *. . . He no longer had any power over me. My love for him was dead. We were divorced. In two days, I was to sail with Richard . . .*

DISSOLVE

INT. HALLWAY—LODGING HOUSE—DAY

114   FULL SHOT—a dilapidated walk-up lodging house with stairwell forming one side, doors the other. Ellen is walking with an old, grimy landlady.

> LANDLADY
> The 'ouse is a little dusty, me lady, but you know 'ow the servants h'are nowadays—if h'it h'ain't one thing, h'it's h'another—
> (indicates door)
> 'Ere h'is 'is room, me lady—and mighty comfortable, too—if me who shouldn't says it.

> ELLEN
> (knocking on door)
> Thank you.

The landlady steps off a little way and stands staring at her, looking as though she will dive for the keyhole the minute Ellen goes in.

> TONY'S VOICE
> (through door)
> Come in.

Ellen enters.

INT. TONY'S ROOM—LODGING HOUSE—DAY

115   FULL SHOT. Tony, in his shirtsleeves, is lolling in an old broken-down bed, his hair uncombed, his face un-

shaven. A whiskey and soda is on the floor beside him. Against one of the walls stands an old upright piano. Tony looks up at Ellen, and rises.

TONY

I'm so glad you came.

ELLEN

I might've known.

TONY

Sorry about that Doctor Jarvis business—but I had to see you.

ELLEN

What do you want?

TONY

Just to say goodbye.

ELLEN

Very well. Goodbye.
(she starts to go)

TONY

Please don't go. There's so much I want to tell you. Won't you sit down, Ellen, please.
(he pushes the piano stool toward her)

ELLEN
(remains standing)
I wish you'd tell me what you want.

TONY

Nothing. You're going away. I may never see you again, and I don't want you to leave hating me.

ELLEN

What difference would that make?

TONY
(standing near piano and hitting keyboard
with one finger)
Not a great deal, I suppose—but after all, we did

have some fun together—once. We were happy at least some of the time.

> ELLEN
> It's too late to talk about it now.
> > (opening door to go)

> TONY
> > (blocking her way)
> I know it. But that is also one of the reasons why I wanted to see you. I wanted to wish you luck in your new marriage. I hope it works out better than ours . . .

> ELLEN
> Thank you. But I really must go now.

> TONY
> Not yet. Please . . . This is the last time I'll ever see you. I want to look at you so I can always remember . . .

From off scene comes the ring of a telephone bell.

> TONY
> > (cont'd)
> . . . the shape of your face—your eyes—your hair—that funny little smile of yours . . .

There is a knock on the door.

> TONY
> > (cont'd)
> . . . the sound of your . . .

The knocking continues. He opens the door, disclosing the landlady behind it.

> TONY
> > (cont'd)
> > (irritably)
> What is it?

> LANDLADY
> The phone—it's for her Ladyship.

ELLEN

For me? I didn't tell anyone I was going to be here . . .

LANDLADY

H'its for Lady Aysgarth. That's you, h'ain't it?

TONY
(stepping aside)

Goodbye, Ellen.

Ellen gives him a look and goes out in the hall.

INT. HALLWAY—LODGING HOUSE—DAY

116 FULL SHOT. Ellen goes to phone hanging on wall.

ELLEN

Hello . . . Hello . . . Hello? . . .
(she hangs up with a puzzled look,
turns to landlady)
Do you know who it was? I couldn't get any answer.

From off scene comes the sound of Tony playing the piano, and continuing through the rest of the scene.

LANDLADY

They must've hanged up on you.

Ellen frowns thoughtfully and starts down the corridor, toward the camera.

LANDLADY
(cont'd)
(points in opposite direction)

This way, ma'am.

ELLEN

Oh . . . Thank you . . .

She turns and goes.

DISSOLVE

EXT. STREET—DAY

117 FULL SHOT—street in front of lodging house. The

door opens and Ellen comes out of the house. Her face is serious and preoccupied.

> ELLEN'S VOICE
> (narrating)
> *. . . I walked out of that house with a strange feeling that something dreadful had happened. That telephone call? . . . I was certain there was someone on the other end who hung up when I answered. I heard the click . . .*

As she hails a passing cab,

DISSOLVE

INT. CHERINO'S—DAY

118   MED. SHOT. It is the same little restaurant where Ellen had her first lunch with Richard. Ellen, sitting by a table standing near a window, is in a pose indicating she's been waiting for quite some time. She glances at her wristwatch.

INSERT   WRISTWATCH: It shows 2:15.

> ELLEN'S VOICE
> *. . . I kept thinking about it all the way to Cherino's to meet Richard. He wasn't there. I waited more than an hour for him, then called his hotel . . .*

DISSOLVE OUT

DISSOLVE IN

INT. TELEPHONE BOOTH AT CHERINO'S—DAY

119   CLOSE SHOT—Ellen, as she hangs up the receiver. Her face is a tragic mask.

> ELLEN'S VOICE
> *. . . The clerk told me he had left without leaving a message or even a forwarding address . . . I realized then that it had been Richard on that phone. Tony must've arranged it somehow to trap me. But what did Richard think?—that I was deceiving him? He must have . . .*

DISSOLVE

EXT. STREET—DAY—(RAIN)

120 FULL SHOT—Ellen. CAMERA TRUCKS with her as she walks aimlessly on, absently bumping into people. She never notices that it begins to rain.

ELLEN'S VOICE

. . . That's why he ran away . . . I couldn't blame him . . . After all, it wasn't his fault that I had been married to Tony. I blamed myself. I should have left him long ago . . . I felt in some way that what had happened was a punishment for my own weakness . . . I tried to gather my thoughts together, but . . .

121 CLOSE SHOT—Ellen's feet, as she keeps wandering around.

ELLEN'S VOICE

. . . all I could think of was how I was going to tell Harriet that we weren't going to Canada after all . . .

DISSOLVE

EXT. SIDEWALK—NIGHT—(RAIN)

122 CLOSE SHOT—Ellen's feet.

ELLEN'S VOICE

. . . I don't know what happened the rest of the day. I must've wandered around in the streets . . .

DISSOLVE OUT

DISSOLVE IN

EXT. BRIDGE ON THE THAMES—NIGHT—
(PROCESS B.G.)

123 MED. SHOT. Ellen walks up to the railing and looks down. A man passes by hurriedly in the background, throwing a curious look at her.

ELLEN'S VOICE

. . . It was already night when I found myself on a bridge staring down at the black water. I suppose I wanted to kill myself. There was nothing to live for any more . . .

124   FULL SHOT (STOCK)—river surface, black and cold, reflecting the bridge lights.

ELLEN'S VOICE

. . . but I didn't have the courage to jump. It looked so cold and wet . . .

125   CLOSE SHOT—Ellen. She shudders and turns her eyes away from the river.

ELLEN'S VOICE

. . . Then, suddenly, all I wanted was to be warm . . . to crawl into bed with a hot water bottle. I went home . . .

As she starts walking,

DISSOLVE

INT. FOYER—ELLEN'S FLAT—NIGHT

126   FULL SHOT. Ellen, wet and bedraggled, is shutting the door behind her when Harriet comes up to her anxiously.

HARRIET

Sir Anthony is here, ma'am—
(flustered and afraid)
I had to let him in—I couldn't stop him, ma'am
. . .

ELLEN

(her face expressionless)
Oh . . . It doesn't matter.

HARRIET

(notices her clothing)
But you're all wet, ma'am . . .

(she goes toward her)
Can I get you something dry? . . .

Ellen dismisses this with a vague gesture, and goes towards
the drawing room.

INT. DRAWING ROOM—ELLEN'S FLAT—NIGHT
127   FULL SHOT. Tony is looking out a window. He is
         shaved and spruce now. He turns when Ellen comes in.

ELLEN
What do you want of me now?

Tony goes towards her, ignoring her question, and sees how
she looks.

TONY
Where've you been, darling? You look half
drowned.

ELLEN
Why don't you leave me alone?

TONY
(leading her by the arm)
Come—sit down here by the fire.
(pushes chair forward and helps her)
Good heavens, Ellen—you're wet to the skin!
(goes to door and calls to Harriet o.s.)
Harriet—get some blankets and make some hot tea.

HARRIET'S VOICE
Yes sir.

Tony turns back to Ellen, who continues to shiver.

TONY
What's happened to you, Monkeyface?

ELLEN
(tonelessly)
Leave me alone—please.

TONY
(ignores this and pours some brandy for her)
Drink this. It'll warm you up a bit.

> (Ellen mechanically drinks it)

There . . .

Harriet enters carrying blankets. Tony takes them from her and places one around Ellen's shoulders.

> HARRIET
> (over action)
> The tea'll be ready in a moment.

> TONY
> (taking off Ellen's shoes and giving
> them to Harriet)
> You'll be lucky if you don't catch pneumonia. Better take those stockings off, too.

As he says this, he makes to pull off her stockings, but Ellen jerks her legs away spasmodically and puts them under her.

> ELLEN

Don't, please.

Harriet throws a curious look at the two, and exits.

> ELLEN
> (cont'd)
> (desperately)
> Please go now—I'm *so* tired.

> TONY
> I can't leave you like this . . . Should I call a doctor?

> ELLEN
> (with a laugh)

Doctor Jarvis?

> TONY
> I know it was a low, shabby trick . . . But I had to do it. I couldn't stand losing you . . . I thought I could— I agreed to the divorce—to everything. But when I actually saw you going off with that

automobile mechanic, I couldn't let you. I realized
that I still loved you . . .

ELLEN

Why do you go on with those lies? Why don't you
leave me alone? . . . Haven't you done enough?

Harriet comes in at this moment with the tea.

TONY

Here's the tea— There—this'll brace you up . . .
(puts brandy into cup; to Harriet, dismissing her)
Thank you, Harriet.

Harriet looks at him and then at Ellen, who makes no sign,
so she leaves rather reluctantly.

TONY
(cont'd)

Here, drink it down.

ELLEN
(tastes it)

You made it too strong.

TONY

Go on, it's good for you.

ELLEN

Are you trying to make me drunk—like Beaky?

TONY

Ellen—that isn't—

ELLEN

Cricket?
(laughs)

But I don't care.
(drinks it down)

I don't care about anything any more.

TONY
(pouring himself one)

That's the spirit.

(drinks it down)
Know what was wrong with our marriage?—You took everything too seriously. Nothing's worth it . . .

ELLEN

You're right—nothing is . . .

TONY
(pours two drinks)
Here's to us.

ELLEN

To us?

TONY

Yes— Aren't you coming back to me?

ELLEN

What for?

TONY

No use arguing, Monkeyface—we belong together.

ELLEN

Why?

TONY

Because that's the hand we've been dealt— And you can't change it.

ELLEN

Because you shuffled the cards?

TONY
(laughs)
That's right. Well? . . .

ELLEN
(raising her glass)
What's the difference?

Their glasses touch, and they drink up.

FADE OUT

FADE IN

EXT. SKY—DAY—(FALL)—(RAIN)—(STOCK)
128   LONG SHOT—a leaden fall sky with heavy windblown
storm clouds.

> ELLEN'S VOICE
> (narrating)
> . . . *Next morning we left for Abbot Monckford. It*
> *really made no difference . . . I wanted to jump*
> *into the river. Going back to Tony was the same*
> *thing. . . . Besides, I didn't have the strength to*
> *struggle any longer . . .*

DISSOLVE

EXT. GARDEN—ABBOT MONCKFORD—DAY—
(FALL)—(RAIN)
129   FULL SHOT—tree whipped by a strong wind of its few
remaining leaves. CAMERA PANS OVER across the
rain-swept bare earth toward the manor house darkly
looming in the background.

> ELLEN'S VOICE
> . . . *But I didn't want a repetition of what had*
> *happened between us that night. I made it clear to*
> *him that we were going to be merely two people living*
> *in the same house . . . Tony didn't object in the*
> *slightest. He could afford to be nice now. By allowing*
> *me to divorce him he had placed my father's estate*
> *in my hands. And now the money was his to spend.*
> *I felt sure that as long as it lasted he would continue*
> *to be nice. But I still didn't know Tony . . .*

DISSOLVE

INT. LIVING ROOM—ABBOT MONCKFORD—DAY
130   FULL SHOT. Ellen, with a warm shawl around her
shoulders, is curled up in a chair by the burning fireplace
reading a book. Harriet enters and gives her a card on
a salver. Ellen looks up and picks up card.

INSERT   CARD. It reads:
          "James A. Forester, Esq.
          Forester and Bentley
          Solicitors"

ELLEN'S VOICE

*. . . One afternoon, just a few days after we had
moved to the country, Harriet told me that there was
someone to see me . . .*

DISSOLVE

INT. LIBRARY—ABBOT MONCKFORD—DAY

131   FULL SHOT. A dignified, gray-haired man, looking
exactly what he is, a lawyer, comes forward as Ellen
enters.

LAWYER

Good afternoon, Lady Aysgarth.

ELLEN

How'dydo—I suppose you want to see my husband. I'm afraid he won't be home till dinner.

LAWYER
(busy with brief case)
Oh, no—he's already signed.

ELLEN

Signed—what?

LAWYER

The will. Er . . . hasn't Sir Anthony told you?

ELLEN
(covering up)
He probably did. I must've forgotten.

LAWYER

It's quite a simple little document—of a so-called
'mutual' type. In case of a demise, he leaves you
all his possessions, and vice versa.

ELLEN
(a little startled)

Oh . . .

LAWYER

Shall I read it to you?

ELLEN

No. No, thanks. I think I know what's in it.

LAWYER
(takes out a pen and indicates)
Very well. You sign right here.

She signs.

ELLEN'S VOICE
(narrating)
. . . It's a rather peculiar sensation to sign one's own death warrant. But that's what the will was . . .

She hands the lawyer his pen, which he closes methodically, then gathers the papers and places them back in his brief case.

ELLEN'S VOICE
(cont'd)
. . . Not that I expected to be killed immediately. I knew he wouldn't do it until he really had to . . .

The lawyer picks up his hat, nods to Ellen and starts out. Ellen looks after him absently.

ELLEN'S VOICE
(cont'd)
. . . If his luck held out, I might live to a ripe old age. And if it didn't . . . well, I didn't really care anyway . . .

DISSOLVE OUT

DISSOLVE IN

INT. HALLWAY—ABBOT MONCKFORD—DAY

132   FULL SHOT. Harriet opens the door to a messenger from the telegraph office. Ellen enters and Harriet hands her telegram. Ellen glances at it and tears it open.

> ELLEN'S VOICE
> . . . *A few weeks later a telegram came. It was addressed merely "Aysgarth." I opened it and discovered it was for Tony . . .*

INSERT   TELEGRAM.

> ELLEN'S VOICE
> (cont'd)
> (over insert)
> . . . *"Thousand pounds on Edgemont at eight to one Newcombe Stakes accepted. This is positively last acceptance without substantial payment on past accounts."* . . . *It was signed: "Wilson."* . . . *Now I knew that I didn't have long to wait . . .*

DISSOLVE

INT. DINING ROOM—ABBOT MONCKFORD—NIGHT

133   FULL SHOT. Tony and Ellen sit opposite each other at sides of long table. The room is gloomily lit by candles. The butler waits on them as they eat without speaking.

> TONY
> (after a pause)
> The new cook seems to know her trade. This beef is excellent.

> ELLEN
> (same casual tone)
> Yes. She's very competent.

> TONY
> (after a pause)
> I wish that wind would let up.

> ELLEN
> It always blows this time of the year.

TONY

Yes, I suppose it does.

ELLEN
(after a pause)

Tony?

TONY

Yes, dear?

ELLEN

When do they run the Newcombe Stakes?

TONY
(surprised)

Next Saturday. Why? . . .

ELLEN

Are you going?

TONY

I thought I might.

ELLEN

Would you mind—if I came along?

This really surprises Tony, and he narrows his eyes, but carries it off lightly.

TONY

No . . . Delighted . . . But—er—since when did you become interested in racing?

ELLEN

I'm not, really. Just a little curious. It's a famous race, isn't it?

TONY

Very. One of the most important of the season.

ELLEN
(to butler)

Will you bring the dessert now, Prentice.

BUTLER

Yes, ma'am.

DISSOLVE

EXT. ENGLISH RACETRACK—DAY

134   LONG SHOT (STOCK)—of the field, showing the grandstands, the crowds, the characteristic bookies, the pork pie salesmen, etc. It is a very gray, miserable day.

ELLEN'S VOICE
(narrating)
. . . As Tony said, the Newcombe Stakes was an important race . . .

135   LONG SHOT (STOCK)—of the track in front of grandstand, as the jockeys parade on their way to the post.

ELLEN'S VOICE
. . . Its outcome was to decide whether I was to live or die . . . I asked him to point Edgemont out to me . . .

136   FULL SHOT—the horse, Edgemont, number five.

ELLEN'S VOICE
. . . He was number five, and looked just like all the others . . . I was a little disappointed. . . .

DISSOLVE OUT

DISSOLVE IN

EXT. STARTING GATE—RACETRACK—DAY—(STOCK)

137   FULL SHOT—jockeys at starting gate. There is the usual confusion caused by some recalcitrant horse that wants to start ahead of the others.

ELLEN'S VOICE
. . . I don't know why, but I thought that he would look different somehow—after all, he was running for rather unusual stakes. . . .

Suddenly the horses start off. Over this comes a roar from the crowd.

CROWD
(excited)
They're off! There they go!

EXT. GRANDSTAND—RACETRACK—DAY

138 MED. CLOSE SHOT. Ellen and Tony in box. Ellen's face is white and rigid as she stares out at track. Tony is rooting excitedly.

> TONY
> (watching through glasses)
> Come, Edgemont! Edgemont! Good boy!
> (to Ellen, without looking at her)
> He's out in front! He's going beautifully!

139 CLOSE SHOT. Ellen. Her eyes are closed and her lips are moving silently, forming the word "Edgemont."

> TONY'S VOICE
> (over scene)
> Come, Edgemont—come!

140 TWO SHOT—Tony and Ellen. Her eyes are still closed.

> TONY
> Keep him there! Keep him on the inside! . . .
> He's swinging too wide! Keep him on the rail!
> . . . Etc.

Tony falls into a desperate rage as the horse begins to lose the race.

> TONY
> (cont'd)
> Whip him, you fool! Use your bat! Boot him! Keep
> him in there!
> (drops glasses)
> Of all the rotten rides!

Ellen opens her eyes and slowly turns her head towards Tony.

> ELLEN
> He . . . lost . . . ?

> TONY
> He threw it away!

He makes a violent gesture, then stops as his eyes meet hers. They stare at each other—both faces tragic. A long pause.

From off scene comes the roar of the crowd, cheering the winner.

>ELLEN
>(low voice)
Shall we . . . go home?

Tony nods, picks up automobile robe and steps aside to let her go out of the box first.

DISSOLVE OUT

DISSOLVE IN

INT. TONY'S CAR—NIGHT—(RAIN)—(PROCESS B.G.)
141   TWO SHOT—Ellen and Tony.

>ELLEN'S VOICE
>(narrating)
>*. . . On the way back we were both silent, busy with our own thoughts. I imagine we were both thinking the same thing . . . Strangely enough, I soon stopped worrying about what was going to happen . . .*

DISSOLVE

EXT. ROAD—NIGHT—(RAIN)
142   CLOSE SHOT—car wheel spinning on wet pavement.

>ELLEN'S VOICE
>*. . . I caught myself thinking about my new hat. I was afraid the rain had ruined it . . .*

DISSOLVE

INT. TONY'S CAR—NIGHT—(RAIN)—(PROCESS B.G.)
143   TWO SHOT—Ellen and Tony. CAMERA SHOOTING in the direction in which the car is moving.

>ELLEN'S VOICE
>*. . . I thought it was rather becoming, and was a little sad that I might never be able to wear it again. . . . Suddenly the car slowed down . . .*

The car slows down. Through the windshield can be seen a fork in the road.

144   REVERSE ANGLE—TWO SHOT—Ellen and Tony.

                    ELLEN
                   (quietly)
      What're you doing, Tony?

                    TONY
                (turning wheel)
      Taking the short cut.

                    ELLEN
      But this isn't it.

                    TONY
             (peers through windshield)
      Yes, it is. I remember that clump of trees.

                    ELLEN
      It's the *next* fork.

                    TONY
             (accelerating car again)
      Nonsense . . .

                    ELLEN
      But, Tony—this road leads to the cliffs. After all,
      I know this country. I've lived here all my life.

                    TONY
                (smiling at her)
      Maybe, but you never did have a sense of direc-
      tion.

Ellen shrugs and makes herself comfortable on the seat.

                 ELLEN'S VOICE
                  (narrating)
      . . . I was sure I was right, but I saw no sense in
      arguing any further. The cliffs were less than two
      miles away—we'd only have to turn around and
      come back . . .

145   CLOSE SHOT—Ellen. Her face grows tense as she realizes that this is it, and her eyes begin to fill with terror.

ELLEN'S VOICE
*. . . Then, suddenly, I knew that I wasn't going to
come back . . . It was going to be an accident . . .
At the last moment he'd jump out and the car would
go over the cliff. . . It was almost two thousand feet
to the bottom . . .*

Suddenly Ellen screams hysterically, and grabs at the wheel.

ELLEN
(cont'd)
Aaah! . . . Stop it! . . . Stop!

146   TWO SHOT—Tony and Ellen. Tony jams on the brake,
tearing her loose from the wheel. The car skids to a stop.

TONY
(angry)
What the devil's the matter with you?

ELLEN
(hysterically)
Not here! Don't do it here! Not here—please,
Tony!

TONY
Do—what?

Ellen collapses, sobbing hysterically against the dashboard.

TONY
(cont'd)
(softly)
What is it, Monkeyface? What's all this about?

ELLEN
(through sobs)
I thought you were going to run the car over the
cliff.

TONY
(looks at her, frowning; coldly)
Really, Ellen, you ought to see a psychiatrist.

(starts car up again)
Your imagination is getting positively morbid.

Ellen lowers her head and closes her eyes, sobbing quietly.

DISSOLVE OUT

DISSOLVE IN

EXT. ABBOT MONCKFORD—NIGHT—(RAIN)
147 FULL SHOT. Tony's car rolls into driveway.

ELLEN'S VOICE
(narrating)
*. . . When I opened my eyes again, we were in front
of the house . . .*

Tony helps Ellen out of the car and up the steps.

ELLEN'S VOICE
(cont'd)
*. . . Tony had to help me out of the car. I was shak-
ing from head to foot . . .*

DISSOLVE

INT. ELLEN'S BEDROOM—ABBOT MONCKFORD—
NIGHT
148 MED. SHOT. Ellen is sitting in a chair shivering as Tony
prepares her bed, fixing the pillows, etc.

ELLEN'S VOICE
*. . . He thought I had caught cold, and insisted that
I go straight to bed. He seemed to be terribly soli-
citous over my health, and was very tender and
kind . . .*

TONY
(turning to her)
Come, darling. I'll help you take those things off.

ELLEN
(shivering)
Nn-No, thanks. I-I can do it myself.

TONY
(looks at her with a little ironic smile)
All right. But do it quickly and get right into bed.
I'll make you a hot toddy, meanwhile. What you
really need is a good night's sleep.

He walks out. Ellen looks up at that, and follows him out
with her eyes.

ELLEN'S VOICE
(narrating over business of undressing and getting into bed. She moves about like an automaton, shivering occasionally with an inner chill)
. . . *Sleep? So that was it. Foolish to have worried
about being driven over a cliff . . . Everyone knew
that lately I had trouble falling asleep, and that
Doctor Soames had given me a sleeping medicine.
What could be simpler than to say that I had accidentally taken too much of it? Besides, it was much
more like Tony to let me die in my own bed . . . I
was perfectly calm. I wasn't frightened any more.
This was what I wanted, and I welcomed it . . .*

Tony comes back in with the hot toddy.

TONY
I really shouldn't've taken you to the races, darling— I'm afraid the Newcombe Stakes was too
much for you—

ELLEN
Yes, I suppose it was.

Tony pauses with the glass in his hand at her bedside.

TONY
Bad race— If Edgemont'd only gotten a better
ride, he'd've won. Rotten luck, losing it.

ELLEN
Yes . . .
(after a pause; looking straight at him)
Aren't you going to give me that?

TONY

Oh, yes—
 (nerving himself and handing her drink)
Here—

ELLEN
(looking straight at him)

Thanks.

Tony watches her tensely as she raises the glass to her lips, her hand trembling. Suddenly she faints and drops the glass.

DISSOLVE

INT. ELLEN'S BEDROOM—ABBOT MONCKFORD—
NIGHT

149   CLOSE SHOT—Dr. Soames, leaning over the bed, stethoscope in his ears.

ELLEN'S VOICE
(narrating)

 . . . *When I came to, I saw Doctor Soames smiling down at me . . .*

DR. SOAMES
(cheerfully)

I say, that was a real long distance faint you pulled on us.

150   MED. SHOT—Ellen and Doctor Soames.

ELLEN
(coming out of it)

Where's . . . Tony?

SOAMES

Don't worry, he's around somewhere. I chased him out. What's the idea—a big, strong girl like you swooning?

ELLEN
(weakly)

I don't know . . . Perhaps I had a little too much excitement today . . .

SOAMES
(laughs)
Excitement? McLaidlaws don't faint from that . . .

Ellen closes her eyes, and turns her head into the pillow.

SOAMES
(cont'd)
I don't know what's the matter with you modern
women. Your mother would've been around to see
me a long time ago.

ELLEN
(trying to understand)
See you?—Why?

SOAMES
Nothing serious, my dear. Just a little baby.

Ellen opens her eyes wide and looks at him incomprehensively.
Soames folds his arms as though he were rocking an imaginary
infant.

SOAMES
(cont'd)
You know—
(imitating a lullaby, and rocking his arm)
Aah—aah!

ELLEN
(hardly audible)
A baby? . . .

Her face slowly grows thoughtful and anguished. Doctor
Soames is amazed at her reaction.

SOAMES
Aren't you glad? I thought you always wanted one.

ELLEN
Did I? . . .

SOAMES
(raises his eyebrows and shrugs; gathering his
stethoscope and thermometer)

Well, young woman—stay in bed for a few days
and keep warm. And send Tony out for a ball of
wool—you'll be knitting in no time.
(he laughs at his own joke, and starts out)

ELLEN

Doctor Soames.

SOAMES
(turning around)
Yes?

ELLEN

You haven't said anything to Tony, have you?

SOAMES

No, not yet.

ELLEN

Please don't.
(he looks at her, questioningly)
I want to tell him myself.

SOAMES
(now beaming at her)
Very well, my dear. Good night.

He exits.

151   CLOSE SHOT. Ellen. She stares into space, thinking.

ELLEN'S VOICE
(narrating)
*. . . I didn't know what to do now. My mind was
in complete confusion. When we were first married
I had wanted children so badly . . . Later, one of
the few things I had to be grateful for was that we
didn't have any . . .*

152   FULL SHOT—Bedroom. Ellen sits up in bed and
combs her hair with her hands in a gesture of complete
indecision.

ELLEN'S VOICE
*. . . What was I to do? Had I the right to sacrifice
another life besides my own? But what kind of a*

child would it be, with Tony for its father? . . . Perhaps it was my duty to let it die with me . . .

She starts getting out of bed.

DISSOLVE

INT. STAIRCASE—ABBOT MONCKFORD—NIGHT

153   FULL SHOT. Ellen, in a dressing gown hastily thrown over her, is stealthily coming down the stairs. As she descends, the sound of Tony playing the piano grows louder—the tune is a variation of Ellen's theme.

ELLEN'S VOICE
. . . There was no one I could ask for advice—and at Miss Doolittle's School for Gentlewomen they taught us nothing about heredity . . .

DISSOLVE

INT. LIBRARY—ABBOT MONCKFORD—NIGHT

154   MED. SHOT. Ellen on the floor before the encyclopedia stand, reading intently. The sound of piano continues.

ELLEN'S VOICE
. . . I went downstairs to see if I could find anything in a book . . .

INSERT: BOOK: Passage reads:

"Generally speaking, heredity determines the physical characteristics of the progeny and its pathological tendencies, such as susceptibility to certain diseases, or in some cases, even their inevitable presence. (vide. Haemophilia) It can also affect, to a limited extent, the psychological make-up. HOWEVER, IT MUST BE SAID THAT TENDENCIES TO VICE AND CRIME FREQUENTLY ATTRIBUTED BY LAY PERSONS TO HEREDITY, DEPEND SOLELY ON THE ENVIRONMENT AND UPBRINGING. PROFESSOR LARSEN, BY PLACING TWO IDENTICAL TWIN BROTHERS IN DIFFERENT ENVIRONMENTS . . ."

Over the INSERT Ellen mumbles indistinctly the introductory paragraph. However, when she gets to "However, it must be said . . ." her voice becomes clear and distinct.

BACK TO SCENE: Ellen reads aloud.

> ELLEN
> (cont'd)
> (reading)
> ". . . demonstrated that while their physical characteristics remained constant, they developed two entirely different personalities. In this connection, it should be noted . . ."

> TONY'S VOICE
> Why aren't you in bed? What're you doing sitting on the floor?

155 ANOTHER ANGLE—to include Tony.

> ELLEN
> (closing book nervously)
> Er . . . I wanted to look something up.

> TONY
> Why didn't you call me? If it was that important, I'd have brought you the book.

Ellen rises and replaces book.

> ELLEN
> Thanks. I found what I wanted.

> TONY
> (suspiciously)
> What was it?

> ELLEN
> Nothing, really . . . er . . . Something about gardening . . . Good night.

Tony stares after her.

> TONY
> (softly)
> Good night.

DISSOLVE

INT. ELLEN'S BEDROOM—ABBOT MONCKFORD—NIGHT

156   FULL SHOT. Ellen enters and locks the door, exhausted. She pauses for a second to catch her breath, then crosses to the bureau and starts packing.

> ELLEN'S VOICE
> (narrating)
> . . . *I had no choice. The child had to live. My only thought was to get out of the house—to run away* . . .

There is a knock on the door. Ellen whirls in a momentary panic.

> ELLEN
> (cont'd)

Yes?

> TONY'S VOICE
> (mild and cheerful)
> It's me, darling. Are you in bed already?

> ELLEN
> (desperately)
> Yes. Yes, I am . . . I was just going to sleep.

She crosses to night table and pulls switch, plunging the room into heavy shadows.

> TONY'S VOICE
> I brought you something. Let me in.

> ELLEN
> No. I don't want anything.

> TONY'S VOICE
> Are you sure you're all right? You sound so funny. Why did you lock the door?

> ELLEN
> I'm all right. See you in the morning. Good night.

She goes to dresser and quickly throws things into valise, trying not to make a sound. Something falls from the dresser, and she freezes.

TONY'S VOICE
What was that?

ELLEN
Nothing . . . nothing.

TONY'S VOICE
You're lying. What's going on in there? You're not in bed.

ELLEN
I am . . . I am in bed.

TONY
Open the door . . .

ELLEN
No, I . . . Please go . . .

TONY
Very well.

Ellen snaps the valise shut and puts her coat on over her night-dress.

ELLEN'S VOICE
. . . I thought he was gone . . .

Suddenly Ellen looks off toward door.

157　CLOSE SHOT—key in lock. It moves slowly, teetering out.

ELLEN'S VOICE
. . . Then I saw the key move . . .

158　MED. SHOT—Ellen, rigid against the bureau.

ELLEN'S VOICE
. . . For a moment, I lost my head. I was completely terror-stricken. Then the door opened . . .

159   CLOSE SHOT—Tony at door. He has a glass of liquid in his hand.

> TONY
> (coldly)
> What's going on here? Get back in bed. You're sick.

> ELLEN'S VOICE
> (narrating)
> *. . . I had to do something. Quick! But I couldn't move. I couldn't take my eyes off that glass in his hand . . .*

> TONY
> You're behaving like a madwoman. What's come over you?

> ELLEN'S VOICE
> *. . . He was coming towards me. Then I remembered. This used to be my father's room. He always kept a gun in the writing desk . . .*

She backs from the bureau towards desk, Tony slowly following her.

> TONY
> Here. Drink this down. It'll quiet your nerves.

> ELLEN
> (wrenches open a desk drawer and
> pulls out a gun)
> Don't come near me!

> TONY
> Drop that gun, and stop being melodramatic!
> (he goes towards her, putting down glass
> on the desk)

> ELLEN
> (backing away)
> Stop, Tony! Stop! . . .

TONY

Give me that—before you hurt yourself.
(he springs forward)

ELLEN
(screaming)

Don't!

She shoots. Tony collapses on the floor. Ellen drops the gun and runs to him.

ELLEN
(cont'd)

Why didn't you stop? I didn't want to . . .

TONY

I guess I should have . . . I didn't think you had it in you.

ELLEN

I had to do it . . . I knew what you . . .

TONY
(cutting in)

You were right. Better spill that stuff— Somebody might drink it.

ELLEN

I would've never done it. But I couldn't let the baby die . . . You didn't know it.

TONY
(amazed)

Monkeyface . . .

ELLEN
(brokenly)

I'm so sorry . . .

TONY

Lay you three to one—it's a boy.
(his eyes close)

Ellen sobs.

DISSOLVE

INT. COURTROOM—DAY
160   CLOSEUP—Ellen in witness box.

ELLEN
. . . That's all he said . . .

She collapses and buries her face in her folded arms, sobbing fitfully.

161   MED. SHOT—Counsel for Defense rising to address Judge.

COUNSEL FOR DEFENSE
If it pleases your Lordship—the defense rests.

Counsel for Defense starts towards Ellen and helps her out of witness box.

162   MED. CLOSE SHOT—Counsel for Crown.

COUNSEL FOR CROWN
(rising)
The Crown also rests, your Lordship.

DISSOLVE

INT. COURTROOM—DAY
163   MED. CLOSE SHOT—Judge.

JUDGE
(as he turns to Ellen)
The defendant will rise and face the Jury.

164   MED. CLOSE SHOT—Ellen, as she braces herself and gets to her feet.

165   FULL SHOT—Jury Box.

JURY FOREMAN
We find the defendant—not guilty.

There is a burst of applause off scene and the sound of the clerk's gavel demanding order. Calls by court attendants: "Order in the Court!"

166   FULL SHOT—Ellen. She steps out of the dock and starts slowly down the middle aisle.

167   MED. SHOT—Richard Kirby in one of the back rows of the courtroom. He rises and, climbing over the legs of seated spectators, hurries toward the aisle.

168   FULL SHOT—Ellen, as Kirby reaches the aisle alongside of her. CAMERA TRUCKS with them as they continue down the aisle.

> RICHARD
> Can you ever forgive me?

> ELLEN
> (turns towards him, startled)
> Richard . . .

> RICHARD
> I came as fast as I could. I thought some of the things I knew might help your defense. But you didn't need my help.

> ELLEN
> I did once—but you weren't there.

> RICHARD
> It was insane of me—but I didn't have time to think. He made it look like an ordinary shakedown—with you as the bait . . . I should've told you that he made me pay him for the divorce . . . And then when I found you in his place, I . . . And by the time I got my senses back, you had already gone away with him . . .

> ELLEN
> It doesn't matter. It's too late now, anyway.

> RICHARD
> I thought so once—remember? But you told me it was never too late.

ELLEN
(half a smile)

Did I?

169   LONG SHOT—REVERSE ANGLE—of courtroom. The huge, massive doors open to let Ellen and Richard through. As they pass through them, another pair of doors in the outer hall swing open to the street— through which gay sunlight pours, as though a promise of future happiness lay outside. The music swells.

FADE OUT

THE END

"A Cool Million"

A Screen Story
with Boris Ingster

O ATSVILLE is in Vermont. The Vermont of nutmegs, blue-
berries and maple sugar. The Vermont of pot-belly
stoves, and cracker barrels. Cal Coolidge's Vermont.

Joe Williams is one of Oatsville's nicest boys, blue-eyed,
fair-haired, with a back as straight and strong as one of his
mother's hickory chairs. A hero out of Horatio Alger.

Only fools laugh at Horatio Alger, and his poor boys who
make good. The wiser man who thinks twice about that ster-
ling author will realize that Alger is to America what Homer
was to the Greeks.

Joe Williams didn't have to think twice. From the day he
went to Oatsville High School, and could understand the Sunday sermon in church, he swallowed Alger's code hook, line
and sinker. Swallowing is too violent a word, perhaps; our Joe
breathed Alger in with the cold, clean, crisp air of Oatsville.

And so, the time came, at last, when he could stop cutting
lawns for quarters and stove wood for widowed ladies. He
had saved a hundred and eighteen dollars and sixty-five cents,
enough to start off for the big city to make his fortune. After
all, hadn't Jeremiah Hanks left Oatsville some thirty years before with even less money and wasn't he now the president
of a big bank?

Oatsville loved Joe in its own undemonstrative, Yankee way.
When the word spread that he was about to set off to make
his fortune, many of the townspeople wished him a heart-felt
God speed.

The principal of the high school went further. He gave Joe
a note of recommendation to Jeremiah Hanks, the banker.
Joe took the note out of politeness, not intending to use it,
for as he told his friends, he did not want to succeed by pull,
but by honesty and industry.

So Joe set off down the pike, carrying his paper suitcase.
Luck was with him. He soon thumbed a ride on a truck. Bubbling over with his dream, Joe tried to explain it to the truck

driver, who turned out to be an uncouth, embittered fellow. When Joe mentioned the cool million he was going to make, the oaf roared with laughter. Joe didn't mind. He put the fellow down for the fool he really was. Laughter would never stop Joe. Nothing short of a machine gun.

Joe was put down on the outskirts of the city. He looked up at the grey canyons of concrete and there was nothing forbidding about them to him. He would conquer and quickly. The world was his oyster.

As Joe started off to find cheap but respectable lodgings, he met a man who was much more friendly and sympathetic than the truck driver. He was very interested in Joe's story and agreed heartily that industry and honesty would turn the trick. That was the way he himself had succeeded. This glib and flashily dressed stranger took Joe to a restaurant for some real apple pie and picked the poor, unsuspecting boy's pocket, removing his little, hard-earned hoard, and quickly left. The restaurant made Joe wash the dishes, six feet of them for a nickel slice of pie.

That night Joe slept in Central Park. Still undaunted, however.

In the park Joe met a tramp, a talkative, worldly fellow. As the two of them watched the wealthy riders along the bridle path on their fancy horses, Joe told him of his hope and ambition. The tramp didn't laugh. He was a civilized man. But he tried to dissuade Joe.

"Go back to Oatsville," he urged. "There you can at least eat oats."

But not our Joe. He tried to show the tramp the logic of his position.

"Just suppose now, I'm walking along a railroad track and a child stumbles in front of an onrushing train. I snatch her from certain death. Her father owns the railroad. He gives me a job. I work hard and someday we're partners."

But the tramp had his own dream. Wall Street. That was where the money was. That was where the millionaires came from. He ought to know. He was wiped out in '21. But he had made three fortunes since.

Joe looked at his torn clothes, too polite to word his doubt.

The tramp explained. The three fortunes were made on paper only—following the stock quotations in old newspapers from the ash barrel. It takes money to make money—or at least credit.

As he went on explaining his fiscal theories, Joe saw an accident on the bridle path. Miss Astorbilt's thoroughbred horse had become frightened and dashed away. Quick as a flash, Joe threw himself headlong into the path of the maddened steed. It knocked him down, but he clung heroically to its bridle. Grooms, rich people all rushed up and helped poor Miss Astorbilt off her mount, who was quieting down but not until he had kicked Joe viciously in the stomach, rendering him unconscious. Everyone was so busy with the young lady that they did not see Joe lying on the ground. They hurried off with the heiress, who was in hysterics. Only the tramp saw Joe. He helped him to a sitting position.

"What happened?" asked Joe.

"They made you a partner!"

As the tramp tried to lift the poor boy to his feet, he saw a cop hurrying towards them. The tramp urged Joe to run, but Joe didn't understand why. He hadn't done anything. The tramp shook his head gravely and dashed into the bushes.

Joe smiled up at the cop, but the cop didn't smile back. He grabbed Joe and shook him.

"You're drunk," he said accusingly.

"I never had a drink of hard liquor in my life."

"Resisting arrest, huh?" growled the cop and clubbed him.

When Joe came to in the station house, the lieutenant gave him a lecture on sobriety without letting Joe get in a single word, then warned him to go back to Oatsville right away, or next time he'd get thirty days.

With that, they threw poor Joe out.

After not eating anything else for a week, Joe decided to swallow his pride and use the note the Sunday School principal gave him. He went to see Mr. Jeremiah Hanks, Oatsville '05, at his bank.

Mr. Hanks was glad to see Joe—glad, so far as a dour, skinflint with an eye, ear and nose only for money could be glad. He agreed with Joe's theories one hundred per cent and

promptly hired him for twelve-fifty a week. Joe was overwhelmed, but he didn't know that the job he was getting
always paid thirty-five.

Laura Conway, one of the girls in the office, showed Joe
the heavy ropes. She was good to look at, a witty, sophisticated big city girl, who had two answers for everything. She
was friendly to Joe until she asked him what he was getting.
Then she got indignant. But Joe stopped her. He was not
interested in the salary. It was merely the first rung on the
ladder of success, which he was determined to mount, rung
by rung, through industry and hard work.

Laura was too startled even to laugh.

But soon everyone in the office was laughing at Joe, even
Otto, the office boy. But soon they stopped laughing, and began taking advantage of Joe's willingness to do anything. Before long he was doing everything nobody else wanted to do.

Mr. Adams, the suspicious, dyspeptic head cashier didn't
like Joe or laugh at him. Mr. Adams' involved bookkeeper's
mind had arrived at the conclusion that Joe was not what he
seemed. He was too good to be true. He went around muttering that Joe was really a shrewd knave and fooling a lot of
them. Just wait . . .

Laura was kind to Joe. She felt badly about the way everyone in the place treated him. He might be a boob, but she
didn't like to see him taken advantage of. She went to dinner
with him and tried to show him her way of seeing the world,
a way that Alger never dreamed of.

But Joe was stubborn and sure in his faith. He was shocked
to hear such disillusionment from the lips of a beautiful lady.
It was she who needed sympathy and help he felt. However,
he got angry when she tried to tell him how his idol, old man
Hanks, really made his money. He knew differently. Success
was the result of hard work.

She had to laugh, although she tried not to. She didn't want
to hurt the poor fool.

Joe took her laughter in his stride. He had a ready answer.

"They laughed at Fulton and his steamboat, Edison and his
electric light, Ford and his horseless carriage. No one will
laugh when he makes a cool million."

Laura apologized, tongue in cheek, perhaps, but yet with

an undernote of sincerity. He was a nice fellow. At her door she kissed him good night.

Joe couldn't sleep on his little cot in his bleak hall-room. He was in love. He was heartbroken because his financial position wouldn't permit him to make a formal proposal. But then he remembered he was on the road to success and fell asleep happily.

The next morning Joe was sure of it when Mr. Hanks called him in and told him he was going to promote him. Mr. Adams, the head cashier, was on his vacation and the assistant was home sick. Until one of them returned, Joe was to do their work—and his own, of course. Although there was no raise involved, Joe was overjoyed at the chance. He didn't know the old skinflint was just saving money and didn't want to put on a new man when he could get three jobs for the price of one.

Joe left his office with his head and heart high. He decided to cut out eating lunch (he hadn't time to anyway) and buy Laura a diamond ring. He asked around the office and they told him Tiffany's was the place to go. He ended up buying one on the installment plan.

That night Joe tried to give Laura the ring. She refused to take it. She wasn't engaged to him and had no intention of being. The good night kiss was his because he was pathetic. Nothing else.

For the first time Joe was really heartbroken. He remained behind that night, after everyone had left, and tried to catch up with his work. His eyes filled with tears as he poured over the long columns of figures in the ledgers. He made several mistakes and caught them. But as the night wore on, he made others and didn't catch them. He didn't even seem to care. A big dent had been made in Joe's faith. Towards morning, as he closed the heavy books, his mind was made up. He was going back to Oatsville.

When Joe told Mr. Hanks, that individual didn't give a darn one way or the other, but asked Joe to stay on until the head cashier returned. Joe agreed. But now his whole attitude was changed. His dream shattered, he refused to be pushed around. When they kidded him about his ambition, he laughed and told them that he had changed his mind.

When Mr. Adams returned from his vacation, he took over without a word of thanks for Joe. He thought Hanks made a mistake in giving Joe such a responsible job. Joe was too sly. In an hour, he found out that he was right. A million dollars was missing. Joe stole it. He dashed into Hanks' office with his ledgers.

Hanks almost went out of his mind. Like the rascal he was, everyone else was a rascal. Joe pulled the wool over his eyes. He should have seen that he was too good to be true, even coming from Oatsville.

Without letting Joe know, he questioned the other employees in the bank. It appeared now that the only one who hadn't suspected Joe all along was Laura. They told Hanks stories about Tiffany's and of how he was always muttering that one day he would have a cool million.

Hanks called in Joe and accused him of stealing the money. Joe denied everything indignantly. This was too much. He was poor but honest. And he was going back to Oatsville. Hanks grabbed him and told him that he wasn't going anywhere until he gave back the million, and then he was going to Sing Sing.

When Hanks realized that he couldn't move Joe with threats, he changed his tactics. He didn't really want to bring any disgrace on Oatsville. He liked Joe. Maybe he did make a mistake— He was a little too young to handle all that money—be given all that responsibility. If he would give the money back, they would forget the whole thing.

Joe still denied everything, and Hanks began to think that he had a very tough customer to handle. He became polite to Joe and when that didn't work, became humble. It wasn't his money. It belonged to widows and orphans. Hanks was just the custodian. But all Joe would say was that he didn't take it.

Hanks asked Joe to please wait until he could have a conference with his bank directors. He ushered Joe into his private office, offered him a cigar and then hurried to call his directors. Joe sat in a big chair, sullen, angry, indignant and inarticulate. He was thinking. The other members of the office staff peered in to get a look at him. The office boy who kicked him down the stairs, called him Mr. Williams. Even Laura began to eye him with new respect.

Joe kept on thinking.

Hanks hurriedly called his partners and his very important law firm. Big limousines dashed to the bank from all corners of Wall Street, and extremely important personages in frock coats arrived in a dither of apprehension. They went immediately into conference about how to get the million back. The important lawyer peeked in at Joe, who sat stonily in his chair, and turned with a sober shake of his head. He said they would never do anything with Joe—he was definitely a tough customer. The best thing to do was make a bargain with him. The others agreed that Joe was very sinister looking, now that he had a million dollars.

Joe was called into the room so that they could dicker with him. They tried to sell Joe the idea of turning back nine hundred thousand and keeping a hundred thousand. But Joe still said he didn't take a nickel, he didn't know what they were talking about. The directors grew more and more desperate. They pointed out to Joe that he had his whole life to live. With a hundred thousand, he could set himself up in business— He shouldn't be a pig and keep it all. After all, it was their money—he should have some consideration for them.

Joe, fed up now, didn't even answer. The bankers offered to take back eight hundred thousand—seven hundred thousand—half, but still Joe refused to make a deal. Finally Jeremiah Hanks, infuriated, called Joe a liar and a thief. Joe rose quietly and punched him on the jaw.

Joe was taken off to the police station, but by the time he reached the station house, the whole city knew about the million dollar robbery. The papers carried it across their front pages—"A COOL MILLION STOLEN."

The first time Joe was arrested, he was pushed around plenty, but now it was a different story. Joe was a millionaire and even the police couldn't help but treat him with respect. One of the most famous criminal lawyers in the city appeared and offered to defend Joe. He immediately put up bail and got Joe out. When Joe wanted to go back to his rooming house, the lawyer put him in a big hotel. When Joe wanted to know who was going to pay for it, the lawyer told him that Joe had a million dollars' worth of credit.

Joe had been thinking hard all the time. He now realized that no one cared how you got your million as long as you had it. And as long as they thought he had it, okay. After all, he wasn't as simple as he seemed. He was a real Yankee. He could dream with the best of them, but when a chance came along he also knew how to grab it.

The lawyer warned him not to make any kind of a deal with the bank or the insurance company. He figured that Joe would get five years, and what was five years in the life of a young man like Joe, when at the end of that time he would have a cool million.

Joe smiled, nodded and fell asleep on his palatial bed, after a double order of apple pie and ice cream.

In the meantime the insurance company sent its ablest investigators to the bank. But the only flaw they could discover in Joe's armor, the only sign of human interest he had ever shown besides the money, was Laura. They immediately approached her and proposed that she aid them for a five per cent commission. Laura accepted the job and said that she could certainly use the money, but she thought they were barking up the wrong tree. Joe was just a simple country yokel. The two investigators shook their heads with admiration. What a smart customer—he didn't even reveal a hint of his true character to the woman he loved. Laura said that maybe she was wrong. After all, Jeremiah Hanks, too, came from Oatsville.

When Laura arrived at Joe's hotel, she found a new Joe. He asked her to dinner, and when she accepted, he signed a voucher for petty cash which the hotel manager delivered himself. Joe took the money without even thanking him.

Now Laura was convinced that he really stole the money. He made her work hard at her job of detecting, taking her from night club to night club, as he lived up to his new-found role of millionaire. All her questions he brushed aside. Even when she told him that she loved him, he laughed and said, "Who do you love, me or the million?"

This was too much for Laura. Tearfully, she told him that she did love him. She confessed that she first started going out with him because the insurance company paid her to. She begged him to give back the money. If he did, she would marry him and go back to Oatsville.

Convinced of her sincerity, Joe also made a confession. He told her that he hadn't a dime. He never stole anything in his life.

She didn't believe him. She got angry and walked out on him.

Suddenly a new and more ominous predicament confronted Joe in the person of Tony, alias the banker, who controlled the bank robbing business. He congratulated Joe on a neat job, and very affably told him that nobody robbed a bank around that town without cutting him in. Since he was a newcomer he would overlook the fact that he pulled the job without consulting him. However, he still wanted his agent's commission. When Joe told him to get the hell out of his room, Tony said it was either his cut of the dough, or else.

Joe threw Tony out of his hotel room, but that night as Joe walked down the street, a big black sedan pulled up and showered him with a spray of machine gun bullets. Joe saved his life by ducking behind an ash barrel. He realized it was serious.

Joe went back to his room and laid there, worried and frightened. But even more heart-rending for him was the fact that Laura wouldn't believe in his innocence.

His old friend, the tramp, appeared. He had read all about Joe in the papers and he congratulated him on his success. Desperately, Joe told him his predicament. The tramp had an idea. Joe had credit, all he had to do was use it. Open an account in a stock brokerage house and play the market with him as coach. Joe told him to go ahead, he didn't care one way or the other.

When the tramp gave Joe's name to the stock broker, he immediately called Hanks. He told Hanks that Joe wanted to open an account. Hanks was overjoyed. At last Joe was giving himself away. He told the broker to play him along and give him twenty-four hours' credit. Joe would have to use some of the stolen money to cover his account, and that would lead the detectives to the hidden cache.

The tramp went to work as Joe lay on his bed and thought

of Laura. While the tramp was yelling "buy this and sell that" into the phone, the door suddenly opened and Tony and his torpedoes came in and grabbed Joe.

The gang took Joe to the back of a warehouse where they put him through a fearful third degree, trying to make him confess where the money was. He would tell them, if he could. But he didn't, and it looked as though he were going to wind up in the bottom of the river.

Finally the insurance company auditors discovered that it was a mistake in bookkeeping that Joe had made. There was no million dollars missing. Joe hadn't stolen anything.

Hanks immediately jumped to the phone and told the broker to cut off Joe's credit. He didn't steal a million dollars. He didn't have a cent.

The broker corrected him. Joe made about eighty thousand in the market.

The papers carried the story. And when Tony and his men learned that Joe really didn't steal the money, they bawled him out for being a phony and kicked him down the stairs—

Into the arms of Laura.

Untitled Outline

THIS IS a story about a racket. One about which nothing has been written so far. Perhaps because it is not a major racket in the sense that bootlegging and extortion are. It doesn't involve enormous sums of money, nor crusading district attorneys who get to be governor on the strength of their fighting it. It is major, however, when one thinks of the type of victim on which it lives—the lonely and helpless of the big cities and the farms.

Sophisticated people are often amused by certain little advertisements tucked away in the personal columns of large newspapers and on the back pages of pulp magazines where they are sandwiched between panaceas for acne endorsements and for miracle-working electrical belts. Worded with an optimistic flamboyance which seems comic to those who are in no need of its services, "friendship clubs" offer to find comrades for the lonely and matrimony for the sex-starved. For a small fee they promise to put a perspective member in touch with friends who will make his or her life joyous, turning their dull, drab existence into a full round of dances and parties, where they will probably meet the husband or wife best suited to them. All over the country, thousands of helpless and depressed souls, in dingy hall bedrooms and faraway farms, read these ads and dream of being popular figures in a romantic social whirl surrounded by gallant swains and ravishing girls. It is on these tragic creatures that the friendship clubs prey, milking them of hard earned dollars and sometimes even exposing them to really horrible dangers.

2.   Most big newspapers have a special type of star reporter whose forte is local color with a comic twist. He is the man who writes about love affairs in the zoo, the home life of a strip tease artist, how it feels to be a peeping Tom, the hawk that lives in the tower of the Empire State Building and hunts pigeons on the steps of the library, etc. etc. It is a tough job because he has to come up with a new one every day and can never repeat.

Earl James is the local color man on one of the biggest papers in New York. He likes the job (so he claims) because he is short of breath and got too tired chasing fires. Local color is nice and stationary, and most of it can be gathered over the telephone, or while reading a newspaper stretched out on his back.

This is just what Earl is doing when we first see him. Couches are not permitted in the office of the Times Dispatch for anyone under city editor, so he is resting on the top of his desk, his long, lean form stretched out, completely at ease, while an office boy, sitting in his chair, is combing a newspaper for likely items.

"A guy in the Bronx," says the office boy, summarizing the story for Earl, "was attacked by a horse, who knocked him down and ate his new panama hat."

"I did one like that last month," Earl says, shaking his head sadly. "—James P. Gilhooey, 37, Queens, was attacked by a sea gull while cleaning a herring in his backyard."

After going over several more items of this type, none of which quite suits the fastidious Earl, the office boy starts reading the advertisements in the agony column—always a fruitful field for local color. He reads about Madame Rena who offers to put anyone in touch with the spirit world at a dollar a touch, a firm of inventors who offer to sell a little device which they guarantee will remove the gold from sea water and make a fortune overnight without stirring from Atlantic City, and several other gilt-edged propositions of like nature, he comes to an advertisement soliciting members for the Golden Friendship Club.

"A friend in need is a friend indeed. Are you lonely? Do you wish you had a beau to squire you to delightful little parties, or a little lady that you might squire? Join the Golden Friendship Club. Send for our illustrated magazine, giving over a hundred photographs of beautiful girls and handsome men, many of them with large fortunes. Don't be timid—hesitate no longer. Join our club and we guarantee to open up joyous vistas for you. Send 25¢ in stamps and we will mail our literature in a plain wrapper, or if you live in this city, call personally and talk over your problems with us. Hearts broken are soon mended at the Golden Friendship Club."

Earl sits bolt upright on his desk.

"That's it!" he shouts. "There's probably a whole series in it."

1. Foreword on racket

2. Introduce newspaper man hero, Earl James, and describe kind of local color and comic reporting in which he specializes. We see him look through the personal column in his usual search for human interest and see him discover the Golden Friendship Club. It looks like a perfect set up to him.

3. Earl James visits the little brownstone house in Brooklyn, where the Golden Friendship Club functions. It is the night of one of their regular dances. He walks in without any one noticing him and watches for a few minutes, meeting several of the Burgess family who run the club. Mrs. Burgess notices his manner and clothes however, before he has a chance to get to work and demands to know who he is. Earl tries to say that he is a lonely man who wants to join the club, but his breezy manner and good clothes make her immediately suspicious. She calls him nothing but a nosey intruder and when he confesses that he is a newspaper man and tries to tell her the publicity will help her business, she becomes cold with rage and orders him out of the place. She says that she knows his stuff and that he is not going to make fun of the simple, kindly people who join her club in the hour of their need. When he still persists in his attempts to get a story, he is thrown out bodily, by several of the more stalwart members of the club.

4. Back at the newspaper, disappointed and a little angry, he bumps into a procession of young journalism students who are being shown over the offices by a professor. They are very serious and rubberneck at the working newspaper men and equipment like a group of tourists being shown through the Louvre. One of the girls is Alice Ronsard. She is the most serious of the group of students and seems to be taking notes on every detail down to the fact that no one takes his hat off. She is a very pretty girl disguised under the prim costume of a girl who graduated with honors from the So. Dakota State University and hasn't been at Columbia School of Journalism long enough to look less like one of her state's prize winning

Aberdeen heifers. She is wearing a tweed suit and white shirt-waist, low heel shoes and woolen stockings and carries a purse made of the hide of a calico pony stuffed with text books, paper, pencils, everything but a linotype machine. Her frown is soberer than any of the other students and her gestures more pretentious than even that of the professor. Earl is amused by the little cavalcade of pilgrims and makes the rounds with them. They stop for a moment at the door of his office and he listens as the professor points out that Earl James is one of the newest manifestations in newspaper writing. Most of the students seem to like Earl's stuff, but Alice Ronsard says that it is her studied opinion that Mr. James is really one of the worst tendencies in modern reporting, and that his stuff is both degrading and nonsensical and that it would be more fitting for it to appear in the back pages of a joke magazine than in a great metropolitan daily.

Earl applauds her little speech and tells her that he agrees—it is men like Earl James who have destroyed the great traditions of a newspaper as fostered by such geniuses as Horace Greeley and Pulitzer. She thanks him quite seriously and starts to follow the others toward a different part of the building. Earl stops her, however, and asks her to step into his office.

She is a little hurt by the trick he played on her, but nevertheless insists on the fact that so far as she is concerned his material is not of a high enough calibre; lecturing him out of a text book, she tells him that newspapers must be raised to a higher level, serious and intelligent, the really important aspects of world affairs, if it is to fulfill its responsibility to its readers. Earl agrees, then asks her if she wants a job—"not as a Washington Correspondent, because that job is being filled by a man with a long white beard, but as a straight, working newspaper stiff." In the same condescending manner she admits that she could use a little practical experience as well as a salary because cattle-business hasn't been so good lately and her father has cut her allowance; besides New York is a very expensive city.

"Swell," Earl says, "you're hired. Come on down to the barroom and I'll tell you the assignment."

In Blake's barroom, which is a typical newspaperman's hangout, Alice hardly fitted. Moreover, she resented the way Earl introduced her to the other tough reporters as the woman who had come along to lead them out of the lush patches of yellow reporting into the cool, green fields of the purer but arid desert of the higher journalism.

Alice is no shrinking violet and she is quite willing to go into the evils and impostures of these men, letting the chips fall where they may. She is fighting the whole room with serious gusto when Earl stops her and the others to tell her what the job is. He wants her to join the Golden Friendship Club and dig up material for a series of articles for him. She can continue school because it is only a part time job, but as he explains with a smile, if she makes good she will have one foot on the first rung of the ladder that leads to covering London for the United Press. She takes it.

5. After Earl has made an appointment to meet her for dinner where he will explain the job in greater detail and take her around to the Golden Friendship Club, Alice hurries back to the sorority house in which she lives near Columbia campus. The other girls who made the tour with her demand to know where she has been, and tell her that Professor Thompson was very angry when they counted the girls on the bus and she wasn't there. They demand to know what happened. She tells them with great pride that she has a job as a reporter and tonight she is going to have dinner with Earl James, the celebrated newspaper man. Not that she cares for his type of writing, but he is nice looking and unquestionably has some talent, even if it is on the garish side. The girls are more excited about her dinner engagement than they are about the job. They insist on lending her clothes, and dressing her up. Alice, too, is very excited, although she tries to hide it, and agrees.

One very smart, sophisticated New York city girl looks her over speculatively and says, "Let's see, what'll you wear? I think that new frock that Betty bought at Elizabeth Hawes will be the basis of your turn-out." Betty objects—she hasn't even worn it herself yet, but one of the other girls points to the motto of their sorority—one for all and all for one—and tonight, she's the one.

6. Earl is waiting for Alice at a table in "21." He is asking

the headwaiter, whom he knows very well, to watch out at the door for a young lady. When the headwaiter asks how he will recognize her, Earl tells him that by the mud on her boots and the straw in her hair.

A few minutes later Alice, smart as a figure in Saks Fifth Avenue window, is led to his table by the headwaiter, who says, "I'll send the other young lady up as soon as she arrives. I've told the doorman to look out for mud and straw."

Earl ignores this, he is staring in astonishment at svelte svengine and soigné Alice. "What the devil is this?" he demands angrily. Alice is astonished. "What are you made up for? Where are the low heeled brogans and the woolen stockings? You're fired!"

Alice is frightfully embarrassed and taken aback. She swerves on her heel and is about to dash out of the place without having said a word when Earl catches her arm and stops her.

"You might as well have a cocktail and dinner—even if you have lost your job."

He makes her sit down, then explains himself. He had hired her because of her appearance that afternoon. Her job was to join the Golden Friendship Club and he had felt sure when he had seen her that they would have let her in without a word, because they only accepted people fresh from the swamps of New Jersey or the plains of the Dakotas. They had thrown him out on first sight. This makes Alice still more angry, but it doesn't spoil her appetite, and they both eat dinner quarreling all the time. Over their brandy Earl hires her again on the condition that she changes out of her glad rags into the store bought clothes and puts on her horn-rimmed glasses and manages to get into the Golden Friendship Club. Tells her what to say: she is alone—no relatives—no friends—lonesome.

7.   The next day after classes, dressed in her most Dakotean outfit, she rings the bell of the Club and is admitted by Mrs. Burgess. Mrs. Burgess is her sweetest when she sees timid Alice. This Mrs. Burgess, the president of the club, is everything that Whistler's Mother was, multiplied by at least seven. She wears a long black dress trimmed with hand crocheted lace, a narrow black velvet ribbon around her neck and a

cameo pinned to the V of her dress. She seems fragile, extremely sympathetic and extremely kind. She gushes all over Alice with her sales talk—

"You want to join our little club? How splendid, sweet child. Friendship is one of the most beautiful things in life. As I often say without friendship, hardly anything is worth while. Here you will find people to share your joys and sorrows with you. And I myself will teach you how life can become rich with fulfillment through friendship."

As Mrs. Burgess pours out the molasses in this way, she leads Alice by the arm into a little office, whose walls are covered with photographs of "friendly gathering, of friendly people." She points out these photographs to Alice (some are of weddings, others of birthdays, and still others of funerals) and tells her that they are proof of what the club offers because the people being married met here in the club and the people being buried are being mourned by other members of the club. In other words, as a member goes down life's long road from marriage to the grave, the blows are softened and the joys made keener by the Golden Friendship Club. As she talks, she sits Alice down in a chair at the desk and hands her some application blanks to be filled out. Alice studies them as Mrs. Burgess talks on and on, ever so sweetly.

The door opens and a man about fifty-eight enters carrying a large batch of mail. He is a well set up Englishman with a ruddy face made ruddy not by the wind but by alcohol. Mrs. Burgess introduces him to Alice as her husband, Colonel Burgess, "late of the 15th Inskilling Dragons." He confides to Alice, clicking his heels and twirling his gray mustache with over-played gallantry. The Colonel is as loquacious as his wife, but instead of being sweet and refined, he is hearty and martial.

After welcoming Alice into their little fold and telling her that just as she is to bring all her little spiritual difficulties to Mrs. Burgess, she should bring all her worldly ones to him. Alice thanks him and after patting her hand gently, he tells her that he must answer his correspondence. As he says this, he shows her the many letters he is holding.

"From my dear friends all over the world," he tells her.

The Colonel goes through the door into another room furnished with a table and a typewriter, several old chairs and a couch on which a young man, Tony Burgess, the son of Colonel and Mrs. Burgess, lies stretched out half-asleep. Next to him is a whiskey bottle.

The Colonel puts the stack of mail on his desk and reaches for the bottle, pouring some into a glass. His son watches him.

"Really, Tony, you've developed some barbarous habits living in Brooklyn. One doesn't drink whiskey directly from a bottle if one is a gentleman."

"Shut up," is his son's quiet reply. The Colonel closes his mouth just as he was about to say something else with an air that shows he is more than a little frightened of his offspring.

"Any cash in the letters?" Tony says, slouching over to the table where the Colonel is sorting the mail.

Tony Burgess is very good-looking. He has an easy, gracious manner with a trace of wildness in it which if it got out of hand might reach a point of hysteria. This wildness is present when he is talking to his father, or his most intimate friends. Otherwise, it is hidden completely by a rather too thick coat of charm.

Tony starts tearing the letters open, some are empty, others have a few crumpled bills, occasionally one of them has a check for a very small sum. Every once in a while, one of the letters yields a lock of hair tied with a ribbon, a photograph of a man or a woman in their best Sunday clothes, all sorts of sentimental little objects. As Tony tears open the envelopes the Colonel sorts these things tenderly. Tony pockets the cash.

"Really, Tony," says the Colonel, chiding him mildly, "after all while I admit that these cheap trinkets are rather in bad taste, still they are symbols of human sentiment, and we should show them a little respect."

Tony, having opened the letters and collected all the cash, goes back to his couch and stretches out on it without replying.

The Colonel looks through the letters, most of which are directed to women. "I don't see one here from that trapper Jake Moran. I wonder if it really pays to continue writing to him. I've already spent more than a dollar in stamps and so far he hasn't sent a thing."

Tony laughs. "Maybe your approach isn't right. What name are you using for him?"

"I signed my letters to Jake, Little Susie Plunkett."

"That's too prim for a trapper," Tony says. "Call yourself Rosa LaRue, and put a little sex in it—maybe he'll come through with a silver fox."

8. In the meantime, Alice has finished making out her application and Mrs. Burgess takes it from her along with ten dollars membership fee. She then shows Alice into the living room in order to introduce her to some of the other members.

A committee meeting for the annual picnic of the Golden Friendship Club is in session. Mrs. Burgess introduces Alice to the members of the committee as a new and charming member and leaves her with them.

The committee consists of five people who all stop work to get acquainted with Alice. They are immediately personal. One buxom lady in a satin dress with a lot of imitation jewelry, her face painted like a twenty-one sheet, tells Alice that she was very popular in Des Moines but when she came to New York she joined the club in order to meet some nice people and low and behold she met Mr. Adams. Mr. Adams is a very large powerfully built man in a Sears and Roebuck suit and a high, stiff Hoover style collar. He tells Alice that he came to find a wife, but that she, pointing to the buxom woman, is really too citified for him, he's afraid, although she is darn pretty. At which the buxom lady is indignant and says that she was raised on a farm and still knows a lot about it. She can still milk cows.

"Not my cows," Mr. Adams says, "with them rings on your fingers."

He then turns to Alice and tells her that she looks strong. He can tell because she has got good teeth—that's always a sign of health in man and beast alike as Doc Sears, the veterinary says. Alice thanks him.

"I'll make some woman a good husband."

The other members of the committee agree, especially one hachet-faced lady of forty winters with a mouth like a purse-seine that has been drawn tight by a steam winch.

"What you need," she tells Mr. Adams, "is a woman of

character and will-power to raise your six children in the way of God. I taught school in the Ozarks for twenty-six years and the only book I used was the Bible."

Mr. Adams laughs gaily. He enjoys their quarreling over him. He considers himself an awful good catch for any woman.

"I'll bet you took a stick to 'em."

"I did," answers the hatchet-faced woman. "And they are better off for it. Among all my students only one was hung and one was pushed off a cliff."

Mr. Adams is much struck with Alice and he turns back to her.

"I don't really need a young woman," he says, "but I would like one—that's if she could tend the children and the small stock around the place. It is a big farm and I've got no time for the chickens, the sheep, the goats and such like. Can you churn butter and make cheese?"

The hatchet-faced lady breaks in again. "Ask her if she writes a nice hand. That's important. And whether she understands how to keep discipline."

"Can she play the pinao?" asks the buxom lady with the painted face. "Life isn't all work. During the long winter nights, Mr. Adams, you'll want a woman who can make the house cheerful with laughter and singing."

Mr. Adams cuts this short by saying, "We go to bed at sun down."

9.   In the room of the photographs, Mrs. Burgess is showing Tony Alice's application. They are both very serious and Mrs. Burgess has dropped all pretense of being Whistler's Mother. She is a hard, cold person. Two items on Alice's application interest both her and Tony very much. One of them is the fact that Alice has no living relatives of any kind, and no friends to whom she writes regularly. The other is the fact that she has saved in the neighborhood of twelve hundred dollars.

"Not bad," Tony says. "Where is she?"

"With the picnic committee. Come along and I'll introduce you."

Mrs. Burgess brings Tony into the parlor. As soon as he

enters, the buxom lady with the paste jewelry goes up to him coquettishly.

"Oh, will you buy a ticket for the picnic from me?"

"I've got a ticket," Tony says coldly, as his mother calls to Alice.

"Come here, darling. I want you to meet one of the most fascinating younger members of our club."

Alice joins Mrs. Burgess and her son, who she introduces as though he were just another member and in no way related to her. Tony immediately puts on all his charm and offers to squire Alice to the picnic. He then talks quite gaily about living in a big city and how much fun it is to know people.

10. Later that evening Alice reports to Earl in his office. She has a notebook full of stuff about Friendship clubs—their economic aspect, their cultural and moral significance and finally even a note on a system of city run clubs which would take care of the problem so badly handled by personal clubs and the haphazard method of such organizations, as the Golden Friendship Club. It is a Sunday editorial, written in the best style of the school of journalism course on civic projects.

Earl lets her talk for a few minutes, then shuts her up with a quick and final, "That's lousy."

Before she can defend herself he says, "Let's go to dinner and I'll make something up."

11. When Alice reports, he is not satisfied with her stuff and she tells him about the picnic, and he tells her how to cover that, because that should be the story he wants, then adds that he'll drop around to the picnic himself and see if he can find out a few things, too.

12. At the picnic Earl sees Tony and Alice, then through some excuse meets the Colonel and a few other comic characters then accidentally overhears Tony and the widow talking. He hears Tony put the Bermuda proposition to the widow and hears her agree to draw the money and go away with him.

13. That night, at dinner, Earl gets whatever material Alice has for him and with the material he has himself, he tells her it is enough for one story. He tells her that she is through and that he will call on her any time he needs an investigator.

She is a little suspicious about the club and tells him there is a bigger story than his little comic squib. He makes believe this is nonsense and at the most it is a little racket for chiseling fifty cents apiece. He insists that she doesn't go around there any more. He insists because he is in love with her. One of the things she drops which makes Earl fire her at once, is the fact that the widow has disappeared.

14.   Earl hangs around the Golden Friendship Club trying to discover something and sees Tony and Alice come out together, apparently enjoying each other's company. He goes up to Alice's that night and asks to see her. He is told that she is no longer living there but has moved to a house in Brooklyn, without leaving a forwarding address. Maybe he can get it from the university in the morning.

15.   Earl is very worried. He goes back to his office and gets the idea of calling the morgue. He finds out that there has been a new female corpse found, goes there and discovers that it is the widow. He gets the university purser on the phone and demands to know what address Alice has moved to, but is told he will have to come around the next morning, the purser is in bed, and it is out of the question. He goes around to the Golden Friendship Club, asks for Alice and is told that they never heard of her. He realizes that he doesn't know what name she used to join.

From there on Alice's predicament and the chase.

LETTERS

To Beatrice Mathieu

Darling Beazel—

This clipping may interest you. Do you remember falling down a flight of steps?

The other day a fellow called Albert "Pete" Lewis came to see me. He is going to Bandol and wanted some advice, about that place and Paris. He is not a bad guy, although a little too cocksure. He may look you up. Don't go out of your way to help him on my account.

Otherwise everything is about the same. Dull . . . I guess that's what's the matter with our generation, eh? for us Life has lost it's savour.

I am working hard but . . . Today I feel like a flop. Sid read the first four chapters of Miss Lonelyhearts and didn't like them very much—too psychological, not concrete enough. He says I ought to put in description of people and things. That's just what I was trying to avoid. I think I'll go to Fadiman at Schuster's some time this month and find out what he thinks. I don't believe he'll like it either. I don't like it much myself. —much.

Well . . .

Love
Pep,
April 12, 1930

To The New York World-Telegram

We have had some experience with the little magazine and think that such a statement as the one recently made by Mr. Frank Shay in connection with Contempo ought not to pass unchallenged.

When he wrote about "panhandling magazines," he was taking a crack at one of the few decent things in American letters. Apparently he is unacquainted with their sponsors and ignorant of the purpose they serve.

As to the sponsors, it would be hard to find greater idealists in the literary world. Invariably they have spent money and given time to what they knew from the start was to be a losing venture. As to purpose, the little magazine in the past has found audiences for such writers as Sherwood Anderson, Ben Hecht, Ernest Hemingway (Little Review); Robert Coates, Malcolm Cowley, Allen Tate, Hart Crane (Transition); Ruth Suckow, Edna Ferber, Glenway Westcott (The Midland)—to mention but a few.

Surely the unpaid writer for that type of magazine has little to complain of, since he and "litrachoor"—but never the sponsors—get anything out of it.

JULIAN L. SHAPIRO,
NATHANAEL WEST.

October 20, 1931

To William Carlos Williams

Dear Bill—
Here's a long list of the kind of stuff I mean.

Arch. McLeish—Rustic poems not the intellectual.

J. Dos Passos—Non-political prose—the big city stuff

J. Herrmann—I've heard a lot about WHAT HAPPENED, how about re-printing a chapter if we can't get anything else as good as THE ENGAGEMENT—Amer. Car.

Eugene Armfield—He's good. Maybe you can get something through R. Johns—should be easy.

Murray Godwin—Do you remember his dream factory stories in transition—what I meant by an American super-realism (?) He's now in New York.

Moe Bragin—Just exactly what we want, I think. His farm stories are great. Has appeared in Hound and H. and Pagany I think. Marvelous stuff.

Caldwell

Dahlberg—Did you read Bottom Dogs—he's pretty good

and right up our alley—The Middle west stuff is the best.
Good Y.M.C.A. stuff, too.

Jo. Herbst (?)

Malcolm Cowley—Poetry about New England graveyards
etc. not the Frenchified symbolist stuff. Prose?

Hart Crane—Like the river part in The Bridge, like the stuff
in Amer. Car.—not Frenchy.

Harold Rosenberg—I don't like his poetry, but he had a
good story in transition—a big city Caldwell story.

Phelps Putnam (?)

Gerald Sykes—have you read his stuff? Too much old
fashioned psychology, some of his stories are very
excellent.

Hemingway

Faulkner

James T. Farrell—the best man writing for the New Review,
I think. Very good Chicago business. Should be easy to
get.

Morley Callahan—any chance of getting some of his Rustic
Canada? Where is stuff appearing? I haven't seen any for a
long time.

Robert Sage (???)

Edmund Wilson—I've heard that he is doing some great
American stuff—his descriptions of cities are swell. Did
you read his job on the Ford factory and on the Empire
State building? Maybe through Kenneth Burke.

Kenneth Burke (???)

Elliot Paul—Isn't he writing about America again?

Robert Coates

Joseph Vogel—American Jews (?) Appeared in Amer. Car.
1929 also 2nd. Amer Car.

Joseph Mitchel—Amer. Car. 1929 (?)

That's all I can think of right now. I suppose most of this stuff is impossible to get. But we might try.

Do you know anybody familiar with Mexican or Spanish American literature? We can get it translated. I've heard that there are some very good indigenous writers down there.

Will you be in New York next week? Let me know.

Yours,
PEP.

late 1931

To Milton Abernethy

April 26th.

Dear Abernethy—

Please pardon the delay.

I would like very much to visit Chapel Hill—I've never been south of Washington, Penn.—but I don't believe I can. I run a hotel and business is lousy. However, if you get to New York—its rather nice in the summer—you can use the place I run. We have plenty of vacant rooms, and I'd be more than happy to have you use a couple of them.

You wanted to know something about me: I'm 28 yrs. old and went to Brown. I got through in 24. I went to Paris for a year in 25 and wrote Balso Snell there but didn't get a publisher until '31. When I came back from Paris I tried to get some "congenial" work, but wound up managing a hotel. I'm a Sunday writer and work slowly, but I expect to finish Miss Lonelyhearts in August. The next number of Contact will have two more excerpts and I wish you would write me what you think of them.

I don't like Contact much. We had an idea in the beginning, but it looks as though we'll drift into the old "regionalism". You know the Blue Denim stuff they print in Pagany and Hound and Horn. No. 1. *Lem Harrington at Cross Purposes:* Sally was sweating like a horse at her weeding and Lem had an erection behind the hydrangea bushes. No. 2: *The Paint Horse:* The Indian came across the meadow leading a restive horse and old Mrs Purdy remembered her youth in the circus with no little regret. No 3: *The White Church:* The old county church looked like a prim little girl in a starched white dress as Jetsy drove by in the Ford on her way to the movies . . . All this followed by a couple of essays entitled TOWARDS A NEW EPISTOMOLOGICAL DIALECTIC and ST. THOMAS VS. IRVING BABBIT. But I suppose anything is better than Jolas and his Anamyths and Psychographs or Putnam and his An International Notebook for the Arts. We're seriously thinking of going Communist in the 3rd no. But I suppose even then we wont find anything to print except lyric stuff about yellow cornfields winding up with "And Ho for the World Revolution."

Are you writing? Wont you send us something.

I think contempo's new format a big improvement.

Yours,

WEST

1932

To William Carlos Williams

Dear Bill—

The way I see the magazine now is:

Mex. Inter.	R. McA.
The Dead Pan	N. West
The Church	J. Shapiro
Sitting in	C. Dejong
Paseo	C. Oneil
Mary	N. Asch
? K. Kelm or better	?
Ten poems	Williams
Over the Green	Caldwell
Poetry?	?
Wine and Water	E. Jaffee

My idea is to concentrate the force of such stories as Mary. Do it obviously—cruelty, irresponsible torture, simply, obviously, casualy told. Not only in but against the American Grain and yet in. Idiomatic pain. Some poetry along the same line, like your dead child in Trans. nothing to die for. More stories. Like Jack Conroy—Rubber Heels—in current Amer. Merc. or story in current (Halper's) New Republic. Conroy offered to contribute; Halper should be easy to get. How about Moe Bragin? The whole mag. to be like a primitive picture.

My reason for wanting to exclude:
Being Exclusive: week, not enough negro against boarding school, not idiomatic, no grain, rather dull.
You Know How . . . : not aware, too accidental, lacks punch, romantic escape—labor is picturesque like the south seas.
19 is: 20 is ÷ A smart idea, but faked. Half the lines meaningless, full of a false awareness, too much trembling on the brink. TOO FAKEY.
Familiar Objects: an adolescent poem of revolt against poetry—no more stars, sez you—too literary—very week.
One: The wrong kind of visions, too subjective and personal—what we want is torture not sickness and no visions except in the form of warnings, sermons, moral and didactic. Ends in the air. Perhaps generalized visions.
Death of a Boy—not as good as Paseo (which contrasts somewhat America and Europe) and might pull our punch—American brutality through lack of moral frame. A different kind of primitive—for another issue.
Poems: F. Fletcher: See America first, omit catalogue of French and Indian names and what have you. Too pretty.

Lets not pull our punches. We don't have too, there's plenty of young men writing the kind of stuff I mean. Farrell in the New Review is what I mean. Mc. A. probably knows him. Achilles Holt and Eugene Armfield are two more c/o Pagany. Your White Mule. Let's not make the mistake Johns makes by being too eclectic. PRIMITIVE AMERICA number, a new beginning, Suckow, Lewis, Dreiser—false begginings because in French Naturalist tradition. Whole hog, hog butcher to the world in the right sense. Just got your book and read first story—just what I mean. I'm grateful. Did you write to Murray Godwin c/o New Repub. his stories of factories are the kind of lyrical relief we need, but not Villa.

Will write in detail about your book and why I think that it is what we need in the mag.

More poetry—there's little I've read that fits. Phelps Putnam, Archibald McLeish, Sometimes Norman Mcleod.

Yours,

PEP

Do you think you could get Charles Sheeler to do the cover, or is it asking too much?

c. April 1932

To William Carlos Williams

May 13th 1932

Dear Bill—

I don't know how to apologize for not answering your notes—Press of business, I guess; and the arrival of my family from the West Coast.

I saw one page of proof, and the type looked better than that used in the 1st issue. It's the same as that used by the Amer. Merc. Gowdy I think. But I haven't seen the cover design or the title page or the story heading—they're really the things that count. Let's hope for the best. Apparently he's using the same lousy printer, however.

The mag. is practicaly the same as you submitted to me. The only additions are a poem by Evan Shipman and another

by Harold Rosenberg. The only substitution is the story
by Bragin for the one by Armfields. Also, I held over the
one by Mangin and part of McAlmon's Mexico. In order to
print the whole of McAlmon it would have to be entirely re-
written—a colossal job. I'll show you the parts I left out and
I'm sure you will agree with me—the craziest awkward con-
structions I have ever seen. Sentences that start Christ knows
where and end Christ knows where, and for no apparent reason with some figures of speech used over and over again. An
ungrammatical Proust without purpose or logic. Every third
sentence would have to be crossed out and every second
word.

Otherwise the mag is the same as you agreed to. 1. Asch
2. West 3. Williams 4. Caldwell 5. McAlmon 6. Shapiro 7. O'Neil
8. Jaffee 9. Reznikoff 10. Cunard 11. Bragin 12. Comment
13. Bib. With the poetry Reeve, Hartley, Shipman, Rosenberg
in between.

I think the thing is a great deal better than the first was. I
feel fairly certain that it will look better.

Abernethy is here, and says you might come into the city
next week. Kamin says we should have some proof by then,
and I'll get it for you. I'd like very much to see you. I agree
that the Wilson story was no good. I spent last evening with
him, and maybe I'll be able to get something better out of
him. I thought his "American Jitters"—what a [   ] title!—
was swell.

I really hope that I haven't made any enemies for you
through the Mss I handled and wish that you would blame
anything that goes wrong on me. But I do believe that many
of the people who send mss assume too much. They seem to
think that having written something the people they send it
to are automatically obligated. Some of them write angry insulting letters ten days after the Mss has been mailed demanding action. I think we're doing as well as can be
expected, however. It's a thankless task.

I'm conscience stricken about not having answered your
letters immediately, but I've been doing a post to pillow act
for the past month or so. Business is lousy and my company
is close to bankruptcy. New money has to be raised or I guess
I'll have to go to Hollywood or start a Brook Farm experi-

ment and wait for THE REVOLUTION, for Lan's sake why don't they hurry up. Lawd's a mercy, how they do stall.

What day next week will you be in N.Y.

Yours,
PEP

Contrite!

To Minna and Milton Abernethy

Feb 17, '33

Dear Minna and Ab:

I was surprised to see the "poem" in print (and most of the others too). If you ask me it's a lousy poem. However, maybe you know best. Flores wrote to say that he wants to re-print it. Maybe I don't know my true worth, but nevertheless it's a lousy poem.

However, have you changed the name of your dog and how are you?

Things are still very bad in New York and getting worse, so grow a good big garden.

Why not write and tell me about some of your new undertakings?

Yours,
PEP

And I expect you to do for me what you did for Dahlberg's Flushing. A lot of reviews to make up for the bad press I expect to get. PEP

To Minna and Milton Abernethy

March 24.

Dear Minna and Ab:

I don't know whether you owe me a letter or not. You probably do, but then I'm known for my goodnature—a goodnatured slob is the way my friends usualy put it.

However, I expect you folks to get behind the event of the

century and Shove. You'll have a copy of Miss L. in a few days and it is an event. Edmund Wilson said it was the best book he had read in three yrs (plese don't quote—it was verbal) and wrote a blurb ending ". . . a minature comic epic." Erskine Caldwell said practicaly the same thing: he too wrote a rave blurb.

I call it THE CANDIDE OF THE TWENTIETH CENTURY, and myself THE SAGE AND WIT OF EAST 56TH ST.

Now, I think your mag. very important because the publishers (as you love me don't mention this complaint to anyone) intend to advertise the book on a very low level, not as serious literature but as a smutty expose of the columnist rackett. SO, by doing for me what you did for Dahlberg, you can aid American letters greatly. I mean several revues and some general noise. I can get revues for you from almost any of the following Bob Brown, W. C. Williams, S. J. Perelman, John Herrmann, Joesephine Herbst. Angel Flores, N. West, possibly Dashiel Hammet.

Also in the N. West Number a half or perhaps full page add. for which I will pay myself by either cash, in kind potatoes or best of all a big due bill of the Sutton Hotel which you can either sell or use yourself.

The book will be out by the 10 of April so keep the space open as you love me. Let me hear from you at once.

PEP

Just to butter you up—your last number was very swell—

1933

To Minna and Milton Abernethy

April 11,

Dear Minnabs—

Bob sent me a copy of the review he sent you. I'd like to suggest the omissions, I've crossed out in pencil.

It looks now as though the only yes-saying to the damn book I can hope for is through youse. Did you see Soskind in the Post—he says I write with my head in a sewer. He thinks the only book Dostoevsky ever wrote is Crime and Punishment.

You didn't write me whether you had read the book and what you thought. Please do.

I am working on an author-review and will mail it to you in a few days.

Angel Flores is writing a review, so is Perelman, and I'll need them because it looks as though your sheet will have to go down the ages as the only paper that said anything decent about the Candide of our era. So there.

I think I'll ask Mike Gold to do the proletarian angle. Or perhaps you'll write to him, and I'll call him up and ask him to do it. He didn't like the book, but he wrote me an interesting letter about it.

I really need your help.

Yours,
PEP

1933

To Minna and Milton Abernethy

Dear Minnab—

By now I suppose you've heard about the deal I got from Liveright.

Despite the fact that they are bankrupt, that they have no books to sell, and that I never received a cent from them and am willing to give up the $400 in royalties that they owe me, they refuse to give me back the copyright to the book. I've been running from lawyer to lawyer, but my contract has no bankruptcy clause and there is nothing that I can do about it.

The book surprised everyone including me—it got swell reviews and even more it started to sell very well, making Macy's best seller list and selling 2000 copies in less than 10 days right in Manhattan without salesmen or promotion of any kind. Liveright has not been functioning as a publishing house for the past six weeks and the book had to make its way by itself.

Everybody, Knopf, Harrison Smith, etc. says that with normal exploitation it might have sold 15,000 copies.

I've been heartsick over the thing as you can imagine, and I'm still sick.

Thank you for the add and the author review—I'm looking forward to the other reviews with great eagerness—

Yours,

PEP

How's the dog? When will I see you?

May? 1933

To Edmund Wilson

July 25—

Dear Wilson—

I expect to be home in a few weeks, about Aug. 10th, and at that time I will try to see if I can do something about a hotel job for your cousin. I don't believe it would be worth trying to do by mail, and I feel that it would be useless to send him somewhere without my speaking to the people first. And as for my own outfit, I've been quarreling with them ever since I left. They owe me some money, and I'm trying to get a settlement. They say that they will only acknowledge the debt if I return to my job. I may have to sue them because, I do not intend to return. You've heard this many times before I know But—I want to write. Why I don't know, but I do, and when I return I shall live on the farm and try to do some short stories and my Horatio Alger book.

There is a funny situation out here now. The sound men are on strike, and the other unions, camera men etc. are evidently going out with them. We "Writers" (a funny thing out here—when anyone asks you what you are you say "Writer") have a new union and a very radical one, organized by such old "movement" men as Howard, Lawson, Ornitz, Weitzenkorn, Caesar, and practically every editor of The Call since Abraham Cahan's day. But there's no chance of our ever striking—behind the baracades we'll go willingly enough, but organized labor action never. I went to a union meeting where there was some big talk, but at the slightest bit of Producer opposition we'll fold like the tents of the Arabs. The strange thing is that almost all the members of the union admit it themselves. Today when I came to work there were pickets in front of the studio, and it felt queer to walk through them. A Writer, one of them shouted, and lip-farted.

See you soon,

WEST

1933

To Minna and Milton Abernethy

July 27th

Dear Minab—

It was only a few days ago that I saw the West edition of your magazine and I am very grateful to you for it. Caldwell showed it to me first, then I received my copies forwarded from New York. It was a goddamned nice thing for you to do.

Yes, I'm in Hollywood; but not permanently or even for long. I will be returning home again in a few more days. This place is not at all what I expected. It isn't very fantastic, just a desert got up to look like Asbury Park. And so far I've bumped into none of the things I expected and was prepared for by reports and plays like Once in a Life Time. The studio I am working Columbia is a highly organized and very practical business place. Five minutes after I arrived I was given an assignment a picture called BLIND DATE and I have been working nine hours a day on it since then with a full day on Saturday.

Otherwise nothing new. Apparently Harcourt does not intend to advertise Miss L. because only fourhundred copies of their edition had been sold. Well, I don't much care; the book did much better than I expected. It has made it possible for me to quit my job. Sometime in August I will return to the east and live on the farm in Erwinna and write.

What's new with you? I hope you have worked yourselves out of your financial difficulties. I will get in touch with you as soon as I return east.

Please keep the news of my quitting the hotel business a secret because there are few people who I don't want to shock quite yet. Especially around the Sutton

As ever yours gratefuly,
WEST

1933

To F. Scott Fitzgerald

September 11th, '34

My dear Mr. Fitzgerald,

You have been kind enough to say that you liked my novel, Miss Lonelyhearts.

I am applying for a Guggenheim Fellowship and I need references for it. I wonder if you would be willing to let me use your name as a reference? It would be enormously valuable to me. I am writing to you, a stranger, because I know very few people, almost none whose names would mean anything to the committee, and apparently the references are the most important part of the application.

As you know, the committee will probably submit my plan for future work to you if you give me permission to use your name as reference. This will be a nuisance, of course, but the plan is a very brief one and you are only obliged to say whether you think it is good or not.

If you can see your way to do this, it will make me very happy.

Sincerely,
NATHANAEL WEST

To Bennett Cerf

Dear Bennet—

Did you get my night letter?

After going over the book carefully here's the way I see the changes you propose:

You're absolutely right about changing Estee to the third person. The first person was left over from another version in which he was really the narrator. But I disagree about taking him out entirely. He is Tod's only contact with "upper Hollywood" and the only person who moves on his mental level. Moreover, I need him for the mechanics of my story as well as its meaning. What I intend to do is eliminate his having been an artist once himself as well as his mock prophecies, and to base his friendship for Tod on a simpler premise. In this way, I'll reduce his importance and make him easier to handle.

I didn't mean the "Europa and Bull-fiddle" episode to be sloppy and drooling. I will cut it down to the nub for you, taking out the part where she kisses the neck of the cello and makes it groan in reply, and only retaining the picture—peppermint towel, deep orange cello, turkey red carpet, peach flesh, etc. I want it for Tod's sake—after all he's a painter and I don't do too much about it. In the new version, the scene will be attractive and not nasty at all.

The Mrs. Schwartzen lesbian scene comes out entirely.

The little black hen definitely has significance. The episode was carefully chosen to show how much Homer is suffering and what a terrible form his torture takes. On re-reading it, however, I realize that I did it too baldly and prolonged it too much. I'll cut it down drastically in length and make it more subtle. Homer probably wouldn't come out with such a plain description of his torment. By understatement and suggestion rather than brutal accent, I feel certain I can make it much less offensive and still retain the horror and the contribution to Homer's final break up.

I hope very much that all this meets with your approval. I do not want to shock just for shocking's sake. By making the woman and cello episode attractive, by taking out the lesbian stuff, and by hinting at the black hen's relation to the gamecocks rather than underlining it, I think your objections will be met.

The date of publication I leave to you. I would prefer October. 1939 is so far away and the times so out of joint and life so precarious. Make it October if you possibly can. The mss. will certainly be in shape within a months time. I intend to do nothing but work on it until I've finished it.

By the way, Sid Perelman tells me that in your conversations with him you didn't like several of the landscape descriptions and felt that they were awkward in some cases and over-written in others. I'm a little worried about some of them myself and would greatly appreciate hearing from you, giving sentence and paragraph if possible.

Thanks again.

Yours,
PEP
May? 1938

To Bennett Cerf

June 7, 1938.

Dear Bennet:

I am making very rapid progress. Should be finished in a couple of weeks.

A few of the nature descriptions are quite flamboyant and I am subduing them.

About the blurb for the jacket—I am not very good at that sort of thing. I am sure someone in your office can do it much better, and I would prefer it that way if possible. I would like to go over it, however.

Should I try to get some blurbs from important people? I hate to do it, but if you think it necessary I will make the attempt. I mean Dotty Parker and so forth. Dash Hammett read it and said—

"I don't like books about Hollywood, but this one is different and held me all the way. A really swell job, with the God damndest set of characters I ever read about."

He said this verbally, so I would like to check with him, if you think you want to use it, when I return to New York.

I expect to be back the first week in August for the rehearsals of my play. It is now called "Blow, Bugle, Blow." Will you be around then? If you are I would like the opportunity of going over the book again with you in detail. There will be time for that, won't there? Even if you bring it out in the fall it won't go to the printers until the end of August, I imagine.

However, I am leaving the publication date entirely up to you and your staff with January as an approximate deadline.

How about the title? Do you like "THE CHEATED"? I have started to wonder if it wasn't a little too pretentious, like most of the Nineteenth Century "The . . . . ." titles. I rather like—"THE GRASS EATERS." Quite a few intelligent people agree on that one.

By the way, I have been shaking out your letters in hopes of finding that tentative contract you spoke of in your first letter. I would like very much to have one. Also the advance; if possible.

Yours,
PEP

To Bennett Cerf

July 11, 1938.

Dear Bennet:

The novel was mailed to you today. I think that this version shows a great deal of improvement over the previous one— in speed, smoothness and consistency of style. I made all the changes you suggested and all those I felt necessary. I think you will find that the "nature" writing is much better now. The "black hen" incident at the end of the book I found impossible to delete, but I toned it down a great deal. It has to be fairly strong if it is to carry the motivation that I need later on.

There is one thing that I am definitely dissatisfied with and that is the title. I have been wracking my brain for a better one than either "The Cheated" or "The Grass Eaters," but so far haven't been very successful. I would like to call it "Days To Come," but, as you know, Lillie Hellman used that on a play. I am going to spend next week trying to find a title so please consider the book as untitled so far. If you or anybody on your staff have any suggestions, I would like to hear them.

See you in August.

As ever,
PEP

To Josephine Conway

Sunday

Dear Jo—

I know my letters have been lousy ones and far and few between, but I've been waiting each time hoping to have something definite to write you about the play. I still haven't anything definite. There is nothing to report except procrastination and most irritating delay. First there was difficulty with the cast. Equity wouldn't let us have Aubrey Mather who was to play Hargreaves because he is English and has to wait six months before going into another play. Susi Lanner who was to play Marie got into a fight with her husband and rushed off to Europe wiring Mayer from the boat half way across. The woman who was going to play Grace decided to have a baby instead. Stanley Ridges is holding out for seven-hundred and fifty, a week which is too much. When a cast was finally lined up, Mayer went to the Shubert's who have a contract to provide a theatre (they own eighteen legit houses or about half the available supply). Shubert told him he could have a house in November sometime, all the houses were booked and double booked (double booked means that after the first booking flops another show is set to go in). For three weeks Mayer argued with Shubert about it. To no avail because Shubert who is a famous thief has a written agreement with Mayer which specifies that Mayer must go into a Shubert house but doesn't specify when, beyond the season 1938–39. Mayer finally got a release from Shubert and went out to look for another house. He found that all the houses were booked double also—the independents that is. It's a terrific season with a show opening almost every night from the fifteenth on. He spent three more weeks and finally was on the verge of making a deal with Grisman, a man who owns five houses, when one of the backers with five thousand dollars in the show suddenly decided that because of the coming war in Europe the play would be a flop. "You can't laugh at war when the newspapers are full of slaughter. You can't show the Germans winning when everyone is on the side of the allies, etc. etc. etc, etc." I think the argument a stupid one but it's his five thousand. Well when that happened I sent a wire to Feldman at once telling him to see Sisk and Frank Davis at Metro about a job for me. And began to prepare to leave here. The day after I sent the telegram, the man with the five grand decided that maybe there wouldn't be a war and maybe there was some reason in the argument that war would help our play by making it front page news and he agreed to put in three of the five he first pledged. Mayer pleaded with me to remain another two weeks while he got a theatre and raised the two grand some where else. He swore he was certain to go into rehearsal by October first. I agreed. I sent another wire to the agents for them to hold up and came out here to the country with Joe to wait for October first. If there isn't a definite theatre and rehearsal date by then I shall leave here without fail on Oct. 2nd. That's the whole story—and a pretty dreary one it is, too. I understand, however—that it's just show business. And that the more trouble, the more certain to be a hit. Ours ought to outrun Tobacco Road.

Otherwise there's nothing to write. I've just fooled away the last six months in barrooms, waiting. In Hollywood I might have made some money and would have at least have gotten some shooting.

How is the money situation with you? Do you need some more vacation dough. Write and tell me at once—you must be running short. If the show does go into rehearsal you'll have to have a still longer vacation. I'll make you make up for it (as though you didn't last year) when I get back. We'll write original plays and novels, poems and short stories and essays at night and work in a studio by day. Anyway, we'll write something.

Everything is O.K. on the novel thank God. It goes into rehearsal (I mean the printers) December tenth and will be out Jan tenth. The publishers think it will do fine.

Write me care of Joe Shrank, Upper Black Eddy, Penna. I expect to be here most of the time while waiting for October first.

Yours,

PEP

September 19, 1938

To Josephine Conway

Dear Jo—

It finally looks as though everything were all set and that rehearsals will start within ten days. The theatre contracts are signed and the casting is going ahead full speed. At least that's what Mayer said on the telephone last Saturday, yesterday. Please pray to God.

We had trouble up until Friday—this time it was a question of more money. One of the backers was definitely out. Finally Joe and I dug up two thousand between us (there goes the Metro money) and Talbot Jennings put in another two to straighten that out. Everything was then signed and we're supposed to be all set. Please don't mention a word of Joe and I having put money in to anyone, and pray like hell as I know you're doing. It may be a case of throwing good money after bad, but I felt I had to do it. I had so much time and money in the damn thing already that I couldn't let it fall through for another thousand bucks as it looked it might. Moreover, I couldn't go back to Hollywood, I felt, after all the talking I did unless the damn thing went on at least, even if it were a flop. I think it's got a good chance, however, bettered in fact by the British double cross of Cheko-slo-vakia—the War scare made the play front news, too. We're doing another re-write right now linking the play up as subtly as possible with the events of the past few weeks.

I'm not worrying even if the show flops and I get back pretty broke. For one thing, Sisk told Gordine that I could work for him whenever I wanted to, absolutely. And also, maybe the Metro thing will be a good credit, especially if Gable plays in it. What do you hear about it?

I had dinner with Bus-Fekete the other night and he wants me to work on his play Porcupine with him—change it to an American background. That's what we may be doing nights when I get back and maybe days too although I hope not.

I am almost certain to be back by the tenth of Nov. Please hold out for me until then. If you need any money don't hesitate to write. This time I won't leave Hollywood for several years and will do my damndest to make a career out there and get more money. Except maybe Alaska for a month.

You must have had a good vacation. What are you doing now—working? With whom and where? Write a long letter with some news and some gossip.

As ever
PEP

My best to your mother—

October 21, 1938

To Bennett Cerf

January 6, 1939

Dear Bennet:

Your note chased me all over, but finally was lowered in through my window by a little man in a leather apron with pointed shoes. Gracious being, the tyke, whose home is on the bottom of the Los Angeles River. This all sounds very cryptic and purposely so, but I have just come out of a story conference here at Universal where I have been working and I feel a little on the cryptic side.

How did you make out with Hammett on the blurb? I guess the answer must have been no or you would have written. Please write and tell me what he said. I am really curious about it. He raved about the book when he read it in the earliest version and promised a blurb at that time—besides which, during one of his blackest hours (the hour lasted five months) when he was locked out of his hotel, I took him into the one I was working in and at the risk of my job, let him live there without paying until he got the money out of "The Thin Man." Well, it's foolish, but those things still bother me. I haven't learned.

How about Miss Parker and her blurb? She promised it, even more fervently than Dash. I suppose that one didn't materialize either. Nevertheless, when the proofs are out, I feel certain that I can get a really good set of them for you. When will the proofs be out? As I understood it, it should be any day now. Write and let me know the definite day of publication, like a good fellow.

How about the spring catalogue? I would like to see what you did with the junk I wrote.

Otherwise, there's nothing new. I've got an idea for another novel that I think is the best idea I've ever had, but God knows when I'll be able to write it. Maybe if I can keep working here this winter I'll save enough to do it. You don't feel like subsidizing it, do you?—not as much as I feel like writing it. Well, I don't blame you. But maybe "The Day of the Locust" (hope springs eternal even if slightly muddied at its source in the San Berdoo Mountains) will click sufficiently for me to afford another one.

Let me hear.

Yours,
PEP

6614 Cahuenga Terrace
Hollywood, Calif.

To Saxe Commins

February 14, 1939

Dear Saxe:

Sid Perelman wrote that he brought you the proofs some time ago. I was hoping that I would hear from you about them, and what you thought about the changes. Why not let me know?

Otherwise, what's new? Do you think you may have the bound proofs pretty soon? Also, what's the jacket going to look like?

This probably sounds like a guy who is having his first book published, but hope springs every two or three years in this human heart, and springs especially hard out here in the sand wastes of San Fernando Valley. So be a good fellow and write all the news about "The Locust."

Give my best to Bennet and Miss Becker.

Sincerely yours,
PEP

P.S. Did you ever read a book called "A Cool Million" that I wrote and that was published by Covici Friede? A lot of people think it is a pretty good one and that the reason it flopped is because it was published much too soon in the race toward Fascism. It came out when no one in this country except a few Jeremiahs like myself, took seriously the possibility of a Fascist America. I wonder if you would help me in this. I would like very much to place it with Blue Seal books or one of those other inexpensive paper backed libraries because I feel that at the present time it might have a very good chance of arousing some interest. Do you know the name of the editor or anyone I could get in touch with in the matter? Or perhaps better (what do you think?), do you know the name of an intelligent agent besides Max Lieber, whom I don't like, who might be interested in submitting "A Cool Million" and trying to work up a deal for me in one of those paper libraries? If you can help me at all in this matter, I would appreciate it extremely.

P

To F. Scott Fitzgerald

April 5, 1939

Dear Scott Fitzgerald:

I'm taking the liberty again of sending you a set of proofs of a new novel.

It took a long time to write while working on westerns and cops and robbers, but reading the proofs I wish it had taken longer.

I never thanked you for your kindness to me in the preface to the Modern Library edition of "The Great Gatsby." When I read it, I got a great lift just at a time when I needed one badly, if I was to go on writing.

Somehow or other I seem to have slipped in between all the "schools." My books meet no needs except my own, their circulation is practically private and I'm lucky to be published. And yet, I only have a desire to remedy all that *before* sitting down to write, once begun I do it my way. I forget the broad sweep, the big canvas, the shot-gun adjectives, the important people, the significant ideas, the lessons to be taught, the epic Thomas Wolfe, the realistic James Farrell—and go on making what one critic called "private and unfunny jokes." Your preface made me feel that they weren't completely private and maybe not even entirely jokes.

Gratefully,
NATHANAEL WEST

6614 Cahuenga Terrace
Hollywood, Calif.

To Edmund Wilson

April 6, 1939

Dear Edmund:

This is a rather late acknowledgement of your book of plays. I have been deep in a body-warm mud hole pleasantly occupied writing an epic tale of a Wall Street customers' man who becomes a post office bandit, tries reform because of love, reverts to crime and finally meets his death on a plowed field to conform with the requirements of the Hays code. Every time I raise above the warm mud to breathe I get batted over the head with a stick with a nail in the end—like last summer in New York with that ill-fated play. There must be something wrong with my kind of comic writing—no warm chuckles and no hearty guffaws, maybe, and distinctly "bad hat." The wrong tone, as they used to say—still do in the Sat. Review.

I guess I don't know what's what, but when I read your three plays, I was even more discouraged than when I left New York in a rain of stones after mine went on. That Sidney Howard or Sam Behrman are great dramatists and the last two plays in your book were never even produced makes me feel as though I were completely without any sense at all, completely without an objective and playing blind man's buff with a trade about which I never knew anything, never could

learn anything, or even suspect anything. Aside from everything else, if that second play of yours isn't "good threatre"
and something like Elmer Rice's "The Left Bank" is "good
theatre" then I'd better stay here in the warm mud with a
weekly check lowered down to me regularly on a string and
stop teasing myself with plans for another play and another
book, etc. I've never been patient enough for the "long
view," and the mud is very soft and heated just right. Why
heave about in it?

One of the final heaves is on its way to you now—the
bound proofs of "The Day of the Locust" which Random is
sending you. Parts of it are bad, especially up front, but the
darn thing took so long to get written and published that I
got sick of it and couldn't fix it any more.

Somehow or other I seem to have slipped in between all
the "schools." My books meet no needs except my own, their
circulation is practically private and I'm lucky to be published.
And yet, I only have a desire to remedy all that *before* sitting
down to write, once begun I do it my way. I forget the broad
sweep, the big canvas, the shot-gun adjectives, the important
people, the significant ideas, the lessons to be taught, the epic
Thomas Wolfe, the realistic James Farrell,—and go on making
what one critic called "private and unfunny jokes." The radical press, although I consider myself on their side, doesn't
like it, and thinks it even fascist sometimes, and the literature
boys, whom I detest, detest me in turn. The highbrow press
finds that I avoid the important things and the lending library
touts in the daily press think me shocking. The proof of all
this is that I've never had the same publisher twice—once
bitten, etc.—because there is nothing to root for in my books
and what is even worse, no rooters. Maybe they're right. My
stuff goes from the presses to the drug stores.

I hope all this doesn't sound too "corny," as Otis Ferguson
would put it, but I've just come back from a story conference
in which I was told that the picture I'm writing lacks significance and sweep—or, as the producer put it—"Why, tell me
why, I dare you, we should spend half a million dollars on it,
what fresh ideas have we got to sell—it isn't funny enough to
make them piss their seats—it isn't sad enough to make them

snuffle, and there's no message for them to carry away. Go back and put a message in it."

Let me hear from you.

I hope you are well and that everything looks decent from where you're sitting these days.

As ever,
PEP

6614 Cahuenga Terrace
Hollywood, Calif.

To Malcolm Cowley

May 11, 1939

Dear Malcolm:

Bennett Cerf sent me a copy of your note to him about "The Day of the Locust." It made me quite a bit happier to hear that you liked the first chapters. I hope you read the rest of it sometime because I think the first five or six chapters are the weakest.

Lately, I have been feeling even more discouraged than usual. The ancient bugaboo of my kind—"why write novels?"—is always before me. I have no particular message for a troubled world (except possibly "beware") and the old standby of "pity and irony" seems like nothing but personal vanity. Why make the continuous sacrifice necessary to produce novels for a non-existent market? The art compulsion of ten years ago is all but vanished.

. . . write out of hope and for a new and better world— But I'm a comic writer and it seems impossible for me to handle any of the "big things" without seeming to laugh or at least smile. Is it possible to contrive a right-about face with one's writing because of a conviction based on a theory? I doubt it. What I mean is that out here we have a strong progressive movement and I devote a great deal of time to it. Yet, although this new novel is about Hollywood, I found it impossible to include any of those activities in it. I made a desperate attempt before giving up. I tried to describe a meeting of the Anti-Nazi League, but it didn't fit and I had to substitute a whorehouse and a dirty film. The terrible sincere struggle of the League came out comic when I touched it and even libelous. Take the "mother" in Steinbeck's swell novel—I want to believe in her and yet inside myself I honestly can't. When not writing a novel—say at a meeting of a committee we have out here to help the migratory worker—I do believe it and try to act on that belief. But at the typewriter by myself I can't. I suppose middle-class upbringing, skeptical schooling, etc. are too powerful a burden for me to throw off—certainly not by an act of will alone.

ALAS!

I hope all this doesn't seem too silly to you—to me it is an ever-present worry and what, in a way, is worse—an enormous temptation to forget the bitter, tedious novels and to spend that time on committees which act on hope and faith without a smile. (It was even a struggle this time for me to leave off the quotation marks.)

How are the wife and child? Are you doing any fishing? I have been laboring on a thing called "I Stole A Million" for George Raft and so missed opening day which was very good this year. I had some great duck and quail shooting, however, when I got back after the play last fall.

As ever,

6614 Cahuenga Terrace
Hollywood, Calif.

To F. Scott Fitzgerald

June 30, 1939

Dear Scott Fitzgerald:

I got your very kind note from Sid Perelman the other day in the mail. Thanks very much.

So far the box score stands: Good reviews—fifteen per cent,

bad reviews—twenty-five per cent, brutal personal attacks, sixty per cent. Sales: practically none.

I'll try another one anyway, I guess.

Gratefully,
NATHANAEL WEST

6614 Cahuenga Terrace
Hollywood, Calif.

To Edmund Wilson

June 30, 1939

Dear Edmund:

Somehow or other I misplaced your letter so I don't know whether you are still at the Chicago University summer school. I am sending this through the New Republic so as not to take any chances.

I have been watching the New Republic for that review of yours, but so far haven't seen it. The fact that you are taking the trouble to review it really means a great deal to me.

The book is what the publisher, at least, calls a definite flop. It will hardly reach a sale of 1400 copies. Right there is the whole reason why I have to continue working in Hollywood. I once tried to work seriously at my craft but was absolutely unable to make even the beginning of a living. At the end of three years and two books I had made the total of $780.00 gross. So it wasn't a matter of making a sacrifice, which I was willing enough to make and would still be willing, but just a clear cut impossibility. I seem to have no market whatsoever and while many people whose opinion I respect are full of sincere praise, the book reviewers disagree, even going so far as to attack the people who do praise my books, and the public is completely apathetic.

I haven't given up, however, by a long shot, and although it may sound strange, am not even discouraged. I have a new book blocked out and have managed to save a little money so that about Christmas time I think I may be able to knock off again and make another attempt. It is for this reason that I am grateful rather than angry at the nice deep mud-lined rut in which I find myself at the moment. The world outside doesn't make it possible for me to even hope to earn a living writing, while here the pay is large (it isn't as large as people think, however) enough for me to have at least three or four months off every year. During the last three years that I have worked here I have managed to get more than eighteen months away.

Please let me hear from you again.

As ever,
PEP

6614 Cahuenga Terrace,
Hollywood, Calif.

To Bob Brown

February
14
1940

Dear Bob:

It was swell to hear from you—and then I immediately lost your letter—therefore this second-hand delivery. I am enclosing a check without an application blank and am looking forward very anxiously to the book. It's a funny thing, but ever since I'd heard you were working at that cooperative college, I've been playing with the idea of offering my services as an instructor for a couple of semesters. Your book, I imagine, must tell all about it.

About working in Hollywood, other guys have asked me from time to time about it and I've always found it extremely difficult to answer. The best I can do to describe the situation is something like this—Southern California is just as cheap or cheaper to live in than Long Island, so that if you haven't some definite financial reason for living on Long Island, it might be a good idea to come out here and take a whack at pictures. The employment situation in the studios has become quite a bit tougher in the last year or so and they are being run a lot more efficiently so far as writers are concerned at least. Wages are down and the length of time one gets to do a script has been cut almost in half. Moreover, they are no longer taking any risks and are shopping for literary material like a set of Uriah Heeps. It might be quite difficult for you to get a job in the studio and begin to draw a salary right off. The way to get started in this business now, aside from a best selling novel or a hit play, is to write originals, a type of composition that includes a plot and characterizations aimed definitely at motion pictures. If you came out I would do my best to show you as much as I know about that sort of thing, and would also do everything I could to help you market it. Once you've sold one or two it would be comparatively easy to get on the payroll. This is the only practical method I know and if you feel that you want to do it, it might turn out to be a good risk. You can't sell originals from the east, but you could come out armed with a couple. If you do take a crack at it, don't make the mistake so many people do of thinking you have to write down for pictures. Look at some of the better ones and try to utilize the best dramatic situations you can think of. What I mean by this is don't fool with spies, gangsters and the usual nonsense. They make plenty of that crap, of course, but they won't buy it from you.

Let me know what you think and write and ask me any other questions you would like to have answered.

Give my very best to Rose.

As ever,
PEP

Of course you can absolutely depend on my doing everything I possibly can to help you break in.

P.

6614 Cahuenga Terrace
Hollywood, Calif.

To Bennett Cerf

February
14
1940

Dear Bennett:

Please forgive my not answering your letter earlier. I have been both ill and busy. The first being a case of the bloody flux or Wilson's influenza, and the latter, a case of the bloody flux or "MEN AGAINST THE SKY," an epic of civilian aviation.

I saw Saxe Cummins on his quick passage through this town and we talked about my new book. I have the entire story clearly in my mind and know just what I intend to do with it and am eager to start. I gave him all the dope in detail and he will relay it to you. Let me know what you think as soon as you think it.

As ever,
PEP

To Bennett Cerf

March
11
1940

Dear Bennett:

I waited a few weeks before answering your letter in order to get all emotion out of my system. You know that crack about "Boy Meets Girl" kind of hurt. Really, I'm not quite that fantastic.

I don't know how Saxe presented my case, but I imagine it must have been a little strong for you to have written such a hard letter. The real reason I asked for money was a psychological one, I suppose. Although I don't get anywhere near two thousand a week, I still have a tremendous sinking feeling in my stomach when I quit a job and leap off into space on the venture of a new novel. By asking you for the money, I wasn't trying to insure myself against financial loss

in any way because even a thousand dollars doesn't come anywhere near doing that, but was really trying to get a sort of
concrete pat on the back to help along my dwindling courage.

As ever,
PEP

To Bennett Cerf

March
30
1940

Dear Bennett:

Your last letter made me feel a great deal better. I realize
that the economics of the thing doesn't make very good sense,
but yet hope springs eternally in my heart, at least. The one
coming up is the one that does it. I have worked the idea out
in my mind in quite a bit of detail and the more I think about
it, the more certain I am that it can be a hell of a book.

So, okay, send on the very airy pat on the back and it will
help at least a little in making me feel that there is some economic sense to what I am going to do.

I expect to be through here within the next few weeks, and
then will go to work.

As ever,
PEP

CHRONOLOGY

NOTE ON THE TEXTS

NOTES

Chronology

1903   Born Nathan Weinstein on October 17, first child of Max
Weinstein and Anna Wallenstein Weinstein, at their home
on East 81st Street in New York City. (Mother was born
in Kovno, Russia, now Kaunas, Lithuania, in 1878, the fifth
of nine children of Lazar Wallenstein and Chaja-Rochel
Wallenstein. Lazar Wallenstein, a prosperous stonemason
and builder, employed Max Weinstein, the fourth of six
children, as one of his workers. Both the Wallenstein and
Weinstein families were Jewish and German-speaking, and
suffered under the anti-Semitic laws and Russification pol-
icies instituted by Tsar Alexander III from 1881 on. In the
late 1880s members of both families began immigrating to
the United States. Max Weinstein joined his brothers in
establishing a successful construction business in New
York City, building tenement houses on the Lower East
Side and later elevator houses and luxury apartments in
upper Manhattan. Anna and Max were married on May
25, 1902, and moved into one of Max's houses at 151 East
81st Street. In later years the family will move repeatedly
into new and more luxurious buildings built by Max's
company.)

1904   Sister Hinda born.

1908–15   Attends P.S. 81, a progressive school which emphasizes ex-
perimentation and individual creativity. Proves a mediocre
pupil, and never earns higher than a "B" for either work
or conduct. Learns German at home. Sister Laura born in
1911. Spends summers with mother and sisters in the country and at the seaside in Connecticut, New York, and New
Jersey, and develops an enduring love of the outdoors.

1915–16   Attends seventh and eighth grade at P.S. 186. Reads Tolstoy, Turgenev, Pushkin, Dostoevsky, Chekhov, Dickens,
Shakespeare, Hardy, Balzac; intersperses literary reading
with frequent issues of *Field and Stream*.

1917–20   Graduates from P.S. 186 and enters De Witt Clinton, one
of the best public high schools in New York City. Fails

freshman year; leaves after three years without graduating. Reads Petronius, Rabelais, Donne, Laforgue, T. S. Eliot, Pound, Yeats, James Branch Cabell, Arthur Machen. With cousin Wally, also 15, plans to run away and enlist in the army in 1918; they are intercepted by their fathers in Grand Central Terminal. Spends summers at Camp Paradox, a Jewish summer camp in the Adirondacks. Lacks skill at sports, in contrast to remarkably athletic cousins; receives nickname "Pep" after sleeping for a whole day following climb of Mount Marcy. Works as assistant on art staff as well as art editor for camp magazine, the *Paradoxian*, signing his name "Nathan 'Pep' Weinstein"; contributes sketches and cartoons satirizing camp activities.

1921   Alters De Witt Clinton transcript in hope of entering college, changing name to Nathaniel Weinstein and adding six credits to the nine and a half he had actually earned. Accepted at Tufts University. Pledges to Phi Epsilon Pi, a Jewish fraternity, and lives in fraternity house. Attends ball games, fraternity parties, and stage plays in Boston. Rarely goes to class and withdraws before end of first full term with failing marks in every subject. Obtains transcript of another Nathan Weinstein, a significantly better student, and uses his record of 57 completed credits to enter Brown University as a second-term sophomore.

1922   Becomes part of social group at Brown he calls the "Bacchanalians"; wears Brooks Brothers suits and is regarded as a "dandy." Joins basketball team, but is cut in January. Meets Sidney Joseph (S. J.) Perelman, who becomes close friend. Excluded from fraternities because he is Jewish, founds the Hanseatic League, a society of the "intellectual elite" who abandon the "ivory tower to sample and reject the cloying sweets of the public fare." With Perelman and others, goes to the movies regularly, attends the theater once or twice a week, and visits The Booke Shop, which specializes in modern literature. Fascinated with religious ritual, reads books on history of religions, mythology, witchcraft, magic, and mysticism. Publishes drawings in Brown's humor magazine, *The Brown Jug*. Withdraws from Brown in the spring. Readmitted in the fall as first-term junior on the strength of fraudulently claimed credits from Tufts.

1923 Does poorly and is frequently absent during fall term, and registers for the spring on probation. Earns one of his three good grades in a course on Greek drama in translation. Essay "Euripides—A Playwright" is published in first number of Brown literary magazine *Casements*, for which he also draws cover. While at Brown, frequently uses name Nathaniel von Wallenstein Weinstein. Becomes an enthusiastic reader of H. L. Mencken's new magazine *The American Mercury*. Contracts gonorrhea; treatment of the disease damages prostate gland and causes recurring pain throughout his life. Works during summer vacation as bricklayer and timekeeper on his father's construction projects.

1924–25 Publishes poetry in *Casements*. Writes and acts in annual St. Patrick's Day musical satirizing Brown undergraduate life. Writes Class Day speech which chronicles the adventures of St. Puce, a flea born in the armpit of Christ. Description in senior yearbook states that "he passes his time in drawing exotic pictures, quoting strange and fanciful poetry, and endeavoring to uplift *Casements*." Develops a special interest in the French and English symbolists; reads Wilde, Pater, Aldous Huxley, Joyce, Flaubert, and also develops interest in American writers including F. Scott Fitzgerald, William Carlos Williams, Hart Crane, and E. E. Cummings. Graduates from Brown in June 1924 and begins work as construction superintendent in his father's business. Hoping to travel to Paris, reads novels about bohemian life by Henri Murger and Francis Carco.

1926 Legally changes name to Nathanael West on August 16. (Continues to use "Weinstein" in family circles until 1932; when William Carlos Williams later asks, "How did you get that name?" West answers, "Horace Greeley said, 'Go West, young man.' So I did.") Goes to Paris in October, a trip financed by uncles Saul and Charles Wallenstein. Meets artist Max Ernst and author Henry Miller; becomes close friend of painter and jazz musician Hilaire Hiler. Works sporadically on first novel, *The Dream Life of Balso Snell*. Considers writing a book of popularized biographies of painters. (Will later claim that he lived in poverty in Paris for several years.)

1927–28   After repeated entreaties by his father, whose construction
           business is encountering financial difficulty, returns home
           in January 1927. Works as night manager at the Kenmore
           Hall Hotel at 145 East 23rd Street. Attempts to enter the
           candy business with a product called "Cactus Candy"
           (abandons efforts after about two years). Offers a free
           room at the Kenmore to Dashiell Hammett, who is com-
           pleting *The Maltese Falcon*. College friends Quentin Reyn-
           olds and I. J. Kapstein share West's social life in Greenwich
           Village speakeasies. Through S. J. Perelman, who has be-
           gun to write for *The New Yorker*, meets staff of the mag-
           azine, including George S. Kaufman, Dorothy Parker, and
           Alexander Woollcott.

1929   Rewrites and completes *The Dream Life of Balso Snell*. In-
           troduced by Perelman to "Susan Chester," a woman who
           writes an advice column for the *Brooklyn Eagle*; she shows
           them letters from readers, which become the basis for *Miss
           Lonelyhearts*. Perelman marries Laura Weinstein, West's
           sister, in July. West meets writer Michael Gold, who en-
           courages him to write for Communist periodicals *New
           Masses* and *The Daily Worker*; also meets Edmund Wilson,
           John Dos Passos, Horace Gregory, Maxwell Bodenheim,
           Edward Dahlberg, and other literary figures. Spends Sun-
           day afternoons in George Brounoff's home discussing
           modern literature with a circle of Jewish intellectuals; reads
           a draft of *Balso Snell* to the group. Introduced by the
           Perelmans to Beatrice ("Beazele") Mathieu, Paris fashion
           writer for *The New Yorker*; at the end of the year, West
           and Mathieu seriously discuss marriage.

1930   Mathieu returns to Paris in February with the understand-
           ing that West will join her in June. West submits *Balso
           Snell* for publication but it is rejected. Begins intensive
           work on *Miss Lonelyhearts*. Continues to worry over finan-
           cial failure, writing to Mathieu: "It's going to be devilish
           hard to be a cheapie." Keeps delaying trip to Paris; finally
           makes arrangements to leave in mid-June, but then cancels
           his ticket, writing to Mathieu, "I guess I'm yellow. I was
           afraid to go out and . . . earn a living writing, hacking
           . . . I feel like, I guess I am, a phoney." Takes position
           in the fall as manager of Sutton Club Hotel at 330 East
           56th Street, a job West describes as an "appointment to
           the position of matron in the Welfare Island home for

retired wealthy prostitutes." Accommodates literary
friends including the Perelmans, Norman Krasna, Dashiell
Hammett, Quentin Reynolds, Edmund Wilson, James T.
Farrell, and Robert Coates. Works over the next several
years on a series of short stories, some never finished, including "The Adventurer," "Mr. Potts of Pottstown,"
"Tibetan Night," "The Impostor," and "Western Union
Boy," but is unable to sell any of them to magazines. In
the fall David Moss and Martin Kamin, who have taken
control of Robert McAlmon's Paris-based Contact Editions, agree to publish *The Dream Life of Balso Snell* after
William Carlos Williams recommends it to them. After-
ward meets Williams and they become close friends. Introduced by his sister Laura to fashion model Alice
Shepard.

1931   *The Dream Life of Balso Snell* published in the summer in
an edition of 500 copies. Writes in advertising leaflet for
the novel: "In his use of the violently disassociated, the
dehumanized marvelous, the deliberately criminal and im-
becilic, he is much like Guillaume Apollinaire, Jarry,
Ribemont-Dessaignes, Raymond Roussel, and certain of
the surrealistes." With boyhood friend Julian Shapiro
(later known as John Sanford), rents cabin in the Adirondacks to work on *Miss Lonelyhearts*. Asked in the fall by
William Carlos Williams to serve as associate editor of a
revived version of *Contact*, the literary magazine Williams
had co-edited with Robert McAlmon in the early 1920s,
to be published by Moss and Kamin.

1932   First number of *Contact*, which appears in February, fea-
tures a chapter from *Miss Lonelyhearts* (chapters continue
to appear in subsequent numbers), along with work by
Williams, S. J. Perelman, E. E. Cummings, and others.
The second number, for which West designs the cover,
appears in May and includes works by West, Williams,
Shapiro, Erskine Caldwell, Charles Reznikoff, Marsden
Hartley, and Nancy Cunard. West writes to Williams:
"Business is lousy and my company is close to bankruptcy.
New money has to be raised or I guess I'll have to go to
Hollywood or start a Brook Farm experiment and wait for
THE REVOLUTION." Kamin asks that the third num-
ber be dedicated to Communist writings, but Williams and
West object strongly; publication ends with the third

number, which includes work by Caldwell, Perelman, James T. Farrell, and Yvor Winters. Father dies suddenly in June from bronchiectasis. West forms close friendship with Alexander King, publisher of satirical magazine *Americana*. Through Williams, West meets novelists John Herrmann and Josephine Herbst; visits them in September at their home in Erwinna, Bucks County, Pennsylvania. Completes *Miss Lonelyhearts* while staying in Frenchtown, New Jersey, near Erwinna, during fall. With the Perelmans, purchases an 83-acre farm outside of Erwinna for $6,000 in December.

1933   Alice Shepard breaks off their informal engagement after she learns that West has spent the night with Lillian Hellman. *Miss Lonelyhearts* is published in April by Horace Liveright in an edition of 2,200 copies; book's jacket features praise from Edmund Wilson, Dashiell Hammett, Erskine Caldwell, and Josephine Herbst. Liveright declares bankruptcy and the publisher's printer seizes all but a few hundred copies of *Miss Lonelyhearts*. West regains rights and the novel is reprinted by Harcourt, Brace in June, but sales are slow after the two-month delay. Sells movie rights to Darryl F. Zanuck of Twentieth Century Pictures for $4,000. In July, magazine *Contempo* devotes a number to essays about *Miss Lonelyhearts* by Williams, Perelman, Herbst, Angel Flores, and Bob Brown. West is hired by Samuel Goldwyn to write script for Hollywood film debut of Russian actress Anna Sten (his work is not used). Accepts screenwriting contract from Columbia Pictures and goes to Los Angeles in July, moving in with the Perelmans; works on unproduced screenplays *Beauty Parlor* and *Return to the Soil*. Writes to Herbst: "This stuff about easy work is all wrong. My hours are from ten in the morning to six at night with a full day on Saturday. They gave me a job to do five minutes after I sat down in my office—a scenario about a beauty parlor—and I'm expected to turn out pages and pages a day." Joins Screen Writers Guild. Contract with Columbia is discontinued at end of August. Film industry newsletter *Harrison's Reports* attacks optioning of *Miss Lonelyhearts*—"I have never read anything to compare in vileness and vulgarity"—and publication's editor conducts letter campaign against novel's filming. "Business Deal," story about Hollywood, published in *Americana* in October.

Returns to Erwinna in the fall; goes hunting regularly with local farmers. Begins new novel *A Cool Million* and completes first draft by November; book is rejected by Harcourt, Brace, which had expressed initial interest. *Advice to the Lovelorn*, film derived from *Miss Lonelyhearts*, opens on December 13 (film bears virtually no resemblance to its source).

1934   *A Cool Million* accepted in March by Covici-Friede. On May 19, West sells movie rights to Columbia Pictures. Begins affair with married woman in Erwinna in the spring. *A Cool Million* is published in June in an edition of 3,000 copies. Reviews are discouraging; few reviewers feel that it lives up to *Miss Lonelyhearts*. West develops idea for a "review or theatrical entertainment based on traditional American literature"; discusses concept with producer John Houseman, but they are unable to get financing and abandon plan after two months of work. Collaborates with Perelman during summer on play *Even Stephen*, but no producers show any interest. Applies in September for a Guggenheim Fellowship in order to write "a novel about the moral ideas of the generation which graduated from college in 1924"; does not receive fellowship, despite recommendations from Malcolm Cowley, Edmund Wilson, George S. Kaufman, and F. Scott Fitzgerald (who calls West a "potential leader in the field of prose fiction"). At year's end, by West's account, the cumulative royalties from his first three novels total $780.

1935   Breaks off affair begun the previous spring, and moves to the Hotel Brevoort in New York; the woman attempts suicide. Meets frequently with novelist James T. Farrell, and at Farrell's urging stands on picket line for striking workers at Ohrbach's and Klein's department stores; spends night in jail after being arrested along with other picketing writers, including Tess Slesinger and Edward Dahlberg. Signs manifesto calling for first annual congress of radical League of American Writers, but does not attend. Returns to Los Angeles in March; unable to find a job, depends on the Perelmans for financial support. During summer and fall, lives at the Pa-Va-Sed apartment near Hollywood Boulevard with extras, stunt men, and midgets. Contracts gonorrhea again, and writes to Perelman: "Even if I got a job now, I couldn't accept it. I can't walk and am in continuous pain . . . I can't work during the day . . . and at night I can't sleep." Frequents Stanley Rose's Hollywood Boulevard bookstore; over the next four years meets there with writers including William Faulkner, John O'Hara, Horace McCoy, John Fante, William Saroyan, F. Scott Fitzgerald, Budd Schulberg, Erskine Caldwell, and Dashiell Hammett.

1936   On January 17 begins working for Republic Productions for $200 a week (salary increases to $250 in May). Moves to apartment at Alta Loma Terrace (will subsequently live in other apartments near Hollywood Boulevard or in the Hollywood Hills, at some distance from the studios). Shares office with Lester Cole, and works with Wells Root, Horace McCoy, and Samuel Ornitz. Collaborates on screenplays including *Ticket to Paradise*, *Follow Your Heart*, *The President's Mystery*, *Gangs of New York*, and *Jim Hanvey—Detective*. Hunts wild boar with William Faulkner in April on Santa Cruz Island. Active in campaign to defend Screen Writers Guild against attempts by Louis B. Mayer, Jack Warner, and other producers to destroy it. Keeps his distance from the Communist Party, with which many of his Hollywood friends are involved. Joins Hollywood Anti-Nazi League; gives talk on the threat of Fascism at meeting of American Artists Congress in the summer. Attends Western Writers Congress (organized by Lincoln Steffens) in November, and reads paper, "Makers of Mass Neuroses," in which he criticizes Hollywood's power to corrupt the audience. Publishes "Bird and Bottle" (an early section of Hollywood novel *The Cheated*, later retitled *The Day of the Locust*) in Steffens' *Pacific Weekly* in November.

1937   Beginning in February, collaborates with screenwriter Joseph Schrank on satirical play about World War I, then titled *Gentleman, the War!*, described by West as an investigation of "the suicidal absurdities of the military mind, the most stupid of all minds"; they copyright third draft of play in November. Continues to work at Republic on screenplays including *Rhythm in the Clouds*, *Ladies in Distress*, *Bachelor Girl*, *Born To Be Wild*, *It Could Happen to You*, *Orphans of the Street*, and *Stormy Weather*. Returning from a hunting trip in Los Banos with Republic producer Leonard Fields, almost sends car over a bridge into an irrigation canal. Nears completion of first draft of *The Day of the Locust*; continues to revise the book over the next two years.

1938   Leaves Republic; works briefly at Columbia on gangster movie *The Squealer*. *The Day of the Locust* accepted by Random House in May; West gets $500 advance and an option on future books. Accepts in June a position with R.K.O. Pictures for eight weeks, completing script for *Five Came Back* (shares screen credit with Jerry Cady and Dalton Trumbo, although little of his work is used in final version). Writes "Flight South," story about the capture of illegal duck hunters, with Gordon Kahn and Wells Root; M.G.M. buys original treatment for $7,500, but it is never produced. Completes final draft of *The Day of the Locust* in July. Returns to New York in August for rehearsals of anti-war play, now titled *Good Hunting*, produced and directed by Jerome Mayer; opening delayed by financial setbacks, and West invests $1,000 to salvage the production. *Good Hunting* opens November 21 at Hudson Theatre, receives mediocre reviews, and closes after two performances. West returns to Hollywood at year's end; joins Universal Studios and works on *The Spirit of Culver*, remake of *Tom Brown of Culver*.

1939   Works on Lester Cole story *I Stole a Million* and receives first important solo screenwriting credit; film is produced in February. Sends bound proofs of *The Day of the Locust* to writers from whom he expects positive reviews, including Fitzgerald, Edmund Wilson, and Aldous Huxley. Remarks in a letter to Edmund Wilson in April: "My books meet no needs except my own . . . I do it my way . . . The radical press, although I consider myself on their side, doesn't like it, and think it even fascist sometimes, and the literature boys, whom I detest, detest me in turn. The highbrow press finds that I avoid the important things and the lending library touts in the daily press think me shocking." *The Day of the Locust* published in May. Reviews are mixed; West writes to F. Scott Fitzgerald: "So far the box score stands: Good reviews—fifteen per cent, bad reviews—twenty-five per cent, brutal personal attacks—sixty per cent. Sales: practically none" (book sells under 1,500 copies). Goes on frequent hunting trips. During trip to Los Banos, California, in October becomes sick; diagnosed with urethritis, spends two weeks in Cedars of Lebanon Hospital. Rejoins R.K.O. in November and begins work with director and screenwriter Boris Ingster (a former associate of Sergei Eisenstein) on adaptation of Frances Iles' novel *Before the Fact*. Writes two films for which he receives solo credit, *Men Against the Sky* and *Let's Make Music*; also works without credit on script for *Stranger on the Third Floor*, experimental crime thriller directed by Ingster. At a dinner party at Lester Cole's house in October, meets Eileen McKenney (subject of her sister Ruth McKenney's sketches for *The New Yorker*, published in 1938 as *My Sister Eileen*). Elected to executive board of Screen Writers Guild in November. Proposes to Eileen in December.

1940   Asks Bennett Cerf of Random House for a $1,000 advance on his next novel; ultimately accepts contract for $250 in April. Marries Eileen on April 19; they honeymoon, July–August, along the McKenzie River in Oregon. Begins work with Boris Ingster in September on an original screen story using the title "A Cool Million"; five studios bid, and Columbia buys it for $10,000 (treatment is never reworked into a script or produced). Ingster and West write another treatment, "Bird in Hand," which they sell for $25,000 to R.K.O.; they are also hired to write *Amateur Angel* for Columbia. At Eileen's urging, West attends Communist study group but finds himself at odds with doctrinaire politics. Moves with Eileen into a new house in North Hollywood in December. F. Scott Fitzgerald dies of a heart attack on December 21 (he had attended a party at the Wests' home the week before). On the afternoon of December 22, while returning from a weekend of duck and quail hunting in Mexico, West runs an intersection stop sign just outside of El Centro, California, and collides with another car. Both West and Eileen are thrown from the car and suffer skull fractures and cerebral contusions (the occupants of the other vehicle survive with serious injuries). Eileen dies in ambulance and West is pronounced dead at Imperial County Hospital at 4:10 P.M. After services at Riverside Chapel in New York, West is buried in Mount Zion Cemetery, Maspeth, Queens, with Eileen's ashes in his coffin.

Note on the Texts

This volume presents the texts of four novels by Nathanael West, *The Dream Life of Balso Snell* (1931), *Miss Lonelyhearts* (1933), *A Cool Million: The Dismantling of Lemuel Pitkin* (1934), and *The Day of the Locust* (1939); six short pieces published by West between 1923 and 1934 (three essays, a short story, a book review, and a promotional leaflet); a selection of 12 writings that were unpublished, and in some cases unfinished, at the time of West's death in 1940 (six short stories and story fragments, a poem, a play, a screenplay, a screen story, and two outlines for future work); and a selection of 29 letters written by West between 1930 and 1940.

West began developing material for *The Dream Life of Balso Snell* as early as 1924, the year he graduated from Brown University. After working on the novel during his stay in Paris in 1926, he wrote a complete draft in New York City between 1927 and 1929, using the title *The Journal of Balso Snell*. He submitted the typed manuscript to Robert McAlmon, the publisher of Contact Editions, a small press in Paris that had earlier published work by Ernest Hemingway and Gertrude Stein, but McAlmon rejected it. (McAlmon later wrote that the work "was too Anatole France for me.") Early in 1930 the novel was also rejected by Brewer, Warren & Putnam, which considered some portions to be blasphemous and obscene. West continued to revise the manuscript and later in 1930 submitted it to Martin Kamin, who, along with David Moss, had recently reached an agreement with McAlmon to take over the Contact Editions imprint. After receiving a favorable appraisal of the book from William Carlos Williams, Kamin and Moss accepted it for publication. *The Dream Life of Balso Snell* was published in New York City by Contact Editions in August 1931 in an edition of 500 numbered copies. There were no other printings in West's lifetime. The present volume prints the text of the Contact edition.

In March 1929 West read some of the letters sent to "Susan Chester," the advice columnist for the *Brooklyn Eagle*. He began writing *Miss Lonelyhearts* early in 1930 and showed 15,000 words from the manuscript to Clifton Fadiman of Simon and Schuster in April 1930 in an unsuccessful attempt to obtain an advance. West continued to work on the novel and in 1932 published five chapters from it in two magazines; these chapters all appeared in revised form in the completed book. "Miss Lonelyhearts and the Lamb," which West intended at the time to be the first chapter in the book, appeared in the February 1932 number of *Contact*. "Miss Lonelyhearts and the Dead Pan" and "Miss Lonelyhearts and the Clean Old Man," both of which are narrated from the first-person perspective of the "Miss Lonelyhearts" character, were published in *Contact* in May 1932. "Miss Lonelyhearts in the Dismal Swamp" appeared in *Contempo*, July 5, 1932, and "Miss Lonelyhearts on a Field Trip" was published in *Contact* in October 1932. West completed the novel in late November 1932 and signed a contract with Liveright, Inc., in February 1933 for its publication in an edition of 2,200 copies. *Miss Lonelyhearts* was published in New York on April 8, 1933, and received several highly favorable reviews; however, Liveright declared bankruptcy as the book was being issued, and the printer refused to release 1,400 copies that had not yet been shipped. Although Harcourt, Brace, and Company agreed on May 26, 1933, to reprint *Miss Lonelyhearts*, using the Liveright plates and substituting a new title page, the novel's sales were adversely affected by the bankruptcy. In 1934 the Liveright plates were also used by the Outlet Publishing Company for a cheap edition of *Miss Lonelyhearts* under the imprint of "Greenberg: Publisher." No other printings were made during West's lifetime. This volume uses the text of the original Liveright printing.

West began writing *A Cool Million* in the fall of 1933. He completed a handwritten first draft in November and submitted the first half of a typewritten second draft to Harcourt, Brace in early December. Although the publisher rejected it, West continued to work on the novel, and in March 1934 it was accepted for publication by Covici-Friede. West revised and rearranged the typescript before sending it to the typesetter and read and corrected galleys. *A Cool Million: The Dismantling of Lemuel Pitkin* was published in New York by Covici-Friede on June 19, 1934, in an edition of 3,000 copies. The novel received mixed reviews and sold poorly; it was not reprinted during West's lifetime. This volume prints the text of the Covici-Friede edition.

West became interested in writing a novel about Hollywood in 1933, when he worked for several weeks as a screenwriter for Columbia Pictures. He returned to California in the spring of 1935 with plans for a book involving an eccentric group of characters on board a chartered yacht and began a draft while living in an apartment hotel near Hollywood Boulevard. Illness, depression, and a severe lack of money made it difficult for him to write at first, but he made more progress on the manuscript after being hired as a screenwriter by Republic Productions in January 1936. An excerpt from the novel, then titled *The Cheated*, was published as "Bird and Bottle" in *Pacific Weekly* on November 10, 1936; in revised and expanded form it became chapter 14 of *The Day of the Locust*. West completed a handwritten first draft, typed a second draft, and then made revisions in subsequent drafts typed for him by his secretary, Josephine Conway. In April 1938 he submitted the novel to Random House, which accepted it for publication on May 17. West made a series of changes, including some suggested by Bennett Cerf of Random House, and submitted a revised manuscript on July 11. He also decided to change the title, and considered "The Grass Eaters," "Cry Wolf," and "The Wrath to Come" before choosing *The Day of the Locust*. West undertook a further series of revisions before the novel was typeset, then made a few alterations while reading proofs early in 1939. *The Day of the Locust* was published in New York by Random House on May 16, 1939, in an edition of 3,000 copies. Although the novel received generally good reviews, only 1,464 copies were sold by February 1940. This volume prints the text of the Random House edition.

None of the six pieces collected in this volume in the section titled "Other Writings" was revised or collected by West after initial publication. "Euripides—A Playwright" was published in *Casements*, the Brown University literary magazine, in July 1923; the text printed here is taken from *Casements*, courtesy Brown University Library. "Through the Hole in the Mundane Millstone" was printed and distributed as a leaflet by Contact Editions in 1931 to promote *The Dream Life of Balso Snell*. Although no copies of the original leaflet are now known to be extant, it was reprinted in *Nathanael West: A Collection of Critical Essays*, edited by Jay Martin (Englewood Cliffs, N.J.: Prentice-Hall, 1971), and in William White, *Nathanael West: A Comprehensive Bibliography* (Kent, Ohio: Kent State University Press, 1975). Since according to White the text printed in the Martin collection introduces three variants in punctuation and italicization, this volume prints the text presented in the White bibliography. The texts of the remaining four pieces in the section are taken from their original periodical publication: "Some Notes on Violence," *Contact*, October 1932; "Some Notes on Miss L.," *Contempo*, May 15, 1933; "Business Deal," *Americana*, October 1933; "Soft Soap for the Barber," *The New Republic*, November 14, 1934.

The 12 pieces collected in this volume in the section titled "Unpublished Writings and Fragments" are believed to have been written between 1930 and 1940 and are arranged chronologically in the probable order of their composition. Some of these writings are extant only in the form of uncorrected and incomplete typescripts or holograph manuscripts. In presenting unpublished texts, this volume accepts West's handwritten and typed revisions and corrects unmistakable typing errors. Unrecoverable or missing material in the typescripts is indicated in this volume by a bracketed space, i.e., [   ].

West is believed to have worked on the stories "The Impostor," "Western Union Boy," "Mr. Potts of Pottstown," and "The Adventurer" in the early 1930s. Two typescript versions of "The Impostor" are in the John Hay Library at Brown University. The first typescript is 22 pages long and was originally titled "The Fake," then retitled "L'Affaire Beano"; the second typescript, an incomplete revision of the first version, is 14 pages long and was titled "L'Affaire Beano" before being retitled "The Impostor." This volume uses the entire revised typescript and a portion of the first typescript as its copy-text for "The Impostor." The text of the revised version is printed here on pp. 411.1–419.38, and the conclusion of the original typescript appears on pp. 419.39–424.20. Courtesy Brown University Library.

The text of "Western Union Boy" printed in this volume is taken from the typescript in the John Hay Library at Brown University, which is the only version of the story known to be extant. There are no corrections or emendations in the typescript, which may have been prepared for submission to magazines (the name and address of Maxim Lieber, West's literary agent, was pasted onto the first page of the typescript). Courtesy Brown University Library.

The only version of "Mr. Potts of Pottstown" known to be extant is a typescript in the John Hay Library, Brown University, that contains both typed and handwritten emendations and which breaks off at the beginning of its seventh numbered section. This volume prints the text of the incomplete typescript. Courtesy Brown University Library.

The text of "The Adventurer" printed in this volume is taken from a 16-page typescript in the John Hay Library at Brown University. This typescript, which contains both handwritten and typed revisions, is the only text known to be extant. No evidence has been located that would indicate whether West ever continued the story past the point at which the typescript ends. Courtesy Brown University Library.

The fragmentary sketch "Three Eskimos" was probably written during or after West's trip to Hollywood in 1933. Although West never completed the sketch, he used its premise in creating the Gingo family, who appear in chapter 17 of *The Day of the Locust*. The text presented in this volume is taken from the holograph manuscript in the Huntington Library, San Marino, California.

West published a shorter, and possibly earlier, version of "Burn the Cities" in *Contempo* on February 21, 1933, under the title "Christmass Poem" (see note 458.1 in this volume). Since no manuscript text of "Burn the Cities" is now known to be extant, this volume prints the text presented in Jay Martin, *Nathanael West: The Art of His Life* (New York: Farrar, Straus and Giroux, 1970), pp. 329–31.

"Tibetan Night" is believed to have been written sometime after the publication in 1933 of *Lost Horizon*, the popular novel about Tibet by James Hilton. This volume prints the text of the typescript in the John Hay Library, Brown University, which is the only text of the story known to be extant. The typescript, which contains one hand-written cancellation, may have been prepared for submission to a magazine; its heading indicates that it was typed at his farm in Pennsylvania, where West moved in the fall of 1933. Courtesy Brown University Library.

West submitted his proposal to the Guggenheim Foundation in the fall of 1934. This volume prints the text of the carbon typescript in the files of the John Simon Guggenheim Memorial Foundation.

In 1936 West met Joseph Schrank, a playwright working for M.G.M., and suggested that they collaborate on a satirical play about World War I. Schrank agreed, and after the two writers had discussed ideas for the play for several weeks, Schrank dictated a 40-page out-line to a secretary. Using the outline, West began writing a first draft in February 1937 and completed it in May. Schrank revised the draft during the summer, and West then wrote a third version in September and October 1937. Jerome Mayer, a Broadway producer, agreed in February 1938 to stage the play, then titled *Gentleman, the War!*, and in the summer of 1938 West and Schrank made further revisions. The play, which had been retitled *Good Hunting*, opened in New York on November 21, 1938, and ran for two performances. This volume prints the text of a photocopy of the typescript of the final version of *Good Hunting* in the Huntington Library (the present location of this type-script has not been determined).

In November 1939 West was hired as a screenwriter by R.K.O. Pictures and assigned to collaborate with Boris Ingster on a film ad-aptation of *Before the Fact*, Frances Iles' 1932 novel. West and Ingster wrote a screenplay in seven weeks, with Ingster concentrating on the narrative structure while West focused on characterization and dia-logue. They subsequently made revisions in scenes 86–87, 100, 104–8, 110, and 119–122; these changes were incorporated in seven retyped pages, dated January 17, 1940, which were inserted into the existing typescript. R.K.O. subsequently assigned *Before the Fact* to director Alfred Hitchcock, who had an entirely new and substantially different screenplay written by Samson Raphaelson, Alma Reville, and Joan Harrison; the resulting film, *Suspicion*, was released in 1941. This vol-ume prints the text of the West and Ingster screenplay from the typescript in the R.K.O. archive.

West and Ingster continued their collaboration and in September 1940 wrote an original screen story together, using "A Cool Million" as their title in the hope that a studio would pay more for a story ostensibly based on a published book. (At the time West expressed confidence that "no one would read the book to check" whether the story he had written with Ingster bore any relation to his 1934 novel.) Columbia Pictures bought the story for $10,000 on September 24, 1940, and assigned it to screenwriter Sidney Buchman, but the studio soon abandoned the project and "A Cool Million" was never filmed. The text printed in this volume is taken from the only version of "A Cool Million" known to be extant, an undated typescript without corrections or revisions in the Huntington Library, San Marino, California.

The material presented in this volume under the heading of "Untitled Outline" was written by West during the summer and autumn of 1940 and may have been intended for use in a new novel. This material is in the form of two separate typescripts, both of which are marked with typed and handwritten changes; the order in which the typescripts were composed is uncertain. The text of one typescript is printed on pp. 755.2–757.3 of this volume, and the text of the other typescript is printed on pp. 757.4–766.25; both texts are taken from the photocopies of the typescripts in the Huntington Library (the present location of the originals of these documents has not been determined).

The final section of this volume contains 29 letters written by West between 1930 and 1940. One letter, signed by West and Julian L. Shapiro, appeared in the New York *World-Telegram* on October 20, 1931, and the text presented here is taken from the newspaper printing. Six letters, addressed to either Milton Abernethy or Milton and Minna Abernethy and dated April 26, 1932, February 17, 1933, March 24, 1933, April 11, 1933, May? 1933, and July 27, 1933, are printed from the originals in the Harry Ransom Humanities Research Center, University of Texas at Austin. The letter to Malcolm Cowley dated May 11, 1939, is printed from the original in the Department of Special Collections of the University Library at the University of California, Los Angeles; the letter to Bob Brown, dated February 14, 1940, is printed from the original in the Bob Brown Collection, Special Collections/Morris Library, Southern Illinois at Carbondale. Two letters to Josephine Conway, dated September 19 and October 21, 1938, are printed from the originals in the Huntington Library. Three letters to William Carlos Williams are courtesy of The Yale Collection of American Literature, Beinecke Rare Book and Manuscript Library, Yale University. Three letters to F. Scott Fitzgerald are from the Fitzgerald Papers, Box 54, Manuscripts Division, Princeton University Library. Published with permission of Princeton University Library. The texts of the remaining 12 letters are printed from the photocopies of the originals in the Huntington Library (the present location of the originals of these letters has not been determined).

This volume presents the texts of the original printings and typescripts chosen for inclusion here, but it does not attempt to reproduce features of their typographic design, such as display capitalization of chapter openings. The texts are printed without change, except for the correction of typographical errors. Spelling, punctuation, and capitalization are often expressive features, and they are not altered, even when inconsistent or irregular. The following is a list of typographical errors in the printed source texts corrected in this volume, cited by page and line number: 6.38, You; 7.30–31, Appolonius; 7.37, Appolonius; 8.26, The; 11.34, life.; 12.37, fragant; 14.19, diary.; 21.6, caterpiller; 23.4, pamplet; 31.10, was his; 35.12, Davenport,; 35.35, Love; 42.1, sucide's; 44.24, Althought; 48.12, "Beagle; 50.2, "Balso; 53.29, tress; 78.17, Krafft-Ebbing; 86.26, desk; 123.37, beds; 172.36, My; 207.10, frantically; 222.20, 6348XM; 223.9, Power's; 252.37, thirty-five year; 301.21, Fay; 310.5, thought; 318.24, principal; 325.9, Quite; 326.37, Lefebvre-Desnouttes; 349.3, Jujutala; 393.13, Shelly; 395.14, others; 396.1, unexpressable; 399.20, occurance; 399.23, that"; 399.23, spite its; 400.11, artisticaly; 401.15, Scandanavians; 401.17, Scandanavians; 401.34, immagery. Errors corrected second printing: 75.24, failure.; 328.39, route; 415.21, recieved; 420.2, him to; 422.30, matress; 430.31, 33, bowel.

Notes

In the notes below, the reference numbers denote page and line of this volume (the line count includes titles and headings). No note is made for material included in standard desk-reference books such as Webster's *Collegiate, Biographical,* and *Geographical* dictionaries. Biblical references are keyed to the King James Version. Quotations from Shakespeare are keyed to *The Riverside Shakespeare,* ed. G. Blakemore Evans (Boston: Houghton Mifflin, 1974). For further background and references to other studies, see: Jay Martin, *Nathanael West: The Art of His Life* (New York: Farrar, Straus and Giroux, 1970) and William White, *Nathanael West: A Comprehensive Bibliography* (Kent, Ohio: Kent State University Press, 1975).

THE DREAM LIFE OF BALSO SNELL

2.1   A. S.]   Alice Shepard.

3.4   *Bergotte*]   A novelist and Marcel's hero in Proust's *A la recherche de temps perdu.*

5.9   O Anus Mirabilis!]   A pun on the Latin phrase *annus mirabilis* (year of wonders).

5.13   Qualis . . . Artifex . . . Pereo]   "What an artist is lost with me!" —the words of Nero shortly before his death in Suetonius' *Nero,* XLIX.1.

5.18–19   O Beer . . . stead.]   Cf. the conclusion of James Joyce's *A Portrait of the Artist as a Young Man* (1916): "Old father, old artificer, stand me now and ever in good stead."

5.29   Tender Buttons]   Cf. Gertrude Stein's *Tender Buttons* (1914).

6.2   Silenus]   An alcoholic satyr in Greek myth who supposedly taught Bacchus to drink.

6.17   *Anywhere Out of the World*]   The title of a prose poem by Charles Baudelaire.

7.4–5   'The Grandeur . . . Rome']   Cf. Edgar Allan Poe, "To Helen," lines 9–10.

8.33   C. M. Doughty's]   Charles Montague Doughty (1843–1926), a British traveler and author of *Travels in Arabia Deserta* (1888) as well as volumes of verse.

9.7   Daudet, . . . bouillabaisse!]   French: Daudet is made of fish soup!

9.25–28   James . . . *whole?*] William James in *Some Problems of Philosophy* (1911), ch. VII, "The One and the Many."

12.29–31   Corpus . . . lave me] Latin: Body of Christ, save me / Blood of Christ, intoxicate me / Water from the side of Christ, wash me.

12.37   Maze at Cnossos] In Greek myth, the extremely complex labyrinth built at Knossos in Crete to imprison the Minotaur.

13.17–18   O Jesu, mi dulcissime!] Latin: O Jesus, sweetest to me!

14.16   letters . . . Sabine farm] Cf. the epistles of Horace; his Sabine farm, near Tibur, was a gift from Maecenas, a Roman patron of the arts.

15.11   Raskolnikov] Central character of Fyodor Dostoevsky's *Crime and Punishment* (1866).

29.13   "What is beauty . . . then?"] Christopher Marlowe, *Tamburlaine the Great* (1590), Pt. I: V.i.160.

30.22–23   Juvenal: "Who . . . Alpibus?"] Satire XIII ("Penalties of Guilt"), line 162.

32.31–14   French poet . . . U blue.] Arthur Rimbaud in "Voyelles" ("Vowels").

32.15   Father Castel] Louis Bertrand Castel (1688–1757), a French Jesuit priest and mathematician who invented an "ocular harpsichord."

32.16–17   Des Esseintes] Central character of Joris Karl Huysmans' 1884 novel *A Rebours* (*Against Nature*).

40.18–19   Mammy, . . . spells Mother.] Cf. Al Jolson's theme song "My Mammy" (1921), words by Joe Young and Sam Lewis, music by Walter Donaldson; Stephen Foster's "My Old Kentucky Home" (1853); and "M-O-T-H-E-R (A Word That Means the World to Me)" (1915), words by Howard Johnson, music by Theodore F. Morse.

41.19   aussi] French: also.

44.34   Werther] Suicidal protagonist of Goethe's *The Sorrows of Young Werther* (1774).

47.2   Bromius! Iacchus!] Surnames of Bacchus, god of the vintage, wine, and drinkers; the roots of both surnames are also related to myths of the underworld.

47.14–15   "A little . . . Pierian spring] Cf. Alexander Pope, "An Essay on Criticism," II.15–16.

47.19   'O esca . . . pulveris!'] Latin: O food for worms! O lumps of clay!

47.20   Dives] Traditional name for the rich man in Luke 16:19, from the word *dives* ("rich man") in The Vulgate, the Latin version of the Bible.

47.33   And where . . . yesteryear?]   "Mais où sont les neiges d'antan" in François Villon's poem "Ballade des dames du temps jadis."

48.7   nourriture des vers!]   French: food for worms.

48.25   born as was Gargantua]   In Rabelais' *La vie très horrificque du grand Gargantua* (1534), the giant is born from his mother's left ear.

50.7–8   Richardson . . . style]   Samuel Richardson's epistolary novels are *Pamela, or Virtue Rewarded* (1740–41) and *Clarissa* (1748).

52.18–19   Golden . . . chimney-sweeps]   Cf. Shakespeare, *Cymbeline*, IV.ii.262–63: "Golden lads and girls all must, / As chimney-sweepers, come to dust."

52.19–20   I turn . . . empty glass]   This and the rhymed lines at 52.31–32 (O how small . . . fair), 52.32–33 (Ah, make . . . descend), and 52.39–40 (And those . . . rain) are from Edward FitzGerald's translation of *The Rubaiyat of Omar Khayyam*.

MISS LONELYHEARTS

59.16   *In sæcula sæculorum*]   For ages of ages (usually translated "for ever and ever").

67.13–14   *Brothers Karamazov* . . . Zossima]   Pt. I, Bk. VI, ch. 3—"Conversations and exhortations of Father Zossima"—in Dostoevsky's novel (1879–80).

105.24   *Mrs. Mills murder*]   The bodies of Mrs. Eleanor Mills and the Rev. Edward Hall were found on the outskirts of New Brunswick, New Jersey, in September 1922. Mrs. Frances Hall, the minister's widow, was eventually indicted for the murders along with her two brothers and a cousin, but all four defendants were acquitted in 1926.

A COOL MILLION

154.20   "Gli . . . gentile."]   He gave him a coin, which made him immediately obliging.

154.22–23   "Si, si, ... giace."]   Yes, yes, . . . This life on earth is like a meadow, eh? The snake lies among the flowers.

155.7   "Qualche . . . signori?"]   What's new, gentlemen?

155.8–10   "Molto . . . danaro no,"]   Much, much . . . We got your letter but not the money.

155.11   "Queste . . . compaesano,"]   I will find those seven medals, compatriot.

176.7   Gay Pay Oo]   The G.P.U., the Soviet state security organization from 1922 until 1934.

176.15   "Der Tag!"]   German: The day!

179.33   Warford House]   Name of a hotel in Frenchtown, New Jersey, where West completed *Miss Lonelyhearts*.

204.11   Third International]   Also known as the Communist International (Comintern), founded by Lenin in 1919 to provide revolutionary Communist leadership to the worldwide socialist movement. It was dissolved in 1943.

223.9   Powers' "Greek Slave"]   A white marble statue (1843) of a nude young woman in chains after her capture by the Turks, by American sculptor Hiram Powers (1805–73).

THE DAY OF THE LOCUST

240.1   For Laura]   Laura Perelman (1911–70), West's sister.

258.19   *"Le Predicament de Marie."*]   French: The Predicament of Marie.

258.36–37   ou LA BONNE DISTRAIT]   or The Distracted Maid.

283.25   *"Jeepers Creepers!*]   Words by Johnny Mercer, music by Harry Warren (1938).

306.16–19   *"Las palmeras . . . se cayo!"*]   Spanish: The palm trees cry for your absence, / The lake dried up —ay! / The fence that was in / The patio also fell down!

306.25–26   *"Pues mi . . . acabo—ay!"*]   Spanish: For my mother took care of them, ay! / Every little thing finished—ay!

307.3–4   *"Tony's . . . wife*]   "Tony's Wife" (1933), words by Harold Adamson, music by Burton Lane.

326.17   "Sargasso Sea."]   Journalist and author Thomas Allibone Janvier, *In the Sargasso Sea* (1898).

329.2   "Sauve qui peut!"]   French: Every man for himself!

335.27–31   *"Mama . . . oil."*]   "Mama Don't Want No Peas and Rice and Coconut Oil," popular Bahamian song; melody attributed to L. Charles (Charlie Lofthouse), with lyrics by L. Wolfe Gilbert (1931).

342.6–10   *"Little . . . day*]   "Little Man, You've Had a Busy Day" (1934), words by Maurice Sigler and Al Hoffman, music by Mabel Wayne.

344.40   t.l.]   Or "trade-last": a compliment, especially one conveyed with the expectation that a compliment will be returned.

359.22–25   *Dreamed . . . vi-paah."*]   "Viper's Drag" (1934), words and music by Fats Waller.

OTHER WRITINGS

393.12   Grilplatzer]   Probably Austrian playwright Franz Grillparzer (1791–
1872).

394.15   I. T. Beckwith . . . says]   The Rev. Isbon Thaddeus Beckwith, a
theologian, professor of Greek, and editor of *The Bacchantes of Euripides* in
the College Series of Greek Authors.

398.14–15   Kurt Schwitters' . . . l'art"]   Schwitter (1887 1948), a German
artist and writer known for his Dadaist collages; "Whatever the artist spits, is
art."

399.22   "Criterion"]   Quarterly literary magazine (1922–39) edited by
T. S. Eliot.

399.22   H.S.D. says . . . story]   Hugh Sykes Davies in "American Peri-
odicals," a review of the February 1932 issue of *Contact*; the "story" is "Miss
Lonelyhearts and the Lamb," an early version of chapter 3 of *Miss Lonelyhearts*.

401.21–23   Williams' description . . . cannonballs.]   William Carlos
Williams, *In the American Grain* (1925), "Jacataqua."

403.11   Balaban & Katz]   Nationwide movie theater chain, begun with a
movie house established in Chicago in 1908 by Burt Balaban (1887–1971) with
his brother Abe Balaban and friend Sam Katz. Burt Balaban became president
of Paramount Pictures in 1936.

407.35   "The Crowd"]   Starkly realistic movie concerning episodes in the
life of a city clerk (M.G.M., 1928), innovatively directed by King Vidor and
starring James Murray and Eleanor Boardman.

407.37   "Dames"]   Musical comedy about a puritanical millionaire's attempt to prevent the opening of a Broadway show (Warner Brothers, 1934),
directed by Ray Enright and starring Joan Blondell, Hugh Herbert, and ZaSu
Pitts.

408.3   Mike Gold]   Pseudonym of Irwin Granich (1893–1967), a literary
critic, editor of *The Liberator*, and author; his essays appeared in *The Daily
Worker* and *New Masses* and his books at this time included the novel *Jews
Without Money* (1930) and story collection *120 Million* (1929).

UNPUBLISHED WRITINGS AND FRAGMENTS

439.40   "Schön! . . . Equis! Delicieux!"]   German: "Beautiful!" . . .
French: "Exquisite! Delightful!"

444.11   7]   West's typescript ends here.

458.1   *Burn the Cities*]   A version titled "Christmass Poem" ran in *Contempo* (Feb. 21, 1933); it reads: "The spread hand is a star with points / The
fist a torch / Workers of the World / Ignite / Burn Jerusalem / Make of

the City of Birth a star / Shaped like a daisy in color a rose / And bring / Not three but one king / The Hammer King to the Babe King / Where nailed to his six-branched tree / Upon the sideboard of a Jew / Marx / Performs the miracles of loaves and fishes // The spread hand is a star with points / The fist a torch / Workers of the World / Unite / Burn Jerusalem".

461.6		Comintern] See note 204.11.

461.26		"Beale Street Blues"] Words and music by W. C. Handy (1917).

461.31		Elizabeth Hawes] New York fashion designer popular in the 1930s.

462.12–13		Hamilton Fish . . . Grover Whalen] Vigorous anti-Communists from New York. Fish (1888–1946) was a U.S. Representative, 1919–45; Whalen (1886–1962) served in various public roles, notably as police commissioner, 1928–30.

467.3		*Joseph Schrank*] Primarily a screenwriter, Schrank was also co-author with Philip Dunning of the Broadway play *Page Miss Glory* (1934) and a chief sketchwriter for the hit musical revue *Pins and Needles* (opened 1937).

467.4		*Cast*] The actors who starred in the play were Aubrey Mather, Nicholas Joy, Estelle Winwood, and George Tobias.

467.29		EGLISE . . . PUCELLES] French: Church of the Twenty Virgins.

469.24		Floyd Gibbons] Gibbons (1887–1939) was an American journalist and World War I correspondent.

501.15–16		gray goose feather] An arrow (winged with gray goose feathers).

505.31		cordon sanitaire] A quarantine barrier.

570.26–27		"Hello . . . Land"] "Hello, Central—Give Me No-Man's Land" (1918), words by Sam M. Lewis and Joe Young, music by Jean Schwartz.

594.18		Ça marche?] French: How is it going?

595.5		Prenez ce fauteuil.] French: Sit down.

621.1		*Before the Fact*] An adaptation of the novel (1932) by Frances Iles (pseudonym of Anthony Berkeley Cox). The script was rewritten for Alfred Hitchcock by Samson Raphaelson, Alma Reville, and Joan Harrison, and produced as *Suspicion* (R.K.O., 1941) starring Cary Grant, Joan Fontaine, and Nigel Bruce. In the film, the heroine discovers that her husband is innocent of murder and they are reconciled; in Iles' novel, she discovers that she is pregnant and, to prevent the birth of a congenitally criminal child, drinks a glass of milk that she knows her husband has poisoned.

654.16		"Fait . . .'dames."] French: Place your bet, gentlemen, ladies.

654.21   Rien ne vas plus!] French: No more bets!

655.5   Rouge . . . impaire] French: Red, twenty-one, odd.

658.17   Dix-huit—rouge—paire.] French: Eighteen—red—even.

706.23   108-110] The folios on the typescript indicate that shots were combined and that this section is a revision of the original scenes 108-110.

759.35   Elizabeth Hawes] See note 461.31.

LETTERS

769.1   *Beatrice Mathieu*] The Paris fashion writer for *The New Yorker* whom West met in the winter of 1929–30.

769.13   Sid] S. J. Perelman (1904–79).

769.28   Contempo] *Contempo: A Review of Books and Personalities* (1931–34), founded at Chapel Hill, North Carolina, and edited by Milton Abernethy with others, including Minna Abernethy.

770.4   (Little Review)] Monthly literary magazine (1914–29) founded in Chicago by Margaret C. Anderson.

770.5   (Transition)] *transition: an international magazine for creative experiment* (1927–30, 1932–38), a Paris-based monthly founded and edited by writer and linguist Eugene Jolas (1894–1952) and Elliot Paul (1891–1958); in 1928 Robert Sage replaced Paul as associate editor. Among its contributors were Gertrude Stein, Carl Jung, and James Joyce, whose "Work in Progress" (later *Finnegans Wake*) first appeared there.

770.6   (The Midland)] Regional magazine (1915–33) published in Iowa City; it merged with *Frontier* to form *Frontier and Midland* (1933–39).

770.16   stuff I mean] West and Williams were planning the new series of *Contact* (see note 772.26).

770.19   J. Herrmann . . . HAPPENED] John Herrmann's novel *What Happens* (1926).

770.21   Amer. Car.] *American Caravan* (1927–36), a yearbook of American literature; its editors included Paul Rosenfeld, Alfred Kreymborg, Lewis Mumford, and Van Wyck Brooks.

770.23   R. Johns] Richard Johns (see following note).

770.28–29   Hound . . . Pagany] Little magazines. *The Hound and Horn: A Harvard Miscellany* (1927–34) was founded in Cambridge and from 1930 headquartered in New York City; its editors included Bernard Bandler, Varian Fry, and Lincoln Kirstein assisted by Allen Tate and Yvor Winters. *Pagany: A Native Quarterly* (1930–33) was founded in Boston and edited by poet Richard Johns (1904–70).

771.16   New Review] Bimonthly little magazine (1931–32) founded in Paris and edited by Samuel Putnam assisted by others including Ezra Pound, Maxwell Bodenheim, and Richard Thomas. It was subtitled "International Note Book for the Arts."

771.19   Callahan] Canadian-born novelist Morley Callaghan (1903–90).

772.10   *Milton Abernethy*] See note 769.28.

772.26   Contact] New York–based little magazine (1920–23; 1932) founded and edited 1920–23 by William Carlos Williams (1883–1963) and Robert McAlmon (1896–1956) and revived in 1932 as *Contact: An American Quarterly* with Williams as editor and West as associate editor; four numbers of the new series were prepared, but only three were published.

773.9–11   Jolas . . . the Arts.] See notes 770.5 and 771.16.

773.24   R. McA.] Robert McAlmon, American author, editor, and founder of Contact Editions in France; see also note 772.26.

773.27–29   C. Dejong . . . Asch] Dutch-born novelist and poet David Cornel De Jong (1905–67), story writer Charles Kendall O'Neill, and novelist Nathan Asch (1902–64), the son of Polish-born novelist Sholem Asch.

773.34   Jaffee] Brooklyn-based story writer Eugene Joffe.

774.1   Succ. . . . P. E. Reeve] "Succumbing" by New York poet Paul Eaton Reeve.

774.4–7   My . . . I. Ehren] "My Country 'Tis of Thee" by Charles Reznikoff (1894–1976), a New York poet associated with the Objectivist group, and the poem "Collect to the Virgin" by Nancy Cunard (1896-1965), an English writer and director of the Hours Press in France who was in New York preparing her anthology *Negro* (pub. 1934). "The Old Furdresser" by Ilya Ehrenberg (1891–1970) did not appear in *Contact*.

774.13–14   Amer. Merc.] *The American Mercury* (1924–80), monthly magazine founded by H. L. Mencken and George Jean Nathan as a successor to their *Smart Set*; from 1930 to 1934, the magazine was known for its scathing critiques of American mass culture.

774.14   (Halper's)] Chicago-born author Albert Halper (1904–84); his first novel, *Union Square*, appeared in 1933.

775.16   Norman Mcleod] American poet Norman Macleod, a good friend of William Carlos Williams.

776.3   Mangin] Probably critic, poet, and editor John Sherry Mangan.

776.15   Jaffee] See note 773.34.

776.16   Bib.] The continuing "Bibliography of the 'Little Magazine'," compiled by David Moss, was a running feature in the new series of *Contact*.

776.40   Brook Farm] Experimental cooperative community (1841–47) near West Roxbury, Massachusetts.

777.7   *Minna . . . Abernethy*] See note 769.28.

777.10   "poem" in print] See note 458.1.

777.23–24   you did for Dahlberg's Flushing] *Contempo* had devoted a number to reviews of Dahlberg's 1932 novel *From Flushing to Calvary* and would devote its July 25, 1933, number to a "critical symposium" on West's *Miss Lonelyhearts.*

778.7   CANDIDE] Voltaire's philosophical novel *Candide, or Optimism* (1759).

778.31   Bob . . . review] American poet Bob (Robert Carlton) Brown (1886–1959) praised West's writing in "Go West, Young Writer!" (*Contempo*, July 25, 1933). Brown's books include *Tahiti* (1915), *My Marjory* (1916), *1450/ 1950* (1929), *Globe-Gliding* (1930), *Readies for Bob Brown's Machine* (1931), a collection of experiments in the use of Brown's "reading machine" by writers including William Carlos Williams, Gertrude Stein, Eugene Jolas, and Robert McAlmon, and *Let There Be Beer!* (1932).

778.34   Soskind] William Soskin, New York *Evening Post* literary editor 1928–33.

779.7   Flores . . . Perelman] Author, editor, and translator Angel Flores' "Miss Lonelyhearts in the Haunted Castle" and S. J. Perelman's "Nathanael West: A Portrait" appeared in *Contempo* (July 25, 1933).

779.11   Mike Gold] See note 408.3.

780.1   Knopf, Harrison Smith] Alfred A. Knopf and Harrison Smith & Robert Haas, New York publishing firms.

780.5   add and author review] In the May 15, 1933, *Contempo.* The advertisement included comments by Erskine Caldwell (1903–87), Robert Coates (1897–1973), Dashiell Hammett (1894–1961), and Josephine Herbst (1897–1969); for West's essay, "Some Notes on Miss L.," see pages 401–2 in this volume.

780.32–33   Howard . . . Caesar] Screenwriters Sidney Howard, John Howard Lawson, Samuel Ornitz, Louis Weitzenkorn, and Arthur Caesar.

781.22   Once . . . Time] *Once in a Lifetime* (1930), a satire of Hollywood by Moss Hart and George S. Kaufman.

782.12   Guggenheim Fellowship] For West's proposal, see page 465 in this volume.

782.28–31   *Bennett Cerf . . . book*] An editor and publisher, Cerf (1898–1971) was founder and president (1927–65) of Random House; the book is *The Day of the Locust.*

784.32   "Blow, Bugle, Blow."] Working title of *Good Hunting* (pages 467–620 in this volume).

786.1   *Josephine Conway*] West's secretary in Hollywood.

786.6–9   the play . . . cast] *Good Hunting* (see page 467 and notes).

787.3   Metro] Metro-Goldwyn-Mayer (M.G.M.), one of the five major Hollywood studios of the 1930s.

787.13   Joe] Joseph Schrank (see note 467.3).

787.18   outrun Tobacco Road] Jack Kirkland's dramatization of Erskine Caldwell's 1932 novel opened on Broadway in 1933 and closed in 1941 after a continuous run of 3,182 performances.

788.31   Bus-Fekete] Playwright and screenwriter Ladislaus Bus-Fekete (also known as Leslie Bush-Fekete).

790.17   *Saxe Commins*] Random House editor to whom West submitted *The Day of the Locust* in April 1938.

790.32   Miss Becker] Belle Becker, an editor at Random House.

791.14   Max Lieber] Literary agent who had tried unsuccessfully to sell West's stories to magazines in the mid-1930s.

792.20   Hays code] The production code to govern the moral content of American films; it was introduced in 1930 by Will Hays, president of the Motion Picture Producers and Distributors of America, became strictly effective in 1934, and continued until 1966.

793.33   Otis Ferguson] Ferguson (1907–43) was a leading film critic.

795.21–22   "I Stole A Million" . . . Raft] West's script was based on a screen story by Lester Cole; the film, directed by Frank Tuttle (Universal, 1939), also starred Clair Trevor and was West's first important solo screen credit.

796.15   New Republic . . . review] Wilson's review of *The Day of the Locust*, "Hollywood Dance of Death," appeared in the July 26, 1939, number.

797.15   *Bob Brown*] See note 778.31.

798.7   Uriah Heeps] Uriah Heep is the sycophantic villain of Charles Dickens' *David Copperfield* (1849–50).

798.28   Rose] Rose Brown, Bob Brown's wife.

799.9   "MEN AGAINST THE SKY"] West wrote the script for this film based on an original story by John Twist. Directed by Leslie Goodwins, it starred Granville Bates, Richard Dix, Paul Hurst, and Grant Withers and was released by R.K.O. Pictures in 1940.

Library of Congress Cataloging-in-Publication Data

West, Nathanael, 1903–1940.
   [Selections. 1997]
   Novels and other writings / Nathanael West.
      p.   cm. — (The Library of America ; 93)
   Contents: The dream life of Balso Snell — Miss
Lonelyhearts — A cool million — The day of the locust —
Other writings — letters.
   ISBN 1–883011–28–0
   I. Title.   II. Title: Dream life of Balso Snell.   III. Title:
Miss Lonelyhearts.   IV. Title: Cool million.   V. Title: Day
of the locust.   VI. Series.
PS3545.E8334A6   1997   96–49007
813′.52—dc21   CIP

THE LIBRARY OF AMERICA SERIES

The Library of America helps to preserve our nation's literary heritage by publishing, and keeping permanently in print, authoritative editions of America's best and most significant writing. An independent nonprofit organization, it was founded in 1979 with seed money from the National Endowment for the Humanities and the Ford Foundation.

This book is set in 10 point Linotron Galliard,
a face designed for photocomposition by Matthew Carter
and based on the sixteenth-century face Granjon. The paper is
acid-free Ecusta Nyalite and meets the requirements for permanence
of the American National Standards Institute. The binding
material is Brillianta, a woven rayon cloth made by
Van Heek-Scholco Textielfabrieken, Holland.
The composition is by The Clarinda
Company. Printing and binding by
R.R.Donnelley & Sons Company.
Designed by Bruce Campbell.